Blue Heaven

&

Three Weeks to Say Goodbye

D0111657

ALSO BY C. J. BOX

Blue Heaven

&

Three Weeks to Say Goodbye

C. J. BOX

MINOTAUR BOOKS

NEW YORK

These are works of fiction. All of the characters, organizations, and events portrayed in these novels are either products of the author's imagination or are used fictitiously.

BLUE HEAVEN. Copyright © 2007 by C. J. Box. THREE WEEKS TO SAY GOODBYE. Copyright © 2008 by C. J. Box. All rights reserved. Printed in the United States of America. For information, address St. Martin's Press, 175 Fifth Avenue, New York, N.Y. 10010.

www.minotaurbooks.com

The Library of Congress Cataloging-in-Publication Data is available upon request.

ISBN 978-1-250-25997-4 (trade paperback)

Our books may be purchased in bulk for promotional, educational, or business use. Please contact your local bookseller or the Macmillan Corporate and Premium Sales Department at 1-800-221-7945, extension 5442, or by email at MacmillanSpecialMarkets@macmillan.com.

First Edition: June 2019

10 9 8 7 6 5 4 3 2

Blue Heaven

For Ann Rittenberg

. . . and Laurie, always

ACKNOWLEDGMENTS

The author would like to acknowledge the fine people of Sandpoint, Idaho, who provided background and hospitality, including Marianne Love and Roley and Janice Schoonover. Thanks to Mark Whitworth in L.A., who first mentioned a place called Blue Heaven.

Sincere appreciation to Ben Sevier and Jennifer Enderlin, who brought this baby home.

This novel would not exist without the patience and perseverance of Ann Rittenberg.

DAY ONE

friday

In countries where associations are free, secret societies are unknown. In America there are factions, but no conspiracies.
—Alexis de Tocqueville, *Democracy in America*, 1835

WELCOME TO THE INLAND NORTHWEST
—sign greeting arrivals at Spokane Airport

Friday, 4:28 P.M.

IF TWELVE-YEAR-OLD Annie Taylor had not chosen to take her little brother William fishing on that particular Friday afternoon in April during the wet North Idaho spring, she never would have seen the execution or looked straight into the eyes of the executioners. But she was angry with her mother.

Before they witnessed the killing, they were pushing through the still-wet willows near Sand Creek, wearing plastic garbage bags to keep their clothes dry. Upturned alder leaves cupped pools of rainwater from that morning, and beaded spiderwebs sagged between branches. When the gray-black fists of storm clouds pushed across the sun, the light muted in the forest and erased the defining edges of the shadows, and the forest plunged into a dispiriting murk. The ground was black, spongy in the forest and sloppy on the trail. Their shoes made sucking sounds as they slogged upstream.

Annie and William had left their home on the edge of town, hitched a ride for a few miles with Fiona, the mail lady, and had been hiking for nearly two hours, looking in vain for calm water.

"Maybe this wasn't such a good idea," ten-year-old William said, raising his voice over the liquid roar of the creek, which was angry and swollen with runoff.

Annie stopped and turned to William, looking him over. A long fly rod poked out from beneath the plastic he wore. He had snagged the tip several times in the branches, and a sprig of pine needles was wedged into one of the line guides.

"You said you wanted to go fishing, so I'm taking you fishing."

"But you don't know anything about it," William said, his eyes widening and his lower lip trembling, which always happened before he began to cry.

"William . . ."

"We should go back."

"William, don't cry."

He looked away. She knew he was trying to stanch it, she could tell by the way he set his mouth. He hated that he cried so easily, so often, that his emotions were so close to the surface. Annie didn't have that problem.

"How many times did Tom tell you he was going to take you fishing?" Annie asked.

William wouldn't meet her eyes. "A bunch," he said.

"How many times has he taken you?"

He said sullenly, "You know."

"Yes, I know."

"I sort of like him," William said.

Annie said, "I sort of don't."

"You don't like anybody."

Annie started to argue, but didn't, thinking: *He may be right.* "I like *you* enough to take you fishing even though I don't know how to fish. Besides, how hard can it be if Tom can do it?"

An impudent smile tugged at the corners of his mouth. "Yeah, I guess," he said.

"Look," she said, raising her plastic bag to show him she was wearing Tom's fishing vest. She had taken it without asking off a peg in their house. "This thing is filled with lures and flies and whatever. We'll just tie them to the end of your line and throw 'em out there. The fish can't be much smarter than Tom, so how hard can it be?"

". . . if Tom can do it," he said, his smile more pronounced.

That was when they heard a motor rev and die, the sound muffled by the roar of the foamy water.

THE BETRAYAL occurred that morning when Tom came downstairs, asked, "What's for breakfast?" Annie and William were at the table dressed for school eating cereal—Sugar Pops for William, Frosted Mini-Wheats for her. Tom asked his question as if it were the most natural thing in the world, but it wasn't. Tom had never been in their home for breakfast before, had never stayed the night. He was wearing the same wrinkled clothes from the night before when he'd shown up after dinner to see their mom, what he called his fishing clothes—baggy trousers that zipped off at the thigh, a loose-fitting shirt with lots of pockets. This was new territory for Annie, and she didn't want to explore it.

Instead, she found herself staring at his large, white bare feet. They looked waxy and pale, like the feet of a corpse, but his toes had little tufts of black hair on their tops, which both fascinated and disgusted her. He slapped them wetly across the linoleum floor.

"Where's your mom keep the coffee?" he asked.

William was frozen to his chair, his eyes wide and unblinking, his spoon poised an inch from his mouth, Sugar Pops bobbing in the milk. William said, "On the counter, in that canister thing."

Tom repeated "canister thing" to himself with good humor and set about making a pot of coffee. Annie bored holes into the back of his fishing shirt with her eyes. Tom was big, buff, always fake-friendly, she thought. He rarely showed up at their house without a gift for them, usually something lame and last-minute like a Slim-Jim meat stick or a yo-yo he bought at the convenience store at the end of the street. But she'd never seen him like this—disheveled, sleepy, sloppy, talking to the two of them for the very first time like they were real people who knew where the coffee was.

"What are you doing here?" she asked.

He turned his head. His eyes were unfocused, bleary. "Making coffee."

"No. I mean in my house."

William finally let the spoon continue its path. His eyes never left Tom's back. A drip of milk snaked down from the corner of his mouth and sat on his chin like a bead of white glue.

Tom said, "Your house? I thought it was your mother's house." *All jolly he is,* she thought angrily.

"Is this *it* for breakfast?" Tom asked, holding up the cereal boxes and raising his eyebrows.

"There's toast," William said, his mouth full. "Mom makes eggs sometimes. And pancakes."

Annie glared at her brother with snake eyes.

"Maybe I'll ask Monica to make me some eggs," Tom mumbled, as much to himself as to them. He poured a cup of coffee before it filled the carafe. Errant drips sizzled on the hot plate.

So it was *Monica,* not *your mother,* Annie thought.

He came to the table, his feet making kissing sounds on the floor, pulled out a chair, and sat down. She could smell her mother on him, which made her feel sick inside.

"That's Mom's chair," she said.

"She won't mind," he said, flashing his false, condescending smile. To him they were children again, although she got the feeling Tom was just a little scared of her. Maybe he realized now what he'd done. Maybe not. He pointedly ignored Annie, who glared at him, and turned to William.

"School, eh?" Tom said, reaching out and tousling the boy's hair. William nodded, his eyes wide.

"Too bad you can't take the day off and go fishing with me. I really got into some nice ones last night before I came over. Fifteen-, sixteen-inch trout. I brought a few to your mom for you guys to have for dinner."

"I want to go," William said, swelling out his chest. "I've never gone fishing, but I think I could do it."

"You bet you could, little man," Tom said, sipping the hot coffee. He gestured toward the cluttered mudroom off the kitchen where he'd hung his fishing vest and stored his fly rod in the corner. "I've got another rod in my truck you could use."

Suddenly, William was squirming in his chair, excited. "Hey, we get out of school early today! Maybe we could go then?"

Tom looked to Annie for clarification.

"Early release," Annie said deadpan. "We're out at noon."

Tom pursed his lips and nodded, his eyes dancing, now totally in control of William. "Maybe I'll pick you up and take you after school, then. I'll ask your mom about it. I can pick you up out front. D'you want to go along, too, Annie?"

She shook her head quickly. *"No."*

"You need to ease up a little," Tom told her, smiling with his mouth only.

"You need to go home," she replied.

Tom was about to say something when her mother came down the stairs, her head turned away from the kitchen and toward the front door. Annie watched her mother walk quickly through the living room and part the curtains, expecting, Annie thought, to confirm that Tom's vehicle was gone. When it wasn't, her mother turned in horror and took it all in: Tom, Annie, and William at the kitchen table. Annie saw the blood drain out of her mother's face, and for a second she felt sorry for her. But only for a second.

"Tommmmm," her mother said, dragging his name out and raising the tone so it was a sentence in itself meaning many things, but mostly, *"Why are you still here?"*

"Don't you need to get to work?" her mother finally said.

Tom was a UPS driver. Annie was used to seeing him in his brown uniform after work. His shirt and shorts were extra tight.

"Yup," Tom said, standing so quickly he sloshed coffee on the table. "I better get going, kids. I'll be late."

Annie watched Tom and her mother exchange glances as Tom hurried past her toward the front door, grabbing his shoes on the way. She thanked God there was no good-bye kiss between them, or she might throw up right there.

"Mom," William said, "Tom's going to take me fishing after school!"

"That's nice, honey," his mom said vacantly.

"Go brush your teeth," Annie said to William, assuming the vacated role of adult. "We've got to go."

William bounded upstairs.

Annie glared at her mother, who said, "Annie . . ."

"Are you going to marry him?"

Her mother sighed, seemed to search for words. She raised her hands slowly, then dropped them to her sides as if the strings had been snipped. That answered Annie's question.

"You told me . . ."

"I *know*," her mother said impatiently, tears in her eyes. "It's hard for you to understand. Someday you'll see, maybe."

Annie got up from the table and took her and William's bowls to the sink, rinsed them out. When she was through, her mother was still standing there, hadn't moved.

"Oh, I understand," Annie said, then gestured toward the stairs. "But William doesn't. He thinks he's got a new dad."

Her mother took a sharp breath as if Annie had slapped her. Annie didn't care.

"We'll talk later," her mother said, as Annie avoided her and went straight outside through the mudroom to wait for William in the yard. She knew her mom would be heartbroken because she hadn't kissed her good-bye. *Too bad,* Annie thought. *Mom had been kissed enough lately.*

AT NOON, Annie waited with William at the front of the school for Tom. They looked for his pickup and never saw it. When a UPS truck came down the block, William pumped his fist and growled, *"YES!"*

But Tom wasn't driving the truck, and it never slowed down.

After taking Tom's fishing rod and vest, Annie and William walked along the damp shoulder of the state highway out of town. Annie led. She knew there was a creek up there somewhere. A woman driving a little yellow pickup pulled over in front of them.

"Where are you two headed with such dogged determination?" the woman asked in a high-pitched little-girl voice. Annie disliked her immediately. She was one of those older women who thought they were young and pert instead of squat and wide.

"Fishing," Annie said. "Up ahead, on the creek."

The woman said her name was Fiona, and she delivered rural mail, and she would be going that direction if they needed a ride. Even though William shook his head no, Annie said, "Thank you."

While they drove deep into the forest and began to see glimpses of a stream through the trees, Fiona never stopped talking. She acted as if she was interested in them, but she wasn't, Annie thought. Fiona was determined to convince them that delivering mail was a very important job and not just anybody could do it. As if she expected Annie to say, "Wow—you deliver the *mail?*" Fiona's perfumed scent was overpowering inside the small cab. Annie's eyes began to water, and she threw an elbow at William, who was pinching his nose shut.

"Can you let us off here?" Annie asked at no particular landmark except that she could see the creek.

"Are you sure this is okay with your folks?" Fiona asked, well after the time she should have.

"Sure," Annie lied.

They thanked her and got out. William was concerned that the fish would be able to smell him because his clothes were now reeking of perfume, but Annie convinced him fish couldn't smell. Not that she knew anything about fish.

MAYBE, ANNIE THOUGHT, the men didn't notice William and her because the dark green plastic they wore over their clothes blended in so well with the color of the heavy brush. Maybe, the men had looked around for another vehicle, and not having seen one, assumed no one else was there, certainly not on foot. But Annie could certainly see *them*; the profiles of four men parked in a white SUV in a campground space.

Everything was wet and dark under the dripping canopy of trees, and it smelled of pine, loam, and the spray of the creek. Other than the white car, the campground looked empty. There was a picnic table next to the SUV, and a low black fire pit.

Annie watched as the driver got out and shut his door, looked around the campsite, then turned back to the vehicle. He was middle-aged or older, lean, fit, and athletic in his movements. He had short white hair and a tanned, thin face. Three more doors opened, and three more men climbed out. They wore casual rain jackets, one wore a ball cap. The man in the ball cap put a six-pack of beer on the picnic table and pulled out four bottles and twisted the tops off, putting the tops into his jacket pocket.

The men seemed to be comfortable with one another, she thought, the way they nodded and smiled and talked. She couldn't hear what they said because of the sound of the rushing creek behind her. The Ball Cap

Man offered bottles of beer to everyone, and took a long drink of his own. They didn't sit down at the table—too wet, she thought—but stood next to each other.

Annie felt William tugging on her arm through the plastic. When she looked over, he gestured back toward the path they had come by, indicating he wanted to go. She gave him a *just-a-minute* nod and turned back to the campsite. It thrilled her to spy on the men. Men fascinated and repulsed her, maybe because her mother attracted so many of them.

What happened next was terrifying.

The Driver circled the group of men, as if returning to the car, then he suddenly wheeled and jabbed a finger into the chest of a wavy-haired man and said something harsh. The wavy-haired man stumbled back a few feet, obviously surprised. As if a signal had been given, both the Ball Cap Man and a tall, dark man stepped back, and stood shoulder to shoulder with the Driver, facing down the wavy-haired man, who pitched his beer bottle aside and held his hands out, palms up, in an innocent gesture.

"Annie . . ." William pleaded.

She saw the Dark Man pull a pistol from behind his back, point it at the Wavy-Haired Man, and fire three times, *pop-pop-pop*. The Wavy-Haired Man staggered backwards until he tripped over the fire pit and fell into the mud.

Annie caught her breath, and her heart seemed to rush up her throat and gag her. She felt a sharp pain in her arm, and for a second she thought that a stray bullet had struck her, but when she glanced down she saw it was William's two-handed grip. He had seen what happened in the campsite, too. It wasn't like television or the movies, where a single shot was a deafening explosion and the victim was hurled backwards, dead, bursts of blood detonating from his clothing. This was just a *pop-pop-pop*, like a string of firecrackers. She couldn't believe what had just happened, couldn't believe it wasn't a prank or a joke or her imagination.

"Annie, let's get out of here!" William cried, and she started to backpedal blindly, toward the creek.

At the water's edge, she looked over her shoulder, realizing they had lost the path and could go no farther.

"No," she yelled at William. "Not this way. Let's get back on the trail!"

He turned to her panicked, eyes wide, his face drained of color. Annie reached for his hand and tugged him along, crashing back through the brush toward the path. When they reached it, she looked back toward the campsite. All three men stood over the Wavy-Haired Man, firing pistols into his body.

Pop-pop-pop-pop-pop.

Suddenly, as if Annie's own gaze had drawn him, the Driver looked up. Their eyes locked, and Annie felt something like ice-cold electricity shoot through her. It burned the tips of her fingers and toes and momentarily froze her shoes to the ground.

William screamed, *"He sees us!"*

SHE RAN like she had never run before, pulling her brother along behind her, yelling, "Stay with me!"

They kept to the trail that paralleled the lazy curves of Sand Creek. The stream was on their left, the dark forest on their right. Wet branches raked her face and tugged at her clothing as she ran. She could hear her own screams as if someone else was making them.

Pop-pop. A thin tree in front of them shook from an impact, and half-opened buds rained down. The men were shooting at them.

William was crying, but he was keeping up. He gripped her hand so tightly she could no longer feel her fingers, but she didn't care. Somewhere, she had lost a shoe in the mud, but she never even considered going back for it, and now her left foot was freezing.

How far were they from the road? She couldn't guess. If they got to the road, there was the chance of getting a ride home with someone.

William jerked to a stop so suddenly that Annie was pulled backwards, falling. Had one of the men grabbed him?

No, she saw. His fly rod had been caught between the trunks of two trees. Rather than let go of it, he was trying to pull it free.

"Drop it, William!" she cried. "Just drop it!"

He continued to struggle as if her words hadn't penetrated. His face was twisted with determination, his tears streaming.

"LET GO!" she screamed, and he did.

She scrambled back to her feet and as she did she saw a shadow pass in the trees on their right. It was the Ball Cap Man, and he had apparently found a parallel trail that might allow him to get ahead so he could cut them off.

"Wait," she said to William, her eyes wide. "We can't keep going this way. Follow me."

She pushed herself through heavy wet undergrowth, straight at the path she had seen the Ball Cap Man running on. She hesitated a moment at the trail, saw no one, and plunged across it between two gnarled wild rosebushes, pulling William behind her. This time, she didn't need to prompt him to keep running.

They were now traveling directly away from the river through heavy timber. Annie let go of her brother's hand, and the two of them scrambled over downed logs and through masses of dead and living brush farther into the shadows. Something low and heavy-bodied, a raccoon maybe, scuttled out of sight and parted the fronds in front of them.

They left the roar of the river behind them, and it got quieter in the forest. At one point they heard a shout below them, somewhere in the trees, one of the men shouting, *"Where did they go, goddammit?"*

"Did you hear that?" William asked.

She stopped, leaned back against the trunk of a massive ponderosa pine, and nodded.

"Do you think they would shoot us if they found us?"

She implored him with her eyes not to talk.

William collapsed next to her, and for a few minutes the only sound in the forest was the steady dripping of the trees and their winded breath. Even as she recovered from exertion, the terror remained. Every tree looked like one of the men. Every shadow looked momentarily like a man with a gun.

She looked down at her brother, who had his head cocked back on the trunk, his mouth slightly open. His clothes were wet and torn. She could see a cut oozing dark blood where a bare knee was exposed by an L-shaped rip. His face was pale white, streaked with dirt.

"I'm sorry I brought you here," she said. "I didn't know what I was doing."

"They killed that man," William said. "They shot him and shot him again."

She didn't say, *They'll do the same to us.* Instead: "If we keep going in this direction, we should find the road."

"What if they're already up there?"

She shrugged, sighed. "I don't know."

"How will we get home?"

"I don't know."

"They just kept shooting him," he said. "I wonder what he did to make them so mad?"

THEY DIDN'T SEE the road so much as sense an opening in the canopy ahead. Annie made William squat down in the wet brush, and they remained still for a few minutes, hoping to hear the sound of a car or truck.

"We're like rabbits," he said, "just sitting here scared."

"Shhh." She thought she heard a motor. "Stay here."

She pushed through the low brush on her hands and knees. She could no longer feel her bare foot, which was cut and bleeding. The grass got thicker as it neared the road, and she crawled on her belly to the edge of it. For the first time since the initial *pop*, she felt a twinge of relief.

Then she felt a tug on her pant leg, and gasped.

"It's just me," William said. "Man, you jumped."

She hissed, "I told you to stay back there."

"No way," he said, crawling up next to her. "What are we doing?"

"We're going to wait until we hear a car," she said. "When it gets close, we're going to jump up and try to get a ride to town."

"What if it's the white car?" he asked.

"Then we keep hiding," she said.

"I thought you heard something."

"I thought I did. Maybe not."

"Hold it," William said, raising his head above the grass, "I hear it too."

ANNIE AND WILLIAM looked at each other as the sound slowly rose, the baritone hum of a motor spiced by the crunching of gravel beneath tires. The vehicle was coming from the wrong direction, from town instead of toward it. But Annie figured that if someone was likely to stop for them, they would be just as likely to turn around and take them home.

And if the vehicle was coming from the direction of town, it was unlikely it could be the white SUV.

She inched forward, parting the grass. She could feel the approach of the vehicle from the ground beneath her, a vibration that made her feel more like an animal than a girl.

She saw an antenna, then the top of a cab of a pickup, then a windshield. She raised her head.

It was a new-model red pickup with a single occupant.

Whooping, she scrambled to her feet and pulled William along with her, and they stood in the road.

At first, she wasn't sure the driver saw her. He was going slowly, and staring out into the trees off to the side instead of at the road. But just as she began to step back toward the shoulder, the pickup slowed and she recognized the driver as Mr. Swann. Mr. Swann had once dated their mother, and although he was much older than she, and it didn't work out, he had not been unkind to them.

As Swann stopped and leaned over and opened the passenger door, Annie Taylor began to weep with absolute relief, her hot tears streaming down her face.

"Whoa," Mr. Swann said, looking them over, "are you two all right? Did you get lost out here?"

"Will you please take us home?" Annie said through her tears.

"What happened?"

"Please take us home," William said. "We saw a man get killed."

"*What?*"

As William climbed into the truck, Annie heard another motor. She looked up the road where it curved to the right and could see a vehicle coming, glimpses of it flashing through the trunks of the trees.

It was the white SUV.

"Get on the floor," she yelled to her brother. "It's *them!*"

"Annie, what's going on here?" Swann asked, frowning.

"They want to kill us!" Annie said, hurtling inside and shutting the door behind her. She cowered with William on the floor of the pickup.

"Oh, come on now," Swann said.

"Please, just drive," Annie said, her voice cracking. "Please just drive ahead."

Swann slid the truck back into gear, and she could feel it moving, hear the gravel start to crunch.

"Maybe I should just stop them and ask them what's going on?" Swann asked. "I'm sure it's a misunderstanding."

"*NO!*" Annie and William howled in unison.

She looked up at Swann as he drove, saw the confusion on his face. What if the men in the SUV waved Swann down to talk? It wasn't unusual on these back roads to see two vehicles stopped side by side as the drivers exchanged information and pleasantries.

"Please don't stop," Annie said again.

"I don't know what's going on," Swann said, "but it has you two scared to death, that's for sure."

Swann pursed his lips and looked ahead. She wished she could see how close the white SUV was, and what the men inside were doing. Instead, she wrapped her arms around William and watched Swann.

"They want me to stop," Swann said, not looking down.

"Don't. Please."

"If I don't stop, they'll wonder why."

Annie felt another imminent, choking cry, and tried to stifle it.

The pickup slowed. She tried to push William down even farther into the floor, and herself as well. She could feel his heart beating, fluttering, where her hand held his chest. She closed her eyes, as if by not seeing the men they couldn't look in and see *her*.

"Afternoon, Mr. Singer," Swann said as he rolled his window down.

"Afternoon," Singer said. Singer was the Driver, Annie guessed. Mr. Swann *knew* him.

Singer said, "Hey, did you see some kids anywhere along the road?"

"They yours?" Swann asked.

"No, not mine. Mine are grown and married, you know that. I don't know who they are. Me and my two compadres here were fishing and horsing around down on the river, and we scared a couple of kids. We were target shooting, and we didn't know they were there. We think they might have thought they saw something they didn't."

"Target shooting?"

"Yeah, we try to get out every couple of months to stay sharp. Anyway, we want to make sure those poor kids know we meant no harm."

Annie cracked an eye to look at Swann. *Don't do it,* she wanted to shout.

"Scared 'em pretty good, eh?" Swann said.

"I'm afraid so. Anyway, we want to find them and let 'em know everything's okay."

"Is everything okay?" Swann asked.

Singer didn't respond.

"It will be when we find those kids," another man said with a trace of a Mexican accent. Annie guessed it was the Dark Man with the mustache.

"So you haven't seen them?" Singer asked again.

Swann hesitated.

Annie closed her eyes again and tried to prepare to die. She didn't hear the bulk of the conversation that followed because it was drowned out by the roar of blood in her ears, although she did hear Swann say someone had come up behind him and was waiting for him to go.

"Yes," Singer had said, "you had better go home now."

She couldn't believe her luck—their luck—when she realized the truck was moving again.

"I think you kids should stay down," Swann said.

Annie asked, "Where are you taking us?"

"My place is just up the road, and I need to make a call."

"Why aren't you taking us home?"

"Because I don't want to run into those boys again," Swann said. "I know them from back on the force, and that story they just told me doesn't make a lot of sense."

"That's because we're telling you the truth," Annie said, feeling the tears well up in her eyes.

"Maybe," Swann said. "Keep your heads down."

Friday, 4:40 P.M.

JESS RAWLINS was doing groundwork with his new horse Chile in the round pen near the corral when a new-model Lexus emerged from the timber on the southern hill and drove down the access road toward his ranch house. It caught him by surprise because he was concentrating so fully on his horse, a fourteen-hand three-year-old red dun. He had fallen into a kind of hyperalert trance, mesmerized by the rhythmic sound and cadence of her hoofbeats. Jess had forgotten how much he loved the sound of hoofbeats, the solid soft pounding rhythm of them, how he could feel them through the ground as the eleven-hundred-pound animal trotted, how the sound lulled him, took him back. A few moments before, when he was lunging her to the right, he'd picked out the sound of a series of sharp rapid-fire percussions along with the thump of her hoofbeats, a snapping sound that alarmed him for a moment before he realized they were from far up the valley and had nothing to do with the gait of his horse. He had stopped her suddenly, and she had turned nicely into an abrupt stop, facing him like she was supposed to, looking at him with both eyes, breathing hard, licking her lips with compliance. He listened and heard no more pops in the distance.

If the wooded valley he lived in was indeed a saddle slope, his house and outbuildings were located just under the pommel. From there, he could see anyone coming down from the state highway toward his ranch. At dusk, he often watched mule deer graze their way to the valley floor to drink at the stream.

He kissed the air and sidestepped to the right, and Chile responded instantly with the correct lead, trotting in a circle to the left on the end of the lead rope Jess held loosely in his left hand. In his right was a stiff coil of rope used to signal the mare, keep the invisible pressure on her to keep moving in a nice smooth stride. Sometimes, to get her attention, he whapped the rope against the leg of his Wranglers. Mostly, though, all he had to do was raise it to get her moving. He had never hit her with it. As Chile circled, Jess stayed on her left flank. Jess was falling madly in love with this horse, a short, stout, heavily muscled little mare with a kind eye and two white socks. People who watched horse races and thought horses should be aquiline and sleek would find Chile ugly. Jess didn't. She was a classic foundation quarter horse, a cow horse. In his peripheral vision, he noted the slow progress of the car.

The Lexus crawled down the access road, the afternoon sun gleaming off the windshield and the chrome grille, the car slowing even more as it neared a cow and calf in the meadow, as if the driver expected the cattle to bolt across the road. There was only one way into the Rawlins Ranch from the state highway, and the road ended at the ranch house.

Jess Rawlins was tall, stiff, all sharp angles: bony elbows and knees, prominent hawklike nose, pronounced cheekbones. The only thing soft about him, his wife Karen told him once, were his eyes and his heart, but not in a good way.

When the Lexus parked between his house and the barn and the driver's side door opened, Jess shot his first glance over while Chile circled. The man who climbed out was slim, well built, with thick blond hair and a bristly mustache. He was wearing khakis and a purple polo shirt that draped well on his frame. He looked like a golfer, Jess thought. No, worse. A Realtor.

Jess brought the coil of rope down sharply, and Chile stopped. Like all horses, it didn't take much to convince her to stop working. Jess liked the way she looked at him, though, waiting for the next command. Sometimes, horses could stare with contempt. Chile, though, respected him. He respected her back. He thought, *We are going to have a long relationship, Chile and me.*

Jess waited for the man to approach the round pen. Then he heard it again, two distinct *pops* from far up the valley. Gunshots. Not an unusual sound at all in North Idaho, where everyone had guns.

The man—his name was Brian Ballard, Jess recognized him from his photo in the real estate pages of the newspaper—appeared not to hear the gunshots. Instead, he stopped on the other side of the railing and put a tasseled loafer on the lower rail and draped his arms over the top rail. As he did it, Jess's eyes slid from Brian Ballard to the Lexus and saw the profile of the passenger inside for the first time. It was her, all right.

"How's it going, Mr. Rawlins?" Ballard asked with false good cheer. "I see you're training a horse there."

"Groundwork," Jess said. "I have to hand it to the new breed of horse trainers out there who stress groundwork above all. They know their stuff, and they're right." He looked over at Brian Ballard: "What do you want?"

Ballard smiled and his eyebrows arched and his mouth pursed. He was uncomfortable, despite the smile. "I don't know much about horses. I'm allergic to them."

"Too bad."

"I'm Brian Ballard, but I guess you know that."

"I do."

"I'm pleased to meet you, finally," Ballard said, nodding toward Jess. "This is a pretty place, all right."

Jess didn't move.

"I saw Herbert Cooper in town this morning. He said you had to lay him off at the ranch."

Herbert Cooper had worked for Jess for thirteen years. The day before, Jess had to tell his longtime foreman that he couldn't pay his wages anymore, that there was not enough income for both bank loan payments and an employee. It was one of the hardest things Jess had ever had to do, and he hadn't slept well. Plus, it was calving season, and he was now on his own.

Jess noticed Ballard looking at Chile. Jess could tell what he was thinking, and it made him angry.

"This horse came to me as payment for leasing out a quarter section for grazing," Jess said, wishing he hadn't said it. There was no need to justify himself, certainly not to this man.

"Oh."

Jess nodded toward the Lexus. "I see Karen in there. She put you up to this?"

Ballard looked back as if confirming it was Karen in his car, even though he knew it was. It took a moment for Ballard to turn back to Jess.

"Let's leave her out of this, if you don't mind. There's no reason you and I can't be gentlemen about this."

Jess said, "There are plenty of reasons. So why don't you get back in your car and get the hell off of my ranch?"

"That's not necessary," Ballard said, his eyes almost pleading. Jess felt sorry for him for a moment. Then it passed.

"You can get out the same way you came in," Jess said. "Remember to close the gate."

"Look," Ballard said, showing Jess the palms of his hands. "Everybody knows the situation out here. It's a struggle, a real hard struggle. You had to let Herbert go, and everybody else is"—he searched for the right word and came up with a wrong one—"*gone*. I've been sending you offers for months now, and you know my reputation. I'm a fair man, and in this case more than generous. I was hoping we could have a discussion man-to-man, feelings aside."

Jess paused, felt his chest tighten. He looked down at his hand and saw that his fingers were white from gripping the lunging rope so tightly that it hurt.

"To have a man-to-man discussion," Jess said, "you need two men. So we're out of luck in your department. I've asked you twice to leave. If I have to say it a third time, it'll be from behind the sights of my Winchester."

Ballard's mouth opened as if to speak, but nothing came out. Jess glared at him, heat rising. Then he took a step forward in order to tie Chile up to the rail. When he moved, Ballard flinched and took his foot off the rail.

"You don't need to threaten me. I can buy this place from you or I can wait and buy it from the bank."

"Git," Jess said.

Brian Ballard backed up, then turned. He said over his shoulder,

"You're making a mistake, Jess. I'll be more than fair, I told you that."

Jess tied up Chile and watched Ballard walk toward his Lexus. He saw Karen turn in her seat toward Ballard as he opened the door. Jess could tell what she was saying by the tilt of her head. He heard Ballard say, "No. You tell him if that's what you want."

Ballard swung into the vehicle and made a U-turn in the gravel, and Jess watched the car drive away for a while up the hill on the access road. It took him a few minutes before his hands stopped trembling.

"We need to get a saddle on you," he told Chile, running his hand along her stout neck.

JESS WATCHED them go over the back of the horse. The afterimage of Karen's profile seemed to hang in the dust whorls left by the tires.

So that was Brian Ballard, the man she left him for. The man she married after him.

He had not fought back when she announced she was leaving, said she had outgrown him and that he not only hadn't kept up but had regressed. Said that just being on the ranch with him made her claustrophobic. That he had to get past what had happened to their son. That he was an anachronism. How could he fight that?

Karen got their savings and the feed store in town, which she promptly sold. And she got the Lincoln and his horse. Sold them, too.

Jess kept the ranch.

THE TREK up the hill and through the timber to the mailbox seemed longer than it ever had, he thought, and his legs felt heavier. For years, Jess never got the mail. Herbert or Margie did it, or another ranch hand, or his wife Karen did it. She used to love to get the mail. Later, he found out why.

To make matters worse, it seemed that more often than not he ran into Fiona Pritzle, the woman who had the rural mail route, at his mailbox. She was a vicious gossip, he thought, the woman who had spread the word when his wife left, and for whom. Fiona would feign concern for his health and well-being, and try to pump him for news and information. Had he heard from his ex-wife? Did he know she had moved back to town? Was it true the ranch was in trouble? So when he heard a vehicle coming up the road, he stopped in the wet foliage. There had been a time when there was little traffic on the road, and Jess knew everyone on it.

In fact, there was a time, in Pend Oreille County, when everybody knew Jess Rawlins and Jess knew everyone else. That was when the lumber mills were running and the silver mines were hiring. It was rough, isolated, fiercely rugged country then, and the people who lived there were subjugated by the mountains, the weather, the deep forests, the isolation, and the unenlightened corporations who came there to extract everything they could, including the goodwill and civility of their employees. The profligate, rough-and-tumble wildness of the environment and atmosphere beat people down. The exception were people like Jess, families like the Rawlinses, who had come from poor stock themselves but managed to build an enterprise—the Rawlins Ranch—rather than simply remove commodities to be shipped elsewhere. They built their own legacy, and by doing it moved up in status and respectability. Unlike the logging company managers and mining executives who were sent to the Idaho panhandle from places like Pennsylvania and West Virginia to do their time and to take as much as they could ruthlessly and efficiently as possible so they could put in for a transfer to a more hospitable post, the Rawlinses built a bulwark and established a heritage that was shared and celebrated.

Jess grew up feeling like a local hero. His grandfather and father had bequeathed the mantle of exceptionalism; that he was of the people, not better than them, but he had a special *something* because his name was Rawlins. The exceptionalism was a result of hard work, honest but tough business dealings, and high moral character.

The Rawlins Ranch was all the more admirable because North Idaho was not optimal cattle country. There were too many trees, not enough prairie and pasture. It rained too much. Unlike the vast ranches to the south or in bordering states Montana, Wyoming, and eastern Oregon, the Rawlins Ranch had to be carved out of the forest and managed carefully like a temperamental machine. They couldn't just let cattle go to forage for themselves for months, like ranchers could do in more wide-open country. If they did, the cattle got lost in the timber. So they moved their herds from park to park, plateau to plateau, keeping careful count. The rain and lushness of the terrain invited hoof-rot and disease born of moisture, so the cattle needed to be inspected and handled more than usual. Jess's grandfather had established the procedure for counting, moving, and inspecting his cattle. From Washington State he'd bought seed bulls who were bred for wet ground and heavy snow. The quality of Rawlins beef became widely praised, and the ranch prospered due to its management. The high price of beef helped, too.

Jess, like his father and grandfather, felt proprietary toward the valley, the community, and the ranch. After serving in the Army, he had no doubt, ever, that he would return. Which he did.

Jess often wondered if he had made the right choice, knowing what he knew now. He also wondered if he'd been the catalyst for things to come, for the decline. Had the spark of exceptionalism died in him? He'd been unable to pass along the sense of eminence he had always felt.

Maybe, he thought, it had just played out.

FIONA PRITZLE, behind the wheel of her little yellow Datsun pickup, had a stern, pinched look on her face until she saw him. The change in her demeanor was instantaneous, though for Jess her self-focused scowl remained as an afterimage, even when she stopped at his mailbox and climbed out and grinned at him. How did she know when he would be there, he wondered? *He* didn't even know from day to day. Fiona had a wide, pockmarked face obscured by heavy makeup. A cloud of perfume was released into the air when she climbed out, and she leaned over the top of the hood, fanning his mail across it as if laying down a winning hand of cards, smiling at him with nice teeth, her best feature. He had, of course, noticed that in the last few months she had been dressing better, putting her hair up, adding lipstick to her mouth. Apparently, she now felt the need not just to deliver his mail but to oversee it.

"Catalogs," she said, "three of 'em today. Two for women's clothing, so you're still on their list even though they don't know . . ."

He looked at her grimly.

"And a property tax notice, again," she said in her little-girl voice, eyeing him suspiciously. "I know I've delivered a couple of these to you already."

He nodded, nothing more.

"Jess, I saw Herbert in town."

"He moved to town," Jess said.

"He waved, but he didn't stop. Is something wrong?"

Damn, he thought. But he repeated, "Just moved to town."

She looked at him suspiciously, then gathered up his mail in a stack and handed it to him.

"This road is getting busy," she said. "I almost rear-ended a vehicle back there when I came around the corner."

He raised his eyebrows, hoping his lack of response would signal her to go away. She had designs on him, he knew. He was over women, though.

"A Cadillac Escalade with three men in it. They were barely crawling down the road, looking into the trees."

He shrugged.

"Brand-new Idaho plates. Probably more transplants."

"There's a lot of them moving up here," he said.

"Most of them are retired cops from L.A.," she said, lowering her voice conspiratorially. "I've heard that there's more than two hundred of them overall, and about a dozen on my route alone."

"How do you know that?"

She puffed up. "I put the pension checks in their mailboxes, and police newsletters, things like that. Some of them meet me every day, like you. A couple of real nice guys, real personable. But some of them are just like hermits or something. Like they don't want to mix with somebody like me. If it wasn't for their mail, I don't know if they'd ever come out of their houses. They call North Idaho 'Blue Heaven' at the LAPD. Did you know that?"

Herbert had told him that, but he didn't want to bring it up. Jess didn't object to the idea of ex-policemen moving in. In fact, if he had to choose the kind of people to move into the valley—not that he *had* a choice—he would have opted for retired police officers. It seemed to him that ex-cops were similar to the original settlers, men like his grandfather. They had been workingmen in crowded cities with blue-collar backgrounds. After years of dealing with the dark underbelly of crowded conditions and the worst of civilization, they'd opted to move to fresh, green country where they could be left alone. *Better ex-cops than actors or dot-com heirs,* he thought. The kind who came in, took over, and transformed the place. There were some of them, for sure. Too many for Jess's taste.

"Hundreds," she said. "Buying up everything. But it sort of makes you feel safer, doesn't it?"

Jess said nothing. She went on, "But I don't like the way some of them keep to themselves, you know? Like they think they're better than everybody else. Why did they move here if they just wanted to keep to themselves? They could have moved anywhere for that. You'd think they'd want to be friendlier, you know, since a lot of them are divorced and all. I mean: *Here I am!*" She did a clumsy little twirl that made Jess cringe. "One of them might steal me away from you, Jess Rawlins, if they pulled their heads out of their butts long enough to, you know, look around. . . ."

Enough, he thought. Seeing Karen had filled him with darkness. He didn't want to talk with Fiona Pritzle, but he didn't want to be rude, either.

"I better get back," he said, gesturing toward his mail as if he couldn't wait to read through it.

"You wouldn't believe how many retirement checks and LAPD newsletters I deliver these days," she said, repeating herself. "They're all up and down this road."

"Then you better get after it," he said cheerfully.

She reacted as if he'd slapped her. "Just being neighborly," she huffed. "I guess I caught you in one of your moods, Jess."

He didn't like it when she used his first name, or that she studied his mail before she gave it to him. She was too familiar with him, he thought. She should be more professional.

Her back tires spit gravel as she roared away. *Maybe if I pick up my mail at night?* he wondered.

He had turned back to his road when he heard another vehicle coming. She was right about the traffic. He looked over his shoulder and saw a red pickup with a male driver. Jess didn't know him. As he passed, the driver appeared to be talking to someone or something in the passenger seat or on the floor, but Jess saw no passengers, and no dog. He waved at the driver, but the driver didn't wave back. These new ones didn't wave back.

As he walked down the hill toward his ranch house, he listened to the silence and the soft watery sound of a breeze in the treetops. He heard no more shots.

Friday, 4:45 P.M.

EDUARDO VILLATORO pressed his nose against the window of the Southwest Airlines flight to Spokane from Los Angeles, via Boise. Below him was an ocean of green broken up only by lozenge-shaped lakes that reflected the sky, and snowcapped mountains that rose in the distance, the tops of the peaks at eye level as the 737 descended. He had only seen so much green once in his life, years before, when he had flown to El Salvador to bring back his mother. But that was jungle, and this was not, and El Salvador had silvery roads slicing through the green and an ocean holding it in, and he could see no roads, and that realization began to create anxiety in him that was only released, slightly, when squares and circles of farmland finally appeared and the flight attendant asked the passengers to put their tray tables in the full-upright and locked position.

He had been keenly aware as he boarded the connecting flight in Boise that he was the only passenger wearing a suit, even though it was his old, lightweight brown one. He had removed his tie on board, folded it neatly, and put it in his pocket. The other passengers, mostly young families and retirees, seemed to pay no attention to him, but in a deliberate way. He was very aware of *them,* and it took him a while to realize why. *He was the only person on the plane who wasn't Anglo.* This phenomenon was new to him, and he couldn't decide what he thought about it. A big part of his success in his career had always been that he didn't stand out. This allowed him to study the people around him and the situations they were in without being observed himself. The last thing he could be called was exotic or flashy, not where he came from. This wholly white world might be a little tough to blend into.

He raised his arm and shot his cuff to look at his new gold watch. He was grateful he didn't need to reset the time, since Spokane was Pacific time as well. He didn't yet know how his watch worked. There were several knobs and buttons, and he assumed he would need to work a combination of them to reset the time, date, alarm, and other functions if he needed to. The dial would light up at night, someone pointed out to him. Unfortunately, he had left the instructions for the watch in the packaging it came in, after he'd opened it and slipped it on to the apparent delight of his former coworkers, who clapped while he did so. They had all contributed to buy the retirement gift, and Celeste, his longtime partner, had taken it to a jeweler to have the back inscribed:

FOR 30 YEARS OF SERVICE

WHILE WAITING for his two bags to arrive on one of three carousels in the airport, Villatoro continued to study the people around him. Families had rejoined, and there was excited chatter. A soldier in desert fatigues had returned from Iraq, greeted by balloons, hand-drawn posters, and his extended family. Villatoro nodded at him, said, "Thank you for your service." The marine nodded back.

If Villatoro were to characterize the residents in a general way, he would say they were plainspoken and blunt. Flinty, maybe. He noted how many of the men wore cowboy hats and big buckles and pointed boots, and how it looked like clothing on them and not a costume. Women and children wore bright colors and opened their mouths wide when they talked, as if it didn't matter to them if anyone heard their conversations. As the bags began to spit out onto the carousel, he saw the flashing of their clear blue eyes.

At the rental car counter, a boy with moussed hair and a starched white shirt and tie told him the company could upgrade his reservation from a compact to a midsize for only five dollars more a day.

"No thank you."

"But it looks like you'll be in the area for a week," the boy said, looking at the reservation on his computer monitor. "You might be more comfortable in a larger car. I'm sure your company would understand."

"No," Villatoro said. "There is no company. I'm retired, as of two days ago. The compact, please."

The boy looked hurt. Villatoro could see a blackboard in the office behind the counter that listed all of the employees by name with check marks to indicate how many upgrades they'd sold. He looked at the boy's name tag, saw his name was Jason, and saw that Jason was leading the pack.

"Arcadia, California," Jason said as he keyed Villatoro's license number and address into the computer. "Never heard of it."

"It's a small town," Villatoro said. "About fifty thousand people."

"Is it near L.A.?"

Villatoro smiled bitterly. "It was swallowed by L.A. like a snack."

The boy didn't know how to answer that, and Villatoro wished he hadn't said it. Too much information.

Jason said, "You wouldn't believe how many folks from L.A. we rent to."

"Really?" Villatoro said.

"A ton of them have moved up here," Jason said, pushing the button to print out the contract. "Have you ever been here before?"

"Spokane?" Villatoro said.

Jason corrected his pronunciation, "It's 'Spoke-Ann,' Mr. Villatoro, not 'Spoke-Cain.' "

"And it's 'Vee-Ah-Toro,' not 'VILLA-toro,' " Villatoro said back, smiling.

WITH HIS KEYS and an agreement for a red Ford Focus in his hand, Villatoro started to pull his bags through the door to the rental lot but stopped until Jason looked over.

"May I please get a map to Kootenai Bay?"

"I'm sorry," Jason said, tearing one off a pad and using a highlighter pen to mark the route. "It's easy. You just take a right out of the airport and follow the signs to I-90 East."

"Thank you," Villatoro said.

Jason handed him the map and a thick, four-color real estate booklet. "I assume you're looking for property."

"No," Villatoro said, taking the booklet anyway, "I'm here on business."

"Really? What do you do? I thought you said you were retired?"

"I am," Villatoro said, not really lying, just not telling the entire story. The boy was more forward than he thought proper.

"Oh," Jason said, puzzled.

As he walked out onto the sun-baked lot, Villatoro thought he'd said half-again too much, and chastised himself.

VILLATORO POINTED his little red Ford Focus toward the mountains to the east and eased onto the interstate through tree-shrouded on-ramps. He passed a large sign and fountain that read:

WELCOME TO THE INLAND NORTHWEST

Spokane itself seemed surprisingly old and industrial, the downtown buildings rising out of the trees with a sense of purpose that had likely been forgotten, Villatoro thought. He saw an exit for Gonzaga University—he had heard of it, something about basketball—and another that said Coeur d'Alene, Idaho, was only fourteen miles away.

As he drove he pushed the scan button on the AM radio in the car. As it swept the stations, he heard snippets of Rush Limbaugh, Laura Schlesinger, Sean Hannity, Bill O'Reilly, and Mark Fuhrman, famous from the O. J. Simpson trial, who obviously had a local talk show. That discovery astonished him.

Acres of outlet malls marked his entrance into Idaho, as well as strip malls that looked just like the strip malls in L.A., with the same fast-food places and convenience stores. He had replaced palm trees with pine trees, but this was all familiar. In a way, he was relieved.

But when he turned north at Coeur d'Alene, the strip malls thinned, and the forest seemed to shoulder its way back toward the road, as if to intimidate the drivers, he thought. It certainly worked with him. Forty miles later, the trees broke, and he was on a long bridge crossing a huge lake, the sun streaming through the windshield with an intensity he wasn't used to. On the other side of the lake, twinkling through a pine forest, was the town of Kootenai Bay, and beyond that, thirty-five miles north, was Canada.

THE DOWNTOWN was small, the vestige of another era, when it was more of a railroad outpost than what it had become. The primary route into Kootenai Bay stretched three tree-covered blocks, then ended with a sharp turn to the left. Old brick buildings—none above two levels—sported signs for snowboards, espresso, bicycling, fishing, real estate. He turned right, away from downtown, dipped under a railroad trestle, and emerged on the lakefront near the Best Western where he had a reservation.

Pulling under a slumping veranda, he uncoiled from the small car and stretched, heard his spine pop with a sound like shuffling cards. The boy at the car rental counter had been right, he thought. A larger car would have been better for his back. As he entered the small lobby, he instinctively hit the remote control lock button on his key ring.

Three people were waiting to check in before him, two large men with crew cuts and a short, heavy woman with big hair and lime green shorts. All three held sixteen-ounce cans of Budweiser and spoke loudly, and he gathered they were in town for some kind of reunion. While he waited, Villatoro looked over the rack of real estate brochures near the door, and took several because they contained maps of the area. When the guests got their keys and left to find their rooms, Villatoro stepped up to the counter.

The check-in clerk was flustered from the three conventioneers, and she blew back a strand of graying hair away from her face and sighed loudly. "You'd think they'd put another person on the desk at check-in time, wouldn't you?" she said. "Especially when there's a Navy ship crew reunion in town."

He shrugged, and smiled. Checking in four guests didn't seem to be an exhausting task.

She nodded at the brochures he had picked up. She was in her late forties, he guessed, and had lived a hard life. Blooms of small threadlike veins mapped her cheeks. Alcohol. Nevertheless, she had an attractive, open face and smile.

She said, "A girlfriend of mine sold her house for $189,000 last week, and the guy who bought it resold it the next day, *the next day,* for $250,000."

"Goodness," Villatoro said.

"Damn right," she said, finding his reservation card. "Makes me wonder what my place is worth. I bought it for forty grand twenty-five years ago."

These people, he thought, talk to you like they've known you all their lives.

"Probably a lot," he said, thinking how familiar it sounded. His own community was filled with tales like that, as longtime homeowners sold their homes to new residents for three or four times what they had originally paid.

"Business or pleasure?" she asked, looking up at him. He felt her eyes sweep over his wrinkled brown suit, his cream-colored shirt, his olive skin.

"Business," he said.

"What kind of business?" she asked pleasantly.

"Unfinished business," he said, a little amused at how it sounded.

"Sounds interesting and mysterious." She laughed. "Come on, fess up."

He felt his face flush. "I'm retired," he said. He was still having trouble actually saying it without being self-conscious. It reminded him of the weeks after his wedding thirty-two years ago, when he stumbled as he introduced Donna as "my wife." It just didn't sound natural at the time, just as retirement didn't sound natural now.

"How long?"

He flushed. "Two days. I was a police detective in Arcadia, California." As soon as he said it he didn't know why he had volunteered the information.

"You have a badge and a gun?" she asked, making conversation.

"Not anymore." He was very conscious of not having either. Like he was walking around without pants. Not that he'd ever drawn his gun, except at the range.

She scribbled something on the reservation card. "You held this with a credit card," she said. "You want to keep it on that card?"

"Yes," he said.

"Do you have a real estate agent yet? I can recommend a couple of good ones."

"Excuse me?"

She looked at him. "I assume you're looking for a house or land up here. You don't need to sneak around. Half of the guests who stay here are looking to buy and retire. And believe me, not all of the real estate agents are trustworthy. There are some real crooks, and they don't care if you're a cop. Or an ex-cop. They're used to ex-cops, believe you me."

"I'm not interested in retiring here," Villatoro said, somewhat defensively.

"Hmmm." She clearly wasn't sure she believed him. "Mr. Mysterious, you are."

"No one ever said that before."

"You seem like a nice guy. How about I cut you a deal, then," she said, almost whispering. "I'll give you the AAA rate instead of the rack rate. Saves you $20 a night."

He wanted to refuse. But $20 a night for six nights would be helpful. "Thank you," he said.

"You bet, Mr. Villatoro."

She pronounced it "VILLA-torro."

IN HIS ROOM, which was on the lower of two floors, Villatoro opened his curtains and looked out. While the hotel itself was tired and dowdy, the view was magnificent. Through a sliding glass door was a lawn that led to a beach, and a marina half-filled with boats. The lake was smooth as a tabletop all the way to the mountains on the other side that were white with snow. The afternoon rain clouds opened up, and columns of sun lined up across the horizon. He expected an orchestra to swell at the sight.

He dug in his pocket for his cell phone and powered it up. He had forgotten to turn it back on after the airplane landed, to check for messages. Maybe something from his wife, he hoped.

There was no signal. He had not even considered this possibility. He tossed the phone on the dresser.

He turned and looked around his room. Nothing special. A television, two double beds with worn bedspreads, a telephone on the desk with a phone book no bigger than a quality paperback beside it. Faded prints of elk, deer, and geese were on the walls.

Sitting on the too-soft bed, he opened his briefcase. After placing the hinged photos of his wife and daughter on the bed stand, he pulled out a manila file and laid it near the pillow. The file was two inches thick, the edges worn, the tab stained by his own fingerprints. The writing on the tab was smeared, but he remembered sitting at his desk, eight years before, and inscribing:

SANTA ANITA RACETRACK
Case File: 90813A

This is what had brought him to Kootenai Bay. This was the unfinished business. This is what had imposed such a strain on his marriage and family and the last few years in the department. The file contained the black cloud that loomed over him, blocking sunshine, preventing him from truly retiring and starting his new life.

Eduardo Villatoro got up and went to the sliding glass door and looked out on the lake and across it to the mountains. What a different world it was than the one he had left that morning. He could not imagine fitting into this world, or wanting to. He *wished* he still had his badge and gun.

Friday, 5:30 P.M.

"THEY SHOULD BE home by now," Monica Taylor said to Tom, who had just come into the kitchen from the living room where he was furtively watching an NBA game with playoff implications. He was wearing his brown UPS uniform shirt untucked over dark shorts. He had muscular legs that were already tan, she noticed. She wished, though, that he didn't shave them. But he had explained that it was what bodybuilders had to do before a competition: shave, wax, and oil.

Tom stopped on his way to the refrigerator and looked at the digital clock on the stove. It said 5:30. He shrugged, opened the refrigerator door. The look of absolute alarm on his face mirrored her own, but for a different reason, and he said, "What, no beer? Do I have to go get some?"

"It's going to be dark in two hours," she said, wiping her hands on a paper towel. "I wonder if I should call somebody."

Three place settings were on the table. Lasagna—Annie's favorite—was baking in the oven. The kitchen smelled of garlic, oregano, tomato sauce, and cheese. Tom had pointed out that she needed another plate. "No," she said, "I don't."

Against her better judgment, she'd let him in the house when he showed up after work and said he was there to apologize for not leaving early that morning. He said when he got up he didn't want to leave. He was trying to flatter her.

He was good at flattering her. That was part of the problem—she liked being flattered, even when she knew better. She'd first heard about Tom when she started work as the manager of her store. The three women who worked the registers out front tittered like schoolgirls when they described the UPS man. His arrival at three-thirty was the highlight of their afternoon, they said. Monica learned why. He was tall, well built, charming, chatty, and single. As he carried the shipments in through the back door, he made a point of flirting with each of the women in turn, complimenting them on their clothes and hair, telling them it looked like they'd lost weight. Monica was on to his act instantly, but she admired his endless good cheer, undeniable charm, and transparent élan, which he soon turned full force on her. Although she tried to deny to herself what she was doing, she found herself checking her hair and lipstick to make sure both were in order before three-thirty. She didn't object when he lingered after his delivery, engaging her in small talk, offering to help stack boxes, move displays, or shovel snow from the sidewalk. Once, he caught a bat that had somehow gotten into the storeroom and impressed her by releasing it outside, unharmed. When the employees on the registers started gossiping about the amount of time Tom was spending in the store, Monica asked him to stick to business. He would, he told her, if he just wasn't so darned attracted to her. When she said she had kids at home, he said he liked kids, and would love to meet them, and hey, how about dinner sometime? That was four months and a dozen dinners ago. Her eyes were open the whole time, until last night, when she deliberately closed them, looked away, and allowed herself a soft moan.

Tom shut the refrigerator door and turned toward her with his arms crossed. His forearms were massive. "I wouldn't worry so much," he said. "When I was growing up here people didn't worry so much. I remember staying out after school fishing, shooting hoops, generally fucking around, until all hours. I'd get home when I got home. If I missed dinner, well, that was my fault. Now, it's a damned federal case if kids just get out of sight for a minute."

"Are you talking about me?" she asked.

He started to say yes, she could tell. But he caught himself. "No, not necessarily. I just mean people in general. Everyone's so goddamned paranoid. We live in such a nanny state now. If a kid is late getting home from school, they put out an Amber Alert. It didn't used to be like this around here. We trusted each other, you know? It pisses me off, is all. She's probably just staying away to make a point," Tom said. "She's a prickly little number."

"Tom," Monica said, measuring her words, "Annie and William had early release today. They should have been home at two if they couldn't go fishing with you."

Something washed over him, the look of a guilty man.

"What?" she asked. "You showed up at the school, didn't you? I assumed they weren't there."

Tom took a deep breath, closed his eyes. "We had two guys out sick today, so they gave me extra routes. I was busier than hell. I guess I forgot."

Monica's face tightened.

"I said 'maybe,'" he pleaded. "I didn't promise anything."

"William thought you did."

He shrugged. "Things happen, Monica."

Monica had spent the day at work in a kind of stupor. All day, her throat felt constricted, and she excused herself to go to the back room and cry. She'd thought about calling the school, asking for Annie. She would explain what happened with Tom, but how could she possibly put it?

Your mom screwed up.

Your mom broke her word.

Your mom drank too much wine with Tom after you and William went to bed and invited him up to her bedroom. He swore he'd get up early and be out of the house by the time you and Willie got up. *He promised!*

But she could hear Annie reply that Monica had sworn she'd never let a man—a stranger—into the family unless it meant they'd really have a father. Annie didn't ask for the vow; Monica had volunteered it. Now she'd betrayed her own children with this man. How could she let herself do it? How could she ever fix things?

Annie was tough and smart beyond her years. The girl was grounded in bedrock and would forgive her eventually. But she wouldn't forget. Willie, though, poor Willie. This was the kind of thing that could scar a child, send him down the wrong path. A breach of trust was a serious thing. Dashed expectations were just as crippling. She'd give anything if only she could somehow erase Willie's memory of the morning when Tom joined them at the breakfast table.

And Tom's way of dealing with it was to say, "Things happen, Monica."

He was an idiot, and it would be easy to blame him for what had happened. But she was the one who'd brought him into their home.

"I need to be alone and wait for my children," she said. "They are probably the only thing I've ever done right."

He responded by visibly softening, and approached her, wrapping his arms around her. She remained stiff, refusing to give in to his physicality. With his grip on the back of her head, he pushed her onto his hard shoulder.

"I'm sorry, honey," he said, cooing into her hair. "They're your kids, so they're important to me, too. Of course you're worried about them."

"I'm sorry, too, Tom," she said. Sorry she'd ever met him.

As he hugged her she opened her eyes and saw her reflection in the glass door of the microwave oven. She was still slim, blond, with oversized eyes and a wide mouth, and an overbite most men liked. She knew she didn't deserve her looks; she had done nothing to earn them. It was the fault of genetics that she looked ten years younger than she was. She wanted to push away and run somewhere. How could he not read her in the slightest?

Tom was talking, saying, "I'd like to think you consider me one of the things you've done right."

She didn't respond, hoped he wouldn't press her for an answer. He didn't.

"It's not often we're alone without your kids here, honey," he said. "We could, you know, use this time just for *us*."

Of course, she knew what he meant, but she couldn't believe he'd said it. She could feel him getting hard against her. He had moved his hips so his erection rubbed her abdomen.

She looked at the clock above the stove—5:45.

"Tom . . ."

He didn't let go.

"Tom," she said, pushing away with more force than necessary, alarmed at the revulsion she felt for the same man who had been in her bed the night before, "why don't you go home now? I need to talk with Annie and William. You shouldn't be here. You've done enough for today."

A shadow passed over his face, and his eyes looked harder than she could ever remember them.

"Okay," he said, flat. "I'll get out of your sight."

She didn't correct him.

"This is all about not taking Willie fishing?" he asked. "Is that what this is about?"

What had she ever seen in him? she wondered. How could she have ever let his looks and steady job cloud the fact—the glaring fact—that he was a self-absorbed ass?

"Go," she said.

Tom rolled his eyes, started to say something, but stopped himself.

"Later, then," he said, heading toward the mudroom and the back door. "You know, it's hard to walk when you get me all riled up like this."

"Don't ever come back," Monica said, her tone flat. "It's over. It's so very over."

He snorted and shook his head in disbelief. "And I came here to apologize."

Turning back to the stove to check the lasagna, she said, "No, I don't think so." The cheese was bubbling and turning brown. She reduced the heat to keep it warm.

"Hey," Tom yelled from the mudroom. "That little bitch took my fishing rod and vest!" He filled the doorframe, his face red, his lovely mouth contorted.

"What?"

"That's a six-hundred-dollar Sage fly rod," he said. "I've got hundreds of dollars of flies in my vest. And the little bitch *took* it."

It was as if the two bulbs in the overhead light had been replaced with red ones. She looked at him through a curtain of deep crimson, thinking she had never seen such an ugly man before.

"Leave," she said, her voice rising into a screech, "and just keep going. Don't you *ever come back in my house!*"

"Oh, I'm coming back," he shouted. "I'm coming back for my rod and vest, goddammit."

"LEAVE!"

For a second, she thought he would come back in after her. But he stayed within the doorjamb, veins popping on his neck and at his temple. Without turning her head and looking, she noted the block of knives on the counter next to her hand.

"Monica," he said, "you're a pretty good fuck. Not great, but good. You've got a nice mouth. But you'll never get any man to stay around here as long as you've got that little bitch here. And that mama's boy, Willie."

It felt as if she had grabbed one of the knives and plunged it into her own chest. She gasped for air.

"GET OUT!" she screamed raggedly.

He shook his head, glaring at her, and went out the door, slamming it behind him.

She put her face in her hands and sobbed, calling him every name she could think of, feeling her heart break, terrified by the fact that she didn't know where her children were and she was utterly alone now.

Knowing it was her fault they were gone.

Friday, 6:15 P.M.

WHAT ANNIE had noticed first, as they'd driven up the road toward Mr. Swann's house, was the smell. Something ripe and bold coursed through the pine-scented air, and it got stronger as they neared his home in the thick trees. He had allowed them to get off the floor once he'd turned from the service road onto his private two-track drive, and Annie had seen what it was that made the odor: hogs.

"There's *my* family," Swann said, smiling. "They know Daddy's home."

"Look at the pigs," William said, leaning over Annie toward the open window of the pickup. "Man, they're excited."

When the hogs saw the red truck coming, they squealed and ran about in their pen, racing up and down a sloppy track, splashing through coffee-with-cream-colored puddles. Annie counted at least twenty hogs, maybe more. One was huge, tan and bristly, and looked to be the size of a small truck. She didn't know hogs could get that big.

"The big one's name is King," Swann said, winking as if he assumed she knew who King was, which she didn't. "I named him after a guy who gave us a lot of trouble once. King won me a blue ribbon at the Pend Oreille County Fair this summer."

"He's *awesome*," William said. "I bet he can eat a lot."

Annie had stopped trembling, although she still felt numb. She couldn't wrap her mind around what she and William had seen at the campsite. Was it possible the man who was shot was still alive? No, she thought, it wasn't. The image of those men standing over him and firing again and again would never leave her. The eyes of the Driver locking on to her own sent a spasm through her, even now.

"Are you okay?" William asked, feeling her shiver.

"Yes," she said, not interested in the hogs the way he was. How could he be interested in hogs after what had just happened? Boys were different, all right. Even William.

Swann had thumbed a remote control, and one of three garage doors had opened. Slowing to a crawl, he'd parked inside. Annie had started to open her door when Swann had said, "Wait just a minute."

She'd waited inside until the door had closed, and watched as Swann had walked back to the window in the garage door and looked down his road. Apparently satisfied that no one had followed them, he'd said, "Okay, you can come out now, kids."

SWANN'S HOME was clean and light, with one big room after another. It was as unlike her mother's house as it could be, Annie thought. He was alone, with his family of hogs, and except for the kitchen and the den, the house seemed not to be lived in at all. There were photos of Mr. Swann in his police uniform above the fireplace, and a framed set of medals and ribbons. Other than that, the walls were bare.

He opened a bag of cookies and poured two glasses of milk and set them on the table, saying, "I'm not used to much company way back here."

Annie wondered if her mother had ever been in the house before, when they were briefly together.

"Just stay here," Swann said. "I need to go make a couple of calls. Eat up. There's more milk in the fridge if you want it."

"Are you going to call our mother?" Annie asked, while William fished three cookies out of the bag.

Swann's expression darkened and became serious. "Not immediately," he said. "If those men figure out who you are—and they might real quickly—the first thing they'll do is go to your house. If your mother knows you're here, she'll probably tell them, or they'll make her tell them. Do you understand what I'm saying to you?"

Annie felt herself nod yes, felt the cold ball of fear knotting in her stomach again.

"I need to make a couple of calls," he said again. He was one of those adults who thought he had to overexplain and overenunciate, as if she and William were an alien species. "There are a couple of guys I know who might have a little bit of an idea what is going on. I don't want to put any of us in more danger than we are now, including your mother."

"Are you going to call the sheriff?" Annie asked. "They'll want to know what happened."

Swann looked at her for a few moments before answering. "After I get a little more information, I'll call the proper authorities," he said.

"I don't know what you mean," she said.

"You'll just have to trust me on this," he said, padding down the hallway to, she presumed, his office. She heard the door close, and the sound of a lock being thrown. *Why did he feel it was necessary to do that?* she wondered.

She turned back to her brother. "How can you eat?"

"I'm hungry," he said, spewing crumbs across the tabletop.

AFTER A few minutes, Annie left the table and washed her hands and face in the kitchen sink. As she dried her face with a dish towel, she looked out the window and watched the sun drop from beneath the clouds and flash a brilliant wink before plunging into the tops of the trees. It would be dark soon. She didn't want to be in Mr. Swann's house in the dark, but she wasn't sure why she felt that way.

The house was still and quiet, something their own home never was. She could hear the hogs grunting outside and the trill of a bird from somewhere in the shadows. Inside, there was only the rhythmic crunching of William finishing off another cookie.

"You should wash up, too," she told William, noticing how filthy his fingers were.

He shrugged a nonresponse and continued eating.

"Mr. Swann is nice," William said. "I'm happy he picked us up."

Annie nodded toward the photos above the fireplace in the living room. "He's a policeman, too."

"He probably has a few guns around here," William said. "I wonder if he'll show them to me?"

"Why do you want to see his guns?"

William arched his eyebrows. "Guns are cool."

Annie glared at him. "Didn't you see what guns did today? To that poor man?"

"That's why *we* need 'em. So that won't happen to us."

"Oh, brother." She didn't want to argue about this.

"I'm ready to go home, though," William said, sitting back. "When do you think he'll take us home?"

Annie looked down the hall at the closed door. "I don't know."

"Maybe we should knock," William said.

Annie shook her head. "I need to find the bathroom," she said.

"Hurry back," William called after her.

She paused at the closed office door as she went down the hall. She could hear Swann's voice inside. It was deep, but she couldn't make out any words, as if he were deliberately speaking softly.

The bathroom was at the end of the hallway. She turned on the lights and shut the door. Like the rest of the house, it was spare and spotless. The only thing on the wall was a fake old sign that said baths cost a nickel and shaves cost a dime. Even the towels were folded neatly and hung over the bar. She thought she could see why Mr. Swann and her mother probably hadn't gotten along.

She looked at herself in the mirror and was shocked at how pale and wild she looked. Her blond hair was tangled, with bits of leaves in it. Her eyes stared back from hollows. Her clothes were crusted with dried mud. There was a scratch across her cheek she didn't remember getting, and it hadn't hurt until just that second, when she saw it. Now it stung.

When she was through, Annie left the bathroom as quietly as she had entered it. Mr. Swann's bedroom was dark and large, and she peeked in. His bed was made neatly, and there were no clothes on the floor.

Even though she knew she shouldn't, she stepped into the room and looked around. The walls were bare except for several framed photos over a dresser. A phone was on a nightstand next to the bed, and she stared at it. What if he was talking to the sheriff? Or her mother?

The phone seemed to draw her, and she put her hand on the receiver. She knew it was wrong, but she wanted to know who he was talking to. As slowly as she could, she lifted the receiver and covered the mouthpiece with her hand.

"You've got him with you now?" Swann asked someone.

"Wrapped up tight," the other man said. "Leakproof packaging."

Swann chuckled nervously.

Who was this, Annie wondered. What did it have to do with anything?

"Everybody's with you?" Swann asked.

"Almost," the man said. "I'm waiting on Gonzo to get back."

"I hope he doesn't take too long. I don't know how long I can keep them entertained."

Annie's eyes shot open wide. *Keep them entertained.*

"Yeah, I know. Wait, I think I see his car now."

"Good."

"Yeah, it's him. We're ready."

"Let's get this over with, then," Swann said. "This is bad, you know?"

"I know. Newkirk is wavering on us. He looks like he's about to shit."

"I don't blame him."

"That was a good move, taking them home with you. God help us if some citizen saw us on the road with them."

Annie eased the phone down and hung it up, which was difficult because her hand was trembling.

She realized when she looked up that her eyes had adjusted to the dark of the room. She could see the photos above the dresser, and she approached them. More shots of Mr. Swann in his police uniform, another of him on a fishing boat somewhere on the ocean or a big lake, and another of a group of men, fellow police officers. She looked carefully at it, and her heart began to race.

Mr. Swann stood in the middle of a group of five men. They had their arms around each other, and several had big grins. But not the Dark Man, who scowled. Singer, the Driver, stared at the camera with the same ice-blue intensity she had seen in his eyes at the campsite. The Ball Cap Man grinned. And the Wavy-Haired Man who had been killed that afternoon looked to be laughing so hard his face was blurred in the photo.

As she ran down the hallway she heard the office door being unlocked by Mr. Swann.

William saw her coming. Luckily, he had left the table and was standing next to the door. He was obviously surprised to see her running so fast, and there must have been something in her face because his eyes widened and his mouth contorted into the look he got before he started to cry.

"Let's go," she hissed at him. *"Run!"*

He didn't argue but threw open the door to the garage. Annie slammed it behind her. She heard Mr. Swann holler "HEY! Where are you going?" from down the hallway.

The garage was completely dark except for the nine blue squares of the garage door windows. She didn't know where the button was for the garage door opener but saw a faint pink glow next to the doorjamb and pushed it. A dull light came on, and the middle door began to open.

"Go!" she yelled, and the two of them ran toward the opening and rolled under it as it rose.

"Stop!" Mr. Swann threw open the door to the garage and snapped on the overhead lights. "Get back here, now!" he yelled after them.

It was raining again. Annie had William's hand, and they ran past the hog pens. A huge mass blasted out of the shadows and hurled itself against the fence and squealed—King—causing them both to veer away and plunge into the dark brush.

As they ran, climbing over downed logs and pushing through bushes that clawed back at them, Annie could hear Mr. Swann shouting back at the house.

"Stop running from me! You'll get lost out there! Get back here, now! I talked to your mother! Everything's okay, *she's coming to get you!*"

"Annie . . ." William gasped, winded.

"He's lying," she answered, not stopping. "He's friends with those men we saw today."

William said something she couldn't understand. It sounded more like an animal noise. He was crying. She stopped and turned to hug him.

"No . . ." he said, pushing her away.

She reached out and grabbed him, holding his thin shoulders in her hands, thrusting her face into his. "William, I heard him talking to them, those men we saw today. Mr. Swann is friends with them. They're on their way up here to find us because we saw them kill that man today. We can't trust *anybody*, do you understand?"

He started to argue but looked away. "I just want to go home," he said in a little-boy voice that stabbed her in the heart.

"We can't go home yet," she said. "That's where they'll look for us first. That's the one thing Mr. Swann told us that wasn't a lie."

"Where do we go, then?"

She pulled him close, wrapping her arms around him, speaking into his ear. "As far away from here as we can get."

Friday, 10:30 P.M.

"OKAY," Ex-Lt. Eric Singer said to Dennis Gonzalez and Jim Newkirk at the rear table in the Sand Creek Bar. "At least we know who they are."

Their names were Annie and William Taylor. Newkirk would rather he didn't know their names because it made what they were trying to do so much more personal.

The Sand Creek Bar was a dark, close, run-down local place just out of Kootenai Bay on the old highway, the kind of place silver miners and loggers used to stop at on their way home. It was a good place for the men to regroup. It had seen better days and stood as a remnant of an earlier time. Now, there were just a few vehicles outside in the gravel parking lot, two pickups and a UPS truck. The Sand Creek offered three kinds of beer on tap—Coors, Bud, and Widmer Hefeweizen from Oregon. Anything else was considered exotic and would be served in dusty bottles from the back. The ceiling bristled with hundreds of knives that had been hurled up there over the years into the sooty paneled wood. Seventy years' worth of pocket knives, hunting knives, fishing knives, survival knives. A few rusty bayonets and an ax in the corner. Occasionally, a knife would drop and stick into a tabletop, the floor, or a drinker's thigh. Newkirk had been told by local friends that the credo of the Sand

Creek was "Drink hard and fast because you never know when you might get cut and die," a maxim that applied to the general atmosphere of North Idaho's rough-and-tumble blue-collar past as well. He'd been there previously a couple of times with his softball team, but Singer and Gonzalez had not. Those two never went anywhere. When he was with them, Newkirk served as their guide even though he hadn't been in the area any longer than either of them.

They'd spent the last three and a half hours patrolling the state highways and old logging roads near Oscar Swann's house, looking for a sign of Annie and William Taylor. They'd found nothing. The timber was so thick and dark in places, they couldn't see into it, even with their spotlight. Some stands were old and dense, so crowded with tree trunks a man would have to turn sidewise to enter and walk through. Those kids could be anywhere in the forest and were small enough to be able to speed through it like rabbits. They would be impossible to find—unless they could have caught them on the move near a road. Swann had shown them their tracks near his pen of hogs, but the pine needles were so thick a quarter mile from his place that the tracks wouldn't hold. They could be anywhere, those kids.

Singer had a police scanner in his SUV, and as they patrolled the forest near Swann's they'd listened to the sheriff's dispatcher. Monica Taylor had called repeatedly. The dispatcher told a deputy of the calls from the mother saying her children weren't home yet from school. The calls were treated as routine, the assumption was the kids would likely show up later that night. There was no sense of urgency yet.

Newkirk felt numb, as if he weren't really there. He was tired, dirty, hungry. He hadn't been home all day. The first glass of beer from the pitcher Gonzalez had brought to the table affected him on an empty stomach. He poured another and topped up Singer's and Gonzalez's glasses. The beer tasted crisp and good.

"This is a critical time," Singer said, keeping his voice low, "before all hell breaks loose. If those kids stop someone for a ride or show up at a house . . ."

"We're fucked," Gonzalez said, finishing the sentence for his former boss.

"Yes."

"Where could they be?" Newkirk asked.

Singer and Gonzalez simply stared at him, as they did whenever he asked an unanswerable question.

"The sheriff probably won't take it seriously until tomorrow," Singer said. "He'll give it some time. It's obvious they think those kids will show up at home tonight."

That was why he'd ordered Swann to go into town and stake out the Taylor house. Swann knew where they lived and could contact Singer via cell phone if the kids showed up. So far, there had been no call.

"I think they're hunkered down in the woods," Gonzalez said. "There's a lot of country out there to get lost in. Nothing but trees all the way to Canada."

While they'd patrolled, Gonzalez had kept remarking on the absence of houses, the lack of lights back in the forest. It struck Newkirk as an odd observation, but understandable given the circumstances. Gonzalez and Singer kept to themselves. They rarely ventured out of their trophy homes, and made it a point not to get to know their neighbors. The thick forest insulated them from human interaction, and their locked gates kept out passersby. Both lived in woodland fortresses with satellite television and Internet, wells for water, backup power generators at the ready. The only time they went to town was to transact necessary business—banking, groceries, whatever—and get back. They socialized with each other and the other ex-cops who'd come up together. Newkirk was different, and proud of it. He was the youngest of them, was married, and had kids at home. Two boys and a girl, all involved in school and sports. Newkirk and Maggie had met other parents, other families. They traveled to soccer and basketball games with locals, had gotten to know and like some of them. Newkirk liked to think of it as "making an effort." In a sense, he felt he was the only one of the ex-officers who actually *lived* here. The others were strangers by choice, although Swann was known to roam around town occasionally. Not Singer or Gonzalez. That's why they were always asking him where to find things, like the Sand Creek Bar.

Newkirk often thought bitterly that Singer and Gonzalez, by keeping to themselves the way they did, could create unwanted suspicion. It was as if they were bunkered in their hilltop mansions, looking down on everyone below them. Especially Singer, who rarely ventured out. It was as if he'd done his time with the human race and had no more use for it. And while people up here minded their own business, they didn't like being held in contempt—they wanted to be liked. Newkirk, for his part, found himself liking them, getting along. Singer, by holding himself above them, could create unnecessary animosity. It just hadn't happened yet.

"So what the fuck do we do?" Gonzalez asked Singer.

"Just let me think," Singer said.

After taking his baseball cap off, running his fingers through his hair, and putting it back on, Newkirk watched Singer. Singer was the man in charge. The lieutenant was the most icily efficient commander Newkirk had ever served under, even in the Army. Singer was the man the department turned to when a case was spiraling in the wrong direction. The man was a fixer, the guy you brought in when a situation had turned into a cluster fuck. Singer brought his calm with him, but the downside of his façade was that palpable feeling of something tightly coiled up just beneath the skin, like a high-tension spring that continued to wind tighter, capable of being released with a snap to strike out like a serpent's head. Newkirk had seen that happen twice and never wanted to see it again. Singer was preternaturally unflusterable, his voice rarely over a whisper. He was the kind of guy who got quieter and colder the worse things got, as if his concentration alone would cut a swath of reason through chaos; that only he was capable of thinking with clarity. Thing was, he was right. When Singer was in charge, like he was now, he was a marvel to watch. There were no wasted motions, no wasted words. He absorbed the vagaries of the situation, processed them, then flicked out commands and expected them to be obeyed. He missed nothing. But there was a profound deep-seated bitterness in Singer, and Newkirk had been there, on the LAPD, as it happened.

There had been a minor scandal, one of many, within the department. That particular one involved the loss of impounded vehicles. Several vocal inner-city leaders had complained to an on-the-make television news reporter that cops were taking or selling cars owned by racial minorities that had been impounded due to traffic violations. The station led with the story for four nights straight, and Singer was assigned the interdepartmental investigation. He determined that the people at fault weren't officers but city contractors charged with towing the vehicles. Despite this finding, the television news reporter had his own agenda and edited Singer's comments in such a way that he sounded not only incompetent, but complicit. The edited report, complete with new questions asked by the reporter that were dubbed in after the interview, aired during sweeps week in Los Angeles, and Singer was referred to as "Stammering Singer" in news columns. The lieutenant, who had never had his reputation questioned before, was furious and asked the department to take action against the reporter and the television station, to at least defend him in public. The outgoing police chief, who later wound up being hired as an expert commentator for the network affiliated with the local station, bunkered down. Singer felt betrayed, and the dedication and passion he had felt toward the department took a 180-degree turn. He was never the same after that, and the quiet and effective hatred he had once focused on criminals and spineless politicians pointed inward toward his employers. Only those close to him—his immediate subordinates—knew of the sea change. Like everything about Singer, the shifting of loyalty from the department to his small circle of men was swift, decisive, and devastating. The LAPD never knew what hit it.

Although Newkirk was physically outmatched by Ex-Sergeant Gonzalez, who sat at the table beside him, it was Singer, a head shorter than Newkirk, he feared the most.

Gonzalez let Singer think and sipped his beer. As always, he had chosen the chair with his back toward the wall so he could keep an eye on everything in front of him. Gonzalez was a big man. He worked out daily in his home gym, and he wore jeans and tight black T-shirts that called attention to his thick arms, barrel chest, and massive hard belly. Gonzo was dark, smoldering, and violent. He fostered his image and persona. He was the kind of police officer, and man, who projected a dark malevolence even when he performed a simple, normal task like opening a door for someone or smiling at a joke. People around him, even strangers, always seemed relieved that Gonzalez had not decided to harm them. He had a way of looking up from hooded eyes that chilled the blood. Gonzalez was never troubled by doubt in his own judgment and never hesitated to follow up with his own kind of justice. He was the creator of the infamous L.A. mutilation known as the "guilty smile," where a man's cheeks were ripped back from the corners of his mouth to his ears. When the victim's face eventually healed, the mutilation made it look like a wide, clownish smile.

Singer had barely touched his beer. Newkirk and Gonzalez had emptied the pitcher, and Gonzo tried to get the attention of the bartender by lifting it whenever he thought the man looked over.

"What we've got to do is get control of the situation," Singer said softly, almost to himself. "We can't wait for things to happen, then react. We've got to get ahead of it so we can steer things in our favor."

"Like waiting for that motherfucker to look over and get us a pitcher," Gonzalez said.

Newkirk sighed. "I'll get it."

He approached the bar. There were only two other drinkers, a skeletal man in stained Carhartts who looked like an old miner, and a much younger man in a brown UPS uniform. Newkirk perched between them and put the pitcher on the bar.

"What was it? Coors?" the bartender asked, rousing himself from where he leaned against the backbar and watched *Sportscenter* on the television mounted to the ceiling.

"Yes," Newkirk said. He shot a glance at the old miner, who nodded at him then went back to watching the television. The UPS man seemed to be waiting for Newkirk to say something. *Oh no,* he thought; *a talker.*

"Don't get too close to me," the UPS man slurred. "I'm radioactive."

"You are?" Newkirk asked pleasantly, but in a way he hoped would be dismissive.

"I'm fucking poison. I might rub off on you, and you don't want that."

Newkirk shifted to look him over. He was built; solid, tight clothes, thick thighs, but a broad friendly face. Newkirk guessed six-two, two-twenty. A brass-colored name tag on his uniform read TOM BOYD. It was unusual to see a package delivery employee in uniform so long after the workday was over. He remembered the truck outside.

"Don't you have to turn your truck in at night?"

Tom snorted. "S'posed to. But instead I pitched camp right here on this stool when I got done with my route. Right, Marty?" he said to the bartender, who had tilted the empty pitcher to fill it with beer from the tap.

"Yes, Tom," the bartender said wearily. Newkirk got the impression Tom had already talked Marty's ear off.

"I'll take care of that pitcher," Tom said, fishing a wad of bills out of his pocket and slapping them on the bar. "And another double Jack for me."

"You sure you need another one?" Marty asked.

"What are you, a bartender or my fucking counselor? A knife could drop out of the sky at any second and kill my poor, pathetic ass. So pour 'em!"

Marty shrugged, and Tom shook his head in drunken exaggeration. "That's right. That's right."

Neither Newkirk nor Marty said anything, not wanting to encourage him.

"I'm poison," Tom said again. "I'm fucking radioactive. Everything I touch turns to crap."

Tom was one of those guys, Newkirk thought, who was practically begging to be asked what was wrong and wouldn't give up until he was.

"Women problems, eh?" Newkirk said, not really interested.

"Is there any other kind? I mean really?"

"Just call her. Let her talk it out and keep your mouth shut while she does. That's what works for me." To emphasize his point, Newkirk raised his hand and rotated the wedding band on his finger.

Tom said, "I *tried* to call her a while ago, and she hung up on me. She said she was waiting for the sheriff to call back and to get off her line. It's bullshit. That kid is just getting back at her by not coming home. I used to do that shit all the time."

Newkirk felt a trill race down his spine. "Why is she waiting for the sheriff to call her?"

"Her kids didn't come home from school," Tom said, rolling his eyes, smiling ruefully. "Somehow, that's *my* fault."

"What did you say her name was?" Newkirk asked, knowing Tom hadn't said it yet.

"Monica."

"Monica Treblehorn? I know her."

"No, Monica Taylor."

"Don't know her," Newkirk said.

"Consider yourself lucky."

"What'd you do?" Newkirk asked conversationally.

"Pissed her off," Tom said. "Forgot to take her little mama's boy fishing, so she fucking threw me out. Threw me right out. Her and that little bitch daughter of hers—they conspired against me."

Boy and girl, Newkirk thought. *Taylor.*

"So they went on their own, huh?" Newkirk said, realizing as he said it that he should have kept quiet. Tom hadn't told him the kids were on their own. But no matter, Tom didn't catch it.

"Took my SIX-HUNDRED-DOLLAR SAGE ROD, too!"

"That sucks, doesn't it?"

"Let me give you a little bit of advice, my friend," Tom said, reaching out and gripping Newkirk's arm. "Don't go out with a woman who has kids."

"I'm married," Newkirk said. "I've got kids of my own."

"Then don't go out with *her,*" Tom said, smiling stupidly. "They'll all conspire against you. They'll win, too. We're outnumbered by the women and the kids and the pansies. We're endangered species, us men, just like that fucking owl that stopped all the logging in the woods."

"Hear hear!" the old miner shouted from the end of the bar, raising his glass.

"Tom," Marty said, handing the pitcher to Newkirk, "advice is frowned on in this place." To Newkirk, Marty said, "Keep it on the tab?" Ignoring Tom Boyd's offer.

"Yes, and buy my new friend here another," Newkirk said.

When he returned to the table, Newkirk said, "You won't believe who I just met. Monica Taylor's boyfriend. And we've got a problem. He said she's waiting for the sheriff to call her back. Things might be moving faster than we thought. I'm guessing they'll form a search team to look for those kids. What if they find them?"

"Jesus Christ," Gonzalez whispered angrily. "Does everybody know?"

"Not like that. He just talked with her," Newkirk said, shaking his head. "He says she threw him out of her house tonight."

Singer looked at Newkirk, his face expressionless. Then, oddly, a tight faint smile.

"This isn't a problem," he said. "It's an opportunity."

"What?"

"See how his mind works?" Gonzalez said with admiration.

———

THEY WAITED until Marty cut Tom off. While Tom pleaded for a last drink, Gonzalez and Singer slipped outside.

Newkirk settled the tab at the bar while Tom stumbled from table to table on his way to the door.

When he got to the parking lot he saw Singer and Gonzo standing with Boyd in the light of the single pole light. Tom was leaning back against the UPS truck. He heard Gonzo say, "You sure you should be driving, mister?"

"I'm fine," Boyd slurred. "Besides, I ain't going home. I'm going to Monica's. We got some things to straighten out."

Newkirk approached them. He could see something square and long protruding from Gonzalez's back jeans pocket. As his eyes adjusted to the gloom, he recognized what it was from his days on the force. It was called a "Stun Monster," 650,000 volts. The department had banned them after some guy died, but that never mattered to Gonzo.

Boyd said, "It's nice of you fellows to help, but I gotta go. Where you guys from, anyway?"

"Guess," Singer said.

Boyd cracked a drunken smile. "I'd guess L.A. Like half the new fuckers up here."

"Right you are," Gonzalez said, stepping toward Boyd as if to assist him into the UPS truck. Newkirk saw the stun gun in Gonzalez's hand and caught a glint of the metal electrodes wink in the lamp's light. Gonzo plunged it into Boyd's neck, and the electricity arced and snapped like furious lightning. Boyd dropped like a sack of rocks half-in and half-out of his driver's door.

Boyd's muscles twitched violently as they pushed him all the way into the truck and dragged him between the rows of parcels in the back. Boyd's leg kicked out spasmodically, and his boot caught Newkirk on the shin, nearly dropping him. Newkirk could smell the awful stench of burnt flesh in the truck from Boyd's neck. The stun gun had short-circuited Boyd's neurotransmitters, so the UPS man had no control over his muscles and limbs. Or sphincter, which released.

"Strong motherfucker," Gonzo grunted, rolling the body over and cuffing him. "Stinky, too."

"You drive," Singer said, handing Gonzo the keys to the UPS truck. "Follow me."

"Cool. I've always wanted to drive one of these things," Gonzo said.

In his white SUV, with the headlights of the UPS truck filling the rearview mirror, Singer turned to Newkirk, said, "This was a gift. Now we can control the situation."

Newkirk had no idea what he was talking about. He shoved his hands under his thighs so Singer couldn't see them shaking.

DAY TWO

saturday

Saturday, 8:45 A.M.

AFTER PULLING two calves during the night, feeding his cattle at 5:00 A.M., and a big breakfast of steak, eggs, and coffee, Jess Rawlins showered and put on a jacket and tie and his best gray Stetson Rancher and went out to start his pickup. The sky was clear of clouds, although mist from the rain the night before hugged the grass and sharpened the smell of alfalfa and cow manure from the hayfield. The clouds would move in again in the afternoon, he guessed. He carried a boot box full of documents and put it on the passenger seat.

JIM HEARNE was waiting for him in the lobby wearing a sport jacket, tie, slacks, and boots. Jess still wasn't used to the new bank building even though it had been there for five years. The new building was impressive, with its big windows and modern furniture, but he preferred the old one, the elegant, cramped, two-story redbrick structure on Main, with its dark interior, muted lights, and hardwood floors. It had once been called the North Idaho Stockman's Bank. That was three name changes ago, before it became First Interstate and was now open on Saturdays. The Rawlins family had banked there since their initial homestead in 1933.

"Jim."

"Jess."

Jim Hearne was in his late forties, stocky, broad-faced, with thinning brown hair and sincere blue eyes. He had once been the exclusive agriculture loan officer, but his duties and titles had multiplied. A bareback rider who had qualified twice for the national finals, he still had a bowlegged hitch in his walk as he led Jess toward his office and shut the door behind them. The Rawlins Ranch had been his college rodeo sponsor.

Jess sat in one of the two chairs facing Hearne's desk and put his boot box of documents in the other. He removed his hat and placed it crown down on the floor next to him. On Hearne's desk was a thick file bound by clips with a tab that read RAWLINS.

"Plenty of moisture lately," Hearne said, sitting down. "That's got to help." Despite the fact that he was now president of the bank, Hearne still handled his old customers personally, and lapsed easily into the old banter. Jess had known him for thirty years, had watched him grow up to become a community leader.

Jess nodded. They both knew why he was here and that Jess wasn't good at small talk.

"Jess, I'm just not sure where to start," Hearne said.

Jess owned and operated a three thousand-acre ranch, one thousand eight hundred acres of it outright and the other one thousand two hundred acres deeded from the forest service, state, and federal Bureau of Land Management. He ran 350 Herefords in a cow/calf operation and sometimes, when the grass was good like this year, took in fifty to one hundred feeder cattle on a lease. It was the second-largest private holding remaining in the county. Hearne knew the herd size, deed arrangements, and layout of the ranch from memory, and didn't need to open his file.

Jess nodded. "There's not much to say. I can't make my payments, and I don't see how that's going to change, Jim. I'm broke. I laid off Herbert Cooper yesterday."

Hearne looked at Jess impassively, but Jess thought he noticed a softening in Hearne's eyes as he spoke.

"Calving is going as well as it ever has," Jess said. "The alfalfa's doing great with this moisture. I've got several calls from folks wanting to pasture their cows on my open meadows. But even with that . . ."

Hearne pursed his lips. Silence hung in the air.

"Everywhere you look," Hearne said, "people are eating beef. Everyone I know, practically, is on that low-carb meat diet. You'd think the prices would rise. That mad cow stuff out of Canada is a red herring."

Jess agreed. This was a never-ending conversation, one they had had before. Meat-processing conglomerates controlled prices and had long-term options on supply. Jess had agreed to those prices years in advance, before the increase in meat consumption, before costs skyrocketed.

"No one held a gun to my head to make me sign those futures contracts," Jess said. "I'm not here to whine."

"I know you're not."

"I'm not here to tell you everything's going to get better, either," Jess said. "It probably won't. But I do know I run a good outfit, and I don't waste your money or mine."

This was as close as Jess would come to asking for a favor, and it made him uncomfortable. He wouldn't have even made the statement if he wasn't still thinking of Herbert Cooper's packing up. He had made Hearne uncomfortable, too, Jess could tell.

"No one ever said that," Hearne said. "I sure as hell didn't."

Jess nodded.

"It's just that the day of the pure cattle outfit in northern Idaho may have passed us by," Hearne said, his face still flushing as he did so.

"I know."

"You're land-rich and cash-poor," Hearne said. "You've probably been following the price of real estate the last couple of years."

"Yup."

"Your place is worth millions, if developed properly," Hearne said morosely, delivering news neither one of them really wanted to hear but had to. "There are ways to get out from under this debt, Jess."

Jess sighed. His back was ramrod straight, but he felt like he was slumping. "I'm no developer."

"You don't have to be," Hearne said. "There are probably a half dozen developers right now who would work with you. I've gotten some calls on it, in fact."

It hurt Jess to know that others knew he was in trouble, that he was a soft target. "I've gotten some calls, too, and offers in the mail. I used to just throw 'em out without even opening them. But the Realtors are getting wise to it and sending 'em in unmarked envelopes. Karen even came out yesterday with her new husband."

"You could diversify," Hearne said. "Look at the Browns." The Brown Ranch was the other remaining family ranch in the area. "One son runs cattle and a meatpacking facility. The other son runs a gravel operation. The daughter operates a guest ranch on the property."

Jess snorted. "I had plans like that once," he said. "You know what happened."

Hearne sat back and sighed. He knew.

The silence groaned.

Hearne said, "None of us who grew up here wants to see you lose that ranch. I sure as hell don't. I think if all of the old ranches are replaced by those five-acre ranchettes, like we're seeing now, the county just won't be the same. But I can't let sentiment run my bank. Those newcomers built this building, and they're sending my kids to college."

Jess wondered why Hearne felt it necessary to tell him that.

"Jess, is there any way you would consider selling some of it? Maybe half? That would buy you some time to figure out the rest and maybe save some of it."

Jess bristled. The thought of being the one to dissolve the operation was a bitter pill. He thought of his grandfather, his father, his mother. They had left him a legacy, and he had screwed it up. The ranch was all he had that defined him, or the Rawlins name. How could he get rid of half of it?

"I'm a rancher," Jess said. "I don't know anything else."

Hearne rubbed his face with his hands. Jess noticed that Hearne's hands were soft. They didn't used to be. He looked down at his own hands. They were brown, gnarled, and weathered.

"We've got to figure something out," Hearne said. "We can't extend any of the loans anymore. I've got directors and auditors who want to know what the hell I'm doing with these bad loans."

"I'm sorry, Jim."

"Don't say that," Hearne said. "I can't stand for you to say that."

The intercom chirped, and Hearne leaned forward and picked up the headset. "I'm in a meeting, Joan."

Jess could hear Joan's muffled voice. Whatever she said had enough import to keep Hearne on the line.

"Oh, I hate to hear that," Hearne said. "Of course they can put it up. Of course they can."

Hearne continued to listen, then glanced over Jess's shoulder into the lobby. "Yeah, I see him. He'll have to wait," and cradled the handset.

"Sorry," Hearne said, his face drained of color.

"No problem. What's the matter?"

"Do you know the Taylor family? Monica Taylor?"

"I've heard the name," Jess said, trying to think of the context.

"She's got two kids, a girl and a boy. Apparently, they're missing."

"Oh, no."

"Been gone since yesterday," Hearne said. "Some other women want to put a poster up of the missing kids in the lobby."

Jess shook his head. "They'll probably turn up."

"Things like this never used to happen," Hearne said. Then, remembering why they were there, the banker said, "Jess, give me a couple of weeks to come up with some options for you. You don't have to take any of them, of course. But we both know you're in default. If I can come up with something to get us out of this mess we're in, I will."

Jess sat back, overwhelmed. "You don't have to do that, Jim."

"I know I don't," Hearne said, deflecting the emotion. "But we've known each other for a long time. I don't want to see your ranch turned into more starter castles for California transplants, either. I want there to be a couple of ranches in this county, too."

Jess stood, clamped on his hat, and extended his hand to Hearne across the desk. "Jim, I . . ."

"Don't say it," Hearne interrupted. "It's good for business, is all. We'll give a lot more loans out to people to live in a place that has ranches, that isn't completely overdeveloped, is all."

Jess said nothing but wanted to embrace the banker who was lying to him.

AS HE OPENED the office door, Jess recognized Fiona Pritzle as one of the women putting up the posters in the lobby. Before he could slink away, she saw him and came rushing over.

"Jess," she said, trapping both of his hands in hers, standing too close, looking up into his eyes, "did you hear about the Taylor children?"

"Just did. It's terrible." Her hands were as dry as parchment.

"I was the one who gave them a ride along Sand Creek yesterday," she said, her eyes shining. "They were going fishing, and I dropped them off. But they didn't come home last night."

"They'll probably show today," he said.

"Oh, with that rushing creek, they could have been swept away and drowned!"

Jess would have had more sympathy for Fiona, but she seemed to be reveling in the fact that she was a major character in the drama and was playing it to the hilt.

"And who knows who could have taken them," she whispered. "There are a lot of people here now we don't know anything about. Who knows how many sexual predators have moved up here?"

Jess winced. "Is there a search team?"

"Thank God, yes," she said. "The sheriff has his deputies out, and people are lining up to volunteer to look for them."

"That's good to hear," he said, gently breaking loose from her grip, at the same time wishing he had more confidence in the new sheriff, who seemed to Jess to be more of a public relations/chamber of commerce type than a lawman. As he thought this, Jess realized he had trapped Hearne in his office because Fiona had blocked him in the doorway.

"It is good," Fiona said. "I heard that a bunch of those retired police officers have volunteered to help the sheriff head up the investigation. They showed up this morning. Isn't that great?"

Jess nodded. "I suspect the new sheriff will welcome their help."

"It shows you that a lot of these newcomers have good hearts," she said. "And they have experience in these kinds of horrible crimes. It's the kind of thing they did all the time in L.A."

"Excuse me," Hearne said, sliding past Jess.

Jess watched as Hearne strode across the lobby and greeted a man sitting in a lounge chair. The man was portly, Hispanic, and well dressed in a light brown suit, Jess noticed.

"Well," Jess said, extricating himself and nodding at the poster Fiona had mounted on the wall, "that's a good thing you're doing. I'll keep an eye out myself since I'm upstream of Sand Creek."

Hearne and the well-dressed man went into Hearne's office, and before the door shut, the banker said, "Take it easy, Jess. I'll call you."

"Thank you, Jim."

Fiona watched the exchange, and Jess could see the wheels spinning in her head.

"Does that mean you get to keep your ranch?" she asked eagerly.

ON HIS WAY out of the lobby doors, Jess paused to look at the poster. MISSING, it said, ANNIE AND WILLIAM TAYLOR. LAST SEEN AT 2:30 P.M. FRIDAY NEAR RILEY CREEK CAMPGROUND ON SAND CREEK. It said Annie was last seen wearing a yellow sweatshirt, jeans, and black sneakers and William was dressed in a short-sleeved black T-shirt, jeans, and red tennis shoes; one of them might be wearing an adult's fly-fishing vest.

The school photos of the children tugged at his heart. Jess thought about how you could see the future personalities of adults in the photos they took when they were children if you cared to look hard. Even now, when he stared at the photos of his son in his home, he could see what he would become. Not that he'd known it at the time, though. But the clues were there, the blueprint. If only he had known.

William smiled broadly, his hair a comma over his forehead, his chin cocked slightly to the side. He looked happy-go-lucky and tragic at the same time. It was Annie who most affected him, and he found himself staring at her likeness, mesmerized by it. She was blond, open-faced, clear-eyed, and looked to be challenging the photographer. But there was something in her eyes and the set of her chin. He immediately liked her and felt an affinity he couldn't explain. Had he met her before? He searched his memory and came up with nothing.

Maybe it wasn't that he'd seen or met her before, but what she represented to him. Maybe her photo made him realize how much he had wanted grandchildren. The thought embarrassed him. It wasn't something he thought about or pined over. In fact, this was the first time it had occurred to him with such force. He wished he could start over somehow, maybe do things differently this time, maybe do things *right*. So instead of an empty house and failing ranch, he would have kids around like these to spend his time with, impart some of his knowledge, tell them they could be . . . exceptional.

He stood back and shook his head at the thought but continued looking at the poster.

Phone numbers for the sheriff's department were written underneath the photos.

As he walked outside, Jess glanced over his shoulder and could see the well-dressed man opening a briefcase and spreading the contents out over Jim Hearne's desk.

Saturday, 9:14 A.M.

MONICA TAYLOR was beside herself. Annie and William had been missing for over twenty hours. She hadn't slept, eaten, showered, or changed clothes since Tom had walked out of her home the evening before. It had been a long night, made worse when smoke rolled out of the oven—she had forgotten about the lasagna—and set off the alarms. She stood on her front lawn, weeping uncontrollably, being comforted by a volunteer fireman, while the rest of the crew charged through her front door with extinguishers and hoses, tracking mud across the carpet and linoleum, to emerge a few minutes later with a black, smoking, unrecognizable pan of black goo. The neighbors who had been outside in their bathrobes or sweats went back inside their houses.

Before the lasagna burned, sheriff's deputies had been there twice, once to hear her initial concerns and again near midnight to obtain photos of the children and descriptions of what they'd been wearing when she saw them last. The difference in their attitudes from the first visit, when one of the deputies had actually tried to pick her up, to the second, when even the flirting deputy averted his eyes and spoke somberly, brought home the growing seriousness of the disappearance.

The sheriff eventually tired of her hourly calls throughout the night, and sent over a doctor, who prescribed Valium. The Valium took the edge off her pain but didn't make it go away. All she had to do was look at the school photos of Annie and William, the frames now clouded with a film of sticky smoke residue, to bring it all back.

She had developed a routine, of sorts, that consisted of walking through the house and out the back door into the yard, circling the house to the left, and reentering through the front door, all the while clutching the cordless phone as if to squeeze it into juice. As she passed the hallway she glanced at herself in the mirror, seeing someone who was almost unrecognizable. The woman who looked back had red-rimmed eyes, sunken cheeks, matted, ratty hair. She seemed to be folding over on herself when she walked. Monica now knew what she would look like when she was old.

When the telephone rang, and it rang often, she would gasp, ask God that it please be one of her children, and punch the TALK button. It was never Annie or William, but the sheriff's office, a concerned neighbor, the local newspaper, or a rural mail carrier named Fiona Pritzle, who told Monica that she, Fiona, was "the last person on earth to see those kids alive." The phrase had nearly buckled Monica's knees, and made her reach out for the wall to steady herself.

Over and over, Monica replayed the morning before, each time revising the situation so Tom left the house before breakfast or, better yet, that he'd never come at all. She hated herself for what happened, and she asked God, over and over, for a second chance to make it right. She thought God, like the sheriff, was likely getting tired of hearing from her lately, especially after all these years when He never even entered her mind. But there would be no more Tom, she vowed. No more *Toms,* period.

Monica had never been blessed with a road map. Her own parents had not provided one, certainly not for a situation like this. She always envied those who seemed to have a map, a plan, a destination, something inside that provided a framework. In times of confusion and despair, she had little to fall back on and no one to call on for advice or support. Certainly not her mother. And who knew where her father was?

It was tough raising two children alone. The men she met were either divorced themselves and loaded with baggage or quirks, married and looking for a fling or an easy out, or immature like Tom. None of them had the potential or desire to be a good father to her children, which was what she yearned for. Annie needed a man in her life, but William needed one even more. Sure, the men she met were interested in Monica. But not Monica *and* her children. She couldn't really blame them, but she did. There had been too many years wasted hoping, too many years of listlessness and paralysis, treading water, hoping some man would throw a lifeline. Monica was well aware of the fact that she was not the only single mother in the world. Her own mother had the same experience, after her father—who called Monica his princess, his angel, his button—had left without saying good-bye. But that's where the similarity ended, because Monica loved *her* children deeply.

But she'd been weak. The desire she'd had for Tom now seemed to have happened in another life. It had been so pointless, so shallow, so selfish. Sure, she'd wanted him in her bed. Once, there had been many. But she wasn't an animal. She'd learned to control herself, not to give in to her basest instinct anymore. There'd been other men—better men— who'd wanted to stay over. The most recent was Oscar Swann. But she'd refused him, and them, explained that her children—their family—came first. Her children needed a father but not simply a male, and certainly not a series of them. Monica knew what that did to children because it had happened to her.

The phone rang in her hand, startling her like it did every time. As she raised it to her mouth, the receiver chirped and the phone went dead. She had forgotten to charge it.

She slammed the telephone into the charging cradle, trying to will it to ring again. It didn't.

For the first time she could remember, her life was absolutely focused: She needed her children back.

SHE WAS at her kitchen table, staring again at the digital time display on the microwave, when Sheriff Ed Carey rapped on the screen door of the mudroom.

"May I come in, Miz Taylor?"

She looked up at him and nodded, not having the energy to speak.

As he entered, she searched his face for some kind of indication of why he was there. She swore that if he wouldn't meet her eyes, if the news he brought was bad news, she would die right there, on the spot. But Carey's face was blank, and maybe a little facetious, as if he were playacting at being concerned but wasn't very good at it.

Sheriff Carey was tall and wore his uniform well, but there wasn't much he could do to disguise the potbelly that stuck straight out from his trunk and strained the buttons on his short-sleeved khaki shirt. When he was inside, he removed his straw cowboy hat and adjusted his belt up, which slipped back down under his gut with his first step.

"I tried to call you earlier," he said, nodding at the phone, the question why she didn't answer hanging in the air.

"The phone was dead," she said, her voice a croak, as if she was using it for the first time. "So that was you."

He nodded and gestured toward a chair.

"Do you have anything to tell me?"

He sat down and looked around for a place that was not dirtied with soot to put his hat down. Finally, he perched it on his knee.

"I need to ask you a few questions," Carey said, and this time he let his eyes slip away from hers.

"Oh, no . . ."

"No, it's not that," he said quickly, realizing what she had leaped to.

"You haven't found them?"

He shook his head. "I wish I had better news, but I don't. What I can tell you is that one of my deputies found some things up by Sand Creek. A fly rod and a shoe stuck in the mud. I was hoping you could identify them."

Her mind raced. Of course she could identify a shoe if it was Annie's or William's. But what was the brand of the fly rod Tom said was missing?

"I could do that," she said. "But I might have to call someone to identify the rod."

"That would be Tom Boyd, I presume?"

"Yes."

Carey nodded, and reached for his breast pocket. "You don't mind if I take a few notes, do you?"

"No, why should I?"

Carey shifted uncomfortably in his chair. He was the new sheriff, barely elected just a few months ago in a close contest. His background was in real estate. She wondered how much he really knew about his job. Forty-nine percent of the county wondered the same thing.

"My deputies think this may be more than, you know, the kids getting lost."

Monica felt as if something were rising in her from a reserve she didn't know she had. She wished the Valium would wear off so she could concentrate better.

"What are you saying to me?"

"Well, Miz Taylor, we've decided to treat this matter as a criminal investigation, not a missing persons case. The rod was found hung up in some brush a hundred yards from the river. The shoe was found in a mudhole farther up the path, and it was easy to see and find. That leads my deputies to believe that whoever lost the shoe—and we think it might have been Annie—could have easily turned around and pulled it out. But she didn't. That indicates that she might have been in a hurry. You know, like she was running from something or somebody."

Monica felt her eyes widen. Her breath came in short bursts.

Carey produced a quart-sized Ziploc bag and held it up to the light. Inside was a muddy shoe. The sight of it seared Monica, welded her to her chair.

"It's Annie's" she said, scarcely raising her voice. "Who were they running from?"

Carey put the shoe on the table and turned his hands, palms up. "That, we don't know. My men have found some prints in the mud up there, but they're bad ones. The rain last night fouled up anything definitive. We're still looking, and my guys are combing the area on a grid, inch by inch."

The world had suddenly made a hard turn and darkened. Throughout the sleepless night, she had envisioned her children lost somewhere in the forest, huddled together in the rain. She had hoped they'd found shelter of some kind and were smart enough to stay put. She had even thought of the creek, thought of them falling into it and being swept away. It was awful, that thought. But she hadn't considered what the sheriff was now telling her. That her children were prey to someone.

"Oh, no . . ."

She stared at the shoe, the smears of mud on the inside of the plastic, the laces broken. As if violence had been packaged in a neat container.

Carey narrowed his eyes and looked at her, studying her. "Miz Taylor, are you going to be okay?"

She shook her head slightly. "No, I'm not. You're telling me that someone was after my children."

"We don't know that yet," he said. "It's speculation based on very little evidence. But we can't rule it out, and we need to cover everything. It could be they'll turn up any minute. Maybe they stayed at a friend's, who knows?"

She continued to shake her head. Her throat constricted. It was difficult to get air. She had given a deputy the names and numbers of all of Annie's and William's friends, and had called their parents herself. None of them had seen her children.

"Miz Taylor, I need to ask you if you know of anyone who may have something against you, or your kids."

"What?"

"Has anyone threatened you? Stalked you? Do you know if your children had any trouble with anyone who might try to scare them or hurt them? They each have a different father, right?"

"Right," she said, wincing at how it sounded. "But neither is around, as you know."

William's father, Billy, had been killed in a prison riot at the Idaho State Correctional Institution in Boise. She had divorced him three years before, while he was on trial for owning and operating four methamphetamine labs, which apparently generated a lot more income for Billy than his struggling construction business. The marriage had been dead by eighteen months after the ceremony but went on for two more years. Billy had been proud of the fact that he fathered a son, but didn't particularly like William and, like Tom, called him a mama's boy. William barely knew or remembered his father, but sometimes talked about him as a mythical being, a stoic and legendary Western outlaw. Monica didn't encourage William's projections but didn't disparage Billy in front of her son because she didn't think it would serve any good purpose. Annie knew Billy for what he was, and rolled her eyes when her brother talked about his father the outlaw. But Billy'd never threatened his son, or Monica, because by the end he simply didn't care about either of them.

Up until a year ago, Annie had assumed Billy was her father, too.

Then she did the math. That had been a bad day for Monica, when Annie asked. When she did, Monica simply said, "He's watching over you." Annie didn't really accept the answer. It was obvious it didn't satisfy her. Monica knew there would be more questions as time went by, and she had dreaded them. Now, Monica hoped Annie would be back so she could answer them.

"Is he dead?" the sheriff asked.

"Something like that. He's incarcerated as well."

The sheriff eyed her closely, withholding judgment. *Yes,* Monica thought, *I'm used to those looks, I know* . . .

"We need to explore every possibility so we can rule things out," Carey said, interrupting Monica's thoughts. "First, and pardon me for being rude, but I assume that your family is fairly low-income. Correct?"

She nodded. It was obvious.

"Anyone you can think of at your place of work? Disgruntled employees?"

"No. Nothing unusual."

He glanced at his notes. "You're the manager of women's casual apparel at the outlet store, correct?"

She nodded. "It provides a steady income and decent health benefits for the kids. It's a meaningless job."

"Any problem with the neighbors?"

She shook her head. She kept her distance from her neighbors except for inevitable pleasantries about the weather or school-related topics. The only thing she could think of was when a single retired bachelor down the block complained about William and Annie cutting across his yard as they walked to school, and she told the sheriff about it. The sheriff made a note.

"What about your extended family? Is there money there? Would a kidnapper have a reason to hold your children for ransom?"

"My mother cleans houses and tends bar in Spokane," Monica said evenly. "My father has been gone for years. We have nothing."

"Any others?"

She thought of her cousin Sandy in Coeur d'Alene, the only cousin she knew. Sandy was married to a city councilman and had four bright kids. She'd invited Monica to picnics and family functions for a while, and used to call to invite her to church. Sandy had even said maybe she could help Monica "meet a nice man." Sandy knew about what happened to Billy, as everyone did. They were decent gestures from a decent woman, but Monica couldn't bring herself to accept. She didn't want to be Sandy's project, or the object of her effort at good works. Monica had been too stubbornly proud to accept help. Sandy rarely called anymore.

So many people—Sandy, the banker Jim Hearne, her neighbor down the street who was always inviting her to church and bingo night—had tried to help her since the divorce, but she never saw it as help at the time. Hearne especially had watched out for her, and had always been there to help in his quiet way. She often saw the attempts as interference, or as pity. That had been a mistake, Monica realized now. Maybe if she'd opened up more, there would have been someone to take William fishing.

The sheriff raised his hand. "Like I said, I need to rule out every possibility. This is bound to be uncomfortable for you."

She nodded again. "Not as uncomfortable as having my children missing."

The sheriff smiled sympathetically, then his eyes hardened. "This Tom Boyd. A neighbor reported that she saw him leaving your house last night. She said he was visibly angry, and she heard him yell and slam your door shut. She said she heard you yelling, too. Was there some kind of disagreement?"

No, she thought. *The sheriff can't be going in this direction*. "We had an argument."

"What about?"

She swallowed. "Tom found out his fishing rod and vest were missing. He thought Annie had taken them. He didn't get along with Annie very well, and I told him to leave."

She knew how that sounded. So: "But I'm sure Tom had nothing to do with it. The kids were gone for a long time already when it happened."

The sheriff asked her for the time of the argument.

"It was around six," she said. "I waited two more hours before I called you."

She could see Carey calculating it in his head. Tom would have had enough time, and enough light, to track down Annie and William.

"Tom called me last night," Monica said. "It was after ten. Maybe ten-thirty. He asked whether my kids had come home."

"How did he sound?"

Monica swallowed. "He was drunk. He was at some bar."

Carey nodded, as if she'd confirmed something. "He was seen last night at the Sand Creek Bar. The bartender said he was inebriated. Still in his uniform, very distraught and upset. They refused to give him more drinks, and he got angry and left around eleven."

Monica seized on the words *inebriated* and *distraught*.

"Someone who knows Tom Boyd says he can have a violent temper," the sheriff said. "He's a bodybuilder, right? Maybe some steroid use? Would you say he has a violent temper, Miz Taylor?"

SHERIFF CAREY asked questions for another half hour. She answered them honestly, and could see how the sheriff was building a case against Tom. No, she didn't know he'd been arrested twice for assault. No, she didn't know Tom's ex-wife had accused him of beating one of his children. How could she not know that, she asked herself. She felt stupid, duped. Again.

"I don't think it was Tom," she said, finally, after the sheriff stood up and slipped his notebook in his pocket. "If it was him, wouldn't he have taken his fly rod back? Isn't that the reason you've come up with why he would even try to find my children?"

"I thought of that, too," Carey said, clamping on his hat. "But it could be your kids lost it before he got there. Or he just couldn't find it in the dark. We'll have to ask him about that," he said ominously.

"I just can't believe it," she said.

Carey stood there, silent, as if he had more to say before he left. She looked up.

"Tom didn't show up for work this morning," Carey said. "His supervisor said he didn't call in, either. Tom's not at his house, and no one saw him come home last night. His truck is still missing. He was supposed to turn it in last night, but he didn't."

"His UPS truck?" she said incredulously.

For the first time, the sheriff almost smiled. "You'd think we'd find a vehicle that distinctive easy enough, wouldn't you?"

"I just can't . . ." She didn't finish, knowing she had said it before.

"I think we'll get this thing wrapped up pretty quickly," the sheriff said. "I hope and pray it will be for the best, but we just don't know. We hope like hell we can find him and bring your kids back, unharmed."

She watched him, waiting for the other shoe to drop.

"I wish I had more men to work this, Miz Taylor. I've only got four deputies for the whole county. Three of 'em are up there on Sand Creek right now, searching it with a state crime-scene team that arrived this morning. I'm starting to get calls from all over. Newspaper reporters, even some producer from Fox News in Spokane. Missing kids are big news, you know. If we can tie Tom Boyd to your kids, we can issue an Amber Alert, but it doesn't meet that standard yet. I looked it up. The first criterion is that law enforcement must confirm that an abduction has taken place. We don't know it to be true. We can't just go panicking everyone this early."

"This early?" she said, astonished.

"Miz Taylor, it hasn't even been twenty-four hours. We don't even consider a person missing until then. Not that the newspeople care. I'm stalling them for now, but they're keeping me busy. Luckily, though, I have an ace in the hole."

"What do you mean?" she asked.

Now, he grinned outright. "Four experienced, seasoned investigators have volunteered to help us. They showed up this morning and asked what they could do. After I talked with 'em, I gave them the authority to run with it, and already things are happening. We're lucky as hell."

She was confused. "Who are they?"

"LAPD's finest," he said. "Retired cops who've worked dozens of situations like this. They told me they want to serve their new community and keep it safe. Within a couple of hours they helped me establish a command center, and they're the ones who figured out Tom Boyd. We're damned glad to have them here, Miz Taylor."

She nodded. For the first time, she felt a lift of encouragement.

"I know you want to stay by the phone," he said, looking around the kitchen. "I think you should, too. But you need some help around here. Some support. Is there anyone we can call to stay with you?"

She had no relatives nearby, and few friends. Sandy was on a cruise with her husband and family. She thought of Jim Hearne, the banker who had always been kind to her, but knew how improper that would seem.

"That woman, Fiona Pritzle, keeps offering to come stay with me," Monica said. "But I don't think I want her help."

Carey agreed. "I'll ask one of the volunteer investigators to come over, if you don't mind. We want to cover all the bases. If someone contacts you with a report on your kids, we want to know right away. We want to screen the call. And, if someone has your kids . . ."

"I don't mind."

"His name is Swann. Ex-Sergeant Swann."

"I know him," Monica said dully.

"Yes, he told me that. He wanted me to ask you if you minded if it was he."

She thought of Swann's kind face and manner, his sonorous voice. He had been obscure, though, and so set in his ways. She felt he was always watching her as a cop watched a subject, not the way a man watched a woman.

"It's okay," she said. "He's a clean freak. Very organized. He'll probably help me out with all of this."

The sheriff snorted and reached out his hand.

"We'll do our best to find your kids, Miz Taylor. I'll ask Mr. Swann to bring you something to eat. I'll call the doctor to come by again as well."

Saturday, 10:14 A.M.

SORRY TO KEEP you waiting," Jim Hearne said to Eduardo Villatoro as he slipped back behind his desk. "That was a local rancher. A friend of mine. A good man."

Villatoro settled into the chair the rancher had just used, his briefcase on his knees. He watched as Hearne gathered up a thick file with the name RAWLINS on the tab and put it on the credenza behind him. Digging in his breast pocket for a card, he leaned forward and handed it to Hearne.

Hearne read it, a glimpse of recognition in his clear blue eyes. "Detective Villatoro of the Arcadia, California, Police Department, now I remember. You called and asked for a meeting a few weeks ago. All the way from Southern California."

"Thank you for meeting with me. I've retired from the department since then."

"Congratulations," Hearne said, his face showing what he was thinking, that the meeting wasn't official after all but of a personal nature. And maybe a waste of Hearne's time.

Hearne said, "Have you ever been to North Idaho before? We say North Idaho, not northern Idaho, by the way."

"I see."

"So, have you ever been here?"

"No."

"How do you like it so far?"

"It's very green," Villatoro said, thinking: *It's very white.*

"Yeah, it's our little piece of heaven," Hearne said.

Villatoro smiled. "It's a very pretty place. Very peaceful, it seems."

Hearne said, "It usually is. We've got a problem going on this morning, though. You probably saw the poster out there. A couple of local kids are missing."

Villatoro had observed it all: the women who arrived with the poster, the loud one with the little-girl voice who told everyone in the bank what had happened, the conversation between the loud woman and the rancher who had left Hearne's office.

"I hope the children are okay," Villatoro said. "I've been struck by how intimate it all is, how local. It's like the town thinks *their* children are missing. It warms my heart to witness such an attitude."

Hearne studied him. Probing for insincerity, Villatoro guessed.

"We do tend to take care of our own," Hearne said. "Maybe it's not like that in L.A.?"

"L.A. is too big," Villatoro said. "It's not as bad as people make it out to be, though. There are some neighborhoods where people look out for one another. But it's just so easy to get swallowed up."

Hearne seemed to be thinking about that, then he looked at Villatoro's card again.

"So, if you're no longer with your police department, what can I do for you? Are you looking to retire here?"

Villatoro looked at Hearne blankly. For a moment, it didn't register what Hearne had said or why he had said it. "No," he said, alarmed, holding up his hand. "No, no. I've got another matter."

"Oh, then I'm sorry. I just assumed."

"I want to complete an investigation I worked on for years. It led me here."

Hearne sat back. "What are you still investigating?"

Snapping open the locks on his briefcase, Villatoro slipped five sheets of paper out of his file and handed them across the desk. They were back and front photocopies of hundred-dollar bills.

The serial numbers for the bills were typed on each one, followed by a series of bank routing numbers that had been highlighted by a yellow marker. Hearne recognized the routing number.

"These came through my bank," Hearne said. "Are they counterfeit?"

"No, they're real."

Hearne raised his eyebrows, as if saying "So?"

Villatoro said, "As you know, there are authorities who electronically scan currency as it flows through the system to check for marked or counterfeit bills. It isn't a perfect system, but when it registers a hit, they increase the frequency of scanning to determine origin. When there are several hits from a single bank, it may be something significant."

"Meaning?"

"I'll start at the beginning. Eight years ago, there was an armed robbery at a horse racing track in my town, which is—or was—outside of Los Angeles. Millions in cash was taken, and a man died during the commission of the crime, one of the guards. As you can guess, it was an inside job, and the employees were convicted and sent to prison by the LAPD. I was assigned to the case and served as the liaison between my small department and the LAPD, which had many more detectives and much greater resources. We turned the investigation over to them even though I objected at the time. It was a decision made by my chief, who is a great lover of outside experts."

"Hold it," Hearne said. "Was this *the* Santa Anita robbery? I read about that."

"Santa Anita Racetrack." Villatoro nodded. "One of the largest employers in Arcadia. My wife worked there at the time and knew many of the employees, as did everyone in town. Yes—$13.5 million in cash was stolen."

"Isn't that where Seabiscuit ran?"

Villatoro said, "Yes. There's a statue of him there."

"My wife made me read that book, and I loved it. We saw the movie, too. I didn't like it as much. I guess they just can't make a good movie about a horse. Horses are too subtle."

Villatoro said, "Do you know about horses?"

"I used to ride in the rodeo," Hearne said. "I do love horses. I miss being around them."

Villatoro said, "Back to the robbery."

"Sorry, go ahead."

He cleared his throat and continued. "Of course, all of the employees who were convicted claimed innocence, but the evidence was too compelling. I've read the court records myself, and I would have convicted them as well if I'd had a vote. One of the former employees gave up the others and testified against them all.

"But there is a big problem. None of the cash was ever recovered, and not one of the people convicted has yet to come forward and say anything, even though they could probably bargain their way out of jail. And for seven years, these people have kept quiet."

"Damn," Hearne said. "That's a long time. They must be tough."

Villatoro waved his hand. "They're not so tough. My wife says the people in prison just weren't the types to do this kind of crime, for what that's worth. To me, though, it's good information. I've met them and talked to them. They're desperate to get out, and they swear they have nothing to tell us."

Hearne frowned.

"We keep waiting," Villatoro said. "I interviewed them every few months, hoping one of them would tell me where the money went. For a long time we thought they'd buried it somewhere. They will get out, probably, in five or six years, maybe more, and I suppose for that kind of reward they could wait. But it doesn't seem like they know. I really feel, in my heart, that if they knew where the money was, they would tell me. One of them should have broken by now, or found God, or just wanted to get out."

"What about the guy who testified against them?"

"Ah," Villatoro said, sighing. "He is no longer with us. He was the victim of a convenience store robbery in L.A. less than a year after the trial. He was there buying milk and was caught in a cross fire between the owner of the store and the criminal who tried to rob it."

"And whoever shot him wasn't caught?"

"Alas, no."

"Interesting," Hearne said. "So what does that all have to do with me and my bank?"

Villatoro gestured toward the photocopies of the hundred-dollar bills. "At the time of the robbery, the cashiers and accountants at the racetrack had a rather efficient procedure for counting the money and accounting for all of it, but an incomplete method for recording the cash. The racetrack didn't have marked bills, like your bank surely does, or dye pacs. You can imagine the sea of cash that washes in during a big day, every twenty minutes or so when bettors come to the windows. The robbery occurred after one of the biggest races of the year, the Southern California Breeders' Cup. It's all computerized, of course, but the cash still needs to match the computer at the end of the day, so it's hand-counted in the back. That takes time. Once the cash matches the computer, armored cars take the cash away to the bank. In the kind of rush they are in to get the cash into the cars, there was no way to mark or record the money in any comprehensive way. The best they could do, at the time, was to randomly record serial numbers. In this case, they recorded the serial number of every fiftieth hundred-dollar bill. Now it's done by scanners, but then it was by hand."

Hearne was listening closely, and urged Villatoro on.

"In the end, we had the serial numbers for 1,377 hundred-dollar bills. The rest were other denominations, or credit card receipts. But most of it was cash, and most of it was in small, circulated bills. Quite literally untraceable."

Hearne looked down at the photocopies of the bills on his desk.

"For three years, not a single hundred-dollar bill with a recorded serial number was reported. Not one," Villatoro said. "Then one came in that had been routed through four different banks. But the bank of origin was yours. We did nothing because one bill means nothing. It could have passed through a dozen people or merchants during that time. I made a copy, though, and kept it in my file. You have a copy of that one there in front of you. Two others surfaced over the years, one from California, then Nevada, the other from Nebraska. There appeared to be no link at all.

"Two months ago, though, four more turned up," Villatoro said. "All four originated from your bank. Those are the four sheets on top. Once this happened, I sensed there might be something to it. I took this information to my liaison contacts in the LAPD, but as far as they were concerned the case was closed. They'd moved on. My department was very small, with only four detectives. We didn't have the budget to send me around the country to follow this up, and my mandatory retirement date was approaching. No other detective wanted to take up the case after I left. But these bills bothered me, and they bother me still. It is my only link to the money stolen, and therefore the criminals. You see, Mr. Hearne, Arcadia is a peaceful place, or at least it used to be. There have never been more than four murders in a year there. Our average for the thirty years I was in the department was two homicides. Only two. And these weren't heinous, mysterious crimes, usually a domestic or easily solved homicide. The bank guard homicide is the only unsolved murder still on our books, and it was assigned to me. I just can't leave without trying to solve it, even if it is on my own time."

Hearne studied the bills, waiting for more.

"I think someone who has access to at least some of the Santa Anita money lives in this area and banks with you," Villatoro said. "I'd like to try and find out who that might be."

"How do you propose to do that?"

Villatoro smiled. "I would like to look at your accounts. Primarily those that were opened four years ago that are still active. I think I may find a name that will jump out at me. Especially if I can trace the name back to California. Then I will have narrowed it down."

Hearne made a face. "You know we can't just turn over a list of our customers to you. That's illegal."

Villatoro nodded his head. "Yes, I know that. But if I can get the proper authorities to request access, I hope you will be cooperative. That's all I ask. And, of course, if you have any idea at the outset who the person might be."

Shaking his head, Hearne handed the photocopies back to Villatoro. "I have no idea. We have hundreds of new accounts, and I'd bet a quarter of them came from California. I really wouldn't have a clue, and if I did, I'm not sure I'd be at liberty to tell you."

"A man died in the robbery, Mr. Hearne. A man with a wife and two children."

Hearne looked away. "That has nothing to do with it, and you know it."

Villatoro sat back. "I'm sorry. I understand."

"Go talk to the sheriff," Hearne said. "His name is Carey. If you make your case to him, he might escort you to a judge who can request an order to see the accounts. Otherwise, there's no more I can do."

An uncomfortable silence hung in the office for a moment, finally broken by Villatoro: "I will certainly see the sheriff. That was my plan all along. But I've learned through experience that often the wisest man in a community, when it comes to assessing the character of others, is the senior official at the most prominent bank. I have learned that often, in these kinds of situations, the bank president or vice president knows where odd amounts of cash come from, and if anything is unusual about their customer's banking habits. Large, regular cash infusions—say just under the ten-thousand-dollar notification cap—usually attract some attention. Especially if there are . . . elements . . . within the community where such amounts of cash are unlikely."

Villatoro felt the banker's stare and waited for him to respond. When he did, Hearne's voice was flat.

"I know what you're suggesting, Mr. Villatoro. You've heard the stories about the white supremacists up here, just like everyone's heard stories. About Aryan Nations and those Nazis. A lot of the country thinks we're no better than rednecks, or racists. You're wondering if those folks bank with us."

"Well, yes."

Hearne swiped his hand through the air. "We ran 'em out of here years ago, Mr. Villatoro. We didn't like 'em any more than you do. We got them the same way the Feds got Al Capone. They didn't pay their taxes. They've been long gone for years, even though the reputation we've got up here never seems to go away."

Villatoro sat for a moment. He believed the heat in Hearne's statements, believed his outrage. He sensed that Hearne would help him. Many bank officers were openly hostile and could drag out an investigation. Hearne didn't seem to be the type to do that.

"Thank you, Mr. Hearne," Villatoro said, shutting his briefcase and standing. "I'm sorry if I insulted you or your community."

"You're forgiven," Hearne said, shaking his hand. "Just make sure to tell your pals in L.A. that we ran those bastards out of here. Besides, this is the last place people like that would want to live these days. Do you realize how many retired police officers have moved here? It's one of the biggest sectors of our retirees."

Villatoro nodded. "I've heard that. One of my best friends on the

LAPD calls this place Blue Heaven. It's interesting that so many retired officers move here. What's the reason, do you think?"

Hearne gestured toward the window. "It's wonderful country, as I'm sure you've noticed. Mountains, lakes, lots of outdoor opportunities. Plus damned cheap land compared to what you're used to. And the culture here is welcoming, I think. The folks around here are tough and independent. They don't ask a lot of questions, and they believe in live and let live. They're not fond of any kind of government or authority, but they're law-and-order types. Everyone has guns, and we're proud of that. As long as you're a good neighbor, they don't care where you came from, what you did, or what your daddy did. Plus, they're blue-collar. Most of 'em were loggers, or miners, or cowboys. I think they feel pretty comfortable with the ex-cops, who are blue-collar at heart. Brother," Hearne said, flushing, "I sound like a chamber of commerce commercial."

"It's okay," Villatoro said. "You've obviously thought a lot about it."

"I want to know my customers," Hearne said, sitting forward and grasping his hands together on his desktop in a gesture that brought the meeting to a near close.

Villatoro turned to open the door, but Hearne cleared his throat. "Before you leave, Mr. Villatoro, I've got a question for you."

"Yes?"

"Is the Santa Anita robbery the real reason you're here?"

Villatoro hesitated before answering. "Yes," he said softly.

Hearne considered it, then said, "Well, good luck. And welcome to Kootenai Bay."

"Thank you. Everyone seems friendly here."

"We are," Hearne said. "Although the guy with the hundred-dollar bills might disagree with that."

"I trust everything we've discussed is confidential?"

"Of course," Hearne said, showing Villatoro out the door, "of course it is."

As Villatoro walked across the lobby toward the door, Hearne called out after him. "The sheriff might be a little busy right now," he said, gesturing toward the poster of Annie and William Taylor. Villatoro looked at it, then back to the banker.

"I don't have that much time," Villatoro said.

AFTER VILLATORO left, Jim Hearne went back into his office and shut the door and leaned with his back to it. This, he knew, was the only place in his office where no one could see him through the windows.

He closed his eyes tightly and breathed deeply. But there was a roar emanating, building within him. His palms were cold, and he reached up and rubbed his face with them.

Villatoro had taken him by surprise. There was a time a few years ago when Hearne thought about what he'd done, or, more accurately, what he *hadn't* done, and the thought kept him awake at night. But like everything, it gradually went away. He thought he'd gotten away with it, since there had been no repercussions. Sure, he'd known better, deep down.

He should have known this day would come.

Saturday, 10:45 A.M.

OSCAR SWANN PARKED his pickup in front of Monica Taylor's house and got out quickly. The pickup was closer than necessary behind a white news van emblazoned with FOX NEWS KUYA SPOKANE on its side. He could see plainly what was happening and was there to stop it.

Monica stood on her front lawn looking aimless and haggard. A young man in dowdy clothes was fitting a video camera on a tripod in front of her, with her house in the background. Near the van, a slim blonde, who seemed scarcely out of college—except for the wolfish look of advanced ambition—held a mirror to her face with one hand and violently raked the other through her hair to make it appear that she had run to the scene. Her bright red lipstick looked like a knife wound slashed across her made-up face, he thought.

He was nearly too late. He should never have taken the time to shower, shave, and put on fresh clothes before he left his house. Singer would tear him apart if he knew that. But the urge to look decent after a long night of driving the roads near his house and staking this one out had left him tired and drained. Plus, he still had a thing for Monica. He remembered the first time he saw her behind the counter of the retail store. She was the best-looking woman he'd run across since he'd moved up there, he thought. After a little small talk, he learned she was single. His cop sense told him she was available if he played it right. Unlike Singer and Gonzalez, Swann couldn't stand endless hours at his own place with only himself and his hogs for company. He had to get out, and he liked to roam the town, saying little but observing everything. Not to the degree of Newkirk, though. Swann thought Newkirk was naïve and reckless, pretending he fit in.

Swann knew better, and he was learning not to mind. Sure, he looked the part. He was a careful observer, and within a year of arriving he'd learned how to dress down to look like a local: T-shirt, open chambray shirt, fleece vest, blue jeans, ball cap. Maybe a couple days of beard. He'd come to the conclusion that although it was possible for country people to move to a city and eventually adapt, it didn't work the other way around. He'd never fully get used to doing without; not having a vast choice of restaurants, grocery stores, shopping, the welcome blanket of anonymity within a white noise soundtrack. Here, they noticed you, talked to you without hesitation, asked where you were from. To deal with that he'd invented a persona and wore it around like he used to wear blue. People knew him here as affable Oscar Swann, retired cop who sought the simple life, raised some hogs, chewed tobacco, and admired the pure country goodness of the natives. They'd never know in his heart he thought of them as jaded Europeans thought of Americans: as childlike, boisterous, loud, too insular to appreciate what they had, too unsophisticated to realize how easy it had been for them. Nevertheless, they seemed to accept him although he learned too late that raising hogs wasn't exactly common. By then he'd come to like it. When he knew Monica, he sensed she'd seen through him, knew intuitively it was an act. He pulled away before she could confront him and confirm it, but that didn't keep him from still wanting her and jumping on this opportunity. He had needs, after all.

"No, no," he said to the newswoman, who had paused in her hair-raking while he strode toward her. "There'll be no interview."

The reporter glared at him. "What do you mean, there'll be no interview? I asked her, and she agreed. She wants to put out a plea for her children."

"Sorry, that won't happen."

The reporter reacted as if he'd slapped her, and she squared off to fight back. "And who in the hell are you?"

"Oscar Swann," he said, extending his hand but looking across the lawn to make sure the camera wasn't rolling yet.

The newswoman didn't reach out. "That name means nothing to me," she said.

"I'm with the task force for the sheriff's department," he said, showing her a laminated graphic of a badge on a lanyard they'd made just that morning. "We've been authorized to help with the investigation. If you want an interview, you need permission from Sheriff Carey. In fact, he's going to hold a press conference in a few hours. But we need you to leave Mrs. Taylor alone for now."

The reporter hesitated, looked at his plastic badge, then his face. He knew he looked fatherly, concerned, avuncular. Trustworthy. He always had.

"Are you a cop? I've never seen you around."

"Retired," he said in a way he thought clipped and official, as if Singer were addressing the media. "Twenty years, Los Angeles Police Department."

"I don't know," she said. "The woman already agreed to speak with us."

"Consider that permission revoked," Swann said. "Let me talk with her."

"Hey . . ." the reporter called after him, but he was already gone.

He positioned himself between the camera and Monica, who had watched the whole thing.

"Oscar," Monica asked, "what's going on?"

He kept his voice low. "Monica, I need to ask you not to speak on camera. This isn't a good idea." He told her about the task force at the sheriff's department, how they'd met and decided to funnel all requests for interviews through the sheriff's department so they could keep some control of the information.

"But why?" she asked, her eyes big. He took a moment to look at her. She was tired, pale, worn-out. There were dark rings around her eyes, and she wore no makeup. Still, though, he thought she was lovely.

"We don't want things to turn into a circus sideshow," he said.

"We've seen it a million times. These people live on rumors and speculation—anything to fill up airtime. They'll dissect every word you say and turn it around to use against you. If we want to do the right thing, we've got to keep a lid on the information we put out and make sure it's straight and accurate. You could accidentally say something that would give all the armchair experts in their studios a reason to suspect *you*. I've seen it happen."

She obviously didn't understand what he was saying, and shrugged. "Me? Why would they think that?"

"Another thing. Look, the person who has your kids might be watching the news. In fact, he'll *probably* be watching. We don't want him to know what we know yet or what leads we're pursuing. You might inadvertently say something that will help keep him from us. We've decided that only the sheriff should speak to the media, that it all be focused on him. That will keep the reporters in one place—the county building—and not camping out here at your house. If they know you won't give them interviews, but the sheriff will, they'll focus on him, not you. That's how we want to play it."

"I'm not sure I understand. I just want to find my kids."

"Monica, you're in the hands of professionals. We've been through this before."

"That means nothing to me."

Swann tried to remain calm, maintain the authoritative voice and demeanor. He could sense the cameraman behind him moving his tripod for a shot of Monica. Countering it, Swann moved to his right to stay between them. "We don't know yet where Annie and William are," he said. "If the person who has them decides to bring them back or contact you, we don't want camera trucks and reporters to scare him off. We also have to think about how things look to the bad guy. We want the face of this investigation to be the sheriff, not the victim. Does that make sense?"

She studied him, then shook her head. "No, not really."

He pointed to the reporter, who had finished with her hair and was standing with her hands on her hips, smoldering. "Look at her. All she wants is a story. She doesn't care about you or your kids."

That seemed to work. Monica assessed the reporter in a different light now, he thought.

"You have to decide to trust me, trust us," he said. "I'm here to help and protect you. Believe me, I've been through these kinds of situations before, we all have. There are ways to do them right, and one of those ways is not to turn this into a media frenzy. Monica, we've got only your best interests—and the welfare of your kids—in mind."

She looked at him as if she wasn't sure about that, but she called, "Later, maybe," to the reporter, and turned back toward her house. He followed her in through the front door and closed and locked it behind them. Through the front window she could see the reporter and the cameraman talking, heatedly, the reporter gesticulating with her hands. He closed the curtains on them.

What he didn't say to Monica was what he was thinking: *And we don't want your children to see you crying for them on television.*

Saturday, 12:20 P.M.

ON HIS way home, Jess Rawlins stopped for lunch at the Bear Trap, which was located halfway between town and the ranch, at an old culmination of logging roads that came down from the mountains. The Bear Trap was a peculiar, idiosyncratic icon: a rambling structure made of logs that had never been as elegant as intended and was now descending into senility. Once a dance hall, boardinghouse, restaurant, and touchstone for loggers and miners (with prostitutes upstairs), the building, once bold, now seemed to be withdrawing in on itself, looking frail and spindly, ready to collapse at an errant sneeze. It had a vast covered porch filled with mismatched weathered rocking chairs, and a hitching post out front that had been hit so many times by trucks pulling in that it leaned over almost to the ground.

Jess's father had once been a steady customer for meals but had boycotted the place when some people from Spokane bought it and attempted to gentrify it, upgrading the kitchen, remodeling the upstairs rooms, closing the credit accounts that were delinquent beyond thirty days, taking chicken-fried steak off the menu, and generally ruining it as far as he was concerned. The Bear Trap changed in character from a local tavern to a tourist stop. Trinkets replaced bullets and fishhooks on the retail shelves. Recently, though, the Spokane owners had thrown in the towel rather than invest any further in the deteriorating structure, and the building had been purchased by a retired crosscut saw foreman and his wife who were trying to make a go of it. Jess stopped there as often as he could, more out of support than desire, each time hoping the food would improve.

As he pulled into the lot he noticed the only other vehicle was a tricked-up SUV with Washington plates, ski racks on top and a bike rack on the rear bumper, a UNIVERSITY OF WASHINGTON decal in the back window, and FREE TIBET and WE VOTE, TOO bumper stickers. Idaho had long been considered a third-world country by Washingtonians, a kind of northwestern Appalachia. Despite the changes in the valley and the influx of new residents, the old perceptions still ran deep.

Inside, it was dark and cluttered, and smelled of decades-old spilled Hamm's beer as well as grease that needed changing out. Jess skipped the tables and went to the bar, waiting for the proprietress, who was busy delivering orders to the four raggedy college-age students occupying a big table in the center of the room. Jess swiveled on his stool and looked at them: two men, two women. They were very loud. The group was obviously passing through. The two men—boys, actually—wore baggy clothes and days-old growths of beard, their hair hanging down over their eyes. One boy had a mass of red hair and light freckles, with a squared-off, oafish jaw. The other was dark, angular, his face slack as if he had just awakened. The girls were young and pretty, one blonde, one brunette, with straight hair parted in the middle. The blonde wore a white tank top and jeans, and the brunette wore a dark T-shirt cut short to expose her belly. A glint of gold winked from a stud through her navel.

As the waitress put down their plates and gathered empty beer glasses, she looked up at Jess with an exasperated expression.

"Another round of beer for my horses!" one of the boys shouted, and the girls giggled, although one of them reached across the table and hit the boy in the arm.

"We're not, like, fucking *horses,*" she squealed.

Jess winced. Of course, he had heard the word before, many times, and used it on occasion. But she was so young, and it came so naturally from her.

He thought of his own son, the first year he had come back from college. He was like that, like those boys. Exuberant, loud, crude, full of himself. For almost a year, Jess Jr. was the smartest human being on the planet, and the people he had grown up with were the most ignorant. He had been charismatic in his way, attractive the way a turbo-charged red convertible is attractive to some girls. Jess had been alarmed by the change in him, but his wife had assured him it was normal. She told Jess their son had been repressed all those years and was now feeling his oats. Her implication was that Jess had been responsible for the repression. But no matter how she characterized the change, Jess still couldn't say truthfully that he liked what Jess Jr. had become. He still didn't. What he didn't know at the time was that he would never see Jess Jr. like that again.

The proprietress came around the bar with her spiral notebook out, eyeing Jess with a plea for understanding and sympathy.

"They're loud," Jess said.

"It's not just that," she whispered. "It's the mouths on them. Hell, I'm used to loggers, and these kids even offend *me*. They said they were on their way to Missoula to visit some friends at the U of M, but they don't seem to be moving very fast. Maybe I'm getting too old for this."

Jess ordered an open-faced roast beef sandwich and a jar—the Bear Trap served nonalcoholic drinks in Mason jars—of iced tea.

While Jess waited for the short-order cook to cover white bread with presliced, shiny cuts of beef, he thought about his meeting with Jim Hearne. Hearne was a good man, no doubt about it. The banker was doing all he could to put off the inevitable and cushion Jess's fall. He might even come up with something that would defer the fate of the ranch on a temporary basis. Jess was out of options, though. There was no way to work himself out of the hole he was in, besides selling the place. And he couldn't yet wrap his mind around that, couldn't yet consider it as a legitimate option.

Behind him, the din increased. A beer glass crashed to the floor, and a girl whooped. The jukebox started up. The college kids were settling in.

"Another beer, barwoman!" one of the boys shouted.

"Give me a sec," she said tersely, sliding the plate in front of Jess. "It's hot," she said.

Jess absently touched the rim of the plate. *No it isn't,* he said to himself.

As the proprietress filled another mug of beer from the tap, Jess overheard one of the boys say, "Dig the white meat on the poster. I could use a little piece of that." And the other boy laughed. "Stop it," one of the girls said, mock-alarmed.

Jess turned to see what they were talking about, saw the poster for the missing Taylor children that had recently been tacked up to a bulletin board, along with years' worth of flyers and notices. No, he thought. They couldn't be referring to *that* poster. It must be something else. Jess turned back to his plate but watched the table in the mirror, his anger rising. It had been the dark boy who had spoken of white meat.

"For sale," the redheaded boy said in a mock rural accent, "two white-trash northern Idaho, um . . . urchins!"

"Urchins!" the other boy repeated, laughing, reveling in the word choice.

"We plumb ran out of uses for 'em when they cut our welfare checks," the redheaded boy continued in the hillbilly accent. *"Since Billy Bob got laid off at the lumber mill, we been eating squirrel and drinking beer. Squirrel don't go as far as it used to . . ."*

The girls were now laughing. Drunk and laughing. They loved the redheaded boy's imitation of a working-class accent, even though the blonde kept saying, "Stop it, stop it, someone will hear you."

"Look at that girl," the dark boy said, pointing toward the flyer. "She'd get a few bucks in a white slave deal, don't you think? Hell, we could sell her to frat boys!"

The girls laughed, the brunette covering her mouth with her hands.

Jess felt dead for a moment, as if someone had hit him with a bat. He couldn't believe they were joking about the Taylor children, and especially the photo of Annie, whose image had broken his heart an hour before. How could they be joking about that? How was it possible? What world did they live in? Where did these kids come from, that a tragedy like this could be fodder for jokes? Sure, the kids were drunk. But how could the girls laugh at that?

Jess looked up to see the proprietress frozen at the beer tap, glaring at the table. Beer spilled out of the mug and poured into the trap. She couldn't believe what she was hearing either, and that the mug was full and spilling over the side didn't register with her. And there was something else, a kind of hurt-puppy look. Jess knew what it was. The college kids were steeped in that old Washington vs. Idaho view. What happened here was beneath them.

He felt something burning in his stomach and behind his eyes, and he slid off the stool. His boots clunked on the hardwood floor as he approached the table of college kids, and they didn't notice him until he was there. Leaning down and placing his hands on the table, he nodded at each of the boys.

"You two," he said. "I need to talk with you outside."

Without waiting for an answer or looking back, Jess straightened up and walked across the restaurant and out the batwing doors. He could hear the redheaded boy say, "What the fuck is wrong with that guy?" and the other say, "We don't have to go anywhere we don't want to," and one of the girls say, "Yeah, we have our rights."

What rights? Jess thought. He remembered when his son returned from college. Jess Jr. had also thought he had all kinds of rights.

Jess waited on the porch with his arms crossed. He didn't want to have to go back in and get them if they didn't come out. He could hear them discussing it, one of the girls telling the boys to stay right where they were, that an old cowboy had no right to tell them what to do.

Finally, the batwing doors swung out and the redheaded boy stepped through them holding a half-drunk mug of beer. The dark boy followed, his face inscrutable in its slackness.

"What's the problem, dude?" the redheaded boy said. "We just want to enjoy our lunch and soak up some local atmosphere, you know?"

Jess didn't know where to start. He glared at them, felt a hot kind of hatred build up in him, felt himself on the razor's edge of violence. But he kept his voice low.

"You were laughing about those missing children in there," Jess said. "That's not appropriate to the situation. I need to ask you to leave."

The redheaded boy started to argue, then looked quickly at his companion, talking about Jess as if he wasn't able to hear him.

"What's wrong with this old dude, man? He's got no right to give us orders like he owns the place . . . we're paying customers, dog."

The dark boy nodded his agreement, but didn't take his eyes off Jess.

There was a hint of uncertainty in his eyes, something the redheaded boy didn't show.

Jess said, "Apparently, while they were telling you how many rights you had at your school, they forgot about teaching you any respect or decorum. What you were saying in there about those missing kids isn't clever or funny, and it pisses me off because I'm from here."

The redheaded boy looked back at Jess, his expression wounded. "Man . . ."

"I'm sixty-three years old," Jess said, his eyes narrowing, his voice getting hard. "More than three times your age. And there are two of you. But if you don't walk back in and get those girls, *right now,* and drive on down the road, I'm going to knock you both into next year."

The boys stared back at him, frozen. Jess had no doubt that if they rushed him, it would all be over quickly, and he would be the worse for it. But in the mood he was in, he wanted them to try.

"We didn't mean nothing . . ." the redheaded boy started to say.

"RIGHT NOW," Jess said through clenched teeth.

The dark boy broke first, saying "Ah, fuck this shit" with resignation and, turning toward the door, grasped the redheaded boy's arm. "Let's go, Jarrod."

"We can take this old fart," redheaded Jarrod said. "He can't throw us out of here. It's a public place."

"Forget it, man," the dark boy said. "He isn't worth it."

Jess let it go. He could grant them a bit of false dignity in their cowardice.

Jess stood to the side on the porch and watched them come out, all four of them glaring at him as they passed. He was pleased that the blond girl at least looked ashamed of herself, ashamed of her companions. The brunette didn't, though. Her face was a mask of righteous indignation. Jess heard the words *white trash* as they climbed into their car and threw gravel as they exited the parking lot. The redheaded boy shouted something as they pulled onto the two-lane, and raised his hand out of the window with his middle finger out.

He finished his lunch, which was cold, while the owner cleaned up the vacated table. The last selection finished on the jukebox, and the only sound in the Bear Trap was the ticking of the clock and the clink of the empty glasses she gathered from the table.

He gestured toward the poster. "This kind of thing is on the news so much these days it probably doesn't even seem real to them."

"They didn't even leave me a tip," the proprietress said as she stacked the dirty plates and glasses behind the bar.

PULLING OFF the road near his mailbox, Jess got his mail and tossed it on the seat next to him. Fiona had placed a Post-It note on an envelope from the county tax assessor with the words "BETTER OPEN THIS!!!" on it.

After changing into his work clothes and replacing his new Stetson with his sweat-stained old one, Jess stuck a pair of fencing pliers in his back pocket and saddled Chile. There was a cold, heavy stone in his belly as he rode up a slate-rock ridge that overlooked the ranch hill on the north side of the near meadow.

Growing up, Jess Rawlins had explored every inch of the ranch within riding distance of the house, and the rest later, on overnights via horseback or dirt bike. He had spent most of his time alone, and he was intimate with the folds of the terrain, the stands of trees, the overhang bank along the creek where he could reach down into the water and, if he was gentle, feel the gills flutter on the three-pound trout that lived there.

The slate-rock ridge was 150 yards from his house. The teeth of the ridge could be seen against the horizon from his porch and from the road, but the slope behind it was obscured from view. It was the perfect place to see but not be seen.

As a boy, Jess had created scenarios where he went into action and saved his family from outside threats. When he was very young he used to imagine Indians attacking. Later, it was escaped criminals or Communists. Aiming down the length of a broom handle or a BB gun, he had hidden himself on the top of the ridge with slate-rock outcroppings, and picked off his targets as they moved down out of the trees into the open ranch yard below. From the outcropping, the main ranch road was in full view as it spilled out of the trees and curved down the hillside in looping switchbacks before straightening for the ranch house. From his perch behind the slate rocks, he would see his mother through the window in her kitchen, but she couldn't see him. She had no idea he was up there saving her, saving the ranch.

Sometimes, he remembered, the situation got so desperate that he would need to counterattack. He would rise to his feet, holler a war cry, and charge down the hill, bobbing and weaving toward the house as his enemies shot at him. Sometimes they hit him, and to make the action realistic, he would splash water from his canteen on the place where the bullet hit, so he could feel the wetness of the blood. He would be practically soaked by the time he made it to the house and dispatched the last of the bad guys, despite his massive and fatal wounds.

At dinner, his mother would ask him why he was wet. He would say, "I *am*?"

Years later, he had shown this place to his son, Jess Jr., even urged the boy to hunker down behind the slabs of slate that poked twelve to fourteen inches through the grassy surface of the ridge like shields. Not that he wanted the boy to create scenarios of his own, but he hoped his son would simply appreciate the view the ridge afforded of the ranch, the land, the open vista bordered by dark trees. His son had looked around, then turned to Jess with a shrug, and asked how long it was until dinner.

HE PICKED his way down the slate-rock ridge, looking out at the newborn calves and their mothers, including the new arrivals from the night before, who were racing around in the fenced-off meadow, bawling, quiet only when they were sleeping or nursing from their mothers. He liked new calves. It was the only time in their lives they were ever clean, and their russet-and-white coloring was vibrant. They smelled fresh.

He rode through them, climbed the other side of the corral fence to the near meadow, and followed the fence to the top of the hill. The barbed wires had sagged between two posts, leaving enough of a gap that the calves could escape if they figured it out. Even so, they wouldn't go far from their mothers, and both mothers and babies would make a god-awful racket trying to reunite. The desperate mothers might cut themselves up on the wire trying to get to their newborns. He dismounted, tightened the wire, and pounded new staples into the posts.

After finishing, he did what he always did, which was to walk along the fence, thumping each post to make sure it was sound, making sure the bottoms hadn't rotted away.

That's when he saw the strip of color hanging from a barb on the second strand from the top.

Jess bent over and looked at it. The yellow strip was no wider than a half inch and an inch long. It wasn't frayed or bleached out by the sun or rain, which meant it was new. Maybe, he thought, one of the search team members had brushed too close to his fence. He remembered the description of the Taylor girl from the poster, that she was last seen wearing a yellow sweatshirt.

Then, in the mud near his boots, he noticed two footprints. One was from a small athletic shoe. The other, slightly larger, was made by a bare foot.

He stood up and looked out over his ranch in the direction the footprints were aimed. They were headed for his barn.

Saturday, 2:50 P.M.

I HEAR someone coming," Annie said, bending forward and clapping her hand over William's mouth and muzzling a long complaint about how hungry he was. William squirmed in protest and reached up to pry her hand away but heard it too: crunching footfalls in loose gravel outside the barn.

IT HAD been Annie's idea to hide in the barn the night before, after they had shinnied through the limp strands of a barbed-wire fence. They had seen the barn roof glowing in the cloud-muted blue moonlight. The barn was situated in an open area at the foot of the slope, a clearing that held back the black wall of trees. There was a house down there, too, in fact two of them, but they were dark and she didn't want to knock on any doors. After what had happened at Mr. Swann's, she didn't trust anyone.

They had held hands as they crossed the ranch yard, stepping as lightly as they could through the gravel, waiting for the charge of barking, snarling cow dogs that never came. Instead, a blocky old Labrador approached them, tail wagging, and licked William's hand.

Luckily, the barn was empty except for a fat cow that stood still and silent in a stall. Half of the barn was filled with pungent hay bales stacked up to the rafters. Annie and William climbed them using the stair-step pattern of stacked bales until they were on the top of the hay. There, she decided, was where they would stop and rest. From the top, she could look down on the floor of the barn and see all of the doors.

"We need to build a nest," she told William.

"Let's call it a fort," he said. "A fort sounds better."

"Okay, a fort."

"I'll protect us," William said. "I got outlaw blood in me."

"You mean Billy? Stop that."

"Dad was an outlaw."

Annie glared at him. "William, your dad was a criminal."

"He was your dad, too."

"I doubt it."

William's eyes misted, his upper lip trembled, and Annie felt bad for what she'd said.

"I'm really sorry. Never mind that," she said. "Let's build our fort."

"I can do it, really," William said through a shuddering breath.

"I know you can," she said.

The bales were heavy, but not so heavy that the two of them couldn't lift six out of the top row by the twine that bound them and stack the bales around the hole they had formed. Their fort was two bales deep into the stack.

Even though William was literally falling asleep as he stood there, Annie coaxed him back down to the ground, where they found a tack room. They carried stiff saddle blankets and a canvas tarp up to their fort and lined its floor with them. William was asleep before Annie could adjust the tarp to cover him.

She made one more trip to the tack room, and found a long, scythe-shaped hay hook and a pitchfork, which she took up to their fort. The pitchfork was now within reach on the top of the bales. The hay hook, with its long shaft and curled tine that looked like a pointed metal question mark, was stuck in the hay at eye level.

Annie had slept fitfully. Every sound—a bird whistling through the rafters, the fat cow shifting her weight or peeing with the sound of a bucket being emptied—scared her and kept her awake. The events of the previous day and night kept replaying in her head, her reminiscence even more vibrant and vivid than what she had actually experienced in the first place. The bright red blood pouring from the chest and face of the Wavy-Haired Man who'd been shot. The smell of pig manure from Mr. Swann's boots as they huddled on the floor of his pickup. The sharp pine needles that scratched at them as they ran through the night, putting several hours between themselves and Mr. Swann's home. William, though, had slept like something dead. When he snored, she prodded him with her elbow to make him stop.

The last thing she remembered, until now, was seeing the muted cream glow from the rising sun through gaps in the east side of the barn.

Someone was coming.

It was much warmer in the barn now, and heat beat down on them from the roof just a few feet over the top of their hay wall. She guessed it was midday, or early afternoon. She threw the tarp back and found herself drenched in sweat. She was thirsty, and her mouth was so dry her lips stuck to her teeth as she tried to talk.

"Here they come," she said thickly.

A LARGE sliding door opened, flooding the barn with light. The sound of it was like a roll of distant thunder. William's eyes widened, and Annie withdrew her hand from his mouth.

Who is it? he mouthed.

She shrugged in reply. She didn't dare rise and peek over the hay bales to see who it was.

"Hello," a man called. "Is someone in here?"

She tried to judge the voice. It didn't sound threatening. But neither had Mr. Swann's.

"I saw some tracks outside," the man said. "They were pointed this direction. If you're in here, speak up."

Annie and William exchanged looks. Annie narrowed her eyes and gestured toward the hay hook and the pitchfork, and William saw them for the first time. He looked back at his sister with admiration.

Annie pulled William to her, and she whispered in his ear. "If he comes up here, we'll have to defend ourselves."

William nodded his understanding.

For a moment, there was no sound at all from below. What was he doing, Annie wondered. Had he left? What if he decided to go into his house and call the sheriff? Or his neighbor, Mr. Swann?

"Annie and Willie, are you in here?" the man asked softly.

Annie's heart raced: *He knew their names!*

She looked at William, who was scowling. He didn't like to be called Willie. He reached up and drew the hay hook out of the bale, and ran his finger along its sharpened tip.

The man below was walking through the barn, and she heard the door to the tack room open and the sound of boots scuffing on the slat-board floor. Then the door closed, and the man called out, even more softly than before.

"Annie and Willie, if you're in here, you can come out. You're probably pretty hungry and thirsty, and I'd guess you've got family who is worried as hell about you. I see I'm missing some blankets and a tarp, and my guess is you needed them to get through the night. That was smart thinking. But I'd bet that a shower and something cool to drink would sound even better right now."

William looked to Annie and made a face, indicating, "It sure would!"

Annie scolded him with her eyes.

"I imagine you two are scared," the man said. "I understand. But I'm not going to do you any harm. My name's Jess Rawlins. I own this ranch."

Suddenly, Annie had doubts. The man's voice seemed kind, and caring. There was a timbre to it she liked. But how could she know he was telling the truth? Or that even if he was a rancher, he wasn't friends with people like Mr. Swann or the executioners?

"I'm coming up there on the top of my hay," Rawlins said, "because if I was a kid your age, that's where I'd go. Plus, it looks like my stack is one row higher today than it was last night when I left it."

William clutched the handle of the hay hook with both hands. Annie slid the pitchfork into their fort from where she had put it the night before. She grasped the rough wooden handle and pointed the rusty curved tines toward the top edge of the hay bales.

They could hear him breathing hard as he climbed the stack, and felt a slight vibration in the closely packed hay from his weight.

"Don't get scared," Rawlins said. "It's going to be okay."

When the long, brown hand reached over the top bale like some kind of crab, William lunged and swung the hook through the air, striking flesh. The man responded with a sharp intake of breath. The point cut through the webbing of the man's hand between his thumb and index finger and opened a gash. Blood spurted from the wound.

Annie's first, instinctive reaction was revulsion. She wanted to run away, but there was nowhere to run. So she swallowed hard, stood with the pitchfork ready, and leaned forward, following the writhing arm down toward a shoulder, then a battered cowboy hat, and a lean, weathered face suspended in a silent scream. She pointed the tines toward his face and tried to scowl.

Rawlins looked back at her, obviously in pain, but his eyes didn't seem to threaten her.

"Damn," Rawlins said. "Why'd you go and do that to my hand? It really hurts."

Annie wasn't sure what to do. She glanced back at William and found him huddled in the corner of the fort, staring at the hand of the rancher pinned with the hook to the bale of hay. A thin line of dark blood coursed down Rawlins's hand and dripped on the tarp. A quarter inch of skin held the hand pinned to the bale. The rancher could pull away and break the skin, and keep climbing. William looked up to her for direction, and she saw the terror in his eyes from what he had done and its implications.

She turned back to Rawlins. His other hand was now on the top bale as well.

"I need to reach over with my free hand and pull that hook out," Rawlins said. "I don't want you jabbing me with that fork, though."

Annie knew she had him, and knew he knew it. So why did she feel so awful?

"You're Annie, right?"

She nodded.

"And Willie?"

"William," her brother corrected.

"Well, Annie and William, I'm glad you're all right. The whole county's looking for you."

Annie shook her head, as if denying the truth of what she had just heard. If everyone was looking for them, maybe it was safe to come out after all.

"Mind if I pull this hook out of my hand?" Rawlins asked.

"We're hungry," Annie said, wishing she could put more sand into her voice. "You can pull it out if you'll take us in and get us something to eat and drink."

Jess Rawlins looked at her with something like amusement. Then he nodded at William. "I was going to offer that anyway," he said. "Luckily, I never liked this hand all that much."

Saturday, 5:34 P.M.

THE BANKER, Jim Hearne, shouldered his way through the knot of men in jackets and ties and women in cocktail dresses and ordered another Scotch and water at the makeshift bar. It was his fourth in barely an hour.

It was the opening night reception for the Kootenai Bay Recreation Center, financed through his bank. He had been the principal officer for the project and was on the board of directors. The Rec Center had a full-size gymnasium, an Olympic-size pool, racquetball courts, aerobics and weight rooms, a climbing wall, sauna rooms, Jacuzzis. Although financed jointly by the bank, the city, and the county initially, enough charter memberships had been sold—primarily to newcomers to the valley—that first-year financial projections would be exceeded. It was the first facility of its kind built in the community, and over two hundred people were touring it, drinks in hand, talking excitedly, slapping him on the back.

Two of the bars were located in the gym, one under the rim of each basketball hoop on opposite ends of the floor. To disguise his intent, which was to become obliterated as clandestinely as possible, Hearne alternated bars each time he ordered a drink so the bartenders and guests wouldn't notice how much he was drinking. As The Banker, he was always being watched, observed, talked about. It came with the territory, and he accepted it. But tonight, there was too much on his mind, too many problems, and a serious one he had to keep entirely to himself.

He circulated through the building, exchanging pleasantries, greeting old friends, welcoming new residents, most of whom were bank customers. He tried hard to remember names because they certainly knew him. If he didn't know their names and couldn't read name tags, he simply said, "Great to see you, thanks for coming," and moved on. He tried not to be drawn into any conversations, most of which were about either the new facility or the missing Taylor children.

The sheriff had held a press conference in the afternoon that was televised on the local affiliates and excerpted nationally. Hearne had watched it nervously, always concerned how his community would be portrayed. He was pleasantly surprised how well the new sheriff presented himself, especially since the banker had not supported Carey in the election, thinking him pompous and unqualified. Carey stressed to the media that it was too early to draw any conclusions, that at this point it was a missing persons investigation, not kidnapping or worse. Carey seemed competent, in charge. Photos of the Taylor children were flashed on the screen along with a hot line number. He explained that he'd tapped the resources of a team of retired big-city police officials to assist him with the investigation. The performance was flawless. Hearne wondered who had coached him.

The makeup of the crowd at the center was interesting to him, and something he was getting used to. Three-quarters of the guests were newcomers to the area, having arrived in the last five years. The remaining quarter were from the area, mainly professional people. It was notable how the newcomers grouped together, and the locals did the same. In only a few instances did he see them mixing. The response to the new facility was different also, he noted. The locals were proud of it almost beyond words, their comments a mixture of awe and reverence, as if saying, "I can't believe what we've done!" The newcomers, on the other hand, were happy with the new facility, but in a different way, as if finally they were receiving something they'd long deserved, something they were used to. As if they had taken another step forward in dragging the hidebound old-timers into the twenty-first century.

But Hearne had trouble mingling, spending much time in either group. As the banker he was sort of a host, so he constantly used that excuse to take his leave, as if pressing matters in another part of the facility pulled him away. His position at the bank and his long history as a resident of the valley gave him knowledge that ran deep. His familiarity with the residents and his customers was a huge asset to the bank, one of the reasons he continued to be promoted every time the institution changed hands. He often felt like the human bridge between the old and the new. His life was a balancing act between ingrained loyalties and newfound wealth, power, and status. But sometimes, like now, he felt he knew too much.

The fact was, Hearne couldn't think of much else than the missing Taylor children and the meetings he had had that morning with Jess Rawlins and Eduardo Villatoro. They all disturbed him, but in different ways. They were moles in a mental Whack-A-Mole game: When he suppressed one the other popped up automatically, as if they were somehow interconnected in a way he couldn't comprehend.

He approached a bar situated in the alcove to the swimming pool and ordered a fifth Scotch. As he sipped it, he looked out on the pool. The black lanes painted on the bottom wavered in the water more than they should. He would have to slow down. But he didn't want to.

"What's wrong with you?"

It was his wife, Laura. He hadn't seen her approach.

"What do you mean?"

"I've been watching you," she said. "You've been running around this place like a chicken with its head cut off. The only places you stop are the bars. Don't think I haven't noticed."

He felt himself flush. Caught.

Laura was a plain-speaking, handsome woman, with strong features and all-seeing eyes. Her skin was dark from being outside so much, riding her horses, working at her stables. She was a horsewoman, a former barrel racer, from a third-generation Idaho family. Despite their rise in status within the community, Laura chose to dress in what was comfortable to her: Western shirts, jeans, sometimes a broomstick skirt and boots, like tonight. She was considered vivacious and home-grown by the locals, and Hearne still saw her that way. Only when she was in a big group of newcomers, with their fashion and trendy haircuts, did he realize how different she looked. He appreciated her sense of tradition, though, and admired how she was comfortable with who she was. Sometimes, though, he wished she would dress up a little, like tonight. Didn't she notice? The thought made him instantly ashamed of himself.

"Are you okay?" she asked. "You seem just a tad distracted," she said in a mischievous way. "My dad would have said you are jumping around like a fart in a skillet."

Hearne almost blurted out his Whack-A-Mole analogy but caught himself. Mentioning it would open doors he wanted kept shut.

"I keep thinking about those Taylor kids," he said, which was true but only part of the reason. "That isn't the kind of thing that happens here."

"Maybe it didn't used to," she said, then gestured toward the crowd. "Before the immigration and all of your new friends."

He smiled sourly. It was a point of contention between them. Laura would have been fine if the valley had remained the way it was when she grew up, small, intimate, rural, eccentric.

"My 'new friends,' as you call them, helped buy your last three horses and the new barn," he said.

"I know. Boy, you are testy tonight."

He looked away, wishing he hadn't said that.

"You had better slow down," she said, nodding toward his glass. "I don't want you falling into the pool in front of all of your . . . customers."

"I will."

"And, Mr. Jim Hearne, don't play coy with me," she said, leaning into him, staring up into his eyes. "I know you. You drink when you're worried, or fretting about something. It never helps, but it's what you do."

"I said . . ."

"Right, the Taylors," she said dismissively.

"Really."

She asked, "Which Taylor are you most worried about? The kids or Monica?"

Hearne felt his neck get hot. Laura had never liked Monica Taylor and harbored suspicions about her. Hearne felt defensive whenever Monica was brought up, even though he had explained the situation to

Laura more than once. He had told Laura Monica thought of him as a father figure because of his friendship with her father. Laura had raised her eyebrows, and asked, "Is that all?" He stammered, said, "Of course. You know what happened."

When Jim Hearne was riding saddle broncs on the college rodeo team, and later on his own when he was sponsored by Rawlins Ranch, his closest friend and traveling companion had been Ty Taylor, Monica's father. Ty was handsome and enigmatic, a star performer, a man who attracted women like a magnet, despite the fact that he was married with a young daughter at home. One of the reasons Hearne partnered with Ty early on was for exactly that reason—where Ty went, women appeared. When Hearne injured his knee and laid off the circuit for a year and returned home, his on-again off-again courtship of Laura got serious, and they married. Ty was the best man, flying home between rodeos in Salinas and Cheyenne to be there.

Hearne finished up his degree in finance while he recovered, but the rodeo was in his blood. Laura didn't like it when he went back to rodeoing and liked it even less when he hooked up again with Ty. Although Hearne was faithful to Laura and tried his best to rein Ty in, he wasn't successful. Ty loved women—as a gender, if not individually—and women loved Ty. When the two cowboys came home together, Hearne watched little Monica look up to her father with unabashed hero worship that broke Hearne's heart, even though it didn't appear to faze Ty. Apparently he was used to that kind of look, Hearne thought at the time.

Ty was severely injured at the Calgary Stampede when his boot caught in his stirrup and he fell, breaking his neck. Hearne stood by his bed in the hospital while they waited for Monica and her mother to get there, and Ty grabbed Hearne's hand and asked him to take care of Monica. Ty didn't care much for his wife, but he said he'd cheated on his daughter, and she didn't deserve a dad like that. He planned to die before they arrived.

But he didn't. Over the next few years, Ty stayed home, recovered, but wasn't able to get medical clearance to rodeo again. So he went back to chasing women throughout North Idaho and eastern Washington. On a warm day in May, he left his family without a word and never came back. Hearne had lost track of him completely over the years, although Ty once called him at the bank to see about a loan "for old times' sake." Hearne hung up on him.

Hearne was no psychologist, but it was easy for him to see how Ty's abandonment affected both Monica and Monica's mother. Her mother became an alcoholic and moved to Spokane, supposedly looking for a permanent job before sending for her daughter. Monica stayed in the area, bouncing around from place to place, growing wilder and more beautiful by the year. Boys were as attracted to Monica as women had been to her father. Monica didn't discourage the attention at all. The most important man in her life had walked away. Others were lining up to step right in. The way Hearne saw it, Monica's mission was to prove to herself she was likable and desirable after all, that her father had made a *huge* mistake. She looked for men who were dazzling, dangerous, and charismatic like her father had been. That she didn't seem to recognize what she was doing, despite her intelligence, was one of life's mysteries to Hearne.

So he had done what he could do, from a distance. He approved a home loan for her after the loan committee turned her down due to insufficient assets. He quietly dismissed overdraft charges on her checking account. When she was seriously overdrawn, he would call her and tell her to move some money into the account and, on occasion, lend her a few hundred when she was strapped. She'd always thanked him for his help very sincerely and never acted as if she was entitled to it.

He liked her, in spite of her reputation and the poor choices she had made. She had come to him the first time she was in trouble, and he'd tried to help her, but helping Monica back in those days was like trying to stop a freight train by standing on the tracks with his palm upraised. Hearne hadn't been surprised when Monica's husband was sent to prison. But even now, he couldn't see her on the street without seeing the face of her in childhood, looking up to her father, unabashed worship on her face. Was he attracted to her? Sure. Every man was. But it wasn't that. She was a casualty, and he had been there when the damage was done. Even though he thought he couldn't do anything about it at the time, he had been there when it happened. Looking back, he felt responsibility for the way things turned out with the Taylors. He should've knocked Ty down, sat on him, and told him to straighten the hell up. Maybe that would have penetrated Ty's thick skull. And even if it hadn't, Hearne would have at least showed Ty he disapproved of the life he was living. Instead, he had stood by, observing, shaking his head, watching Ty wreck his own family. Then going off with Ty to the next rodeo. Laura thought he was nuts for thinking he could have done anything to stop the situation, and said so.

"They'll find those kids," Laura said, breaking into his reverie. "I'm sure they'll turn up at somebody's house or something."

"I hope so," Hearne said. He couldn't imagine what it would be like to have children missing. The Hearnes had a son and a daughter, both married and moved away. Their lives had revolved around their children while they grew up. Imagining them missing when they were young was incomprehensible.

But, of course, it wasn't only that. He thought of Jess Rawlins, how he could see no way to save him, either. Jess was, in Hearne's mind, the conscience of the valley as he was growing up. Jess had taken Hearne under his wing and treated him as if he were his own son. Jess had never asked for anything for his sponsorship other than "to do us proud." Us, meaning the valley. Jess was stubborn, independent, but intrinsically fair. That his own family had failed the way it did was a tragedy, Hearne thought, and he blamed Karen, Jess's ex-wife. Hearne knew things about Karen, about her personal bank account and growing balance while the ranch accounts went dry, about her many dinners with men other than Jess, about her secret life. Karen had drained off the cash flow of the ranch, and Jess never knew it. Hearne had been duty-bound to keep quiet about it for years. A banker had no right to reveal that kind of information without the permission of the account holder. After Karen finally left Jess, and Jess was devastated, Hearne felt immensely guilty for not softening the blow. He could have taken Jess out for a cup of coffee, or taken Karen, and talked to them about what he knew. It would have been an ethical breach, but it would have been the right thing to do, he saw in retrospect. Jess had not recovered from the financial or emotional loss, and now his ranch was literally on the block.

And it wasn't that Jim Hearne was immune to ethical breaches, and that's what troubled him most. The meeting with Mr. Villatoro had laid bare Hearne's own deception, even though Villatoro didn't yet know it. Hearne knew his own actions—or lack of them—had brought Eduardo Villatoro to North Idaho.

He recalled his first meeting with Eric Singer, who had flown up from Los Angeles to meet with him and make an offer. The timing of the visit was opportune, just days after the board of directors meeting where the chairman decided the only way to keep the bank viable and growing was to change their strategy from low-return and high-maintenance agricultural loans to commercial finance. The bank needed to grow up and out, increase its cash deposits exponentially, and aggressively get ahead of the development boom that was starting to occur at the time. Since Hearne was in charge of ag loans, he saw the writing on the wall. So when Eric Singer walked into his office, it was as if fate had sent a messenger.

Hearne's first impression of Singer was not good. He didn't like the man's superior demeanor and thought his attitude toward the community was condescending. He told Hearne he sought isolation, cheap land, and a live-and-let-live attitude. Rather than being put off by the reputation Kootenai Bay had of harboring white supremacists, Singer seemed drawn to it, saying he'd had his fill of "political fucking correctness." Hearne remembered biting his tongue as Singer talked, weighing a defense of his home against the prospect of lucrative new accounts. Singer was not the first retired LAPD officer to find his way to North Idaho, nor the last. But unlike the others Hearne had met, Singer promised to bring up a small but well-heeled group of colleagues with him if Hearne was willing to make the conditions right.

Hearne made the conditions right. Singer delivered. Hearne was promoted personally by the chairman of the board. But it haunted him still.

He knew too much, as The Banker. He wished he didn't. But it was too late for that kind of thinking.

Despite the disapproving look Laura was giving him, Hearne put the empty glass on the bar and ordered another.

Saturday, 6:18 P.M.

THE COMMAND CENTER for the disappearance of the Taylor children had been established in a modern conference room off the Kootenai Bay City Council chambers, down the hall from Sheriff Ed Carey's office. Off-duty dispatchers had been called in to help set it up with telephones, computers, a fax machine, along with a coffeemaker and mini refrigerator. The straight-backed chairs surrounding the long table had been replaced with the comfortable, ergonomic chairs used by council members for their meetings. Ex-Lt. Eric Singer, the volunteer in charge of the effort, had long since used his sleeve to wipe the whiteboard clean of past council business. He stood at the board with a fistful of different-colored pens.

Ex-Officer Newkirk was slumped at the foot of the table, looking vacantly away from the whiteboard through a window at the city council chambers, at the nameplates of each absent council member. He felt ill, his skin gritty. His stomach was acting up, and despite the fact that he hadn't had breakfast or lunch and there was a cold-cut tray in front of him, he wasn't hungry. The scenario that was playing out in front of him was the last thing in the world he wanted to be involved in. This was the situation that had kept him awake at night for years. This, right here, was the reason he had ulcers.

"Are we ready?" Singer asked, pulling the cap from a green pen.

"Ready," Gonzalez said, adjusting a legal pad filled with scribbles in front of him. He began to read, and Singer started writing on the whiteboard. The marker squeaked as he wrote, and it filled the room with a watered-down airplane-glue smell.

"When we're done here, I want you to go get the sheriff," Singer said, pausing and looking over his shoulder. "Newkirk?"

Newkirk wasn't paying attention, and Gonzalez leaned over and whapped him on the arm with the back of his hand, saying, "Wake the fuck up."

Newkirk wheeled in his chair, startled. "What?"

"The lieutenant was talking to you."

"I asked you if you would go down and get the sheriff when I'm done here," Singer said quietly, enunciating every word in an exaggerated way. "We need his approval to proceed."

"Okay."

"Are you okay, Newkirk?" Singer asked, his ice-blue eyes unblinking. "You with us here?"

Newkirk nodded, then looked to Gonzalez and nodded again.

"You better be," Gonzalez said.

Singer lifted the marker to his nose. "Ah, it smells like a briefing room in here, doesn't it?"

They were in control.

AS NEWKIRK entered the Pend Oreille County Sheriff's office, he noticed a paunchy man in a brown suit waiting in the reception area. Newkirk nodded at the man, then told the receptionist that Singer was ready in the command center.

"The command center, Officer Newkirk?" the receptionist asked.

"The conference room," Newkirk said, an edge in his voice. "We're calling it the command center now until we get those kids back."

The receptionist flushed, turned in her chair, and walked back toward the sheriff's office.

"It's a good thing you are doing," the man in the brown suit said to Newkirk. "Very community-minded."

"What?" Newkirk turned, adjusted his ball cap, and studied the man. A man wearing a suit in the sheriff's office on a Saturday evening. He looked out of place, enough so that Newkirk's antennae went up.

"I heard your name. You are among the volunteers who have come forward. You used to be with the LAPD," Villatoro said pleasantly, a statement more than a question.

"That's no secret. You a lawyer?"

"No."

"You have some kind of interest in this case?"

The man shook his head. "I'm here on another matter." The man stood and extended his hand. "Eduardo Villatoro."

Newkirk didn't reach out immediately. It grated on him when Latins gave their names with Spanish pronunciation, rolling the "r's" and playing up the accents. Gangbangers would do that, even though most of them were second- or third-generation American. He felt his street cop dead-eye stare take over. Usually, when he did that, the other person in the situation would reveal himself, talk too much.

"I'm here to see the sheriff as well," Villatoro said. "But it's after six. I was wondering how long you might be with him before I can talk with him."

"About what?"

"Another matter."

Newkirk continued the dead-eye. "Fine, don't tell me. I doubt it's as important as this one."

"I have no doubt of that," Villatoro said, holding his hands palms up and widening his eyes to try and clear the air. Newkirk liked that.

"What is this other matter?" Newkirk said, letting sarcasm creep into the question.

Villatoro smiled. "You are right. It isn't as important as the community service you are performing here. I was just wondering if I should wait for the sheriff this evening or come back tomorrow. That's why I was asking."

This dark guy made Newkirk uncomfortable, and he wasn't sure he knew why.

"Come back tomorrow," Newkirk said.

Villatoro nodded and seemed a little cowed. Good, Newkirk thought. He needed to be knocked down a peg.

The receptionist came out of the sheriff's office, and said to Newkirk, "He's finishing up a call and will be with you shortly."

"I'll wait."

He watched Villatoro dig for his wallet and approach the receptionist.

"I would like to leave this card," Villatoro said. "I'll be in early tomorrow morning to see the sheriff."

The receptionist took the card without looking at it and placed it on her desk. She watched the light blink out on her handset.

"He's through," she said.

Sheriff Carey came out of his office a moment later, looking haggard. His eyes were deep-set, his hair mussed. He was a worried man, Newkirk realized. Cops were one way or the other, he knew. Men like Singer got a case like this and were energized by it like it was new, fresh blood pumping through their veins. But for people like Carey, and Newkirk himself, it was just the opposite. It wore them down.

"That was the FBI in Boise," Carey said. "They want to know if we're ready to call them in. I told them to give us a day or two since we should have things wrapped up by then. I hope."

Newkirk nodded. Singer would be interested in that, since he had advised the sheriff early on to keep the Feds at bay.

"So you're ready for me?"

"Yes, we are. In the command center."

Newkirk noticed that Villatoro had slipped out during the exchange.

"Okay, then," Carey said, heaving a weight-of-the-world sigh.

"Sheriff . . ." the receptionist called after him.

"Yes, you can go home now, Marlene."

Newkirk waited a moment while Marlene cleared her desk and the sheriff strode down the hall toward the conference room. When Marlene turned around, he reached over and plucked the business card from her desk and slipped it into his back pocket.

ON THE WHITEBOARD, in green, Singer had written TIMELINE. Under the heading, each fact of the case was bulleted next to the military time it had occurred. The children had left school the day before, Friday, at noon on early release. Between noon and 15:35, when the mailwoman Fiona Pritzle had picked them up on the road and dropped them near Sand Creek, they had presumably gone home, taken the fishing rod and vest, and set out on foot. Monica Taylor became concerned about their absence at 17:30. Her fight with Tom Boyd had occurred at 18:00. She called the sheriff's department at 19:00, after first contacting friends and neighbors. Boyd staggered from the Sand Creek Bar at 23:30 and hadn't been seen since.

Singer ran his finger down the list, noting when the rod and shoe had been found near the river.

Newkirk watched the sheriff as Carey listened to Singer. Carey leaned back against the conference table, with Newkirk on one side and Gonzalez on the other. The other volunteer, Swann, had left hours before to go to Monica Taylor's home.

"Our last timeline entry was 08:10 this morning," Singer said, looking pained. "We've got nothing since then." He pointed at a figure he had written and underlined: "These kids have been missing for twenty-seven hours."

His words seemed to hit Carey like individual slaps.

"Our experience," Singer said, nodding toward the other ex–LAPD officers in the room, "is that once we pass twenty-four, we've got a problem."

"I *know* we've got a problem," Carey said.

"Word is out," Singer said. "Everybody knows we've got missing kids. Everyone's looking for them. But there have been no solid leads or sightings since we found that shoe and the fishing rod."

Carey swallowed.

"We've got people volunteering to join search teams up the wazoo," Singer said, gesturing toward Gonzalez. "Gonzo's been keeping a list of names, addresses, telephone numbers. There are three teams of ten out there now, combing through the woods on a grid from where that shoe was found. It's slow but thorough. So far, we've got nothing."

"I know."

"Sheriff, in your experience, how long would it take for a body to surface on Sand Creek? Assuming the person drowned?"

The sheriff shook his head. "It's not very deep, but it's fast with runoff. The creek completely shallows out before it empties into the lake, so there's no chance any bodies floated all that way. It's only eighteen inches deep at the mouth. So all we're talking about is four miles of creek before it empties into the lake."

Singer looked concerned. "Is it possible the bodies got caught under debris? Or got sucked into, I don't know, some kind of deep pool?"

"It's possible but unlikely," Carey said sadly. "It just isn't that deep anywhere."

Singer looked thoughtful. He rubbed his chin with his hand. Then: "Let's continue."

Singer had written SUSPECTS in red, and ASSIGNMENTS in black.

Under suspects were Tom Boyd, Monica Taylor, Fiona Pritzle, transient unknown, and "area pedophile."

"Can you think of any others?" Singer asked.

"I'd scratch the mother and the mail lady off the list," Carey said. "The mother's just too upset. And that mail lady was the one who called us. If she had something to do with it, she could have just kept her mouth shut and nobody would even know those kids went up Sand Creek in the first place."

Singer gestured to Gonzalez. "Gonzo?"

Gonzalez cleared his throat. "I had a guy once who came into the station and said he'd seen a man lure a kid, a young white male, into his car in East L.A. Later, a call came in reporting a missing kid that matched the description. We turned that city upside down looking for the vehicle the witness described. He even had a partial plate number. But we never found it. Two years later, a naked kid escaped from a house and ran down the street screaming that some guy was raping and torturing him. Turns out the perp was the guy who had been the witness on the other case, and that he had tortured and killed a half dozen boys. He had reported the first one just for the thrill of it, to see how we worked."

Carey visibly shivered. Newkirk could almost read his mind, like he was saying to himself, *So this is what the big leagues are like.* "Still, I can't imagine Fiona Pritzle . . ."

"Let's not scratch her off just yet," Singer said. He pointed to TRANSIENT UNKNOWN. "This is the hardest one. It could be a guy who is passing through, or maybe on a sales route. Who knows? I'd have your guys start interviewing citizens at motels and boardinghouses, B&Bs, asking owners if they've got—or had—anybody suspicious staying with them. We should assume they checked out today, probably first thing this morning, so I'd get a list on that. I can't imagine the guy hanging around."

Carey pulled his notebook from his pocket, and wrote that down. Newkirk noticed that the sheriff tried to stop his hand from trembling, but his writing was wavery. When he was through, he put his hands in his pockets to hide them.

"Area pedophile," Singer said. "A little easier. I'm sure you've got a list of registrations, right?"

Carey nodded. Newkirk remembered that one of the platforms Carey had run on was aggressively keeping up the known pedophile list.

"There are a couple of names on it, last time I looked," he said. "I think one of them might have moved away, though. We notified all of his neighbors, which really pissed him off."

"Then I'd key on the other name," Singer said casually. Carey made a note.

"Then we've got Tom Boyd," Singer said, drawing a star by the name. "He's got priors. He's probably on steroids. He had a fight with the kids' mother, and he was mad at the kids. He never turned in his truck last night, and now he's missing. When he left the Taylor house, he likely had an idea where two kids might go fishing. M, M, and O."

Carey looked up. Newkirk could tell he was trying not to reveal that he didn't know what the acronym meant.

"Motive, method, and opportunity."

Carey nodded, visibly grateful that Singer had let him off the hook so easily.

Next to the list of suspects were ASSIGNMENTS.

MONICA TAYLOR—Swann

COMMAND—Singer, Newkirk

GROUND SEARCH—Department

TRANSIENT UNKNOWN—Department

AREA PEDOPHILE—Department

TOM BOYD—Gonzalez

FIONA PRITZLE—Newkirk

LIAISON WITH STATE, FEDS—Sheriff, Singer

"This is only a recommendation," Singer said softly, "based on a cumulative seventy-six years of experience in this room. But you're the sheriff, and we're just volunteers trying to help out. You need to make the call."

Carey didn't hesitate. "Looks good to me."

Singer didn't smile, didn't pat the sheriff on the back.

"Then we should go to work," Singer said.

AFTER THE SHERIFF left the room, Singer looked to Gonzalez.

"Hook, line, sinker," Gonzalez said. "He reminds me that democracy works, though. A county full of idiots elects an idiot to be their chief law enforcement officer. Fuckin' rube."

Newkirk saw smile lines form at the edges of Singer's blue eyes, even though the ex-lieutenant didn't grin. There was no need for him, or anyone, to say more at the moment. Newkirk turned away, studied the city council chambers some more, thinking: *I'm going to throw up.*

Singer said, "Take it easy on the sheriff. He's perfect. He's our media strategy. Just look at him—he comes across great on camera. Sincerity just drips off him. Doesn't he look like he might burst into tears any second? They love that, it's good television. I mean, if it comes to that. Right now, we want to wrap things up quick so we don't have to worry about it."

"Thinking ahead," Gonzalez said to Newkirk, nodding at Singer. "That's what he does, think ahead."

Singer flipped open a cell phone and punched a number on speed dial.

"Swannee? Has there been any contact from the kids yet?"

A beat of silence as Singer listened. Then: "Shit. I'm losing patience. At least things are going well on this end. The sheriff signed off on our action plan."

Newkirk thought, if a third party heard this phone conversation, they would be none the wiser. Singer and Swann were careful. They'd had years to practice saying things that got their message across but could not be considered incriminating. It sounded like Singer was concerned for the welfare of the Taylor children, and was angry there had been no progress on their disappearance, which is exactly what Singer, and the other ex-officers, were supposedly there for.

"Yes," Singer said. "Gonzo's heading up the investigation into Tom Boyd. Just like we talked about. Newkirk?"

Newkirk looked up to see Singer staring at him. "Newkirk is assisting me at command central. He's also assigned to follow up on that Fiona Pritzle woman."

Singer listened for a moment, moving his eyes off Newkirk. Newkirk wondered what Swann was saying.

"No, he's okay," Singer said in a low voice.

No, I'm not, Newkirk thought.

"You don't look so good, Officer Newkirk."

"I'm fine," Newkirk lied, and thought: This is the nightmare, all right. The one where something happens that could threaten them, reveal them, and lead to something else, something worse, another crime. Even Singer, the master at controlling these kinds of things, may get swamped by the sheer magnitude of it. And the only way to keep ahead of the situation, to circumvent discovery and revelation, was to think and become truly evil, to become the antithesis of everything he believed in, everything he reached back for to justify his actions, all of the reasons he had become a cop in the first place. A cop: one of the good guys, a valuable part of a thin blue line that kept the scumbags at bay.

"The fuck is the matter with you, Newkirk?" Gonzalez said. "In for a penny, in for a pound. That was the deal."

That was the deal. But . . .

"What are the odds on a couple of kids being there?" Newkirk asked. "Right there, where they could see everything? Ten minutes either way, or a mile down the road, and we wouldn't be here now." If his own kids were missing . . . he couldn't even imagine how he'd feel.

Singer shrugged. "We can't change the situation now. We can only deal with what we've got. Forget that odds business, Officer. It's like trying to figure out why anything happens. You can't do that. If the asshole on that street corner hadn't had a video camera with him, nobody would have ever heard of Rodney King and there wouldn't have been riots, murders, and beatings. We can't play that game."

"Fucking game," Gonzalez said.

"I just wish it wasn't kids," Newkirk said.

"Oh, Jesus." Gonzalez rolled his eyes.

"We all wish that," Singer said, his voice dropping to a whisper. "Nobody likes it. None of us."

You saw her face, Newkirk wanted to say. She had a beautiful, wide-open face. And her eyes, big as they were, got even wider as she looked at them and seconds lapsed. She had seen something no child, no little girl, should ever have to see. She would be forever tainted. They had poisoned her, and the little boy. Ruined them.

"How many kids did you save?" Singer asked suddenly.

"What?"

"As a cop. Working the streets. All those domestic violence calls. You worked hundreds of them. You ever tally the kids you saved when you busted some scumbag father or live-in? Or took some crackhead whore in so her kids could be taken in by social services? How many, you think?"

Newkirk paused, thinking back, couldn't even count them. "Hundreds," he said.

"Hundreds," Singer repeated solemnly. Then he cocked his head to the side, his eyes fixed on Newkirk. "Don't worry. I'm not going to even suggest that because you saved so many kids these two don't mean anything. But if they surface, and they talk, we go down. Simple as that. Between you, me, Gonzo, and Swann, we've saved and protected thousands of citizens. The same people who spit on us and riot like animals with half an excuse. We were the only adults in the room. The politicians and the media pandered to those animals, gave them what they wanted, cooed over their problems. Only us—the police—could keep the lid bolted down. We did *good*, Newkirk. We waded into the shit swamp and saved people's lives so they could later bash in a truck driver's head with a cinder block in the middle of the afternoon, on the street, and slap high fives about it. And so the media could say the riots were caused not by rioters, but because of the situation we created. Like those people had no choice but to act like animals. Like they had no responsibility for their own actions. That was our thanks, my friend. *We* were the ones being portrayed as the criminals."

Newkirk said nothing.

"What was our reward?" Singer continued. "The Feds came in to oversee our department like *we* were the problem. No, we earned what we've got now," Singer said, his voice a whisper. "We can't let anyone, even kids, take that away from us."

"That was the deal," Gonzalez said.

Newkirk nodded weakly.

Gonzalez suddenly leaned forward and placed a huge hand on Newkirk's knee and squeezed with surprising force. His black eyes burned. "Don't fuck this up for me," he said softly but with absolute menace. "Let me tell you what this is all about. My grandfather crossed the border into Texas every day of his adult life to pick beans. He never spoke English and couldn't read Spanish. All he knew was to work hard and keep his mouth shut so what he did would benefit his kids and grandkids. Every day, when he came to work over the checkpoint, they made him strip naked so they could spray him down with pure DDT so he wouldn't bring his filthy Mexican lice into their pure white country. He brought my dad with him a couple of times to see what he did to support his family, but my dad saw only the humiliation of a good man. It burned in my dad, and when he told me how they treated my granddad, he cried. My old man and my mom worked the fields of the San Joaquin Valley and supported me so I could go to the academy. They never spoke English either, but they made sure I did. Look at me now, Newkirk. *Look at me.*"

Newkirk didn't dare look away, didn't dare blink.

"Look where I live, what I've fucking got. I own more than the entire village my grandfather came from combined. I can take care of the people who took care of me. It's the goddamned American dream, and you're not going to fuck it up for me, understand? I ain't going backwards now that I'm here. Do you understand?"

"Yes."

"You fucking better. You know what happened to Rodale when he forgot the deal we all made."

Newkirk nodded.

"You in?" Singer asked. Everything rode on the answer.

"I'm in."

Then he remembered the business card in his back pocket.

"ARCADIA POLICE DEPARTMENT," Singer said, fingering the card. "Eduardo Villatoro, Detective. Then he handwrote 'Retired' under it. From our old stomping grounds."

Gonzalez asked, "You know him?"

"I know him," Singer said. "Actually, I know of him, because I always avoided meeting with him in person. He's that pain-in-the-ass local who kept coming around asking questions. He couldn't recognize a stone wall if he drove into it. Either that, or he didn't care."

Newkirk said, "This could be bad."

Singer shook his head, dismissing the notion.

"What if he's here because of, you know?"

"Then we'll handle him," Singer said calmly.

"*Eduardo Villatoro!*" Gonzalez said in heavily accented English, rolling his tongue around the name, just like Villatoro had done.

"He's an ex–small-town cop," Singer said, handing the card back to Newkirk.

Gonzalez said, "Maybe he wants to retire here. He's probably worn-out from a lot of big cases in his career like getting kittens out of trees and shit like that. It means zilch. Let's not get paranoid. We've got a couple of young'uns to locate first."

Something banged the door, and the three ex-cops exchanged glances. Singer signaled for Newkirk to check out the sound.

Newkirk approached the door silently, then quickly grabbed the doorknob and threw it back.

A janitor stood in the hallway, pulling a mop back from where he had hit the bottom of the door. There were rainbow-colored arcs of soapy mop water on the linoleum floor. Newkirk saw the man jump when he opened the door, and take an involuntary step back. The janitor looked to be in his midthirties, a trustee judging by his orange jail-bird jumpsuit. Stringy brown hair coursed to his thin shoulders. Unfocused—and alarmed—eyes moved from Newkirk to Singer to Gonzalez.

"What do you want?" Gonzalez asked from behind the table. He had folded his arms across his chest in front of him so they looked even bigger than they were.

"Nothin'," the janitor said. "Jes' cleanin'."

"You hear anything?" Singer asked conversationally. "What's your name, anyway?"

"J.J."

"What about the first part of my question?"

J.J. looked to Newkirk for help, found none, then lowered his head so his hair obscured his face.

"I'm jes' cleanin'. I didn't hear nothin'. I didn't even know there was anybody in here."

"Not that there was anything to hear," Singer said. "We're assisting with the investigation into those two missing kids."

The janitor nodded, which consisted of his hair bobbing up and down.

"Take it easy, J.J.," Singer said. Newkirk closed the door.

"You boys are paranoid, all right," Gonzalez said, showing his white teeth. "We got it under control as best we can. And we've got that sheriff dicked."

NEWKIRK NEVER TIRED of driving his car up the long, paved, heavily wooded road to his home and seeing it emerge through the trees. It was a mansion, his mansion, even though it was neocolonial and looked out of place among the huge log structures that were being built throughout the county. The only thing he liked better than seeing it in the daylight was seeing it lit up at night. It had been three and a half years since the house was complete, and he still couldn't believe he lived there.

Three cars were in the circular driveway: his wife's Land Rover, his sons' Taurus, and the old pickup he used for cargo. The Taurus was parked in the place Newkirk reserved for himself, so he entered his home peeved. Sometimes, he thought his family didn't appreciate what they had now, that it had all come so easily. They had no idea what kind of sacrifices he'd made to create this new life, what he'd done so his boys could grow up as Tom Sawyer instead of 50 Cent. Singer and the others, they just wanted to get out for themselves from careers that had become disgusting and intolerable. Newkirk got out for his family, to save them. He wished they knew that, wished they appreciated what they had now.

The boys and his daughter were at the kitchen table, already eating dinner. His wife, Maggie, looked up and glared at him. Newkirk noted the empty place setting that had been for him.

It was only then that he remembered Maggie telling him to be home early to have a family dinner with his kids since getting everyone together was so rare these days, with spring baseball practice and ten-year-old Lindsey's soccer and all.

"Ah, jeez . . ." Newkirk moaned. "I totally forgot."

The boys looked at their food. They knew their mother was angry, and they didn't want to get into the middle of the fight.

"I guess you did," Maggie said. She was slight, pale, with red hair and green eyes that could flash like jewelry when she was angry, like now.

"I was at the sheriff's office . . ."

"And you were going to call," she finished for him.

He eased the door closed behind him. It was quiet in the house. Most of all, he felt bad for his kids. His sons could take it, he thought, they were in their teens and totally absorbed in sports, girls, iPods. Lindsey, though, she could break his heart. Lindsey worshipped her dad. She'd known only the Good Dad, the one in Idaho. She never knew what he used to be like, what he used to bring home.

Maggie pushed her chair back and approached him.

"Do you realize how hard it is to plan anything?" she asked. He looked at her. She was livid. "The one night I ask you to be home at a certain time, you can't bring yourself to do it. The one night!"

Newkirk stepped back, then leveled his eyes on her.

"Look, I'm sorry I forgot. But there are some kids missing, and I volunteered to help find them. I've been down at the sheriff's office with Lieutenant Singer, and Sergeant Gonzalez . . ."

She rolled her eyes when she heard the names.

"What?"

Her eyes filled with tears. "Jim, I thought that was the life we left. You promised me. You *promised* me."

He wanted to say, *Don't you care about those kids?* but couldn't bring himself to say it. Not with what he knew.

"So are you home now?" she asked.

He paused. "No, I'm here long enough to get a change of clothes. I'm likely to be down there all night."

Maggie's face tightened, and her eyes widened, making her head resemble a skull. She turned on her heel and walked straight to the bathroom off the living room. The slam of the door echoed throughout the house.

Newkirk stood there, his face red. Jason, his youngest son, shot a glance at him.

"There's some steak left if you want it."

Newkirk instead turned to Josh, the seventeen-year-old. "When you're through with dinner, I want you to move your car. You're in my place."

Josh sighed. "Okay."

"I'll see you kids tomorrow," Newkirk said, going up the stairs to his bedroom for his clothes. "Tell your mother I had to go."

Saturday, 6:20 P.M.

JESS RAWLINS cleaned the wound again in the sink and looked clinically at the hole in his hand. It was good that it bled so freely, he knew, because punctures like that should bleed out and wash away potential infection with it. He flexed his hand, cringed at how much it hurt, and stuck it back under the cold running water.

Annie and William Taylor sat at the dining room table, watching him, looking guilty. They looked smaller at the table than they had in the barn. Annie's feet—one with a shoe and the other dirty and bare—hardly touched the floor. William swung his legs, filled with nervous energy. William looked at him furtively, Jess noticed, not full on, like Annie. He was probably afraid he would be in trouble for the wound, Jess thought. Some kids had strange reactions to the revelation that they were capable of physically hurting adults.

"Let me get this bandaged, and I'll get some food going," Jess said. "Then we'll call the sheriff and let him know I found his strays."

"Sorry about your hand," Annie said.

"I'll live. You are pretty good with a hay hook. Ever consider stacking hay?"

"No. Besides, William did it."

Jess looked at William, who reacted with a mixture of fear and pride.

"You know," Jess said, "I almost got into it with a couple of college boys this afternoon who could've probably put me in a world of pain, but they didn't. It took a ten-year-old boy to do real damage."

William beamed now, until Annie shot him a glance. "You should apologize."

"I said I was sorry," he said. To Jess, he said, "My dad was an outlaw. Maybe that's why I did it."

Jess thought that over, said, "I'm not sure you want to be too proud of that."

William looked hurt, and Annie looked vindicated.

"But you swing a mean hay hook," Jess said quickly. William smiled. Annie didn't.

William asked, "What are you cooking?"

"Breakfast. Pancakes, steak, and eggs. Is that okay with you two?"

"It's almost dark out," Annie said. "Why are you going to cook breakfast at night?"

He looked at her. Her eyes were fixed on him. He thought he noted a kernel of hardness in them beyond her years, like she'd seen a lot in her brief life and was used to being disappointed. Jess felt a pang. There was something about her, all right. He recalled how he felt when he saw her photo on the poster the first time, and the anger that rushed through him when he heard the college kids making their stupid jokes. He felt some kind of affinity for her right off. He didn't want to disappoint her.

"Because," Jess said, "I know how to cook breakfast for kids. I used to do it. I haven't cooked for more than one for a while now, and I'm out of practice. That's why."

"Where are your kids?" William asked.

"Only one son," Jess said. "Gone. Grown up." He winced as he rubbed the wound with salve, applied a square of thick gauze to the entrance and exit, and wrapped white medical tape around his hand to hold the bandages in place. When he had a good, tight wrap, he reached up and tore the tape off with his teeth. He could hear Annie admonish William in a whisper, saying the rancher was pretty old, so of course his son was gone. He was "probably really old, like forty," she hissed.

"Okay, I'm calling now. Yup," Jess said, gingerly taking the handset from the wall with his bandaged hand, "you kids created quite an uproar in town. They've got posters up, and even some volunteers, ex-policemen, are looking for you. Your mother must be worried sick about you."

Annie and William exchanged looks.

He didn't know whether to dial 911 or the regular sheriff's department number. He decided on the latter, and thumbed through the directory for the county listings. It struck Jess, once again, that all of his friends were dead or gone. The realization had come to him suddenly a few months before, and it reared again now, filling him with unwanted nostalgia and simple dread. The county had changed while he hadn't. There had been a time when there were a dozen good men and women—neighbors—he could trust to give him counsel on this situation. Not anymore. They were all dead, or bought out and in Arizona.

As he punched the numbers, he saw Annie, who had left the table, reach up with a dirty hand and pull the phone cradle down, ending the dial tone.

He looked at her, puzzled.

"Mister," she said, "is Mr. Swann with them? The police, I mean?"

"I don't know him," Jess said. "Could be."

"Tell him, Annie," William urged from the table.

"Tell me what?"

She said, "You don't know what we saw. We saw some men kill another man. Down by the river. We saw their faces, and they saw ours."

Jess looked at her, hard.

While she talked—the words rushed out, and William interjected things to abet her story—she never took her hand down from the cradle of the telephone. Jess still held the handset, but listened. A cold-blooded murder, followed by a chase, a close call with a Mr. Swann, the biggest pigs she had ever seen, fleeing through the dark, wet forest to the barn.

Jess had his doubts. "But, Annie," he said gently, "I haven't heard anything about a man being shot to death. That sort of thing doesn't happen here, and if it did, I'd have heard about it."

Annie shook her head from side to side, pleading, "That's what we saw. Me and William. We saw them shoot that man over and over again, then they saw us and chased us. They *shot* at us!"

"But how do you know Mr. Swann wanted to hurt you, too?"

"I heard him talking on the telephone," she said. "I told you that."

"But you don't know who he was talking to," Jess said. "You might have thought he was saying one thing when he really was talking about something else. Why would those men want to hurt you?"

As he said it, he thought again of that kernel of hardness, how it had already made her wary and distrustful. It was sad. Kids experienced so much, so early, these days. . . .

"What if you call the sheriff and those men come after us again? They know we can recognize them," she said, her eyes misting. "What will you do if that happens?"

He started to say he would talk directly to the sheriff, explain the situation and the reason for her fears, get things sorted out. But her face showed such raw desperation, such fear, that he couldn't make himself say it. She was so sure of what she'd seen, and what had happened. But a murder in Pend Oreille County would be big news. Fiona Pritzle would have tracked Jess down like a dog just to be the first one to break the news, and she hadn't. Search teams had been all over the banks of the river looking for Annie and William, and they would have found a body in a public campground. Somebody surely would have reported a missing man. It didn't make sense. He wasn't sure what to do. Maybe feed the kids, clean them up, wait until they fell asleep—they were no doubt exhausted—and call?

But wasn't that what Swann had done to them, if Annie's story was true? Hadn't Swann betrayed them in that way? He didn't want to give them a reason to run again, to further frighten them. People could be trusted, he wanted to show them. This was a good place after all.

"Your story is pretty believable," he said, finally. "But you can't just *live* here. You need to get home and see your mom. You might even need to have a doctor look at you both, to make sure you're all right."

"We're fine," Annie said. "We'll live in the barn in that cave if we have to."

"It's a *fort*," William corrected.

"You're not living in the barn," Jess said, furrowing his brow.

A minute passed. Annie kept her hand on the cradle.

"How about I call your mother?" Jess said. "I'll let her know you're okay. That way she won't be suffering any longer, and I'm sure she'll know what to do."

Jess could see Annie trying to think it through. He could see she wanted to say yes, but something pulled at her as well.

"We're mad at her," Annie said.

"You may be," Jess said, "but I'm sure she loves you and she misses you. You know how moms are."

Annie wanted to argue, Jess could tell. But she didn't. She let her fingers slide off the cradle, and Jess heard the dial tone.

"What's your phone number?"

THE CORDLESS PHONE burred in Monica Taylor's hand, and she looked at it as if it were a snake. Swann entered from the kitchen at the sound. He had said he would have to screen any calls. The local telephone exchange was monitoring the line, he said, and would be able to track the Pen register and trace the source, if necessary.

Every time the telephone rang, panic rose from her belly and momentarily paralyzed her. It could be good news about her children, and she desperately wanted that. But it could be the worst possible news of all.

"Monica," Swann asked, "are you going to give me that?"

It rang.

"Why do you have to answer my calls?"

"We've been over that. In case it's kidnappers . . . or a crank call. Sickos like to prey on people in your situation, especially when it gets on the local news."

It rang again.

Swann approached her and held out his hand. Reluctantly, she handed him the phone.

"Monica Taylor's," he said.

She watched his face for some kind of inkling, some kind of reaction. She could tell from the low range of the voice on the other end that it was a man.

"Yes, she's here," Swann said. "Who is calling?"

Swann waited a moment. Monica couldn't hear the caller.

"Hello?" Swann said.

The caller spoke, and she recognized it as a question by the way his voice rose at the end.

"This is Sergeant Oscar Swann, LAPD, retired. I'm assisting Ms. Taylor. Again, who is calling?"

A hum of a voice. Swann nodded, said "yes" a few times. Then: "I'm afraid I can't help you with that. I have no authority there. I'd suggest you call the sheriff."

Swann punched the telephone off.

"Nothing?" Monica asked, already knowing the answer by his demeanor.

Swann shook his head and put the phone down on the table. "Some rancher. I didn't get his name. First, he wanted you, to tell you he hopes your kids get found real soon. But what he was really calling about, he said, was that one of the volunteer search crews knocked down part of his fence and some cows got out. He's wondering who will pay for the damage, and you heard what I advised him."

"Mmmmm."

"Jesus," Swann said. "You'd think with all that's going on that he'd wait a little bit before bitching about a fence."

Monica blankly agreed, but her mind was elsewhere. Why, she wondered, did Swann feel the need to screen calls? If there really were kidnappers, wouldn't it be best if they thought the police weren't quite so involved? Like his answering her telephone for her?

But then she realized what was likely happening. Swann, or the sheriff, or the volunteers, really didn't believe it was a kidnapping. They assumed the worst had happened. Swann was there to deflect the initial blow, to get the news and deliver it to her gently because he knew her.

Monica Taylor tried to close her eyes and sleep right there, but she couldn't. She thought, *Some rancher?* There weren't many of them around in the area anymore. She wondered if it was possible . . .

ANNIE HAD WATCHED Jess Rawlins place the call and had listened to everything he said. No doubt, Jess thought, she had seen his face flush red.

"You lied," she said.

"Yes, I did."

"Why?"

"Because," Jess said, rubbing his eyes with his left hand, "Swann answered the telephone."

"He's at our house?"

"Answered the phone."

"So now do you believe us?" she asked, challenging him.

I don't know what to believe, he thought but didn't say. "I've got to think about it."

"Is my mother all right?" William asked.

"I don't know. I didn't talk with her."

Annie turned away to William, her expression hopeful. "We can't talk to her yet, William. That would get us all in trouble."

In trouble, Jess thought, *a kid's term. As if she would be grounded or something.*

"I know," William mumbled, rolling his eyes.

Jess hadn't moved. He was trying to think, trying to put things together. Swann could be what he claimed to be: a volunteer with big-city police experience helping out a bereaved mother and an inept sheriff (although the ex-policeman hadn't said as much). Swann could have an entirely different take on what Annie claimed had happened in his house. Maybe he had been looking out for their safety by talking to people he knew before he called the sheriff, and Annie misinterpreted his conversation. Maybe Jess was buying into a child's haunted delusion when he should be the adult, thinking clearly, notifying the authorities so the whole county could breathe a collective sigh of relief. Not to mention their mother. He was glad he hadn't given his name.

And, he thought, if a murder had been committed, given the atmosphere of the last two days, wouldn't it be possible that the sheriff would keep a lid on it? If for no other reason than not to further panic a jittery community? Or, even more likely, Annie and William had thought they had seen something they really hadn't, and their active imaginations had taken over.

He wasn't sure what to do. If the children in his kitchen were his own, what would he do?

"You two go down the hall and get cleaned up," he said, finally. "There are towels in the hall closet. In the back bedroom are some boxes of old clothes, from when my son lived here. There might even be some shoes that fit, Annie. I'm going to cook you some dinner while you clean up, and then we'll figure out what our next move is."

He spoke with authority, and was almost surprised when both children nodded and went down the hallway.

There were always steaks in the freezer, and he pulled a package down to thaw in the microwave. He knew he had eggs. He had not made pancakes for over ten years, but he hadn't forgotten how.

He heard the shower turn on, then a brief argument over who went first. Annie won, as he thought she might.

JESS WASHED and dried the dishes after dinner, still amazed how much the children had eaten and how much they had liked it. During the meal, he had found himself simply watching them at the table, enjoying the way they dug into their food with unabashed enthusiasm. At one point, William had looked up, and said, "Mister, you sure can cook."

"Too bad that's the only thing I can cook," he had said, smiling.

William shrugged and went back to eating.

Now, as he put the plates into the drying rack, Jess said, "You kids must have been starving." When no response came, he turned and found them both asleep in their chairs. Annie was slumped forward on the table, her head in her arms. William was splayed out as if shot, his hands limp at his sides, his head tilted back, his mouth open.

Jess carried them one by one into a spare bedroom. Years ago, it had been his son's room. How small the kids were, he thought, how frail. But he'd forgotten how heavy a deeply sleeping child could be. Calves, which weighed twice as much, were easier to lift and carry. The bedding had probably not been changed for years, but he doubted it would matter much to them. He hadn't exactly been expecting company, after all. Jess put Annie's head near the headboard, William's head near the footboard, and pulled blankets over them both. He knew they would be more comfortable with their new clothes off, but it wasn't something he wanted to do.

Leaning against the doorjamb, he looked at them while they slept. It had been a long time since there had been children in the house. They brought a fresh smell with them, something else he had forgotten.

What in the hell was he doing? he asked himself.

Saturday, 7:45 P.M.

VILLATORO SAT on one of his two lumpy beds and ate his dinner from a sack between his knees. Two McDonald's hamburgers, fries, and the second of a six-pack of beer he had picked up at a convenience store. He ate voraciously, wishing he had ordered more since it was late and he had skipped lunch, wishing he had gone into a real sit-down restaurant instead of driving the streets of Kootenai Bay, trying to decide what looked good and eventually giving up. The prospect of eating alone had daunted him, so he drove until he found the McDonald's north of town and went through the drive-through. French fries and beer didn't go down well together, and he knew he would suffer for it later.

Beyond the sliding glass door of the room he could hear teenagers out on the sandy shore of the lake, laughing and sometimes singing snippets of songs. He wondered if they knew how good they had it here. He doubted it, though. Kids always wanted out, no matter where they were. A freight train rattled through town to the south, shaking the walls.

The television was on with the news out of Spokane, Washington. The disappearance of the Taylor children led the broadcast, but the anchor and the in-the-field reporters knew nothing more than Villatoro did simply from being in the bank and in the sheriff's department that day. He leaned forward, though, when an attractive blond reporter interviewed Sheriff Ed Carey. Carey looked sincere and deeply concerned, and said he was doing everything he could to locate the children: following every lead, pursuing every angle.

"I've heard it said that you've assembled what amounts to a Dream Team to help locate the missing Taylor children," the reporter said, and thrust her microphone at the sheriff.

Villatoro noticed a hint of a smile on the sheriff's mouth, a whisper of relief, as if this was the only good news he could convey.

"That's right," he said. "We're blessed in our community to have plenty of retired police officers who have worked situations like this before. They have years of experience, and they've volunteered their services to the department and the community."

"That's great," the reporter said, beaming.

Carey nodded. "They're working tirelessly, without compensation. We've greatly expanded the scope of our investigation with the service of these men, and we're proceeding in the most professional way possible."

The reporter threw it back to the anchor, who closed the story by saying: "The volunteers are reportedly retired police officers from the Los Angeles Police Department. . . ."

Villatoro paused, a hamburger poised in the air. He wondered how many ex-cops had volunteered to form the task force. And besides Newkirk, who were the others?

AFTER CHECKING his watch and assuming she was still awake, he called his wife, Donna. She picked up quickly, and he visualized her in bed, under the covers with her knees propped up and a book open. He apologized for not calling the night before, and she told him how his mother was driving her crazy.

"Where are you again?" she asked. "Ohio? Iowa?"

"Idaho," he said gently. "Almost in Canada."

"Isn't that where potatoes come from?"

"I think so, yes. But not this far north. Here there are mountains and lakes. It's very beautiful, and very . . . isolated."

"Would I like it?"

"For a while, I think. There's not much shopping and not many places to eat."

He told her about the missing children, and she said she thought she'd seen something on the news about it. But it could have been *other* missing children, she said. It was such a common story these days, she said. So many missing children it was hard to keep up with them.

Donna was Anglo. In the last ten years she had put on a great deal of weight and was constantly fighting to slim down. Villatoro had told her, repeatedly, truthfully, that it didn't matter to him. His mother had made the situation worse, though, when she announced at breakfast two weeks before that she was making them a new comforter for their bed. "I decided it will be a light one," his Salvadoran mother had said, "because big people create their own heat." Donna had been mortified, and had been depressed ever since.

"Have you heard from Carrie?" he asked, inadvertently glancing at the framed photo he had brought of their family. Their daughter, their beautiful, dark, loving daughter, was going to college, majoring in cinematography. Her departure had left a hole in the house that Donna and his mother couldn't fill.

"An e-mail," Donna said. "She needs money for some kind of film club."

"Then send it to her," he said automatically.

He listened while Donna replayed her day: breakfast with Mama, grocery shopping, fighting with the dry cleaners. The city had turned off the water for two hours that afternoon while repairing the street.

He realized, too late, that she had asked him a question while his mind was elsewhere.

"What?"

"I asked you when you thought you'd be back."

"I don't know," he said. "A few more days. I have a feeling I'm getting close. It's more than a feeling, in fact."

"You've said that before." She sighed.

"This time, though . . ."

"This obsession, it's not healthy."

It was more than an obsession. They had had this discussion many times before.

"Why is this so important to you?" she asked. "You need to find out what it's like to be retired. You haven't even tried yet."

"I'm not ready."

"I talked to the Chows down the street," she said. Arcadia was 50 percent Asian. "Mr. Chow retired a month ago and they just bought a big RV. They're going to tour the country. They're like a couple of kids, they're so excited."

"Is that what you think we should do?"

Hesitation. "No, not really."

He faked a laugh, hoping to defuse the topic. He had explained it before to her. She had said she understood. But if she did, it didn't stop her from bringing it up again.

For eight years since the robbery, he had lived with the case. It was the only open murder investigation within the department, and it had been his responsibility. Retirement didn't change that. Villatoro had always taken his responsibilities seriously, even if no one else seemed to take theirs with the same passion. He took good police work seriously, and considered it a calling, like the priesthood. He knew most of his fellow officers didn't think that way, and he never could understand that. They would have been just as happy and content working as building inspectors or within the city's recreation department.

He had been shocked when his chief agreed to turn over the investigation to the LAPD and assigned Villatoro a peripheral liaison role in it. The officers he dealt with from L.A. were much more interested in going to Santa Anita and betting the horses than they were in solving the murder of the guard. The L.A. detectives treated their very few days in Arcadia like holidays from their offices, with long lunches, storytelling, and very few questions for him. This bothered Villatoro on two counts. One was that despite the convictions of the racetrack employees, the men who murdered the guard had never been caught. The detectives didn't seem very concerned about that. They were used to messy, unfinished cases. To them it was about putting in their time, filing a few reports to grow the file, winning a couple of races at the track. The other thing that consistently bothered Villatoro—in fact, it ate at him like a cancer—was that these men were the vanguard of a sprawling, dirty, indefinable city that continued to grow, continued to reach farther out, overwhelming small communities like Arcadia and sucking them in until what remained had no resemblance to what there once was. He saw his fellow officers and neighbors change to adapt, lowering their standards, letting their responsibility to the community and each other slip away into the maw of the beast. Arcadia was no longer the small, sun-baked city it had once been. Now, it was just another colony.

Villatoro was a proud man, despite his humble nature. He noticed how the L.A. cops shot glances at one another when he spoke, was stung when they disregarded his suggestions about following up on the marked bills. One of the detectives, after being told about the second bill traced back to Idaho, said, "Do you have any idea what my caseload is like? Get fucking real, man."

Villatoro reflected on what he'd said to his wife, and decided he'd been wrong. It wasn't that he wasn't ready to retire. He was. But the single unsolved murder was like a hot coal in his belly. It burned. He had told Donna this.

There was the widow of the slain guard, and her children. No one—not the prosecutors, not the judges, not the L.A. detectives—had met the widow, as Villatoro had. She deserved justice, and only he could deliver it.

He told his wife good night and that he loved her.

HE SAT BACK on his bed with the television on but the volume turned down, and thought of his last visit to Santa Anita Racetrack.

He had done it yearly, ever since the robbery, long after the L.A. detectives stopped going to Arcadia pretending to investigate. He chose days when no races were held, when the old, stately place was still and silent. The last time he had been there was the week before, on an unseasonably hot day, ninety-four degrees in April.

Parking his car in the huge, empty lot, he had walked across the hot asphalt with beads of sweat forming on his upper lip. The stadium was blue and massive; heat shimmered and distorted the palm trees and the hills that framed the track. He had loved the place, the feel of it, ever since he took his daughter there for equestrian events during the summer of 1989. It had the look and feel of lost elegance, of a fifties Los Angeles that was bursting with energy, pride, and money. A gentler, more civilized, more humane time, when the issues were water and wider highways and Arcadia had been a sleepy, tree-lined village, like Kootenai Bay was now.

He had found an open gate, as he did each visit. The maintenance men never seemed to lock it, as if he were meant to enter. Walking through Seabiscuit Court on a red concrete path, across manicured lawns with empty tents and tables for guests, he glanced at the statue of the horse, the bronzes of famous jockeys, the monument to George Woolf. The grounds were more of a garden than a racetrack, which was something else he liked. It soothed him. Birds chirped in flowering trees, making the lawns in front of the stadium seem tropical.

The escalator was not turned on, so he climbed the steps, and was sweating hard when he reached the top. He walked though the Front-Runner Restaurant, with its white linen tablecloths and silver place settings, to the Turf Club. From there, he could see everything. The oval track was laid out in front of him, the infield so green it burned his eyes. But the track was eerily empty, not a single employee or horse to be seen.

He turned in the entranceway, and once again ran through the events of that day in May, eight years earlier.

The cash had been counted by a dozen employees in the administrative offices, directly below the stands, in a windowless office. Two armored bank cars idled outside the office, on a service road that was gated on both sides and manned by armed guards. When the cash was counted and accounts reconciled, it was banded and placed in heavy canvas bags, with each bag holding $900,000 to $1 million in cash as well as computer-generated bank deposit slips. There were fourteen bags in all. On a signal, the office doors were opened by the guards, and bonded staff from the bank cars entered to pick up the bags of cash, which were secured with steel cable and clasp locks. On that day, eight bags were placed in the first armored car and six in the second. The driver of the second armored car was a young father of two children named Steve Nichols.

As always, the armored cars waited until the last race of the day commenced. They timed it that way so the cars could slip away from the facility before the races were completed and thousands of customers left for their cars. Plus, for public relations reasons, the owners of the track didn't like the idea of vehicles filled with betting losses leaving at the same time as the patrons.

When the roar went up from the packed house, guards manually opened the front gate, and the armored cars rumbled away, taking an employee-only road obscured from the fans by banks of trees. They emerged at the far end of the parking lot, where heat waves now almost entirely obscured a sign for PURRFECT AUTO SERVICE.

Villatoro walked to the south end of the stadium and looked over the railing, so he could see Huntington Drive. He visualized the two armored cars, unnoticed by thousands of cheering customers who were watching the final race, proceed east. Past Holy Angels School, past Salter Stadium.

On that day, the vehicles stopped for the red light at Huntington and Santa Anita Boulevard. From there, they planned to turn left and drive a short distance to the on-ramp to I-210, and west toward L.A. and the bank. But at that intersection, something happened.

A man walking his dog along Huntington witnessed it from a quarter of a mile away. He testified later that he could see thick rolls of yellow-brown smoke pour out of the shooting ports of the armored cars, followed by the scene of armed guards throwing open the rear doors onto the street. The police investigation said that canisters of tear gas hidden within the bags of cash were triggered by remote control. The guards rolled in agony on the pavement, the gas now so thick in the air that the witness couldn't see much else. What he heard, though, was the sound of engines roaring, squealing tires, and a moment later, the sharp crack of gunshots. The speculation was that the robbers had been parked in the lot of the H. N. & Francis C. Berger Foundation building on the other side of the intersection, and that two cars (of unknown description) converged on the armored vehicles. The robbers were armed and probably wore gas masks, or they couldn't have entered the smoking vehicles to remove the cash bags or kill Steve Nichols, the driver of the second car.

The only witness to the crime, the dog walker, had turned his back to run and couldn't see the cars tear away, or say whether they escaped west to L.A. or east to San Bernadino on the freeway.

No vehicles were ever recovered that could be tied to the robbery, since no reliable description of the cars was ever made.

Because of the placement of the tear gas bombs, the counting room staff was immediately isolated and questioned. The police determined that several of the employees were involved, and a witness came forth to name names. Despite protestations of innocence by the counting room employees, three people were convicted and imprisoned. The head cashier, a woman named Anita, dubbed by the evening newscasts as "Anita of Santa Anita," was sentenced first.

Villatoro met Steve Nichols's widow six months after the robbery. She was young, pretty, with a toddler, and eight months pregnant at the time. Nichols had worked two jobs to be able to afford the small home in Tustin. His death had brought her a little life insurance money, but that would soon be gone. So would the house. She had pleaded with Villatoro to help her, and he could do nothing. As he left the house that day and skirted the FOR SALE sign in the yard, he had made another promise to himself. He would find the man who had killed her husband.

But no one ever came forth with the names of the men in the two cars who had taken the money, killed Steve Nichols, and escaped. Those imprisoned either refused, or, as Villatoro now suspected, *did not know* the identities of those men. And no one had come forward to shed any light on who they were.

DESPITE THE HOUR, Villatoro pulled the telephone to the edge of the nightstand. Even though it was the weekend, he called his former partner, Celeste, and left a message on her cell phone.

"Celeste, I'm sorry about the time and the day, but will you please go into the office on Sunday and pull all of the Santa Anita files? I need you to go through them to see if you can find the name Newkirk." He spelled it out. "I don't know his first name, although I suspect he was a police officer with the LAPD. It may be in our formal reports, or it may be written on a piece of scratch paper, or in the margin on something. I don't know for sure. I wish I could remember. But the name is familiar, somehow."

He paused. "If you find it, call me immediately. And whether you reach me or not, cross-reference that name to everything in the case. The investigation, the trial, the after-trial. Anything and everything. I realize what I'm asking you for is beyond what I should, now that I've retired. You don't have to help me, and there are no hard feelings if you don't. But I don't know where else to turn, and I want to solve this. I know you do, too."

He paused again. "Thank you, Celeste."

Why, he wondered, was the name familiar? What was it about that chance encounter in the sheriff's office that gnawed at him? Maybe he was wrong. Maybe it was just the fact that Newkirk was the first person he had met so far in North Idaho who looked at him suspiciously. Sure, others looked at him because he didn't fit, and he didn't. But Newkirk had eyed him coldly, *assessed* him. Newkirk stood back and hadn't offered his hand, as if discouraging any more familiarity.

And he was the first person Villatoro had met who, after initial pleasantries, had not asked, "So, how do you like it here?"

A knock on the door startled him. Villatoro rolled off the bed, used his palms to flatten the wrinkles on his shirt, and tucked his shirttails into his trousers. There was no peephole, so he opened the door a crack.

It was the receptionist from the front desk with a bucket of ice.

"Hello," he said. "I didn't order any ice."

She looked up and smiled conspiratorially. "We could put some in a glass, and pour some bourbon over it, and we'd have a cocktail."

He could feel his face flush. Even though he was blocking the door, he could see her look into the room, making sure he was alone.

"You seem like a very nice man," she said.

"A nice married man," he said.

She laughed huskily. "I'm not asking you to get a divorce. I just thought you might want to have a drink with me. I just finished my shift."

He didn't know what to say. She was so open, and so bold. And she wasn't as unattractive as his first impression of her had been, now that she was off duty.

She read his face, and smiled. "Some other time, eh?"

"Perhaps," he said.

"You know where I am," she said, handing him the bucket. He watched her walk down the hallway. Nice walk, he thought. He found himself wondering what she had looked like twenty years before. She paused at the end of the hall, looked back at him over her shoulder, and winked. He waved with a flutter of his fingers and shut the door.

He carried the ice bucket into his room and placed it absently on the desk, his mind spinning.

After pacing back and forth, he made a decision: He would sleep in the other double bed tonight. Maybe it wouldn't be as lumpy.

He lay in the dark, flustered, but a little excited. It had been years since a woman . . .

Clicking on the bed lamp, he addressed the photo of his wife and daughter. "Sorry, Donna. Don't worry," he said, before turning the light off.

Real sleep was still hours away.

Saturday, 10:23 P.M.

NEWKIRK WAS in the backseat of Singer's white Escalade, looking between the heads of Singer and Gonzalez at the sweep of headlights in the trees. They were on a well-graded dirt road, climbing a series of S-turns in the timber, en route to Gonzalez's home. Singer suddenly tapped the brakes to let a doe and fawn run across the road, and Newkirk lurched forward, grasping at the front seat for support.

"Didn't see her," Singer said. "Sorry, Newkirk."

Gonzalez said, "I saw her eyes reflect back, but it was too late to say anything. Why don't they just cross the road when they hear you coming? They wait until you're right on top of them to decide to run. Fucking deer."

"There's a lot of them," Singer said.

After a beat, Gonzalez said, "You notice how every animal has different-colored eyes when light hits them? Deer are green. I seen a coyote up here, and his eyes were blue. Rabbits are yellow. I seen some orange eyes a couple of nights ago up here on my road, but I still don't know what the animal was."

"Badger," Newkirk said. "My boys and I spotlighted a badger once, and his eyes were orange."

"Fucking badger," Gonzalez said.

GONZALEZ LIVED on a hilltop, in a home that perched over a cliff and afforded a vast, breathtaking view of a dark forest valley and the moonlit mountains eighty miles away. From the deck, Newkirk could see a kidney-shaped lake far below that mirrored the stars and moon. Like all of them, Gonzalez lived in a home that would have been unattainable ten years before, something beyond their dreams. The house alone would have cost 7 or 8 million in L.A., and that didn't include the eighty acres that went with it.

Singer stepped out through the open sliding glass door and handed Newkirk a beer as he joined him at the rail.

"You know the name of that lake?" Newkirk asked.

"No, I don't."

"There are so many lakes up here. I've tried to learn their names."

"Gonzo's Lake," Singer said. "We can call it that."

Newkirk took a sip of the beer. It bothered him, once again, that Singer and Gonzalez had no real interest about where they lived.

"You know what the deal is when we go downstairs," Singer said. "You and I don't talk. No matter what happens or what's said, we don't talk. We don't want him to know how many of us there are, or who we are. We don't want him to hear our voices again, or he'll put things together."

"And Gonzo is okay with that?"

"Sure he is."

Newkirk took a deep breath, looked away.

"Yes," Singer said, acknowledging Newkirk's concern, "we're taking a calculated risk here. We're using Boyd to create a plausible diversion that will pull the search teams out of the woods. We need to get them out before they find something, and we need to change the story from missing kids to finding Tom Boyd. With the sheriff's office and community attention on Boyd, the odds go way down that the Taylor kids will be found by law enforcement and put into protective custody—or be interviewed on network TV, for Christ's sake. And if the focus is on Boyd, we can use the time we just bought on doing good police work to locate those kids. Just good, solid, professional police work, meaning chasing up every lead, interviewing every possible witness, using our training. It always works, Newkirk, it always works. This way, we'll find them before some idiot deputy does."

"What if a citizen finds them?" Newkirk asked.

"We've set it up so we're the first responders," Singer said. "We'll get there first. Then we'll deal with it."

"But Boyd . . ."

"Don't worry," Singer said. "We'll keep him alive. We might need him again."

Newkirk felt a chill that had nothing to do with the night air.

THEY WENT down the stairs into the basement, Gonzalez in front of them, clomping loudly. Newkirk followed Singer down, replicating Singer's gentle steps. The man in the basement would probably sense there was more than one of them, but he wouldn't know how many for sure. As he followed, Newkirk heard his stomach gurgle. The dread he felt grew stronger. So did the odor. Urine, feces, sweat, fear.

At the landing, Singer turned and made a face at Newkirk, then drew a handkerchief out and tied it over his nose and mouth. Newkirk didn't have a cloth, so he raised his arm and pressed his face into his sleeve.

Gonzalez snapped on a light, a bare bulb in a fixture attached to the upper floor joists. The basement was unfinished except for a framed-out spare bedroom and bathroom on the north wall. The floor was bare concrete.

Tom Boyd shouted, "Who's there?" His voice was muffled because of the cloth sack tied over his head. Burn marks from a Taser stun gun, like snakebites, could be seen just under the collar of Boyd's light brown uniform shirt. Newkirk was glad he couldn't see the man's face.

"Remember me?" Gonzalez said in a fake voice. Newkirk recognized it as what Gonzalez called his "whitey-white" voice, the one he'd used to mock supervisors and politicos back on the force. Gonzo was a great mimic, master of eight or nine dialects. He used to read departmental memos in the locker room in that whitey-white, just-returned-from-a-weekend-in-the-Hamptons voice, and always got big laughs. But it was horrible now, Newkirk thought.

"You probably thought I had forgotten about you down here, Mr. UPS man. But I was busy all day."

"I know who you are," Boyd said. "You're those cops."

Singer and Newkirk exchanged glances.

Boyd was in a stout straight-backed wooden chair. His hands had been triple Flex-cuffed behind his back, to assure that the heavily muscled man couldn't break free. His thick torso was tied to the chair with tight bands of climbing rope, his bare ankles Flex-cuffed to the chair legs. Newkirk could see where the cuffs dug deeply into Boyd's skin. The seat of the chair and the inside of Boyd's dark UPS uniform shorts were sodden where he'd been forced to foul himself. For some reason, Gonzalez had removed Boyd's shoes. When Newkirk saw why, he almost retched.

Gonzalez had glued Boyd's feet to the floor with construction adhesive.

"Jesus, man, I gotta open a window," Gonzalez said. "You really stink up a party."

"Please," Boyd pleaded, his head slumping forward. "I don't know what you think I did. I don't know why you're doing this to me. . . ."

As Gonzalez opened casement windows, Newkirk looked everywhere but at Tom Boyd. He would never need to look again, he thought. The image was seared into him.

There was a workbench attached to the basement wall. On the bench were a video camera bag, Boyd's shoes, a half-empty box of department Flex-cuffs, and an open toolbox. Newkirk could see the glue gun Gonzalez had used to attach Boyd's feet to the floor.

"We're going to start where we left off early this morning," Gonzalez said, taking a stool from the workbench and moving it near Boyd. He perched on the stool so he was above the man. "You know those kids pretty well. I want to know where they would go if they were trying to hide. Where would they run?"

A sob came from inside the cloth sack. "I told you I don't know . . . I don't know. If I knew, I'd tell you. I thought they'd run to their mother's house, I told you that. I don't know of any relatives around, I don't know their friends. I never fucking paid any attention to them, you know?"

Gonzalez turned and looked at Singer, then shrugged.

Singer nodded. Newkirk wondered what the exchange signified.

He had seen worse. There was a house in Santa Monica the police had used for a while. They called it "Justice Ranch." Newkirk had been there on several occasions. Justice Ranch was a last resort, used to elicit information from scumbags when every legal avenue had been used or blocked. It wasn't a place to get confessions that could be used in court, because neither the cops nor the victims wanted to go to court. It was a house of torture, the place where Gonzalez often performed the "guilty smile." Newkirk became acquainted with both when a judge released a child rapist on a procedural technicality three days before another missing boy was reported. The rapist was picked up in an unmarked car and taken to the Justice Ranch. Gonzo had been there waiting for him. He called himself the Head Wrangler, but instead of tack he had a toolbox. No one ever heard from the rapist again. Then the Feds came in and shut it down.

But that was different, Newkirk thought. He had always been confident that the suspects taken into that house were guilty, even if the cops couldn't get enough proof for a conviction in court. And if the suspects weren't guilty of that particular crime, they were guilty of others. No doubt about it. But this was a whole other deal. Tom Boyd was just a local yahoo. It made him sick.

"Look, I'll be straight with you," Gonzalez said, leaving his stool for the workbench. "I kind of believe you don't know where those kids went. I *kind* of believe it. But I'm not a hundred percent. I need to be a hundred percent to reach my comfort level."

Newkirk tried not to listen to Boyd, who was begging. Crying and begging at the same time. Saying all the same things, over and over. Offering to do anything, pay anything.

"Anything?" Gonzalez asked, pausing. "Would you bite your own penis off, for example?"

Newkirk winced.

Boyd croaked, "Just about anything."

"Ah, that's different. I said I needed a hundred percent. You're not giving me that."

Boyd moaned and thrashed his head back and forth. "What do you want? What is it you fucking want?"

Gonzalez walked across the concrete and rattled through the tool box. He removed a pair of needle-nosed pliers. "I need one hundred percent compliance."

"To do what?"

Gonzalez glanced over at Singer, and Singer raised his eyebrows, as if saying, *This is going to be easy.*

"I want you to confess."

"WHAT?"

"I want you to confess that you took those kids and killed them because you were pissed off at their mother, and your brain was fucked up with steroids at the time."

Boyd moaned again, and the moan turned into a sob.

"You can say it was an accident," Gonzalez said, raising his whitey-white voice. "That you didn't intend to hurt them at all. You sort of blacked out, and when you came to they were dead."

"I can't . . ."

"Oh yes, you can, Mr. UPS man."

"You'll kill me after I say it."

"No," Gonzalez said, shaking his head. "That's not going to happen if you confess, but it sure as hell will if you don't. If you cooperate with me, Mr. UPS man, I'll put you in the back of a car and you'll be driven to Las Vegas, where you can start a whole new life. That's the place to start over, Las Vegas, *where dreams can come true.* I'm not going to give you money, or a new name, nothing. You're on your own. A guy like you, with all those muscles, should be able to find a job pretty easy. They like muscle down there. Big muscles and little lizard brains look good on a résumé in Vegas. And you can't ever come back here, you understand?"

Boyd was silent.

Even though Newkirk knew Gonzalez was lying, it had been a convincing performance. Newkirk again looked away, afraid he would get sick.

"I can't confess to that," Boyd said.

Gonzalez sighed theatrically. Then he snapped the pliers together in the air a few times, *clack-clack-clack,* and bent down to Tom Boyd's naked feet, saying, "How many toenails does a guy really need?"

Newkirk didn't care if Singer saw him close his eyes and cover his ears with his hands to drown out the scream.

JIM HEARNE sat straight up in bed, his eyes wide open, his breath shallow. He could feel his heart racing in his chest, something that always scared him. His father had died at age thirty-eight from a heart attack that came out of nowhere.

He felt Laura's cool hand on his bare stomach. "Jim, what's wrong? Are you all right?"

"In a minute . . ." he said, gasping.

He breathed deeply, tried to will his heart to slow down. He'd tried not to dwell on the Taylors, Jess, and Villatoro. After the reception, he'd kept himself busy, mindlessly chain-sawing dead limbs from the orchard, stacking them in a pile higher than his head, burning them as the sun faded. Being physically tired had been good, because he was ready to go straight to bed after two more quick cocktails.

But in the night it had all come back.

Should he just call Villatoro? Come clean? Risk his career?

Or should he call Singer and tell him, if nothing else, to close his accounts and move his business to another bank? Try to wash his hands of everything now?

The timing would be poor, he conceded. Singer was suddenly a local hero, leading the inept sheriff's office in the search to find the Taylor children. Singer could make trouble for him, too, if he chose to. And what did that matter, if Singer did move his accounts? The board of directors would note the loss and ask questions. And moving them wouldn't negate the fact that he'd established them in the first place, which was the problem, wasn't it?

What did I set in motion?

DAY THREE

sunday

Sunday, 2:18 A.M.

IF ANYTHING, the second night was even harder than the first for Monica Taylor. The sedatives helped, reducing the peaks of her emotions, smoothing things out a little, but beneath the blanket the pills pulled over her there was still the relentless fact that her children were missing.

She lay fully clothed on the bed in her darkened bedroom, trying not to roll her head over and look at the time on the digital clock radio. She needed sleep. Her muscles and joints ached for it. But it was more soothing to stare into the darkness with her eyes open than to close them and enter drug-induced, horrific nightmares involving Annie and William and every possible scenario of what could have happened to them.

How many hours now? She couldn't count, for some reason. Nearly forty, she knew that much. She remembered reading a story in the newspaper about a three-year-old boy who had disappeared from a campsite near Missoula the year before. He was found three days later shivering but healthy on a logging trail. He had survived by eating rose hips and drinking creek water. Three nights was a long time, but the boy had made it. Annie and William were smart. The second night wasn't even over yet. They would figure out rose hips, if they had to, whatever *they* were. Or they'd find a cabin, or they'd build a shelter.

She knew, somehow, that they were still alive. She just knew it.

She replayed the last argument with Tom, the slamming door now sounding like a gunshot. She still couldn't believe he had anything to do with the disappearance of her children, but the sheriff seemed to. How could she have not seen that in him if it was true? How could he have been capable of such evil? And if he didn't have anything to do with it, where in the hell was he?

She sat up, wide-awake. She needed desperately to talk to someone.

Monica padded through the living room past Swann, who was sleeping under a light blanket on the couch. The phone was on the stand next to him, and she plucked it out of the cradle as quietly as she could and took it back into the bedroom and dialed.

As she expected, it was picked up on the first ring. Her mother would have just gotten home from the bar she worked at near the airport.

"Mom, it's Monica."

Hesitation. A long breathy draw on a cigarette. "I'm not surprised you're calling at this hour."

Monica pictured her mother in her apartment bedroom, lying on top of her bed in a housecoat with a Scotch and water on the rocks on the nightstand and the television at the foot of the bed flashing washed-out colors on the close walls. She would be watching TV through the V of her naked, misshapen feet, swelled from standing all night behind the bar.

Monica asked, "Are you alone?"

"What kind of question is that?"

"I just wanted to be able to talk freely."

Her mother laughed a bitter laugh, and Monica could hear the years of smoke and liquor and disappointment in the sound. "I say whatever I want whenever I want. I don't care anymore if somebody hears me or what they think about it. I'm beyond all that. It's one of the perks you get when you get old, Monica. I may not have my looks or a pension, but I feel it's my perfect right to be rude if I want to. I've been around the block so many times my tires are bald. I deserve it. And yes, to answer your question. I'm alone as always."

"Not always," Monica said, remembering all of the men.

"Now, girlie."

"Mom, Annie and William are missing."

"I heard. It's all over the news. I seen their pictures all over on the TV in the bar. It's a damn shame. I didn't even recognize them at first."

"Mom . . ."

Monica talked softly, hoping not to wake Swann in the next room. She pressed the receiver close to her ear, though, because her mother had a loud voice that carried through a room. Over the years, her voice had become a grating bray, without inflection or subtlety. Monica wished she knew how to turn down the volume on her phone.

"That reporter who bought me drinks asked me if I was related to you, since my name is Taylor. I told him 'She used to be my daughter, but she ain't no more.'"

Monica closed her eyes. "You didn't talk to a reporter, did you?"

The long suck of the cigarette. Then: "Not at first, anyhow."

"Oh, no. What did you say?"

"Honey, I told him I lost track of you years ago, or more precisely that you shut me out. That I hadn't seen my grandbabies in four years."

Monica remembered the last time her mother showed up to see her "grandbabies." She was drunk and had been driven to Kootenai Bay by a seedy barfly in a porkpie hat who stood in the living room waiting for an invitation to sit down that he never received. Her mother asked Monica right in front of Annie and William for a loan to get her through the month. The barfly leered at eight-year-old Annie, and Monica threw them both out.

Her mother said, "I told him things like this don't just happen in a vacuum. They might seem like they do, but they don't."

"What are you talking about?"

"You probably brought it on somehow with your damned attitude, that sense of entitlement you always have. What kind of man are you with now, anyway?"

Monica was speechless.

"Your daddy always thought you were a little queenie. He'd bring you presents and pile them high in your room. But what did he bring me? Nothing, is what. He brought me nothing but a bucketful of trouble," she said, her voice rising, getting harder.

"This has nothing to do with him, Mom. This has nothing to do with anyone. This is about William and Annie. They're innocent. They did nothing wrong."

"Not what I heard on the news."

"They did nothing wrong," Monica said through clenched teeth.

"Someone is at fault, and it ain't me."

"Please don't," Monica said. "I feel so alone, and you aren't helping. This isn't about you."

"You called me. So it's about me."

"Not this time. I need support to get me through this."

"You shoulda' thought of that before."

"Mom . . ."

"It's time you quit trying to pretend you're something you're not. Who do you think you're fooling? I know you're wild. I seen it, remember? I was there. Now you act like it never happened, like you're Miss Priss. I know you better. So do you. Anybody with eyes could see this coming."

"Please, not now."

"It all has to do with him. Your daddy. You're just too worshipful to see it."

"I wish you hadn't talked to a reporter," Monica said in a whisper.

"I got bills, girlie."

"He *paid* you?"

"That and the drinks."

Monica lowered the phone to her lap and shook her head. She could hear her mother say, "I'm tired. I can't talk no more. I got to work tomorrow."

"Mom," Monica said, raising the phone, "this is about my children."

Her mother blew out a long stream of smoke and for a second, Monica thought she could smell it through the phone. "I don't even know 'em," her mother said.

"This should have happened to you, not me."

"But it didn't, did it?"

Monica pushed the OFF button.

AS MONICA sat on her bed with the phone in her hand, she replayed the conversation with her mother over in her mind, hoping it had been a bad dream, knowing it wasn't. Hot tears streamed down her face, and she wiped them away with the back of her hand.

Suddenly, she wanted Swann out of the house. She wanted to be alone. It wasn't anything he had said or done in particular, but she was becoming more and more uncomfortable around him. Maybe it was the way he looked at her with what she thought was a mixture of malevolence and predation. Where there should be pity, there was, she thought, overfamiliarity. As if he knew how things were going to end, and he was there as another actor in her drama. As if he knew more than he let on.

She had asked him earlier why he looked at her in that way, and he'd played dumb, gotten defensive, reminding her how he was volunteering his time, how he didn't have to get involved at all. She'd let it drop.

But who kept calling him on his cell phone? Why did he immediately leave the room after seeing who was calling on the phone display? Why were his conversations so monosyllabic? And why, when she asked him who had called, were his explanations so lame?

And, she realized with a sudden shudder that broke through the Valium blanket, why was he standing in the doorway to her bedroom, *right now?*

"What are you doing?" she croaked, her voice thick with exhaustion.

He cleared his throat, spoke quietly. "I thought I heard something. I wanted to make sure you were all right."

"I was talking to my mother."

"I wondered where the phone went. Here, give it to me in case somebody calls."

Meekly, she handed it to him. But he didn't leave her bedroom.

"Is that all you wanted?" she asked.

He paused.

"Get out of my room."

Swann didn't respond, but simply withdrew, as if he had never really been there at all. She heard his footsteps in the hallway.

Groggy, she climbed out of bed and closed her door. She remembered closing it tight earlier, she thought, but maybe she hadn't.

This time, she locked it.

Sunday, 3:15 A.M.

THE PREGNANT COW stood with her legs braced in the stall, her muscles quivering, her eyes wide, her breath heavy and rhythmic. It took effort for her to turn her head and look back at Jess, who sat on an up-turned bucket just out of kicking range.

"Just relax, sweetie," Jess said, hoping the calf wasn't breech. "It'll be all right."

The only sound in the barn, besides the labored breathing, was the *grumble-mumble* sound of grass hay being chewed. There were two more pregnant cows in the barn, and Jess noticed they would look over at the laboring cow with impassive eyes, stare for a moment, then go back to eating.

The sliding door squeaked as it opened a few inches. Jess slitted his eyes at the sound. He saw a shock of blond hair, and Annie's face peering in.

"What are you doing?" she asked.

"What are *you* doing? You should be sleeping."

Annie pushed the door open a few more inches and stepped in. She wore oversized pants and a hooded sweatshirt that was several sizes too big. The clothes were familiar to Jess; seeing them tripped something in him.

"I woke up and couldn't find you," she said. "I was afraid you'd left us. Then I looked out and saw the light out here."

"Why do you think I'd leave?"

She shrugged. He noticed her feet were bare.

"Couldn't you find any shoes?"

"I'm all right."

Jess noted that the cow in labor had now swung her head around the other way, so she could see Annie.

"I've got a cow here about to calve any minute," Jess said.

"What time is it?"

He looked at his wristwatch. "It's after three in the morning," he said.

She shivered. Jess stood up and found another empty bucket and an old Army blanket in the tack room. "Come on over here, if you want. Have a sit, Annie. You can wrap your feet in this blanket."

Annie nodded and joined him. Despite the oversized clothing, he was again amazed at how small she was. He watched her wrap the blanket around her bare feet.

"Have you ever seen a calf being born?"

"No."

"Have you ever seen anything like that?"

"A boy down the street had a dog who had puppies," she said. "I saw them before they had their eyes open. I thought they looked like a bunch of mice."

"This can get pretty, um, basic," Jess said. "You'll have to decide how long you want to stay."

She paused for a long time. He could see how exhausted she was. Her eyelids were at half-mast. "I'll stay for a while."

"It's nice to have some company," he said.

"You told Mr. Swann something about a fence. I didn't understand. Was my mother there when you called?"

"We covered that. I assume she was there, but I don't know for sure. In fact, I'm not sure I did the right thing at all."

"What are you going to do now?"

He looked at her. "I'm going to help this cow."

"No, I mean tomorrow. What are you going to do?"

He rubbed the gray stubble on his chin. "I guess I'll drive into town, see if I can find out what's going on without showing my hand."

She was obviously confused.

"I mean, I won't tell anyone you're here until I can determine that it's safe to tell someone. If the sheriff is open to it, without those ex-cops around, I could give him the word. But I'll need to do a little groundwork first."

"Groundwork? You talk funny," she said.

"I'll do some *investigating*," he said patiently. "I'll find out if it's okay to tell the sheriff and your mother you're here. I'm still a little confused why nobody has said anything about a man who got shot. There's something wrong with that whole deal."

"We saw him."

"I know you think you did."

"No," she said, leaning forward on the bucket. "We *saw* it. I could take you there, to the exact place it happened. I could draw you a picture of the men who did it."

"You could?"

"I can draw."

"Then tomorrow, after breakfast, I'd like you to do just that."

"Okay."

After a few minutes of silence, she asked, "Do you have to do this every night?"

"I do this time of year. It's calving season. The rest of the year I can pretty much sleep like a normal person. Unless the cows knock down a fence, or one of 'em gets sick or injured, or something like that. Ranching can be a twenty-four-hour job, Annie."

"My mom has a job," she said. "She works at a store. Sometimes she has to work at night, but she doesn't have to work at four in the morning."

Another long silence. Jess watched the cow. She was starting to dilate. A wet stream ran down one of her legs.

"Won't be long now," he said.

"Where is your wife?" Annie asked.

Jess snorted. "That's to the point."

"So where is she?"

Annie asked her questions in a matter-of-fact way. When he answered, she didn't cluck, didn't hang her head, didn't feign concern. She just wanted to know what was what, why he was alone.

"She left me." It just hung there, and he didn't like it. He didn't like saying the words, either. In fact, it was the first time he had ever said them. "I guess she figured there wasn't much of a future on this place, and she was probably right," he said. "She is an ambitious woman, and when our son was gone, she didn't have much to do. I could have changed a little more, I guess. I thought I was too old to change, and that I was still the man she married. I guess I thought wrong."

"Where's your son?"

"Jess Junior? He's around," Jess said. "He's sick, though. Spent some time in rehab, spent some time in jail. Got mixed up with drugs, bad ones. He's not all there anymore, is what I'm trying to say. It's not a good story."

Jeez, he thought. *Why am I telling all of this to a little girl?*

"Why didn't you have more kids?"

"I wanted more," Jess said. "A couple more, at least. Maybe a little girl or two. I asked her about having more, and she said she didn't want to bring another child into this world. But she meant the ranch, I know now. She meant *me.*"

He realized he had said too much and turned his head away.

"You do all of this ranch stuff by yourself?"

"I do now," Jess said. "I had to let my foreman go a couple of days ago."

"What if you get sick or something?"

"Then things don't get done."

"That's not fair."

"It's plenty fair," he said. "Why wouldn't it be? Folks aren't entitled to a living."

"It just doesn't sound right," she said, a little more unsure of herself.

"I'm not saying it's right. I said it was fair."

She paused, something else on her mind. "I'm pretty sure Billy wasn't my father. He's William's father, not mine. Someday, I want to find out where I come from. I know I come from somewhere." She looked up at him.

Jess had no clue how to respond to that.

Her probing eyes finally slipped from his face and back to the cow. "What's that?"

"That's the first sign of a little one trying to get out, and mama is trying to ease it out so she can meet it."

A gush of liquid burst forth, and it hit the packed dirt with a splash and beaded in the dust.

"Here we go," Jess said, grunting to his feet and pulling on latex gloves. "Help me welcome a brand-new cow to the world, Annie."

"Wow," she said. "A brand-new cow. It's pretty gross."

"Life is messy," Jess said, meaning one thing but realizing it sounded like something else.

Sunday, 7:05 A.M.

WHEN THE sun broke over the mountains, Villatoro was in his compact on a two-lane state highway headed west, trying to get a better sense of where he was, what this place was about. His back was stiff from sleeping in the too-soft bed, and his belly rumbled with hunger. He'd been awake since five, spent an hour drinking the entire pot of bad weak coffee from the motel room coffeemaker and watching cable exercise shows in his bed. He skirted the lakeshore, plunged into shadow and mist, and emerged on a straightaway and an ancient bridge over the inlet of the lake. Dark, forested mountains rose sharply on his left. The road was bordered by heavy brush and knee-high grass beaded with dew, and when the sun cascaded over the peaks, it ignited the droplets, creating fields of sparks. The air smelled of damp pine.

He got a better read on the area as he distanced himself from the town of Kootenai Bay. It was a community in transition, with a new population and culture superimposing itself over another. Older, smaller homes were near the road. Many of them had lawn decorations made of massive old circular saw blades with alpine scenes painted on them. There was something quaint, but tired, about the older homes, no doubt occupied by past generations of families who worked in the original extraction industries of logging and mining. These homes had postage-stamp lawns, small white fences, and a sense of humility about them, a conscious effort by the owners not to overreach. Then there were the huge new glass-and-log homes with sweeping grounds, gleaming new SUVs parked in circular driveways, and attractive new signs out front with names like "Duck Creek Ranch," "Elkhorn Estate," "Spruce Casa." And HOMESITE FOR SALE signs everywhere. A whole new community was forming around the skeleton of the old one. Golf courses were being constructed. Quaint shops and espresso bars occupied old storefronts that still had fading painted signs on their porticos reading GENERAL STORE or NIGHTCRAWLERS.

Within sight of the Montana border, he turned around and drove back. There was more traffic on the road now, and more human activity. Newspapers were being delivered, four-wheel-drive pickups were parked in front of restaurants for breakfast, the drivers pausing to finish cigarettes before entering. By contrast, thin, bronzed women of indeterminate age, some with dogs on leashes, jogged along the lakeshore in tight, colorful clothing, iPod earbuds wired to their heads.

As he reentered town, he checked his watch. It was still too early for Celeste to have come to work if she got the message from him the night before, and therefore much too soon to expect any information on Newkirk. He drove downtown, and swung into a space behind a battered pickup across from an old-fashioned diner called the Panhandle Cafe.

As he killed the engine and reached for his keys, he looked up through the windshield and gasped. The massive round face of a bear stared straight at him from six feet away.

It took a moment to realize what he was looking at, and for his heart to stop whumping. It was a bear, all right, in the bed of the pickup in front of him. Despite open eyes and a gray tongue that lolled out of its mouth, the bear was dead, its head propped up and over the tailgate on the back of the truck. The dead bear's front paws were arranged on either side of its head, making it look like the animal was trying to climb out.

Once his breathing returned to normal, Villatoro opened the car door and slid out, never taking his eyes off the face of the dead bear. He saw now that a long thick stream of maroon blood ran from the bottom of the tailgate of the pickup to the street and had pooled in the gutter.

"Spring bear hunt," someone said behind him, and Villatoro instinctively jumped, slamming the car door behind him. He was instantly ashamed of his reaction.

"Sorry," the man said. "Didn't mean to scare you."

It was a mature man in his late fifties or early sixties, thin, wearing a stained cowboy hat and light denim jacket. One of his hands was bandaged. Villatoro recognized him as the rancher who had preceded him with Jim Hearne at the bank. He didn't recall the bandage from the day before. They had not been introduced then, and Villatoro wasn't sure the man recognized him. *What was the name on the file Hearne had put away? Rawlings?*

"I'm fine now," Villatoro said. "I just looked up and there was that bear. . . ."

"I know," the man said. "I wish they wouldn't do that, but it's sort of a tradition around here. When a hunter gets a bear, he's obligated to drive it into town and buy a round for the house."

Villatoro nodded toward the Panhandle Cafe across the street. "Is that a good place to get breakfast?"

"Yup, it is. It's not as good as it used to be, though. But it's still sort of the place where the old-timers like me gather in the morning."

"Do people here go to church on Sunday?"

The rancher paused. "Yup, they do. I'm usually there myself, but not today."

"Just wondering. It seems like a community of faith. I used to live in a place like this."

The rancher looked at him with a hint of suspicion.

Villatoro turned again to the bear. "Do people here eat bear meat?"

The man shrugged. "Some folks make sausage out of it. It kinda tastes like pork. I've never been very fond of it myself."

Villatoro shuddered. He wished the bear's eyes were closed, at least. It bothered him that the tongue was exposed. If he were ever found dead, Villatoro thought, he hoped his tongue wouldn't be sticking out like that, swelled up, looking like he was sucking on a gray sausage.

"Well, thanks," Villatoro said, and crossed the street toward the restaurant. Before entering, he dropped two quarters into a newspaper machine and took the last copy of the *Kootenai Bay Chronicle*. As he did so, he glanced over his shoulder. The man in the cowboy hat was still across the street, examining the bear. He looked back at the man's truck, and saw the name RAWLINS RANCHES painted on the door.

Right, Villatoro said to himself. *Rawlins.*

THERE WAS a time, years ago, when the big round table in the corner of the Panhandle was reserved most mornings for ranchers. Jess had first taken a place there as a boy, with his father. Jess could still remember his elation when his father motioned him over from where he sat at the counter and cleared a space for his son on the half-moon-shaped vinyl seat. It meant something to be invited to sit with the adults, and they all knew it, and they grumbled good-naturedly when they shifted to the left, making a place for him. They teased him a little about the hot chocolate he brought with him, and offered to fill his mug with strong coffee instead. He let them. He knew enough to sit silently, to defer, to listen. The talk was of cattle prices, noxious weeds, predators, politics, cattle buyers. But that was a long time ago. How different it had been when Jess had duplicated the gesture with his own son. Jess Jr. had refused to come over, instead rolling his eyes and turning his back to the table. The other ranchers in the booth had all seen what had happened, and they suddenly found their cups of coffee fascinating to look at. Jess was humiliated. It was the first of many more humiliations to come involving his son.

The table was now occupied by a large family of visitors to the area, who obviously planned a day of hiking, judging by their high-tech boots and garb.

Jess took a stool at the counter and put his hat crown down on the bar. A knot of men talked loudly at the end of the counter, surrounding a young man with a beard who had blood on his shirt. The bear hunter.

"What can I get you?" the hunter asked Jess after wiping beer foam from his mustache.

"Coffee's fine," Jess said.

"Nothing stronger? I got a bear out there."

"I saw it," Jess said. "Congratulations, but coffee's fine." Not saying: *I already cooked and ate breakfast a while ago with a couple of missing kids.*

VILLATORO WATCHED the exchange from a booth while he waited for his coffee. There was something about Rawlins he admired. There was a quiet dignity about him, something solid and old-fashioned. He wished he had introduced himself, but the dead bear had shaken him to his bones. He would do so after breakfast.

The former detective ordered and spread the newspaper open in front of him. The issue was dominated with stories about the disappearance of the Taylor children. Their photos, the same ones he had seen in the bank and on flyers in the sheriff's office, were reproduced on the front page. A photo of the woman he'd seen clutching at Rawlins—she was identified as Rural Postal Contractor Fiona Pritzle—was featured under the headline THE LAST TO SEE THE CHILDREN. He read a little of the interview. Pritzle said that she'd "had a feeling that something wasn't right" when she'd dropped off the siblings to go fishing. "I should have gone with my best instincts and just taken those kids home to their mother," she said. She blamed herself but was quoted in such a way that she deflected it: ". . . But I just figured that there was no way those kids would have just taken off like that without their mother's permission and approval."

That poor mother, Villatoro thought, shaking his head. *That's all she needs.* He searched through the paper for a photo of Monica Taylor and found one on the next page. Monica Taylor was an attractive woman, but she'd refused to be interviewed by the *Chronicle.* Instead, a volunteer named Oscar Swann, who identified himself as her spokesman, said she was under medication and was too distraught to make a statement.

The name Swann was familiar to Villatoro. He felt himself take several quick, shallow breaths. Could it be that two of them were up here? Would that be coincidence? He didn't buy it.

Villatoro underlined the name in the newspaper before reading further. Sheriff Ed Carey was quoted extensively. It was the same interview Villatoro had seen the night before on the Spokane news. Carey made several references to his investigative team.

He read:

> When asked for more detail on what has been referred to as
> a "Dream Team" rumored to be made up of retired police offi-

cers from the LAPD, Carey said the volunteers had selflessly given their time and expertise to the case, and that he, and the residents of the county, would be forever in their debt. When pressed, Carey refused to reveal the names of the volunteer investigators but said they were being led by a former senior officer who had been involved in dozens of high-profile investigations.

JESS WAS reading the same article after deliberately covering up Fiona Pritzle's face with his coffee cup.

Swann was describing himself as Monica Taylor's spokesman? What in the hell did *that* mean? As he thought it over, his coffee turned bitter and cold in his mouth. If what Annie and William told him was true, Swann had ingratiated himself with their mother so he could head off or prevent any contact with her by them. He would be there if one of them called, probably answering the telephone.

Jesus, Jess thought.

On the television in the corner, the now-familiar photos of Annie and William Taylor were shown, followed by a graphic with a map of the state of Idaho. The room hushed as everyone turned toward the screen. A reporter doing a live shot followed the graphic. He was standing in the middle of the street in Kootenai Bay, holding a microphone and talking straight into the camera. Over the reporter's shoulder was the sign for the restaurant.

"That son of a bitch is right outside," the bear hunter said. "If I walked out the front door, you guys could see me on Fox News!"

"We've seen enough of you already," his buddy said.

Jess had a momentous decision to make. Seeing Annie's and William's faces on national news triggered it. Either he believed those kids or he didn't. And either way, he was harboring them, telling no one, while the entire nation worried and searched for them. By not reporting their presence immediately, he had crossed a line. Every minute he kept his secret was another minute he was more guilty. But he had to know more about the situation. Jess had always thought for himself. Hell, everybody did up here. Who could blame him for waiting and listening to make sure he was doing the right thing?

The world was different now, all right. Twenty-four-hour news channels told everyone what to think, what they should be concerned about. If those news networks decided the disappearance of the Taylor children was big news, there was no way he could keep them hidden much longer. He just hoped he could figure out what was what before that happened.

Turning in Annie and William would be the easy thing to do. He could hope for the best and wish things worked out. But who would he be turning them in to? Swann?

"SHERIFF," THE WAITRESS behind the counter greeted Carey. "What can I get you?"

Like every set of eyes in the place, Villatoro's watched the sheriff enter the restaurant, walk wearily to the counter, and take a stool. As the rancher next to him had done, Carey took off his hat and placed it on the counter. Even the bear hunter and his friends had stopped talking.

"I guess I should eat, even though I ain't hungry," Carey said. "Eggs over easy, ham, coffee, wheat toast."

The waitress scribbled and took the order into the kitchen.

The sheriff sat with his shoulders slumped, his uniform shirt wrinkled, his face unshaven. His eyes were dark and hollowed. He held his coffee mug with both hands and sipped it cautiously.

"Any news, Sheriff?" the bear hunter asked from the end of the counter.

Carey sighed. "Nope." Then, as if he realized how hopeless he had sounded, he said, "We're working on it, though."

JESS TRIED to keep his own voice calm. He spoke softly. "What's the deal with the volunteers? Are they really ex-cops?"

Carey eyed Jess with cool eyes, as if trying to determine whether he was a supporter or in the 49 percent who had voted against him.

"And you'd be . . ."

"Jess Rawlins."

"That's right," the sheriff said, pretending he remembered.

"I've got a ranch north of town, not far from Sand Creek."

"Right. It's not all that far from where the Taylor kids disappeared."

"Over ten miles away," Jess said, feeling defensiveness creep into his voice.

The sheriff heard it as well and looked stricken. "That's not what I meant . . . I wasn't implying anything."

Jess shrugged it off. "Your volunteers?"

Carey was grateful to move on. "Yes, they're all ex-cops. LAPD retirees, but not all that long in the tooth."

"How many of them are there?"

"Four are working with me directly. But another couple dozen on search teams."

Jess nodded. Annie had made the drawing he had asked her for on the kitchen table. The sketch was folded in his pocket. The caricatures were rudimentary: a thin man with white hair and blue eyes, another wearing a ball cap, the third bigger, darker, with a black mustache. Three of them, not four. Then Jess remembered Swann.

"Did they all know each other before this?" Jess asked.

"I think so," Carey said. "They seem pretty familiar with each other. They all pretty much agree who the leader is, anyway."

"Who is that?"

"A man named Singer. Used to be a lieutenant, from what I understand."

"This guy Swann," Jess asked, tapping the newspaper with his finger, trying not to convey his trepidation, "the paper says he's the spokesman for Monica Taylor. How'd that come to be?"

Carey's antenna seemed to go up, Jess thought. Maybe he was asking too many questions.

"Do you know him?" Carey asked.

"I've heard his name," Jess said truthfully.

"Well, apparently he's friends with the mother. He volunteered to stay with her in case somebody calls. But with the exposure this thing is getting in the press, he might spend most of his time keeping reporters away from her. I really can't spare a man for that."

Jess nodded. "This is kind of a crazy question, but is this the only big case you're working on right now? I heard a wild rumor about a possible murder in the county."

Carey's eyebrows shot up, and he seemed to examine Jess in a whole new way that said, *This old man is a nutcase.*

He kept his voice down, as Jess had done. "Where in the hell did you hear *that*?"

"You know how people talk."

"And where was this murder supposed to have occurred?"

"By the river."

Carey shook his head. A vein had enlarged in his temple, and Jess could see the sheriff's heartbeat.

"I wish they'd stick to real life, goddammit."

"So, no other big crime in the area?"

Carey reached over and tapped the newspaper, as Jess had. His eyes were both angry and pleading. "Isn't this enough right now?"

The waitress emerged from the kitchen with Carey's breakfast and topped off their coffee.

"If you'll excuse me . . ." Carey said, turning to his plate and stabbing egg yolks with points of toast.

Jess sat back. He hadn't noticed another man enter the restaurant and walk straight toward the sheriff.

BUT VILLATORO saw him. It was Newkirk. Newkirk approached the sheriff and threw an arm over his back so he could tell him something private.

JESS KEPT his eyes averted but listened carefully. The man had whispered something about a videotape. The man wore a ball cap.

"How'd we get it, Newkirk?" Carey asked, his toast poised in the air between his plate and his mouth.

"Somebody dropped it by this morning. We found it in a grocery sack near the front door of the station. Nobody saw who left it."

"Have you looked at it?"

Newkirk solemnly nodded his head. "It's something you need to see, Sheriff."

"Do I have time to finish my breakfast?"

"No, I don't think so."

Carey called for the waitress to box up his breakfast.

"Who's on it? Are the kids on it?"

Newkirk looked quickly around the room before answering. He seemed suddenly agitated, and Jess followed his line of sight. Newkirk was looking at the dark man in the booth who was eating his breakfast, the man who had been startled by the bear across the street.

AFTER NEWKIRK ushered the sheriff out, Jess withdrew the sketch. There he was, the one in the ball cap. He stood, threw down two dollars, and slid off his stool. He was clamping his hat on his head and leaving when the man in the booth intercepted him.

"I didn't introduce myself earlier. I'm Eduardo Villatoro."

"Jess Rawlins."

"May I buy you a cup of coffee?" Villatoro asked, gesturing to the empty seat in his booth.

"I'm kind of coffeed out, thanks."

"May I ask you a question?"

"Shoot."

"I overheard you talking with the sheriff. He mentioned the name of a man he's working with, an ex-lieutenant. What was the man's name again?"

"He said it was Singer."

Villatoro's eyes narrowed. *Singer.* Now there were three.

"You know him?"

"Yes. This name I know for sure."

Jess tried to read Villatoro's face, wondering what he meant by that.

"I guess I will have that cup of coffee," Jess said.

Sunday, 9:55 A.M.

THE FIRST THIRTY seconds of the videotape was of a Seattle Sea-hawks football playoff game from the previous season. As the quarter-back pulled back to pass, the screen faded into snowy static, there was an audible pop, then it was filled with a starkly lighted head-and-shoulders shot of a man in an otherwise dark room.

"My name is Tom Boyd. . . ."

They were in the command center with the door closed. Newkirk stood in the back of the room, watching over the sheriff's shoulder. Newkirk's belly was on fire, and his eyes watered from the taste of acid in his throat that wanted to come up. He had not seen the video before now because he had refused to watch it being filmed the night before. Instead, he had stayed upstairs on the deck drinking Wild Turkey and looking at the reflection of the stars on the faraway lake. All he knew was that it had taken a long time. Nine tries before they got it right, Gonzalez said later. Newkirk had rolled home at 4:30 A.M. His bedroom door was locked, blankets and a pillow on the couch in the entertain-ment room. Even his dog avoided him.

"I work for United Parcel Service here in Kootenai Bay, and I got to get something off my chest before I split the country for good. . . ."

Boyd looked terrible on the tape, Newkirk thought. His face was white and drawn, his eyes gleamed and looked vacant at the same time. Newkirk noticed that either Singer or Gonzo had buttoned the man's shirt up to the collar to hide the Taser burns. But when Boyd turned his head slightly while talking, Newkirk thought he could see the top edge of one. Would anyone else see it if they weren't looking for it? He felt a hot surge in his throat and turned away. He needed cold water fast.

"I didn't mean to hurt those kids. I don't even remember how it happened. I mean, what caused it. It was like I was there one minute, and I didn't wake up until after it happened. Like I blacked out, or something. I feel real bad about it. . . ."

The sheriff moaned, "Aw, shit." Newkirk looked at Carey. The man had looked bad at breakfast, but nothing like he did now. It was as if the sheriff were collapsing into himself. His shoulders slumped, and his hands fell limply to his sides.

"I ain't saying where the bodies are at, only that you won't likely ever find them. All I can say is they didn't suffer nearly as much as I am now. I'm sorry, of course. They didn't deserve it. Maybe if their mother would'a taught them not to steal, but I ain't completely blaming her, either. She needs help, but I ain't the one to give it."

Boyd paused, swallowed as if it hurt him, then continued.

"Don't bother looking for me, either. By the time you see this, I'll be so far away you'll never find me. All I can say is I wish it never would have happened, and it'll never happen again. I'm through with the drugs and the alcohol."

For the first time, Boyd glanced away from the camera lens, then returned to it. To Newkirk, the reason was obvious: Boyd was looking for approval. But would anyone else see it that way?

"That's it. I'm gone."

You sure are, Newkirk thought.

The tape once again faded into snow before the game returned. The room was filled with the sound of the announcers describing a replay. No one else spoke for several minutes.

Finally, Singer walked to the VCR and monitor and paused it. "Do you want to see it again?" he asked the sheriff.

"Jesus," the sheriff said. "No, I don't want to see it again right now."

"Looks like we've got our guy," Singer said. "Whether we'll be able to find him is another thing."

"Those poor kids. My God."

"The tape belonged to Boyd, no doubt about it," Singer said. "He kept a library of Seahawk games from last year. Eighteen tapes, all the same brand, lined up in order on his bookshelf. The last one was missing, which is the one we just looked at. So was his video camera, but he left the case for it."

"Maybe we should get some dogs," Gonzalez said. "We could get the scent from clothes at the mother's house and send the dogs out near the river. I'm guessing that's where we'll find the bodies. I don't know the situation around here, but we used to have some dog guys available we could call in."

Carey seemed incapable of moving or speaking. He stared at the frozen screen.

"Sheriff?" Singer asked gently.

"The mother needs to know," Carey said. "I don't look forward to that conversation."

Singer screwed up his face in sympathy. Newkirk felt another violent surge. Again, he fought to keep it down. He looked away, at the empty council chambers, hoping that not seeing Singer, Gonzalez, or Carey would settle his flaming stomach.

"We could call Swann," Singer said. "He could break the news."

The sheriff looked troubled. "No. That's something I should do."

"Swann knows her," Singer said. "It might be better coming from him."

Carey considered it. "You're probably right."

Coward, Newkirk thought.

"Time to issue an Amber Alert and call in the FBI," Carey said. "We've got a suspect now, but this is beyond us. Boyd is probably halfway across Nevada or in Canada by now."

Singer's eyes flared, but so quickly that Newkirk wasn't sure the sheriff even noticed.

"No FBI," Singer said. "Do you know how they come in and completely take over a case? I've been there, believe me. The most dangerous place to be on earth is between an FBI spokesman and a television camera. They make the locals come off as incompetent and lame. There's nothing the Feds can do that we've not already thought of."

Carey shook his head. "We need somebody to analyze the tape. Maybe they can figure out where it was shot, or see something in it we can't see."

Newkirk was surprised by the sheriff's determination and mortified by the sudden turn things had taken. Singer had been sure Carey would defer to him.

"Why does it matter where he took it?" Singer asked. "What matters is what he said. He confessed, Sheriff. We've got our man. Now we've got to concentrate on finding Boyd and locating those bodies. The FBI can't really help with that here. You know this county better than they ever will."

Carey cleared his throat. "It doesn't feel right to me that Boyd here would confess on a tape and, in effect, dare us to come find him. He doesn't seem proud of what he did. He feels like shit, and he sure looks like shit. Maybe he had to do it to clear his conscience, but why not just turn himself in? He's no hardened criminal. He's just a local boy gone bad."

"Sheriff . . ."

Carey looked at Singer. "That's right. Last I looked, I was still the sheriff around here. It makes sense to me to bring in some expertise."

To an outsider, Newkirk thought, it might look like the sheriff had won. But Singer's face was calm, impassive. As if he were considering what the sheriff said and thinking it over. But Newkirk knew Singer and knew that Singer was at his most dangerous when he appeared serene.

"Okay," Singer said, chancing a small smile. "You're the sheriff. We're here to help, not to tell you what to do. But please realize that when the FBI comes in, it will no longer be your show. The Feds will look at everything. The way the investigation was run, how you manage your office, everything. If they don't find Boyd or those bodies, they'll say it's because the investigation was botched in the early stages. They'll hold hourly press conferences to feed the networks their raw meat, and you'll end up getting the blame. You don't deserve that, Sheriff Carey. You've done nothing wrong. You've worked your ass off, just like we have. But in the end, however it goes, there will be people out there, voters, who will think you waited until the case was botched before you called in the cavalry. Didn't you say you won with fifty-one percent of the vote? How many votes would swing it back? Less than a hundred, I'd guess. How many people will think you fucked up, even though you didn't? I haven't been here all that many years, but I've been around long enough to know that the citizens aren't fond of federal involvement. They're an independent bunch up here. Why elect a sheriff when all he's going to do is bring in Federales when he doesn't know what to do next?"

Carey listened in silence, never taking his eyes off Singer. Finally, Carey shifted and looked at Gonzalez, who was sitting back in his chair, arms crossed, obviously disappointed with him. The sheriff turned back to Newkirk, who said, "Do what you need to do, Sheriff."

"Twelve hours," Carey said, standing up. "You've got that time to clear things up. There's a guy down in Coeur d'Alene with bloodhounds we contract with. And we'll need to reissue the APB for Boyd along with the Amber Alert, to make sure everybody in the country is looking for him. We'll say we suspect him to be armed and dangerous. But if we don't have Boyd or those bodies in twelve hours, I'm calling in the FBI."

"Fair enough," Singer said.

Newkirk found himself staring at Singer. *What was he thinking? What did a day really matter?*

Carey left the room and shut the door, only to reopen it and lean in. "You'll ask Swann to break the news to the mother?"

"I will," Singer said. "I'd hold off on any public announcement about the confession, though. At least until tomorrow, if we can."

"I'll tell the press about the alert," Carey agreed. "Until then, we'll have to see more and more stories about the white supremacists who used to be here."

SINGER WAITED until the sheriff was back in his office down the hall before addressing Gonzalez and Newkirk.

"That means we've got today to find those kids."

"Son of a bitch," Gonzalez said. "Maybe the tape was a bad idea."

Singer shook his head. "No, no, it wasn't. There's no doubt in that sheriff's mind who did it now. That was the purpose of the tape, after all."

"What if the FBI looks at it?" Newkirk asked. "What if they figure out where it was made? Or they see Boyd looking to Gonzo to see if he's said everything right? I thought I could see that stun-gun burn when he turned his head."

Singer responded with a cold stare. Newkirk stopped talking.

"We've handed the sheriff a confession, Newkirk. We gave him a fucking slam dunk. He'll think about it and realize it's better to close this thing than to keep it open."

"What if he doesn't? He seemed pretty determined."

"Then we'll deal with it," Singer said. "We'll stay ahead of him. It's not that hard."

"Where are those fucking kids?" Gonzalez asked rhetorically, looking at the map of the county pushpinned to the wall. "Maybe they *are* dead by now. How long could a couple of kids survive out there in those woods and not be seen by anybody?"

Singer's voice dropped to a whisper. "It could be that somebody is hiding them. If so, we've got to find out who."

"What if they *are* found?" Newkirk asked.

Singer snapped back, "If they show up, we're in perfect position to take care of it. We'll be able to get to them before they can yap. We've got a man with their mother, remember? You think they'd talk if they knew what could happen to her if they did? There is no way they'd be out of our control long enough to fuck us over.

"But I'd rather not have to go that route," Singer said, abruptly changing his line of thought. "It's too messy. Someday, one of them would talk. So we've got to get out and find them, *now*. They're out there somewhere, we know that. We've got to deal with this *now*."

Gonzalez agreed. Newkirk said nothing.

"Gentlemen, make sure your cell phones are charged up. After we take care of the package, I want both of you out in the field. Start with where we last saw them, Swann's place. I've kept the volunteer search teams out of that area so far. They've all been concentrating on the river, where we know those kids can't be. So start at Swann's. Go house to house. Start checking buildings. They could be hiding in some old shack or abandoned barn."

Newkirk suddenly remembered he was supposed to pick up his sons after baseball practice that evening. Jeez . . .

Singer was on his cell with Swann. He gestured to Gonzalez. "Swann can meet you at his place in forty-five minutes. Can you deliver the package by then?"

Gonzalez nodded. "Same as before?"

"Yes."

"How much can they eat, for Christ's sake?"

Singer smiled. "They can eat a lot, Gonzo."

"Isn't it inhumane to feed them meat laced with steroids?" Gonzalez laughed. "It won't be organic pork anymore."

"Hold it," Newkirk said, stepping forward. "What aren't you telling me?"

Singer said, "Mr. Boyd expired on us."

"He wasn't so tough after all," Gonzalez said. "He died of fright or something. I found him dead this morning."

Newkirk let that sink in. Gonzalez put his hands out, palms up, in a what-can-you-do? gesture.

"You were too rough," Newkirk said to him.

Gonzalez shrugged.

To Singer, Newkirk said, "You said you were going to keep him alive."

"We'll deal with it," Singer said dismissively. Then: "Go fill in for Swann at the mother's house while Swann is away. Don't let her answer the phone or talk to anyone without you clearing it. In fact, just keep her the fuck away from everybody. Swann will be back soon enough to relieve you."

Newkirk nodded his head. Like Gonzalez, he instinctively patted his weapon under his jacket and his cell phone in his shirt pocket. He had an urge to seat his nightstick in his service belt, but of course he no longer had one.

"Oh," Singer said to Swann on the cell, "tell her Tom Boyd confessed. That ought to keep her locked away in her room for a while."

He snapped the phone closed and dropped it in his pocket.

"Newkirk, you with us?" Singer asked suddenly.

"What do you mean?"

"You're not wavering, are you?"

"No. It's just that I had things to do tonight."

Gonzalez snorted.

"This is a little more important, don't you think?" Singer asked, stepping across the room and throwing an arm over Newkirk's shoulder. Despite the gesture, Newkirk could feel Singer's fingers digging hard into his neck. "I'll get us through this, Newkirk. Then everything will be like it was, and we can forget about it and move on."

"Okay."

"Trust me," Singer said. "It's under control." Newkirk could feel Singer's fingers stop digging and relax. Singer tousled Newkirk's hair, knocking his cap off.

"Keep your cell phone on," Singer said.

Suddenly, a thought came to Newkirk, something he had meant to tell Singer earlier.

"I saw that Barney Fife dude again this morning, at the restaurant. The ex-cop from Arcadia."

"Villatoro?"

"He was sitting there watching everything. The fucker makes me nervous, Lieutenant. There's something about him."

"I'm running a check on him," Singer said. "He'll likely turn out to be trouble."

Gonzalez actually laughed. "Good. More trouble. The hits just keep on coming."

NEWKIRK MADE it to the bathroom before he threw up. As he cleaned his face with a wet paper towel, he looked in the mirror and saw the janitor trustee, the same one who had bumped the door with his mop the night before.

"What the fuck are you looking at?" Newkirk asked.

"Nothing," the janitor said. "I guess I gotta clean that up."

"I guess you do," Newkirk said, going out the door, wiping his mouth with his sleeve.

Sunday, 10:15 A.M.

MONICA TAYLOR took the news with a calmness that surprised her, and told Swann, simply: "I don't believe it."

"What do you mean you don't believe it?" Swann said, closing his cell phone. "He confessed on *videotape*."

Monica shook her head. "No."

Swann's eyes were unblinking. "Why would he lie about something like this? What could possess *you* not to believe it?"

She didn't know, and she didn't care. And it wasn't about Tom Boyd at all, she thought. It was about the feeling she had when she'd awakened that morning. She couldn't explain it to herself, much less to Swann. But she had awakened simply knowing that her children were still alive. It was as if, for the first time, she had recognized an invisible cord that connected her to Annie and William that had always been there. She was sure it hadn't been severed. They were still out there. Probably scared, probably alone. Possibly hurt. But they were still out there.

"Do you want to see the tape?" Swann asked, his voice rising. "We could go down to the station right now, and you can watch it."

"I don't want to see it."

Swann sighed angrily and turned away. Monica sipped her coffee. She had refused to take the prescribed medication that morning. Her head was clearing. She could see Swann near the stove, see him thinking while holding his phone. Was he weighing whether to call someone back?

He turned back to her. "Denial is a powerful emotion, I realize that," he said. "It's a natural first reaction. At some point, though, you need to accept the truth, Monica, as hard as that may be."

"I don't have to accept anything, Oscar."

Again, his eyes bulged, and he turned away. It seemed odd, she thought. He was dealing with her intransigence not with sympathy or pity but with anger. She thought: *As if I wasn't playing the game correctly.* She almost smiled to herself, thinking, *I've never played any game correctly. That's been my problem. Maybe this time, it's my advantage.*

"Maybe I can ask the sheriff's office to make a copy and bring it here," Swann said, mostly to himself. "You've got a VCR, right?"

"I do," she said. "But it doesn't matter."

"Is it Boyd?" Swann asked. "Is that your problem? Do you think the guy just isn't capable of this?"

She didn't answer. She knew Tom was capable of anything when he was angry.

"Do you still love the guy, or what?"

"I never loved him, I realize now," she said. "Not the kind of love I have for my children."

Swann started to speak, then drew back. He simply stared at her, as if she were a mutant, devoid of appropriate human emotion.

"What was the name of that rancher you talked to yesterday? Do you remember?" she asked.

"What does that have to do with anything?" Swann said. "Besides, he didn't give me a name."

"Why did you open my door last night?" she asked.

The question derailed him. "What?"

"Why were you standing in my room?"

Swann leaned back on the kitchen counter, still looking at her in that way. "I was making sure you were all right."

She smiled slightly. "Really?"

"Yes, really."

"You weren't hoping I would invite you into my bed?"

She watched him carefully, saw his neck flush.

"You're nuts, lady," he said, but he couldn't meet her eyes.

"That's what I thought," she said.

How could a man who seemed to be as kind and mature as Swann portrayed himself even think of bedding a mother whose children were missing? Why would his reaction to telling her about the murder of her children be anger when she didn't fall apart?

Was he really there to protect her, to provide guidance and comfort? Or was Swann there to keep her imprisoned? And if so, why? What did he know?

Monica held all of this in. She hoped her face didn't betray what she was thinking. She hoped she wasn't nuts, after all.

Swann anticipated the doorbell ringing in the front room and was moving toward it before it did. Monica waited, frozen with her thoughts, as she heard a brief conversation on the threshold.

Swann ushered a man younger than himself into the kitchen. The visitor looked at her cautiously.

"This is Officer Newkirk," Swann said. "He'll be staying with you for a couple of hours while I attend to some business at home. He knows the situation, and he's a good guy. He's here to help you, Monica."

She looked Newkirk over. He was shorter than Swann, with a shock of dirty blond hair sticking out from beneath his baseball cap. He looked strained, and pale, but his eyes had the same hardness Swann's did. Another ex-cop. She noted his wedding ring.

"You're my new jailer?" Monica asked.

Newkirk looked quickly to Swann for an explanation. Swann shook his head sadly.

"She just found out about the videotape," Swann said. "She's shaken up by it."

Newkirk nodded as if he understood. "I'm here to do anything I can," he said.

"Who exactly are you helping?" Monica asked.

Again, Newkirk looked to Swann for an explanation.

"She needs to take her medication," Swann said like a grumpy father.

"You can talk directly to me, Mr. Swann. I'm right here. You don't have to talk about me like I'm not."

Swann sighed again and zipped up his jacket to leave. "See if you can get her to take her meds. If you can't, call the doctor and ask him to come over. She needs rest."

"I'm perfectly fine," Monica said.

"Good luck," Swann told Newkirk before leaving. "Keep her off the phone, and if the press comes, don't let them see her."

Sunday, 10:17 A.M.

JESS RAWLINS and Eduardo Villatoro left the restaurant together after Villatoro had insisted on paying the tab. Jess was aware of the ex-cop behind him as he walked across the street toward his pickup.

"Nice morning," Jess said, stopping on the center line and looking around at the mountains on all sides. There was no traffic. The sky was clear of clouds, and endlessly blue. The sun had yet to take charge of the day, although its intensity warmed his exposed skin.

"Very nice," Villatoro answered. He could see the news crew from Fox News packing their cameras and sound equipment into their van down the street. The reporter who had been on-screen earlier stood to the side, brushing his hair in a mirror.

They had spent the last half hour probing each other, Jess knew. He had learned why Villatoro was in Kootenai Bay and had listened to the details of the robbery at Santa Anita. He had believed the man when he said he thought he was getting close to something and how important it was to him to solve the case. Jess had listened patiently, trying not to let his mind wander to his ranch, where the children were, or to the implications of his current situation. He had waited until the end of the robbery story, where it would logically loop back to the present, to hear what Villatoro had to say about the ex-cops who were helping the sheriff with the investigation. Jess didn't want to tip his hand and ask too quickly about them.

When it came to Singer, Villatoro had not provided as much information as Jess had hoped. Lieutenant Singer was a familiar name to Villatoro because he'd been involved in the investigation of the Santa Anita robbery in a peripheral way. He wasn't the lead investigator, but one of the prime administrative hurdles. Newkirk was connected to the investigation as well, Villatoro said. He was pretty sure Newkirk was one of the team assigned to the case. There were others, Villatoro said. He was waiting for the names, and their ties to the case. There was something else, too. He just couldn't connect it yet.

"There is simply too much coincidence," Villatoro had said, "that two of the names involved in Santa Anita are now here, of all places. Don't you think?"

Jess had said he didn't know. And he didn't. "I don't like the idea of bad cops up here," he said. "I don't like the idea of bad cops, period."

Villatoro agreed. "I hope in my heart that's not the case," he said. "I've worked with police officers all of my life. For the most part, they've been dedicated and honest. Sure, there were some lazy ones. But truly bad cops—no. The idea disturbs me, and I hope it's wrong."

"Yup."

"There were some officers I didn't like, and who didn't like me. Too many of the cops I worked with out of L.A. looked down on me and my department. They thought we were small-timers. We probably were, but we were very close to our community at one time. It's not like that anymore. It's hard to adjust to being swallowed up, I guess. I see that happening here."

Jess said, "I'm not one to oppose change. No offense, but my granddad changed this place when he moved here and started the ranch. I'd be selfish if I thought, 'Now that I'm here, no one else has a right to be.' Live and let live, that's what I think."

Villatoro nodded. "That's a good attitude to have. I admire that."

"I just want the new ones to have some respect for what was here before they got here," Jess said. "Hell, if I moved to Los Angeles, I wouldn't expect 'em to put a cow in every yard and elk in the parks just so I could feel more comfortable."

Smiling, Villatoro said, "We agree about respect."

"Damned right. Maybe it's also having a sense of history," Jess said.

"And duty," Villatoro said. "There is duty. I can still repeat the last words of the Peace Officers Code of Ethics, even though I haven't said it out loud for thirty years."

Jess raised his eyebrows "Let's hear it then."

Villatoro said, "I know that I alone am responsible for my own standard of professional performance and will take every reasonable opportunity to enhance and improve my level of knowledge and competence. I will constantly strive to achieve these objectives and ideals, dedicating myself before God to my chosen profession—law enforcement."

"Too bad you retired," Jess said.

"I haven't retired from that. Not yet."

Jess thought how unusual it was to have a talk with a man about these subjects. Especially a man he'd met for the first time. That there were others who thought this way made him feel good. He liked this Eduardo Villatoro, but he couldn't tip his hand about the children, not yet.

Crossing the street, Jess had decided that if nothing else, Villatoro could be an outside resource. If Jess couldn't work with the sheriff's department, which he was more and more sure he couldn't because they were compromised, he would need to contact someone else. Villatoro might be a man he could trust.

As he approached his pickup, Jess slipped his hand into his pocket to make sure Villatoro's card was there. The man had written down the number of his motel and his room as well. In turn, Jess had given Villatoro the number for his ranch.

"I hope I can talk to you from time to time as my investigation continues," Villatoro said. "It's good to have a local expert who knows how things work. I hope you don't mind. This is a foreign place to me."

Jess turned. "I don't mind. Just don't ask me to gossip about my neighbors. I won't do that."

"I wouldn't dream of asking," Villatoro said, flashing a smile. "It is just that I see this place as, I don't know, a million trees with a few people walking around in them. I can't see the whole picture, it is too strange. It would be like if you were dropped in the middle of East L.A. with no one to help you out. You wouldn't know what to do, where to go, what was proper. There are predators there, too," he said, gesturing toward the bear, "but they wear colors and carry guns. It's so different."

Jess said nothing. He had always thought it was easier for rural people to live in a city than lifelong city dwellers to move to the country.

"For example," Villatoro said, gesturing to the eastern range, "when I look at that mountain there, all I see is a mountain with trees all over it. There is probably more to it, but that's all I can see."

Jess turned to see where Villatoro was pointing. "That's Webb Mountain," Jess said. "See where there's that big sweep of green on it that's lighter than the rest? Kind of a mosaic? Those are aspens. There was a forest fire up there twenty years ago, and aspens grow back first. Eventually, the pines will overtake the aspens, but it'll take centuries. There was some talk about putting in a ski resort on Webb Mountain, but the developers got chased away by the environmentalists. It's good bear habitat. I'd guess that's where our hunter here got his bear this morning."

He looked around to see Villatoro smiling. "That's what I mean," the ex-detective said. "I see a mountain that looks like every other mountain of a hundred in every direction. You see history and a story."

Jess reached for his door handle, then thought better of it. He could walk where he needed to go.

"This is why this is such an amazing country," Villatoro said. "It is so big, and so different. One will never know all of it."

Jess suppressed a grin of his own. "You're an interesting man, Mr. Villatoro."

"I'm a fish out of water, is what I am. But I'm a determined fish."

"That you are," Jess said. "I kinda feel the same way myself."

They shook hands.

BECAUSE THE county building was only two blocks away, Jess decided to walk. He needed a few minutes to think, to put his plan together. He was overwhelmed and confused. Things seemed to be swirling around him, keeping him off-balance. It had begun when Herbert, his ranch foreman, left and disrupted a routine he had gotten used to. With all of the problems a rancher had to face—weather, prices, natural disasters, regulations, trespassers, bad employees—any kind of routine was a necessity. Tasks needed to be done at certain times. A ranch couldn't be run by the seat of one's pants. But with Herbert gone and the appearance of the children—and their dangerous story—he felt cut loose from his moorings. He was adrift and unsure of himself.

Whether or not the murder had been reported—or whether it had even happened—everything else he had learned that morning seemed to lean toward Annie and William's version of events. The thought that the murderers were ex-cops who had moved in quickly to shape and control events would fit. Placing a man with the mother to guard her would fit, too. But without a body, what the children had told him could be dismissed as the result of overactive imaginations. It all hinged on a murder that apparently hadn't happened, on a dead man who wasn't missed by anyone.

Jess thought of the implications of his situation and felt a stab in his chest. If what Annie and William had told him turned out not to be true, he was guilty of a great fraud on the community, and possibly even a crime. Every hour that went by that he kept his secret was another cruel hour for the mother.

And what was on the videotape Newkirk had whispered about to the sheriff?

What held him back from walking into the sheriff's office and telling them he knew where the missing children were and leading them to his ranch? It was simple, he realized. He believed Annie.

But he still wasn't sure. He needed more information. What was on the videotape? He had to find out. Then, he would make his decision.

AS HE PASSED by the realty office, Jess quickened his pace, but she saw him.

"Jess?"

He slowed, debated whether to stop or resume his march. He wished he would have taken his pickup to the sheriff's office and avoided this possibility.

"Jess?"

He stopped on the sidewalk and shoved his hands in his pockets, looking at her under the brim of his hat. God, she looked good. Trim, fit, wearing black slacks, a white shirt and blazer. Her lipstick was a smoky shade he had never seen before, and her dark hair was pulled back. No gray; she must have dyed it. She had never looked that good on the ranch.

"Hello, Karen."

"I was surprised to look out and see you walk by."

"Working on Sunday, huh?"

"We've got a closing at eleven. I'm waiting for the buyers. Hey— what did you do to your hand?"

"Accident with a hay hook," he said, hoping that would suffice.

She stopped on the sidewalk and awkwardly crossed her arms in front of her. He didn't expect a hug, but it seemed odd to talk with her from five feet away. It felt like a mile.

"What are you doing in town?" she asked.

"Going to the county building."

She pursed her lips. "They're closed today."

"Not the Sheriff's Office."

"Oh," she said, looking him over, obviously wondering what would come next.

"I wanted to see if there was any news on the Taylor kids." Not a lie at all.

"Isn't that terrible?" she said, shaking her head. "Nobody I've talked to can remember such a thing happening here before. I hope they find them, and they're okay. It's awful."

Jess said, "Yup."

"You came all of the way into town to ask about them?" She was eyeing him closely.

He sputtered, "Had breakfast at the Panhandle, and thought I'd check while I was here."

"Is that the only reason you're going there?"

He knew what she was asking and looked away. He hadn't thought of that. A familiar brand of guilt crept in. He didn't know what to say. The silence went on a beat too long.

"Talking has always been a problem for you, hasn't it?"

He felt his palms begin to sweat in his pockets. Thankfully, she changed the subject back.

"Monica Taylor," she said. "I heard some things about her."

He looked back.

"I heard she gets around," she said. "Her ex-husband was in prison, you know. She's got a little bit of a reputation."

"Reputations come and go," Jess said, too quickly.

Her face darkened. "What is that supposed to mean?"

"Nothing. Forget it."

"Can't you let this thing go? It's been three years now."

He looked at his boots, then at the sky. *No,* he thought, *I can't.* It wasn't that he wanted her back, not now. It was the years of deception before the betrayal. The secret letters, the calls, the liaisons, the men. How could he just move on? How did other people do it? In retrospect, Karen's darkness was simply stronger than his thin strand of generational hope, and she'd overpowered him.

The door to the office opened, and Karen's new husband, Brian Ballard, stepped out. He was dressed as he had been Friday: open shirt, jacket, creased Dockers, tasseled loafers.

"Everything okay out here?" he asked, too cheerfully. "Are you asking Jess about the property?"

"We hadn't gotten to that yet," Karen said, not taking her eyes off Jess.

"I'm not selling unless I have to," Jess said. "Nothing's changed."

Brian put his arm around Karen, pulling her into him as if to say, *mine.* "You know, this doesn't have to be an adversarial thing. We would work with you."

"I'm busy right now," Jess said.

Brian looked to Karen for an explanation. She watched Jess. She looked at him in that focused way he remembered, as if by staring at his face she could suck his thoughts out. "Jess, what's wrong?" she asked. "I can tell there's something wrong."

He didn't dare speak.

"Nothing," he said. "I've got to go."

LEAVING HIS BELT, Leatherman tool, pocketknife, and change with the woman running the security check, Jess entered the sheriff's office and stood at the counter. He wasn't sure what, or who, he was looking for. Someone sympathetic, maybe. Someone he knew.

He stepped aside as three men in their late fifties or early sixties came down the hall to retrieve their belongings. It was obvious they were angry about something.

One said, "That's bullshit."

Another said, "There's no way they've got enough guys. The sheriff is always whining about manpower, but he turns us away."

The third said, "How could they have enough help? It's that asshole Singer, I'd bet. I heard stories about that guy."

The first man looked up while stuffing his wallet back into his pockets and saw Jess waiting for them to come through the security check.

"Sorry, I didn't mean to make you wait."

"Are you fellows here to volunteer?" Jess asked. "Are you policemen, too?"

"Retired," the second man said. "LAPD. But the sheriff didn't even meet with us. He had his secretary come out and tell us to leave our names, but he didn't need our help right now. Can you believe that shit, with two missing kids?"

Jess thought it was more than interesting.

THE RECEPTIONIST told him the sheriff was in, but not available. Before Jess could ask why, she said, "He's sleeping at his desk. The poor man's exhausted. He just held a press conference to announce the Amber Alert. Now everybody in the country is looking for Tom Boyd and those poor children. You've heard what happened, I assume. Is this an emergency?"

Was it? He wasn't sure.

Tom Boyd. He'd heard the name. "The UPS man?" Jess asked incredulously.

"That's him," she said.

Across the room he recognized Buddy Millen, a sheriff's deputy who had once worked on a hay crew on the Rawlins Ranch. Buddy waved, and Jess waved back, then went through the batwing doors on the side of the counter and took a seat at the deputy's desk.

"I was just thinking about you," Buddy said. "I've been on a search team not far from your ranch, looking for those little kids. Every time I see those hayfields of yours, my back starts to hurt."

Buddy looked tired, and Jess noted that his uniform was dirty from the search.

"Why were those men out there turned away?" Jess asked. "They were retired police officers volunteering to help."

"They're not the first to be turned away," Buddy said. "Half the retirees up here have been in."

"So why did the sheriff say no?"

Buddy shrugged. "Singer's call. He had enough people out there already, I guess. He's calling the shots. Personally, I think it's bullshit. We ought to have hundreds of searchers out there."

"That's what they thought, too," Jess said.

"Look, I'm just finishing up here, then I'm going to go home and crash. I've been up for thirty-six hours."

"No luck, huh?" Jess asked.

Buddy shook his head sadly. Then he glanced around the room, and leaned forward to Jess. "I shouldn't be telling you this, but things are moving fast. We're on to something. A local guy confessed on camera."

Jess sat back. "Really? The UPS guy?" The videotape.

Buddy nodded. "Unfortunately, we're changing our mission from looking for lost kids to looking for bodies. It's awful. But please keep it confidential. There won't be an announcement until tomorrow."

Jess tried to keep the confusion off his face, tried to stanch his impulse to say, *They're okay, Buddy.* But what did this mean that Tom Boyd had confessed? To what?

Okay, Jess thought. *Buddy is a good guy. Buddy can be trusted. Maybe he can help sort things out.*

"Buddy . . ."

The telephone rang on the desk. Buddy held up one hand, palm out, and snatched the receiver with the other. Jess waited, trying to form his words, wondering if it wouldn't be a good idea to take Buddy outside somewhere, away from the office, to tell him. Maybe feel him out a little bit, maybe get more information about the confession that had now changed everything and made a confusing situation even more confusing.

Buddy made reassuring sounds to the caller and jotted down an address on a pad.

"Okay, ma'am. Does he have a cell phone? Have you tried his hotel?"

Buddy looked over at Jess and wiggled his eyebrows while the caller talked.

"We can't really file a missing person's case until he's been gone twenty-four hours," Buddy said. "I'm sorry. In 99.9 percent of these situations, everything turns out all right. But I'll make a note of it and give the information to the sheriff. I'll personally follow up with you first thing tomorrow morning. But when he shows up, please remember to call us and let us know right away, okay?"

Buddy cradled the phone and scribbled some more on his pad. "A wife says her husband was supposed to be back from a steelhead fishing trip last night, but he hasn't shown up. She wants us to go out and search for him, as if we don't have enough on our plate right now. I'll bet he's back by tonight. He probably got stuck in the mud or broke down, or more likely he had a little too much fun in some honky-tonk or strip club. And I'll lay you odds she forgets to call us and tell us he's back."

The words hit Jess like a hammer blow. He knew he flinched. Luckily, Buddy hadn't seen it.

A man was missing.

He decided to invite Buddy for a cup of coffee.

Buddy said, "She said he's a retired police officer, and he'd never be late without calling."

"Was he one of those L.A. cops?" Jess asked, his mouth suddenly dry.

"That's what she said. Why?"

Jess couldn't think of a lie. He wasn't good at them. Instead, he glanced at the pad Buddy had scribbled on. He memorized the name that was written on it.

"No matter," Jess said.

WITH HIS STOMACH in turmoil, Jess found the men's room. He splashed cold water on his face and dried off with a paper towel. He felt weak, and his legs were rubbery, his wounded hand throbbed.

He heard the splashing of a mop in a bucket and saw the janitor behind him. Jess closed his eyes for a moment. It was too much for him right now.

The janitor swirled his mop, kept his head down with his long hair covering his face and his shoulders hunched like a man who wanted not to be noticed.

"J.J.?"

The mop stopped. Slowly, the janitor looked up. Eyes looked out through the strings of hair. Jess thought of how he had observed earlier that you could see the characteristics of the future adult in the photographed face of a child. Not that he'd recognized it at the time, but when he looked at the old photos, the grade-school photos, he could see it now. The boy was disconnected early, already on a destructive path. He was born with a form of sickness that was always there, lurking, but didn't show itself until he was in his late teens, and it hadn't erupted until his first year of college. The doctors said it was paranoid schizophrenia, and other names Jess couldn't recall. The boy had always had quirks—talking to himself, brushing his teeth until they bled, refusing from age twelve on to be touched. Then it got worse: hallucinations, rages, the drowning of a litter of barn kittens because the mother cat supposedly had tried to smother him while he slept. He opted to use chemicals to try to change the world around him, to bring it into line with what he perceived it to be. He had succeeded, to some extent. J.J. had never been meant to join the ranchers at the breakfast table.

"Jess Junior, do you recognize me?"

His son stared at him dully. The medication he was on that allowed him to work while incarcerated rendered him passive and emotionless. But without it, he would hurt himself and others.

"Dad."

"How are you doing, son?"

A slight, simple smile. "Not good."

"You're working hard, it looks like."

J.J. nodded. "Jes' moppin'."

Jess tried to sound encouraging. "Are things going all right?"

It took a moment, but J.J. began to sweep his woolly head from side to side. Jess stepped forward, but J.J. held the mop out to keep him back. "Don' you touch me."

"I won't, son. I remember how you hate that. What's wrong?"

Jess waited a full minute for his question to penetrate and for J.J. to form an answer. His struggle to put thoughts together to speak broke Jess's heart.

"There's some bad men here, Dad."

"In the jail, sure."

"No," J.J. said, making his eyes big, shaking his head from side to side in an exaggerated way.

"Do you mean the ex-cops?" Jess said, and withdrew the sketch Annie had made and unfolded it, showing it to J.J. "Is this them?" Jess asked, already knowing the answer by the look of alarm in his son's face.

J.J. gave an exaggerated nod. "They're really bad."

"Son," Jess said, feeling his eyes mist, "I believe you."

"Don' touch me."

"I won't, son."

AFTER RETRIEVING his possessions, Jess found a pay telephone in the lobby of the county building. He tried to shove aside his devastation from seeing Karen and their damaged son on the same morning. He dug Villatoro's card out of his pocket while he dialed, and was transferred to the motel room. The line was busy, so he left a message.

"Mr. Villatoro, this is Jess Rawlins. I don't know what it means yet, but maybe you should check on another name. It's another ex-cop. I've got his name here. . . ."

As he spoke, Jess thought things had become much more clear and much, much worse. He knew for sure now which side he was on.

Sunday, 11:40 A.M.

NEWKIRK ROOTED through Monica Taylor's refrigerator not because he was hungry but because he knew he should eat. His body was starved for something besides Wild Turkey. His hands shook as he pushed a half-full gallon of milk aside on the shelf and looked for something he could warm up. He checked the freezer. Aside from containers of juice and ice trays, there was only a large, aluminum foil–covered pan. He tapped it: frozen solid.

He was unsettled from a telephone conversation he had just had with his wife. She was coldly furious with him when he told her he likely wouldn't be home for a while. She reminded him of their son's spring baseball practice, and of previous plans to spend the day preparing her vegetable garden. It all sounded so trivial, he thought, given the situation right now. It reminded him of the bad old days on the force, when he was on a high-stakes assignment and she would be angry with him because he wouldn't be home to watch television with her. Now, it was happening again. It was exactly what he thought he had left behind in L.A., the tension, the resentment, the fights. Everything was back again. As for his wife, who was showcased in a home she could have only imagined years before, who didn't have to work outside the home, whose idea of a tough day was to take an exercise class at the gym or turn over the soil in her vegetable garden, well, *fuck her.* She didn't know what he was going through—she couldn't see any farther than her own false eyelashes.

Monica Taylor was in the living room, sitting alone and alert on the couch, staring at who-knows-what. She seemed frustratingly serene. There was something wrong with her, he thought, to be that way, given the circumstances. She was also more attractive than he thought she would be. Now that she was so sure that her children were alive some- where, she was intolerable. Plus, he didn't trust her. It was almost as if she knew what they were up to, but there was no way she could know that.

He slammed the refrigerator door shut so hard that he heard a bottle break inside. "Don't you have anything here to eat?"

"Excuse me?"

"I'm starving," he said, charging into the living room. "I haven't had a normal meal in two days. All you've got in the refrigerator is milk, salad, and eggs. Do you have something I could eat?"

She said, distracted, "I think there are some cans of soup in the pantry."

"What's that in the freezer? There's something in a casserole dish. Is it something I can thaw out?"

She turned and looked directly at him. "Leave that alone. It's lasagna I made yesterday and froze. Lasagna is Annie's favorite, and I'm saving it for when they're back. The first one got burned up Friday night."

Newkirk snorted, "Jesus, lady."

His cell phone burred and he drew it out and looked at it. Singer calling. He went back into the kitchen and closed the door.

"How is it going there?" Singer asked.

Newkirk sighed. "Okay. She's nuts, though. She insists her kids are coming back."

A pause. "They aren't."

Newkirk felt a flutter of both terror and relief. "Did something happen?"

"No, not yet. But I have confidence that you and Gonzo will find them. The more I think about it, the more I agree with Monica Taylor. Those kids are somewhere hiding out. We've got to find them."

"I thought for a second there . . ."

"No. But we're in control. I just heard from Gonzo. The package was delivered to Swann, and Swann is overseeing disposal. He should be heading back to the house within an hour or so to relieve you."

Newkirk tried not to think of what Swann was disposing of.

"I told Gonzo to start on the house-to-house. He's got a couple of good maps from the sheriff's office, with every residence and building in the county. He's going to start visiting people one by one, working out from Sand Creek. When Swann gets back, I want you to recon with Gonzo and do the same."

"Do you want us to work together or separately?"

"I'll leave that call up to Gonzo," Singer said. "My guess is you'll split up but stay in the same vicinity. That way, you'll be able to cover twice as much ground, but you'll be close enough to each other to provide backup if necessary. I think it's just a matter of time before we find them."

Newkirk didn't need to ask what would happen if they did. As he listened, he cracked the door to check on Monica Taylor. She was still sitting there, hands in her lap, relief on her face.

"I'm kind of looking forward to getting out there," Newkirk said. "This lady is creeping me out."

Singer laughed softly. "Swann can handle her. Don't worry."

"I wish this thing was over with," Newkirk said, immediately regretting he had confided in Singer. "You know what I mean."

A long pause. "Are you still solid?"

"Sure, it isn't that." But it was.

"Stay tough, Newkirk. We're only as strong as our weakest link."

"Believe me, I know."

"It'll be over when we find those kids," Singer said. "So let's concentrate on that."

"Yes, sir."

"Oh, I nearly forgot. I heard back from my contacts about your guy Villatoro."

"And . . ."

"You're right. We may have more trouble than I thought. He was the lead investigator for the Arcadia PD on the Santa Anita robbery. That's where I'd heard his name. He used to give our guys headaches."

"Fuck."

"No doubt our former friend's indiscretions brought him here. So we were right about that."

Newkirk didn't care whether they'd been right or not. *What's done is done,* he thought. But now they had a new, serious problem, one Singer had predicted long before if anyone went off the reservation and got sloppy.

"What are we going to do about him?" Newkirk asked, anticipating the answer.

"I'm not sure yet." A note of hesitation, which was unusual in Singer. "He's retired, so he's not here in any official capacity. He's got no juice, so he can't make any demands. I know he's not making any progress with the sheriff. He might just give up and go away, if we're lucky. But we need to keep an eye on him. A very discreet eye, if you know what I mean."

"Hmmm-hmmm."

"Before you join Gonzo, take a quick run around town. Take a look at motel registers for his name so we can nail down his location. If anybody asks, just tell them you're doing follow-up for the sheriff for his sexual predator list. See when he plans to check out. Call me, and we'll go from there."

"Okay."

"Try not to let him see you," Singer said. "He's seen you a couple of times already, and we don't want him to put anything together."

Why don't you check out the registers, then? Newkirk wanted to ask. *He hasn't seen you before.*

"Are you okay with that?" Singer was asking.

"Sure," Newkirk sighed.

"Be discreet," Singer said again. "Then go help Gonzo. Let's wrap this thing up."

"Ten-four," Newkirk said, and closed the phone.

WHILE NEWKIRK was in the bathroom, Monica stared at the telephone and made up her mind. She would call the man she thought could help, who'd helped her before. If nothing else, maybe he could calm her down, soothe her, tell her everything would be all right. He owed her, after all, and she'd not reminded him of it in twelve years.

She crossed the room and snatched the phone out of the cradle. There was no reason to use the phone book. She had memorized the number years before, had intended to dial it a hundred times and never had.

"What do you think you're doing?" Newkirk asked her, coming out of the bathroom, speaking loud enough to be heard over the sound of the flush.

"Making a call."

"To who?"

"None of your business."

"Stay the hell off the line," he said, snatching the phone from her and slamming it back in the cradle. "You need to keep the line clear in case someone calls who knows about your kids." Newkirk's face was red, his eyes dark.

"Are you helping me or guarding me?" she asked.

"Take it up with Swann," he said.

"Maybe I should go find that reporter and tell her I'm being held prisoner in my own house."

"You're not going anywhere," Newkirk said. "We're trying to keep you out of the spotlight so the investigation can proceed to its conclusion. Didn't Swann tell you that? There'll be time for press conferences and other shit once this is over. You don't want to be gone if a call comes through about your kids, do you?"

She glared at him, tried to see through his words. She wondered why he was suddenly sweating.

Sunday, 11:41 A.M.

VILLATORO'S HEART leaped when the receptionist at the motel handed him a sheaf of documents that had been faxed from his old office by Celeste throughout the morning. The receptionist eyed him with amusement as he shuffled through the papers, and said her invitation would still be open for tonight, if he was interested.

"Pardon me?" he said.

"You heard me." She gestured toward the documents she had handed him. "Man, I've never seen a guy so excited to work on a Sunday."

He found himself beaming at her.

"I couldn't help but notice that most of them are lists of names of policemen," she said coyly. "Do they have something to do with the reason you're here?"

Villatoro was too elated to be angry with her for snooping. "Yes, maybe. I have to look them over first."

"Some of those guys I know," she said. "Everybody stays here while they're looking for property in the area. I get to know quite a few of them, at least by name. If you wanted me to, I could look back through a few years of registrations. . . ."

"You don't mind doing that?" he asked.

"Hey, there's not much going on," she said, and winked. "I need something to do to pass the time before we have a cocktail tonight."

He hesitated, and ruled against his instinct. "Thank you for the help," he said. She smiled at him and brushed her hair back.

DISAPPOINTMENT SET IN as he read over the documents. There were duty rosters, lists of security personnel at Santa Anita, copies of clippings from the *L.A. Times,* police reports he had already read and reread a dozen times.

Newkirk had been at Santa Anita Racetrack that day, all right. Along with three other off-duty policemen, Newkirk had been hired to provide security in the counting room. It was common for the track to hire off-duty cops, and Newkirk was one of the regulars on race days. Villatoro read Newkirk's affidavit, one he had read before, which was why the name was familiar. Officer Newkirk stated he had not seen any irregularities during the counting by track personnel and could not provide any information beyond the routine procedure he had witnessed dozens of times before. The cash was counted and banded, a staffer had recorded the serial numbers of select hundred-dollar bills, and the cash had been stuffed into the canvas bags and locked with the balance sheets attached. He had recognized the men in the armored car crew, exchanged friendly insults and pleasantries with them, and stood outside while the truck rumbled away during the roar of the final race.

This was nothing notable, really. That Newkirk was at the track on the day of the robbery and also now living in Kootenai Bay was interesting, a coincidence, but evidence of nothing. Villatoro read the names of the other three off-duty cops, a man and two women officers, hoping to see a name he recognized, but he didn't. Anthony Rodale, Pam Gosink, Maureen Droz. None of them connected to anything else he could find.

Lieutenant Singer's name showed up in several more documents Celeste had faxed. Singer had served as the liaison between the LAPD and the California Department of Criminal Investigation on the case. He had been quoted occasionally in the *Times,* saying that the investigation was proceeding. It was Singer who announced before a press conference that one of the track employees had come forward to name the others and that arrests had been made. It was also Singer who had been quoted announcing, "with profound regret," the untimely and unrelated murder of the star witness in a convenience story robbery. Villatoro had never met Singer. Singer had been remote, unapproachable, always too busy to accompany his officers to Arcadia. And Villatoro remembered something else. The LAPD detectives, who would joke about anything and anybody, never joked about Lieutenant Singer.

Villatoro thought Singer and Newkirk were both connected to Santa Anita in different ways, and both now lived in North Idaho. Villatoro felt a flutter, but the more he thought about it, the more he discounted his excitement. Sure, it was little more than coincidence now. But how many police officers were involved in the Santa Anita investigation in some way? Hundreds, Villatoro knew. How many ex-cops had retired and moved to Blue Heaven? Hundreds. And Swann's name had yet to appear on the documents.

He sat back in his uncomfortable chair and stared at the ceiling. He could interview Newkirk and Singer, he supposed. Maybe he could get something out of them, something more. But he remembered the look of suspicion on Newkirk's face, and dismissed the idea. Villatoro had no authority, and he couldn't compel the men to talk to him. So far, he didn't have enough information to go to the sheriff to ask for a subpoena. Ex-cops knew the law and would know immediately to get lawyers to indefinitely delay or prevent interviews. They could easily outlast him since he needed to get back, and they were staying. They knew how the game was played.

Again, the idea of bad cops disturbed him deeply. It was so rare, in his experience, to find a truly bad one. In a city of 3.5 million people, there were 9,350 Los Angeles police officers. How many were corrupt? How many were outright criminals? It defied logic that there were none.

The telephone rang and startled him. It was Celeste. Her tone was anticipatory, excited. He thanked her sincerely for giving up her Sunday, and church, to come into the office and fax him the documents.

"Are we getting closer?" she asked.

"Closer," he said. "But we don't have enough yet to do anything. Officer Newkirk and Lieutenant Singer are up here, but that really doesn't mean anything yet. An officer named Swann is up here and involved with them, but I don't see any connection between him and either the crime or the investigation."

"Is there anything else I can send you?" she asked.

She sounded disappointed. He felt he had let her down. "I don't even know what to ask for," he said. "I have my files here, and you're sure you've gone through everything we have to match up their names?"

She said she was sure, and was a little insulted by the question. She'd been at the station since four that morning, she said. Again, he apologized.

"There is one more thing," she said, "but it doesn't come from the files."

"Yes . . ."

"I did a simple Google search just a few minutes ago, typing in both of their names. I found something called the SoCal Retired Peace Officers Foundation, or SRPOF. It's a nonprofit group. According to the public filing, it's an organization, a 501(c)3 that exists to provide scholarships to police officers' children, grants to widows, things like that. Both Singer and Newkirk are officers on the board."

Villatoro thought about it and couldn't figure out a reason why the SRPOF information would be helpful.

Then: "Where is it incorporated?"

"Let's see," Celeste said, obviously scrolling down her screen. "Burbank," she said. Then she hesitated. "And Pend Oreille County, Idaho."

That made him sit up.

"When was it formed?"

She gave him the date of the filing with the Secretary of State's Office. SRPOF had been created two months prior to the Santa Anita robbery.

"How is the organization funded? Does it say?" he asked.

He could hear her fingers tapping the keyboard.

"Voluntary contributions," she said. "It doesn't look like they've got a membership set up."

His mind was spinning. "Voluntary contributions from, I assume, other police officers."

"I would guess so."

"Contributions that would come in cash, in small denominations, I would guess. Officers throwing bills into a hat that was passed around the squad room, something like that."

"I don't know, but I suppose so."

"Is there a list of contributors?"

"Not here," she said. "I don't know where I would find that without contacting the organization."

"Who would likely not provide it," Villatoro said, feeling his excitement return, "because there are no contributors. It's a perfect way to launder a lot of money in small bills. Slowly, over time, cash-only deposits can be made that supposedly come from random collections."

Celeste was quiet for a moment. "I don't follow."

"This has been one of the things I've always been puzzled by," Villatoro said. "How could the robbers use all of that money without being noticed by anyone? Banks notice when all-cash deposits are made, especially of large sums. They have to report them if they're over a certain amount. But if the money is deposited over a long period of time, in fairly small amounts, say a few thousand dollars at a time, the bad guys have covered themselves. Especially if it's understood that the cash came from small contributors to a charity. It's perfect."

Celeste was getting it. She said, "My God, Eduardo . . ."

"But the plan wouldn't work if someone didn't deposit the money as he was supposed to, and spent some of it. Especially if the bills were marked. That would be the thing that aroused suspicion, if several of those bills came from the same location."

While he talked, Villatoro thumbed through his file for the copies of the marked hundred-dollar bills.

"We may have something," he said, trying to keep his feelings out of his voice. "Who are the other officers?"

She read him the list.

Eric Singer, President. Oscar Swann, Vice President. Dennis Gonzalez, Second Vice President. Robert Newkirk, Secretary. Anthony Rodale, Treasurer.

Bells in his head went off at the names. He had her read him the names a second time, and check the spelling.

"My guess would be that the officers of this organization are well paid," Villatoro said. "The IRS may be interested in that. And we've connected Officer Swann now as well."

"Are they all up there?" she asked.

"Three of them are, for sure. Newkirk, Singer, and Swann. I need to find out about the other two."

He could hear her shuffling through papers. She told him to hold on while she checked something.

"I'm looking at the LAPD duty rosters for that day," she said, and he knew without thinking which day she was referring to. "Swann was on duty. Newkirk, Singer, Gonzalez, and Rodale were off duty. We know Rodale and Newkirk were working security in the counting room."

Villatoro slapped his desk with his open palm. Two of the officers of the SRPOF were in the counting room. Two others were off duty. The dog-walking witness said there were at least two robbers who entered the armored car and killed Steve Nichols. They could have been Singer and Gonzalez. That would leave Swann, who had been on duty. The getaway cars had fled onto the freeway and literally vanished. That had also been a puzzle for Villatoro. But if the cars had a police escort . . .

"Good work, Celeste," he said. "Good, good work. Please tell the chief we may be close."

VILLATORO STOOD, and his knees popped and his back crackled. His mind spun with possibilities. Finally, finally, things were connecting. Or were they? He knew there were likely to be holes, lapses in logic. What had he overlooked? He needed time to sort it all through, connect the dots that were growing bigger and closer to one another on the page.

Then he realized something. He had heard there were four ex-cops helping out the Taylor investigation. What about the fifth? It could be explained if the two cases were wholly unrelated, of course. But what if they weren't?

He couldn't stay in his room. He was too excited. He threw open his door and walked down the hallway, not even noticing the intensity of the high-altitude sun streaming in from the windows.

"Mr. Villatoro," the receptionist called when she saw him. "Are you all right?"

"I'm fine," he said, approaching and grasping her hand with both of his. "I'm more than fine. It's a beautiful day."

She blushed and kept her hand there. Suddenly embarrassed, he let go first.

"I've got those names for you," she said.

"I had forgotten," he said.

She held a small piece of paper above her head, out of his grasp. "Drinks tonight?" she said.

"Yes, of course." He had no choice.

"Wonderful," she said, handing him the paper.

He read the names. Singer, Gonzalez, Swann, Newkirk.

He slowly closed his eyes. Another link.

But what about Rodale? The phone book, he thought. He would simply look up Rodale in the telephone book and go see him. Maybe Rodale had had a falling-out with the others. If so, it might be a perfect opportunity to talk to him. But he'd need to find him first. He'd left the directory in his car that morning, when he'd used it for the maps inside as he was driving.

Villatoro turned and bounded out through the glass door to the parking lot. He saw Newkirk pull in before the ex-cop could open his door.

There you are, Villatoro said to himself, *checking up on me.*

The genuine surprise on Newkirk's boyish face fit well with the scenario Villatoro had developed that morning. The ex-cop was shocked to see him standing in front of him. Why would he be shocked if he was just another retiree, minding his own business?

"Hello, Mr. Newkirk."

"Hey." Newkirk was obviously trying to come up with a good excuse why he was there. Although Newkirk's face quickly flattened into the dead-eye cop stare, there had been a second where Villatoro sensed both fear and confusion.

"What can I help you with, Mr. Newkirk?"

"How do you know my name?"

"I recognize it from my investigation," Villatoro said, stopping himself from saying more. Newkirk had flinched, and Villatoro noted the impact. He didn't like chance encounters like this. Villatoro was a man of planning, of thinking things through. Especially when there was so much at stake and so much he still didn't know. But he recognized this as a remarkable opportunity. Newkirk was surprised by his presence and his manner, and perhaps he would give something away if Villatoro pressed on.

Newkirk stepped forward, his eyes hard. "What are you saying?"

"What I am saying, Mr. Newkirk, is that it's not too late for you to save yourself. I'm no longer an officer of the law. I can't arrest you, and I don't necessarily want to arrest you. I was the lead investigator for the Arcadia Police Department. I've spent the last eight years of my life looking into this crime. I'd like to find the killers, and the money, or at least as much as there is left."

"*What?*"

Newkirk was off-balance, taken aback. *Keep going,* Villatoro thought.

"When I first saw you I thought I saw a man with a conscience, Mr. Newkirk. I noticed the wedding band on your finger. It looks like mine. Work with me to solve this crime. If you do, I'll do everything I can to keep you out of the trouble that will come."

"I don't know what you're talking about," Newkirk sputtered.

"Ah, I think you do. You were a police officer, and a good one. You know as well as anyone that deals can be struck that benefit all of the parties. But the chance to help voluntarily lasts only so long. If you don't take your single opportunity, well, who knows what will happen?"

Villatoro could see Newkirk's mind working, see the veins in his temple throb.

"You've got a family, a good life here. Would providing assistance in my case help preserve that? Are there some things you can tell me that would benefit you and your family?" Villatoro said. "You'll need to decide. I would guess that your conscience is troubling you, and this is the way to cleanse it."

To Villatoro's mild surprise, Newkirk appeared to be listening.

"It's Sunday. Tomorrow, I will make a call to my contact at the FBI," Villatoro said. "So you need to make your decision tonight, my friend."

"I still don't know what you're talking about," Newkirk said without conviction.

"Think hard, Mr. Newkirk. Go see your family. Look at them. Then decide."

Newkirk started to speak, then pulled back.

"Think hard," Villatoro said softly. "Contact me here and we'll talk."

"I've got something to say right now."

"Yes?"

"Fuck off, mister."

He watched Newkirk slide into his car and drive away.

When he was out of sight, Villatoro breathed in deeply. His knees felt weak. It wasn't what Newkirk said that struck him. It was what he *didn't* say.

Newkirk didn't ask Villatoro what specific case he was investigating. He didn't ask what happened in Arcadia that would have brought him here. He didn't mention that he'd been at the racetrack that day. And he didn't ask why the FBI was going to be called.

IN HIS ROOM, Villatoro opened the phone book on his knees. The name he was looking for didn't have a listing. He thumbed through the book for Singer, Newkirk, Gonzalez, and Swann as well. All unlisted. As he searched, he saw his message light blinking. Donna? Celeste? Would Newkirk be calling already?

The message had been left an hour before, when Villatoro had been on the phone with Celeste.

"Mr. Villatoro, this is Jess Rawlins. I don't know what it means yet, but maybe you should check on another name. It's another ex-cop. I've got his name here. Tony Rodale. That's R-O-D-A-L-E. His wife called the sheriff and reported him missing. I've got an address."

Sunday, 12:59 P.M.

THE ANCIENT TELEVISION in Jess Rawlins's home received only three channels, and of those, only one came in clearly. An older satellite dish was outside on a concrete pad, and an electronic box sat on top of the set. Annie watched William try to figure out how to manipulate the blocky old remote control to access the satellite. He wanted to watch cartoons.

"This is driving me *crazy*," William said, pointing the remote at the set and the box and pushing button after button. "How can that old guy live like this? Without good TV? I can't even get Nickelodeon."

"Keep trying," Annie said. "You'll figure it out."

"I wonder if all of the wires are connected from that dish out there? Maybe something is busted?"

"Stay inside," she said. "You heard what he said before he left. Keep the curtains closed and the lights off. We're not supposed to go outside."

William made a face. "If I can't get this TV to work, I'm going out there."

"No you're not."

"No you're not," he mocked.

She took the remote from him and looked at it. There was a button marked SAT, and she pushed it. The snow cleared on the screen to reveal a Spanish soap opera.

"What did you do?" William cried. "Give me that!"

She handed it over as he scrolled through the channels. "He's not as big a hick as I thought he was," William said.

Annie got up off the couch and went into the kitchen. Before he left, the rancher had locked the doors and windows and told them not to open them unless they were sure it was him. Annie was surprised to hear him say that it was the first time he had ever locked the front door. The rancher had to spray the lock with some kind of lubricant to get the bolt to work.

She looked through the kitchen cabinets and refrigerator. Crackers, spices, oatmeal, tea, and coffee in the cabinets, frozen packages of ground beef and steaks in the freezer. She'd never seen so many tins of chili powder in her life. Mr. Rawlins had said he would bring groceries back to the ranch when he returned from town, and he had asked what Annie and William liked to eat. Annie had scribbled a list and given it to him, and he had read it, smiled, and put it in the pocket of his long-sleeved, snap-buttoned shirt.

"When will you be back?" she had asked.

"Early afternoon, I reckon," he said. "And remember, keep the doors locked and everything shut off."

"You told me that three times already."

Jess had looked at her. "Well, I hope one of 'em took."

WILLIAM YELLED, "Annie, come look at this!"

He had found the Fox News channel, and on the screen was a photo. She hardly recognized him, he looked so bad.

"Why is Tom on TV?" William asked, trying to find the volume button to turn it up.

"Why are our pictures on TV?" he asked, as Annie's and William's school photos filled the screen over a scrolling graphic that read AMBER ALERT.

MORE THAN once, Annie had considered calling her mother. She had gone as far as lifting the receiver and hearing the dial tone before talking herself out of it. With their pictures on television, Annie considered it again now.

What would it hurt to call? To say, "We're all right, and we love you, Mom." To hear her mother's voice? But Mr. Rawlins had said Swann was there, in their home, and she couldn't bear to think of him answering the telephone.

She hoped that when Mr. Rawlins returned he would have a plan of some kind to get them home where they belonged. He seemed to be on their side, but with his own doubts. Would he turn on them, like Mr. Swann had? It was possible, but she didn't think so. He seemed to believe them, in his slow way. And he seemed to like her. Annie had caught him looking at her with a soft, sad expression, as if he were seeing her but thinking of someone else. She felt Mr. Rawlins was someone she and William could trust. Besides, they had no other place to run.

"Hey, Annie, come look at *this*!" William called again from the living room.

"What now?" she said as she found him poised in front of an opened dark wood cabinet.

"This is awesome," he said, stepping aside so she could look inside.

Rifles and shotguns, seven of them altogether, stood in a rack. Boxes of bullets and shells were stacked near their butts. William reached for one of the rifles, and Annie stopped him.

"Leave them alone," she said, pushing his hand down.

"But they're cool," he said. "I wonder why he has so many?"

"He's a rancher. Ranchers have lots of guns."

"Yeah, for bears and stuff," he said, his eyes wide. "I wonder if he'll show me how they work?"

She shrugged. "I guess you can ask him." She wished Mr. Rawlins had a lock of some kind on the guns. It was obvious William was fascinated with them, and she didn't trust her brother not to take them out and play with them if he thought he could get away with it.

"I could help protect us," William said soberly. "So if he needs to go to town again, we'll be safe."

She reached across him to shut the cabinet door.

"No," he said, stopping her. "Look at this one."

Before she could intervene, he reached in and snatched a rifle with a lever action. The rifle was obviously old, with the barrel rubbed silver and scratches in the wood of the stock.

"This looks like something a cowboy would use," he said, pulling it out. "It's heavier than I thought." There was writing on the barrel. "What does it say?"

Annie read the stamping. "Manufactured by the Winchester Repeating Arms Company. New Haven, Conn."

"Con?"

"Connecticut. Patented August 21, 1884. Nickel Steel Barrel. Twenty-five-35 WCF. I don't know what that means."

"Wow, I wonder if it's too old to shoot."

"I don't know," she said. "Put it away."

"Annie . . ."

"Put it away, *now*."

He did, taking his time to fit it into the rack. "You have to admit it's a cool old gun," he said.

She closed the gun cabinet.

"There's something else," William said, walking across the living room to an old rolltop desk. "Wait until you see this."

"You shouldn't be snooping," she said as she followed.

"Oh, like you didn't snoop at Mr. Swann's, right?"

He pulled open one of the drawers of the desk. In it was a framed photo of a much younger Mr. Rawlins, very much younger, wearing an Army uniform and a peaked cap. Mr. Rawlins stared right through the camera, as if he wanted to show how serious he was. Inside the drawer were hinged boxes containing war medals.

William opened them. "He was an Army sharpshooter," he said, showing her the medal. "He also got this silver star thing here. There are a couple of other ones, but I don't know what they mean."

She touched the silver star medal with her fingertips.

"Maybe he's cooler than we thought," William said.

"I wonder where he got these?"

"We need to ask him," William said. "I bet he's got some stories."

When they heard the sound of a motor, they looked at each other, then furiously shut the hinged boxes, returned the medals, and shut the drawer.

William went to the window and inched the curtain aside before she could tell him not to.

"Someone's coming down the road," he said. "But I don't think it's Mr. Rawlins."

THEY HID under the desk with their arms wrapped around their shins, looking out.

"I wonder who it is," William whispered.

"Could you see anything?"

"Just a black truck."

"How many people were in it?"

"I couldn't tell."

"I wish you hadn't pulled the curtain back like that."

"They couldn't see me."

"How do you know that? Next time, just look through the slit between the curtains, okay?"

William started to argue, then stopped himself. "Okay," he said.

The motor grew louder, then stopped. A car door slammed shut.

"They're right outside," Annie said. Then she realized: "The TV! You left it on!"

William scrambled out from beneath the desk and found the remote on the coffee table. He pointed it at the screen and started pushing buttons. Before he found the power button, he inadvertently hit the volume, and the sound of a cartoon roared through the empty house, then went silent. Annie sucked in her breath as she watched William drop the remote and rapidly crawl on his hands and knees to rejoin her.

"Sorry," he whispered.

She glared at him.

They heard a heavy knock on the front door that rattled dishes in the kitchen.

"Hello, hello!"

They looked at each other. A man with a deep voice.

"Hellooooo. Open up. It's the Kootenai Bay police."

What should we do? William asked with his eyes.

Annie put a finger to her lips.

"Hey, I heard the TV. Please open up. I need to ask you some questions."

She recognized the slight Mexican accent as belonging to the man who had spoken to Mr. Swann while they cowered on the floor of his truck.

William dropped his face into his hands. Annie patted his back to reassure him.

"Helloooo in there." The pounding on the door was brutal.

Next, she heard the doorknob rattle. He was trying to get in. Then silence.

She felt William trying to burrow backward farther into the shadows beneath the desk. She heard him sniff; he was holding back tears.

A form passed by one of the curtained windows in the living room, and she could see his silhouette clearly. It was him. She recognized him as one of the killers, the dark one. He was a stocky man, with a big head and mustache. She didn't want to tell William.

The man passed by a second window, then came back, filling it. Through the curtain, the points of his elbows stuck out like wings. He had pressed his face against the glass and was trying to look into the house through the slit in the curtain, using his hands to frame his eyes. Since she couldn't see him, she assumed he couldn't see her. But it took a few seconds of terror to realize it.

At last, he moved on. His heavy shoes clumped on the porch, then went silent. A few seconds later gravel crunched on the side of the house.

He was going to try the back door.

She tried to remember if it was locked. Mr. Rawlins had said something about locking the doors, but she hadn't seen him go to the back of the house.

"William," she whispered. "Get ready to run."

The back door rattled but didn't open. It was locked after all. Then, again, a heavy pounding. "Wake up in there," the man shouted. "It's the police!"

She wondered how easy it would be for the man to break down the door. Pretty easy, she thought. He was a big man, and the door didn't seem to be very thick.

Then he was gone. There was no sound.

Had he left?

No, she thought. She hadn't heard the engine start up.

His shadow again filled the window. There was a squeak, a cracking of paint. He was trying to open it.

After a few moments of pushing he gave up. He sighed heavily, and moved to the next window.

"I'm going to get a gun," William said through tears.

"No," she whispered back. "You don't even know how to load it."

"I've seen it on TV."

She thought of all the boxes of cartridges they had seen in the gun cabinet. How would he know which bullets fit into which guns? He wouldn't.

The man couldn't open the second window, either. Thank God Mr. Rawlins had locked them.

She saw the man turn, and pat his jacket. Then, the chirp of a phone.

"Newkirk," the man said, "where the fuck are you?"

Sunday, 1:04 P.M.

FOR TWENTY MINUTES, clutching the shopping list Annie had made, Jess pushed his cart down grocery aisles he had never been down before. Everything looked unfamiliar. Twice, he had to ask a stocker where to find items on the list. Frosted Flakes, juice boxes, frozen pizza rolls, string cheese, bagels. Things he had never seen, eaten, or purchased.

As he shopped, he was still reeling from the revelations of the morning, his chance encounters with Karen and J.J. If he thought he was unmoored from his foundation while he drove into town that morning, it was nothing like he felt now in a grocery store he thought he knew but that now seemed strange and foreign to him. The only thing in his cart he recognized was the can of Copenhagen chewing tobacco. That was for him.

He rolled his cart into the checkout line. There had never been so many colorful boxes in his cart before. He found himself looking forward to seeing the children again, cooking for them. He had always wanted grandchildren, and he had once looked forward to it. This was kind of like that, he thought. There was no reason, after all they'd gone through, that he couldn't spoil them a little. Tonight, he'd read the packages and figure out how to cook frozen pizza rolls—whatever they were—if that's what they wanted.

Then he'd need to figure out just what in the hell he was going to do about them.

Someone bumped him gently in the back with a cart, and he looked over his shoulder to see a beaming Fiona Pritzle. "Hey, good-lookin'," she said in her little-girl voice.

He nodded a greeting as his heart sank.

"Did you see the newspaper today, Jess? They interviewed me about the Taylor kids. There's a picture, too."

He looked in her cart and saw a dozen copies of the paper along with frozen pizzas, a case of Diet Coke, and little boxes of cosmetics.

"Would you like one of these?" she asked, handing him a copy of the paper.

"I've seen it."

"What do you think of the picture? I think they could have shot me with better lighting, myself. I've got shadows on my face."

"It's fine," he said, wishing the woman in front of him would quit fishing in her purse and find her checkbook. Why was it that some women were always unprepared to actually *pay* for their purchases at the register, as if it had never occurred to them before?

"It's a pretty good story, though," she said. "Amazingly accurate. I asked to see it before they put it in the paper, but they said they didn't do that.

"I've got an interview scheduled tomorrow with CNN, and a request from Fox News. They're fighting over me. They're both on their way and should be here tonight some time. This is really turning into a big deal since they issued the Amber Alert," she said, tossing her hair as if this information gave her validation as an insider. "I'm also expecting to hear from the Spokane television station. They've been covering this story pretty good, and I'm sure they want to talk to the last person who saw the kids alive. I need to get home and check my messages, although I did give them my cell phone number. My luck would be they will call me tomorrow, when I'm on television or on my route."

As she spoke, she fished her phone out of her purse and looked at it. "No messages as of now," she said.

Jess was thinking about how she said *the last person who saw the kids alive.*

"So you don't think the Taylor kids will be found?" he asked. The woman ahead of him had finally located her checkbook but was arguing about the price of a head of lettuce.

Fiona's eyes got huge, and she shook her head in an exaggerated way. Then she shinnied around her cart so she could whisper into Jess's ear.

"I don't want to say too much because, you know, I'm now considered sort of an expert in this case," she said, peering around the store as if looking for spies, "but I think a sexual predator has them. Or had them. I think it's just a matter of time before the bodies show up. And I wouldn't be a bit surprised if they find out those kids have been . . . violated."

Jess leaned away from her as she talked, and squinted at her. "A sexual predator?"

"Don't talk so loudly," she said, wiggling a stubby finger in his face. "Somebody will overhear us."

"Sir?"

Jess turned. The checkout clerk was ready for him, and he gratefully pushed his cart forward.

As he unloaded it onto the belt, he could feel Fiona Pritzle studying him.

"String cheese? Juice boxes? What are you doing with those?"

Jess felt his face flush. He couldn't think of a way to explain it.

He looked up at her. "Wanted to try some new things," he said. "I'm in a rut." He was also a poor liar.

She stared back at him, her eyes narrow.

"I had a bunch of coupons," he said. That one crashed, too.

He paid in cash and left her standing there. As he pushed his cart toward the door, blood rushing in his ears, his face hot, he heard her ask the checkout clerk if she had seen the newspaper today.

AS HE DROVE out of Kootenai Bay, Jess surveyed the northwestern sky and saw the blunt shapes of thunderheads nosing over the mountains. It had been clear and warm all day, but rain was coming again. The barometric pressure would change, and it was likely at least two of the cows would calve tonight. He still had a fence line to check. These thoughts were hardwired into him, the result of routine and experience. The fence could wait, but there was nothing he could do to postpone the calves. He hoped he could get some sleep before they came, though.

And he prayed the children would be at his house, where they should be, and that everything was okay. He pushed aside a mild panic at the thought of them being gone or harmed.

He stopped at his gate as he always did before realizing that someone had left it open. He quickly got back in his truck, drove over the cattle guard, and shut the gate behind him. Who had come onto his ranch? His immediate thought was that the trespasser wasn't local. Locals closed gates. When he topped the hill and cleared the trees, he could see his home below and he felt a rush of anxiety and ice-cold fear. A vehicle he didn't recognize, a black pickup, was parked at a rakish angle on the circular drive. A dark man he had never seen before stood on his porch with his hand to his face—talking on a cell phone?—with his other arm gesturing in the air. Jess recognized him from the drawing Annie had made. It was the big one, with the mustache.

The rancher accelerated, and his fear was replaced by anger. The house looked to be as he left it: locked up tight. The doors were closed and the curtains drawn. The children must still be inside, he thought, probably scared out of their minds. Who was this man, this trespasser, who strode along his porch with such contempt and familiarity?

Jess slowed and parked behind the black pickup. The man on the porch had now seen him, and he was closing his phone and glowering. The man stopped, his arms folded across his massive chest, waiting for Jess.

He spoke before Jess could. "Is this your place?"

Jess shut his door, leaving the groceries inside. The man on the porch exuded menace. He outweighed Jess by at least forty pounds, and he was younger. The rancher stopped and leaned forward on the hood of his truck. The motor ticked as it cooled. Jess usually had his Winchester in his gun rack for coyotes, but he had taken it out to clean it several days before and had forgotten to put it back in.

"This is my ranch," Jess said. "The question is what *you're* doing on it."

The man snorted. "I'm with the sheriff's department. If you haven't heard, there are a couple of local kids missing."

"I've never seen you before."

"Ah," the man said. "I'm sure you haven't. I'm helping out the department as a volunteer. Several of us are assisting Sheriff Carey with the investigation."

As he spoke, Jess looked at the man's reflection in the living room window. He could see the butt of a pistol poking out from his belt behind his back.

"You're one of the cops, then," Jess said. "Do you have a name?"

"Dennis Gonzalez. Sergeant Dennis Gonzalez. LAPD."

"Not anymore."

Gonzalez smirked and rolled his eyes. He showed his teeth under his bushy mustache. "No, not anymore. But that don't matter. We're working with your sheriff."

"I heard. So what are you doing trespassing here?"

"Trespassing?" he said, the smile growing wider. But his eyes remained black and hard. "You need to watch that language, mister. We're going house to house looking for any sign of those kids. This place is on my list."

To Jess's horror, he saw the curtain part behind Gonzalez, and William's blue eyes in the window. William was looking at Gonzalez's gun. To William, Jess wanted to shout: *"Get away from there."* To Gonzalez, Jess wanted to plead, *"Don't turn around."*

Jess sighed. "All right, then. I'm back. You can go now."

"Not so fast. I heard activity inside when I drove up. I'd like to have a look around."

"It's just me here," Jess said, hoping his face didn't reflect his anxiety. "My foreman left a few days ago. I'm running the place by myself."

"No wife inside?"

"Divorced."

"You and me both, brother," Gonzalez said. "So if nobody is in there, why not invite me in for a cup of coffee or something?"

"I've got work to do."

"On a Sunday?"

Jess nodded. "Yup. Couple of cows about to calve."

Gonzalez studied his face. "I'd really like to take a look around this place so I can scratch it off my list. I'd like to take a look in your barn, and in that house across the lot there. I want to make sure I wasn't hearing things when I drove up."

"You were," Jess said.

For a moment, a tense silence hung in the air. Jess shot a glance at the window. Gonzalez noticed it, and looked behind him. Thank God, William was gone.

"Let me get this straight," Gonzalez said, turning back around. "Are you denying me the opportunity to look around here? I'm here to clear you off my list as a kidnapper. Do you understand how suspicious this sounds?"

The word *kidnapper* hit Jess hard, and he tried not to flinch. Could he let Gonzalez look around? The man would find nothing in the barn because he probably didn't know what to look for—the missing hay hook and horse blanket, the arrangement of bales on the top of the stack—but how could he let him inside of his house? Even if the kids were hiding, there would be telltale signs: shoes in the mudroom, too many dishes in the sink, unmade beds.

"That's what I'm saying," Jess said. "You're trespassing on my ranch without a warrant. I didn't even get a call from the sheriff saying you were coming out. This is my place, and my family's had it for three generations. Nobody has the right to trespass on my ranch."

Gonzalez laughed harshly. "You're a fucking piece of work, old man. If we were in L.A. . . ."

"We aren't," Jess interrupted. "We're on my ranch. Now get off, and don't come back without the sheriff and a piece of paper that says you can search here."

The wide, insincere smile faded. "You could make your life a lot easier if you let me look around, *compadre.*"

"I'm used to a hard life," Jess said. "Now get off."

Something flashed in Gonzalez's eyes, and for a second Jess expected the man to bolt off the porch and jam the gun into his face. He wished he was armed himself. But the moment passed, and Gonzalez looked up at the rain clouds forming over the rancher's head.

"I'll be back here," Gonzalez said, stepping off the porch and walking slowly to his pickup. "You and me are going to tangle. You could have avoided it, but you had to go get all fucking cowboy on me."

Jess said nothing. He kept his palms firmly on the hood of the truck so they wouldn't shake.

Gonzalez opened his truck door and looked back. "You people. You're too stupid to know what you've just done, old man," he said, and the smile came back, which chilled Jess to his boot soles. "I'll be seeing you."

"Don't threaten me," Jess said, his voice firm and low.

"I don't threaten. I advise."

"Close the gate on the way out this time," Jess said. "I've got cattle. If they get out, I'll press charges."

"You'll press . . ." Gonzalez said, but didn't finish the sentence because he was chuckling.

Jess watched the pickup drive up the road and into the trees. Slowly, he withdrew his hands from the hood, leaving long wet streaks.

"HE WAS one of them, wasn't he?" Jess asked, unpacking the groceries in the kitchen.

Annie and William stood in the doorway to the living room, their faces pale white. They had obviously heard the exchange.

"Yes," Annie said. "We thought he was going to come in and find us."

Jess swung around and pointed a trembling finger at William. "You nearly got yourself hurt and your sister hurt along with you by looking out that window like that. When I tell you to stay inside and not look out, I mean it!"

William stood still, but mist filled his eyes.

"I'm sorry," he said, his mouth curling down, even though he was fighting it.

"Ah, man," Jess said, walking across the kitchen and pulling Annie and William into his legs. "I'm just glad you're all right. It's okay, Willie. It's okay."

"William," the boy said, his voice muffled by the hug.

"Is he coming back?" Annie asked.

Jess released them and squatted so he could look at both children in the eye. "I think so, yes."

"What are we going to do?"

"I don't know yet," he said. "I'm thinking it over."

"You could show me how to shoot one of those guns in there," William said. "You could show me and Annie."

Jess looked at him, about to argue. Then he didn't.

"For right now, let's get you two something to eat," he said instead.

Sunday, 4:03 P.M.

JIM HEARNE sat in a recliner with the newspaper opened on his lap and a Seattle Mariners game droning on in front of him. He didn't know the inning, the score, or who they were playing. Instead, he stared at something between where he sat and the television set, a wall he could not see through, a wall he had invented, a wall that seemed to get thicker and harder to ignore since that morning, when it came to be.

The wall—he started to think of it as a barrier to everything else—began to grow while he and Laura were in church. It wasn't the minister's sermon that triggered it, and it wasn't the surroundings. It was the fact that for the first time in two and a half days, his mind was empty, partially due to the massive hangover from which he was suffering. The void was filled with thoughts of his meeting with Eduardo Villatoro and what he had read in the newspaper about the effort to find the missing Taylor children. About the ex-cops from L.A. who were heading up the task force. About his own role in everything, his responsibility.

As if seeing things for the first time, Hearne looked around the room he was in. It was a magnificent living room, with high ceilings, slate tile floors covered with expensive rugs, an entertainment center so advanced that he had no idea what it was capable of. Through the huge picture window was a long, sloping lawn that led down to a small tree-bordered lake, his wooden fishing boat turned upside down on the bank. He could hear Laura in the kitchen, cooking and talking to her mother, who was in a controlled-living complex in Spokane. The aroma of Sunday dinner filled his home. She was frying chicken, his favorite, doing it the old-fashioned Southern way by soaking the pieces in buttermilk first, then coating them, then chilling them in the buttermilk again. It took all afternoon. He wished he could get excited about it, but eating was the last thing on his mind.

Hearne felt like an imposter in his own home. A real businessman should live there, he thought, not him. Someone who would not feel the conflict he felt about what was happening in the valley, someone who could justify his participation in it. Hearne, despite the home, the lake, the property, and his status, felt like a piss-poor rodeo cowboy who had made a pact with the Devil. He needed to stop fretting, and do something about it.

He stood up and stretched, heard his back pop like a string of muf-fled firecrackers. The old injuries set in when he remained still for too long, as he had today, and it took a moment of painful stretching to loosen up. There were three telephones in the house: one in the kitchen where Laura was, one in the bedroom, and one in his home office. Tucking the folded newspaper under his arm, he leaned into the kitchen and breathed in the full brunt of the meal in progress until Laura turned from the stove and saw him. She had the telephone clamped between her shoulder and jaw so that her hands were free. She raised her eye-brows as if to say, "Yes?"

"Will you be much longer?"

"My mother," she mouthed.

"Tell her hello from me," he said. "Will you be on the line much longer?"

Laura shot an impatient look at him and covered the receiver.

"She's on a roll about a dance they had at the center last night," she said. "We talk every Sunday afternoon, as you know. What's the crisis?"

"No crisis," he said, lying. "Don't worry about it."

He heard her call after him as he walked back through the living room, grabbed his cell from where he'd left it on the bookcase, and went outside.

Afternoon rain clouds were moving across the sky, blocking out the sun, and he could sense the moisture coming. The pine trees smelled especially sharp, as if their bite was being held close to the ground by the low pressure.

The article in the newspaper listed a telephone number to reach the task force to report any information regarding the Taylor children. Hearne had nothing to report, but he assumed it would be the best way to reach who he needed to talk with. He punched the numbers into his cell phone, and the call was answered after three rings by a female receptionist.

"I'd like to speak to Lieutenant Singer, please."

"Please hold while I put you through."

Hearne was placed on hold for a moment, listened to a scratchy rendition of "The Night They Drove Old Dixie Down," then: "This is Singer." The man's voice was flat and businesslike.

"Lieutenant Singer, this is Jim Hearne," he said.

No response.

"Your banker," he reminded, after a beat.

"I know who you are." Deadpan, slightly annoyed.

"I was hoping we could have a few minutes to talk."

"Why? I'm busy right now, as you can imagine."

"It's about a retired detective from California. From Arcadia, wherever that is. He was in my office asking about cash deposits and certain bills that have surfaced that apparently were marked. The bills were traced back to my bank."

The cold silence on the other end of the call unnerved Hearne. "Lieutenant Singer?"

"I'm here."

"I think we should get together and talk about this situation."

"Why?" Singer said quickly, his voice dropping.

"Well . . ." Hearne wasn't sure what to say.

"Well what?"

"I'm sure he'll be back. It won't take him long to identify certain accounts, and he'll want to know about them." Hearne didn't like how he sounded, like a weak coconspirator. He wanted Singer to say something to assure him there was nothing to worry about.

Finally: "Listen to me carefully, Mr. Banker," Singer said, almost whispering. Hearne found himself clicking the volume button on his cell phone so he could hear. "Do not say a thing to that man right now. Not a thing."

"But . . ."

"But nothing, Mr. Banker. As far as you're concerned, you don't have any idea what he's talking about. Or better yet, you're simply unavailable for a meeting. He can't hang around here forever. He'll go away."

Hearne couldn't get past the words, *He'll go away.*

"We'll talk when this is over," Singer said. "We'll get everything straightened out. Is that a deal?"

Hearne looked at his cell phone as if it had switched sides and turned against him. Then he closed it, ending the call.

WHEN HE turned back to the house, Laura was standing in the doorway.

"Since when do you make calls out on the lawn?" she asked.

He shrugged and tried to shoulder past her, but she stepped in his way. "Jim?"

Enough, he thought. Enough holding things in. He reached up and grasped her gently by the shoulders, looked straight into her eyes. He could see that she was prepared for anything but scared at the same time.

"I've put us in a situation," he said. "At the bank. Now it's coming back to kick me in the ass. I may be in a lot of trouble."

She searched his face for more.

"Actually," he said, sweeping a hand around the grounds, "I may have put us both and all we have in trouble."

"What did you do, Jim?" she asked.

"It's not what I did," he said. "It's what I didn't do. I looked the other way when I knew better, which is just as bad. I let something happen without stopping it, without asking the right questions. I did it because I knew if I looked away, deliberately, it would lead to a lot more business, and that's what happened. But I knew better. I knew something wasn't right."

She slowly shook her head. Would she press him for details?

"Jim," she said, "that's not like you." It hurt more than anything else she could have said.

He dropped his head, couldn't look into her eyes. "Laura, I need your permission to try and square this, knowing that I might not be able to do it. What's at risk is my job and our reputation."

She sighed, which surprised him. "You've always cared a lot more about our status than I have," she said. "I'd be just as happy in our old house, with the valley more like the way it was when we grew up. I know I can't turn the clock back, and neither can you. But I wouldn't mind if we weren't always in the middle of making it grow bigger and inviting everyone in. I'm not sure it's worth it. It doesn't matter how nice our house is in order to cook Sunday dinner."

He slowly raised his head, amazed at her, in love with her.

"Do what you need to do to make things right," she said.

"Then I'm going to miss dinner," he said.

"It'll keep 'til you get back."

Sunday, 5:15 P.M.

WHILE ANNIE AND WILLIAM ate at the table, Jess thumbed through the phone book in the Federal Government listings and found the number for the FBI office in Boise. He looked at his watch. Five-fifteen on Sunday night. Would anyone even be there? Turning his back on the Taylor kids, he dialed and got a recorded message:

"You've reached the Boise District Office for the Federal Bureau of Investigation. Our normal office hours are eight to five Monday through Friday. If this is an emergency, please hang up and dial 911 to contact local authorities. If it isn't an emergency, please stay on the line and leave a message. A special agent will return your call as soon as possible."

When he heard the beep, Jess hesitated for a moment. Then, in a hushed voice, he gave his name, number, and said he knew something about the missing Taylor children.

He hung up, not at all sure he had done the right thing. Would the agent call him back directly, or contact the sheriff and the ex-cops first? If the latter happened, everything could go to hell. He stared at the receiver, wishing he could retrieve and erase the message somehow. He should have hung up and waited until tomorrow, when he could talk to a real person. This wasn't like him, being impulsive. But he had to do something. Gonzalez on his own porch had unnerved him. They would suspect him now, and he was sure they'd come back.

THE CHILDREN seemed to be as comfortable as they'd been since they arrived, Jess thought. They sat in the living room, surfing through television channels. He found himself staring at them from the doorway in the kitchen, wishing he could be as carefree. Annie looked over and smiled at him, then turned back to the television.

Something had happened, he thought. Because they had overheard the exchange with Gonzalez, the children trusted him completely now. They thought he could take care of them. Jess wasn't so sure about that. He needed help, and some kind of plan. He didn't know where to turn.

He thought of the man he'd had breakfast with, Villatoro. Jess could tell Villatoro had connections, knew people in law enforcement on the outside. Maybe even their home telephone numbers. Perhaps the ex-detective could put him in contact with a friendly FBI agent who could circumvent a call to the sheriff? Jess dug the card out of his pocket again, called the motel, and again got voice mail. Jess cursed to himself, and left a message asking Villatoro to call him whenever he got back to his room.

Who else could help? Buddy?

He looked up the deputy's number and called. The phone was busy. Probably off the hook, Jess thought, while the man slept.

Jess paced his kitchen, washed and dried the dishes, stared at his watch and the telephone that didn't ring.

Maybe, he thought, Sheriff Carey would believe him if he could talk to the man without the ex-cops around. Maybe. He would need to try, and he couldn't chance waiting until morning. By that time, the ex-cops might be coming back to his house or the FBI might be in contact with them. It would need to be tonight.

And as he looked again at the Taylor children sprawled on his couch, he thought: *Don't let them down. You've already overseen the destruction of one family, your own. Don't let it happen again.*

They needed to reunite with their mother, and she needed to know they were all right. Those kids trusted him to protect them. He would do his best, or die trying. He had nothing to lose.

———

"I'M GOING to be gone for a while," he told them, after muting the volume on the television so he could get their complete attention. "I need to go to town."

"Tonight?" Annie asked. "Are you going to leave us here?"

He nodded. "I have to."

"What if that man comes back?"

Jess paused. "Annie, I'm going to show you how to operate a shotgun. If anybody besides me comes into this house tonight, I want you to know how to use it."

Annie nodded slightly. William looked at her with obvious jealousy.

Jess opened his gun cabinet, withdrew his twenty-gauge over and under, and broke it open. "I taught my son how to hunt with this gun," he said. "Just remember it's not a toy. Come here, and I'll show you how it works. . . ."

BEFORE HE LEFT, Jess went back to the gun cabinet. He looked at each weapon, doing a quick checklist of pluses and minuses associated with each. He quickly dismissed his scoped hunting rifles. They were good at long range, of course, but were unwieldy if the target was close or moving fast. The bolt actions made them slow to reload, and he'd be limited to three or four cartridges. The shotguns were devastating at close range and didn't require perfect aim, which is why he showed Annie how to fire one. But beyond fifty yards they lost stopping power. He needed a weapon that would fill both needs, long and short, and most important, something he was comfortable with.

Jess withdrew the .25-35 Winchester. It had been his grandfather's gun, a tough little open-sight saddle carbine that held seven cartridges. High-velocity, small-bore, simple, and reliable. He had shot his first deer with it when he was a boy, and had kept it for J.J., who had never showed interest. As he held the weapon, it felt like an old friend, with a tie to the past.

He loaded it as the children watched. "Remember what we talked about," he said, shoving in cartridge after cartridge. "If somebody besides me comes into this house, point the shotgun at the thickest part of

his body and pull the trigger. Don't forget about flipping off the safety
first. Whether you hit him or not, I want you two running and out of
here the second after you fire. Annie, where will I find you if you have
to run and hide?"

"The old corral up in the trees behind the house," she repeated.

"Good. Are you up for this, William?"

William nodded. Jess had the impression William was looking forward to it and would be disappointed if Gonzalez didn't come back.

"Okay, then," Jess said. "Keep the doors and windows locked, and
the curtains pulled. If anybody comes, don't look out at them."

Annie and William said they understood.

Jess winked at them. "I won't be long," he said.

The Winchester would not leave his side until this thing was done.

Sunday, 5:30 P.M

WHAT IN the hell do you think you're doing?" Swann asked Monica sharply.

She was packing, throwing clothes into a small suitcase on her bed. Her clothes, Annie's clothes, William's clothes. They would surely need a change of clothing. She was startled, hadn't realized Swann was in the hallway watching her.

"I've got to get out."

"You're not going anywhere."

"I'm smothering to death in this house. I feel like your prisoner. Why can't I leave?"

"What if they call?" Swann asked, sputtering. He had the same pan-icked reaction Newkirk had shown earlier when she told him she wanted to leave. That told her all she needed to know.

"What if who calls, Oscar? I thought you were all convinced Tom took them? Since when is Tom a *they*?"

Swann hesitated. She could see him biting his lip.

"Maybe I'll talk to the reporters down at the county building, make a plea for my children." She said it to test him.

Her destination, she had decided, was outside of town. But she didn't want to tell him of her suspicion. That confirmed in her mind that the situation had changed. *Swann,* she thought, *is not here to help me.*

"Monica, sit the fuck down."

His command froze her. She could tell by his face that, if necessary, he would cross the room and make her stay.

"This is for the best," he said. "You have to trust me on this."

She weighed his words against the crazy look in his eye, the set of his shoulders, his clenched fists.

"I don't trust you at all," she said.

He raised one of his fists, opened his hand. Her car keys were in them.

"You're not going anywhere," he said.

Sunday, 5:49 P.M.

THE HOME of Anthony and Julie Rodale was magnificent, Villatoro thought. A huge new log home built with a southern exposure and lots of windows, soft underground lights marking the driveway and pathway, thick Indian throw rugs on the hardwood floor, and a cathedral ceiling in the great room that made him feel insignificant. The heads of mounted mule deer and elk flanked the stone fireplace, a half dozen colorful lacquered fish—he guessed steelhead, although he had never seen one—glowed in the light from the chandelier.

Julie Rodale had been watching *60 Minutes* on television when he arrived, sitting in an overstuffed chair just a few feet in front of the wide screen, eating a large bowl of macaroni and cheese. She still dug into it unself-consciously as they spoke, sometimes making him wait for an answer while she chewed.

Julie Rodale was tall and blond, with a round face and full cheeks. By the way her clothes strained at their buttons, he guessed she was either newly heavy or had simply refused to admit that she needed a new, more matronly style of dress. She was not hesitant to talk with him.

"You said you were a detective?" she asked. "I thought you were with the sheriff's office when you drove up. I'm waiting to hear something on my husband, Tony."

Villatoro took notes on a small pad he'd found in his motel, mainly to be doing something. It was his experience that people tended to talk more and say more when the questioner appeared to be hanging on every word and taking notes. She didn't seem to care that he wasn't with the local police or was retired, only that he was interested in what she had to say.

"You said he went steelhead fishing."

"Yeah." She rolled her eyes toward the mounted fish on the wall. "He lives for it. Every weekend, at least. All winter he buys equipment and reads fishing magazines, and all spring, summer, and fall he goes fishing. I tried it with him a couple of times, even took a book to read, but I thought it was boring, boring, boring."

"Does he often go alone?"

She shoveled in a mouthful of macaroni while nodding. "Not all the time. Sometimes he convinces a buddy to go with him. Jim Newkirk goes along sometimes, but you know, he's got kids at home, and he just can't get away as much as Tony. Nobody can, it's ridiculous."

Villatoro noted Newkirk's name.

He tried to keep his tone soft and conversational. "He was supposed to be back this morning?"

"If not last night," she said, chewing. "He said he had something to do on Monday, so I would have expected him back by now. I'm starting to get pretty pissed off."

"Are you worried about him?"

"Not really," she said, shaking her head. "He's a tough guy. He always takes his service weapon with him. That's not what I'm worried about. I just think he got his truck stuck somewhere, or he got lost, or he hit the bottle. I tell him to take his cell phone, but he always claims he goes too far away to get a signal.

"A woman gets lonely being a fishing widow," she said. "That's what I call myself, a fishing widow. See all those fish on the wall? That's nothing. You should see our basement. You want to see it?"

"That's okay," Villatoro said. "I don't want to take too much of your time."

"Do I look busy?" She laughed.

"So you've been here four years?" he asked.

"You mean in the house or in Idaho?"

"Both."

"Yeah, four years. We moved up here just after Tony took early retirement from the force. I would have moved anywhere, after all of those years of wondering if he was going to get shot, or beat up, or something. It was such a relief, you know?"

"My wife knows that feeling."

She scooped in a large forkful. "I didn't think you looked like you were from around here."

He smiled. "So several of you, I mean several retired officers, all came out here at the same time. Is Tony friends with the others? You mentioned Newkirk."

For the first time, Julie hesitated for a moment. "Why are you asking me about his friends?"

"I'm curious. I heard several of them were helping your county sheriff with the Taylor case. But obviously, Tony isn't involved in that."

She laughed. "Believe me, if he wasn't fishing, he'd be with them. Tony likes hanging out with all of his old cop buddies. You'd think he'd be sick of them after all of those years, but that's not the case."

Villatoro shifted in his chair. "Aren't they all involved in some kind of charity together?"

"Yeah, something. I don't know much about it. They have meetings every once in a while. Tony don't say much about it, though. You mean Lieutenant Singer and Sergeant Gonzalez, right?"

"Do they get along okay? Are they friends?" Villatoro was hoping that Rodale was estranged from the other ex-cops, that being the reason why he had not volunteered with them. If he was having trouble with them, Villatoro reasoned, perhaps he would be easier to talk to than the others.

"I think so," she said, without conviction.

"Was he a little angry with them recently?"

She blew out a long stream of breath to clear a strand of hair from her face. "I'd say he's been irritable lately. He wouldn't really say why. But come to think of it, he's been pissy since their last meeting a couple of weeks ago. Maybe something was said, I don't know. Tony doesn't talk about that stuff."

"Right. Have you called them to see if they know anything about where Tony went?"

"Sure I did. Yesterday. But all they knew is that he said he was going fishing."

"So they all knew that? They weren't surprised when you called?"

She paused, fork in midair: "No, why should they be? They all sounded concerned. Lieutenant Singer especially. He said he didn't think it was ever a good idea to go fishing or hunting by yourself. I said, 'Amen, Brother Singer.' Why do you ask?"

"No reason," he said, and quickly changed the subject. "This is quite a place you've got here," Villatoro said. "I bet it would cost a few million back home."

"More than that," she said, grinning. "Tony did well with his pension. He also did really well with investments. All those years, I had no idea he was buying stocks and stuff. But when he told me he wanted to take early retirement, he said he's been building up this . . . fortune . . . in the stock market. He said he got out before the bubble burst, and we could afford a home like this."

Villatoro watched her carefully. She spoke without guile. She obviously believed her husband came into their wealth through legitimate means.

"He did well," Villatoro said, looking around. "My wife Donna would kill for a home like this."

She smiled in a proprietary way. "The man shocked me. Really shocked me. I didn't know he had any interest at all in stocks or anything. I didn't even know about this fishing thing until we moved up here. That just goes to show you that you can live with somebody for twenty years and not really know them, you know?"

She sat back and sighed. "I have to admit, though, I sometimes miss the old neighborhood. There was nothing special about it, just a street with a lot of forty-year-old houses on it. But I miss hearing kids out on the street, and the block parties we would sometimes have in the summer. It was chaos, but I miss being a part of it. I guess I miss neighbors. All I ever hear up here is birds. That gets a little boring at times. I'd like to have a reason to charge out of the house to see what's going on, you know?"

Villatoro stood up and closed his pad. He felt sorry for her, with her big house and big body and big bowl of macaroni and cheese. She seemed like a nice, normal woman, someone his wife would be friends with.

"I know what you mean," he said, and thanked her and said he would let himself out.

"Stick around," she said. "You can watch me pound that guy when he finally gets home. I'll glue a damned cell phone on his forehead for the next time."

THE SKY FLASHED and there was a rumble of thunder as Villatoro approached his car in the driveway. The storm clouds had shut a curtain over the dusk sun, making it darker than it should be. The air was moist, and he expected rain any minute.

Tony Rodale, who had been working security at Santa Anita with Jim Newkirk on the day of the robbery, who sought early retirement, who was the treasurer for the SoCal Retired Peace Officers Foundation and therefore in charge of making cash deposits into their account, was missing. If he showed up, Villatoro wanted to meet him. There had to be a reason why only four of the five ex-cops had volunteered to help the sheriff together, and the fifth went his own way. Maybe an argument between them, maybe dissension. Maybe, Villatoro conceded, Rodale just wanted to go fishing.

There was a flash of lightning and a thunderclap that seemed to sway the treetops with its power, and sheets of heavy rain lashed through the trees. There was no buildup to the rain, it just came, furiously. He switched his wipers to high and turned on his headlights.

He was so consumed with his thoughts and the driving rain as he drove that when his headlights swept over a parked car nearly blocking the road to Rodale's home near the two-lane, he reacted late and almost sideswiped it, missing the car by inches. He braked a few feet beyond it and glanced up into his rearview mirror.

The driver's door opened on the car he had almost hit, and the dome light came on. Newkirk got out. The ex-cop was lit in the red glow of Villatoro's taillights, and he walked out of the view of the mirror and tapped on the passenger-side window.

After searching for the window switch in the rental car, Villatoro found it, pressed it, and the window whirred down. Newkirk leaned in. "I've been thinking about what you told me in the parking lot. I think we need to talk."

"Do you want to meet somewhere?" Villatoro could smell the whiskey on Newkirk's breath.

Newkirk shook his head. "No place is safe. I don't want us to be seen together."

Villatoro found himself gripping the wheel so tightly that his knuckles were white. Slowly, he let go and relaxed them.

"Too many people know my car," Newkirk said. "Let's go in yours."

"The car is not very big."

Newkirk looked down. The passenger seat was covered with maps, files, paper. "Clean that off and I'll get in."

"I'm not sure . . ."

"Do you want to talk or not? Make up your mind. I don't like standing out here where someone could drive by and see me. Besides, I'm getting soaked."

Villatoro realized what an opportunity this could be. It could crack the case. But he was scared. There was another lightning flash and a low-throated roar of thunder. He gathered up the papers and tossed them over the headrest into the tiny backseat, and Newkirk swung in heavily and closed the door. Steam rose from his clothing.

"Where are we going?" Villatoro asked.

"Just drive," Newkirk said.

Villatoro put the car into gear, and they slid out onto the state high-way. Large raindrops hit the windshield like balls of spit.

"I'm going to show you where the bodies are buried," Newkirk said, "so to speak."

Sunday, 6:25 P.M.

JESS ENTERED Kootenai Bay under a strobing pyrotechnic display of lightning, and the rain fell hard and steady, creating a jungle drumbeat within the pickup. A close flash of lightning lit the cab, leaving the afterimage of his Winchester, muzzle down, on the seat next to him.

Sheriff Ed Carey lived in a modest ranch house in an older neighborhood not far from downtown. Streetlamps on the corners lit up the falling rain in the orbs of their halos and created blue lightning bolts on the wet streets. Carey's county Blazer was parked in his driveway. A white SUV Jess didn't recognize was also in front of the house. A white SUV? Like the one Annie and William had seen?

Behind Carey's Blazer was a small yellow pickup. Jess frowned, familiar with it from his daily encounters. What in the hell was Fiona Pritzle doing at the sheriff's home at this time of night?

He drove by slowly, saw that the curtains were open and the lights on. He continued down the block and parked under a dark canopy of old cottonwood trees, as far away from the streetlights as he could get.

Jess had a yellow cowboy slicker rolled up behind the seat, but he decided to leave it there. The yellow would stand out, even in the dark. He'd just get wet.

Leaving the Winchester in the truck, he walked toward Carey's house in the rain, stumbling once on a section of sidewalk that had risen and buckled from a tree root.

He didn't know whether to knock, ring the bell, or try to figure out what Fiona was doing there first. As he approached the house, a thin stream of rainwater poured from his hat brim. He could hear nothing from inside because of the sound of the rain coursing through the trees and hitting the street and sidewalk with a sound like applause.

Rather than walk up the sidewalk to the front door and lighted porch, Jess cut across the grass of Carey's next-door neighbor toward the corner of the sheriff's house. There was a picture window in front of the house and a smaller window on the side that was open except for a storm screen. Aiming for the opened window and the shadows beside it, he felt the suck of soft mud beneath his boots. *Christ,* he thought, *I'm walking across their newly planted garden. I'll apologize later.*

Jess stood to the side of the open window in the mud, slightly under the eave of the roof so the rain didn't hit him. He looked out from the shadows and saw no cars on the street, no neighbors looking out of their windows at the rain.

The sound of Fiona Pritzle's sharp, high-pitched voice cut through the rain like a razor through fabric.

"There's always been something odd about him, don't you think?" Fiona was saying. "I've really noticed it lately. Like he's got a secret life, and he doesn't want anybody to know it."

Jess took a chance and looked in the window. He hoped like hell he wouldn't be entering anyone's view.

Fiona sat in the middle of the room, perched on the edge of a chair that must have been brought in from the kitchen table. Her hands were clamped between her thighs. She leaned forward toward Carey, who sat on his couch in a T-shirt and sweatpants, his hair uncombed. Jess could see the side of his face, and he looked troubled or irritated. Since it was Fiona sitting there talking, Jess figured both were likely. A man Jess didn't recognize at first was in an overstuffed chair across from Carey listening to Fiona. He was trim and compact, with close-cropped silver hair. His bearing suggested authority, his face a mask of world-weariness except for his eyes, which studied Fiona with a kind of manic fascination. Jess could see his face in three-quarter profile and identified him from Annie's drawing. It was Singer.

"He seems, you know, evasive," Fiona said. "I try to be friendly and sweet as pie, but he always seems to be somewhere else, you know? Like he has other things on his mind."

Singer turned to Carey, ignoring Fiona, and said, "Do you know him, Sheriff? Is he familiar to you? Gonzo had a problem this afternoon with a rancher who wouldn't let him search his property. Is this the same guy?"

"I know him," Carey said. "In fact, I sat next to him at breakfast at the Panhandle just this morning, Mr. Singer. He did ask a few questions about the investigation, as I recall."

Jesus, Jess thought, *they're talking about me. What is Fiona up to?* Jess withdrew from the front of the window but pressed his shoulder against the siding next to it so he could hear better and not be seen.

Fiona said, "You know as well as me what's happened out there over the past few years. First, his wife left him. You know about his son. He's a tragedy, just a tragedy. Something *obviously* happened to him."

Carey said to Singer, "He's the trustee who mops the floor at the station. You've probably seen him around."

"I've seen him," Singer said.

Jess couldn't believe what he was hearing.

Fiona continued, "Why else would an old single man be buying food that only little kids eat?"

"That's not much to go on, Fiona," the sheriff said.

Her voice rose. "But think about it. His ranch is failing. His son is a mess. His wife leaves him, but he shows absolutely no interest in the opposite sex. I mean, single lonely man, available woman"—Jess could imagine her gesturing to herself—"and he doesn't do anything? At first I thought it was me, but maybe it's because he has other interests, you know? Even his employee left him recently, I found out. He's completely by himself out there. Who knows what he's up to? Maybe he's got those kids, and he's holding them prisoner!"

"Fiona . . ." The sheriff was skeptical. He turned to Singer. "What's this do to our theory about Tom Boyd?"

Singer shook his head quickly. "Not much."

Carey paused, waiting for clarification.

"We've got the tape," Singer said. "Boyd's missing. That part of our theory still holds."

"So where does this rancher fit in, if at all?"

Jess was frozen where he stood, stunned.

"I've read a lot of magazine articles about sexual predators," Fiona interjected, her voice rising. "It *grows* in them. Just grows in them until they get the opportunity to gratify it. I've never thought before how much he fits the profile. Look"—she dropped her tone again—"he gets mail in large envelopes without any return addresses on them. Maybe that's how he gets his pornography?"

No, Jess thought absently. *That's how developers send offers these days, knowing I won't open them if I know where they came from. Jesus . . .*

"I'm surprised you haven't looked to make sure," Carey said, deadpan.

"I can't believe you said that," she sniffed. "That's a huge insult. I could lose my job with the postal service if I did, you know."

Fiona suddenly got an idea and nearly shot out of her seat. "Hold it! Maybe that's how he met Tom Boyd? UPS delivers out there, you know. Maybe the two of them struck up a friendship based on a common interest," she paused dramatically, "*pedophilia.* I've read where those people seek each other out."

Jess didn't know what to do. Burst in, set the record straight? He was so flummoxed he didn't even know if he could speak clearly. But how would he explain the groceries without telling them the rest or coming up with some kind of lie? What if the sheriff held him, or arrested him on the spot? Singer could send that dark ex-cop, Gonzalez, back to his house to find the Taylor children. He wished Singer weren't there, because he might have a chance of clearing himself if it was just Fiona and the sheriff, because obviously Carey didn't give Fiona much credibility. But with Singer there . . .

"You can either do something, or I'll call my contacts at the networks," Fiona threatened. "I'm sure they'd find this new development very interesting."

Jess walked away from the window. The rain pounded his hat. He was angry, and getting angrier. He swung into the cab of his pickup, started the motor, and roared down the street, not caring if anyone could hear him leave.

Sunday, 6:56 P.M.

JESS COULD see J.J. through the locked front doors of the county courthouse. As usual in his orange one-piece trustee jumpsuit, J.J. was cleaning, spraying banisters with disinfectant, rubbing the wood until it glowed. Jess rapped hard on the glass of the door. Inside, J.J. looked up, but in the wrong direction. Jess rapped again, hitting the glass so hard it stung his knuckles. J.J.'s head swiveled, and his eyes narrowed when he saw Jess. There was something canine in the way J.J. looked at him.

"J.J., I need to talk with you," Jess shouted. The rain pounded the street behind him and sluiced through the gutters.

J.J. shrugged, couldn't hear him. But he let the cloth fall from his hands and walked slowly across the floor to the doors.

Jess could see J.J.'s mouth. "Locked."

Who had a key? Jess wondered. He needed to talk with his son.

Jess pulled futilely on the doors, rattling them. J.J. watched as if he expected alarms to go off. He shook his head, scared to open them from the inside.

"Hold on," Jess said, raising his hand, and turned for his pickup that was parked on the street. He returned with the rifle. J.J. saw it, and backed away, his eyes wide.

Jess used the butt of it to break through a panel of glass on the door. No alarm sounded. He reached through the hole and pulled back on the bar, opening the door.

"I don't mean to scare you," Jess told J.J. as he stepped inside and let the door wheeze shut.

"I could get in trouble," J.J. said. Jess noticed that J.J.'s voice was clearer than usual. It had a deep timbre to it that was usually missing. Jess knew what that indicated. This is when a window sometimes opened, if briefly, a window of illumination. It didn't last long.

"J.J., I think you can help me," Jess said, then rephrased it: "I need your help."

"You broke the door. Man, I'm going to get in trouble now."

"Tell them I did it."

J.J. nodded.

"You seem okay. Are you okay?"

"Not really, no," J.J. said, shaking his head. "I gotta go back for my meds. What time is it?"

Jess looked at his wristwatch. "Nearly seven."

"I'm late. I shoulda been back to the ward. They're gonna come looking for me."

Jess tried to calm himself. If he was calm, J.J. was more likely to respond.

J.J. said, "When my meds wear off my own sick brain starts taking over. I see shit I know can't really be there."

"I know that, son," Jess said, stepping closer. J.J. recoiled.

"Don't worry," Jess said, "I won't touch you."

"It isn't you," J.J. said. "It's your germs. I can't get dirty, like these floors. I clean them and clean them, but the people here, they make them filthy again every day. They bring their filth in with them from the outside. I can't win."

Jess breathed deeply. He felt a pang for taking advantage this way.

"J.J., tell me about the ex-cops. There are four of them. You've been around them here. Are they good?"

"No." Emphatic, spittle flying.

"Are they honest?"

"NO!"

"What have you heard?"

"They want to find those kids," J. J. said.

Jess grimaced. Of course they wanted to find the Taylors.

"They want to hurt them," J. J. said. "And they called Monica a *bitch*."

"Monica Taylor?" Jess asked, taken aback by J. J.'s familiarity with her. "You know her?"

J. J. smiled a dark and secret smile. It reminded Jess of the way J. J. used to be, before all of this happened. That wasn't necessarily good.

"She's a pretty woman," his son said. "She was wild."

This startled Jess. "What do you mean? How did you know her?"

"Some things I remember like they happened yesterday. I remember Monica that way."

Jess had more questions, but didn't want to take J. J. down a path they'd get lost on. He didn't know how long this rare sliver of clarity would last, and he had to use it.

"About the ex-cops. Why don't you tell the sheriff?" Jess asked.

"He won't believe me. I don't want to get in trouble. I like this job, cleaning. I can't stay in my cell. It's filthy and disgusting, germs fester there. I need to be *out*. Away from the nightmares . . ." J. J. looked away.

"J. J., stay with me," Jess admonished gently. "I know you can leave here anytime you want. You've done your time. You can just walk out whenever you want."

"Man, I need my meds, Dad."

Dad. He called him dad. Jess felt his chest well up.

"Come with me," Jess said suddenly. "Let's get you out of here."

"Really?"

"Really."

A slight smile. "I want to see the ranch. And Mom."

Jess didn't want to explain. Not yet. Now, he just wanted to get J. J. away from there. With what he knew, his son was in danger from the ex-cops and possibly the sheriff. J. J. didn't know that, but Jess couldn't leave him there to find out. Jess's mind whirled, and he felt a tumble of emotions. This had been the first real conversation he had had with his son in over ten years. He was elated, while at the same time he wondered if J. J. had been in there all along, waiting to come out. And Jess had neglected to try.

Jess backed up and opened the door. "Come on, son," he said gently.

J.J. stiffened. He seemed to grow taller as he became more rigid. His hands, which had hung at his sides, curled into claws.

"No."

"What do you mean?" Jess said.

"I can't go out there. It's too filthy."

"It's raining," Jess said, hoping that would make more sense to J.J. than it did to him.

"NO!" J.J. shouted like a five-year-old, and stomped his boot. "No, Dad! I can't."

Jess paused at the door, his heart breaking. J.J. had backed up across the floor and retrieved his cleaning cloth. He rubbed a desktop with it violently, scattering a stack of papers to the floor.

"Damn it!" J.J. seethed, snatching the papers up to put them back. They kept slipping out of his fingers to flutter back to the floor.

"I'll come back for you, son," Jess said. "You've really been a lot of help to me. You did a good thing, talking to me. But don't tell anyone what we talked about, okay? Please?"

J.J. was furiously trying to snatch the pages from the tile.

"I miss you, son."

J.J. didn't look up. He was gone again.

"DAMN IT!" he screamed.

Jess turned and walked away, the rain slashing him. He paused at his pickup and gazed back. J.J. kept his head down, picking up papers and dropping them like a demon.

Sunday, 7:16 P.M.

MONICA LOOKED up when the doorbell rang, and Swann scrambled to his feet from the couch. He had been on his cell phone with someone, another of his secret calls. Something about going back to his house again that night; Swann didn't seem to want to do it.

They had not spoken since Swann showed her that he had her keys. She was simply waiting now, biding her time. When he left the room, she'd be out the door. She could borrow a car from a neighbor. Or get a ride with someone. But she wanted him to think he'd talked her out of that idea, so she sat silently. Let him think she'd reconsidered.

"You expecting someone?" he asked as he neared the door.

"Of course not," she said, hoping it was news of Annie and William.

Swann bent and looked out the peephole. "Some man," he said, then opened the door.

Monica didn't recognize the wet cowboy on the front porch. He looked angry, though, the way he squinted inside like a gunfighter, like the sun was in his eyes.

"What can we do for you?" Swann asked.

"Are you Monica Taylor?" the man asked, shouting louder than he needed to, not acknowledging Swann. The rainfall was steady and loud behind him.

Intuitively, she knew it was about her children. She nodded.

"Then you must be Swann," the man said, reaching back for something that was out of sight. Then he strode into the house holding a rifle in both of his hands. Before Swann could reach for the pistol in his belt, the man clubbed Swann hard in the face with the butt of the rifle. Swann staggered back, blood already gushing from his nose, his hands grasping at air, his feet tangling with her magazine rack. He fell into the wall, sliding down partway, taking a framed photograph of Annie with him. His elbow rested on the top of the couch and stopped him from falling all of the way to the floor. The man was in the living room now, straddling Swann, and to Monica's horror, he reared back and clubbed Swann again in the head with a short, powerful stroke. Swann went limp, and rolled with his face to the wall, his weight pushing the couch out, and he crashed behind it on the floor. All she could see of Swann were the soles of his shoes. The rest of him was wedged behind the couch.

The cowboy bent over and came up with Swann's pistol, which he shoved into the front pocket of his Wranglers. Then he looked up, caught his breath.

Monica had not screamed, but had withdrawn into her chair, her feet under her, her fists at her mouth.

"He'll live," the man said, nodding his hat brim toward Swann. Then he looked right at her. "I'm Jess Rawlins. I'm here to take you to your kids."

At the sound of his name, Monica felt her throat constrict. Jess Rawlins. She'd always known of this man. And here he was, in her own living room, there to rescue her.

Sunday, 8:21 P.M.

JIM HEARNE felt panic growing as the rain receded into cold mist and hung suspended in the air above the pavement of streets, and his tires sluiced through standing puddles. Something was going on in his town late on a Sunday night, but he hadn't yet been able to figure out exactly what it was, how big it was, or how many people were involved. As with the feeling he had had in his living room, when he suddenly felt like an imposter in his own home, he drove through Kootenai Bay under the strong impression that despite the recognizable buildings and layout, he was a stranger in this town.

He swung his Suburban into the county building lot and parked it next to Sheriff Carey's Blazer. He was grateful for locating the sheriff, since the two other men he had tried to find earlier had been gone. Lieutenant Singer was not at the task force room in the county building, or at his home. And Eduardo Villatoro had not been back to his hotel room since late afternoon.

Hearne got out of his vehicle and tried to calm himself by inhaling the moist air deeply into his lungs. He looked at his watch. He had accomplished exactly nothing for all of his running around, except to confirm that whatever was happening was happening someplace else, and he had no idea where that might be. Now he thought he might be in the right place, judging by the three network satellite trucks that took up most of the parking lot at the front of the building. There was a hive of activity. It was obvious they had all arrived within minutes of each other, and technicians were out on the pavement, jockeying for position. Some unfurled thick cables that snaked across the asphalt. Hearne recognized a celebrity reporter brightly lit by a portable bank of lights, and thought he looked shorter, thinner, and more frail than he did on TV. The man seemed to be waiting for somebody to tell him something in his earpiece. Looking at the trucks, the bustle of men and women, he feared for Kootenai Bay.

Avoiding the news crews, which had situated themselves so the front doors and sign on the county building would be visible in the background for camera shots, he walked around to the back, where the dispatcher was located. The door was open, as it should be, but the dispatcher—a heavyset woman with a bright red helmet of hair—looked up in alarm through thick lenses. She wasn't used to visitors walking into the building, and unlike most people in town, she didn't recognize him.

He said, "Is the sheriff in? I saw his vehicle out front."

"I think he's in for a minute," she said, looking around, her eyes winking like crazy behind the glasses, "but I think he's going to go home. Is this something that can wait until morning?"

Hearne felt a surge of impatience. "Do you think I would be here at this time of night if it was something that could wait? Where is he? In his office?" he asked, pushing through the batwing doors on the side of the reception desk, striding past her.

"Yes, but you should wait until I call him. . . ." she said, her voice trailing off.

Sheriff Carey was in the act of hanging up his telephone. His office blazed with lights, even though the rest of the department was dark. When Hearne stepped into the doorway, Carey looked up slowly, without expression. It didn't seem to surprise him that the local banker was in his office late on Sunday night. He looked terrible, Hearne thought, completely unlike the confident man holding the press conference the day before.

"Sheriff, are you okay?"

Carey nodded slowly. His eyes seemed moist, oily. The dark circles surrounding them looked painted on. "Hello, Mr. Hearne."

Hearne reached across the sheriff's desk to greet him. Carey's hand was chilly and without strength.

"Sheriff, you look like hell."

Carey smiled slightly, sadly. "I'm real tired, Mr. Hearne."

"Call me Jim. I won't keep you. I'm just trying to figure a couple of things out, and I hoped you could help me."

"Pretty late for that."

"I know," Hearne said, not knowing if the sheriff meant the time of night or the situation in general. He looked hard at Carey and saw a man who was physically and emotionally spent. This was not the time to confess. That would have to be later.

"When I ran for sheriff, I really didn't think there would be nights like this," Carey said softly, looking at a place just above Hearne's left shoulder. "I don't think I'm . . . *equipped* for this sort of thing. There's too much going on. I'm in over my head, Jim. I just want to go home and get into my bed and never wake up, you know?" Hearne didn't know what to say. He barely knew the man, and what he knew wasn't encouraging. He didn't expect to be witness to what appeared to be a breakdown in progress.

"Can I get you something? Coffee?" Hearne asked lamely.

Carey shook his head. "A bullet in the brain might help."

When Hearne's eyes widened, Carey held up his hand. "Just kidding," he said. "Sort of." He gestured outside with a nod. "Those people out there want a statement from me. Now, it's big-time."

Carey began to tell Hearne what had been happening for the last three days, from the missing Taylor children to the confession of Tom Boyd, from the creation of the task force, to the call he had just received from a deputy reporting the severe beating of Oscar Swann. Not only that, but Monica Taylor was missing from her house, taken by a man who fit the description of Jess Rawlins. "Fiona Pritzle suspects Rawlins as well," Carey said. Hearne was stunned by it all.

"How could this all be happening?" Hearne asked, finally. "It's like I don't know this place anymore."

Carey shook his head. "Me neither."

Hearne thought about it for a minute, his mind whirling, filled with possibilities, all of them dark. "Sheriff, do you know where Singer is right now? Or the rest of the task force, for that matter?"

Carey shook his head no. Like everything, he seemed to be saying, the task force was out of his control.

"How can they just be gone?" Hearne asked. "Are they at the hospital, with Swann?"

Carey shrugged. "Maybe. I don't know."

"What about Eduardo Villatoro? The detective? Do you know where he is?"

Carey shrugged again.

Hearne sat forward in his chair, angry. "Look, Sheriff, I realize it's tough right now. You probably haven't slept in two days. But damn it, you're the sheriff. You can't just sit here."

Carey looked back, his eyes dead.

"And what you told me about Jess Rawlins. I don't believe it. I've known Jess all my life. There is no way—NO WAY—he's involved in the disappearance of those kids. Anybody who knows him knows that. Fiona Pritzle is a common gossip, the worst kind. Do you think Singer and the others believed her, for Christ's sake?"

The sheriff looked away. "Maybe," he conceded.

Hearne stood up. "You've got to set them right! Get ahold of them, and tell them Jess is a good man and Fiona Pritzle is crazy. Tell those reporters out there before they broadcast these allegations to the whole country. Look, I came here tonight because four years ago I opened an account at the bank I shouldn't have opened. It was right as the L.A. cops discovered us. I looked the other way at the time, I admit it. I should have asked more questions, but I wanted the business. But I didn't hand over the keys to this whole valley. None of us have. It's still ours, we just need to reclaim it. It's time to show some leadership. That's why the people elected you *sheriff!*"

Hearne heard himself yelling, something he rarely if ever did. But instead of getting through to Carey, waking him up, his shouting had the opposite effect. Carey seemed to withdraw further, saying nothing.

Hearne looked around. The red-helmeted dispatcher stood in the doorway, her mouth open, her eyes blinking so fast they blurred.

"Sheriff, I heard shouting," she said.

"It's okay," Carey said, so wearily even Hearne felt sorry for the man. "Just go back to work."

When the dispatcher left, Hearne tied to calm his voice. "So you don't know where anybody is?"

Carey shook his head. "Singer might be at the hospital, what I'd guess."

"Okay, then," Hearne said, standing. "Please, I'm asking you to get in touch with Singer. Tell him Jess Rawlins is a good guy. Don't let the press run with this. We can't have anything happen that shouldn't."

Carey nodded blankly.

Hearne turned toward the doorway.

"Jim," Carey said. Hearne looked over his shoulder. "I'm turning the whole thing over to the state and the Feds. I've called them, and they'll be here by morning. I know it's only been two days, but this thing is just too damned big for me."

"That's probably overdue," Hearne said. "I'm surprised you waited. And Sheriff, I'd suggest you get a grip on yourself. Go home and take a shower and shave. Try to act professional."

Carey looked up, his eyes far away. "I'll try," he said.

HEARNE TRIED to contact Jess Rawlins on his cell phone as he drove away from the county building toward the hospital. No one picked up, and Jess didn't have voice mail. He wanted to tell Jess what was happening, warn him what some suspected due to Fiona Pritzle's gossip. The thought of Jess Rawlins being suspected as a kidnapper or child molester turned Hearne's stomach.

On his way out of town he decided to stop by the hospital, see if he could locate Singer. Hearne felt a compelling need to tell Singer their business relationship was over, that it was time to let the chips fall where they may. Despite everything that was going on, and Singer's heroic role in the task force, Hearne desperately wanted to sever their relationship. It would be his first step back to respectability, even though it would also be an invitation to bank examiners to question his judgment, and the board of directors to discuss his continued employment.

He parked his car at the back of the hospital and left it running while he retrieved his cell phone to call Laura, to tell her he would be even later than he thought. While it rang, he looked at the way the word EMERGENCY from the red neon sign above the entrance reflected backwards and upside down on the hood of his car, the colors lighting up beads of rain.

"Hi, honey," she said by way of greeting. Her voice sounded tired.

"Sorry to call so late," he said, still looking at the reflection. "I'm going to run out to Jess Rawlins's ranch before I come home."

"Jess? Is he okay?"

"I think so," he said, and tried to briefly tell her what he knew. As he talked, and she listened sympathetically (she had always disliked Fiona Pritzle), he almost didn't notice the subtle change in the light reflection on his hood as a form passed in front of his car. Looking out the rain-streaked side window, he continued to talk as the form—a man wearing what appeared to be hospital whites with a heavily bandaged head— staggered between the row of cars, reaching from car to car to steady himself and maintain his balance.

"My God," Hearne said suddenly to Laura. "You won't believe who just walked by the car and didn't even see me."

"Who?"

"That ex-cop I told you about. The one who was beaten. Oscar Swann."

"You're kidding."

"I'm not," he said distractedly, watching Swann lurch from car to car, now bending at each, looking inside. For what?

Hearne knew the answer when Swann opened the door of an aged red compact and the dome light came on. He watched the ex-officer painfully bend himself into the driver's seat and heard the rough whine of an out-of-tune motor start up.

"He's stealing a car," Hearne said. He heard Laura gasp.

"I'm following him," he said, knowing her protestation would be next.

SWANN APPEARED to be going home. Hearne held well back, and faded even farther when Swann drove the stolen car beyond the city limits onto the wooded state highway that led to his house. The banker could see taillights in glimpses as Swann cornered or there was a clearing in the dark trees.

Why would the man simply walk out of the hospital like that? And steal a car?

Hearne had his cell phone on his lap and watched as the signal bars decreased until the NO SERVICE prompt flashed. Wherever he was going, whatever he was going to do now, he would be out of touch unless he could find or borrow a land line. He wished he'd have asked Laura to call the sheriff, then thought how pointless that would have been given the condition the sheriff was in when he left the office.

It took half an hour for Swann's brake lights to flash before he began the turn from the highway onto the two-track that led to his house. Hearne saw the flash, pulled to the side of the road, and cut his headlights. He waited until Swann's car had vanished into the trees before turning his own lights back on and following.

HEARNE HAD never been to Swann's house, and he knew he was on legal thin ice the moment he entered private property and began to climb the drive. He had no intention of confronting Swann, or even of approaching the house. All he wanted to do was see where the road took him, see that Swann had settled in (he hoped), and proceed to Jess Rawlins's place.

Hearne felt equal parts thrilled and terrified by what he was doing. But the pure happenstance of seeing Swann in the parking lot and following him to his home had given him a purpose in a night where his ineffectiveness bludgeoned him blow after blow. Maybe following Swann would lead to nothing. In that case, only Laura would know.

When he could see a dull glow of lights through the trees, Hearne cut his own and pulled over. He didn't want to drive right to Swann's house.

He killed the engine and slid outside, careful not to slam the door. As he walked through the trees toward the lights, his eyes adjusted to the darkness, and the tree trunks he had not seen earlier emerged from the gloom. The forest floor was spongy with moisture, and he walked carefully so he wouldn't slip and fall.

He could hear movement, a drumbeat of footfalls, so he stopped and tried to see. A deer. His heart was racing in his chest, and he could actually hear it when he paused.

Seventy-five yards up the hill, Swann's house was bright with lights both inside and out. In addition to the red car Swann had stolen, Hearne recognized Singer's white SUV. There was also a shiny black pickup with chrome wheels. He immediately guessed the whole task force was there, at Swann's house. Hearne felt real fear. Swann's house seemed like a very odd choice for a meeting, when the group of ex-cops had the entire sheriff's department and all of the county's resources at their disposal. Something wasn't right.

Fright gripped him, seemed to make his legs heavy and his movements slow. He walked close enough to a large pen to see movement in there: pigs. A massive hog false-charged him, grunting. Hearne jumped back, tripped over a tree root, and broke his fall with his elbows. While he lay in the mud he could hear the shallow, staccato breathing of the hog and smell its putrid hot breath.

His thighs were illuminated by a shaft of light from the house that slipped through the panels on the fence. As he scrambled back to his feet, his phone fell out of his shirt pocket and bounced off his knee and landed a few feet in front of him, in a pool of light.

As he stepped out of the shadows to retrieve it, the front door of Swann's house was thrown open. Hearne froze and watched as three men—he recognized the profiles of Singer, Swann, and Gonzalez—stepped out onto the front porch. Could they possibly see him?

Hearne couldn't breathe. He looked from the phone in the light to the men up on the porch. If he could see his phone in the light, they could too. They looked in his direction. He could see no weapons drawn.

Then Singer turned to Swann and said something he couldn't hear while gesturing in Hearne's direction. It was then Hearne realized the two men were looking down the dark road and not at him. Like they were waiting for someone. His breath returned, but it rattled in his throat.

Hearne backed up farther into the shadows but didn't take his eyes off Singer and Swann. He prayed he wouldn't step on a dry branch under the tree canopy, or trip again in the mud. He would leave the phone. He had no choice.

BLUE HEAVEN

———

AS HEARNE felt his way through the trees toward his car, he thought about the accounts at the bank, the ones he had opened for Singer, the accounts that grew quickly with all-cash deposits, each deposit barely under the ten-thousand-dollar figure that would require the bank to notify the IRS. Hearne had advised his head teller not to worry about it, that the money came from donations all the way out in Los Angeles, that it was for a good cause. But he'd known from his first meeting with Lieutenant Singer and Tony Rodale that something didn't quite fit. An initial deposit for $9,780 in tens and twenties? An additional deposit of $9,670 the next day, and the next?

Jim Hearne knew his culpability. He knew that by looking the other way he had opened the door to all of this, that his small transgression had begun a cascade of trouble and misunderstanding.

He had to warn Jess Rawlins. The ranch was just a few miles away. He would go there first.

Sunday, 8:32 P.M.

SINCE JESS and Monica had cleared Kootenai Bay and headed north, the rain had been sporadic. She had brought nothing with her except a jacket from the closet because he had told her to leave quickly. The Winchester was between them on the bench seat, muzzle down, a smear of Swann's blood on its butt plate.

In spare, halting language, he had filled her in. How her children had shown up in his barn, defended themselves, told him their story. Where things stood now.

"What are we going to do?" she had asked. "How will we keep my children safe?"

"I don't know," he said.

She was calm, he thought, not skeptical of him from the minute he had appeared in her door. She seemed to trust him immediately. He wondered to what he owed this pleasure, since they had never met. It was almost as if she knew him somehow. He had stolen glances at her as he drove, looked at her profile. She was attractive but obviously exhausted. Her skin reflected light blue in the passing cones of pole lights, the hollows of her eyes and cheeks were shadowed. Her voice was soft when she said, "I knew they were alive. I don't know how, but I knew it."

It made him feel good to know he was bringing her together with her children. She seemed to want nothing more than to be with them.

He thought of what Karen had said about her, that she had a bad reputation. How Fiona Pritzle had denigrated her ability as a mother by saying in the newspaper, ". . . But I just figured that there was no way those kids would have just taken off like that without their mother's permission and approval."

Consider the source, Jess thought. He knew nothing about the woman in the seat next to him except that she wanted to be with her kids. The rest didn't matter.

"You're familiar to me," she said, "even though we've barely met. I've always thought of you as what was old, tough, and good about this valley, before everything changed."

He looked at her, puzzled, said, "You've got the 'old' part right, anyway."

AS HE PULLED in front of his house, he told Monica to wait for a minute in the truck.

She started to protest.

"Look," he said, "Annie is sitting in there holding a shotgun. I told her not to open the door unless she was sure it was me. If she panics and something goes wrong, I don't want her to shoot her own mother."

"Annie has a gun?" Monica said, her jaw dropping.

Jess suddenly smiled.

"What's so funny?" she asked.

"I don't even want to say it," he mumbled.

"What?"

"When you asked me that I thought of *Annie Get Your Gun.* I don't know why I thought that was funny."

"I don't think it's very funny now," Monica said, but in a self-mocking way he liked.

Jess walked up to his door and knocked hard on it. "Annie and William," he said, "it's Jess Rawlins. I've got your mom with me."

Out of the corner of his eye, Jess saw the living room curtain pull back and William's face, cautious at first, break into a grin when he saw his mother in the cab of the pickup.

JESS STAYED out of the middle of the reunion and went into the kitchen to make coffee after he saw Monica sink to her knees, crying, and take both of her children into her arms. He heard William and Annie talking over each other, retelling the story about the murder they had witnessed and Mr. Swann, about the dark man who had come to the house that afternoon. How Jess Rawlins had taken care of them.

Halfway into measuring coffee for the pot, he remembered the shotgun in the living room and went to get it. He tried not to stare at the Taylors, who had now settled on the couch, with William clinging to his mother, his head in her lap, Annie next to her, talking a mile a minute. Boy, that girl could talk. Monica looked different, as if she were glowing from within. William looked more like a little boy, her child, and he didn't seem to care if Jess saw him hugging his mother like he'd never let go. This scene, this snapshot, Jess thought, made what he had done to Swann worth it.

Jess put the shotgun next to the Winchester on the kitchen table, wondering if Monica took her coffee with cream or sugar, lamenting that even if she did, there hadn't been any cream in the house in four years.

As their talking subsided in the living room, he noticed the silence from the roof. The rain had stopped. He parted the curtain over the sink and looked out. There were pools of rainwater in the ranch yard reflecting stars as the sky cleared. Beyond the ranch yard was the muddy ribbon of road that led into the wooded hills and the locked gate. He recalled Gonzalez standing on the porch, and Swann bloodied and stunned behind the couch in Monica Taylor's house. And there were two others involved in the shooting Annie and William had witnessed, making four in all.

That chain and lock on the front gate would mean nothing to four armed ex-cops who had already murdered and had conspired to manipulate every event since the children had seen the execution. These were men who had not only infiltrated but literally taken over local law enforcement.

Then he felt a presence next to him, his waist being squeezed, and he looked down and saw Annie, her wide-open face turned up to him.

He couldn't speak, so he didn't. Instead, he reached down and mussed her hair gently, then cupped her chin in his palm.

"I'm so glad she's here," Annie said. "Thank you for bringing her. I'm so happy it's all over."

Jess, feeling his lips purse, his own eyes sting from holding back tears, thought, *It's not over, Annie. Not even close.*

Sunday, 9:36 P.M.

THE SMELL inside the car was of bourbon, rain, and burning dust from the heater/defroster that hadn't been used in a while. Villatoro tried to adjust the level of the fan to keep the glass from fogging up inside. Newkirk, damp, drunk, and agitated, had fogged the glass.

After leaving Rodale's driveway, Newkirk said, "Go that way," pointing to Villatoro's left with the mouth of the open pint of Wild Turkey he'd produced from his jacket. Villatoro turned the wheel, heard the hiss of water spraying from beneath his tires on the undercarriage of the little car. He wasn't sure what road they were on, or which direction they were going. Everything looked the same to him; dark wet trees bordering the road like walls, wet asphalt, no lights. It wasn't until Villatoro recognized the same sharp corner and turnout for the second time that he realized they'd been going in circles for over two hours. It alarmed him, and he said, "Where exactly are we headed?"

"Want some?" Newkirk asked, handing over the bottle.

"No thank you."

"Better take some. You'll need it."

"You've kept me driving for half the night."

"I'm thinking."

Because the retired detective wanted Newkirk to talk, he took the bottle and sipped from it. The bourbon was sweet and fiery at the same time. It burned his lips, which were chapped from the altitude, the intense sun, and the thin air.

"Pull over here," Newkirk said.

"Here? Why?"

"Just do it and get out."

Villatoro did as he was told. Newkirk got out of the car at the same time. Both men left their doors open. *What?* Villatoro wondered. *Does he want to drive?*

"Put your hands on the hood, feet back and spread 'em," Newkirk said. "You know the drill."

"This isn't necessary. . . ."

"Do it," Newkirk said. "What I'm going to tell you is for your ears only. I've got to make sure you're unarmed, and that you're not wearing a wire."

"I'm retired."

"So you say."

Villatoro complied, placing his palms on wet sheet metal. Newkirk stepped behind him, expertly frisked him from his collar and shoulders to his shoes. Villatoro felt Newkirk roll his socks down.

"What are you doing down there?"

"Making sure you don't have a throw-down," Newkirk said, standing up, satisfied that he was clean.

A throw-down? Villatoro thought. The fact that Newkirk had even thought of that said a lot about where Newkirk was coming from. Villatoro had never considered carrying an illegal weapon in all of his years in the department. There had been no need. Obviously, Newkirk came from a different world, where throw-downs were common.

"Sorry," Newkirk said, "I needed to be sure."

Villatoro climbed back in the car and glanced at the digital clock on the dashboard. He thought of the desk clerk at the motel. She was waiting for him, and he felt bad about that.

Newkirk raised the bottle and drank from it. "Harsh shit, man," he said, and wiped his mouth with his sleeve.

Villatoro said, "So, you want to talk?"

He could feel Newkirk looking at him, staring at the side of his head.

"No. I just didn't want to drink alone. Don't be a dumb fuck."

Villatoro clamped his jaws. *Just let the man talk. Don't screw it up by prompting him.*

Moments passed as they drove. Newkirk drank again, then settled back into his seat. Villatoro kept his eyes on the road.

"I wanted to be the best cop on the force," Newkirk said. "I didn't have notions like I was gonna change the world or anything, but I wanted to do my job the best I could, and take care of my family. But mainly I wanted to be a great cop. I wanted to look in the mirror every night when I got home and say, 'Man, you are a *good* fucking policeman.'"

Villatoro nodded as he scaled back the fan of the defroster.

"I was like everybody, I tried too hard at first. When I saw a crack baby or human beings who treated other human beings like pieces of shit, I let it get to me. I thought I could reason with those people, show 'em somebody cared. But you know what I learned? I learned that the best thing you could do, overall, was arrest as many of 'em as you could and follow through, make sure they went to prison. I learned that maybe, maybe, ten percent of 'em might go straight, and ten percent was all I could hope for. I didn't even care what ten percent it was, or if it was five percent, as long as I was doing my job. Just fill the prisons, keep those scumbags away from the good people, that's what I wanted to do. And I did a damned good job of it, even though it was a war zone out on the streets. You have no idea what it was like."

"No, I don't."

"But you can't talk about this stuff with anybody except other cops," Newkirk said, talking over Villatoro. "You can't come home for dinner, and say, 'Gee, Maggie dear, how was your day? Did you go shopping? How was first grade, Josh? Dad had an interesting day today. I found the corpse of an eleven-month-old baby in a Dumpster with cigarette burns all over her body.'"

Villatoro shot him a look. Newkirk's eyes reflected green from the dashboard lights. He was staring straight ahead, talking as much to himself as to Villatoro.

"You know what it's like trying to raise a family with kids on a cop's salary. The wife had to work, and my kids were babies. Day care, the whole stupid thing. Day-care workers who were not much better than the assholes I was arresting out on the streets. In fact, some of them I *saw* on the street. I started thinking I needed to get my little boys and my daughter away from a place like that. So I started applying for jobs in places I thought I'd like to live—you know, Montana, Wyoming, places with space. But the cop jobs out here paid less than what I was making. I started thinking I'd never get out of there, you know? That I'd turn into one of those lifers, one of those guys who can tell you how much pension they've got built up to the penny if you wake 'em up in the middle of the night."

Villatoro didn't say, *You knew what the job paid when you applied for it.* He wanted Newkirk to keep talking.

"So that's when I discovered the world of off-duty security work." Newkirk smiled. "I found out I could just about double my income if I was willing to wear the uniform and be a rent-a-cop. It was a lot of extra hours, but damn, we started to swim out from under it. The debts, I mean. See, my wife likes to live beyond our means, and I can't say no when it comes to the kids. So I worked security a lot."

"At Santa Anita," Villatoro said.

"Among other places. But yeah, Santa Anita was the most steady. In the counting room, but you knew that." The way he said it made the hairs stand up on Villatoro's neck. He began to believe that Newkirk thought he knew more than he did. In order not to dispel the notion, Villatoro told himself to keep his comments to a minimum.

Newkirk took a long swallow, then rubbed his eyes. "At that point, I was still damned proud to be a cop. I was *proud* of the LAPD. Despite what you see here in front of you," he said, gesturing to himself, "I still think they're one of the best departments in the country. There are thousands of dedicated men and women, risking their lives every day they go out. They're good people, man. They're tough and honest, with a couple of exceptions. Too bad everybody points out the few bad ones and makes us all out to be fucking criminals. They say it's better now, too. That the new chief is cleaning things up. That'd be good if it's true. But the city's still a fucking cesspool, and the department needs twice as many cops. Hell, we need three times as many cops. But the taxpayers don't want to pay the bill for them."

Villatoro waited a moment, then said, "Santa Anita."

"Is that all you care about?" Newkirk sneered.

"No, it's not all," Villatoro said, trying to sound conversational. "But I've spent the last eight years trying to figure out what happened there."

Newkirk laughed. "Me too."

Villatoro started to think they were getting nowhere, when Newkirk sighed and said, "It was a pretty good gig, basically just standing around, like so much copwork. We didn't even open the doors until the security truck got there. Then we just stepped aside and guarded the perimeter while they loaded the trucks. We stuck around until all of the paying customers cleared out, then went home. A good gig, me and Rodale. We worked it all the time together. They liked us, we liked them.

"Gonzalez was our sergeant," Newkirk said. "Everybody respected and feared the guy. He used to give us a lot of shit about working security at Santa Anita, saying we must have a couple of dollies out there to want to work it so much."

Villatoro made the connection without saying anything. Gonzalez was one of the names on the list, one of the officers of the 501(c)3, one of the volunteers helping the county sheriff.

"Gonzo was great because he didn't give a shit about anything. He always did what was righteous, whether it was PC or not. I could tell you stories about Gonzo that would curl your hair if you had any. You ever hear of a 'guilty smile'?"

Villatoro said, "No."

"Remind me to tell you about it later. Let's just say when he took some scumbag into the Justice Ranch, the scumbag deserved whatever he got, okay?"

Villatoro had read something about an investigation into a place called the Justice House, but had never heard the results of the inquiry.

"Singer was our commanding officer, over Gonzo," Newkirk said. "Singer was the toughest motherfucker in the department, even though he never shouts, never yells. He defended his officers to the death, though. He'd go to the mat for them, and he was so cool under pressure that the brass would always come get him whenever the situation was too hot to handle. There wasn't a guy in our division who wouldn't take a bullet for Lieutenant Singer or Gonzo. They were, like, *mythical*.

"So when Gonzo invited me and Rodale for beers at a cop bar one night, after we'd been working security at Santa Anita for a year or so, we thought that was pretty cool, so we went. Swann was there, too—it was the first time we met him. After a few cocktails, Gonzo started asking us how we would rob the place if we were bad guys—you know, what the best scenario would be to take the place down."

Villatoro found himself looking over.

Newkirk curled his lip. "It's not like that, man. It was just a conversation. You know how cops do it all the time, try to figure out how bad guys would do a job, so they can *prevent* it, you know? Sometimes you've got to think like a criminal to stop a criminal. Besides, it wasn't like it was real money out there, like people needed it to feed their families. It was gambling losses. The idiots had already lost it, so it couldn't have been all that important to them. Gambling money, you know, like all of that cash the state collects from lotteries and shit like that."

"But it belonged to someone," Villatoro heard himself say. "It belonged to the owners of the track."

Newkirk laughed. "Like they didn't have insurance? You expect me to give a shit about an insurance company? Everybody hates those guys. Turn here."

"Where are we going?" Villatoro asked, taking another dark two-lane highway.

"Just driving. I told you that."

Villatoro tried not to sigh, tried not to show that he was beginning to get a bad feeling about this.

Newkirk drank. Then: "Nobody was supposed to get hurt. Shit. That wasn't the plan."

At last, Villatoro thought. Newkirk had admitted being involved. This is what he had worked years to hear.

"Me and Rodale figured out the part about putting the gas canisters in the money bags. That way, they could be set off by remote control when the truck stopped at the intersection.

"To start out, we had this big idea that Gonzo and Singer would bust into the counting room wearing masks and make everybody get on the floor. Shit, we had even worked out a deal where Gonzo would pistol-whip Rodale or me to make it look real. But the chances of them driving off after doing that and not being seen by someone or getting caught weren't good. So Swann thought of the idea of waiting until the security truck was off the park, robbing it there away from everything. It was the best idea, and we went with it."

"So it was Singer's idea in the first place?" Villatoro asked.

"Shit, I don't know whether it was Singer or Gonzo. It didn't matter. But Singer was in charge, thank God. He wasn't the kind of guy to rush into anything, either. We talked about the robbery and planned it for a year and a half. We had meetings where we went over everything and tried to shoot parts down. We did a couple of run-throughs at night so we could walk the route and time everything. Once we decided on the perfect plan, it was still another four or five months before we decided to do it. Singer didn't even want to try it until he could figure out how to launder the money. I hadn't even thought about it, but Singer was so fucking smart. He said the only thing worse than robbing a place these days was figuring out what to do with all of the cash, because nobody uses cash anymore. That's when he came up with the idea to create a foundation and to make all of us officers in it. We'd hide the cash and dribble it into legit accounts, not deposit it all at once. Pay ourselves in officer's salaries and big bonuses. It was fucking brilliant."

Villatoro wished he was wearing a wire. But if nothing else, even if he never gained Newkirk's trust, even if the ex-cop later denied everything, Villatoro would know how the robbery happened, who had been involved, where the money was.

"Also," Newkirk said, tapping the dashboard with the mouth of the bottle, "we had to wait until all of the stars lined up perfectly. A big cash day at the track, me and Rodale on security, Singer and Gonzo off duty so they could trigger the gas and rush the truck, Swann on patrol so he could escort the getaway vehicle to the auto salvage yard, where it was crushed. Remember, no one ever found a car?"

"I remember."

Newkirk chuckled. "Swann drove Singer and Gonzo and $13.5 million in cash back to L.A. in a police van we took the seats out of and dropped them off at their houses. Imagine that."

Villatoro whistled. "But a security guard got killed."

Newkirk seemed to darken. "Yeah, that still pisses me off. Some yahoo tried to be a cowboy. Gonzo had to take him out."

"His name was Steve Nichols," Villatoro said. "He had a wife and two children."

Newkirk didn't respond at first, just stared out the windshield. "That wasn't supposed to happen," he said.

The ex-cop remained silent while Villatoro drove. Finally, Villatoro said, "What about the guy, the employee, who fingered the other employees in the counting room? Why did he do that if he wasn't involved?"

Newkirk shrugged. He seemed to be losing enthusiasm for telling the rest of the story. "Singer's boy," he said. "The lieutenant had something really incriminating on the guy—totally unrelated to the track. Pictures of him dealing drugs, or with boy prostitutes or something. I never did know what it was exactly, but it was bad enough that the guy did what Singer told him."

"But the employee died before he had a chance to testify in court," Villatoro said.

"Yeah, wasn't that convenient?" Newkirk said darkly. "He gets caught in a cross fire while he's buying a pack of cigarettes at a 7-Eleven. The clerk gets popped, the witness gets popped, and the robber empties the cash drawer and escapes scot-free. All they can see on the security tape is a big masked guy in black walking in and blasting away."

Villatoro let it sink in. "Gonzalez?" he asked.

Newkirk nodded slightly. "And Swann was the investigating officer."

Jesus, Villatoro thought. *It's worse than I imagined.*

"Creating the charity was a master stroke, I agree," Villatoro said. "Making small deposits in a bank in northern Idaho never attracted any attention at all for years. The only problem was tracing a few of the hundred-dollar bills back to here. You must not have realized that some of them could be traced to the robbery."

Newkirk turned, his face screwed up in contempt. "*Of course* we knew about the serial numbers on some of the hundreds. Me and Rodale were in the counting room, remember? We knew about that. Do you think we're stupid?"

"No," Villatoro said, feeling outright fear rise up in his chest. He tried not to show it.

"That's where Tony Rodale screwed the pooch," Newkirk said, his voice rising, his eyes flashing with either anger or tears, Villatoro couldn't tell which. "He was the treasurer. He made the deposits. Singer had it all worked out. On a schedule, Tony made a cash deposit supposedly collected from random cops in L.A. and other places. But we knew about the hundreds, how a few of 'em were marked. So Tony's job was to get in his car and drive all around the country to break the hundred-dollar bills in restaurants, or gas stations, or bars, or wherever. He told his wife he was going fishing, but his job was to cash the hundreds and deposit the change later. That's all he fucking had to do."

Now, Villatoro started to understand. He thought of the mounted steelhead on Rodale's wall, thought of the years Rodale had deceived his wife about his absences. Thought of the places of origin from some of the marked bills that had been identified, California, Nevada, Nebraska. All within a day or two driving distance of Kootenai Bay, but far enough from each other that no pattern could be established.

"But the asshole got greedy," Newkirk said. "Singer noticed that some of the deposits were off, and figured Tony was skimming, which he was. The idiot was using some of the hundreds to bet on football, of all things, with some lowlife bookie in Coeur d'Alene. Tony wouldn't admit it, of course, but Singer found the bookie and shook him down and proved it to us."

Newkirk leaned across the car so his face was inches from Villatoro. When he talked, Villatoro could smell his sour whiskey breath.

"Tony risked *everything*. Not just for himself, but for all of us by paying his debts to a bookie in stolen hundred-dollar bills. *Our* money. When Singer found out he was afraid it would be a matter of time before someone like you came up here, tracing those bills back."

"And here I am," Villatoro said, not sure why he'd spoken.

"Here you fucking are," Newkirk said, as if in pain.

"But where is Tony Rodale?"

Newkirk started to speak, then looked away. Beads of sweat sparkled on his forehead. The anguished look on his face was lit by dash lights.

"That's what I'm going to show you," Newkirk said.

"Oh no," Villatoro whispered. "You killed him."

"Not just me. All of us. The agreement was we all put a couple into him, so we were all equally responsible. All of us except for Swann, who was late."

Another murder, Villatoro thought. It was too overwhelming to process. Steve Nichols, the inside witness, the convenience store clerk. Now, one of their own.

"It might have worked, too," Newkirk was saying, "except that those two fucking kids saw us take Tony out. Hey, keep driving."

Villatoro hadn't realized he had slowed the car to a crawl. Things were connecting in a way he had not anticipated. He felt as if all of the blood had drained from his hands and face.

"The Taylor children," Villatoro said. "Oh, my God."

"Everything keeps getting worse," Newkirk said, and this time there were real tears streaking down his face. "One crime, one perfectly planned crime. We were set for life. Then Tony fucked up, and those kids saw us, then the UPS guy. I feel like I'm already in hell." His voice cracked. "In fact, I think hell would feel nice and cool to me right now."

Villatoro sped up but realized his hands were shaking. He had trouble staying in his lane. What did Newkirk's reference to a UPS man mean?

"This is so much bigger than I had imagined," he said.

Newkirk's reaction surprised him. The ex-cop laughed bitterly, then wiped tears from his face with his sleeve before reaching behind him to withdraw his black semiautomatic. He aimed it at Villatoro, shoving the muzzle into his neck.

"It's about to get bigger," Newkirk said softly, his voice sincere. "I'm sorry I've got to do this, man. Especially since you were a cop yourself." It was as if Newkirk could not force himself to stop what he was doing, what was in motion, even though perhaps he wanted to.

"Slow down and turn here," Newkirk said, nodding toward a wet black mailbox on the side of the pavement marking a dirt road.

"What are you doing?" Villatoro asked, his voice stronger than he thought it would be.

"Turn here," Newkirk said, with more force.

"Someone is coming," Villatoro said, nodding toward a pair of headlights approaching a quarter mile away on the highway.

"Shit, I wonder who that is."

"They'll see us," Villatoro said. "They'll see the gun."

Newkirk lowered the weapon but jammed it into Villatoro's jacket beneath his armpit. He hissed, "I said *turn*, goddammit."

The road he wanted them to take was a two-lane dirt road pooled with rainwater that inclined up the hill into the trees.

"I don't think this little car will make it," Villatoro said. "We don't have any clearance, and the road goes up the hill."

"Take it fast," Newkirk said, clearly worried. "Don't slow down."

"Go!" Newkirk yelled, jamming the gun hard into Villatoro's ribs. "Go, now!"

As Villatoro floored it and drove up the hill, the rear tires fishtailing in mud, he recalled the name on the mailbox near the road, the name of the owner of the house they would soon be approaching: SWANN.

With a strange kind of calm, perhaps the calm of shock, Villatoro thought, *I'm going to die.*

Sunday, 10:01 P.M.

JESS WAS picking up the telephone to try to reach Buddy again when he saw the lights of a car blinking through trees on his access road. He hung up the receiver and walked across the kitchen for his rifle, glancing into the living room, where Monica, Annie, and William were huddled up on the couch, talking softly.

He leaned into the room. "Turn off the lights and don't open the door unless it's me," he said calmly. "Someone is coming down the hill." He reprimanded himself for not taking a chain up to the gate and locking it closed.

Monica turned her face to him. It drained of color.

"There's only one car," Jess said. "Please, now. Turn off the lights."

Annie disentangled from her mother and bounded across the room to flip the light switch. On the way back, she turned off the table lamp.

"It may not be anything," Jess said, trying to reassure them.

"Where are you going?" William asked. "Are you coming back?"

"Sure," Jess said, picking up the Winchester, turning off the lights in the kitchen, and feeling his way through the mudroom to the screen door.

HIS BOOTS crunched in the gravel as he walked across the ranch yard. The pole light in the corrals threw a pool of blue that lengthened and deepened the shadows. Jess didn't have time to turn it off, judging by how quickly the car was approaching. So he walked away from it, to the side of the barn. From there, in deep shadow, he should be able to see the car and who was in it as well as the front of the house. Noticing that someone had left a light on in the bathroom, he cursed silently.

The car approached quickly, and there was a flash of brake lights before the engine was shut off. Jess timed the sound of working the lever action on the rifle to the car door's opening. Looking down at his rifle, he saw a wink of brass as the cartridge slid into the chamber. He raised the rifle but didn't aim.

As the door opened, the interior lights of the car showed one occupant, not three or four. The occupant was Jim Hearne.

Jess frowned in the dark, puzzled.

Hearne stepped out of the vehicle but kept the door open. The banker faced the front of Rawlins's house, and called, "Jess? Jess Rawlins? Are you in there?"

"Behind you," Jess said from the shadow.

The sound of his voice made Hearne spin and duck. "You scared me," said Hearne.

"What do you need?" Jess asked, stepping out from the side of the barn but remaining in the shadows. While he wanted to trust Jim, he didn't want to expose himself just yet.

"Jess, most of your lights are off, and I didn't know if you were home. You didn't answer when I called earlier. You've got to hear what's going on."

Jess lowered the Winchester and approached Hearne. He saw Hearne's eyes shift to the rifle.

"Jesus, Jess—were you going to shoot me?"

"Maybe. Let's go inside."

"SO ALL of 'em are up there now," Jess said, shaking his head and sipping from the mug of coffee he had just brewed.

"All except for Newkirk—I didn't see him. But it was obvious they were waiting for someone."

"Then what?"

Hearne shrugged. Again, he turned in his chair and looked through the doorway into the living room, where the Taylors were. "I still can't believe they're here," he said softly. "What a relief."

Jess nodded. He was rehashing what Hearne had told him about the sheriff giving up, about the FBI coming, about Fiona Pritzle and her damned gossip. About the conclave of the ex-cops at Swann's house.

"Maybe we should gather everyone up," Hearne said, gesturing toward the Taylors, "and make a run to town."

"Where would we go?"

Hearne thought for a second. "Maybe if the sheriff saw everyone together . . ."

Jess shook his head. "What if we can't find him? What if he calls in Singer? No, I feel safer here until we know what's going on. All we have to do is hunker down and wait until the morning, from what you're telling me. We can explain everything to the Feds when they get here."

Hearne said, "Maybe we could go to my house?"

"Either way, we would need to drive straight down the state highway, right in front of Swann's place. What if they put up a roadblock? Or have a couple of men in the trees waiting for us?"

"I hadn't thought of that," Hearne said sullenly.

"I know one thing," Jess said, standing up and tossing the rest of his coffee into the sink. "I don't like speculation. We'll just drive ourselves crazy with it."

"So what are you going to do?"

"I'm going to see what those boys are up to," Jess said.

JESS HEARD Hearne come outside behind him. He turned, said, "Keep that shotgun handy while I'm gone."

"You're going up there? To Swann's house? What if they see you coming?"

Jess grinned. "I'm not going to drive."

It took Hearne a few beats to understand. Then: "I'll help you saddle up."

IN THE BARN, Jess shoved his rifle into the saddle scabbard and swung up on Chile. Hearne stepped aside, nearly backing into the pregnant cow in the stall.

"I can get there quicker overland," Jess said, turning his horse toward the open stall door. "Straight across my meadows and up into the timber on the side of Swann's place. They'll be looking for headlights, not a rider."

"If you aren't back in an hour," Hearne said, "I'm going to pile the Taylors into my car and go to town."

"That sounds like a plan," Jess said over his shoulder as he walked the red dun out of the barn. "Hand me that length of chain there so I can lock the gate on my way. And in the meanwhile, keep an eye on that cow. She's ready to pop."

AFTER LOOPING the chain around the gate and snapping two big locks through the links, Jess turned Chile around and goosed her into the trees until they emerged in a meadow, where he spurred her on. The sound of hoofbeats in the dark lulled and energized Jess at the same time. He asked Chile to settle into a slow lope, trusting his horse to see in the dark better than he could. Nevertheless, he clamped his hat down tight and hunched forward in the saddle in case a tree branch tried to dismount him. The rain had begun to drizzle again.

He rode across the meadow and up into the dripping pine trees. As they climbed, he glanced over his shoulder at his house down in the saddle slope, picturing the Taylors on the couch in the dark and Hearne sitting on the porch with the shotgun across his lap, looking very much not like a banker.

Sunday, 10:32 P.M.

THE LITTLE CAR made it up the hill and the road leveled out. Villatoro could see the lone porch light of a house blinking through the trees. He could no longer feel his fingers, or his feet. A sense of utter calm sedated him.

"Stop here," Newkirk said.

When he did, Newkirk leaned over him and pulled out the keys. "Get out."

Villatoro opened the door and unfolded himself. Cold rain stung his face and sizzled through the trees. There was some kind of pen in front of him, and huge, dark forms scuttled behind the slats of a fence. He heard a grunting noise that sounded like a man, then a squeal. Pigs. They were pigs.

A big man, Gonzalez, wearing a raincoat and pointing a pistol at him, stepped out from the shadows near a shed.

Gonzalez said, "Good job, Newkirk."

"I've got a wife and a daughter," Villatoro said. His voice seemed to be coming from someone else.

Gonzalez stopped and leveled his gun with two hands, the muzzle a few feet from Villatoro's face.

He heard Newkirk say, "Sorry, man."

He heard Gonzalez say, "You going to do this or am I?"

He heard Newkirk say, with a choke in his voice, "You do it."

"You never should have come out here, old man," Gonzalez said to Villatoro. "You should have stayed in the minor leagues. Shit, you're retired, right? What's wrong with you?"

Villatoro looked up and saw a silver ring hanging in the dark inches from his eye. It was the mouth of the muzzle. He wondered if he should strike out, try to hit someone, try to kick someone, try to run. But he had never been a fighter. The two fights he had had as a youth had both ended badly, with him cowering on the ground while being punched and spit upon. He didn't have the mind of a fighter, preferring reason to force. In thirty years, he'd never been attacked or forced to draw his weapon. *Oh,* he thought, *if I could live my life again I would learn how to fight!* He had a strange thought: *Do I keep my eyes open or do I close them?* Hot tears stung his eyes, and he angrily wiped them away.

"Fuck this," Gonzalez said, and the ring dropped away. "You need to finish the job you started. That's what the lieutenant told you, right?"

"I guess," Newkirk said, sighing.

"Then finish it."

Villatoro felt his stomach begin to boil sourly and hoped he wouldn't get sick.

"Take care of this guy," Gonzalez said, turning toward the house and walking away. "Take care of this fake cop." Then he laughed softly. Villatoro was humiliated, and angry. But most of all, he was terrified.

Villatoro felt Newkirk's gun in the small of his back, pushing him forward.

"Walk down to the end of the pen along the rails," Newkirk said, his voice weak. "And don't look back at me."

He's going to shoot me in the back of the head. That's better than in the face.

As he stumbled forward, he sensed one of the hogs, the huge one, walking along with him on the other side of the fence. He could hear the pig grunt a little with each breath.

Villatoro's shoe caught in a root, and he staggered, but Newkirk grabbed the collar of his shirt and held him up. "Watch where you're going, goddamn you."

"Sorry."

"Shut up!"

Newkirk pushed him ahead until they were under a canopy of trees at the corner of the corral. He kept his hand on Villatoro's collar, guiding him ahead. It was dry there. Villatoro could feel the crunch of pine needles under his soles although the tree dripped all around them.

Any second now. He could barely hear the drip of the trees because of the roar in his ears. And something else . . .

"Mister, I'm ready to shoot your eye out of the back of your head."

It was not Newkirk who spoke, Villatoro realized. It was a voice from the trees, from the dark. The voice was deep and familiar, but Villatoro couldn't place it, and for a moment he thought it was his own imagination, his brain trying to give him a second or two of false hope.

But Villatoro felt the gun twitch on the small of his back and heard Newkirk say, "Who is it?"

Another sound, the snort of a horse somewhere in the dark cover of the trees.

"The guy who's about to blow your head off."

Villatoro felt Newkirk's grip harden on his collar, but the gun left his back. There really was someone out there! And the voice, it was that rancher he had talked to at breakfast. Rawlins.

The gun returned, this time pressed to Villatoro's temple.

"I don't know who you are," Newkirk said, his voice rising, "but if you don't back off, he's a dead man."

"He's a dead man anyway from the look of things," the rancher said. "So fire away. Then there'll be two dead. Simple as that."

Villatoro tried to look in the direction from which he thought the voice was coming, but the gun against his head prevented movement. At any moment he expected to feel and hear an explosion, experience a flash of orange lights and his body dropping away. But Newkirk did nothing.

"Who are you?" Newkirk asked, his voice weak.

"Tell you what," Rawlins said. "No harm, no foul. Let the guy go and step back, and I'll let you walk away."

Villatoro could almost feel Newkirk thinking about it, weighing the odds. Villatoro wanted to speak, but couldn't find his voice anywhere.

"I can't just go back," Newkirk said, sounding like a little boy.

"Let him go, and I'll let you fire your gun in the dirt," Rawlins said.

"They'll think you did your job, and I'll never tell. Neither will Mr. Villatoro."

He pronounced my name correctly, Villatoro thought.

"It will never work," Newkirk said.

"I don't think there's a choice in the matter."

"They'll find out."

"Too bad for you if they do."

"But . . ."

Villatoro felt the grip on his collar loosen, felt the absence of the gun on the side of his head although the place where it had been pressed seemed to burn on his skin. Then he was free. He chanced a step forward, and nothing happened.

"Keep walking, Eduardo," Rawlins said. "Don't stop, don't turn around."

Villatoro did as he was told. He emerged from the canopy, felt cold raindrops on the top of his head. Nothing had ever felt better. He kept walking. From the dark, a hand gripped his forearm and pulled him into the warm flank of a damp horse.

"Go ahead and shoot," Rawlins said to Newkirk, "but don't even think about raising the weapon again."

The explosion was sharp but muffled, and Villatoro felt his knees tremble at the sound of it. But there were no more shots.

"Go back to the house now," Rawlins said to Newkirk.

Finally, Villatoro turned to see a glimpse of Newkirk's back as he walked away into the foliage. The big pig shadowed him along the rail, grunting for food, agitated.

"Climb up," the rancher said in a whisper, offering his hand.

"I never rode a horse," Villatoro said.

"You won't be riding. You'll be hanging on to me."

Sunday, 10:55 P.M.

IT STOPPED raining," Newkirk said to Gonzalez.

"No shit," Gonzalez replied.

They were on the deck of Swann's house, sitting on metal lawn furniture under the eave. Newkirk was still shaking, but he watched the red end of Gonzo's cigar, watched it brighten as the ex-sergeant sucked on it, the glow bright enough to light up his eyes.

Lieutenant Singer and Swann were inside, Swann talking. Newkirk could hear the pigs grunting and squealing, hungry. Those damn pigs were going to give him away. If Gonzo walked down there and couldn't find the body . . .

"That guy from Arcadia must taste good," Gonzo said, and Newkirk felt a wave of relief since Gonzalez had mistaken the sound. "Did he give you any trouble?"

"No."

"I'll never understand that, especially from an ex-cop. Me, I'd fight until my last breath. I'd be like that knight in Monty Python, you know? Cut off my arm, and I'd keep coming; cut off my leg, I wouldn't give a fuck. I wouldn't let somebody just take me out and shoot me in the head."

Newkirk grunted.

"One shot to the brain, right?"

"Yeah."

"I just heard one shot. But it was raining."

Newkirk was drunk but not drunk enough. Violent shivers coursed through him, making his pectorals twitch. He tried not to think about Villatoro and what had happened. He wanted to be able to do what he used to do on the force in a bad situation. Like the time he was first on the scene to a gangland slaying, four bodies tied up with electrical cords, multiple shotgun wounds to their heads. He'd been able to think of himself in the third person then. It wasn't him who walked through the warehouse, through the blood, it was someone else who knew to call for backup in a calm voice. Just like it wasn't him that evening who gained Villatoro's confidence, or told him everything for the sole purpose of getting the man to Swann's place. It was someone else *playing* him, acting out a role, reading the script he'd been handed. Not him. He wasn't evil. He had a wife and kids, and he coached soccer. He had even come to like that small-town detective a little. And to turn Villatoro over to the guy in the dark without a fight, then to keep silent about it? Well, that wasn't him, either. What he couldn't decide was whether his action was based in virtue or cowardice or something else. Maybe depression. But enough of that kind of thinking.

"What's Singer planning in there?" Newkirk asked, taking a long pull from the bottle he'd brought with him.

"He's figuring things out," Gonzalez said, irritated. "He's the planner. You know that. You asked me the same question five minutes ago. You're starting to make me nervous, Newkirk. Just shut up if you don't have anything to say."

Newkirk was glad Gonzalez couldn't see him in the dark, couldn't see the mixture of hate and self-revulsion he was sure was on his face.

"You better cool it with the boozing, too," his old boss said, his voice dropping with concern. "We might have to go into action tonight again. You need to be sharp."

"I thought I'd just let you do the killing," Newkirk said, surprised that he verbalized it. Sure, he was thinking that, but he didn't mean to actually say it.

"What the fuck does that mean?" Gonzalez said, instantly hostile.

"Nothing."

Gonzalez turned in his chair, put his huge forearms on the table between them. "You think I like it? Is that what you think?"

Newkirk wanted to take back his words, but he couldn't. "No, I don't think that. Forget I said anything."

"But you said it, asshole," Gonzalez said, his voice rising. "So you meant it. That's what you think, that I like shooting guys in the head. You think I like that, don't you?"

Newkirk shook his head hard, tried to get his wits back. There was too much alcohol in him. "No, really, I . . ."

Gonzalez was across the table and his hand shot out. Before Newkirk could pull back, a thumb jammed into his mouth between his teeth and cheek, and he felt Gonzalez clamp down with his fingers and twist as if he were trying to tear his face off. Newkirk groaned and gagged, turned his head in the direction of the twist, his head driven down into the tabletop.

Gonzalez was now standing over him, bending down, his mouth inches from Newkirk's ear. The thumb was still in his mouth; the pressure and pain were excruciating.

"Don't you dare get sanctimonious on me, Newkirk," Gonzalez hissed. "Don't you fucking dare. You're in this as deep as I am, as deep as all of us. None of us like what's happened. I had nothing against that guy . . . except the fact that he wanted to put me into prison. He wanted to take my new life away from me. I like my life, Newkirk. I'll do anything to keep it. And if that means shooting a sanctimonious prick like *you* in the head, I'll do that, too."

Newkirk blinked away tears and tried not to make a sound. The thumb in his mouth tasted of metal and tobacco. He wanted to be still, let the moment pass, give Gonzalez a moment to cool down.

"I'm sorry," Newkirk said after a beat. Or tried to say. But it sounded like a croaked moan with the thumb in his mouth.

Gonzalez relieved the pressure, and Newkirk sat back up.

"I said I'm sorry," Newkirk said. "I mean it. It was the bourbon talking."

"Yeah," Gonzalez said, drying his wet hand on his pants, his anger receding. "But the bourbon used your mouth."

They heard a chair being pushed back from the table inside. "Somebody's coming," Newkirk said.

"It better be Singer," Gonzalez said, standing.

Singer stepped out onto the porch. "Did you solve our problem?" he asked Newkirk, all business.

"Solved," Gonzalez said. "The pigs are happy."

Singer's face went dead as he listened. "You cut him up?"

Newkirk choked as he spoke. "Nah."

"I told you to cut him up."

"When I shot him, he fell back into the pen," Newkirk lied. "The pigs were all over him. I didn't want to go in there with him."

Singer looked away, obviously angry. "What did you do with his car?"

Gonzalez said, "It's in the garage for now, right next to the UPS truck. We can take it to the chop shop in Spokane later."

"Was he any trouble?" Singer asked Newkirk.

"Nah, he drove right up here."

"Anyone see you?"

"No," Newkirk said. No need to complicate things further.

Singer narrowed his eyes at Newkirk. "What happened to your face?"

Newkirk reached up and rubbed his jaw. He could either tell Singer what had happened or pull his weapon and shoot Gonzalez right now in a preemptive strike. Or he could do neither, which is what he chose.

Gonzalez stepped back and threw an arm around Newkirk, crushing him into his hard barrel chest. "Emotions were running a little high, Lieutenant. We had a little scrap, but everything's cool now, isn't it, Newkirk?"

Newkirk nodded, lowered his eyes away from Singer's fixed stare, and said, "Yup. We're cool."

Singer moved his eyes from Newkirk to Gonzalez, back to Newkirk. It was impossible to tell what he was thinking.

"Okay, let's meet," Singer said, turning on his heel and going inside.

THE LIEUTENANT strode behind the kitchen table and turned toward them as they entered. Swann looked bad. Singer said, "He's got a broken nose and cheekbone and a busted jaw. Somebody worked him over and took Monica Taylor."

"Shit!" Gonzalez said, hard and fast.

Newkirk thought he knew who had done it.

"The sheriff's in a panic," Singer continued, his voice so calm it reminded Newkirk of the rhythm of a bedtime story. "He's contacted the state DCI and the Feds. I tried to talk him out of it, but I was unsuccessful. The sheriff thinks he's got a double kidnapping on his hands. The Feds will be here first thing tomorrow in a chopper."

Newkirk tried to concentrate on what Singer was saying, tried to put it into context and think ahead.

"Who did it?" Gonzalez asked Swann.

Swann's face was half-again its normal size. He had trouble talking but said, "Tall thin old guy, maybe sixty, sixty-five, wearing a cowboy hat. He had a lever-action rifle with him, that's what he used on me."

Newkirk thought, *Yes, sounds like him.*

"Why'd he take the woman?" Newkirk asked instead, which resulted in a laser-beam stare from Singer.

"I don't know why he took the woman," Singer said. "But I've got a pretty good guess. Have you been drinking, Newkirk?"

Newkirk felt his face get hot. "Some," he said.

"Are you okay to work?"

"Yes," Newkirk said, his voice thick.

"He'll be fine," Gonzalez said, trying to smooth things over between them in his brutish way. "He can follow orders and pop a cap in some old cowboy's ass, if that's what we need him to do."

Again, Singer looked from Gonzalez to Newkirk. Analyzing them, dissecting them. Coming to some kind of conclusion that was inscrutable.

"You remember Fiona Pritzle?" Singer asked. Before they could answer, he continued. "She's the one who gave the Taylor kids a ride to go fishing. She's a gossip, a local busybody, but she showed up at the sheriff's house earlier tonight with an interesting story. She said she saw a local rancher in the grocery store buying food that only kids eat, but the guy doesn't have any kids. She says he lives up the valley, about eight miles from the Sand Creek campground. The sheriff knows the citizen, named Rawlins. Jess Rawlins, our cowboy. Anyway, Pritzle thinks Rawlins may have the kids. She thinks he's an old pervert. The sheriff wasn't buying it at the time. I'm sure he'll tell the Feds about him, though."

"Rawlins," Gonzalez said, turning the name over in his mouth. "I ran into that old fucker today. He threw me off his ranch, said I couldn't search it without a warrant. I wouldn't mind seeing him again. We have issues."

Newkirk kept quiet.

Singer was motionless for a moment, looking at something beyond Newkirk but not really looking at anything at all. Thinking, building a plan.

"He's got them," Singer said. "He's got the kids, and he's got Monica Taylor."

He paused to let the fact sink in. "Obviously," Singer said, in a tone as reasonable as it was icy, "we've got to get him before the Feds and the state cops come in. We've got to force a confrontation. What happens is the rancher gets killed, and the Taylors go down in the cross fire. The dead rancher later gets pinned with the whole thing: kidnapping, sex crimes, murder. We don't hit the kids ourselves, we use the rancher's gun to shoot them."

"Jesus," Gonzalez whispered.

Newkirk couldn't say anything if he wanted to. He was too busy trying to stop the surge of sour whiskey from coming back up.

"What do we do when we've got a hostage situation?" Singer asked.

Silence.

Then Singer slammed his palm down on the kitchen table so hard that glassware tinkled in the cupboards. "Gentlemen," Singer said, his voice sharp and straight like a razor's edge, "what do we do when we've got a hostage situation?"

Newkirk gagged, then stumbled to the kitchen sink and threw up. He felt their eyes on his back but didn't turn around until he had gulped down two glasses of water. Finally, he said over his shoulder, "Cut off power and electricity. Try to force them out into the open."

"Right," Singer said, satisfied.

Newkirk turned around, leaned against the counter, wiped his mouth and eyes with his sleeve.

Singer leaned toward Gonzalez: "Do you recall when you were there earlier where the power lines are that lead to the ranch?"

"Yeah. They're along the highway."

"First things first, then," Singer said. "Gonzo, go out into the garage with Swann and you two grab his toolbox, then get over to that rancher's gate, fast. Use your vehicle to block the exit so they can't get out and can't get around you through the trees. Figure out where phone lines are—I'm sure they're on the highway right-of-way with the power. Go now."

"I'm out of here," Gonzalez said, scrambling. Swann stumbled along behind him.

"We'll meet you there," Singer said, turning to Newkirk. "I want you to follow me in the UPS truck."

Newkirk shook his head, puzzled. "Why?"

"We want it close," Singer said. "Close enough to the ranch to take it down there when everything's over. It'll help us build the legacy of Jess Rawlins."

Sunday, 11:17 P.M.

I THOUGHT for a minute you were going to let Newkirk shoot me," Villatoro said.

"Nope," Jess said. "It was a bluff."

"It was a good bluff," Villatoro said emphatically. "I believed you."

"Mr. Villatoro, you'll need to keep your voice down a little," Jess said softly over his shoulder as he rode. "Sound carries out here. We don't want them to hear us."

"I'm sorry," Villatoro whispered. "My nerves are jangling."

"Mine, too."

They were deep in the timber, the mare picking her way over downed logs and between crowded stands of dripping trees. More than once, Jess had to duck and caution Villatoro to do the same as they passed under overhanging branches. They were on his ranch now, he could feel the comfort of it. His passenger clutched him so tightly around his ribs that at times he had trouble breathing and had to ask Villatoro to ease up. The Winchester lay across the pommel of the saddle. Although the moon was still behind clouds, the sky was clearing, and muted shafts of moonlight shone through the branches and blued the barrel of the rifle.

Villatoro whispered, "Will your horse carry both of us all the way back?"

"Hope so."

"I still can't believe I'm on a horse."

"Kind of uncomfortable, isn't it?"

"I hope I don't fall off."

"Me too."

Villatoro sighed, as if everything that had happened was settling in, exhausting him suddenly. "Jesus," he moaned. "What a night. All those years in the department, and nothing ever happened like that. I feel foolish for not fighting back, but what could I have done?"

"Not much," Jess said over his shoulder. "I've been thinking. Hearne's right. As soon as we get back let's pack everybody into his car and my truck and get the hell to Kootenai Bay. We'll get through this. We'll go straight to the sheriff and the media and try to make our case. I'd rather those kids were there than here tonight."

Villatoro took a cautious breath before asking, "What kids?"

Jess explained.

All Villatoro could say was, "My God."

JESS COULD feel Chile getting tired, slowing down, stumbling where earlier she was surefooted. But she didn't protest with a crow-hop, or try to shrug them off. *She's a gamer,* he thought. He admired her character.

"Let's dismount and lead her for a while so she can catch her breath," Jess said, pulling her to a stop.

"I'd guess the both of us are pretty heavy."

Jess agreed and nodded in the dark and felt Villatoro slide clumsily off Chile's back. When he was clear, Jess swung out of the saddle and shoved his hand between the horse's flank and the saddle blanket, where it was hot and moist with sweat.

"Soon as she cools down, we can ride her in," Jess said in a low whisper, leading her by the reins. Villatoro walked alongside with a hand on the saddle because Chile and Jess knew where they were headed, and he didn't.

Above them, in the trees, was a sweep of light.

"What was that?" Villatoro asked.

Jess put a gloved finger against his lips and shushed him. "Head-lights," Jess whispered.

They stopped and listened. Far above them and to the east, Jess could hear a motor and the crunching of gravel under tires. There was the squeak of brakes being applied, a surge of the engine, then another squeak before the motor was killed.

"They blocked the gate," Jess said.

In a swath of moonlight, he could see Villatoro bury his face in his hands in despair.

Sunday, 11:59 P.M.

VILLATORO AND HEARNE sat at the kitchen table drinking coffee. The shotgun was on the table as well, along with a box of shells. In hushed tones, Villatoro was telling Hearne about the encounter in the trees at Swann's place, and Hearne kept shooting glances at Jess while he did it. Jess sipped his coffee with his back to the kitchen counter and half listened.

Annie and William were asleep on the couch in the living room under the same blanket. Monica rifled through Jess's refrigerator and cupboards looking for ingredients so she could make lasagna, but she couldn't find noodles or cheese and gave up. She said she wanted to cook something because she was too nervous to sleep.

"So it's all coming together," Hearne said, sitting back as if he were in a loan officers' meeting. "They robbed Santa Anita, all five of them, and moved up here. Then Rodale screwed up, and they executed him for it, but Annie and William happened to be witnesses. That set everything in motion."

Monica had settled on baking a cake, and Jess watched her as she looked again and again at the directions on the back of the cake mix box. He could tell she was distracted, that she was doing something just to be doing it. Who would want to eat cake?

Villatoro turned to Jess. "What are we going to do? Those men are killers."

Hearne said, "The sheriff told me he called the FBI. They'll be here tomorrow morning. Like Jess said, all we can do is wait it out until we can tell our story. But the ex-cops have probably figured out where you are and who is here," he said, gesturing with his head toward the sleeping children. "They'll want to silence them—and us—before we talk."

Villatoro looked at his wristwatch. "I wish there was someone we could call." Celeste should be home and could get the ball rolling urging local law enforcement to contact the FBI or Idaho authorities. Then he thought of Donna, waking her up, telling her what was going on. She would go hysterical. Plus, there was nothing she could do to help. But it was important, he thought, to tell her he loved her. That he always had.

Jess said, "I wish I knew the names of those ex-cops, the ones who got turned away when they tried to volunteer. I would guess they'd want to help us out. There are plenty of good ones up here, I think. They'd be pretty pissed off if they knew what these guys were doing."

While they talked, Jess noticed that Monica kept looking at him as well as Hearne, as if measuring something besides cake mix.

"Do you have an idea?" Jess asked her.

She shook her head. "Not about that." Then she looked hard at him. "Jess, I'd like to talk with you."

Jess felt uncomfortable that she was calling him away from Villatoro and Hearne.

Hearne felt it, too, and said, "Excuse me, I'm going to call my wife. I want her to know I'm safe."

"That's a good idea," Villatoro said, rising from the table. "You call, then I'll call Celeste and then my wife." He said it with a tone that barely disguised what he meant, which was, *in case we never see them again.*

"We can step outside," Jess said to Monica.

As she started for the mudroom and the door, Hearne turned around with the receiver in his hand. "There's no dial tone."

Jess froze. He knew what that meant.

Villatoro said, "They've cut the line."

Jess said to Hearne, "Try your cell phone."

"It's gone," Hearne said, gesturing with empty hands. "I lost it at Swann's."

"What about you?" Jess asked Villatoro.

He shrugged. "Mine never worked up here in the first place. Wrong company."

"So we're blocked in, and we can't communicate," Jess said flatly. "I've had better days."

In midsentence, the lights went out. From the living room, Jess heard Annie scream.

DAY FOUR

monday

Monday, 1:24 A.M.

CARRYING TWO HISSING Coleman lanterns, Jess entered the house from the barn. He put one lantern on the table and held the other up at shoulder height, so he could see the faces of everyone shining back at him. Monica held both William and Annie in front of her. Hearne sat at the table. Villatoro was behind him, holding the shotgun.

To Hearne, Jess said, "Can you still ride?"

"I haven't forgotten how."

Jess nodded outside. "Then take Chile into town. She's still saddled, and that way you can avoid the road. You might be able to get to Sheriff Carey before daylight. Maybe you can convince him to get his men together and get out here."

Hearne nodded, went to the gun cabinet, and pulled out another shotgun. "Should I take this?"

"Yup."

Jess turned to Villatoro and the Taylors. "I'm not running. This is my place. I'll know if they try to come because there's only one way in with a vehicle."

No one said a word. They were waiting for more from him, he realized.

"I know every inch of this ranch, and they don't," Jess said. "That's our only advantage. We're going to hold our ground. Don't worry, I've been preparing for it all of my life."

"But you're old, Jess." It was Annie, who sounded concerned. He didn't even know she was there.

"*Annie!*" Monica said.

"Hell, let her be." Jess laughed. "She may be right."

AS JESS pulled Chile's flank strap tight and adjusted the stirrups for the shorter-legged Hearne, the banker said, "Jess, let's make a pact."

Jess finished, turned.

Hearne said, "If I don't make it, promise me you'll take care of Annie and see her through. William and Monica, too."

Jess tried to read Hearne's face, but couldn't get past the resolve in it.

"I'll do the same if something happens here to you," Hearne said.

"You trying to tell me something?" Jess asked.

Hearne simply looked at him, said, "I mean it, Jess."

"Then okay," Jess said after a beat. The pact seemed noble and worthwhile, he thought. He held out his hand, and Hearne shook it.

"Remember," Jess said, "trust your horse to find the way in the dark."

OUTSIDE, JESS stood with Villatoro on the front porch and watched Jim Hearne wheel on Chile and ride off into the dark. He could hear hoofbeats drum and recede into the meadow.

Jess handed the weapon he had taken from Swann to Villatoro. "You probably know more about handguns than I do."

"I never shot anyone," Villatoro said.

"You mean you can't, or you never have?"

"I never have."

"But you can do it if you need to?"

Villatoro didn't hesitate. "Absolutely. Emphatically. Yes, I'm willing. I vowed to myself up in those trees that if I had another chance, I would fight."

"Good." Jess placed his hand on the man's shoulder in an effort to reassure him.

Villatoro said, "My wife will never believe this. All those years, and I never had a gun pulled on me. I always wondered what I'd do if that happened, and now I know. I just stood there and waited for the bullet. I'm ashamed of myself."

Jess looked up at the saddle slope hill where the access road was, saw no headlights, said, "Don't be. Everybody freezes up sometime. Look at the bright side—you may get a second chance to get it right."

Villatoro chuckled uncomfortably. "Some bright side," he said.

Monday, 2:30 A.M.

MONICA FOUND JESS in the barn, sitting on an upturned bucket, the Winchester across his knees, a lantern hissing and throwing out warm yellow light. In the stall in front of him was a hugely pregnant cow, legs splayed, tail twitching with pain. She could hear the cow's shallow breathing.

"I was wondering where you went," she said. "I got the kids down again and realized you weren't in the kitchen. Then I saw the light out here."

She wore a heavy canvas ranch coat she had found hanging from a peg in the mudroom. It smelled of campfire smoke and hay.

Jess looked over at her. "These cows, they don't pay much attention to the news of the day or our situation. They just keep having little ones no matter what I think about it or how much else I have to do."

"I don't know how you can concentrate on this right now."

Jess shrugged. "Doing something normal helps me think."

Monica stepped inside the barn, pulling the coat tight against the damp chill. "Is she okay?"

Jess squinted at the stall. "I'm worried about a breech with this one," he said. "She had a breech baby last year, so I'm afraid it might happen again."

"How close is she?"

"Any minute," he said.

"And if the baby is breech?"

He held up a long rubber glove. "Then I have to reach in there and pull the calf around so it can come out. If that won't work, I need to pull it out piece by piece."

She flinched and nodded, looking at the moist and inflamed birth canal, then back at the glove.

"It's a messy business," he said, in response to her facial expression, which had given her away. Then he nodded at a bucket near him. "You can sit down, if you'd like. Annie used that bucket last night to watch the same thing."

"Annie watched a cow being born?" Monica asked, moving toward the rancher. "How'd she take it? She didn't say anything to me."

"She's pretty tough," the rancher said. "She's a good kid, if you don't mind me saying that."

Monica smiled and sat down. The bucket rocked a little, and she reached out for his arm to steady herself. She noticed how he stiffened at her touch.

"Of course I don't mind," she said, righting her balance. "She really likes you. So does William. He said you should come live with us when this is over."

She looked over to gauge his reaction, and was rewarded with a look of surprise that almost made her laugh.

"He said *that*?"

"Yes. He told me when I tucked him in."

Jess shook his head, looked down at his dusty boots. She couldn't tell what he was thinking, whether he was flattered or horrified.

"Jess," she said, screwing up her courage, "what I wanted to talk to you about before . . ."

"Yes?"

She took in a breath and held it, then blew it out long. "I've known a lot of men in my life. I can't think of one of them who would have done what you did."

He wouldn't look over at her, and she noticed how his ears turned red. He mumbled, "There's a couple more. One inside the house, and the other on horseback right now."

"I can't tell you how much I appreciate it," she continued. "You've risked everything for me, and you never even met me. Annie and William have never had a man like you in their lives before."

He continued to stare at the cow. The vein in his temple pulsed. She noticed the wetness in his eyes.

"Jess, are you okay?"

"I'm fine," he said.

"What do you think of what I just said?"

He shook his head slowly. "It's real nice."

There was a beat of silence while she waited for more.

"My wife always said talking was a problem for me," he said sheepishly.

She was touched, and she reached for his arm again. "I don't mean to make you uncomfortable. Especially after all you've done for us. You brought me together with my children. You don't need to talk."

"I don't mind talking to you," he said, his face red. "It's just that I can't think of the right words to say."

It took her a few moments to summon the courage for what would come next. He picked up on the hesitation, and glanced at her but didn't stare, making it easier for her. She said, "Jess, there's something you might want to know. I know there've been rumors over the years about me, and I want to clear them up."

She said, "Thirteen years ago"—he turned to her as she said the number, a puzzled look on his face—"I was seventeen and I thought I was a pretty hot little number. Actually, I *was* a hot little number. I wanted to grow up fast. So, along with three friends, we went to Spokane on a Friday night, to the university because we'd been invited to a frat party. At the time, it sounded incredibly adult and exciting . . . *college boys,* you know."

Jess nodded. It was obvious he was a little uneasy with the story thus far but was too polite not to hear it out to see where it went.

"Not long after we got there, my friends and I got separated from each other, and even though I was the hot little number, I was a little scared because I was out of my league. There were so many people who knew each other, and a lot of drinking. I'd had way too much myself. Luckily, though, there was a boy I recognized at the party. A boy from around here. Even though we really didn't know each other very well—he was three years ahead of me in school—it was great to see a familiar face. And he was a very nice boy, very friendly, very handsome. Smart, too. It was exciting. I wanted to find my stupid friends so they could see how well I made out, you know? So he said he'd take me through the frat house and we'd try and find them. And if we couldn't find them there, we'd go from party to party on campus until we did."

She saw Jess shake his head, probably not even realizing he was doing it. Did he disapprove? What? She continued.

"I was head over heels being with him. I wanted to *acquire* him, and I wanted him to acquire me. He was an amazing boy, the most charismatic man I'd met other than my dad. He lit up a room when he walked into it, and I wanted him, and I told him so. No college boy can resist that, trust me. That boy and I spent the next two days together locked up in his room. It was magical. You could just look at him and know something big was going to happen with this boy—like he was on the verge of something. I found out later what that was, but at the time I didn't see it. I don't think anyone did. Finally, my friends came and found me and practically had to drag me back to the Kootenai Bay.

"I still wanted to see him, so I called him. I was scared to death that I'd say 'This is Monica,' and he'd say 'Who?' But when I called the frat house they were evasive. They said he wasn't there anymore, but they wouldn't tell me how to reach him. It was weird. At first, I thought they knew who I was, and they were trying to shield him from me, but that didn't make sense. Then I figured, well, stupid frat boys. He probably left the fraternity and went to another one, and they didn't want to admit he'd left or something. I started to get worried. So I called the one friend who'd always been there to help me out and told him the situation, that I was scared something had happened to this boy. We drove to Spokane, and that's when I found out my man had gotten sick . . . mentally. That he'd had some kind of real severe breakdown the week before and gotten arrested."

When she looked at Jess, he was staring at her with an intensity she hadn't seen before.

"Jess, the boy was Jess Jr."

"He told me he knew you."

"Was that all he said?"

Jess swallowed. "He said you were wild. You aren't going to tell me Annie is my granddaughter, are you?"

She hesitated for a beat.

"No, I'm not. Annie is Jim Hearne's daughter."

Jess was speechless.

"He was the friend I called to take me to Spokane to try and find out what happened to J. J. He was my father's best friend, and I think he felt he owed something to me and to you. But one thing led to another. Neither of us planned it, and afterward, Jim felt horrible. He said he'd get a divorce if I wanted him to, even though he loved his wife, because he'd betrayed her with his friend's daughter. I told him never to say that again, and to go home to Laura. I never told him I was pregnant. I let him think the baby—Annie—was J. J.'s. But she wasn't. J. J. never completed the act, but Jim did. So I know for sure. In a way, I think he knows, too, but he's been too frightened all these years to ask. If you're wondering why the local banker is on that horse right now, I think you've got your answer."

"My God," Jess said. "Now I know what Hearne was trying to tell me."

She said, "I'm no victim. He didn't take advantage of me like it sounds. He gave in to *me*. I was like that then. But I didn't want to ruin a good man or bust up a marriage. I had *some* dignity, I guess. And Annie is such a joy, such a wonderful, wonderful girl. I'm blessed to be her mother. She's a freak of nature because she's special, and better than both her parents, I think."

She tried to guess what he was thinking. It was as if he couldn't quite process what she had told him, and she couldn't tell if he was relieved or disappointed.

"I wanted to tell someone so many times," she said, "but I didn't. I guess I was waiting for the right time, and that never came. When I was married there was certainly no point. My husband never knew who Annie's father was. I kept that from him. So it's amazing to me how things worked out. It's like there was a reason we were brought together tonight, and the least I could do was let you know."

He smiled sadly. "I was kind of hoping you were going to tell me I had a grandchild."

"I'm sorry she isn't."

"It doesn't matter," he said, excited. "I like 'em just the same."

She laughed at that, and he smiled. "Jess, I don't know how much you've heard about me," she said, seeing his eyes flinch and knowing he had heard, "but I've made a vow to myself during all of this that I'm going to keep: My kids come first. If there is anything good at all to come out of all of this, it's that I've learned that lesson. No more Tom Boyds, no more J.J.s, no more Jim Hearnes, no more anyone. Annie and William come first. I've made that promise with God."

He nodded. "I think that's good."

"I think that's good," she mocked good-naturedly, causing him to smile again. "Yes, it is. I need to make my own way in the world without relying on any man to make things happen for me. I think that's possible, don't you?"

"Sure," he said. "Might as well try."

"I'll prove it can be done," she said, holding up her hand over her heart as if taking a pledge. "I may have to take the kids and move to somewhere I don't have any history, but I'll prove it can be done."

He flinched again, which surprised her.

"What's wrong with that?" she asked.

He looked down. "Nothing, I guess."

"What, Jess?"

He looked at his boots, at the cow, at the bare lightbulb, anywhere but at her. Then, when he turned his head and looked at her full on, he said, "However things work out, I'd kind of like to keep up with Annie and William. We can pretend they're my grandkids."

This time, it was Monica who was speechless.

"My own family got pretty screwed up," he said. "I'd like to help your kids if I can, maybe make up for the damage I've caused around here."

She reached up and blotted her tears with the rolled-up cuff of the barn coat. She was surprised that he continued.

"This place," he said, gesturing toward the open barn door but meaning the ranch, "is the only thing I've got that connects me to my own father and mother, and to my granddad, who homesteaded it. They passed along a pretty good thing. They said to work hard and pass it on to my own kids. That'll never happen. It doesn't look like I can keep it, or leave it to anyone. Developers want it, and they'll likely get it. It belongs more to the bank than it does to me.

"So," he said, "there'll be nothing for me to pass on. I'll leave no mark on this valley. But if I can help out Annie and William, maybe help them get a leg up, well, that'll be fine. It means I've got something to live for. I've got someone to defend. That means . . . everything."

He turned away, the expression on his face telling her he thought he had said too much. But he hadn't, and she leaned over and hugged him, buried her face into his neck, said, "You're a good man, Jess. You're such a good man," and meant it, feeling such affection for him, wondering why she hadn't called him years before to see how J.J. was doing, thinking how sometimes, it was the hardest men who were the softest.

Monday, 2:41 A.M.

JIM HEARNE thought, *It feels good to sit a horse again.*

He had slowed Chile to a walk once they entered the timber on the other side of the meadow. He wanted both to conserve her energy and give her the opportunity to pick her way through the gnarled undergrowth. She could see much better than he could in the dark beneath the closed kettle lid of the tree branches, so he gave her her head and let her go. She picked through the downed timber, placing each front step carefully, her back feet knowing instinctively how to mirror the movement to keep them going forward. He also slowed her down because he knew there was a barbed-wire fence ahead somewhere, the fence that separated the Rawlins place from forest service land. She would likely see it before he would.

She was purposeful, he liked that. He could see why Jess liked this horse. She was the kind of horse that was best if she had a job: cutting cattle, herding, or, in this case, delivering him to Kootenai Bay. He was glad he had a purpose, too, that he was doing something that might save the lives of the Taylors, Villatoro, and Jess. It was the least he could do. He was glad it involved doing something physical. He didn't want to have the time to think about how his own actions had incubated the whole situation, how he was culpable. He was finally doing something good, doing something right, for Monica and Annie. This ride was his ride of redemption. When he thought about those words, he smiled. Man . . .

The rain had stopped, and the sounds of the forest returned: chattering squirrels warning of his arrival, the crunch of pine needles beneath the hooves of the horse, the panicked scuttling of creatures he never saw getting out of his way. Sitting the horse connected him to the ground, made him part of it. He could feel the softness or hardness of the ground transmitted up her legs through the saddle. It was as if sinews had reached up through the dirt and reattached themselves to him. He had forgotten about the feeling of being connected. It wasn't something he felt in his car.

Could he convince the sheriff? He thought he could. Simply the fact that he was riding into town on a horse should tell Carey something.

HE COULD feel Chile hesitate, feel her muscles bunch beneath his thighs, and in a moment he could see the four thin ribbons of barbed wire coursing down through the trees ahead of him. At the fence he turned her to the right, uphill, parallel to the fence, and walked her up a slope looking for a gate. If he couldn't find one, Hearne would need to do the old cowboy trick of detaching the wire from the posts to stand on while leading the horse over. It was a tricky maneuver that sometimes spooked horses because they thought the wire was water and felt a need to bolt or jump.

The trees cleared into a grassy mountain park washed blue with starlight. The sky opened. He could see better, but he couldn't see a gate.

Hearne was studying the fence line with such intensity that he almost didn't realize that the forest sounds had stopped and left only the soft footfalls of his horse and the creak of the leather saddle. Something had silenced the sounds. He saw that Chile was looking ahead, her ears alert, her eyes wide, her nostrils flared as if to woof.

Above, in the black timber on the other side of the meadow, a twig snapped.

Hearne signaled Chile to stop with a tug on her reins, and he sat the saddle, trying to make his eyes pierce the darkness of the stand of trees.

He thought, *The fence line goes all the way up to the road. If someone were to walk the perimeter of the ranch, they would likely use the fence line as their guide.*

The voice came from the trees. "You need some help, mister?"

It was deep and had a Mexican inflection. Hearne froze.

The shotgun was deep in the saddle scabbard under his right leg, the butt poking out from the sleeve of leather. Hearne leaned back in the saddle, letting his right hand drop to his side. He felt the metal butt plate and slid his fingers around the stock.

Chile crow-hopped as a form emerged from the dark trees. The movement caught Hearne off guard, and he scrambled in the saddle for balance, but a light from a flashlight blinded him. There was a metallic click, and he never heard the shot.

Monday, 4:08 A.M.

As THE CLOUDS parted to reveal a cream wash of hard, white stars, Newkirk felt a hangover of epic proportions forming in the back of his brain. His mouth was dry and tasted of whiskey and Gonzalez's thumb, and his eyes burned for sleep. He looked at his wristwatch. Gonzalez had been gone for hours.

Newkirk and Singer were in the white Escalade, backed up into a stand of trees, pointed at the locked gate to the Rawlins Ranch. Their lights were off and the windows open, and they were far enough off the highway that they wouldn't be seen by anyone on the road. Before leaving to scout the ranch house below, Gonzalez had parked his vehicle beside them. Swann was in Gonzalez's pickup, slumped against the door. His sudden appearance at his home had surprised them all. Swann smelled of antiseptic, blood, and panic. Cuts on his face were stitched closed, and dark bruises were forming under his eyes. Newkirk thought Swann should have stayed in the hospital because the sight of him was sickening. But Singer welcomed the display of loyalty and had clapped Swann on the back. Now, though, Swann was sleeping and, Newkirk thought, useless.

Before joining Singer in his Escalade, Newkirk had parked the UPS truck deep into the trees down a logging road ten minutes from the ranch gate.

Gonzalez had taken the handheld radio and his scoped .308 Winchester rifle. Above them, resting on pine branches and swinging in the slight northern breeze, were the power and telephone lines Gonzalez had cut away from the utility pole hours earlier. Both Singer and Newkirk thought they had heard a muffled gunshot in the distance, and had waited for a second shot to confirm it that never came. Singer had tried to raise Gonzalez on his handheld, but there was no response. Singer assumed Gonzo had squelched the receiver, and they had no choice but to simply sit and wait.

Newkirk shifted in the seat and moaned involuntarily, his head pounding like the drumbeat of a marching band. Singer looked over at him, and he saw a slight curl of disdain on the lieutenant's lips, knew the man despised weakness.

"You gonna make it?" Singer asked.

"I'm fine."

"You need to hang in there. Drink some water."

"Water'd be good," Newkirk said, reaching for a canteen. He fought a crazy urge to confess he'd not killed Villatoro, that he'd let the rancher take him. Just to see the rage and confusion on Singer's sanctimonious face. But he stanched it, like he did his thirst.

Singer had a police scanner and radio mounted under his dashboard. It had been silent for most of the night. There was nothing going on in town other than town cops calling in the ends of their shifts, and a license check of an abandoned car left in a bar parking lot. Singer told Newkirk he had been concerned the sheriff would call his men together to form a team for an early-morning meeting, but it hadn't happened. Apparently, Carey was simply going to wait for the Feds to arrive, brief them on the situation concerning Monica Taylor and the missing children, and turn the whole case over to them. That Singer had been able to persuade the sheriff to put that off this long was a major victory for them.

On the bench seat between Singer and Newkirk was a detailed topo map of the area that included the Rawlins Ranch. On the map was a handheld, the volume down and the squelch minimized. Gonzalez had its twin out there somewhere in the dark. Singer's cell phone was on but silent next to the handheld.

Newkirk couldn't figure out what Singer was thinking. The plan the lieutenant had come up with had been simple: cut the power and phone, set up at the gate, wait for Rawlins to come to them. When the rancher got out of his truck to unlock the chain, they would cut him down in a cross fire. Then, using the rancher's rifle, they'd take care of the Taylors, implicating Rawlins. Newkirk would get the UPS truck and drive it down and hide it in the rancher's barn. That way, there would be a link between Boyd and the rancher—two secret pedophiles, one who kidnapped and delivered the children and the other who abused and murdered them. Just like Fiona Pritzle's theory, only a little more lurid. Then call it all in to the sheriff after it was over; say, "It happened so fast, we had no choice but to return fire."

But the rancher never came. And Newkirk knew that the rancher had Villatoro, so that might complicate things. But Singer didn't know that.

Newkirk noticed Singer looking at his own wristwatch with more frequency as the night went on. If the lieutenant was worried, he didn't show it. But he never showed anything.

When the handheld chirped, Newkirk jumped, causing the pounding to resume in his head.

Singer snatched the receiver, whispered, "Gonzo? Is that you?"

A beat. "It's me. I'm approaching the gate. Don't let Newkirk shoot me."

A moment later, Newkirk saw a dark form emerge from the shadows of the heavy timber, a glint of a rifle barrel in the starlight as Gonzalez climbed through the barbed wire of the fence. Then the sergeant was at the driver's side window, next to Singer.

Gonzalez said, "I walked the fence line and ran into your banker. Who the hell knows why he was out there, he surprised the shit out of me. I thought it was that cowboy trying to get away on his own on horseback. He won't be a problem for us no more."

"Jesus," Newkirk said.

Gonzo's teeth reflected blue as he smiled. "One shot and he went down. The horse ran off. I guess you didn't hear the shot, eh?"

"We heard it," Singer said, distracted. Then: "I didn't expect that. I didn't think Hearne would be around. How did *that* happen?"

Gonzalez shrugged. "Who knows? There's always something."

Newkirk thought, *There's more . . .*

"I went down the road until I could see the house," Gonzo said softly. "I thought I saw a light once through a window, but when I looked through the scope I couldn't see anything. The house is dark, and nobody's moving that I could see."

"Is the rancher's pickup there at the house?"

Gonzo nodded. "It's parked in front. He's there, all right. Another car is there, too. I'd guess it was the banker's."

"Maybe they're sleeping," Newkirk said, his voice a croak. "Maybe they don't even know they don't have power. Maybe the Taylors aren't even there."

Singer and Gonzalez both looked at him, said nothing, dismissing him. Newkirk closed his eyes, tried to shut out the hurt of humiliation, tone down the pounding in his head.

"Could you see another way out, besides this road?" Singer said. "The map shows a road out to the south, but it's a hell of a long way to get to the highway."

Gonzalez shook his head. "You mean if they walked out? Or took another vehicle? I don't think so. There's a big meadow in back of the house, and I could see it pretty good through the scope. I couldn't see anybody on foot, and I didn't hear any motors."

Singer processed the information, rubbed his nose with his index finger while he did so.

The radio came to life. "This is USGID-4 in Boise for Sheriff Ed Carey. Come in, Sheriff Carey."

"The chopper pilot," Singer said, looking at the radio.

"This is Sheriff Carey." He sounded wide-awake, Newkirk thought.

"The chopper's fueled and ready, and we've got clearance," the pilot said. "We've got just about everybody on board."

"Well," Carey said, "come on up. I'll start a pot of coffee. When do you think you'll be here?"

The pilot said, "ETA is 0600."

"About an hour then," Carey said.

"Roger that."

"An hour," Singer repeated.

"I wonder if Carey told him about this place?" Gonzo asked.

Singer shrugged. "I doubt it. That would make too much sense."

"What if they come over the top of us on the way to town? I think we'd be right on their flight path," Gonzo said. "Or fly straight here? Shit."

Singer rubbed his nose again. "We can use this to our advantage," he said.

Newkirk wondered how.

Snatching the mike from the cradle, Singer keyed it and spoke, "Sheriff, this is Singer. Do you read me?"

"Yes, Lieutenant," Carey answered. "I didn't realize you were on the frequency."

Newkirk listened for skepticism or anger in Carey's tone. He heard neither, only a profound bone-weariness.

"Yes, Sheriff," Singer said. "I've been monitoring communications. Right now, our position is directly across from the Rawlins Ranch. We think he has them in his house."

Silence. Newkirk could imagine Carey, suddenly confused, wondering what to do next.

"Sheriff, we've cut off the power and communications to the subject's home. We're waiting for him to come out."

"For God's sake, Lieutenant," Carey sputtered, "who authorized you to do that? Who do you have there with you?"

Newkirk saw the faint smile form on Singer's lips. "Sergeant Gonzalez and Officer Newkirk are with me. Officer Swann is here, too. He checked himself out of the hospital so he could be of service. As for authorization, no one, sir. We took it upon ourselves as deputized officers. We want to make sure the subject doesn't escape before you and the FBI arrive."

"What if he's listening to us now?" Carey said.

"I repeat, all power and communications have been cut off. There's no way he can hear us, Sheriff."

"Oh, yes, you said that. I don't know, Lieutenant . . ."

"Would you like us to withdraw, sir?" Singer asked reasonably. "We can do so, but we risk the possibility of the subject escaping, or further hurting those kids and the mother. But we'll withdraw if you give us the command, sir."

Newkirk found himself marveling at Singer's ability to turn Carey any way he wanted. The sheriff couldn't risk making another mistake.

"I'm just not comfortable with you up there," Carey said, his voice hesitant. "We don't know if we've got the right guy."

"Again, sir," Singer said, "we will withdraw upon your command."

"You shouldn't have gone up there in the first place without talking with me."

"I'm aware of that, sir. It was a decision we made after we saw Mr. Swann in the hospital, beaten within an inch of his life by the subject."

Gonzalez turned away from Singer's window, and Newkirk could hear him snort with laughter.

The radio remained silent for a few moments. Then: "Okay, Lieutenant. But stay put. Do not engage the subject in any way until we get there. I repeat, do not engage the subject."

Singer looked up, made an exaggerated face of disappointment. "Roger that, Sheriff. We will remain in place without engagement unless the subject confronts us."

"Hey, I didn't say anything about . . ."

"Roger that, Sheriff," Singer said, talking over him, then hanging up the mike and reducing the volume to zero.

"Okay," Singer said, looking at his watch. "We've got about an hour before dawn."

Singer looked up. "Gonzo, you ready?"

Gonzalez nodded. Newkirk could see starlight reflect from his teeth. "Newkirk?"

"Sure, Lieutenant."

"We've been given our hunting license," Singer said. "Let's go finish this. Gonzo, do you have the bolt cutters in your truck?"

Monday, 4:55 A.M.

JESS NOW LAY on top of the rock ridge he had explored as a child, amid the slate, the dampness of the grass long since soaked into his jeans and ranch coat. His scoped .270 hunting rifle was next to him, as was the Winchester .25-35 saddle carbine and a box of bullets. He watched the sky lighten, felt the dawn breeze start to move along the ground with an icy pulse. He thought about how Monica and Hearne had been connected all of these years. How he'd hoped, as Monica told him the story, that it had been J.J. He was surprised how he'd unburdened himself to her in the barn like that. How his words had tumbled out as if he'd rehearsed them. Of course he'd said too much. But by saying what he had he felt somehow cleaner now, pleased he had a mission. It felt good.

His heart hardened when he saw the riderless horse cantering across the meadow toward the barn. He could see the saddle had slipped upside down, and could see the stirrups flapping as the horse ran. He knew how unlikely it was that Jim Hearne, ex–rodeo cowboy, had been bucked off.

Jess knew what it meant. He thought about Annie, and Monica. Jim Hearne had been a good man.

But now, they were on their own.

———

A BRANCH snapped up in the timber, in the direction of the road. Shortly after, a rock was dislodged, and he heard it tumble down the hill until it stopped with a *pock* sound against a tree trunk. He didn't see anyone in the darkness of the timber, but he knew someone was up there, scouting.

Now there was a ping of metal, faint but distinct. And familiar. It was the sound of a link of chain being cut.

A moment later came the throaty sound of engines starting. Jess shifted where he lay and studied the timber where the road was. No headlights winked through the trees. Either the vehicles hadn't begun to come down the road, or they were rolling with their headlights off. He guessed the latter.

He looked quickly toward his house. It was dark and still. He wondered if Monica and Villatoro could hear the vehicles idling.

There was no way to stop it now.

Monday, 5:10 A.M.

NEWKIRK NERVOUSLY rubbed his thumb along the wooden hand-grip of the shotgun on the seat next to him. It was still too dark to make out the two-track road, and the trees on each side of him were so dark and tall that it felt like he was moving through a tunnel. They were creeping down the hill, the Escalade in four-wheel-drive low so the lieutenant wouldn't have to apply the brakes and flash brake lights. How could Singer even see where he was going?

The AR-15, a fully automatic rifle with a banana clip, was on the seat as well, next to Singer.

A pine branch scraped the side of the Escalade and showered needles through the open passenger window. Newkirk brushed them from his lap, and Singer corrected the wheel to the left.

Then, almost imperceptibly, Newkirk could tell they'd cleared the trees. The terrain opened up in front of them, lightened, but it was still too dark to see clearly. The sky to the east was gunmetal gray, though, as dawn approached.

Singer brought the vehicle to a gentle stop, having to tap the brakes.

Newkirk looked back, hoping Gonzalez had seen the flash of light and wouldn't drive right into them.

"We'll wait here until we can see better," Singer whispered, almost imperceptibly.

JESS WATCHED the two vehicles emerge from the timber and stop, saw a blink of a brake light. Even though they were there, as he expected they would be, a part of him couldn't believe it was actually happening.

Nosing the .270 over a piece of slate, he looked at the trucks through his rifle scope, thankful that it gathered more light than his naked eye. The white of the first vehicle was more pronounced against the dark, but he still couldn't see inside. Minutes went by before he thought he could make out two forms in the front of the white car, and another two in the pickup behind it.

The crosshairs rested on the driver's side window of the white SUV. It was too far for an accurate shot. Nevertheless, he worked the bolt of the rifle and chambered a round. The sound of the bolt action in the still morning jarred him, but he didn't think it could be heard by the men in the trucks.

NEWKIRK CHECKED the time obsessively. He felt cold all over, and his nose ran freely. The ranch house, the barn, the other outbuildings began to take shape at the bottom of the hill. To their left was a grassy ridge with broken rocks on top. On their right was a gentle saddle slope with black fingers of pine reaching down the hill.

He looked over at Singer, who sat still, his eyes surveying the valley below. The man was so cool, Newkirk thought. Newkirk wished it would rub off.

A shiver started in his chest, ran up his neck, made his teeth chatter. He clamped his mouth shut, waiting for the shiver to run out. It had nothing to do with the cold.

JESS BREATHED in a long, quivering breath. The crosshairs trembled on the driver's side window. He realized he had been holding his position too long, that his legs and arms were cramping up, causing him to shake. He tried to relax, tried to breathe normally to steady himself, flatten out his aim.

When had he last sighted in the rifle? He couldn't remember. Jesus. It might be completely off.

Again, he glanced down at his house. No movement, no light. Good.

In the barn, the calf he had delivered the night before bawled for its mother.

Then the vehicles were moving forward, down the switchback. The white SUV was picking up speed, the men inside not nearly so worried about stealth now. The black pickup, the same vehicle Jess had seen the day before in front of his house, was right behind it.

There was a curve in the road about 250 yards away from Jess, where the intruders would need to slow down to make the turn safely. It would be close enough for a decent shot, but not a sure shot. Jess pulled the stock tight to his shoulder, eased his eye to the scope, saw the crosshairs bounce around on the side of Singer's face. He pulled the trigger and nothing happened.

"Shit!" he said, remembering to thumb the safety off. But by the time he did and sighted through the scope again, the trucks had turned away from the curve and were barreling down the road away from him. He couldn't believe he'd made such an amateur mistake in such a critical circumstance, and was furious with himself.

NEWKIRK REACHED up through the open window and clamped onto the roof with his hand to steady himself as Singer upshifted and the engine roared and they reached the bottom of the hill where the road straightened out. He saw the ranch house fill the windshield and Singer drove toward it. Gonzalez and Swann shot past them in the pickup on Newkirk's side.

Both vehicles slid to a stop in the gravel, facing the front door of the house.

Training took over now, and Newkirk bailed out of the Escalade, keeping the open passenger door between him and the structure, aiming his shotgun at the front door of the house over the lip of the open window. In his peripheral vision, he saw Singer do the same after snapping back the bolt to arm the AR-15.

Gonzalez was out of his pickup, racking a shell into the chamber of his shotgun, the sound as sharp and dangerous as anything Newkirk had ever heard. Swann had stayed inside.

While Newkirk and Singer covered him, Gonzalez jogged across the lawn, up the porch steps, and flattened himself against the wall of the house next to the door. Newkirk shot a glance at the picture window. The curtains were pulled closed except for a narrow space between them. Another window on the far side of the house was covered inside with tightly drawn blinds. There was no movement behind either of the windows.

Gonzalez held his shotgun at port arms, then spun and used the butt of it to pound the front door.

"Jess Rawlins! This is the sheriff's department. Come out of the house right now!"

The sound of the pounding and Gonzalez's deep voice cut through the silence of the morning.

Newkirk racked the pump on his own shotgun, aimed again at the front door. Waited.

Gonzalez shot a glance to Singer, asking with his eyes, What now?

Singer nodded: *Do it again.*

This time, Gonzalez pounded the door so hard with the shotgun, Newkirk expected the glass to fall out of the panes of the window. He saw Swann open the truck door and slide out, stand unsteadily on the lawn with a pistol in his hand.

"Jess Rawlins! We need you to come out right now! RIGHT FUCKING NOW!"

Nothing. The pounding echoed back from the wall of timber to the north.

"Jesus Christ," Gonzalez said, looking again at Singer. Swann limped across the lawn, climbed the steps to the porch, and struggled toward the corner of the house.

Newkirk thinking, *They're not there. No one's inside. The chopper's on the way. We're fucked, but thank God it's over. Thank God for that. But no . . .*

Gonzalez stepped away from the front of the house, and for a second Newkirk expected the sergeant to try to kick the door down. But he must have decided against it, because he turned and took a step toward the picture window.

Newkirk watched as Gonzalez leaned over, trying to see through the slit in the curtains.

JESS WATCHED it all through the scope on his rifle, the safety off this time for sure. He had not taken a breath since Gonzalez had pounded on the door the second time and the sound washed up and over him.

Gonzalez was in front of the window, leading with his head, trying to see in. Jess was surprised to see that Swann was with them. His head was bandaged, and he appeared to be wearing a hospital smock.

Jess whispered, "Now."

INSIDE THE front room, Eduardo Villatoro sighted down the barrel of the shotgun at the shadow on the other side of the curtain, put the front bead on the bridge of Gonzalez's nose through the glass, and fired.

NEWKIRK HEARD the boom, saw Gonzalez's head snap back and come apart at the same time, shards of glass cascading through the air, the shotgun clattering on the porch. The sergeant took two steps straight back away from the house and hit the railing and crashed through it. He fell in the grass with his arms outstretched over his head, his boots still up on the porch, shards of glass dropping from the window in a delayed reaction.

Swann cried out and flung himself against the outside of the house, near the door but away from the window. He held his pistol with both hands, the muzzle pointed down, ready to react.

"Goddammit!" Singer said, standing, raising the AR-15, and the morning was filled with a long, furious ripping sound as he raked the house on both sides of the window from right to left, then back again.

ANNIE HAD peered out from behind the cast-iron stove, where she and William had hidden, in time to see Villatoro raise the shotgun and fire. Her mother pulled her back down. After the blast, which was much louder than anything Annie had anticipated, her mother gathered her and William closer as bullets ripped through the walls, a few clanging off the stove behind which they hid.

PLACING THE crosshairs between Singer's shoulder blades, Jess squeezed the trigger. The rifle bucked, the scope jerked upward, over the top of the roof of his house. He quickly worked the bolt and peered back down the scope, saw Singer arching as if stretching his back, slowly turning around to face him, holding his weapon out away from his body.

Did I miss? No—Jess could see a bloom of dark red blood on Singer's coat and a spray of it across the hood of the white SUV.

Jess quickly found Newkirk in the scope. The man was crouched, looking up, searching the ridge for the source of the shot. Newkirk looked confused, and very human. Jess shot him, saw Newkirk fall back into the door of the car, then roll away, under the car, out of sight.

When Jess swung the rifle back to Singer, Singer was gone, probably hiding under the SUV.

And where was Swann? Jess couldn't see him on the porch.

NEWKIRK FELT as though someone had kicked him in the stomach so hard it took his breath away. He rolled under the car until his shoulder thumped the front differential, where he stopped.

The engine radiated heat above him, the grass was icy and wet beneath him. Slowly, the kicked feeling receded, and something burned. He imagined a red-hot poker pressed against his bare stomach. He knew what it was. He'd been shot. He always wondered what it would feel like to be gutshot, to have a bullet rip through his soft organs, opening up their fluid contents to mix together inside of him.

From where he was stuck under the car, he rolled his head back, looked around.

Gonzalez's body was in the grass ten feet away. Steam rose from the mass of pulp that used to be his face. He could still make out half of Gonzo's mustache, though. The other half was somewhere else.

He flopped his head the other way. Singer had pulled himself up again. His boots were there, near the front of the car.

"Newkirk, goddammit," Singer was saying, his voice filling with liquid, "I'm hit. Where are you? I need cover fire."

Newkirk kept his mouth shut, for once. He wondered where his shotgun was. Instead, he drew his service weapon, racked the slide, held it tight to him.

He was in the third person again, where he longed to be, hovering over the body of the man wedged beneath the car, watching, shaking his head with disappointment, relieved that it was all happening to somebody else.

Monday, Newkirk thought. It was Monday morning. The boys and Lindsey should be getting ready to go to school. Wouldn't they be ashamed to know where their father was right now?

The car rocked, and another shot boomed down from the ridge. Then another. This time he heard breaking glass, and it cascaded down around him in the grass.

A long rip from Singer's AR-15 made his ears ring.

Where had Swann disappeared to?

JESS HAD SWITCHED to the .25-35 when he was out of cartridges with the .270. As he levered in the first shell, there was an angry burst as bullets hit and ricocheted off the plates of slate and cut branches from trees in back of him. Something stung his face, and he reached up, saw the blood on his fingers. He rolled to his side, then pushed the barrel of the saddle carbine through a V in the rock.

Without the scope, he could barely see Singer's coat through the broken windows of the SUV, but he could see it, and he fired.

Jess thought, *I'm shooting men, but it doesn't feel like it.* He'd never had a wide-open shot in Southeast Asia, not like this. He could not think of the men down there as human beings but as enemy targets. Targets who would do harm to the children, Monica, him, his ranch . . .

ANNIE HEARD the back door smash in but didn't see Swann until he jerked her out from behind the stove by her hair. She screamed and struggled, kicking at the floor, heard William burst into tears, and shout "NO!," saw her mother wheel and both of her hands go up, pleading.

Villatoro had been crouching behind a desk, but he rose when he heard the scream.

"Drop that shotgun or everybody dies," Swann said to Villatoro.

Villatoro hesitated but dropped the shotgun on the floor.

Swann said, "You were supposed to be dead. That fucking Newkirk . . ." He shot Villatoro twice—*bangbang*—and the retired detective collapsed in a heap on the floor.

"Oscar, don't hurt her, don't hurt her," her mother pleaded. "Take me if you need to take someone. Don't hurt Annie anymore."

Swann turned his attention to Monica and didn't respond so much as growl, and he lifted Annie to her feet by her hair and pressed the muzzle of the hot pistol into her neck.

"Oscar, please . . ." her mother cried.

"Shut up," Swann said. "I've got to use her to get out of here, to get that rancher."

Monica glanced at the shotgun Villatoro had dropped on the floor, and Annie felt Swann tighten his grip on her and saw the pistol rise over her shoulder and aim at her mother. Villatoro was still.

Swann said, "Back off now into that room back there and take your boy. I'm going to lock you in because I may need you for later. But if you try and get out, she dies, you all die."

NEWKIRK HEARD another bullet hit Singer, a punching sound, heard it go *thump* like when a baseball hits a batter. Saw Singer suddenly drop back into view, on the ground with him again, Singer squirming like he was trying to get ants out of his clothes. Inside the house there had been two quick gunshots. Newkirk thought, *Hell has broken loose.*

Newkirk and Singer were eye to eye. Singer's coat was drenched with red. Newkirk could smell it, hot and metallic. Bright red blood foamed from Singer's mouth and nostrils as he tried to breathe, but his eyes were blue and sharp, fixed on Newkirk.

"You hid," Singer said, spitting blood as he talked. "You fucking hid. . . ."

"It never should have gone this far," Newkirk said.

"We deserved it, we *earned* it!" Singer said in a rage. He sounded like he was drowning inside, and he probably was, Newkirk thought.

Singer's lungs were filling up with his own blood. Bad way to go, but he wished he'd quit talking and twitching.

"It wasn't worth it," Newkirk said. He raised his weapon and shot Singer in the forehead.

Singer stopped squirming.

"There," Newkirk said. "Enough."

Then he heard the sound of a car coming down the road, and the faraway beating of a helicopter.

But behind him, the front door to the ranch house burst open, and there stood Swann, holding the little girl with his gun to her head, his mutilated face twisted in agony and fear.

"HEY, RANCHER!" Swann yelled toward the ridge, his voice cutting through the sudden morning stillness. "I've got the little girl here. I want you to stand up and throw down your weapon. We can work this out so nobody else gets hurt." As he yelled, Annie could feel his arm tighten around her neck and the muzzle of the pistol press hard through her hair, biting into her temple.

Annie thought, *If Jess goes for it, he's a dead man. He should stay put. Look what happened to Mr. Villatoro when he listened to Swann.* She hoped William wouldn't try something stupid to save her and get himself hurt.

"You need to answer me!" Swann shouted, his voice cracking, revealing his fear. Annie craned her neck to see that the shouting had stretched Swann's face, popped several of his stitches. Blood streamed down his face and dripped from his chin onto the top of his collar. It was soaking through his shirt onto her neck. It felt hot, like oil dripping from beneath a car. *Be tough,* she thought. *Show grit. No crying.* She was more angry than scared, and if he loosened his grip, she would fight her way free like a wildcat.

She felt Swann take a sudden gasping breath of alarm. She turned back around and couldn't believe what she saw.

Jess Rawlins was running down the hill toward them, still holding his rifle, the barrel flashing in the morning sun.

"What are you doing, old man?" Swann yelled out. "You need to stop right now and drop the weapon. STOP!"

Swann jerked the pistol from her head, pointed it unsteadily out in front of them at Jess, and fired off three quick shots. She flinched with every explosion. Jess Rawlins jerked and stumbled, but didn't stop coming.

The old rancher was close enough now that Annie could hear the sound of his boots crunching in the gravel.

Swann suddenly threw her aside like a doll so he could set his feet and grip his pistol to aim with two hands. He fired again, four shots in quick succession. At least two she could tell were hits. There were blotches of blood on the front of Jess's jacket, but the man's face and his look of pure determination hadn't changed a bit.

When the rancher finally stopped it was to raise his rifle from twenty yards away, aim calmly, and shoot Oscar Swann squarely between the eyes. Swann dropped straight back into the doorway, his pistol thumping on the porch. Annie rolled away, unhurt.

MONICA ROLLED the dresser drawer as hard as she could into the locked door of the bedroom, and it swung open, the lock broken. She stepped over Villatoro's body and grabbed William's hand, pulling him through the living room behind her. She saw Swann's trunk in the doorway. He was flat on his back, blood pouring from his ears, pooling on the floorboards. Annie was scrambling to her feet and running off the porch, toward someone out in the yard.

Monica heard it. The sound of a helicopter approaching, blades thumping bass.

She stepped over Swann's body and saw everything at once. Singer, dead on the grass in front of his car. Gonzalez, splayed out and steaming, his face and most of his head gone.

The helicopter sliding over the southern hill, flying so low it was kicking up dirt and branches, coming straight toward the house. The sheriff's SUV, siren suddenly whooping, speeding down the two-track toward the ranch, followed by two other departmental vehicles and an ambulance.

Jess slumped in the yard, sitting down, his rifle cast aside, his bare head bowed as if he were sleeping, his hat off, upturned in the grass next to his legs. Annie running toward him, her arms outstretched.

———

THE LAST THING Newkirk saw before he turned the pistol on himself was Monica Taylor and her two kids down on the ground with the rancher, hugging him, wailing, keeping him still in the grass as the sheriff bore down on them.

may

I have no hesitation in saying that although the American woman never leaves her domestic sphere and is in some respects very dependent within it, nowhere does she enjoy a higher station. And if anyone asks me what I think the chief cause of the extraordinary prosperity and growing power of this nation, I should answer that it is due to the superiority of their women.
—*Alexis de Tocqueville*

JESS RAWLINS ALMOST DIED three times in the helicopter before he finally stabilized, although there were periods when he wasn't sure just which side of that line he was on. That was a month ago.

Now, he seemed to be emerging from his trauma, if only for a while. There were things he just knew had happened, without recalling the details. The ride in a helicopter, EMTs in flight suits prying his eyes open, asking him questions, talking about him as if he weren't there. Villatoro lying next to him on one side, Hearne on the other. Both either asleep or gone. *My team,* Jess had thought. Jess's world going black and wonderfully white twice while in the air, once while landing. The white was ethereal, welcoming. But turning back each time, thanks to the electric shocks that restarted his heart. Then surgery, doctors, bright lights, more surgery, the prick of needles on the undersides of his forearms, the sharp smells of antiseptic and his own blood, the tinny sound of bullets that had been removed from his body being dropped into metal trays.

In the midst of the surgeries, there had been a long parade of faces, voices, one after the other, some he knew, some he didn't, some he wished he didn't. He would try to sit up to meet and greet the people who were there to see him, but his legs wouldn't cooperate. He would be able to speak, smile, talk things out sometimes. Not always, but sometimes. There were instances when he could see them and hear them clearly, and his mind was active, but he couldn't will his lips to move. He hated that.

But there were things he could recall clearly.

Monica, wearing many different outfits, even changing her hair, telling him to get well, pull through, she needed him to live, it was important.

Sheriff Carey, hat in hand, talking to his own boots, apologizing as much to himself as to Jess, Buddy with him, looking from Carey to Jess. Carey saying, "They're mounting a recall petition to get rid of me. The whole damned valley. I'll resign before they throw me out, though." Buddy saying, "Our old sheriff says he wants the job back."

Karen and Brian, Karen shaking her head as if she just *knew* this kind of thing would happen, Brian consoling her for her loss, putting his arm around her, gently trying to steer her out of the room before she broke down. Karen saying she didn't know how she would deal with it if Jess died now that he was such a hero, wondering out loud why he'd never shown this kind of heroism with her before, saying this was so . . . unsatisfying.

J.J., escorted by Buddy, breaking Jess's heart when he reached out and touched his hand through the sheets before recoiling, Jess knowing how hard it was for his son to do that, thinking at the time it was best J.J. not even know about Monica and Hearne, the best thing for everybody concerned. J.J. making Jess's heart soar when he said he was feeling better, that he'd like to try to come back to the ranch and reenter the world to see how it worked out, that he missed the place and his father more than he realized.

Doctors showing other doctors where the five bullets had hit, reenacting the trajectory of the one that had really done the damage when it broke his collarbone and angled down, nicked a lung, exited through his spine. The others, two in the thigh, one of which turned out to be the real bleeder, one in his neck that passed straight through, and a really painful one in his butt, kind of embarrassing, mostly. That one ached the most. Then it didn't.

Three surprising visits, although they didn't seem surprising at all at the time.

Fiona Pritzle, darkening the doorway, flowers in her hand, saying, "How are you doing, my big guy?" Jess, coming out of himself, hurling a bedside water bottle at her, missing and hitting the top of the doorjamb, the water spraying everywhere. Fiona scuttling away, the nurses rushing in to calm him, get him settled back in the bed, reinserting the tubes in his arm.

Jim Hearne, in jeans and cowboy boots instead of his banker's suit, apologizing to Jess for not making it into town. Saying, "It wasn't the first time I didn't finish a ride, I guess."

"I'm proud of you," Jess said. "You tried."

"Didn't try hard enough," Hearne said sheepishly. "There's nothing I wanted more than to be the hero."

"You're a hero," Jess said.

"No," he said, looking away, moisture in his eyes. "I betrayed Laura. I wish I could tell Laura one more time that I love her."

It took him a few moments to collect himself, then, "I betrayed people who looked up to me, and I betrayed myself. And in the end, I didn't come through for Annie and Monica. I wish I could talk to them, clear the air."

"That's not necessary," Jess said. "They know you did your best. That's what they'll remember. You gave your life for them."

"Doesn't seem like enough," Hearne said.

"What more is there?" Jess asked.

Jim Newkirk came into his room after dark, wearing a ball cap. He looked fine, the picture of health. Newkirk stood at the foot of the bed and wouldn't meet Jess's eyes.

"I thought you were dead," Jess had said.

Newkirk looked out the window. "I am. I just wanted to see how you were doing."

"Not very damned good."

"Better than me."

Jess said, "Life's messy, isn't it?"

Newkirk had haunted eyes. "It's hard, all right. But maybe a man can live with himself if he makes the right decisions. If he does what he knows is right. Things may not work out, but at least he can live with himself."

Jess fell asleep and never saw Newkirk again. But he had a feeling he'd see Hearne.

EDUARDO VILLATORO, on crutches, wearing his brown suit. Introducing Jess to his wife, Donna, and his mother. They had flown up from Southern California, Villatoro said, and had stayed with him at the motel but were now at Julie Rodale's house, keeping Julie company.

"Julie has convinced Donna to consider moving here," Villatoro said, raising his eyebrows in disbelief. "We might even do it. I should enjoy my retirement, don't you think? Maybe I'll buy a horse."

"Great," Jess said, smiling. "Another ex-cop moving here."

After Donna and his mother left, Villatoro told Jess the wrongfully convicted Santa Anita employees were being released from prison. He also said the FBI had figured out everything, even how the ex-cops used pigs to dispose of the bodies—Anthony Rodale, Tom Boyd—and analysis of the pig manure confirmed it all. Thanking Jess again for saving him from that. Saying oddly, Jess thought, that he admired how Jess could look at a mountain and know the story about it.

Laura Hearne, Jim's wife, came to see Jess and brought the RAWLINS file with her. She said she knew the situation with Jess's ranch had troubled Jim greatly, and felt she owed it to the memory of her husband to finish the job he'd started. She'd done some research, she said. Her idea was to donate the ranch to the State of Idaho on the condition it be kept intact.

"Poor Jim," Jess said. "I miss him."

Tears flooded her eyes, but she didn't cry. She was a tough old girl. Country people were more used to the cycle of life and death; they experienced it every day.

"I miss him, too," she said, looking up at Jess. "I always knew about Monica, even though he never told me. He didn't have to. I forgave him years ago, but I never told him that. I wish now I had told him."

Jess nodded, thinking Hearne would have liked to have known that and hoped he knew it now.

Jess told her to forget about the donation. He had a better idea. When he told her, she responded with a devilish look, said she'd help with the details because Jim would have wanted her to.

"I just wish he hadn't died feeling guilty," she said later. "That eats at me."

"He didn't, in the end," Jess assured her. "He was doing the right thing, and he was on a horse again. He loved you. He told me."

What Jess didn't say was *when* Hearne had told him.

This time, she cried.

JESS AWOKE, his head clearer than it had been since he'd arrived in the hospital, whenever that was. The pain was simply gone. Everything, gone. No feeling below his chest. He rolled his head over on the pillow. Sun streamed through the window and warmed his face. The room was filled with flowers, which was probably why, he thought, he kept dreaming he was in a garden.

Annie sat in a chair at the side of the bed.

"Shouldn't you be in school?" Jess asked.

Annie looked up. She seemed older, somehow. More serious.

"Is this really you?" she asked.

"Yup."

"It's hard to tell. Sometimes you're there, and sometimes you're not."

"I'm here," he said. "I think." He could feel the sun, and it felt real. The lack of pain was certainly real.

"We've been coming here every day for two weeks," Annie said. "My mom brings us after school."

"Two weeks? I had no idea," he said. "It's May, then."

"I guess so."

He tried to recall the days, the weeks. It was impossible to sort out. He knew what he knew: the faces, the visits, the explanations from people living and dead. Maybe, when he was strong again, he could sort it all out.

Annie glanced toward the door, then rose and leaned to Jess. "Mrs. Hearne told us what you did."

Jess worked his hand out from beneath the covers and reached out to her. He was shocked at how spindly his arm looked, how gnarled and old his fingers had become. Nevertheless, she took his hand in hers. She didn't seem to mind. Jess felt a twitch of a smile. "What does your mom think about that?"

"She can't believe it."

He snorted, anticipating pain. Astonished, he said, "It used to hurt to laugh. Now it doesn't."

"Why did you do it?" Annie asked, demanding an answer.

Jess said, "Because you're tough. You can handle it. You'll do well."

She nodded. No point in arguing that.

Jess said, "You agree with me, then."

"Annie." It was Monica, entering the room, her face flushed. "Jess, I'm sorry," Monica said. "You know Annie." Monica glared at her daughter, who smiled back.

Jess looked up at her. It was good to see her again.

"She's a pistol," Jess said, his voice thick.

"Jess, we need to talk about what you're doing. Laura Hearne talked with us and explained how it all works. She's been an angel, considering the circumstances. She says she'll help us every way she can, just like Jim would have done. She's a remarkable woman."

"I agree," Jess said.

"But I still don't understand why."

Jess nodded. "Annie knows," he said, looking at Annie, who nodded, as if they were sharing a secret.

"You might want to rethink this when you're well," Monica said. "You're pretty busted up."

Not just that, Jess wanted to say. He lowered his eyes, looked at the contours of his body under the blanket, the way the sheets draped away from his knees and trunk. He wanted to see a fitter version of himself, but it was not to be.

Annie was still squeezing his hand. "Like Laura told you, Annie, I don't care what you do with it as long as you benefit from it. You can sell it to developers, or divide it up, whatever you want to do. Jim had some good ideas on how to keep most of it intact. He was a smart man, and Laura is just as smart. You and your mom should listen to what she has to say."

Annie flushed and rolled her eyes, saying, "Jeez."

Monica moved further into the room and put her hands on Annie's shoulders. "This is a lot for Annie to understand right now. I can't believe it myself. You'll likely want to change your mind when you get better," she said, chuckling softly.

Jess reached up and brushed a strand of hair out of Annie's face. She had tears in her eyes. She knew.

He felt suddenly exhausted and happy, as if he'd just had a huge meal in the middle of the day. He felt sleep reaching up and pulling him back to somewhere dark, shadowed, and peaceful, and when he opened his eyes, it was light again, and he was riding Chile, his legs firm and strong, the sun high, the sky cloudless, and the air smelled of pine and cattle.

Three Weeks to Say Goodbye

To Marc and Jenny
. . . and Laurie, always

Acknowledgments

The author would like to thank those who provided background, suggestions, careful reading, and inspiration for this novel, including Allison Herron Lee, Ann Rittenberg, Laurie Box, Molly Box, Becky Box, and the wonderful team at St. Martin's Minotaur—Matthew Baldacci, Andrew Martin, Hector Dejean, and, especially, the peerless Jennifer Enderlin.

The bloodthirsty hate the upright,
and they seek the life of the righteous.
An unjust man is an abomination to the just,
and he who is upright
is an abomination to the wicked.

—Proverbs 29:10, 27

Denver

One

It was Saturday morning, November 3, and the first thing I noticed when I entered my office was that my telephone message light was blinking. Since I'd left the building late the night before, it meant someone had called my extension during the night. Odd.

My name is Jack McGuane. I was thirty-four years old at the time. Melissa, my wife, was the same age. I assume you've heard my name, or seen my image on the news, although with everything going on in the world I can understand if you missed me the first time. Our story, in the big scheme of things, is a drop in the river.

I was a Travel Development Specialist for the Denver Metro Convention and Visitors Bureau, the city agency charged with bidding on and hosting conventions and encouraging tourism to Denver. Every city has one. I worked hard, often staying late and, if necessary, coming in on a Saturday. It's important to me that I work hard, even in a bureaucratic environment where it's not necessarily encouraged or rewarded. You see, I'm not the smartest guy in the world, or the best educated. My background doesn't suit me for the job. But my ace in the hole is that I work harder than anyone around me, even when I don't have to. I am the bane of an office filled with bureaucrats, and I'm proud of it. It's the only thing I've got.

Before doing anything, though, I punched the button to retrieve my voice mail.

"Jack, this is Julie Perala. At the agency . . ."

I stared at the speaker. Her voice was tight, cautious, not the confident and compassionate Julie Perala from the adoption agency Melissa and I had spent hours with while we went through the long process of adopting Angelina, our nine-month-old. My first thought was that we somehow owed them more money.

"Jack, I hate to call you at work on a Friday. I hope you get this and can call me back right away. I need to talk with you immediately—before Sunday, if possible."

She left the agency number and her cell-phone number, and I wrote them down.

Then: "Jack, I'm so sorry."

After a few beats of silence, as if she wanted to say more but wouldn't or couldn't, she hung up.

I sat back in my chair, then listened to the message again and checked the time stamp. It had arrived at 8:45 Friday evening.

I tried the agency number first, not surprised that it went straight to voice mail. Then I called her cell.

"Yes?"

"Julie, this is Jack McGuane."

"Oh."

"You said to call immediately. You've got me scared here with your message. What's going on?"

"You don't know?"

"How would I know? Know what?"

There was anger and panic in her voice.

"Martin Dearborn hasn't called you? He's your attorney, isn't he? Our lawyers were supposed to call him. Oh dear."

My heart sped up, and the receiver became slick in my hand. "Julie, I don't know *anything*. Dearborn never called. Please, what is this about?"

"God, I hate to be the one to tell you."

"Tell me what?"

A beat. "The biological father wants Angelina back."

I made her repeat it in case I hadn't heard correctly. She did.

"So what if he wants her back," I said. "We adopted her. She's our daughter now. Who cares what he wants?"

"You don't understand—it's complicated."

I pictured Melissa and Angelina at home having a lazy Saturday morning. "Of course we'll work this out," I said. "This is all some kind of big misunderstanding. It'll all be fine." Despite my words, my mouth tasted like metal.

Said Julie, "The birth father never signed away parental custody, Jack. The mother did, but the father didn't. It's a terrible situation. Your lawyer should have explained all of this to you. I don't want to be the one going over legalities because I'm not qualified. As I said, it's complicated . . ."

"This cannot be happening," I said.

"I'm so sorry."

"It doesn't make sense," I said. "She's been with us nine months. The birth mother *selected* us."

"I know. I was there."

"Tell me how to make this go away," I said, sitting up in my chair, leaning over the desk. "Do we pay off the kid, or what?"

Julie was silent for a long time.

"Julie, are you there?"

"I'm here."

"Meet me at your agency *now*."

"I can't."

"You can't or you won't?"

"I can't. I shouldn't even be talking with you. I should never have called. The lawyers and my executives said not to make direct contact, but I felt I had to."

"Why didn't you call us at home?"

"I got cold feet," she said. "You don't know how much I wished I could erase that message I left for you."

"I appreciate that," I said, "but you can't walk away. I need to understand what you're saying. You've got to work with me to make this kid go away. You owe us that."

I heard a series of staccato sounds and thought the connection was going bad. Then I realized she was crying.

Finally, she said, "There's a restaurant near here called Sunrise Sunset. On South Wadsworth. I can meet you there in an hour."

"I might be a little late. I've got to run home and get Melissa. She'll want to hear this. And on such short notice, we'll probably have Angelina with us."

"I was hoping . . ." Her voice trailed off.

"Hoping what? That I wouldn't bring them?"

"Yes. It makes it harder . . . I was hoping maybe you and I could meet alone."

I slammed the phone down. Stunned, I wrote down the address of the restaurant.

I SENSED LINDA VAN Gear's arrival before she leaned into my office. She had a presence that preceded her. It could also be called very strong perfume, which she seemed to push ahead in front of her, like a surging trio of small, leashed dogs. Linda was my boss.

She was an imposing, no-nonsense woman, a force of nature. Melissa once referred to Linda as "a caricature of a broad." Linda was brash, made-up, coiffed with a swept-back helmet of stiff hair like the overlapping armored plates of a prehistoric dinosaur. She looked like she wore suits with shoulder pads, but they were her shoulders. Her lips were red, red, red, and there was usually a lipstick line across the front of her teeth, which she moistened often with darts from a pointed tongue. Linda, like a lot of the people who worked international tourism marketing, had once had dreams of being an actress or at least some kind of indefinable celebrity, someone who judged amateurs on a reality singing show. Linda was not well liked by the women in our office or by many in the tourism industry, but I got along with her. I got a kick out of her because everything about her was out front in spades.

"Hello, darlin'," she said, sticking her head in the doorway, "I see you found the leads."

I hadn't even noticed them, but they were there: a bulging manila envelope filled with business cards that smelled of her perfume, cigarette smoke, and spilled wine.

"They're right here."

"Couple of hot ones in there," she said with mock enthusiasm. "They'll singe your fingers when you touch them. Let's meet on them in a half an hour." She squinted, looking me over, asked, "Are you okay?"

"No I'm not."

I didn't really want to get into details, but felt I needed to explain the situation to her in order to postpone the meeting.

She listened with glistening eyes. She loved this kind of thing, I realized. She loved *drama,* and I was providing it.

"Some boy wants custody of your baby?" she asked.

"Yes, but I'm going to fight it."

"The baby obsession skipped this broad," she said. "I guess I never really understood it." She shook her head. She had no children and had made it clear she never wanted any.

I nodded like I understood. Fragile ground, here.

She said, "Look, you know I'm leaving for Taiwan with the governor Monday. We've got to get together before then. Hell, I dragged my jet-lagged ass out of bed just to meet you here this morning. We *need* to meet."

"We will," I said. "Let me call you as soon as I talk to Julie Perala. That's all I ask."

"That's a lot," she said, clearly angry.

"I'll call," I said. "I'll even come meet you at your house if you want."

"Plan on it," she said, turning on her heel and clicking down the hallway, her shoes sounding like manic sticks on the rim of a drum in the empty hallway.

MELISSA WAS ON THE FLOOR with Angelina when I came in the door. Before I could speak, Melissa said, "What's wrong?"

"Julie Perala called. She says there's a problem with the adoption."

Melissa went white, and she looked from me to Angelina and back.

"She said the father wants her back."

"Back?" Melissa said, her voice rising in volume, "Back? *He's never even seen her!*"

I met Melissa when we were both students at Montana State University thirteen years before. She was a lean jade-eyed brunette—attractive, smart, athletic, earthy, self-confident—with high cheekbones and a full, expressive mouth that tended to betray whatever she was thinking. She *sparkled*. I was drawn to her immediately in a crazy, almost chemical way. I could sense when she entered a crowded room even before I could see her. She was taken at the time, though, involved in a long-term relationship with the star running back. They were a remarkably handsome couple, and I despised him for no reason other than she was his. Still, I pined for her. The thought of her kept me awake at night. When their breakup became news, I told my friend Cody, "I'm going to marry her." He said, "In your dreams," and I said, "Yes, in my dreams." He said, "You've got it bad," and urged me to forget about her and go out and get drunk and get laid. Instead, I asked her out and became Mr. Rebound. She thought I was solid and amusing. I found, to my delight, that I could make her laugh. All I ever wanted to do, all I still want to do all these years later, is make her happy. After we'd been married three years, she said she wanted children. That was the next step, the next easy, logical step. Or so we thought.

The look on her face now crushed me and angered me and made me want to pound someone.

I walked over and picked up Angelina, who squealed. Until this little girl entered our lives, I didn't know how much I could care. She was beautiful—dark-haired, cherubic. Her eyes were big and *wide open*—as if she were always in a state of delighted surprise. Hair that stuck straight up in spots when she woke up from a nap. Four pearly teeth, two top, two bottom. She had a wonderful laugh that started deep in her belly, then took over her entire body. Her laugh was infectious, and we'd start laughing, too, which made her laugh even harder, until she was limp. She laughed so hard we actually asked our pediatrician if there was a problem, and he just shook his head at us. Recently, she'd learned to say "Da" and "Ma." The way she looked at me, like I was the greatest and strongest creature on the planet, made me want to save and protect her from anything and anybody. She was my little girl, and like Melissa, she made me think differently about my place on earth. In her eyes, I was a god who as yet could do no wrong. I was a giant—her giant. I wanted to never disappoint her. And as the bearer of this news, I felt I had.

I THOUGHT I'D MISUNDERSTOOD the address or name of the meeting place as we entered because I couldn't locate Julie Perala at any of the tables or booths. I was lifting the cell to call her when I saw her wave from a private room in the back used for meetings and parties. I pocketed the phone.

Julie Perala was broad-faced and broad-hipped, with soft eyes and a comforting professional smile. There was something both compassionate and pragmatic about her, and we had liked her instantly when we met with her so many months before for our orientation. She seemed especially sensitive to our situation without being cloying, and was by far more knowledgeable about "placements" than anyone else we had met at other agencies. Nothing made her happier to be alive, she told us, than a placement where all three parties were perfectly served—the birth mother, the adoptive parents, and the child. She was to be trusted, and we trusted her. I also noticed, at times when she let her guard down, a ribald sense of humor. I had the feeling she'd be a hoot with a few drinks in her.

"Coffee?" she asked. "I've already had breakfast."

"No thanks," I said, pausing.

Melissa held Angelina tight to her and glared at Julie Perala with eyes I hoped would never be aimed at me.

"I know the manager," she said, answering a question I was about to ask, "and knew I could get this room in the back. Please close the door."

I did, and sat down as she was pouring coffee from a thermos carafe.

"I'm taking a real chance meeting with you," she said, not meeting my eyes, concentrating on pouring. "The agency would kill me if they knew. We've all been advised to communicate only through the lawyers now."

"But," I said, prompting her.

"But I like you and Melissa very much. You're good, normal people. I know you love Angelina. I felt I owed you a frank discussion."

"I appreciate that."

Melissa continued to glare.

Julie said, "If this comes back to bite me, well, I'll be very disappointed. But I hoped we could talk without lawyers around, at least this once."

"Go ahead," I said.

It took her a moment to form her words. "I can't tell you how bad I feel about this situation," she said. "This should never happen to a nice couple like you."

"I agree."

"We shouldn't have kept it a secret from you that Judge John Moreland contacted us three months ago," she said. "Our hope was we could settle it internally, and we offered to do exactly that. Our hope was you would never be troubled about it at all, that you wouldn't even know."

"Who is Judge Moreland?" I asked. "The biological father?"

"No, no. The biological father is his son, Garrett. Garrett is a senior at Cherry Creek High School. He's eighteen years old."

"Unbelievable," I said.

She shrugged and showed her palms to me. "I agree. But if we'd been able to resolve it internally, we wouldn't be here now. There wouldn't be a problem at all."

I said, "*Ninety-nine percent.* Remember when you used that figure when I asked about the birth father signing away his parental rights?"

Her face clouded. "I remember. And it's true. It really is. I've been involved in nearly a thousand placements in my life, and this is the first time this has ever happened. We just didn't think it could."

"Didn't you say you tried to find the birth father?" Melissa asked bitterly. "Didn't you say he'd agreed to sign the papers?"

She nodded.

"What happened?"

"We tracked him down in the Netherlands, where he was on vacation with his mother. He was staying with his mother's relatives, I guess. I didn't talk with him, but a coworker did. She explained the situation to him, and she said he was surprised. He agreed to sign away custody and he gave us a fax number where he could be reached. We sent the papers over."

"But he never signed them," I said.

"We dropped the ball," she said. "The woman who'd made contact left the agency. If any of us had had any inkling at all that he would refuse to sign, we would have kept you abreast of the situation. But as far as we knew, it was his wish not to be a parent. We can't coerce him, you know. We can't pressure. It has to be his decision."

My anger was building to the point that I had to look away from her.

"Legally, we covered our bases," she said sympathetically, almost apologetically to us. "We placed public notices for him and did everything we're required to do. Not having the signed papers isn't that unusual, because the family court judge always—and I mean always—awards full custody to the adoptive parents in a case like this. After all, we can't let a nonresponsive birth father hold up a placement, can we?"

"Did you contact Garrett's father?" I asked. "Is that how he got involved?"

"We normally don't contact the parents of the birth father. That's considered coercive."

"But you knew about him? You knew about John Moreland?"

"No."

"Interesting that his mother didn't know, since she was with him overseas when your agency contacted him. How could she *not* know?"

Julie shrugged. "It doesn't make sense to me, but a lot about this situation makes no sense. Maybe she knew but didn't want to tell her husband. Why—I don't know."

I said, "So this Judge Moreland entered the picture after Garrett told him?"

"As far as I know, yes."

"And that's when Moreland's lawyers contacted the agency?"

She looked down. "Yes. The letter came from them with less than ten days left in the public notice period. If they'd waited just two more weeks, custody would have been granted to you by the family court. It was bad timing for you."

"It sure was," I said sarcastically.

"If you and Melissa choose not to fight the Moreland claim, our agency will do everything in our power to make the situation right for you."

"Meaning what?" Melissa asked.

She took a quick breath and raised her eyes to meet Melissa's. "I've been a party to the meetings we've had with our executives and our lawyers. I know we would immediately refund all fees and arrange, free of charge, for a new placement. You would be moved to the top of the priority list for a new baby. And we'd offer a very large settlement to you and Melissa and our apologies. That's if we can keep this whole thing out of court and out of the news. I think you'd agree with me that the last thing anyone would want to do is discourage children's chances of future placements with loving families who might be scared out of adoption by this situation."

"This can't be happening," Melissa said, as much to herself as to Julie Perala.

"Why didn't your lawyers contact our lawyer about these meetings?" I said. "Isn't that how it's supposed to work?"

"I thought they had," she said.

"We've heard nothing."

She shrugged. "I'm not a lawyer."

"Neither is ours, apparently," I said, spitting it out.

"You don't understand," Melissa said. "We can't lose our baby."

Julie started to speak, then bit her lip and looked away.

"We can't lose our baby," Melissa said again, but this time her voice was close to a shout.

"Judge Moreland is a powerful man," Julie said softly. "I get the impression he's used to getting what he wants."

"Tell me about him," I asked. "Tell me what kind of man I'm up against."

"He's a wealthy man," she said. "His wife has the fortune, from what I understand. Judges aren't paid that much, I guess. He owns lots of real estate. I'm telling you this because you mentioned something about buying off Garrett. I hate to say it, but I don't think you could. And the judge comes across as such a nice man. He's handsome, confident. He's the kind of man you instantly like, and you hope he likes you because you don't want to displease him, you know?"

I said, "Julie, when I think of you all having these meetings and talking about us it makes me ill."

She nodded, then looked away again. "We discussed what his options were. He was very concerned about doing things the right way so as not to hurt you and Melissa."

"How kind," Melissa said.

"Tell me, Julie," I said, "how do you live with yourself?"

She put her face in her hands and cried. I couldn't help it—I felt terrible for making her cry again. But I didn't take my words back.

Finally, she grabbed a napkin and wiped the tears from her eyes, smearing eyeliner down her cheek, making it look like a faded scar.

Melissa stood up with Angelina. "I've got to change her diaper," she said, and left the room. "We'll be back."

For a moment we just sat there not looking at each other.

"There's one thing you can help us with," I said.

"What?"

"If you were Melissa and me, would you fight this in court? Knowing what you know, do we have a prayer?"

She shook her head sadly, said, "The best you could hope for, I think, is some kind of joint custody that a judge would decree. But I don't think either of you would be happy with that. And if I were you, I'd pray to God your baby is raised by John and Kellie—that Garrett is kept as far away from the baby as possible."

I felt my skin crawl. "Why do you say that?"

She shook her head. "There's something wrong with that boy. He scares me. And it isn't anything I can quite put my finger on—there's just something wrong about him."

"Oh God," I said.

She pursed her lips and looked down at her hands. "It's like the temperature in the room goes down ten degrees when he enters. There's no warmth. He seems bloodless and cunning. I wouldn't trust him with a child—or anyone."

I felt myself tingling. I leaned forward, "I understand what you're saying, but do you have anything I can use? Have you heard anything about Garrett we can investigate to prove what a bad father he'd be?"

She was still, her hands mindlessly caressing her coffee mug on both sides. Thinking.

She said, "I think there's been some trouble at school," she said. "Once, when we were meeting with John, he got a call from someone at Garrett's high school, and he had to cut the meeting short. I don't know who called or what it was about, but the judge was quite upset."

"This happened within the last month?" I asked, trying not to show my anger that the Morelands and the agency had been meeting behind our backs in secret.

"Yes."

"Anything else?"

"One thing, but it's no more solid than the first. When we were looking over your placement application with them . . ."

I took in an angry breath, but she continued.

". . . the judge pointed out you owned a dog."

"Harry."

"The judge said they couldn't have pets because Garrett couldn't get along with them. I thought that was an odd choice of words. Not that he was allergic to them, or wouldn't take care of them or something, but that *he couldn't get along with them*. When he said it, I could see he wished he hadn't."

"Is that all?" I asked.

"Yes," she said. "And it all sounds so baseless when I say it."

"Thank you," I said. "At least it gives me something to go on. But it also makes me feel a little sick."

"Yes," she said, then she lifted her chin and looked at me. "I think the only answer is somehow to convince Garrett to sign the papers giving up his parental rights," she said.

She took a deep breath to compose herself, mumbling that she hated to cry in front of others.

"Maybe he needs some *strong* persuading," she said, letting an angry edge into her voice.

"Meaning?"

"Meaning," she said, leaning across the table, her eyes flashing, "if Angelina were my daughter, I'd hire a couple of mean-ass bikers or wranglers and have them scare the living shit out of Garrett so he's only more than happy to sign anything put in front of him. He needs the kind of persuading that makes him think his father's determination is the least of his concerns."

I sat back. *That* had come from left field, but obviously it was something she'd been thinking about.

"I'm speaking hypothetically, of course," she said. "Not as a representative of the agency or a placement professional."

"Of course," I said. "Could he be scared?"

She thought for a moment before whispering, "I think so."

ON THE WAY HOME, I said to Melissa, "You're taking this much more calmly than I thought possible."

"I'm not calm at all," she said. "I'm dead inside. But this does explain why we have a phone message from Judge Moreland. He says he's coming over tomorrow afternoon with his son."

"Jesus," I said.

"What should we do?"

"I'm going to go see Martin Dearborn," I said. "I'm going to his house. Don't call the judge back. In fact, keep the phone off the hook. I'll call you on your cell, so keep it with you. The judge may put off coming to our house if he isn't sure we got the message, and we don't respond."

She laughed—a chilling, uncharacteristic laugh I'd never heard before and never wanted to hear again. It was a false laugh filled with horror and defeat. She said, "You know how they say your life passes before your eyes before you die?"

"Yes."

"That's happening now."

MARTIN DEARBORN, OUR ATTORNEY for the adoption, was in his driveway wearing a gold-and-black Colorado Buffaloes sweater and loading seat cushions and blankets into the back of his Mercedes M-Class SUV when I drove up in my ten-year-old Jeep Cherokee. I remembered the CU alumni awards on the wall of his office and noted the CU license-plate frame. Dearborn was plump and sandy-haired and wore thick glasses that made his light brown eyes look bigger than they were. He had a large head and a deep bass voice and ham-sized hands. He squinted when I jammed my Jeep into park because he obviously didn't recognize the vehicle or the driver—at first.

When I jumped out, I saw something pass over his face that told me he knew why I was there but didn't want to admit it.

His wife, a too-thin woman with a pinched face, also decked out in Buffs colors, came out of the garage, saw me approaching, and said, "Who is *that?*"

Martin gestured for her to go back inside. He tried hard to blank his eyes and face as I came up the driveway, but he wasn't successful.

His wife theatrically looked at her wristwatch, and he said, "I know. We'll make it in time for kickoff."

She said, "It isn't kickoff I'm worried about. It's the preparty."

He said, "We'll make it, don't worry."

She stomped back into the garage.

"Jack," he said, "this can wait until office hours on Monday. My wife and I are . . ."

"You son of a bitch, how long were you going to wait to tell us?"

"Monday. During regular office hours. That's when we *work,* Jack."

"Monday's too late, and you know it."

"Look," he said, lowering his voice into his official lawyer tone, the one he used to impress Melissa and me, "I've been in the Springs on a big civil case. I wasn't able to return the calls to them during the day because we were in court."

I stepped close enough to him that he flinched. "You didn't have breaks? You don't have paralegals who could make the call on your behalf?"

He looked away.

"Damn, you look guilty," I said. "You've got to get us out of this, and I mean now. This guy and his son are coming to our house tomorrow."

His voice wasn't as low when he spoke. "I'd advise you to be civil. He's got the law on his side, I'm afraid."

I reached out and grabbed a handful of CU sweatshirt, then quickly let it go. I couldn't help myself. From the garage I heard Dearborn's wife say, "Honey, do I need to call the police?"

"No," he said. "It's okay."

I said, "So you know all about it, then. I'd advise *you* to pretend you're an attorney—our attorney. We need to go to court right now and do something. Isn't there a restraining order or something? Can't we prevent this from happening?"

"I'd have to research it," he said, uncomfortable.

"We don't have the time."

He turned to me, his face flushed. "Jack, he's a sitting federal judge. He's been appointed by the president and confirmed by the Senate. Don't you think he knows the law? Hell, he makes it."

"So that's it, then," I said.

"Our firm has cases scheduled before him next month, Jack. Big cases. Million-dollar cases with national implications. I've got a real conflict here."

I shook my head. I wanted to smash him. His wife was still in the garage, and I noticed she had a telephone, ready to call the police. She pointed to it with her other hand, and mouthed "9-1-1."

"Is he aware I'm your counsel?" Dearborn asked.

"No," I said, "because you haven't done a damned thing. How would he know?"

"You need to calm down," he said. "And I'm afraid you need to get a new attorney. I'm not your man for this case. He's best friends with the mayor and the governor, for Christ's sake. And his name has come up for the Tenth Circuit and higher."

"So what are you saying?"

"That he not only knows the law, he knows how to work the law. This is inside baseball, Jack. You never told me you were going up against Judge Moreland."

"I didn't know."

"I think you should calm down and look at this from his point of view."

"I think you're fired," I said, even though he'd resigned.

"Good."

"Nine-one-one," his wife said, holding up the phone like a totem.

I DROVE TO LINDA Van Gear's town house in an angry fog. I found her wearing sweats with her hair down, shuttling between a fish tank in the living room to the toilet in the bathroom carrying dead fish one at a time. Her town house was a shambles.

"This is what happens when you travel for a living and you ask your neighbor to feed your fish and he forgets and goes skiing '*because the powder was awesome, dude,*'" she said angrily. "You come back to a tank full of dead objects."

I told her my situation had grown much worse since I'd seen her last, and I needed to cancel my scheduled trip to World Tourism Bourse in Berlin in a week.

That stopped her cold, and she stood there with a pale and dripping angel fish in a little net.

"So you want to send someone else to WTB, then?"

"Yes."

"Whom do you suggest?"

Our department consisted of the two of us. I suggested Rita Greene-Bellardo, a new employee who served as executive assistant but seemed to have little to do.

"Pregnant," Linda said. "I just heard. She's gonna have her baby and take the maternity leave and quit. I heard her telling a girlfriend that was her plan. We can't depend on her to follow up."

I floated the name of Pete Maxfield, who headed the media-relations department. Pete sometimes worked with international journalists and might have some experience he could use at the show. Linda didn't like Pete, though.

"Honey," she said, "Pete is a hound dog. He'd spend the whole time drinking German beer and trying to get some deaf, dumb, and blind German girl to come to his room at the hotel, or he'd blow the entertainment budget on prostitutes. This is our biggest and most important market. We don't just send people for the sake of sending someone. The only choice we have is me, and you know it."

I did, but I didn't want to ask.

"I'll be in Taiwan," she said. "I can't be both places."

I knew where this was headed.

"You *need* to have that big meeting with Malcolm Harris," she said.

Malcolm Harris was the iconic UK owner of a travel company called AmeriCan Adventures—a play on America and Canada—which sent thousands of British tourists to North America on custom-designed package tours. AmeriCan was the number one tour operator to Denver and the Mountain West, and thus a very important client. Our marching orders were to treat him like a god, despite his reputation as being quarrelsome, cantankerous, and smug about his claims that he knew more about America than practically any American he'd ever met. He expected to be fawned over, wined and dined, and he was. Any requests he made were immediately first priority in our office and across destination promotion bureaus throughout the region. Linda was infamous for attaching herself to him like Velcro when she worked the European market, hanging on his every word, laughing at his asides, and beholding him with what was described by one of her detractors as "Nancy Reagan eyes."

She said, "As you know, he's thinking of establishing a U.S. reservations office and call center to handle his tours," she said. "We're talking hundreds of jobs. He's looking at three cities—New York, L.A., and Denver. We're the front-runner because of our location. If we got that office here, the mayor would love us because he could say our tourism efforts not only bring in tourists but jobs. I'm sure he's meeting with reps from L.A. and New York. If you just *don't show up* in Berlin to convince him to choose Denver, we may lose out on this."

There was an uncomfortable pause. I said, "Does the mayor know about this, then?"

"It was in my report to him last month. His chief of staff sent me an e-mail about it last week, asking if we'd landed AmeriCan yet."

I let her go on.

"Honey," she said finally, "do you realize that every time the city gets a budget hit, and they're looking for places to cut, someone always suggests international tourism promotion? We're the easy ones to dump because they think we have these glamorous jobs and jet all around the world. We're easy to dump, you know? Tab Jones has no love for us, but he sees us as a means for him to travel the world, so he's not given the department the ax. But every time there's a budget crunch, I go to the mat and fight for us. I show them facts and figures, and this time when we were on the chopping block I told them about the possibility AmeriCan might open up a company here. Tab and the mayor got all excited about that because tourists are ghosts, but a building and jobs are something he can take credit for. Are you hearing me?"

"Yes," I said.

"If you don't go, honey, we can kiss this department and your job goodbye. And I *need* this job."

"I do, too."

I wasn't kidding. Since Melissa had quit her job to stay home with our daughter, we were literally one paycheck away from not making our mortgage payment. The loan we had was one of those bad ones, one of the worst decisions we'd made. We had *no* cushion. If I lost my job, Jesus, I didn't know where we'd be. Especially given the situation we were in, possibly trying to prove in court what great parents we were. My job was *everything*.

She stepped back, sized me up, said, "So you understand me, then?"

"Yes," I said. "I'll be going to Germany and meeting with Malcolm Harris."

"Good man, Jack," she said. "I knew you'd come around. Let's get going on those leads now."

As I gathered up the work and stuffed it into my briefcase, Linda said, "Aren't there other babies out there?"

"Not an option," I said back with heat. "It's not like trading her in for a new model," thinking: *How can she not understand?*

She waved dismissively, "Well, good luck with the baby thing."

THE BABY THING.

We had tried everything to get pregnant. Melissa studied up on the medical literature, threw herself into reproductive studies with a single-minded will as only she can do, reading everything from the library, on the Internet, becoming as well versed in the subject as any doctor and better than most. Having sex became my second job. Melissa drew pink hearts on our wall calendar to chart our couplings. There were a lot of hearts. We had sex every morning for three weeks straight and every other evening in one magnificent stretch run. Once, when we were able to have lunch together downtown, she showed up with bare legs in a dress and told me over sandwiches that she wasn't wearing underwear and that she'd rented a dayroom in a hotel next door. I could barely eat. I was equally aroused and alarmed, pointing out to her (tepidly, I admit) that with my job at the CVB it was possible someone might recognize me and assume the tryst was something it was not. She laughed and shook it off, then led me outside by the hand. In the elevator on the way to our floor, she started disrobing. I got hard, and she squeezed me through my pants. She said, "So you're getting into it, then?"

But it was never about me not getting into it. I was. And I was, and am, wildly attracted to my wife. She's my *ideal*. That she seemed to think—deep down—that she no longer did it for me and for some reason that was why we couldn't conceive was as startling as it was desperate. I told her repeatedly she drove me wild. She said, "Then why can't we have a baby, Jack?"

THE DOCTOR'S NAME WAS KIMMEL. He was thin, athletic, and fastidious in appearance. When we finally sat down with him at the clinic to review the tests, he confirmed what she had already determined: It was me.

"Let me put it this way," the doctor said, turning slightly on his stool in my direction but not really facing me. "Imagine, if you will, that you are a machine gunner but not a good one. In fact, a lousy one. The worst one in the entire Corps."

Kimmel paused to let that sink in.

"So I'm shooting blanks," I said. "Thank you, Mr. Bedside Manner."

He nodded, first to me, then to Melissa.

I felt Melissa's eyes brush across the side of my face.

"There are alternatives, of course," Kimmel said. "In this day and age, there really isn't male infertility anymore. We can isolate a single sperm." He explained procedures, drugs, in vitro fertilization.

We were hopeful. We tried them all, one after the other. For years. Melissa had three miscarriages. Our marriage became tense and our time together frustrating. There were long, silent meals and times we would be in the same room for hours and not look at each other. She secretly blamed me, I secretly blamed her. Her emotions were raw and increasingly close to the surface. Sometimes I caught her looking at me as if she was assessing my manhood and character, and I'd lash back with something sarcastic and cruel that I immediately regretted. I suggested once that maybe if we didn't try so hard, maybe if we didn't make our entire life's mission to conceive a child, we could be happy again. She didn't speak to me for weeks after that. I thought she might even leave me.

Finally, she said, "Let's adopt."

We really didn't discuss it. I trusted her judgment, and adoption is a good thing. And I had my wife back, and the clouds that had been building for years in our lives broke up and sunlight poured through.

Julie Perala at the agency explained to us that there were three kinds of adoption: international, closed, and open. We chose open. But there were levels of openness as well, from meeting the birth mother (our preference) to agreeing on visitation with the birth mother and her family.

The birth mother was a fifteen-year-old named Brittany. She was pale, freckled, and slightly overweight even before the pregnancy. Every other word from her was "like," as in, "I'm, like, gaining weight," or "It's, like, a *drag* to get morning sickness." The reasons she gave the agency for choosing us included the fact that we were fairly young, childless, and we looked "calm" and "outdoorsy." We overlooked Brittany's arrogance at times. She knew she had what Melissa wanted. Brittany was fertile, and she assumed Melissa wasn't, so she took on a superior air. Once, though, when Melissa left the room, I leaned toward Brittany and said, "It isn't her. It's *me*."

Even though, frankly, with our unexplained infertility it was most likely both of us somehow. But I didn't tell Brittany that.

Terms regarding adoption are something we're both sensitive about now, especially Melissa. Often, the wrong thing is said in all innocence, but it can cut deeply. For example, Brittany is the birth mother, not the "real" mother or the "natural" mother or the "biological" mother. Melissa is Angelina's mother. Period. Brittany didn't "give her baby up for adoption," she placed the baby with adoptive parents. People have a natural instinct to pry. I try not to hold that against them when they ask, "Where did she get those dark eyes?" (since mine are blue and Melissa's are green) or "Her hair is so thick and dark!" when mine is reddish brown and Melissa's is light brown. We'd learned to answer, vaguely, "It runs in the family." We weren't lying. We just weren't saying *whose* family.

In retrospect, we could have asked more questions about the birth father. But we were assured by the agency and from Melissa's discussions with Brittany that the boy was no longer in the picture. Brittany wouldn't even say his name other than to call him "Sperm Boy" and say he refused to take her calls. She never mentioned that he was out of the country, which led us to believe she hadn't known where he was. He meant nothing to her, she told Melissa. She'd been drunk and in the backseat of Sperm Boy's nice car. One thing led to another.

Angelina turned six, seven, and eight months old. She was healthy, cheerful, loving. She began to form the words "Ma" and "Da." She loved Harry, our old black Lab and my last carryover from bachelorhood, who began to sleep under her crib to protect her. Everything was right with the world.

Then it wasn't.

THERE IS AN ABSOLUTE irredeemable beauty to pure routine, for if there wasn't, I'm not sure we could have gotten through that evening when I finally got home.

We ate, I'm sure.

We might have watched television.

I do remember halfheartedly playing with Angelina on the floor. She loved her Fisher-Price barn set. Angelina got all of the other animals as well as the farmer and his wife, and I was the cow and the cow only. Angelina's menagerie spent all of their time telling the cow what to do. The cow spent all of his (her?) time trying to make Angelina laugh. But my heart wasn't in it.

I also remember a disjointed, fierce "They'll never take her away" discussion Melissa and I had. We were in the midst of it when Melissa walked over to the telephone in the kitchen and hung it up on the receiver to check and see if there were any more messages. I watched her eyes widen and her mouth purse, and she pressed the speaker button.

The voice was male, mature, and sympathetic:

"Jack and Melissa, I hate to place this call. This is Judge John Moreland. I know you're aware of why I'm calling and believe me, this is just about as difficult for me as it is for you. No one ever in his or her life expects to be in a situation like this. For that I am deeply, *deeply* sorry. But I hope you appreciate the situation my family has found ourselves in as well. Angelina is our first granddaughter, and my son's child. I assume you are checking messages, even though you aren't picking up the phone. We will be at your house tomorrow at 11:00 A.M. Don't worry—we're coming simply to meet you and to talk. There's no reason to panic or overreact. It'll be a conversation among adults who find themselves in a bitterly tough situation through no fault of their own."

Melissa and I exchanged glances. I could see relief flood into her face, and her shoulders relaxed.

Then he said: "The county sheriff is aware of my visit tomorrow. I'm sorry I had to contact him, but I thought it best for all concerned—especially the baby—that our meeting be under the auspices of the authorities. Don't worry—he won't be with us. But he'll be available if the situation turns sour. Not that I expect it to. I admire and respect you both. And I think a reasonable solution to our dilemma is at hand. I hope you'll hear me out, and I hope you will welcome our visit.

"God bless and good night, and we'll see you tomorrow."

Click.

THAT NIGHT, as we lay in bed not sleeping, I slid out of the bed and padded over to the closet. On the top shelf of our closet, hidden by a ball of loose old clothing, was my grandfather's single-action Colt .45 Peacemaker revolver. The Gun that Won the West. I wish I could say he gave it to me in some kind of intergenerational ceremony loaded with symbolism and meaning, but the fact is I stole it while I helped my father move Grandpa from his house in White Sulfur Springs to a nursing home in Billings. He never knew it was missing and never asked about it at the time. Later, as he slipped deeper into dementia, the nurses said he called out for his weapon, but they had no intention of locating it for him.

The revolver was blunt and heavy, with a six-inch barrel. It was loaded with five ancient cartridges. The firing pin rested on an empty cylinder to prevent accidents. The handgrip was made of ash, polished smooth by years of handling. The cylinder was rubbed clean of blueing from being drawn and put back into a leather holster hundreds of times.

"What are you doing?" Melissa asked.

"Nothing," I said.

Two

On Sunday, Melissa looked both beautiful and scared. She had a smattering of freckles across her nose and cheeks I'd always found girl-like and attractive. Her hair was shoulder length and the cut sophisticated. She'd spent hours wondering what to wear, trying on outfit after outfit to find a combination that would give her confidence and strength. She'd agonized over whether to wear panty hose but decided against it. She'd chosen a simple white sleeveless top, a sweater, and beige skirt. Her legs looked long, firm, and tan. She wanted to look nice, but not too nice. Not so nice that the birth father would hold it against her, she said.

I wore jeans, a dress shirt that showed some wear, and a navy blazer. Nice but not too nice. Melissa had asked me to change from my old cowboy boots to loafers, saying she didn't want them to think me a redneck. When it comes to such matters, I learned long ago to defer. I think that deferring is one of the secrets to a happy marriage.

Angelina was in a white ruffled dress with red polka dots. She looked like a doll—jet-black hair, creamy skin, chubby cheeks, and those startling dark eyes. I loved it that our new baby loved me, and looked at me without a hint of what was going on around her, about her.

"Those bastards," I said, "putting us through this." My voice was harsh, and Angelina balled her fists and took a breath, ready to cry.

"No, it's okay, honey," I cooed. "It's okay." But it wasn't. Nevertheless, she relaxed. She believed me as I lied to her, which broke my heart. Melissa took her upstairs for her morning nap. I hoped that when she awoke our lives would be normal again, that she'd never have to learn about what almost happened.

OUTSIDE OUR HOME, a blue late-model Cadillac SUV slowed to a crawl on the street and swung into our driveway. I could see two people inside.

Garrett Moreland, son of the judge and supposed birth father of Angelina, got out first and looked at our house with an expression I can only describe as amused disdain.

GARRETT MORELAND WAS DARK, tall, chiseled, with raven-dark hair and striking eyes like brown glass marbles balanced on a whalebone shelf. Seeing Angelina's eyes mounted in this man-boy's face made my heart clench, and I could taste a spurt of something rotten in my mouth. Garrett had an abnormally long neck and prominent Adam's apple that bobbed up and down as his jaw muscles worked like taut cords while he surveyed the front of our home. His skin was pale white, his mouth a thin-lipped red cut that looked like a razor slash a second before it oozed blood. He was dressed like an eighteen-year-old forced to go to church—chinos, loafers, an open-collar button-down shirt and a slightly too-big blazer that was probably his father's. As he stood there he bent slightly forward, rocking on the balls of his feet, with his hands held at his sides and the crown of his head bent so he was looking at the house from under his eyebrows and I thought, *He looks demonic.*

John Moreland was tall as well, and movie-star handsome. In his mid-to-late forties, he had a pleasant boyish face and longish brown hair combed in a long comma over his forehead. He looked like a hip Presbyterian minister, a man who was used to being noticed, a man supremely comfortable in his own skin; he was the deacon, the Rotary president, the former Peace Corps volunteer still remembered and worshipped back in the third-world village. His tan suit draped nicely, and he wore a cream-colored dress shirt. He was lightly tanned and had a mole on his cheek where a model would pencil a beauty mark. There was confidence in his attitude and walk, and a significant exchange of . . . *something* . . . as Moreland and Garrett Moreland glanced at each other before knocking on our door.

I heard Melissa come down the stairs.

"It's them," she said. "I saw them from upstairs."

I nodded.

"They're good-looking men," she said. "I can see why she went out with Garrett."

I looked at her, tried to remember the last time she'd made a comment like that.

"My heart sank when I saw them get out," she muttered under her breath. "I so wanted to hate them on sight."

"You don't?"

She shook her head quickly while she patted down her clothes and put on her game face. "I hate why they're here," she said. She took my face in her hands. "Remember what we talked about. Stay cool—control your temper. The last thing we want to do right now is to anger them—especially Garrett. We need him to sign the papers. Don't give him a reason to withhold his signature one second longer than necessary."

"Got it," I said.

"Are you sure?"

"I'm sure."

John Moreland smiled broadly when we opened the door. He had a disarming, sloppy smile, but he seemed nervous behind it. He carried a bulging white paper sack in one hand that he seemed to have forgotten he had. It hadn't occurred to me they would be nervous, too. The fact made me feel better.

We stepped aside and asked them to come in. Boy, we were gracious. Melissa asked if they wanted coffee. Moreland said he would like a cup. Garrett shook his head sullenly. I couldn't read him at first. He wouldn't meet my eyes, and his movements and attitude seemed designed to put distance between him and everyone else in the room.

"Please sit down," I said, gesturing toward the couch with the coffee table in front of it. I had moved two of our big chairs to the other side for Melissa and me. The chairs were slightly taller than the couch, and I wanted a scenario where Moreland and Garrett would need to sit closely together and look up at us. I'd learned this from business meetings. It gave us a psychological advantage.

Unfortunately, Moreland didn't bite on my seating arrangement, and acted as if he hadn't seen me point to the couch. He sat in one of the chairs. Garrett shambled over to the couch and sat down heavily with undisguised contempt for his father. Or me. Or something.

Melissa saw the situation the minute she came back from the kitchen. She could either sit in the chair in the dominant position or settle in next to Garrett. Her hesitation was obvious, and I filled it by taking the couch. She had cups on a tray I'd never seen before, which slightly annoyed me. Moreland took his coffee.

"I brought this for you, a little gift," he said, handing the bag to me. I looked inside and saw sticky pastries of some kind. I handed the bag to Melissa, and she looked inside, said "Thank you" to Moreland, and went back into the kitchen to put them on a plate, which she brought back out.

I broke the awkward silence by turning to Garrett, saying, "It's nice to meet you. You're a senior this year, right?" Showing I knew a little about him.

Garrett said, "Yeah, a senior," with a slight curl of his lip.

In social situations, Melissa always led the way. I turned to her and saw that despite the smile, her face had drained of blood. She was terrified to speak, to get to the matter at hand. I did my best to carry on, to maintain the slight edge I thought I'd gained by addressing Garrett.

There was some small talk about the weather (cooling), the traffic on the way to our subdivision (light since it was the weekend). Moreland had a deep sonorous voice with a homey Southern accent. I tried to place it and guessed either Tennessee or North Carolina. He had a way of looking directly at us when he talked that had the effect of putting me at ease. Garrett said nothing. Melissa either.

"The roads should be fine until the game tonight," I said. "Then it'll be bumper-to-bumper on I-25 for a while."

Moreland smiled knowingly and nodded. "We've got season tickets. I haven't missed the Broncos playing the Raiders in fifteen years. As far as I'm concerned, the Broncos can't beat them by enough." He looked at me empathetically, "Tell me you're not a Raiders fan and I've just insulted you."

"I'm not a Raiders fan," I said, wishing for a moment I was.

"Well," Moreland said, smiling, "we've certainly got that in common. I've learned since I came out here to go to school at CU in Boulder how special the Broncos are to those of us who live here. The Broncos are our touchstone, our way of establishing a common bond and interest. Even people who don't like football follow the Broncos, since a win means everyone will be in a fine mood to start the week and a loss means snarling drivers and grumpy service in the stores."

With that, control of the situation ebbed away from me and flowed to John Moreland.

I tried to take my cues from Melissa, but she wasn't helping me. Instead, she observed both Moreland and Garrett closely. Mostly Garrett. No doubt she was seeing similarities in his features to Angelina, or perhaps she was trying to imagine him as father material. I noticed Garrett stealing looks at her as well when he thought she wasn't paying attention. Long, predatory looks that took her in from her feet in sandals, up her bare legs, quickly over her hands in her lap to her breasts under the sleeveless white top and sweater. I tried hard not to let it bother me.

"I think we should get to it," I said, probably too abruptly. *Enough with the small talk. Enough with the staring at my wife.*

"Yes," Moreland said, almost sadly.

Even though no one really moved, it felt as if everyone's gears shifted, and the room suddenly became sterile. Melissa sat up straighter, as did Moreland. Only Garrett, who continued to lounge on the couch with his arm thrown over the backrest, continued observing something on the ceiling when he wasn't examining Melissa.

"We understand," I said, "you've contacted the adoption agency in regard to our daughter Angelina."

Moreland nodded.

"According to Mrs. Perala at the agency, Garrett doesn't want to sign the papers giving us full custody of Angelina. This came as an unbelievable shock to us. The agency said this was the first time this has ever happened to them. Of course, you can imagine this is something we never even thought possible, that someone could wait eighteen months, then step forward."

Garrett wouldn't meet my eyes. He alternated between studying the ceiling light fixtures and flicking glances at my wife. Moreland was still, but I could tell by a rapid pulsing in his temple he was becoming agitated.

"Mr. Moreland," I said, "we love Angelina, and she loves us. We are the only parents she's ever known. The birth mother selected us from several very deserving couples, and we've done everything we can to provide a loving house and family. Look around you. Melissa resigned from her job so she could stay home with the baby and provide full-time care. Melissa is Angelina's mother." I didn't say what should have come next, that I was her father. No reason at this point to alienate Garrett when I had the inkling he was on our side.

"We hope now that you and Garrett have met us and seen our home that you will consider signing the papers," I said.

I liked the way Moreland seemed to listen to me as I spoke, and noted that his eyes swept around the room when I mentioned our home.

I was encouraged when he said, "You have a very nice home, and I don't doubt your sincerity."

Then it came.

"*But . . .*"

In my peripheral vision, I could see Melissa squirm. Her hands tightened on the arms of her chair.

". . . we have a different view."

Moreland gestured toward Garrett. "My son made a very terrible mistake. I am ashamed of him. His mother, Kellie, is ashamed of him. He is ashamed of himself. This is a black mark on our family, this be-havior. He had some bad friends at the time, and they encouraged this kind of thing. They are no longer his friends. That's why we sent him away for a while. We wanted him to get his head on straight, grow up into a man. But Garrett, and our family, can't avoid our responsibilities or the consequences of his stupid actions while he was younger. It is a situation we must deal with ourselves, within our family. We want to raise our child in our family."

I couldn't find words to speak. *Our child.*

"Mr. and Mrs. McGuane," Moreland said, leaning forward in the chair and looking from Melissa to me and back to Melissa, "I'm a federal judge, as I think you know. I'm known as a fair judge, and a tough one. I believe in accountability and being responsible for one's behavior. If there's one thing I want to pass along to my son, it's that there are consequences in life. It's vitally important that we bear responsibility. Garrett is responsible for the conception and birth of this baby.

"Please don't misunderstand what I'm saying," Moreland said in a conciliatory tone. "I have nothing against you or your wife. It is obvious you love the baby, and you've provided a wonderful home in a wonderful neighborhood. I am sorry this has to happen. I am truly, truly sorry. We didn't know about our granddaughter until I found the letters from the adoption agency in Garrett's room. He hadn't even opened them," he said, shooting a withering look at his son, who rolled his eyes. Then back to us: "Surely there are other babies?"

He sounded almost reasonable in his words if not his intent.

Come on, Melissa, I wanted to plead. *Say something here.* Instead, she studied Moreland with cold but curious intensity.

"Mr. Moreland," I said as softly as I could, "what you're asking is not possible. Angelina has been our daughter for nine months, and that doesn't include the seven months prior to that we were with the birth mother awaiting delivery. We've bonded as a family. I don't need to point out that during all of that time we never even knew Garrett, or you. If you had concerns, we would have reached out to you. To come here now is just unreasonable."

Moreland nodded in sympathy. He said, "I know this is going to be hard for you. I also know the financial outlay you've made."

I felt myself begin to squirm.

"I've done some research, Mr. and Mrs. McGuane. I know that it likely cost you over $25,000 to transact the adoption. I know Mrs. McGuane is no longer working outside the home, which is admirable. And Mr. McGuane, I know that a salary of $57,500 is not very much to maintain a house like this and a family. I'm sympathetic

36

to both of you, but we know how deeply you are in debt, and that is not a pleasant place to be. I'm prepared to cover all of your costs, plus what it would take to adopt another child."

I felt violated by his knowledge. Our careful staging for the meeting was gone just like that. Poof. I shot a look at Melissa. Her face was an alabaster mask. Her eyes were pinched and hard, a look I'd never seen. A look that emboldened me and terrified me at the same time. I was amazed she had remained silent. I'm amazed I didn't leap across the table at him.

"It's not about money," I said. "It's much, much too late for that. Maybe if you'd come to us before Angelina was born . . ."

"I didn't know," Moreland said, his voice rising with anger, but not at us. He looked at his son with pure contempt. "Garrett was out of the country with his mother for several months. He never told us anything about it. If he had, we wouldn't be here now."

Melissa said to Garrett, "Where were you?" Her voice was leaden.

Garrett didn't seem to realize she was talking to him.

"He was in the Netherlands and England visiting relatives," Moreland answered for him. "Kellie's extended family and just being tourists. We learned of this," he gestured to us, "only two months ago."

In my peripheral vision, I saw Garrett roll his eyes.

"Did you know she was pregnant?" Melissa asked Garrett.

Garrett looked at Melissa with a half smile and shrugged in a way that said, "*Whatever.*"

I leaned forward in my chair until I had Moreland's attention, and said, "This is not about you. It's not about your son. It's not about us. This is about Angelina and what's best for her." Trying to drive a wedge between father and son.

Moreland paused a long time before saying, "It is about the baby, I agree. But the baby is part of my family, our family, despite my son's behavior. The baby is our blood and our responsibility, not yours. We must right this wrong."

It was later when I realized Moreland, the entire time he was in our home, never once said "Angelina." Always *the baby*.

I looked at Garrett. He was ignoring us, his eyes fixed on Melissa, who had caught him this time and stared back. The intensity of their gaze seemed to sizzle through the air. I couldn't stand it another second.

"Garrett," I said.

Nothing.

"*Garrett.*"

Slowly, he turned his head toward me. Contemptuous.

"I have to ask you a question."

He raised his eyebrows.

"Do you really want to be a father? Do you really want to change your life right now? Do you realize how much work it is to be a father, to care for and support a baby?"

Moreland spoke for him once again. "Kellie and I will raise the baby. She will be our granddaughter and our daughter. Garrett will go to college to become a lawyer or a doctor, and when he's married and has a home, he will take the child in with him."

"I asked Garrett," I said.

"He has nothing to say about it," Moreland said, heat in his voice. "We have discussed this in our family, and that is the way it will be."

Garrett watched me as his father spoke to read my reaction.

"So where is your wife in this?" Melissa asked Judge Moreland. "Why didn't she come with you?"

"She was too uncomfortable," Moreland said, tight-lipped.

"She doesn't want to meet us?" Melissa asked, bitterness in her voice.

Moreland flushed and looked at his shoes. "She's embarrassed."

It sounded like a lie.

He changed the subject, saying, "I'd like to see the baby."

Melissa said, "She's asleep."

"I won't wake her."

Melissa looked to me with horrified desperation.

"Maybe it would be best not to see her now," I said.

"I want to see her. I want to see what she looks like," he said firmly.

Standoff. And no one spoke for a full minute. My insides churned, and I realized the palms of my hands were icy cold and dry. The confidence I'd had when the meeting began was gone. It seemed as though the room we sat in had tilted slightly and become unfamiliar.

Melissa sighed. "I'll take you up there."

"Are you sure?" I asked. Were we conceding anything? I wasn't sure. Maybe Melissa thought if Moreland saw Angelina asleep in her crib, in her room, in our house, he would soften to our position. After all, the discussion so far had been abstract. Seeing the baby might help us.

"Sure," she said.

I turned to Garrett. "Do you want to go?"

Garrett shook his head. "That's okay," he said. "I'd like a Coke or something, though. Do you have a Coke?"

He didn't want to see her. That buoyed me. While Melissa led Moreland up the stairs, I went into the kitchen for the drink. Melissa kept a stash of Diet Coke in the back of the refrigerator. I filled an empty glass with ice from the icemaker and took the can and glass back into the living room. Garrett was standing at the mantel, looking at photos of our wedding, my parents on the ranch, Melissa's family at their reunion last summer at the Broadmoor in Colorado Springs, Angelina as an infant in Melissa's arms.

Over the baby monitor, I could hear the door to Angelina's room open.

I handed the can and the glass to Garrett. He took the can without a word. That he'd stayed downstairs gave me an opening.

"You don't really want to be a father, do you?"

"Not really."

"So it's your father?"

"He has ideas of his own."

"Can you talk him out of it?"

"I don't think so."

"Will you try?"

Garrett looked at me blankly. Something in his eyes disturbed me. It was as if he saw me as someone who couldn't possibly understand him, and I was not worth an explanation.

"Just sign the papers," I said. "There's nothing your parents can do if you sign them."

He smiled that half smile.

"I'll do what I can for you if you sign them," I said, having no idea what I could possibly do for him.

"My father is very rich," he said. "I don't need you."

"You might if you sign the papers," I said, trying to engage him man-to-man again. "Look, we've all made mistakes. None of us is perfect. Being a father changes your life, believe me. It's a good thing, but you need to be ready for it. There's a lot you need to give up. Your life is no longer your own. You lose your freedom. Plus, it's the right thing to do, and I think you know that."

He nodded while I spoke, and his eyes glistened. He was hearing me, and it seemed like he wanted to hear more. I got the strange feeling, though, that he wasn't offering me encouragement as much as egging me on.

Over the monitor, I heard Melissa say, "Don't touch her." Her tone startled me.

"I just want to turn her over and look at her face," Moreland said.

"I'll do it," Melissa said.

I could hear Angelina's covers rustle, and heard a murmur.

"There," Melissa said.

I realized both Garrett and I were staring at the monitor, straining to hear ever word, every sound.

"Ah," Moreland said. "She's beautiful. She looks like her father and me."

Silence from Melissa.

"See that little birthmark on her calf? I have that birthmark. It's a sign of being a Moreland."

"No!" Melissa said.

What was he doing?

He said, "I want to pick her up."

"I said no."

"Okay, okay," Moreland said. "I'll let her sleep. Can I take a photo of her at least? To show Kellie?"

"Please, I'd rather you didn't," Melissa said, sighing.

"Just a photo? Just one?"

Her silence was taken as acquiescence by both Moreland and me. I heard the click of a digital camera.

"I want to look at her for a few more moments."

Melissa said, "Just look. That's all."

I put the glass of ice on the coffee table and prepared to go upstairs. My hands were trembling and knotted into fists, and I felt myself on the verge of losing control. If he said anything more, took more photos, touched her . . .

"Please, Mrs. McGuane . . ." the judge said. "Don't make this harder than it already is."

Melissa said, "She's my baby, and you want to take her away from me."

"I understand how you must feel," he said gently.

I took a deep breath, tried to calm myself. It had been a long time since I'd been as angry. I wondered what I would have done up there. I thought again of the Colt .45. And I knew that Melissa and I had entered a whole new place, where everything was different.

I noticed Garrett watching me, a smirk on his face.

"What were you going to do?" he asked.

"Nothing," I said.

"I bet nothing."

"You don't want to see the baby, do you?" I asked.

"No," he said, with that lazy curl of his lip.

"Sign the papers," I said.

"You have a nice wife," Garrett said. "I like her."

His demeanor changed from the smirk back to stoic as Melissa and Moreland came down the stairs. His eyes were on Melissa, not his father.

"Maybe I'll come over and watch the Bronco game with you," Garrett said.

"What?" I was stunned once again.

"I should probably get to know you better," he said, his eyes still on Melissa. "We should hang out."

I didn't know how to react to that. I could tell by their faces that both Melissa and Moreland had missed the exchange.

Moreland stopped on the landing and shook Melissa's hand.

"Thank you," he said. "She's beautiful."

"She is," Melissa said, letting a tiny smile escape despite herself. "And she's ours," she added.

"Ah, we need to resolve this."

"No," Melissa said. "There's nothing to resolve."

Damn, I admired her for her toughness. Simply no.

Moreland turned to me. In response, I nodded toward Melissa as if to say, *It's out of my hands. The answer is no.*

"Come along, Garrett," Moreland said. And to us, "Thank you for the coffee. It was nice to meet you."

Garrett drained his Coke and handed the empty can to me,

letting Moreland walk by until he was out of earshot. He had an incredulous look on his face, as if he couldn't believe his sudden good fortune.

"What?" I asked.

The corners of his mouth tugged upwards and his pupils dilated and I could almost hear him say to himself, *I own you people now, don't I? You don't dare do anything or say anything that will make me mad, or I won't sign the papers.*

Then he smiled outright, and something danced behind his eyes. I felt a chill roll down my back.

"Son?" Moreland opened the front door and Garrett ambled out, shooting a look at me as he went by. "Later," he said.

Moreland said to Melissa, "I need to do some thinking. You are very impressive people. But . . ."

There it was again, that *but.*

"The circumstances of this issue are black-and-white. I've reviewed the case law, and met with lawyer friends well versed in family law. The birth mother signed away her parental rights, but the father—Garrett—didn't. Garrett should be the custodian of the baby, simple as that. No court would disagree. Regardless," he said, waving the legal argument aside though he'd made his point, "I still feel we can work together. You obviously have feelings for the baby, and you've acted in good faith. There may be some wiggle room we'd agree to. Maybe you could visit her occasionally and be a positive part of her life, like an aunt and uncle. But the fact is the baby is our blood, and she legally belongs to us. One can't diminish that fact. Blood is blood, the law is the law. Any judge can see we have the means to take excellent care of her and a wonderful home environment."

"What does that mean?" Melissa asked. "That we don't?"

"Of course you've done your best," Moreland said, not without sympathy.

"We love Angelina," Melissa said, a note of panic showing.

John Moreland nodded and pursed his lips.

"Think about having Garrett sign the papers," I said. "You say we can adopt another baby and Garrett needs to accept responsibility. Maybe *he* can visit her on occasion. Maybe Garrett can be the uncle."

I felt Melissa's eyes bore into me. She wanted nothing to do with either of them.

"Ah, compromise," Moreland said, toasting me without a glass as his way of acknowledging what I'd said. "That's not going to happen. I just hope we can resolve this among ourselves, without a protracted legal struggle you'd eventually lose. That would make it tougher and more emotionally draining on you and the baby. In fact, it could be cruel to her, since the outcome is certain, and your ability to pay lawyers is finite.

"Look," he said gently, "I know this is tough on you right now, and your head is probably spinning. But my offer still stands. There are other babies to adopt, and I can help make that happen. There are thousands of babies out there who could be nurtured and loved in a home like yours. My offer still stands to make things right for you.

"Let's talk about timing. While we have every right to demand the baby right here and now, that wouldn't be compassionate. And we want to avoid any scene of sheriff's cars rolling up to your house with lights on and having them forcibly return the child. So we'll give you three weeks to say goodbye—until the end of the month. That's a Sunday. That should give you enough time to get new adoption proceedings under way—with my help—and to say goodbye to the child. I've already notified the sheriff of the date, and he and his team are available. He won't come unless he has to, so please don't make him have to. That's the best we can do, I'm sorry. Three weeks."

Garrett stood there, his face stoic, giving no signal of what he was thinking.

"Well," Moreland said, "we had best be going. Go Broncos, I guess," he said. "At least we can agree on that, right?"

He closed the door behind him. Melissa joined me at the window. There didn't seem to be much oxygen in the room. We watched Garrett climb into the passenger seat, close the door, stare straight ahead. Moreland paused before reaching for the door handle to gaze at our house, as if making a decision that pained him. He looked remorseful, but at the same time he had a determined set to his face. My heart sank. I knew then he would never change his mind.

But he couldn't leave yet. My friend Cody had chosen that moment to pull up to our house in his police department Crown Victoria and unwittingly block the judge's car in the driveway. The judge stood there with his hands on his hips, glaring at him. Cody was oblivious. He swung out of his car and opened the trunk, his always-present cigarette dancing in his mouth. I could hear the loud twang of country music from the Crown Vic's radio. Cody grabbed the power drill he had borrowed months before and finally remembered to return as well as a twelve-pack of cheap beer and turned toward the house. That was when he saw the judge, and the judge saw him.

I couldn't hear their exchange of words, but it was obvious Cody was apologizing all over himself and backing up. He threw the drill and beer into the trunk and quickly backed up to let the judge and Garrett out.

Melissa saw none of it because her face was buried in my chest.

"This can't be happening," she cried.

"I know."

She looked at me fiercely. I've never seen such absolute manic conviction. "Swear to me, Jack, that you'll do everything you can to save our baby from them."

I nodded, squeezed her tighter.

"*Swear it to me!*"

"I swear," I said. "I promise." My stomach churned.

Cody let himself in the front door. His sandy-colored hair was uncombed, and he wore stained sweats. "Jesus Christ, I hope that judge didn't recognize me out there. I'm not supposed to use the car

45

when I'm off duty to run errands. What was he doing here, anyway? Hey, what's wrong with you two? You look like you've seen a ghost."

From the other room, we heard Angelina stir over the baby monitor. We listened as the baby yawned, gurgled, sighed. We heard the crib squeak as she tried to pull herself up. She said, "Ma . . ."

Three

Two minutes into the first quarter of the Broncos game that evening, I heard the bass burbling of a car motor outside in my driveway. Melissa was upstairs bathing Angelina.

The doorbell rang.

There were three of them: Garrett, a young Hispanic covered in tattoos who looked like a gangster, and an emaciated red-haired Caucasian who was dressed in the same hip-hop style as the Hispanic. Garrett's bright yellow H3 Hummer was parked in the driveway, looking like the muscle-bound older uncle of my Jeep Cherokee.

Garrett said *hey* in an overly familiar way. Then: "I hope you don't mind that I brought my friends Luis and Stevie." They'd come, Garrett said, to hang out.

I said nothing.

"Problem?" he asked, wide-eyed and mocking. Stevie smirked.

Luis said, "Hey, *amigo*," and nodded at me with a dead-eye stare.

Garrett and Luis sat on the same couch Garrett had occupied

earlier in the day. Stevie sat on the arm. Stevie's body language suggested he was subservient to them. The three boys watched the game in utter silence, not commenting on anything. I can't say they looked bored, because they were alert and didn't miss a thing. They both watched Melissa come downstairs and go into the kitchen and close the door. And I caught the "*See? What did I tell you?*" look Garrett gave Luis after she was gone.

Luis was shorter and darker than Garrett, with a blunt pug face that looked like it had been hammered in. He wore an oversized white T-shirt with an even larger open long-sleeved plaid shirt over it and massive cargo pants. He had close-cropped black hair and dull black eyes, and a tattoo on his neck below his jaw reading "Sur-13." Unlaced and oversized heavy boots with Vibram soles were splayed out in front of him. Stevie wore the same oversized clothing as well as a red bandana on his head. But his haircut, perfect teeth, and expensive new sneakers gave him away as a rich kid pretending to be a gangster. I could see Stevie as Garrett's friend. But Luis was the real deal and didn't seem to fit.

During a commercial for curing erectile dysfunction, I asked, "Garrett, is there anything you want to talk with me about?"

He looked at me sincerely, said, "Yes, there is."

I nodded, urging him on.

"I'd like a cold drink. Another one of those Cokes would be just fine. I'd bet my friends could use a cold drink, too."

"I'd like a beer, man," Luis said, grinning, showing gold teeth.

"Me too," Stevie said with a slight—and false—Mexican accent intonation.

I shook my head. Unbelievable.

"Maybe some snacks," Garrett said. "Chips and dip? Nachos? Don't you have snacks during a game?"

"We always have snacks," Luis said. "We like snacks during a game." Mocking me.

I cursed under my breath and went out to get soft drinks.

No beer for Luis or Stevie, though, and no damned snacks. Back in the living room, I could hear them chuckling. I had to close my eyes and take deep breaths to keep a handle on my anger.

DURING THE THIRD QUARTER, I asked Garrett if he'd thought about signing the papers.

"I haven't thought about it," Garrett said dismissively. "You need to talk to my father about that."

I detected an intransigent smirk on Luis's face when Garrett spoke.

"Does he always speak for you?"

"On this he does."

"Why?"

He locked eyes with me, and I felt a chill that made the hair on my arms rise.

"We have an agreement," he said.

Before I could ask what it was, Melissa came out of the kitchen to go upstairs to go to bed and Garrett's eyes and attention went with her.

Harry, our old Labrador, padded in from the kitchen. Garrett recoiled and sat back in the couch.

"He's harmless," I said, smiling. "Harry loves everybody."

"Can you please get him away?" Garrett asked me, his voice leaden.

"Sure," I said, puzzled. I am always surprised when someone doesn't like dogs. I put Harry out into the backyard. When I returned, the boys hadn't moved, although Garrett had a lingering look of what I can only describe as disgust on his face.

"Somebody allergic?" I asked.

"No," Garrett said in a way that signaled he no longer wanted to discuss the matter.

"He don't like dogs," Luis said. "Me, I got four. Fighting dogs, man. Nobody gives my dogs any shit."

"Do you mind if I use your bathroom?" Garrett asked.

"It's upstairs and to the left," I said, wondering if his plan was to sneak a peek at Melissa in Angelina's bedroom. But he was in and out quickly. As he came down the stairs, Luis said, "I'm next, man."

With Luis upstairs, I turned to Garrett. I ignored Stevie. "What do you want from us?" I asked. "Why did you bring your friends here?" I knew I was gripping the arms of the chair too hard.

"What, you don't like Mexicans?" Garrett asked innocently. "Does Luis make you nervous?"

"It's not that."

"Seemed like it to me. What do you think, Stevie?"

Stevie said, "Seemed like it to me, too."

Garrett smiled to me, "You remind me of my stepmom. She doesn't like Luis either."

"Your stepmom?"

"Yeah. My real mother died. Kellie's my stepmom."

"She's fine, too," Stevie said.

"We both know you gotta be nice to me," Garrett said, "or there's no way I sign the papers. You gotta be real nice. I know it's killing you, but hey."

"What kind of game are you playing?" I asked.

"No game," he said.

"Do you have any intention of signing?"

He shrugged. "I'm still thinking about it. It depends how nice you are to me and my friends. If you insult me or them, well, you won't get what you want."

I wanted to throw myself across the room and slam my fist into his mouth, but instead I gripped the arms of the chair tighter.

He looked up as Luis finally came down the stairs, his face oddly flushed.

"All through?" Garrett asked him.

"Yeah," he said. Then, to me, "There's something wrong with your toilet, man. You need to get that fixed."

"There's nothing wrong with . . ."

"We need to go," Garrett said, smiling at me. "I've got school tomorrow, you know?" To his friend, he said, "Ready, Luis?"

"Catch you later," Garrett said to me under his breath. They let themselves out. I heard the Hummer fire up. The three of them sat there for a few minutes in the dark with the motor running and a tricked-out muffler pounding out a deep beat. I shut the lights off inside to signal to them to leave and so I could watch them. I couldn't see them well, but it appeared by the way their heads bobbed that they were talking and laughing, which enraged me. Finally, the car backed out of the driveway and slowly, slowly, went down the street.

As their car rumbled away, Melissa cried out from upstairs, "Jack!"

Stained brown water pulsed out of the toilet bowl, flooding the carpet. The smell was horrific. A floating mass of feces bobbed in the water, breaking apart, pieces of it cascading over the rim.

"I'll call a plumber," I said.

"Call Cody," Melissa said, gagging. "Call Brian, too."

Four

I GREW UP ON a series of ranches in Montana. I remember each one clearly. What I mean is I remember the layout of each place, where the buildings were, the corrals, the hiding places. The ranches were near Ekalaka in eastern Montana, Billings, Great Falls, Townsend, Helena. My father was a ranch foreman, and he moved us around with his jobs. I wish I could say he moved up, but he didn't. Some ranches were better than others, but all seemed to have owners my dad couldn't get along with. He had his own ideas about cows, horses, and range management, and if the owner didn't completely agree with everything he wanted to do, my father would tell my mother that he and the owner "didn't see eye to eye" and my mother would sigh and they'd start asking around until he found another job. Once the new job was in the bag, he would angrily quit the old one, pack all of our possessions in the pickup and stock trailer, and we'd go off to the next ranch. My only constant was my parents, and as I grew older I became ashamed of them.

I've since reconsidered in part, and I feel guilty for being ashamed. They were simple people from another era and mind-set. They were the Joads. They worked hard and didn't even look up as the world passed them by. They rarely read books, and their conversation was about land, food, and weather. My dad didn't buy a color television set until he no longer had a choice. But in many ways they gave me gifts I just didn't recognize or appreciate at the time. They gave me perspective. I am the only person I know who grew up *outside*. I know hard work and suffering because that's what my family specialized in. When my coworkers complain about long hours or the amount of paper on their desks, I contrast it with calving time during a spring blizzard where if you don't get the newborn to the barn within minutes, it will freeze to death in midbawl.

I simply wasn't hardwired for ranch work. I fixed fence, branded, docked, vaccinated, fed hay out of wagons and pickups to starving cattle in the winter. But it just didn't take. I was never surly or disrespectful toward my dad and his occupation, just disinterested. He gave up on me early on as a future ranch foreman or competent hand. My mother withheld affection except for unexpected and oddly inappropriate moments. I remember once when I was walking down the dirt road to the school bus stop, and I realized she was running after me. I stopped and ducked, covering my head with my arms, expecting a beating and wondering what I'd done wrong. Instead, she smothered me in her arms, kissed the top of my head, said with tears in her eyes, *Oh, you're my world, you're my everything my wonderful, wonderful boy.* She was still kissing and hugging me when the bus pulled up filled with hooting rural kids hanging out of the windows. When I got home that night I asked her what had come over her, and she went pale and looked back at me with wide-eyed horror for bringing it up in front of my father. Only now do I understand the depth of parental love she revealed to me. I feel it myself when I look at Angelina and know that no matter what happens, I'll love her.

I used to take refuge in the theory that my mother secretly cheered for me to get away. Now that I have, I'm not so sure I was right about her secret wishes. Instead, I think she saw me as her surrogate for rebellion against her husband and her life in general. Not to say she was mean—she wasn't. But she was born with a dark cloud over her head that got darker as she aged. I've reconciled myself to that.

The only place we lasted more than two years was on the HS Bar between Townsend and Helena. The owner, whom I only met once, was a millionaire investor who lived in Connecticut. He was blustery, fast-talking, and abrasive. He showed up on the ranch in cowboy clothes that were inspired by *Bonanza* and looked more like a costume than real clothing. I didn't like him—he called me "Jake" instead of Jack—but due to his poor health, a bitter divorce, and problems with the SEC, we didn't see or hear much from him. Therefore, my dad said he was the best owner he'd ever worked for, and he got along with him. They saw "eye to eye," my dad said, meaning the owner never spoke to him. During those years, I took the bus into Helena High. I was a Bengal. On the way to town we picked up Cody Hoyt in East Helena, which was on the wrong side of the tracks. Cody and I became great friends. Later, we met Brian Eastman and the three of us clicked, probably because none of us really belonged to any other established group. Brian's father was a Presbyterian minister in Helena.

We hunted, fished, hiked, and chased girls together. Even early on, it was obvious Brian was destined for great things. All of the girls loved Brian. He was their best friend and confidant. Cody and I met girls through Brian because none of them ever seemed good enough for him. At least, that's what we thought at the time.

After high school, Brian and I went off to college. Brian to the University of Denver on a scholarship. I went to Montana State in Bozeman on financial aid and student loans that would hang over my head for ten years. When I took my twenty-year-old pickup to

Bozeman, I knew I would never return to the HS Bar or whatever ranch my parents were managing. Cody stayed around Helena and worked both construction and on ranches, pulling a six-month stint on the HS Bar working for my dad. He told me later that working for my dad convinced him to enroll in the police academy so he'd never have to work for such a mean old son of a bitch for the rest of his life.

I waited until Melissa and I were engaged before introducing her to my parents so as not to scare her off. My dad took a long look at her, turned to my mom, said, "She's too good for him." Melissa's parents, who lived in Billings at the time and were not yet divorced, felt the same way. With those hot winds of confidence filling our sails, we drove to Las Vegas with Brian and Cody in Brian's car, littering the highways with empty beer cans all the way to Nevada. While nursing screaming hangovers, my friends served as best men and witness to the wedding that took place at Chapel of the Dunes in Glitter Gulch.

I got my degree in journalism, which turned out to be practically worthless, and started as a reporter at the *Billings Gazette*. Mainly, I worked as an assistant in graphics making a dollar over minimum wage. We lived in a trailer out by MetraPark, within sight and smell of the livestock they brought in for auctions, sharing the place with two dogs who just showed up and stayed. Melissa landed better than I did, and went from assistant in reservations at a local hotel to assistant general manager to general manager within two years. When an opening came up at the Billings Convention and Visitor's Bureau, she convinced me to apply and used her connections to talk me up. Her reputation was so good the CVB board assumed her husband might be worthwhile, so they hired me. After a few years, I did stints in Bozeman and Casper, Wyoming, learning the travel industry. I started to feel like my father, moving about from place to place.

Brian stayed in Denver after graduation and was a highly successful real-estate developer who had quickly become prominent and high-profile within the community. He was also on the board of the Denver CVB, and suggested to Linda Van Gear, Vice President of Tourism, to hire me.

So we moved to the big city.

Cody bounced around in law enforcement from place to place as well, from small town to small town in Wyoming and Montana, then to Loveland, Colorado. His name began to pop up in the *Denver Post* and *Rocky Mountain News* in newspaper articles in connection with several high-profile crimes, including the kidnapping, rape, and murder of a college coed by an illegal Mexican immigrant. The article in the *News* referred to him as a "relentless investigator." He married and divorced twice. He eventually signed on with the Denver Police Department, and had recently been promoted to detective first class in the Criminal Investigations Division. Cody was the lead investigator who had arrested Aubrey Coates, the man known in the newspapers as the "Monster of Desolation Canyon."

We chose Denver like so many others. I meet very few people in Denver who are from Denver, or from Colorado. There is little sense of shared history or culture. Relationships and connections are as deep as the piddling South Platte River that trickles through the city.

"YOU COULD PROBABLY SWEAR out some kind of vandalism complaint and I'm sure they know it," Cody Hoyt said later that night. "It isn't whether you've got reason to press charges, it's whether you've got the guts to take them on and piss them off."

Cody came right over, as did Brian. Larry of LARRY'S 24/7 EMERGENCY PLUMBING was still upstairs.

Cody still wore the same sweats he'd had on earlier that day, and he hadn't shaved. He smelled of beer, cigarette smoke, and sweat, and he said he'd spent the evening watching the game at a cop bar near police headquarters on Cherokee Street after dropping off the drill earlier. As he grew older, Cody was looking more and more like his father, a notorious drinker and Vietnam War vet with a bulbous nose and kettle-sized potbelly who did odd jobs throughout the county from a ramshackle panel van. The semiautomatic pistol he had clipped to the waistband of his sweatpants gave me pause and created an air of seriousness and purpose our living room had been lacking, I thought.

Brian, on the other hand, wore chinos, tasseled loafers with no socks, and an untucked pale blue dress shirt. His hair was receding and had been reduced to a tight swoosh high on his forehead. He had penetrating hazel eyes. He'd lost even more weight from when I'd seen him last and was beginning to resemble a hanger for his fine clothes.

Melissa had asked if they wanted anything before settling down in a chair. Cody asked for a beer. Brian wanted ice water with "a little slice of lemon."

"I'm sure it was Luis," I said. "He was in the bathroom a long time. I'm not sure Garrett didn't put him up to it, though."

"Disgusting," Brian said. "*Animals.*"

"The 'Sur-13' tattoo you described," Cody said, "that's for Sureños 13—the local chapter of a nationwide gang. You see the gang graffiti all over the south side and downtown. We know all about them—they deal most of the meth in Colorado. I'll check out this Luis dude with the gang task force, see if they know him."

"Why would Luis be with Garrett," I asked, "and vice versa? Stevie is a white kid, too."

Cody said, "We're seeing it more and more. Rich white kids slumming with the Mexican gangsters. They want some of that power and cool to rub off on them. It's just like white rappers, trying to be something they're not. The Mexican gangs are the kings of Denver, just like every other city in the West and Southwest."

I asked, "What's in it for the gangsters?"

"Connections," Cody said. "Access to schools and neighborhoods where there are plenty of kids with disposable income. Plus, Luis is probably smart. He knows Garrett's dad is a federal judge. That connection could help him and his buddies somewhere down the road."

"Something else," I said. "The remote control for the television is missing. They must have taken it when I got them the drinks."

"That was nice of you," Cody said sarcastically.

"We were nice to them because we didn't want to start out as adversaries," Melissa said. "We hoped they'd see reason once they met us and saw the home we've established for Angelina . . ."

Brian and Cody nodded sympathetically.

Cody glanced down at his notes, said, "So did Garrett say anything you could consider threatening?"

"No."

"But he indicated you better be nice to him or he wouldn't sign the papers?"

"Yes."

"Melissa, did you hear that exchange?" Cody asked.

"No."

He turned back to me. "So it's your word against his."

I shook my head. "It wasn't just what they said, it was how they acted. Like they were sharing a big joke being here. They kept looking at each other like they'd burst out laughing anytime."

"It was really uncomfortable," Melissa said. "Garrett stares at me like I'm a piece of meat."

That agitated Brian, who leaned forward and gripped his knees with his hands. He was protective of Melissa and had been since our marriage. We were, he said, his surrogate family since he'd never have one of his own. He and Melissa talked on the telephone every few days. Long, aimless conversations punctuated by her laughter and her mock-outraged cries of "Brian!" when he said something catty or off-color. He had been there for her after the miscarriages, and he had a rapport with her I sometimes envied. She was still amazed that in all of those years growing up I hadn't realized he was gay, since she'd known the first time she met him. He was, Melissa said, her best friend. Brian's partner was an architect named Barry. They'd been together for several years and lived in a hip loft apartment in the heart of the city. Barry was hard to get to know, I thought. I found him stiff and standoffish, but he hit it off with Melissa right away. I didn't see Barry much.

Melissa once told me she always suspected Cody was conflicted in his feelings toward his old friend since Brian had become so successful—and more flamboyant in his personal life. I shrugged it off and attributed Cody's attitude to the cynicism so many cops held toward businessmen. Cody had grown up reciting the Honoré de Balzac line (even though he didn't know it was Honoré de Balzac), "Behind every great fortune there is a crime." I think he believed it. And he probably attributed it to both John Moreland *and* Brian.

Brian looked at me with anger. "Why did you just *let* them in?"

"I thought maybe Garrett wanted to talk," I said. "I hoped he'd offer to sign away custody. But he never even mentioned it until I brought it up."

"You can't prove they took the remote, though," Cody said.

"I know I had it when the game started," I said. "I went to the kitchen while they were here, and that's when I assume they took it."

"Why would they want a remote control they can't use?" Cody asked.

"A trophy," Brian said. "It's symbolic. It's like they are taking control away from you. Is anything else missing?"

Melissa and I looked around the living room. It was possible something else was gone, but I couldn't be sure. I still had the lingering feeling from our meeting earlier in the day that our house was unfamiliar to me.

Melissa's eyes paused on the mantel, and I saw the blood drain from her face. She quickly got up and went to the fireplace.

"The photo of Angelina and me in the hospital," she said.

"Garrett was looking at that earlier today," I said. "I saw him."

"Maybe he wanted a photo of his daughter," Brian said.

"His birth daughter," I corrected. Melissa was sensitive to terms.

"Or maybe," Cody said, "he wanted a photo of Melissa."

The thought made me clench my fists.

Larry the plumber cleared his throat while he came down the stairs. He was shaking his head and smiling. "All fixed," he said. "Happens all the time when you've got toddlers."

Melissa and I exchanged puzzled looks.

"I should start a museum collection of the things I've found in toilets," Larry said, standing on the landing and finishing up his invoice on a clipboard. "Barbie dolls, socks, shoes. One kid tried to flush a whole apple because he didn't want his mom to know he didn't eat it. Problem is, the only people interested in what we find in toilets is other plumbers."

"We don't have a toddler," Melissa said.

"You don't?" Larry said, looking up. "That's strange."

Then he saw Harry and he laughed. "Next to toddlers, it's the Labradors who drop things in toilets."

"What was it?" I asked.

"Your remote control," Larry said. "It was wedged down in there and it's ruined, I'm afraid. Unless you want me to clean it off and try to get it working again."

"That's okay," I said.

"It's still a mess up there," Larry said, handing me the bill. I tried not to gasp when I saw the amount—nearly $400.

"You pay dearly for twenty-four/seven emergency calls," Larry said, trying to sound breezy, "especially on game night after I've had a few cold Coors and gone to bed early."

As Larry left the house and climbed into his panel van in the driveway, Brian said, "The symbolism continues. He took your control and he and his buddy flushed it down the toilet and crapped on it. Exactly what kind of kid are you dealing with?"

CODY SAID, "LET'S COME up with a plan."

We were up until two in the morning. It took an hour for the four of us to strip the rugs and hose them down outside and to clean the bathroom floor. Brian wore a bandana over his nose and mouth, but we could hear him saying, over and over, "Animals." Before we started cleaning, Brian took photos of the mess with his digital camera and put the camera in his pocket.

Brian thought we needed a new attorney since I'd fired Dearborn. We needed a bulldog, Brian said, someone who would "go after the Morelands and drop a nuclear bomb on them."

"We can't afford someone like that," I said. "We're strapped as it is with the house, the adoption. We don't have Melissa's income anymore."

"I was wondering if that would come up," she said more heatedly than I could have anticipated.

Before I could explain myself, she said, "We can sell the house. I can go back to work. I've gotten calls from Marriott and Radisson . . ."

"I'll help you out," offered Brian. "Don't worry about money. In fact, let me be your advocate in this whole mess."

He leaned forward, his voice dropped an octave. His business voice. "Since I've been in Denver I've met a hell of a lot of people, and a bunch of them owe me favors. It's a big city, yes, and it's growing like crazy, but that's at the margins. At its core it's still a small town run by a cabal of old-timers, developers, and politicians. There are levers of power, and I know how to work them. I've been doing it for years. I know city councilmen and media people, and you know I'm familiar with the mayor's inner circle. If word gets out I'm fronting for you, this changes your problem into an *issue*. That's the last thing the powers that be want."

"Thank you, Brian," Melissa said, her eyes glistening with tears.

I didn't know what to say. No one in my life had ever said the words *Don't worry about money*.

"No," Cody said. "I don't think it's the best plan. Even with a loan and a new attorney . . ."

"I never said 'loan,'" Brian said sharply to Cody.

". . . you're still up against Judge John Moreland," Cody continued, dismissing Brian just as curtly. "Moreland is a judge, and he's connected in more ways than you can know. He can hire teams of lawyers to tie you up and drain you for years. Plus, any judge would determine he could provide real well for the baby while you two get deeper and deeper in debt."

"It's just not right," Brian said through clenched teeth.

"No, it ain't," Cody said, not without sympathy. "But the fact is Garrett didn't sign away custody, right? He may be a thieving, humping little scumbag, but he has the law on his side. And lots of luck finding a good lawyer who wants to take on a sitting judge. Particularly this sitting judge."

Melissa sighed, sat back. Her eyes were rimmed with red. There was a set to her mouth that indicated she was fighting back tears. "It's so unfair. We don't deserve this. We did everything right. I'll fight them to my last breath," she said, almost spitting the words out. "I'll do anything, say anything, to keep my daughter. If I need to act like I'm flirting with Garrett—I will."

I winced.

"Somehow," she said, "we've got to convince him to sign the papers. I can't believe he has any interest at all in Angelina. He doesn't want to be a father although I can't figure out what his game is. Maybe he's just using this situation to intimidate us."

"Sounds like he likes *you*," Brian said to her.

"We can't confront him," she said. "We've got to find a way to convince him to come around."

"This is headed the same direction Julie Perala suggested," I said.

She turned to me. "You can continue to be nice to him, can't you? At least pretend you don't hate him until we can figure out how to persuade him?"

"After what he did tonight?" I asked, gesturing upstairs. "He's not just calculating. He's evil. I looked into his eyes and got chills."

"That'll play well in court," Cody said, rolling his eyes. "Don't you know there is no such thing as evil in this day and age? In our politically correct city? Man, you've got to get out more."

Brian said to Cody, "Some of us call it tolerance and diversity, Cody. It's thought of as progress."

Cody blew out a stream of breath, said, "Progress, my ass."

"Please," Brian said, "let's deal with the issue at hand, okay?"

"It's not Garrett," Melissa said, ignoring them. "It's his father. If we could separate them, and I could just talk with Garrett . . ."

"No," I said. "I don't think it's a good idea."

She said, "Maybe if I talked with him or showed him how much care is required for an infant, it would scare him off. Maybe he needs to see some dirty diapers or throw-up on a bib and he'd realize he's in way over his head even if his parents are actually raising her."

"But he didn't want to see her," I said. "There's a reason for that. You're assuming he's reasonable. I didn't see any of that."

"You think he's *evil*," Cody sneered.

"Garrett doesn't want to confront the situation in real life," she said. "He wants to avoid her. Maybe if he actually saw her . . ."

"I don't know," Brian said, shaking his head.

I agreed.

Melissa took a moment to look at each of us in turn.

"Guys," she said, "we need to think of Angelina's best interests most of all here. If the worst possibly happens, she might end up with them. I'm not saying that should happen, but we can't just dismiss the possibility out of hand. John Moreland seemed pretty determined to me. And if the worst comes about, I don't want to poison Angelina's relationship with them."

There were several beats of silence. I was conflicted.

"You're amazing," Brian said to Melissa in a whisper.

She was. I was astonished she was mine.

But a cold fear worked its way through my insides. If the worst-possible scenario came true, if the Morelands somehow got Angelina, I knew it would destroy Melissa. And after all we'd gone through, it would destroy *us*.

"I won't let it happen," I said.

She looked at me and smiled sadly.

"I won't," I said.

"Jesus," Cody said, standing, "I need another beer."

"WHAT MORE DO WE KNOW about John Moreland?" Melissa asked rhetorically. "He's the key."

Cody shifted on the couch as if clearing the space around him before he spoke. Brian cut in.

"I've met him a few times. At society functions and charity events. I hate to say it, but he seems like an incredibly normal, nice guy. He's best buddies with the mayor, and he's really well connected to both U.S. senators, the attorney general, and even the president. What I've heard is he's on a fast-track to something bigger. U.S. circuit, maybe higher. He just exudes competence and confidence, you know?"

Melissa shook her head. "We know."

"He's married to Kellie," I said. "Garrett referred to Kellie as his stepmom. He said his real mother was dead."

Brian sat back, screwed up his face. "I've seen Kellie. She's a blond bombshell."

"I wonder where the Sureños 13 connection comes in?" Cody said.

"Anyway," Brian said, "I can start asking around in my circles. It's amazing what you can find out about people at a higher level, you know? At cocktail parties and charity events. Get these people a few drinks in them, and all sorts of deep dark secrets start coming out. It's no different than Helena, you guys—just bigger. Maybe I can find out that he's not so perfect after all, and we'll have a little ammunition to go after him."

Melissa and I nodded, knowing Brian was an excellent gossip who could dish with anyone on earth. Attractive married women— like Melissa, come to think of it—seemed compelled to spill secrets to him because his delight in hearing them was reward in itself.

"Be careful you don't ask the wrong people and have it come back on Jack and Melissa," Cody said, "or me. I work for the city, and occassionally I have to testify in Judge Moreland's court. I got to know him when he was a U.S. Attorney and I was working joint task forces."

Cody had complained to me over the years that he was frequently assigned to multi-agency task forces involving the feds, state investigators, and the Denver Police Department. He had a problem with the bureaucracy, procedure, and territoriality of the FBI, and clashed with them. But because Cody was good at his job and didn't care about making friends, he personally broke cases and let the feds take the credit as long as they left him alone. Cody had never played well with others.

"What's he like in court?" I asked Cody. "He described himself as tough and fair. And obviously he has a thing about accountability if he'd put his family and ours through this."

Cody nodded. "All judges describe themselves that way, so don't put too much stock in it. But I'd say Judge Moreland loves being a judge, maybe too much. He's a great judge to have if you've got a defendant he hates right out of the box because he'll throw the book at him. We kind of know which way the decision is going to go right off the bat by the procedural moves Moreland makes to get to the outcome he wants to get to. If he thinks the defendant is a scumbag, he'll make sure there's federal prison time. If for some reason he thinks we've got the wrong guy, there's nothing we can do to convince him otherwise.

"Judges are supposed to hear the arguments," Cody continued, "research the law, and make a judgment based on the facts presented. Moreland does that, but he prejudges the case, and most of us think he holds himself above the law. That's great if he agrees with us, but it sucks when he doesn't. But most of the time he's procop, and that's all we care about."

Cody said, "I'm testifying in his court tomorrow on the Coates case. You know, the Monster of Desolation Canyon. Maybe you ought to come to the courtroom and see the guy in action. Court's in session at one."

"Will I learn anything?" I asked.

"You'll learn what you're up against," Cody said in a way that gave me no confidence.

There were a few uncomfortable beats of silence. Brian broke it, saying, "Garrett is the one, Melissa. Garrett's got to have some kind of history if he comes off the way you two describe him. I mean, you say he exudes evil, and he shows up tonight with a gangbanger. Maybe if we found out more about Garrett, we could convince a court he's absolutely not father material, despite what Judge Daddy says."

Cody nodded. "Might be tough, though. If he's got a juvie record, it could be sealed."

"To a detective?" Brian asked, smiling wickedly. "To the star maverick detective who got fed up with working with the feds and finally arrested the Monster? I bet that detective has ways to take a look at the file."

I cautiously checked Cody out. I didn't want to pressure him.

"I'll make some discreet calls," he said. "But I've absolutely got to stay away from any kind of investigation of the judge himself. I've got to stay completely clean. Can you imagine what would happen to me and the department if word got out I was investigating a sitting judge on my own? Shit, I'd get sent back to Montana or worse."

Brian shuddered. The last place he ever wanted to go was home.

"Okay then," Brian said, a gleam in his eye, slapping his knees. "We have a plan and less than a month to implement it. I'll find out what I can about the judge, Cody will check on the kid. Jack and Melissa, you keep doing what you're doing. Hire a good lawyer and fight the bastards as long as you can. In the meanwhile, I think you should swear out a complaint against Garrett and Luis for that stunt they pulled here tonight."

Cody held up his hand. "If you do that, you can't implicate me in any way. And I think it's a stupid idea."

"Why?" Brian said, hurt.

Melissa jumped in. "We don't want to antagonize Garrett. Not yet. We want to try and win him over first."

Brian looked at me with a *what-can-you-do?* look.

WHEN BRIAN AND MELISSA went upstairs to look in on Angelina, Cody came out of the kitchen with another beer.

"You sure you want that?" I asked. "You've got to testify tomorrow, right?"

Cody shrugged and popped the top. "We're going to nail that Coates son of a bitch. We've got the Monster of Desolation Canyon dead to rights. I'm not worried, even though the feds are mad at me for breaking it. But I do hope the judge didn't recognize me in front of your house. If he knows we're friends . . ."

"What?"

He shrugged. "I'm not sure."

Cody took a long pull off the beer, and we sat in silence for a few moments. Then he leaned forward and spoke softly to me. "I know Brian means well, but . . . well, I can see him running his mouth to all his society friends. They'll eat this up. And if Judge

Moreland hears about a concerted effort to dig up dirt on him or his son, he might really lower the boom on you two—and maybe me."

"Meaning what?" I asked, a little angry.

"Maybe he takes back his offer to get you another baby. That's a pretty generous offer, Jack."

"Melissa would never consider it, Cody," I said. "Neither would I."

"Sometimes you've got to get the best deal you can, is all I'm saying. You know I've got a son of my own, right?"

"*What?*"

Cody wiped his mouth with his sleeve. "Yeah—the result of a little drunken tryst up in Fort Collins when I was working undercover. A barmaid name of Rae Ann. She's married now to her second husband, but I send her money for little Justin every month. On my salary it's a hit, but whatever."

"You never told us," I said.

He shrugged. "It happens. But that's not my point. My point is Justin and I are getting close now that he's turned six. Those first five years he was just a baby. He could have been any baby, to be honest. Now he's a real person, you know? He likes baseball and rocks. But for those first five years, he was just kind of a little fat . . . *thing*. Babies aren't people until they grow up, is what I've learned."

I shook my head. "I don't follow."

He killed the beer. "I guess I'm saying for a man, babies are babies. You could get another one, and she'd grow up to be a person. Hell, maybe you'd love her more than you love Angelina now. You just don't know. If you have the chance to get another baby, you and Melissa will raise a winner, is what I'm saying."

I saw a flash of red in front of my eyes. "Cody, I think it's late, and you're drunk. So shut up. Now."

He raised his hand, "I'm just saying . . ."

"I know what you're saying. Stop it. It's not an option."

"You might want to give it some thought, Jack."

"It's not an option."

He started to argue more when Melissa and Brian appeared on the stairs.

"Enough," I cautioned Cody.

"Okay," he said. "So, will I see you tomorrow?"

At that moment I didn't care if I ever saw Cody again.

"Call me," Brian said to Melissa as he hugged her goodbye.

"I will," she said. She was as exhausted as me, and showing it. Tears welled again in her eyes.

"Too bad we can't just call Uncle Jeter to take care of things." Cody laughed. "He'd love to drive down here and kick some ass."

I smiled at the thought. Jeter Hoyt was a legend when we were growing up in Helena. One of the reasons no one ever touched Cody, Brian, or me was because Jeter Hoyt was Cody's uncle, and stories about him were the kind told only in furtive whispers after the storyteller had glanced over his shoulder to see who was in the room.

When they were gone, Melissa said, "You have some good friends."

I said, "*We* have some good friends." I didn't tell her what Cody had said.

WE'D BEEN IN BED AN HOUR. Melissa had tucked the covers around Angelina and whispered something to her that didn't come over the monitor. Our daughter's sleeping breath provided the sound track in our room. I was sleeping fitfully.

AT 4:00 A.M. I heard the burbling sound of a motor cruising by on the street. I recognized it as Garrett's car.

I imagined him out there with Luis, looking at our house as they crawled by, the photo between them on the seat.

Monday, November 5

Twenty Days to Go

Five

ANGELINA WOKE US UP very early Monday morning, but in the most pleasant way possible.

"Listen to her," I said. "She's singing."

"It's not really a song," Melissa said. "She's just happy."

We listened to Angelina coo and say nonsense words over the monitor. Melissa's face, as she listened, was a picture of momentary serenity.

"Did you get any sleep?" I asked Melissa.

"Not much," she said.

"Me either."

THE COURTROOM OF JUDGE John Moreland in the Alfred A. Arraj United States Courthouse on 19th Street was spacious and blond–wood paneled and lit with recessed lighting that created an atmosphere of serious decorum. I got to the crowded courtroom and found a seat in the second-to-last row, just in time to see Detective Cody Hoyt take the stand. Large faded murals done in the Depression era depicting Colorado history—silver and gold miners, railroaders, Pikes Peak—lined the walls. The scenes reminded me that Colorado had a go-go, get-rich-quick beginning that was being replicated by the most recent wave of newcomers—like me—who came here not because of family ties or culture but because there was opportunity.

The acoustics inside the courtroom were amazing. Despite the size of the room and the number of spectators, I could hear the muffled clicking of the court reporter's fingers on her keyboard from her desk near the bench, the shuffle of paper as the Assistant U.S. Attorney reviewed her notes on a yellow legal pad, and the labored breathing of the defendant, Aubrey Coates, forty-three, accused of the kidnapping, sexual assault, and murder of Courtney Wingate, age five, who went missing from a playground area at the Desolation Canyon Campground where Coates was employed as a campground host. Because the campground was located within a national forest, the trial was taking place in federal court.

Although I'd spent some time in courtrooms in Billings as a journalist—I covered the infamous trial where the two Crow Indian brothers and their meth-addict girlfriends went on the weeklong crime spree across southern Montana and northern Wyoming and murdered a ranch couple along the way—Judge Moreland's courtroom had a slick sense of process about it that probably came from the no-nonsense, clipped way he moved things along. He didn't shout, or gesticulate, but when he spoke, everyone listened. He was charismatic and in total command. I couldn't keep my eyes off him in the way one can't keep one's eyes off a great actor—Denzel Washington, say—even when he isn't speaking or the focus of attention. I wasn't the only one so afflicted. If Moreland raised an eyebrow while a lawyer asked a question, that lawyer got the vapors, and the opposing attorneys acted smug. Of course, I observed him to see if

I could learn anything about him, to size him up, to find a weakness. If he saw me enter the room, he showed no sign of recognition. I was still buzzing from the events of the night before. There was a black ball of dread in my belly that seemed to be pushing upward into my lungs, leaving me short of breath.

I was seated next to a large and well-dressed black woman in a floral-print dress and with a fleshy wide face who seemed unrelated to the players. I continued to survey the courtroom. Cops, reporters I recognized from local television and cable news, plenty of observers attracted by the lurid nature of the case itself, including, I assumed, my new companion next to me. Then I found myself staring at the back of the head of Aubrey Coates himself, sitting at a table facing the judge.

"That there's the Monster," the woman next to me said, leaning my way. Her bare chocolate arm radiated heat as she pressed into me, and her breath smelled of mint and cigarettes. "He turns around and looks back every once in a while, seeing who is here," she whispered. "I think he likes the attention because he is a sick, sick man. When he looked at me I gave him one of these . . ." She instantly sat back with attitude and gave me a wicked dead-eye glare. "That look usually freezes folks where they walk. But he just kind of smiled at me."

I'd seen photos of Aubrey Coates in the newspaper. Of course, the photos were prior to his haircut and shave. Now he sat slumped, small, in an ill-fitting suit jacket. He had tufts of gray hair over large ears, and when he turned his head to whisper something to his lawyer, I saw a hawkish and heavily veined nose, protruding lips, and a pointy chin. When he turned back, his bald dome reflected the light from the walls in a checkerboard pattern on the side of his head. I thought of the nature of evil, how sometimes you could just see it and sense it.

"He did it," she said, nodding. "No doubt in my mind. And he did a lot more, too."

I held out my hand. "Jack."

"Olive," she said, her large hands enveloping mine. "Ask me anything. I know everybody in his room. This is what I do—observe trials."

"Do you know Coates's defense attorney?" I asked, looking at a rotund man sitting next to Coates with an easy smile and manner.

She nodded, and her eyes widened. "He's got the best—Bertram Ludik. I don't know how that little worm can afford him. I think if Charles Manson had hired Bertie Ludik, he'd be out there sticking forks into people to this day!"

"Come on," I said.

"You watch," she said. Then: "Luckily, Judge Moreland won't allow Bertie to be Bertie."

"That guy I know," I said, chinning toward Cody, who was approaching the stand.

"Detective Hoyt," she whispered sympathetically. "I'd like to take that man home and hug him and tell him everything will be all right."

"Why?" I asked, perplexed.

"He's a troubled soul," she said. "Look at him. A great detective, but a troubled soul."

He's just hungover, I thought.

Cody was wearing a dark blue suit that gathered under his arms, a white shirt, and a solid but faded red tie. He looked courtroom savvy but disheveled at the same time. He shambled when he walked and raked his fingers back through his hair, messing it up. When he sat down in the witness chair, his eyes took in the room in a world-weary way that said "I'M A COP. JUST LET ME DO MY JOB." I nodded at him, but I'm not sure he saw me.

Judge Moreland said, "The witness is reminded he is still under oath."

"I understand, Your Honor."

"Miss Blair," Judge Moreland said to the Assistant U.S. Attorney, an attractive redhead who had been huddled in conference with the U.S. Attorney at the prosecution table, "you may continue to question the witness."

"Thank you, Your Honor," she said, standing, holding the legal pad at her side as she approached the podium. "I have just a few more questions."

Moreland gestured impatiently for her to begin.

"Detective Hoyt," she said, flipping back the pages on her pad, "you said Friday before the weekend recess that when you apprehended the defendant on the morning of June 8 last summer, he was in the process of destroying evidence . . ."

HERE'S WHAT I KNEW about Aubrey Coates, the Monster of Desolation Canyon.

Every summer, children vanish. Over the last decade children had gone missing while on vacation with their families in the Mountain West.

It happens quite a lot in the mountains. Often, the families are having picnics and reunions and suddenly someone realizes that one of the kids didn't show up for dinner. Sometimes the children got lost, sometimes they washed into rivers, sometimes they got mad at their siblings and "ran away," and sometimes they climbed into the wrong car. Most are found. I remember when my dad and I volunteered to search for a missing little boy who'd wandered away from a campsite near the Gates of the Mountains Wilderness north of Helena. We took horses, and I remember it as a great and serious adventure combing the trails and riverbanks calling out "Jarrod!" for two days. Until Jarrod was found less than a mile away from where he'd vanished and confessed he'd gotten turned around in the forest and fallen asleep. He admitted hiding from volunteer rescue people as they walked and rode by because they were strangers, and he had been taught not to talk to strangers—even those calling his name.

But in some isolated instances the children were never found. These children vanished from isolated locations in Colorado (Grand Junction, Pueblo, Trinidad), Utah (Wasatch, St. George), Wyoming (Rock Springs, Pinedale). Boys and girls, all under the age of twelve. In nearly every instance, the parents said the child was there one minute and gone the next. The places the children were last seen were playgrounds, near streams, on hiking trails. Then poof—they were gone.

In retrospect, when one looks at the instances of these particular missing children over the years, you can see a pattern, and the authorities are blamed for not seeing what should have been in plain sight. But that's unfair, as Cody explained to me. The children went missing in three states over ten years. The only "pattern" was that they vanished from campsites or in undeveloped areas. There were no calling cards left, no evidence of where the children were taken, and nothing left behind. All occurred in different jurisdictions, with different sets of law-enforcement personnel. The FBI was never called in because linkage wasn't discovered until after the fact. None of the parents were ever contacted for ransom or taunted. No one confessed or implicated others. And none of the bodies was ever found.

Aubrey Coates, who worked as a temporary replacement for campground hosts, was questioned on four different occasions because he had his trailer parked in the areas where the children went missing. In each instance, Coates answered all questions asked and was cooperative. More than once, Coates volunteered to help search for the missing children. He had no arrests, and his name didn't exist on any sexual-predator lists. National Forest Service staffing personnel in all three states knew him to be a kind of eccentric loner with his battered Airstream trailer that bristled with television and Internet satellite dishes and antennae, but he was considered experienced and reliable. Whenever a host got ill, or went on vacation, Coates was contacted to fill in. His job consisted of collecting overnight fees, keeping the campgrounds clean and neat, making sure campers didn't overstay their limits, and providing advice and assistance to campers in states where camping is part of the common cultural fabric. In twenty years of being a campground host, only two complaints had been filed against him. The complaints—parents in one instance felt he leered at their children, and someone accused him of being rude because he angrily refused to come outside his trailer ("What was he *doing* in there?") when a camping family wanted to borrow a tire pump— were minor and filed in two different states six years apart.

Coates covered his tracks very well. Three of the missing children were taken *after* the regular campground hosts had returned, so his name never came up.

Worst of all, Cody told me, was that the seven children prior to Courtney Wingate was an arbitrary number. The actual number of children Coates took could be ten, or twenty, or fifty. In the three decades across the West—years Coates has not accounted for—Cody said there were over seventy missing-children cases open from Nebraska to California. And dozens more in western Canada.

Why just seven? Because the police found photos of seven missing children on Aubrey Coates's laptop computer. If there had been others—and Cody thought Coates had been successful in destroying electronic records on a server located in the trailer as well as most of the laptop—Cody and the computer specialists brought in on the case couldn't find them.

After initially filing charges against Coates for the disappearance of all seven children in the hope Coates would bargain with them—lesser charges in exchange for a confession or the locations of the bodies— the federal prosecutor ran into a brick wall because Coates admitted nothing and proclaimed his innocence. After a few months, the charges were pared down to the disappearance of Courtney Wingate, who vanished most recently, in Desolation Canyon, where Coates had served as temporary campground host. Several digital photos of Courtney were found on Coates's laptop, and her parents identified him as lurking around their campsite the night before she disappeared.

As Cody and the prosecutor walked the jury through a Power-Point presentation of the photos found on Coates's computer—evidence Coates had been targeting the little girl for some time, including shots of her riding a big plastic three-wheeler and outside at an unidentifiable location with pine trees in the background—I found her parents behind the prosecutor's table. It was painful to imagine what they were going through. Crystal Wingate, Courtney's mother, was thin, pinched, hard, with the wizened face of a woman who'd seen tough times, none tougher than this. Donnie Wingate, who worked construction, had a big mustache and mut-tonchops, and he looked very uncomfortable being indoors. He was so tense as the photos were shown that I could see cords in his neck popping out. Donnie looked big enough and capable enough to step over the rail barrier and snap Aubrey Coates's neck before the bailiff could stop him. I wished he would. He glared at the back of Coates's head as Cody explained the other photos he'd found on the laptop and the extensive—but sabotaged—array of electronics they'd discovered in Coates's trailer.

Cody testified for another hour and a half, much of it a summary and recap of his all-day session on Friday. I was riveted. In unambiguous language and with a manner that had been honed doing exactly this in years of courtroom appearances, Cody let himself be led by Assistant U.S. Attorney Blair. The U.S. Attorney himself—tall, bald, athletic—looked on with obvious approval.

Cody built his case methodically from the initial missing child call from the Wingates to his suspicion when he arrived at the scene at the request of the county sheriff and first saw the campground tender's trailer with so much electronic capability.

He said, "Coates's trailer reminded me of one of those communications units our military uses overseas. You know, the ones that can transmit audio and visual data to some commander all the way in Florida or Nevada, so they can give orders on the battlefield in real time. There were dishes and antennae all over the trailer, and a generator outside if his campground power source wasn't enough. So I asked myself why a man who wanted to be so connected to the Internet in such an immediate way would choose to be in an isolated campground when he could be in Denver, or any city. It started with that."

Without consulting his notes, Cody told the jury how, with that question in mind, he started his investigation of Aubrey Coates. The more he learned about Coates's habits and travels and the missing children that corresponded with his locations, the more he suspected Coates of taking Courtney. The records of Coates's satellite Internet provider showed patterns of massive activity, sometimes thousands of megabytes of data being uploaded and downloaded. Most of the activity took place from 2:00 A.M. to 6:00 A.M.

"The Internet activity fit the profile of someone involved in child pornography," Cody said. "And he was not only receiving streaming-video files and other high-density material, but he was transmitting it—uploading it—as well."

Aubrey Coates himself sat stock-still during Cody's damaging testimony. He didn't shake his head or roll his eyes but seemed to watch and listen carefully. It wasn't Coates who bothered me, though. Bertram Ludik seemed to behold Cody with amusement and barely disguised scorn. And as Cody built his case—convincingly, I thought, and so did Olive—the more agitated Ludik became. Once, when he sighed loudly, Judge Moreland shot a look in his direction that shut him up.

Blair read from her pad. "So when you entered the defendant's trailer on June 8 with the federal search warrant, what did you observe?"

Cody said, "We found the defendant in the process of destroying his electronic files. The video camera had been wiped clean, and the memory sticks for his still cameras were missing. He'd already burned a bunch of magazines in a trash barrel next to the trailer, material which through analysis was later identified as photos and magazines containing graphic child pornography. Obviously, he had somehow learned of the raid in advance, but we were still able to find enough evidence to arrest him."

Blair introduced the exhibits—charred photos and magazine pages in plastic envelopes. Members of the jury passed the evidence from one to the other. Several jurors looked visibly sickened by what they saw, and one lowered her glasses to the tip of her nose and glared at Coates with undisguised contempt.

"And the computers?" she asked, returning to her podium. "What did you find?"

"The photos of Courtney Wingate we showed to the jury," Cody said, "and photos of six other missing children."

When Cody said it, there were audible gasps in the courtroom. Heads of jurors swiveled toward Coates, who still sat impassively. It was a defining moment. How Donnie Wingate restrained himself is a mystery to me.

Blair concluded her questions but asked the judge for the right to follow up with Cody later, which the judge granted. As she walked to her table, there was a noticeable spring in her step. I think at that moment if the courtroom were polled—jury included—the vote would have been unanimous to find a rope and hang Aubrey Coates right there and then.

That is, until Bertram Ludik stood up, cleared his throat, shook his head sadly at Cody as if admonishing a child, and walked to the podium stiff-armed and stiff-legged, like a bear.

AT FIRST, I couldn't understand where Ludik was headed, and I didn't listen closely. Cody's testimony had taken everyone in the room up a roller coaster and plunged them down, me included. My mind wandered. Ludik's questions were procedural. When the search warrant was applied for, when it was granted. The exact time of the raid. How the items found inside Coates's trailer were cataloged. How many officers were present and the duties of each. Several times, Ludik messed up names of officers, and Cody had to correct him. Cody's patience with Ludik was impressive, I thought. He was gentle and professional, and I could see that the jurors liked him. Ludik seemed confused and disorganized. His questions bounced all over the place, and he paused after Cody's answers as if searching on his notepad for what to ask next to fill the time. When I looked to Olive with amusement, wondering what she had seen in the past of Bertram Ludik that so impressed her, she looked back and shrugged.

I looked at my watch, wondering how long it would go before Judge Moreland concluded the session for the day. I reconstructed my meeting with Julie Perala and the black ball of dread returned. My mind drifted back to yesterday.

I was jolted back to the courtroom when Blair bolted to her feet, saying, "Objection, Your Honor! Mr. Ludik's line of questioning is without foundation."

I looked to Olive. She had heard his question and was straining to hear more.

"What?" I asked her.

"Bertram asked Cody something about the laptop."

"Approach the bench," Judge Moreland said, clearly irritated with Ludik.

The discussion between the attorneys and the judge was heated. Judge Moreland covered his microphone with his hand while they argued. The U.S. Attorney heard enough from the table that he joined in the discussion. I had no idea, of course, what was being said.

Because Cody was in the witness box, he could obviously hear snippets of the argument. Although his face didn't change expression, it drained of color, and he seemed to be staring at something over our heads as if watching his life pass by. I recognized the look, and it scared me because I'd seen it before. When we were in high school together, Brian's father gathered the three of us, sat us down in his den, and asked which one of us had broken into his wet bar and taken two bottles of bourbon. I knew it wasn't me, and I guessed it wasn't Brian. Cody was the guilty party and looked it and finally confessed.

What, I wondered, was he guilty of now?

JUDGE MORELAND SENT the attorneys away. The U.S. Attorney looked furious and sat back down in a huff. Assistant U.S. Attorney Blair seemed tight as a bowstring, and she glared at Cody, her jaws clenched. Ludik, meanwhile, smiled at the jury as he walked back to the podium. I realized now Ludik's opening act of stumbling and disorganization had been a ruse, a way of getting Cody off his guard. His questions were now crisp, and his tone contemptuous.

"Detective Hoyt, I need you to clarify something for me."

Cody nodded. Then, before he could be reminded by the judge to speak so the reporter could hear him, said, "Yes."

"During the raid on my client's trailer, your report indicates 108 items of so-called evidence were taken."

"I believe that's correct," Cody said.

"I need better than your belief, Detective. You can check your notes or read the file. Don't worry, I can wait."

I knew Cody well enough to know he was angry, but he internalized it. It was the face and attitude he used to adopt when he played middle linebacker in high school, just before he fired through the offensive line and crushed somebody. He flipped through the pages of the case file until he found what he was looking for.

"Yes. There were 108 items of evidence."

"And these items of evidence were logged in at the Denver Police Department facility, correct?"

"Correct."

"But this was a joint federal and local task force. Why weren't the items taken to the federal facility, as per normal procedure in this kind of investigation?"

Cody cleared his throat and glared at Ludik. "Because the feds are nine-to-fivers. I *knew* our building would be open."

"So you not only arrested my client without informing or involving your federal partners, you took the so-called evidence to your friends downtown as well?"

"Yes I did," Cody said.

"Interesting. Now back to the evidence itself. At the DPD, each item is given a description and assigned a specific number, correct?"

"Correct."

"Each and every item. Each piece of charred paper from the trash barrel, everything."

"Correct."

"I've looked this list over many times, Detective, and I can't seem to find the description or number for the hard drive of the server in my client's trailer."

Cody looked up at Ludik.

"Did I miss something?" Ludik asked.

"No. There was no hard drive."

"What?"

"I said there was no hard drive. Coates destroyed it or hid it before we could have it analyzed."

Ludik rubbed his face. "Detective, I'm a Luddite when it comes to computers. My wife calls me 'Luddite Ludik'"—this caused some titters from the jury—"so please forgive me if I have to ask you to explain obvious things."

Judge Moreland, bless him, cut Ludik off at the pass. "Mr. Ludik, please get to the point or drop it," he said sternly.

"Yes, Your Honor. Sorry. Detective Hoyt, correct me if I'm wrong, but a hard drive is like the brains of a computer, correct? Where all of the files, all of the memories are kept?"

"Yes."

"Without the hard drive, a computer is nothing more than a nonfunctional piece of machinery, correct?"

"Yes."

"So without the hard drive of my client's server, there is no way to know what the computer was used for or where my client went in his midnight forays onto the Internet?"

"Correct."

"Same with the missing memory sticks for the digital cameras?"

"Yes."

"So all that you supposedly have to connect my client to the disappearance of poor Courtney are photos of her not on the missing hard drive from the computer supposedly used in the middle of the night or from the cameras found in his trailer, but from my client's laptop computer, correct?"

"Correct." Cody's voice was flat.

"And the photos of poor Courtney we saw earlier, they're from the laptop?"

"Yes."

"And the other photos of the missing children, they're from the laptop as well?"

"Yes."

"So did you find other things on the laptop connecting my client to child pornography? Like movies, or other disturbing photos?"

"No."

Blair was again on her feet. "Your Honor, this is going nowhere. Physical evidence of child pornography was found in the trash barrel outside the defendant's trailer!"

Ludik said to Moreland, "We don't dispute that, Your Honor. But no one has testified in this courtroom that they saw my client burning anything. There are no address labels on the magazines, and no subscription or postal records have been introduced that prove my client owned or used that material. For all we know, it could have been put in the barrel outside my client's trailer by someone else.

"Or," Ludik said, taking a theatrical step toward Cody in the witness box, "it could have even been placed there by a third party and burned just before the raid itself."

"OBJECTION!" This was from the U.S. Attorney himself, who until this moment had not been involved in the proceedings. "This is nothing but reckless speculation!"

"Get up here," Judge Moreland said angrily to the attorneys. "Now!"

The conference was brief and intense. Moreland was animated. He shook his finger at Ludik and told the U.S. Attorney loud enough for me to hear to "back off." I found myself admiring the way he ran the courtroom. And wondering what in the hell was happening.

When Ludik returned to the podium, he wasted no time.

"Detective Hoyt, back to the laptop. It is listed as 'Evidentiary Item #6' on the list, correct?"

Cody said, "Correct."

"Let me ask you something as an experienced detective and investigator. Did you find anything about the photos themselves to be unusual or odd?"

Cody hesitated. "I'm not sure what you're asking."

But I did. And it had occurred to me earlier when we saw them but didn't hit home until now. I felt sick inside. Olive, who suddenly got it as well, reached out and grasped my sleeve.

"The photos of the children," Ludik said. "In all of them, the children are at their homes or with their families. They are the kinds of photos all parents take of their kids. We all have these kinds of photos on our desks. Isn't that correct, Detective?"

"I'm not sure," Cody said.

"Get to the point," Judge Moreland said.

"I will do that now, Your Honor," Ludik said deferentially. But he hesitated and looked down, as if gathering strength, as if preparing himself to do something he really didn't want to do, but I recognized it as stage acting.

"Detective Hoyt," Ludik said, "before we go back to that, let me draw your attention once again to the list of evidence gathered at my client's trailer. Do you agree that there are 108 pieces of so-called evidence?"

"Yes."

"Now, please turn to another document in your file, Detective Hoyt. This is the check-in sheet from the evidence room at the Denver Police Department dated June 8. Can you find it?"

Cody took his time. Finally, he grunted.

"Look at it closely, Detective Hoyt. It's basically a copy of the other sheet, but there is a number on the right of each item of evidence where it's been officially received by the sergeant in charge of the room. As each piece of evidence is entered, the sergeant assigns it a specific inventory number and date, correct?"

Another grunt.

"As I read the document, Detective Hoyt, there is one piece of evidence not registered by the sergeant on June 8. It's *on* the list, but it isn't noted until June 12—four days later. Do you see the item, Detective Hoyt? I'm referring to evidentiary item number 6, the laptop. It appears that the laptop was collected from my client's trailer on June 8 but wasn't checked into the authorities until June 12. Is that what you see as well, Detective Hoyt?"

"Yes." Barely audible.

"And whose initials are those near the check-in entry on June 12, Detective Hoyt?"

"Mine."

"So did the sergeant in charge of the evidence room make a stupid error, or was there really a four-day gap between when the laptop was taken and when it was checked in?"

Cody fixed a dead-eye stare on Ludik.

"Detective Hoyt, did you answer the question?"

Cody mumbled something I couldn't hear. The whispering and murmuring in the courtroom among the spectators and the reporters drowned it out.

Judge Moreland called for quiet. When he had it, he turned to Cody, said, "Detective Hoyt, please answer the question."

"I had the laptop in my custody," Cody said.

"You did?" Ludik asked, false astonished. "Is that normal? Isn't that a breach of departmental regulations?"

Cody said, "I wanted to see what was on it. I was doing my job."

"Your job," Ludik repeated with sarcasm. "So you're a computer expert? You're qualified to root through a suspect's computer on your own for four days? Four days when real experts could have been going through it? And where were you doing this technical work—in your private Bat Cave?"

Blair was on her feet. "Judge, that's argumentative! He's harassing the witness."

Olive whispered, "The judge is letting Bertie get away with stuff I can't believe. He must be really mad at the detective, is all I can figure."

Uh-oh. I tried to make eye contact with Cody, but he wouldn't look up.

Cody glared at Ludik. His eyes burned red, his mouth was pinched tight.

Ludik apologized, then: "I'll rephrase, Your Honor. Detective Hoyt, where were you on the weekend of June 9 and 10 immediately following the raid in Desolation Canyon? And where were you Monday, June 11, when the Denver PD log shows that you didn't report for duty?"

Cody broke his glare from Ludik and looked to Blair and the U.S. Attorney, expecting something, help maybe. None came. The two of them were glaring at each other, obviously wondering who had missed this detail if it were true.

"Detective Hoyt?" the Judge prompted.

"Evergreen," Cody said. The town of Evergreen was in the mountains via I-70.

"In a hotel in Evergreen?" Ludik asked innocently.

"No," Cody answered.

"Where, then?"

"Where do you think I was?" Cody asked, baring his teeth at Ludik. "You seem to know everything, and you like drawing it out."

"You were in jail, weren't you, Detective Hoyt? Arrested for public intoxication Friday night, June 8. You were in the Evergreen town jail until Monday morning, weren't you?"

Cody said, "I was. I was celebrating our arrest of Aubrey Coates, and things got out of hand, I guess."

"You guess?"

"They got out of hand."

Olive whispered to me, "My God. *They didn't know!*"

Blair stood and asked for a recess. Moreland denied it.

Ludik shook his head sadly, as if it troubled him that the prosecution's case—all those hours of preparation, all those press conferences announcing the capture of the Monster, all of the witnesses leading up to this moment—were an unfortunate waste of time.

"So where was the laptop while you were in jail, Detective Hoyt?"

"In my car. Locked in the trunk."

"Are you sure? Could you somehow see your car out the window of the jail cell?"

"Your Honor!" Blair said, standing up, her voice high-pitched. "He's once again harassing the witness."

"It's a legitimate question," Judge Moreland answered, disappointment in Cody written across his face. He seemed the most letdown of all. "And one the witness will answer."

Not "Detective Hoyt," but *the witness.*

"Of course I couldn't see it," Cody said.

"So," Ludik said, "for two and a half days the crucial piece of evidence in this case—the piece of evidence the prosecution is counting on to send my client to prison for the rest of his life—was in the trunk of your car in a parking lot outside of a bar in Ever-green, Colorado?"

Cody tried to swallow, and it looked like it hurt. "No one tam-pered with it," he said.

"Oh? And how can you be sure?"

Cody looked away. "It wasn't tampered with," he said, without emotion.

Ludik moved in for the kill. "Detective Hoyt, let me follow up on a question that I brought up earlier—something that's been bothering me ever since I saw the evidence against my client. You say you're an expert in pedophiles and their behavior, that's why you targeted my client. But don't you find it strange that the photos he supposedly had on his laptop computer of the seven missing children were not porno-graphic or suggestive in any way? That they were candid shots taken mainly by their parents? That, in fact, the photos *were the same ones cir-culated by the various police departments in their missing persons alerts?*"

Blair, despite herself, let out a little gasp. The U.S. Attorney turned sidewise in his chair, away from Cody. Aubrey Coates slowly leaned back in his chair and looked over his shoulder at the Wingate family, as if saying, "*See?*"

"Detective Hoyt," Ludik asked, after the judge hit his gavel to once again quiet the room, "did you download those photos from your own police files onto my client's laptop?"

"No!" Cody nearly jumped from the witness stand. The bailiff took a step toward him, and the judge ordered Cody to sit down.

"Maybe Monday afternoon, after you were released from the Evergreen town jail and before you transferred custody of the laptop in question to the evidence room?" Ludik asked.

"I said no," Cody growled.

"But you can't honestly tell the jury that someone else might not have taken the laptop from your car and done it during the weekend?"

Cody shook his head.

"What, Detective Hoyt?"

"I can't say with certainty, but . . ."

"Detective Hoyt, can you recall an important case where the chain of custody of the key piece of evidence was broken quite so badly?" Ludik asked.

Cody sputtered. "We'll find that hard drive," he said. "And when we do, it won't matter. That man," Cody said, rising again, pointing at Aubrey Coates, who smiled back at him, "kidnapped and killed at least seven innocent children. You can't turn him loose to kill more!"

Judge Moreland, furious, said, "Detective, sit down and shut up, or you'll be arrested right here for contempt of my court." Turning to the jury, the judge said, "Please disregard what the witness just said. He was out of line, and what he said cannot be considered in your deliberations."

"No more questions at this time, Your Honor," Ludik said, flipping back the pages of his pad.

Judge Moreland said, "Miss Blair, redirect?"

Blair appeared stunned and angry. Her voice was weak. "We may have some more questions later, Your Honor. Right now . . . well, it's getting late in the day."

Moreland snapped, "I'll make the decisions to recess for the day, if you don't mind. I don't need your help to read the clock. Now, do you have any more questions for the witness?"

"Not at this time." Cowed.

"Bailiff," Judge Moreland said through gritted teeth, "please escort this witness off the stand."

As Cody was led through the courtroom with the bailiff at his shoulder, all eyes were on him. As he passed me our eyes met, and Cody angrily shook his head.

"Mother of God," Olive said. "I've never seen anything like that before."

I followed Cody out into the hallway. A few of his fellow cops were approaching him, trying to console him. He brushed them aside barking "Leave me alone!" and charged toward the glass doors. A couple of reporters shouted questions, which he ignored.

I caught the door as it closed and pushed it back open.

"Cody!"

He didn't turn around, just kept stomping down the stairs toward the street.

"Cody!"

On the sidewalk, he paused, and I caught up with him. I'd never seen him so furious. The skin of his face was pulled back, slitting his eyes and making his mouth a snarl.

"*That motherfucker!*" Cody hissed. "I'd like to go back in there and cap him!"

"Ludik?"

"No," Cody said, shaking me off as well. "Moreland. He fucked me. He just fucked me. And he fucked the families of all those kids."

"Cody," I said, as my friend knocked my hand off his sleeve. "It was Ludik . . ."

"You don't understand anything," Cody said. "You don't know how these things work. The judge could have steered it back my way or granted that recess so the prosecutors could regroup. He let it go when he could have stopped it. The prosecution was so stunned they couldn't think of anything to say. The judge can do anything he wants, and *he let it go on.*"

I found myself in the ridiculous circumstance of wanting to defend the man who was trying to take our baby away.

"Leave me alone!" Cody barked as I reached out for him again, and for a moment I thought he was going to cap *me.* I watched him walk into the street without even glancing at the oncoming cars, who braked so they wouldn't splatter my friend, the suddenly disgraced detective, across Bannock Street.

IT WAS DARK and spitting hard little balls of snow when I arrived home. I'd called Melissa and started to tell her what had happened in the courtroom when she cut me off, saying, "It's all over the news. They say he's being suspended." She said Brian had been at our house most of the afternoon, and they'd been following the case for hours, switching from channel to channel. Cody's demolition had become a sensation.

I parked in the driveway next to Brian's Lexus and killed the motor. The falling snow sounded like sand as it bounced off the hood and roof of the Jeep. I sat for a moment, suddenly exhausted, very much confused.

I felt a hundred years old as I willed myself to open the door and get out. The snow stung my exposed face and hands. I was numb, and not paying attention to the rhythmic thumping of hip-hop music from the street and the sound of a motor that should have been familiar and should have warned me.

As I reached for the handle on our front door the hip-hop suddenly rose in volume. Later, I realized it was because the car had stopped at the curb, and the passenger rolled down his window and aimed the gun out.

The popping was muffled by the snow, and I was hit twice in the back. I turned on my heel and was struck in the face, hot liquid splashing into my open eyes, blinding me.

I could hear laughing over the roaring in my ears as the car sped away.

Six

PAINTBALLS. I'D BEEN SHOT four times with a paintball gun. The color of the paint: yellow. The people who shot me? Garrett or Luis or Stevie, I couldn't be sure.

Melissa called the police while I wiped paint off my face with a kitchen towel. It took several minutes for my heart to slow down, for the adrenaline that had coursed through me to dissipate. My hands shook as I wiped the paint from my eyes and ears. My terror faded and was replaced by anger.

The police officer who responded, who was in his midtwenties, Hispanic, with a wisp of a mustache and a belly straining at the buttons on his uniform shirt, wrote down my statement and took photos of the paint hits on the back of my coat. He shook his head while he did it, saying I wasn't the first.

"There were quite a few similar instances this past summer," he told us. "Kids compete by seeing how many citizens they can 'kill' in a given amount of time and tally it up. They get more points for a 'kill' in a good neighborhood, like this one. We've caught a few of them. Some are gangsta wannabes, but mostly they're just normal knuckleheads."

I bit my tongue, and Melissa and I exchanged glances.

He continued, "But you didn't actually see them, right? Or get a description of the vehicle or a license plate?"

"I was blinded by the paint," I said. "I told you that."

"We'll follow up and let you know if we find anything," the officer said in a tone that meant we would never see him or hear from him again.

WHILE WE ATE—Brian had fetched Chinese takeout—Brian slid his chair back and drew his cell phone out of his breast pocket. "I called Cody earlier and left a message for him to call or come by. He's not answering."

"I hope he doesn't do anything to hurt himself," I said, "or anyone else."

I rehashed the trial for them, and Melissa shook her head sadly. "Poor Cody," she said. "Do you think Ludik really thinks Cody set up the Monster?"

"Hard to say," I said. "But he injected enough doubt into the proceedings, I don't see how they'll get a conviction now. He even had me wondering if Cody or some of his fellow cops might have planted some of the evidence. Not that I don't think Coates is guilty of something—I'm sure he is. I just don't know if they've got enough evidence that isn't tainted to convict him."

Melissa shuddered. "If he goes free, no parent in Colorado will be able to sleep at night."

"And everyone will hate Detective Cody Hoyt," Brian said, not without a vicious little note of glee.

"I doubt Coates will be able to infiltrate himself again, though," I said, ignoring Brian. "Everybody will be on the lookout for the guy."

"Don't be so sure," Brian said. "If he is found innocent, there'll be nothing in his record. He might even be able to sue to get his job back. You can't prevent a man from getting a job because the cops may have set him up, you know."

"Cody didn't set him up, I'm sure," Melissa said, scoffing.

Brian steepled his fingers on the table and gazed over them at her. "Cody is capable of doing things you might not approve of," he said. "In fact, I would say it's possible they targeted this Coates guy and maybe did some things to make their case stronger. It wouldn't be the first time that's ever happened. And we know our Cody isn't pure as the driven snow."

"Brian!" Melissa said, angry.

"He isn't," Brian said. "I'm sorry, Melissa. But Cody takes pride in putting bad men in prison, and he doesn't mind cutting corners if he needs to. He's told me that. Once, he showed me what he called his 'throw-down' gun. It was a pistol with the serial numbers filed off he would have handy if he ever needed it."

Melissa shook her head and looked to me for support.

I shrugged. Cody, in confidence, had told me as much before.

Things happened on the street, on both sides, that were under the radar. Cody had told me about some of them. According to Cody, since Mayor Halladay had been elected and had started building housing for the homeless and declared Denver to be a Sanctuary City, we'd been flooded with the indigent and illegal workers, mainly undocumented Mexicans. The gangs preyed on the new populace and sold them drugs and protection. The police, according the Cody, did their best to keep a lid on the situation without calling attention to the sharp rise in crime. When Denver was named host for a major political party convention, word came down from the mayor's office to "get those people off the streets." An unofficial crackdown was under way. The level of tension between the newcomers, the gangs, the police, and the mayor's office was rising. The police, if Cody was an indication of the rest of the force, felt the mayor was "embracing diversity" on the one hand and issuing under-the-table orders to clear out the riffraff on the other. While acting on the mayor's wishes, individual officers knew that if a brutality accusation was made or an incident captured by a ubiquitous cell-phone camera of a cop pounding on a homeless man or a minority, the mayor would side with the alleged victim because Mayor Halladay was a champion of the downtrodden, according to his spokesmen. Brian had once been very close to Halladay, before he was mayor. They'd been involved in business ventures together, but they'd had a falling-out, and their relationship was no longer cordial.

"Cody might bend the rules," I said, "but he'd never set up an innocent man. And he'd only cross the line in this case if he thought he was punishing a monster who might do it again. That's why he was so mad at Moreland. It wasn't about Cody. It was about the fact that Coates might go free and hurt more kids."

"Speaking of Judge Moreland," Brian said, withdrawing a sheaf of papers from his jacket pocket, "Melissa and I have been doing some detective work of our own."

"Let's hear it," I said.

"I'm going to go put pajamas on Angelina," Melissa said. "I'll be back in a few minutes."

While she was gone, Brian said, "It's amazing what one can find out using Google and a few well-placed friends in the right offices. Plus, there are a couple of wonderful high-society gossips who love to dish."

With that, he outlined Moreland's professional and marital history:

"In 1980," Brian read, "John Moreland graduated from Ridgeview High School in Asheville, North Carolina. He was an outstanding student, first in his class. President of the debate team, quarterback, yadda-yadda. An only child, from what I could find. His parents are deceased."

"Really? He doesn't seem that old."

"He's forty-five. His parents died in a car accident when John was eighteen. I read the clippings. The police said John's dad must have fallen asleep while he was driving home and drove head-on into a tree. Both parents were killed on impact, and Mrs. Moreland was thrown thirty feet through the windshield. There was some speculation that someone might have forced them off the road, but no one was ever charged."

"Was Moreland a suspect?"

"My first thought. But he didn't appear to be. He was at home with his girlfriend, waiting for his parents to get there. His girl-friend's name was Dorrie Pence, and she confirmed his where-abouts. Remember that name, Dorrie Pence."

I nodded.

"I'm still looking into this," Brian said. "All I can get from the newspapers was it was a tragic accident. The whole community came to the funeral, and there were fund-raisers for Moreland, that kind of thing. I've got some real estate contacts in North Carolina, and I've put out some feelers to them to find out if they ever heard anything. In my experience, real-estate folks have their fingers into everything in the community—who might be moving, who might be divorcing and selling, that kind of thing. A lot of times they know more about what's going on than the local cops. I mean, I know more about what's going on in Denver than that doofus cop who was here, if you know what I mean."

"Go on," I said, seeing Brian was still clearly enjoying this.

"Okay, well, he came to Colorado right after he left North Carolina. He attended the University of Colorado on academic scholar-ships but he had plenty of life-insurance money from the deaths of his parents. He was never a poor college student, that's for sure. He gradu-ated with a major in political science. Then off to Harvard Law School, where he graduated magna cum laude—of course. He was twenty-four, and he married his high-school sweetie, Dorrie Pence, in Denver."

"Ah," I said. "Dorrie provided the alibi, and he married her."

"Right-o," Brian said. "Garrett was born in 1989. No other

children. An only child, like his daddy. Anyway, Moreland was in private practice in Denver for the next few years. He was a very highly regarded criminal-defense attorney before switching over to civil litigation. He was named one of the ten best litigators in the nation, yadda-yadda. From what I can find out, he was one of those men who just shines at everything he does. He was appointed United States Attorney and held that position for the next five years. But here's where it gets interesting."

Melissa came back downstairs with Angelina in soft yellow pajamas with feet in them. She looked darling, and seemed to be mimicking Brian with her chatter. I took her and held her while Brian went on.

"In 2001, Dorrie dies tragically in a hiking accident in the mountains. John and Garrett were with her, and they were apparently hiking a trail in a canyon when the path gave way. She fell sixty feet and bashed her head in on some rocks. John and Garrett saw the whole thing, but they weren't able to save her. And it turns out she was six months pregnant at the time with their second child."

Melissa and I exchanged looks.

"Were they sure it was an accident?" I asked.

Brian nodded. "There's nothing in any of the news articles about it that suggested anything otherwise. In fact, Moreland is described as distraught and devastated. There isn't much about Garrett, but he would have been only twelve at the time. Big funeral, lots of city fathers and politicians in attendance. Yadda-yadda."

"So both his parents and his first wife die in accidents," I said. "How strange. How many people do we know who've died in accidents? I can't think of any."

"Your uncle Pete," Melissa said. "Didn't he die in a boat accident? Drown or something?"

"There's one," I said.

"Do we know anything about Dorrie?" Melissa asked. "Did anyone know her very well?"

"Not many," Brian said. "Judge Moreland was—and is—at all of the Denver society events and fund-raisers. I've seen him myself—he's a fixture. But apparently she didn't like the limelight, according to my gossips. She went back to the church big-time, apparently. She was a Catholic when they married, and she became very involved in the church here. Going to Mass every morning, that kind of involved. She was, well, very plain-looking from the wedding photo in the newspaper. John looked like some kind of movie star, and he married a homely girl on the heavy side. Later, she got *very* heavy. My best gossip described her as shy, overweight, and uncomfortable in a crowd. She and the judge were a mismatched pair."

Melissa snorted. "She sounds inconvenient to a man on the make."

"It gets better," Brian said. "John Moreland married ex-model and heir to a cosmetics fortune Kellie Southards almost twelve months to the day Dorrie died. It was a massive wedding. And that same year—2002—he was appointed to the United States District Court for the District of Colorado."

"One year seems a little quick to me," Melissa said, "for a man who was distraught and devastated."

"Interesting," I said, my mind racing. "But don't forget that all we're doing is speculating here. And we are talking about a judge who seems incredibly well liked and well connected. We might be jumping to conclusions."

"And now we get to Garrett," Brian said. "I'll let Melissa take it from here."

"GARRETT MORELAND SEEMS LIKE a very bright and a very troubled young man," Melissa said. "I don't think that information will come as any surprise to us. I also learned it is very difficult to get any background on a juvenile through official channels."

"How did you get what you got?" I asked, impressed.

"A friend of a friend I used to work with downtown is a counselor at Garrett's high school in Cherry Creek. We had coffee this afternoon while you were at the trial. At first, she was very coy about talking specifically about Garrett because she's not supposed to, you know. But when I told her the situation we're in"—she nodded toward Angelina in my arms—"she started telling me things. I'm sworn to secrecy, of course. But what she told me about Garrett makes me even more determined to fight them, Jack."

"Not that you were wavering before," I said.

"No. But I think we're dealing with a very sick boy."

"What did you find out?" I asked, chilled.

"Garrett had a reputation before he even got to high school," she said, digging the pad she used for grocery lists out of the diaper bag near her feet. "He wasn't an unknown quantity. There was an incident in middle school that made the rounds and she heard about it from a fellow counselor. Apparently, the middle-school counselor knew Garrett quite well because he'd talked to the boy after the death of his mother the year before. He said he thought the boy was hollow inside, and he couldn't get through to him to get him to grieve properly. Anyway, since Garrett knew the counselor, he went to see him one day to complain that his friends wouldn't have anything to do with him anymore and he wanted the school to punish them. He gave the counselor a list of four boys who should be punished."

I shook my head.

"The counselor asked why the friends should be punished, and Garrett told him they wouldn't walk to school with him anymore, that they ditched him whenever they could."

"Kid stuff," I said, remembering how casually cruel young teenagers could be.

Melissa said, "Next to each of the boys' names Garrett had written suggested punishments. He said two of the boys should be branded with a hot iron. He said one of them should be forced to wear girls' clothes for a month. And the last should be castrated."

Brian whistled.

"The counselor was alarmed and took the list to the vice principal. Keep in mind this was two years after the Columbine massacre, so school officials were ultrasensitive to anything that resembled a threat. But apparently the vice principal knew Garrett's father, and they agreed to handle the situation quietly. John Moreland and the vice principal gathered the four boys and Garrett together in a conference room and asked them to talk it out, to work out their problems. What it came down to was the four boys thought Garrett was weird and scary. Garrett was reprimanded for making the list, but he wasn't disciplined in any way. The counselor was furious at the outcome, and told his colleague—the woman I had coffee with—about it when Garrett moved on to high school.

"In high school," Melissa said, "there were disturbing writings. Garrett was—or is—interested in creative writing, and he wrote several fantastically violent plays and short stories. The counselor I had coffee with had read them and agreed with the English teacher that they crossed the line. Torture, beheadings, that kind of thing. He was very interested in criminal behavior. She talked to Garrett about this, but Garrett said he had the right of free speech, especially since he was an artist. He said he would get his father involved if the school tried to stop him from being an artist."

I said, "I thought these were the kinds of things that got kids bounced out of school these days," recounting stories I'd heard and read about students who were expelled for things like bringing a plastic butter knife to school in their lunch sacks.

"They do," Brian said, "but apparently it depends on who you are. And who your father is."

Melissa said, "The counselor said Garrett brought in books he'd found in the school library filled with violence and violent images, and movies he'd rented at Blockbuster which were just as graphic as what he'd written. He built a case that his work wasn't any worse than what anybody could get their hands on just about anywhere."

"A future criminal defense attorney," I said, thinking of Ludik's performance that day.

"So nothing was done with Garrett," Melissa said. "This empowered him, according to the counselor. And so did his money, which he flashed around the school constantly. He always has the best car, the best clothes, the best computer. He was the first kid at Cherry Creek to have an iPhone—that kind of thing. Other kids resent him for it, but they also want to be around him because he was always willing to pay for lunch, or give them rides, or buy them alcohol."

"This is where his gang connection comes in," Brian said.

Melissa nodded. "The counselor said when Garrett was a junior, he started showing up to basketball and football games with gang members from downtown. They were like his posse. Garrett played it up. The gang connections gave him power. So here was a kid who had both money and power in high school and nobody—including the teachers or the counselor—took him on. The school started having some serious drug problems that year as well, and the counselor suspected Garrett's gang pals of selling crystal meth and other drugs to students."

"A criminal-defense attorney and a gang kingpin," Brian said. "That's a deadly combination."

"Can we prove this?" I asked.

Melissa said, "In a court of law? Like in front of a judge if we could get a custody hearing to keep Angelina?"

"Yes," I said, feeling hopeful for the first time.

"There have to be quite a few students in that high school who would say the same things the counselor told me," she said.

Brian nodded, excited. "With the right bulldog lawyer and a parade of kids and teachers who know Garrett, I could see a judge ruling that you should keep Angelina for her own well-being and safety."

I wanted to believe him.

"Think about it, Jack," Brian said. "You've got a man whose parents and first wife died mysteriously and a son who comes across like Little Scarface. What court would rule they should get a baby girl because of a ridiculous technicality?"

"And maybe it doesn't even have to go that far," Melissa said. "Maybe we talk with Judge Moreland and tell him what we know. I'm sure he doesn't want this all aired in a courtroom. It might be enough to make him go away."

WE STAYED UP LATE after Angelina was put to bed and Brian kept us optimistic and hopeful. He was able to get Melissa to laugh at his jokes, and it was a wonderful sound to hear. It was as if days and nights of built-up terrors and fears were being released.

BRIAN WAS PULLING ON his coat to leave when there was a knock on the door. Melissa and Brian froze and looked at me. I glanced at the clock: 1:20.

A combination of fear and rage not far under the surface revealed itself. Were the boys back? If so, this time I wouldn't be humiliated. I ran upstairs and got the .45.

"Jack!" Melissa said, seeing the weapon in my fist.

"They may have paintball guns," I said, "but I have the real thing."

"Oooh," Brian said, shaking his head, "I don't know . . ."

But I'd already thrown open the front door, ready and willing to level the Colt at Garrett's or Luis's face.

Cody slumped against the threshold, his face flushed, his eyes watery. There was snow on his shoulders and head.

"Go ahead," he slurred, "shoot me."

I put the gun aside, and Brian and I helped him in. He could barely walk, and we steered him toward the couch. The smell of bourbon on him was strong. He sat down in a heap.

Melissa said, "Cody, you're covered in blood. Are you hurt?"

I hadn't even noticed, but now I saw it: dark floral patterns of blood on his pant legs and down the front of his coat. His knuckles were bloody, the skin peeled back.

"I'm just fucking dandy," Cody said, "but that kid out there in the Hummer with the paintball gun isn't doing so hot."

Seven

LIKE SPRING SNOWSTORMS IN the Rockies, late-fall snowstorms often had a particular kind of all-encompassing intensity and volume that could make you slip out of your everyday life, look around, and say, "Do we have enough groceries in the house?"

But that night, when Cody showed up at our house drunk and bloody, the snow didn't divert attention from where we were but steered it back from our brief little respite of hope, and made everything more focused and harder-edged.

BRIAN WAS IN THE PASSENGER SEAT of my Jeep as we slowly circled the block looking for the kid or vehicle Cody described. The snow was falling in white-capped vertical waves of poker chip–sized flakes. The volume of snow muted outside sound and haloed the streetlights. It wasn't cold enough yet that the snow wouldn't melt, but it was falling so hard and so fast that it didn't get the chance. Cottony balls of it bunched on the hood of the car and rested on the tops of the blades of the wipers.

A few lights were on behind closed curtains in our neighbors' homes, and three or four porch lights. Falling snow, like fat summer miller moths, swirled in the glow one second and vanished the next as the neighborhood went black.

"Uh-oh," Brian said. "What happened?"

"Power's out," I said. "Maybe the storm took a line down."

"Wonderful. The hits just keep on coming."

"Jesus," I said. "What did Cody say before he passed out?"

"Something about nearly rear-ending a car that was coming down the street with its lights off," Brian said. "Then he saw who was inside and followed them."

"Did he say where?" I asked, my voice pinched with desperation. There weren't any unfamiliar cars on the curbs or in the driveways of my neighbors. Those that were there had at least six inches of snow on them, making the models hard to pick out in the dark.

"He was hard to understand," Brian said. "Bombed out of his mind. What I heard was that he pulled the car over and the boys in it tried to run away but he caught one of them. He's so out of it, though, that I can't even be sure he wasn't hallucinating."

"That blood on him wasn't a hallucination," I said.

"But we don't know if it happened here, is what I'm saying," Brian said. "I still think we should have called the cops, let *them* look for the boy and the car."

"And get Cody arrested," I said.

"Maybe he *needs* to be arrested."

"You heard Melissa."

Brian sighed. "By not calling them have we already broken the law?"

"I'm not sure," I said.

"But we know we *should,* right?"

"I guess so."

"But we aren't going to, are we?"

"No."

I CRAWLED THE JEEP down the length of my subdivision street and took a left at the next block, passing under a darkened streetlight. In the dark and in the snow, my own neighborhood seemed unfamiliar. It was the same odd feeling I'd had on Sunday when Judge Moreland showed up at my home and somehow turned it into a place I didn't know or feel very comfortable in.

"There," Brian said, pointing through the windshield.

Halfway up the next block, Garrett's H3 Hummer was parked with a front tire on the sidewalk and the back end angled out toward the street. The headlights of my Jeep washed across the length of vehicle, revealing no one inside. I slowly drove on.

"I didn't see anyone inside," Brian said. "Where did they go?"

"Cody said one took off. But where's the other one?"

I didn't want to stop in the street and train my headlights on the Hummer in case any of my neighbors were looking out. In the dark, I wouldn't be able to see them, and they might recognize me or my Jeep. I wondered if anyone had noticed the H3—it was not exactly a model that would melt into the scenery—or called the police. For sure, I thought, someone had contacted the power company by now.

At the end of the block I flipped a U and cruised back.

"Not too fast," Brian said, "I'm looking."

"There he is," I said, pointing.

"Where?"

"*There . . .*"

The heap of clothing was about ten feet from the sidewalk on the lawn of an unfamiliar house. The pile of clothing was dark but substantial and flecked with snow. There was just a glimpse as we passed by, but I thought I saw a bloody face with the wisp of a mustache. A snow-covered FOR SALE sign with a local Realtor name was planted in the grass. Even though there was no power, the house looked absolutely still, and there was a good likelihood, I thought, that no one was inside.

"Luis," I said. "Not Garrett. Luis."

"Oh man, oh man," Brian said, grabbing my arm. "What are we going to do?"

"I'm not sure."

"Is he dead? If he isn't, he'll freeze soon enough."

"I know."

"And where's Garrett?"

I looked around, shaking my head. "Let me find a place to park. I've got to think."

"Jeez," Brian said, using an expression I hadn't heard from him since we'd been in high school. "If the lights come back on . . . if the cops show up . . . if Garrett comes back . . ."

"I *know!*"

I drove the length of the block again and turned around, nestling the tires of the Jeep against the curb and killing the lights and the engine. Garrett's Hummer was fifty yards up the street. Luis was motionless, looking like a dark sooty smudge against the snow. As my eyes adjusted with the headlights off, I could make out tracks in the snow from the driver's side of the vehicle leading up the street, into the shadows. Where Garrett had run.

"What if he's still alive?" Brian asked, nodding toward Luis, his voice high-pitched.

I wished I could drum up some sympathy, but all I knew of Luis was what he did in the bathroom of my home and the paintball attack. Plus, he was associated with the kid who wanted to take my daughter away from us. The very idea of him made me angry. In a prosperous city like Denver, which was booming economically and offering opportunities to anyone who sought them, Luis had opted to belong to a violent street gang that sold drugs. It wasn't like he didn't have choices. And I didn't mind right then if he went away. I didn't really mind if he died. But could I sit there and watch him die?

Yes.

But I didn't want Cody to be implicated.

As I reached down for my door handle I noticed a glow in the snowfall down the street. I paused. The falling snow started to light up yellow like shooting sparks. Headlights. A car coming.

"Slump down," I said, and we both slid forward in our seats.

"Man oh man," Brian whispered. "What do we say if it's the cops?"

"If they don't see us, we don't have to say anything," I said.

"I'm well-known in this town, Jack," Brian said. "I've got a lot of friends and a lot of enemies. If I get caught out here, there's no way it doesn't make the papers."

"I know. Don't forget who *I* work for."

"Yes, but . . ."

"But *what?*" I barked at Brian. "You're more important? You've got more money?"

"Honestly, yes on both counts," Brian said. "But I also won't be in a position to help you and Melissa."

Nice save, I thought.

I kept my head high enough that I could see through a slot beneath the top of the steering wheel and the dashboard. It suddenly occurred to me that the Jeep might be the only vehicle on the street not blanketed by snow, that we would be obvious. It was snowing harder. Flakes were sticking to the glass and beginning to cover the hood. Still, my Jeep was at least an inch behind in snow covering.

The approaching car appeared and swung behind the Hummer, keeping its headlights on. It was an older model low-rider four-door sedan, definitely not a police car. It was the kind of tricked-up American classic some Hispanics preferred. Three doors opened at the same time, and the dome light lit up. Garrett was in the passenger seat. The driver and occupant in the backseat were Hispanic, wearing oversized coats, trousers, big, tan, unlaced boots.

"Garrett and the gangsters," I whispered to Brian. "They've come back for Luis."

"Do they see us?"

"Not yet."

The .45 was on the seat next to my thigh, and I spider-crawled my hand across the upholstery until I found the smooth wooden grip. I cracked my window so I could hear them out there.

The driver and Garrett ran to where Luis lay and shouted at him to get up.

"Fucking get up, man . . ." the driver said, nudging Luis with his boot. "Get the fuck up, Bro . . ."

The gangster from the backseat stood next to the car, acting as lookout. He kept his hands in his pockets, and I instinctively thought he had a gun or two. He looked up the block and down, eyes brushing over my Jeep. His face was dead, impassive, a round pie tin with a soul patch and heavily lidded eyes.

Garrett and the driver tugged on Luis, eventually pulling him to his feet. They draped his arms around their shoulders and guided him toward the car. I thought I saw Luis's legs move under their own power, helping them, but I couldn't be sure. His head slumped on his coat as they got him to the car. When they lowered him into the backseat I could see blood on his face and clothes from the dome light. My impression was Luis was alive—barely.

I did see Garrett's face, though, and it was hideous, contorted with rage. He said something about a paint gun, and the lookout left the car and found it on the lawn and brought it back. It had been them, all right.

"Okay," Garrett said, slamming the back door and stepping away.

The driver swung into his car and the lookout jumped in next to him. Garrett started for his Hummer, keys in his hand.

As he reached for his door handle he suddenly froze and turned toward me, squinting.

"Oh no," I whispered.

"What?"

"I think he sees us." I lifted the .45 and put it on my lap. Suddenly, stupidly, I couldn't remember if the revolver was single-action or double-action. Did I have to cock it, or could I just pull the trigger? Christ . . .

The sedan made a slow turn in the snow and started down the street from the direction it had come. Its taillights looked pink in the falling snow.

Garrett still stood near the door of his H3. I could see his mind work, looking over his shoulder at his friends departing and again at my Jeep. His backup was gone, and he wasn't sure. I thought again of my car sitting there at the curb looking sleek and dark without nearly the amount of snow on it as the other vehicles up and down the street, sticking out like a sore thumb. Had Garrett paid any attention to what I drove? Had he seen the Jeep in my driveway?

He walked toward us in the dark down the middle of the street like a gunfighter. Twenty yards away. Reaching behind him for something tucked into his belt with one hand. With his other he flipped open his cell phone and raised it. I could see the glow of it shadow the handsome features of his face. Probably calling the sedan back, I thought.

I cocked the revolver, the cylinder turning, a fat bullet poised in the chamber. Aim for the thickest part of him, I remembered from deer and elk hunting in Montana, and if you need to, fire again and again.

Garrett was ten yards away but had slowed and was bending forward, trying to see into our car.

At that moment, the power was restored and the streetlights crackled and lit up. Porch lights blinked on up and down the block. Interior lamps lit up.

"It's Christmas," Brian whispered. Because we'd grown used to total darkness, the lights seemed more intense than they should have.

"For us it is," I said, as Garrett wheeled, jogged to his Hummer, and roared away.

Brian sat up and took a deep breath. I could feel my heart pounding, whumping in my chest.

"Would you have used that?" Brian asked, gesturing toward the .45.

"Yes."

"I'm glad you didn't," Brian said.

I wasn't so sure.

THE SNOW WAS STILL FALLING outside our bedroom window when I slipped into bed. I was tired, exhausted, and had taken three Advils to blunt the effects of an oncoming headache. Brian left as soon as we got back to the house, saying he hoped his hands would stop shaking so he could drive. Cody was downstairs snoring on the couch. Melissa had gotten his shoes and jacket off and covered him with a quilt.

I tried not to wake her, but of course she was not asleep.

"What happened out there?" she asked. I told her, leaving nothing out.

"I hate him," she said, referring to Luis, "but I wouldn't want anyone to freeze to death although I've read it's just like going to sleep. It isn't painful."

I wasn't sure how to respond.

"Will Garrett connect Cody to us?" she asked. "Does he know Cody is our friend? Will he blame us for what happened?"

"I don't know. I suppose it depends on whether Cody said anything to them or just started pounding on Luis."

"I'd bet he said something."

"We can ask him tomorrow—if he even remembers."

"Oh, Jack, it's gone from bad to worse."

I nodded even though she couldn't see me in the dark. She sidled over under the covers and put her warm palm on my chest.

"You showered again," she said. "Why?"

"I felt dirty, I guess."

"What time is it?"

"Almost three."

"Are you going to work tomorrow?"

"I've got to."

She put her head on my shoulder. Her hair smelled nice. "I wish you could just stay home. We could have a snow day—just our family."

"And Cody," I reminded her.

"And Cody." She laughed gently.

I glanced out the window. The snow had lightened considerably.

"We could just stay home and be a family," she said, repeating herself.

I kissed her on the mouth. She kissed back, but broke it off.

"Not that," she said, "not now. I just want to be held, that's all."

I held her.

We could hear Angelina stir and cry out over the baby monitor. Melissa was instantly alert, and she ducked under my arm and swung her bare legs out of bed.

"What?"

"She's having a bad dream," Melissa said, standing and pulling on her robe. "She's been having them since the Morelands showed up on Sunday. I don't know whether she's sensing something from me or what. I'm going to get her."

Melissa left, and I heard Angelina whimper and the sound broke my heart. Over the monitor, I could hear the springs of the crib mattress squeak as Melissa picked her up and cooed at her.

"I think I'll let her sleep with us for a while," Melissa whispered as she came back in the bedroom. I made room, and Melissa lowered Angelina between us. The baby was still sleeping. In the ambient light from the window she looked peaceful and content. Her long lashes were exquisite, and her little rosebud mouth formed a pleasant smile. Her breath was slight, little puffs of sweet air. I brushed her round warm cheek lightly with the backs of my fingers. So soft. She was just so *small*.

"Don't roll over and crush her," Melissa said.

I was always scared about that, and I edged farther away.

"We've got three weeks," she said. "And you'll be gone one of them."

"I'll be back sooner than that," I said. "I'll be back as soon as I have that meeting with Malcolm Harris."

"Still . . ."

"I'm more optimistic," I said, "after what you and Brian found out tonight. The judge and his son aren't so all-perfect and all-powerful after all."

"I was talking with Cody about that while you and Brian were out," Melissa said. "He might have just been out of it, but he wasn't very encouraging."

"What do you mean?" I asked, alarmed.

"I told him what we'd found out, and he just shook his head, and said, '*Third-party gossip shit. None of it would work in court.*'" She tried to imitate his particular sarcastic cadence of speech.

"But we're just getting started," I said. "We still need to prove everything."

"What if we can't?" she said. "Rumors are cheap. It's different when we try to *prove* these things."

"We don't have to prove that Moreland's parents and wife died mysteriously," I said.

"But it's nothing, really, when you think about it. The judge was never charged or even suspected of anything as far as we know. And Garrett just comes across as a moody teenager. What's so strange about that?"

"Cody said this?" I asked, getting angry.

"No," she said. "I was thinking about it. He's right. We don't have anything but a bunch of rumors. We can't go up against a powerful judge and his son with just a pack of stories. Somehow, we have to prove something—anything."

The minutes ticked by. The more I thought about it, the more I realized she was right. The last vestiges of the hope I'd had earlier skulked out of the room as if ashamed.

"Honey," I said, "there is no point getting a lawyer and going to court. We may find out something about them, but now Garrett has an attempted murder on *us*."

She sighed. "Maybe Brian can find out something more solid. He said he'd dig deeper."

It was as if she didn't hear what I'd just said.

She said, "And I can follow up on the school incidents, but all we've got right now is what a counselor says she heard from another counselor. If I were a judge I wouldn't even listen to us."

"I should have shot the son of a bitch," I said.

"Jack, don't say that. If you did, you'd get put into prison. This baby needs a father, and I need a husband."

Still . . .

"I HAD A STRANGE THOUGHT," Melissa said after a while. "Luis was somebody's baby. And Garrett was a baby once, too."

"It is a strange thought," I said.

"Jack, I love you," she said.

"I love you, too."

"What's going to happen now?" she said.

"I don't know."

"We've got to protect this child," she said.

"Yes."

"You were brave tonight."

I liked hearing that because I never thought of myself as

particularly brave. I wanted her to think of me as a man of courage, and I vowed not to give her a reason to think otherwise. I had never before that moment thought in those terms, although every man, I think, wonders what he'd do when it comes down to a fight-or-flight decision.

"I'm going to leave you two alone," I said, getting out of bed. "I'm still too wired to sleep. I'll be back. I'll try not to wake you up when I come in."

Melissa was already falling asleep, an arm stretched lightly over Angelina. At the doorway I stopped and looked back. My wife and my daughter in my bed, both breathing softly.

I KEPT THE LIGHTS OFF in the family room and turned on the television. Since our remote had been stolen and ruined, I'd learned where to power it up on the set itself. It was tuned to CNN. I was too lazy and disinterested to surf through more channels using the buttons on the set and I sat down in my chair. The light from the set flickered on Cody under the blanket on the couch. Periodically, he would make me jump with thunderous flatulence or a racking snort. I could smell old bourbon in the room, as if it were seeping through his skin. I smiled as I contrasted Angelina and Cody, and wondered what it was about age that made the odors so much worse.

Over the news anchor's shoulder on the screen were the graphics MONSTER OF DESOLATION CANYON and the booking photo of Aubrey Coates. They cut away to a local correspondent named Erin somebody doing a standup in front of the courthouse hours earlier as the snow began to fall.

"The case against Aubrey Coates was dealt a major blow today in the Denver courtroom of Judge John Moreland," the attractive dark-haired lady said, "when . . ."

I half watched, half listened. Cody was shown stomping out of the courtroom, snarling at the camera. I couldn't help but glance over at his broad back on the couch.

The segment ended as the reporter said, "I'd bet you a bag of donuts that unless the prosecutors have something powerful and unexpected up their sleeves, Aubrey Coates is going to walk. Back to you, Anderson."

Anderson said, "That was recorded earlier tonight. And Erin, a bag of glazed donuts will be just fine."

"*Motherfucker . . .*" Cody growled in his sleep, tossing about violently.

Friday, November 9

Sixteen Days to Go

Eight

THREE DAYS PASSED. THERE was nothing in the papers about Luis. I had no idea if he was dead or alive. There were no police visits, no calls from Garrett or John Moreland. It was as if that night had never happened. I could say I felt relief with each passing day, but it wasn't like that at all. Instead, I felt the tension mounting, anticipating their next attack, wondering this time if it would be with real bullets. And never doubting that it would come.

While women can generally intuit the subtle feelings and motivations of other human interactions better than men, men instinctively know one thing: when they're at war. What shocked me was how smoothly I slipped from the bank into the full current.

ON FRIDAY, I went to the office early to tie up loose ends. I wasn't the only person at the bureau, despite the early hour. Jim Doogan, the mayor's chief of staff, flashed by in the hallway but made a point of pausing in front of my open door and looking in.

I waved hello.

"Let me get a cup of coffee," he said, and continued down the hall.

I smiled. Doogan couldn't even wave back until he had coffee.

Doogan was a curious man—he looked just like his name. Late fifties, Irish, beefy, red-faced with short-cropped red hair speckled with gray. He was a blunt object, so different from the mayor, who was young, thin, handsome if effete, so filled with energy one expected shooting sparks from his enthusiasm to start a fire in the wastebasket. But Doogan was necessary. Someone had to scare off sycophants and interest groups who wanted too much of the mayor's time. Someone had to run interference and fix things out of public view. Doogan was the man sent in to tell someone who'd met with the mayor and claimed Halladay had promised them something to tell them no, the mayor had simply *acknowledged* the problem. I'd always kind of liked Doogan. There was nothing slick about him. He reminded me of men in Montana—cattle buyers, country commissioners, who, when they bested you, would throw an arm around your shoulder and offer to buy you a beer.

Apparently, the mayor was having his monthly breakfast meeting with our bureau president, H. R. "Tab" Jones. Before being appointed to the bureau, Jones was the mayor's campaign manager and chief fund-raiser. Jones was tall, loud, slick, and from what I gathered from longtime staff, not as intolerable as past presidents. Jones came from banking and had no background in tourism promotion, which never stopped him. In staff meetings, he threw around hot business buzzwords and catchphrases—"metrics," "skill sets," "paradigm," "worldview"—but he often used them incorrectly. He urged us to "push the envelope" and "think outside the box." Behind his desk were dozens of current business and motivational books which, I noticed, had uncracked spines.

Doogan finally came back with a cup of coffee and entered my office, shutting the door behind him. He'd never done that before. I looked up and leaned back in my chair. His aftershave smelled sharp.

He shook his head and pursed his lips, as if what he was about to tell me saddened him.

"Brian Eastman?" he said simply. "Not a good idea."

And with that he was out the door before I could ask him how he knew so quickly, or more important, how the *mayor* knew.

LATER, LINDA LEANED INTO my office after an executive staff meeting, asked, "What on earth did you do to piss off the mayor?"

"What do you mean?"

She said Tab Jones told her Mayor Halladay specifically asked him about me.

"He asked if you were competent or some kind of loose cannon," she said. "The mayor asked if you could turn out to be a liability. Tab said he defended you and our department, but I think that's horseshit. I think he . . ." she delivered a devastatingly accurate imitation of Jones's best executive voice, "*expressed shock and concern and assured the mayor he'd look into it.*" She reverted to her real voice. "Meaning, in all likelihood, your days could be numbered. Which leads me back to my first question: What on earth did you do to piss him off?"

I suddenly felt cold. I desperately needed this job.

"I didn't do anything to the mayor," I said. "But it's possible John Moreland said something to him." Wondering, did Garrett tell his father what happened Monday night? Or did he lie, make up some story about how he'd come to our house to see Angelina and was jumped by a maniac, his friend left to die in a vacant yard? Did our friendship with Cody, the disgraced cop, or Brian, who'd had a sour business relationship with the major before he was mayor, bring about this sudden interest in me? Were Brian's inquiries hitting soft spots? Or was it all Judge Moreland?

And I realized the Morelands didn't need bullets, or paintballs, to attack. Breakfast with the mayor accomplished the same purpose.

"Keep your nose clean," Linda said, studying me, the wheels spinning in her head. "I can't afford to lose you right now. I'm not sure we'd be able to hire a replacement, the way things are going with our budget. And even if we could, it could take months, and we don't have months. The trade-show season is upon us."

"I'll do my best," I said. "I always do."

She nodded, agreeing with me, but still with that look. The look of a racehorse owner assessing a promising colt who'd just come up lame.

MY FLIGHT TO BERLIN was to be Sunday, two days away, with arrival at Tegal at 7:05 A.M. Monday. The suitcase was nearly packed upstairs in our room, my briefcase heavy with my laptop, lead sheets, business cards, brochures, a six-pack of Coors beer for Malcolm Harris, who loved the stuff. I would be gone a week, returning the following Saturday. In my mind, I must admit, I was already halfway out the door.

I had tried to convince Melissa to take Angelina and stay with her mother in Seattle while I was gone, but she'd have none of it. Melissa was still smoldering about her parents' divorce and disliked her mother's new husband. Even given the circumstances, she didn't want to see her mother "hat in hand," as she put it.

CODY STAYED AT OUR HOUSE. He slept on the couch at night and watched television and helped around the house during the day. He's better at fixing things than I am, plus he had the time. He rehung a couple of sagging doors, fixed the toilet so it would stop running, and painted the kitchen. Melissa said he took breaks only to follow the Coates trial on TV and smoke cigarettes on the deck. He told her he couldn't remember what he said to Luis that night, but he had a feeling he "went all Dirty Harry on his ass." He asked if he could stay with us until the reporters camped out around his house gave up and went away, and we agreed. Melissa appreciated his help and companionship, and I liked the idea of his being there with his weapons and training and capacity for violence in case Garrett and his boys showed up again.

Saturday, November 10

Fifteen Days to Go

Nine

AFTER BRIAN HAD LEFT THE night of Cody's confrontation with Luis, we didn't see him for the rest of the week. He was in New York, Chicago, St. Louis, and the Bay Area on business. He kept in touch with Melissa by text messaging her from airports between flights. She kept the messages and showed them to me when I got home from work. I reviewed them over coffee Saturday morning.

LEARNING MORE AND MORE THINGS ABOUT THE JUDGE. CAN'T WAIT TO TELL YOU.

And,

TALKED TO ONE OF MY FRIENDS WHO DABBLES ON THE DARK SIDE. HE SAID THERE MIGHT BE SOME PHOTOS THAT WILL BRING THE JUDGE DOWN. I'LL FOLLOW UP. IT MAY COST US SOME CASH.

"Photos of *what?*" I asked.

"I texted him back," she said. "He hasn't replied."

She sighed. "You know how dramatic he can be. He won't just tell us, he'll want to show us."

Cody stood in the doorway in a paint-splattered T-shirt and a three-day growth of beard. He'd overheard.

"Let's take a drive downtown," he said to me.

"Do you mind?" I asked Melissa.

"No," she said, "as long as you'll bring dinner home and not drink too much. Remember, you've got an early-morning flight tomorrow."

As if I didn't know.

IN SEVERAL NATIONAL SURVEYS, Denver has been cited as the least-overweight large city in the country, usually neck and neck with Portland. Health and recreation is a religion. I know this because I sell it overseas. In contrast, Cody sucked on his cigarette with a kind of junkie intensity, sat back in the seat, closed his eyes, and slowly blew the smoke out. He smoked with such needy and obvious pleasure that he made me wish I was a smoker.

On workdays, there was traffic. Lots of traffic. On those days I compared the street we lived on out in the western suburbs to a tiny seasonal creek, like the one that used to flow through the ranch my father managed for a while near Great Falls. Like that creek, our street/creek trickled into a busier residential street (or stream, in my analogy) which poured into a tributary (C-470) of a great rushing river (Interstate 70 to I-25) toward downtown. Once I became a part of the river hurtling down the valley toward the high-rises, stadiums, and inner city, I became a different animal, a fish fearing for his life. Currents of traffic coursed across lanes while the entire river picked up speed and volume. Outlets (exits) lessened the pressure only temporarily, because inlets (entrance ramps) produced greater flows. I was a little fish in an ocean of them. At night, like a spawning salmon, I would navigate the powerful river of traffic back to my sandy creek bed of origin where Melissa and nine-month-old Angelina would be waiting for me, and all would be right with the world.

Saturday-morning traffic was sparse on Interstate 70 into the city, although the situation was different westbound into the mountains. Several ski areas were already open because of the early snow and the snow they'd made from machines, and I'd never seen so many Volvos, Land Rovers, and Subaru Outbacks with skis or boards on top in my life. I imagined the occupants inside to be listening to Dave Matthews if they were under forty and John Denver if they were over.

We took I-25 to the Speer Boulevard exit and plunged into downtown, past the gentrified lofts near Pepsi Center and Coors Field, empty except for the homeless on the 16th Street Mall.

We parked in a lot that cost five dollars in a still-seedy part of downtown the developers hadn't gotten to yet. Not that Cody paid. Instead, he badged the attendant as he strode past the booth. The attendant—tattooed, pierced, reeking of smoke—recoiled as if he were a vampire and Cody's shield was a crucifix. I followed my friend to Shelby's Bar and Grill on 18th. I knew it as a cop hangout.

The waitress knew him and bowed like a subject before her king, but with a smirk on her face to project her sarcasm. "Your throne is ready, sir," she said.

Cody grunted and sat down heavily in a dark booth. I took the other side.

"Hit you both?" the waitress asked Cody.

"Jameson's," he said to her. "Three of 'em."

To Cody, I said, "Three?"

When she went to the bar, Cody dug into his pocket for his pack of cigarettes, said, "I've got a guy coming in to meet with us. I hope he still shows up, given my current status with the department."

"About that," I said. "How is the trial going?"

"It's all over but the shouting," he said. "The defense rested without calling a witness. The jury's sequestered for the weekend, and Monday they'll all come in and set that bastard free."

I shook my head. "So there was nothing else on him?"

"We had enough," Cody said, lighting up. "We had more than enough." He inhaled and blew a long stream of smoke at the NO SMOKING sign above our booth. The ban was statewide.

"You want to ask me if I set him up," Cody said.

I didn't say yes, I didn't say no.

And he didn't answer.

Cody's cell phone burred, and he went through a comic ritual of patting all of his clothing with the cigarette dancing in his mouth before he found it in his breast pocket and pulled it out.

"Yeah, we're here," Cody said to the phone. "And I already ordered, so come on in."

He closed the phone and put it on the table so he wouldn't lose it again. "Jason Torkleson just came up to detectives last week," he said. "They assigned him to my squad. He's bright-eyed and bushy-tailed, like all of us were when we started. Before he could get bogged down with a caseload or get co-opted by the lieutenant, I asked him to research Garrett Moreland and Luis and Sur-13 and put together a background report."

The door opened and sunlight streamed into the dark room and a slender young man with pale skin and deep red hair came in grasping a manila folder. He was wearing a track suit, and he looked fit, as if he'd completed his morning workout shortly before the meeting.

"Is that him?" I asked.

Cody bent over and craned around the side of the high-backed booth and waved Torkleson over.

"Obviously, they're still talking to me," Cody mumbled.

After introductions, Torkleson sat down on my side so he could face Cody and present his findings to him. The file was on the table. The waitress delivered the three drinks, and Cody took his from her hand before she had the chance to set it down. He drank deeply, said "Aaaaugh," and slowly lowered it. I sipped mine. It burned nicely.

"Starting early, eh?" Torkleson said.

Cody sang a line from a Louis Jordan song, "*What's the use of getting sober, when you're gonna get drunk again . . .*" and laughed. I did, too. Cody had been growling that line for ten years.

"Maybe I'll pass," Torkleson said.

Cody's expression went dead, and he beheld Torkleson with heavy-lidded eyes. "What, you keeping in shape?"

"Actually, yes."

Cody said, "The word 'actually' is overused these days, and when it's used, it's not used correctly. You youngsters say 'actually' nearly as much as you use the word 'like' and 'basically.' They're all unnecessary words the way you use them. Both are incorrect usage, according to my Helena High English teacher Ms. Lesa Washenfelder. Right, Jack?"

I nodded solely so Cody would move on.

To Torkleson, Cody growled, "Now drink your fucking drink."

Torkleson sat back as if slapped. It took a beat, but he reached for his drink and sipped it gingerly, his eyes flinching at the taste.

The file just sat there.

"Aren't you going to look at it?" Torkleson asked.

"Later," Cody said. "Give me the gist."

Torkleson looked at me, then back to Cody.

"He's all right," Cody assured him. "Anything you tell me he can hear."

Torkleson tapped the folder. "I wish I had more in there, but there wasn't that much information available. Garrett Moreland is the son of Judge John Moreland, but I think you already knew that."

"We did," Cody said, working his fingers on the tabletop like a blackjack player wanting another hit from the dealer. "Give me more."

"Garrett's mother . . ."

"We know that, go on."

"There's no rap sheet and as far as I can tell no juvie record."

"Damn."

"The only thing I could link to Garrett was his name showed up a couple of times on cross tabs—he's listed as a known associate of a couple of gangbangers. I found that surprising."

"Go on."

"Sureño 13. I printed out all the info on them I could find in our files. *Sureños* is a Spanish word for Southerner . . ."

Cody held up his hand. "You don't need to go into all of that if it's in the file. I know all about Sur-13, from the fact that it was born in the California prison system and has now spread into all fifty states, that the thirteen refers to the thirteenth letter of the alphabet—M—which stands for Mexican Mafia. The gang identifies with the color blue, members have three tattooed dots on their knuckles, and as an organized crime gang they handle most of the meth and heroin in Colorado."

Torkleson nodded.

"What we're interested in is how a good Cherry Creek High School boy got mixed up with them, and why," Cody said.

"That I can't tell you," Torkleson said, tapping the file on the table. "What we do have are a half dozen photos of him—Garrett—with known members of Sur-13 going in and out of the Appaloosa Club down on Zuni Street. You know about the Appaloosa?"

Cody nodded. Even I had heard of the Appaloosa Club. The reason I knew about it was because it was on a block downtown the bureau made sure we steered journalists and other guests away from. Somehow, the area had been missed by the urban developers and probably would be in the near future. The buildings on it were dilapidated. Tattoo parlors, bars, and a couple of liquor stores with bars on the windows. In the middle of all of them was the Appaloosa, easily identified at night because the patrons had smashed most of the ancient red neon tubes above the door so it read P-OO. I'd heard from Cody that patrolling cops often took a detour around the club so as not to have bricks rained on their cruisers.

"There are some undercover shots of your boy inside the club, too. He looks like he belongs—he doesn't stand out like some of the adventurous white girls who show up there every now and then looking for trouble. But if Garrett is welcome and comfortable in the Appaloosa, we know he's in deep with these guys."

"That's it?" Cody said. "A few pictures?"

"I'm afraid so."

Cody sighed. I expected him to upbraid Torkleson, but he didn't. The new detective seemed to have gathered all he could within the department even though it gave us little we didn't already know.

"I wish I had more," Torkleson said, reading Cody's body language. "Juvie stuff is hard to get without a warrant, even though I have a few buddies downtown. My impression is there was really nothing to get—that Garrett has kept himself clean. And the other name you gave me, 'Luis,' well, you can just throw that section in the file away."

Cody honed in on that. "What do you mean?"

Torkleson said, "If the subject you wanted intel on is Pablo 'Luis' Cadena, known associate of Garrett Moreland and vice versa, well, he's no more. His body was found a couple of days ago in the South Platte. He'd been stomped and beaten. The coroner said he was dead before he was dumped."

I stared at Cody, willing him to look back. But he didn't. I realized Cody didn't want to give any hint of alarm away to Torkleson, and Cody's face was a mask. Under the table, I felt the nudge of a boot—Cody telling me to look away from him and keep my mouth shut. I did.

"Any suspects?" Cody asked.

Torkleson shook his head. "Nothing. Cadena had a sheet as long as your arm. The homicide's being categorized as 'gang-related' and was handed over to the task force."

"I hadn't heard anything about it," Cody said.

"You haven't been in," Torkleson said, looking away to spare each of them the embarrassment. "And it's not exactly front-page news when a gangbanger is found dead these days."

Cody finished his drink and signaled for another. He seemed not to have heard what Torkleson said. "So," Cody said, "what's the word on me in the department these days?"

Torkleson used the question as a reason to push back and stand up to leave. "Actually, basically, to the brass you're like dead meat, buddy."

AS WE WALKED BACK to my Jeep two drinks (for Cody) later and Torkleson long gone, Cody said he'd personally protect Melissa and Angelina while I was away.

"Are you up for that?" I asked.

He shot a hurt look at me.

"I don't mean the drinking," I said defensively. "I meant whether or not your schedule allowed it."

"I don't *have* a fucking schedule until my hearing," Cody said.

We got into the car and shut the doors. I was overwhelmed and could feel my chest constrict.

"Aren't you going to start the motor?" Cody asked.

"We got away with it," I said.

Cody looked straight ahead.

"Cody . . ."

He turned on me. "I heard you. And Jack, this isn't something we will ever talk about again. *Ever.* What's done is done. Tell me you didn't tell Melissa what happened."

"Not all of it," I lied.

"Good. Don't."

Then: "Who are we kidding here? You tell her everything, don't you?"

"Yes."

He sighed heavily. "You may want to rethink that," he said.

WE DIDN'T TALK FOR TEN MINUTES while I drove home. Cody was smoldering, thinking, and smoking.

"This deal with Luis tells me a lot," he said, finally. "It should tell you a lot as well. That Garrett decided to dump Luis's body and make it look like a neighborhood hit—it's interesting. Especially considering what he *could* have done, like either calling the cops that night or going to the press with it. But what this tells me is Garrett didn't want it out that he was cruising your street with Luis."

I shook my head, not following.

"If Garrett reported the beating, the question would be asked why he was there in the first place. Angelina would have had to come up, and that would have sucked Judge Moreland into the story. Either Garrett didn't want his dad involved—or to know he was there—or the good judge didn't want it known. So instead, they covered it up the way they did."

"I don't get it."

"I don't either entirely," Cody said. "But what this tells us is there is a lot more going on than we know. There's a reason—or reasons—they would risk dumping Luis's body rather than have the spotlight turned on them right now. Which makes me wonder what in the hell they don't want found out, especially since they claim to be on the right and legal side of this adoption business."

I said, "Maybe Garrett and Moreland aren't talking. Maybe they're operating independently of each other."

Cody shook his head. "I can't buy that. I'd bet money they're communicating, coordinating their moves."

I thought about that.

He said, "What this also means is they've chosen to go below the radar, just as we have. We are no longer operating above the surface. Which means we're really in dangerous fucking territory."

We cruised back downtown into the old warehouse and industrial section. There were no pedestrians on the sidewalks and few vehicles. This was the area where Jack Kerouac and Neal Cassady used to hang out in the 1950s when Kerouac was "researching" the beat travelogue that would become *On the Road*. The construction cranes that hovered over LoDo like praying mantises had not yet perched here, but it was only a matter of time. The old tobacco, wool, and dry-goods warehouses would soon be condos and retail stores.

"I realize what you're doing, and I appreciate it," I said, finally. "You'll never know how much I appreciate it. You're going above and beyond."

"I know," he said, his eyes half-lidded. "But you're my best friend. If I can't help you out, what good am I? You and me and Brian—we've got to watch out for each other. We're just Montana boys in the big city even though Brian pretends he isn't."

The sentiment touched me and surprised me.

"Is this the drink talking?"

"Partially."

"Well, I appreciate it anyway."

He snorted.

"Damn, you're cynical."

He took a deep drag on his cigarette. "You have no idea," he said.

ON THE WAY BACK to my house, Cody leaned back and put his head on the headrest and closed his eyes.

"One more thing," he said.

"What?"

"Remember when I told you I wouldn't go after the judge? That I couldn't go after him?"

"Yes."

Cody flicked his fingers as if tossing aside something small and dead. "Forget that. That ended in the courtroom. I'm going to war with that motherfucker."

Then he slipped off into sleep and his head bobbed while I drove. I thought, *This man will watch over Melissa and Angelina?*

WHEN WE GOT BACK to my house, Cody's head popped up, and he seemed perfectly sober and lucid.

"I guess I conked out," he said without a slur.

"Would you like some dinner?" I forgot I was supposed to pick up something. "We can order a pizza."

"Naw, I'm fine. I've got to sneak down to my place and get some clothes."

"Should I tell Melissa you'll be here all next week?"

"Tell her whatever you want. Just make sure she's okay with that."

"Cody . . ."

He waved me away. "Don't worry," he said.

I walked him to his car.

"You'll be back in a week, right?" he asked.

I said yes.

"By the time I see you next, I will have talked with my uncle Jeter," Cody said.

I froze.

"Don't worry. I'm just making sure he's still around and available if we need him."

"Don't you know someone around here who could do the job?" I asked, uncomfortable with the fact that I'd acquiesced, that this all just seemed so inevitable. That I'd said "the job" like some kind of low-rent mobster.

"I know people," he said. "But for something like this, I can only trust blood relations. I can't risk somebody talking, and neither can you."

"Jeez," I said, "I don't know."

"I'm just checking on availability," he said. "That's as far as I'll go. If you want to talk to Jeter, you'll have to make that decision yourself."

I nodded.

Cody grinned at me, then held out his hand. "Have a good trip," he said. "And don't worry about anything. She'll be safer with me around than she is with you, for God's sake."

I think he meant it to be a joke.

LATE THAT NIGHT, Brian called. He said, "Get Melissa on the phone—you've both got to hear this."

"Where are you?" I asked while Melissa scrambled to the other room to grab the extension.

"San Diego. Seventy-two degrees constantly. I don't even know why they have weathermen."

Melissa picked up, and Brian launched, speaking in his rat-a-tat-tat manner, "I talked to a friend of a friend who went to high school in Asheville with John Moreland. He didn't paint a happy picture of our boy growing up. Apparently, John was the unwanted son of his wild-about-town teenage mother, who gave the child to her older sister and her husband, the Morelands. Just *gave* John to them. Apparently it wasn't all that unusual down there. So John grows up in this tight-assed, repressive household where his 'mother' is actually his aunt and his 'father' is his uncle. They go to court and get John's name changed to Moreland—I don't know what it was before and it doesn't matter. Anyway, John hates his parents. He doesn't say a lot about them in high school, other than they '*try to keep him down,*' whatever that means, but my friend's friend thinks it has to do with his ambition. Maybe they wouldn't sign scholarship or financial aid applications, something like that, but I'm just speculating. But when they pass on as a result of that car wreck, well, our boy not only gets two insurance-policy payoffs, but the whole world of financial aid must have opened up to him. That's how he could afford to leave and go to CU. And he just washed his hands of his upbringing, from what I understand. Never went back to North Carolina for reunions or anything like that. Never went back to visit the graves of his parents, according to my source.

"So," Brian said, "we're dealing with one cold bastard."

"But he had an alibi the night of the crash," I said. "You told us that."

"And he brought his alibi with him to Colorado," Brian said. "Later, he married her. And later, she died, too."

Berlin

Monday, November 12

Thirteen Days to Go

Ten

TEGAL AIRPORT WAS AS it always was—too small, bustling, confusing, metallic, and round. Gray-white morning light seeped through windows that seemed dirty but weren't—it was the quality of the light itself—and I waited for my luggage at a squeaking, lurching, stop-start-stop carousel in a crowd so dense there was no way not to touch shoulders with others and be jostled. I was still lost in the familiar fuzzy twilight of jet lag. I had the feeling of being alone in my head, looking out through dry and bloodshot eyes. My skin felt gritty. I needed a place where I could regroup and shower.

Arriving passengers were a mix of Euros from the east and west on business, North Africans in flowing robes, large extended families of Turks. The crowd was veined with distinct groups of four or five who were no doubt arriving to attend WTB, as I was. Jamaicans, Thais, Argentines, Cubans—all sticking together, waiting not only for their luggage but their display booths, boxes of tourism brochures printed in German, and in the case of the Cubans their cigar-making gear so they could hand-roll smokes for select German tour operators. Everybody in the world sought the well-heeled and determined German travel market. We all wanted these people who got five to six weeks of mandated vacation time, who thought of travel as a right and not a privilege, who many times knew more about us and our geography and culture than we knew ourselves.

It was easy to pick out the Americans, with our open and animated faces, our loud talking as if no one else could understand English, our inadvertent and instinctive élan that so annoys others. A contingent from Las Vegas, including tanned men with dark, slicked-back hair and showgirls who, without their costumes and feathers, were simply too tall, pale, and thin, looked like a Mafia excursion to Tahoe or Atlantic City that had taken the wrong airplane.

As I checked my wristwatch to see how long we'd been waiting for our luggage, I thought I heard my name called out and raised my head. I recognized no faces and decided it was simply a similar-sounding word barked out in another language. Then, in an English accent, "Jack! Are you lost, my boy?"

Malcolm Harris of AmeriCan Adventures, wearing a tailored English suit with his trench coat folded over his forearm, clapped me on the shoulder from behind.

"I almost didn't recognize you," I said, trying to snap out of my dreamlike state so as to be as sharp as possible for the most important tour operator to our area. "The last time I saw you, you were wearing jeans and a cowboy hat and sitting on a horse." I remembered how much he'd loved playing cowboy on a dude ranch.

Malcolm Harris was pale, with thin black hair and a twitchy smile that slid back to reveal two rows of bad teeth. His suit hid his paunch. His sharp nose was discolored with the red and blue road map of a serious drinker and there was a strand of sweat beads along the top of his upper lip.

Harris tipped his head back and laughed. "I wish I were back out in Colorado now instead of this bloody place."

"Me too," I said.

"So, when did you get in?"

They always ask "So, when did you get in?" even though it was obvious I had just arrived.

I said, "I'm just hoping my luggage got here with me."

Then I recalled Linda Van Gear's first maxim of tourism marketing: *It is always about them. It is never about you.*

"It's good to see you," I said. "You're looking very good. Do you have a booth at the show?"

"It's good to be seen," he said as an aside. "No, I never get a booth here. You think I want to talk to bloody Germans?" He whispered that last part, but not quietly enough, I thought. "No, I'm here because it's the best place to see all of you and get some business done. All of you all in one place—it's brilliant, even though I despise Berlin. And the whole bloody Fatherland, for that matter. They have no sense of humor here, and that's just to start with."

I quickly looked around to see if we were being overheard. I locked eyes with a green-uniformed *Polizei* who looked back at me, dead-eyed.

"Where are you staying?" he asked.

"The Savoy. On Fassenstraße."

He nodded with recognition. "Fine place. I know it. English ownership. Still have that great cigar bar?"

"I think so."

"Brilliant. How about I meet you there tonight, and we go to dinner afterwards. Your treat." And he laughed.

"Perfect," I said enthusiastically, thinking I would rather put a bullet in my head—or at least get some sleep.

"Seven o'clock then," he said, patting my shoulder again. "I was hoping I'd see you. I have a lot of questions for you—important concerns. All on the QT, of course."

I nodded as if I knew what he was talking about.

The carousel belt groaned, and luggage appeared. The crowds

rushed the apparatus, as if their items would appear sooner as a result of their aggression.

"I've got to get out of this hellhole," Harris said, sneering at the crowd and patting the carry-on he'd brought with him from London. "See you at seven, then."

I reached out to shake his hand goodbye, but he'd already shouldered his way through a family of Turks toward the exit. The *Polizei* who'd overheard his remarks watched him the entire way, burning eyeholes into the back of his suit jacket.

THERE WERE SKIFFS OF dirty snow in the shadows between buildings and along the River Spree as my cream-colored Mercedes taxi—something I still got a thrill from, a Mercedes taxi—sliced through the traffic of midmorning. The skies were leaden. Through breaks in the trees, I could see sky cranes in the east bobbing their heads like prehistoric ocean birds.

I looked at my wristwatch again. It was 2:30 A.M. at home. I couldn't wait to call. I envisioned Melissa and Angelina sleeping in their beds, and Cody tossing and turning on the couch. And—it came out of nowhere—Garrett Moreland sitting in his Hummer down the block, watching my house in the dark.

I straightened up and shook my head, trying to shed the image.

The taxi driver was observing me in his rearview, and when I locked eyes with him, he looked away.

THE HOTEL WAS FILLED with WTB people from countries all over the world. My room wasn't ready, so I stored my luggage and shoved my hands in my pockets and went for a woe-is-me walk along the Kurfürstendamm, the main shopping street in Berlin, known as the Ku'Damm and pronounced "Koo-Dahm." High-end stores, restaurants, bustle. I couldn't believe there were still peddlers selling pieces of the Wall, whose last authentic remnants disappeared nearly twenty years before, as well as ersatz East German caps and "*Stasi*" binoculars made in Asia. Jet-black-skinned Africans sold jewelry and knockoffs on blankets that could be gathered up in two seconds' notice if a *Polizei* strolled down the block. There were women shopping in furs and carrying bags, and the smell of cigarette smoke hung in the cold damp air. The smell reminded me of Cody.

Something I couldn't explain nagged at me. I blamed the jet lag for my inability to determine what it was, but it was like a pebble in my shoe I couldn't locate and discard.

Berlin still had a sort of prewar men-in-hats-women-with-shoulder-pads feel to it, although every year, it seemed, there were fewer Germans and more North Africans, Turks, and Arabs on the streets.

I walked as far as the big department store, the KaDaWe, before crossing the street and working my way back. Unlike home, where we'd been watching every penny for months since we'd adopted our baby, I was on the bureau expense account now. My wallet was flush with euros, and my CVB credit card was primed and ready. I couldn't go crazy, but I could eat an early lunch of white sausages with a beer in sight of the Broken Tooth, a bombed-out church the Berliners had chosen not to reconstruct after WWII.

As I sat and ate and drank I tried to figure out what was bothering me about my walk, what I'd seen that had set me on edge. Finally, as I sat back and waited for the bored waiter to bring me back my change and the hated receipt, I realized it wasn't what I'd seen on the street but what I *hadn't* seen that was eating at me.

Children. There were no children. Obviously, the older kids would be in school. But in the entirety of my walk I hadn't come upon a single stroller or young mother with a baby. It was as if it were a street, a city, filled only with adults. I thought how strange, how horrible it would be to live in a world without children. Until that moment, the notion had never even occurred to me. Here in Berlin, because of the choices they'd made for whatever reason, there were no little ones to punctuate the day with noise and harmless chaos. Instead, there was a sense of quiet and antiseptic order.

As I folded my receipt into my wallet, I withdrew a photo of Angelina taken a few months ago. In it, she was beaming and reaching out for the camera to try and gum the lens.

Even though it was just a photo, she was the only child in sight, and they were trying to take her away from us, to turn our house—our lives—into cold and quiet Berlin.

DESPITE WHAT LINDA VAN GEAR had said about my job being in danger, I decided I would rebook a flight home the next day after my meeting with Harris. I feared for my wife and my daughter, and I already missed them. Linda would be angry, but if I returned with the AmeriCan deal in hand, she'd get over it.

When I got back to the hotel I had a message from Malcolm Harris. He needed to postpone our dinner meeting until the end of the week. Something had come up, and he needed to return to London for several days.

I balled up the message and threw it across the hotel lobby.

Eleven

FOR THE NEXT FOUR days, I was in hell. Waiting for Malcolm Harris to return to Berlin was torture. I was in bad humor—annoyed with cloying tour operators and journalists and the kissy-kissy greetings of Europeans (one cheek or two, two cheeks or three—it was maddening) and cigarette smoke and crowds. Our Colorado shell-scheme looked good from the outside but was held together with wires and tape and everything about my job and my life right then felt as false and cheap and ready to collapse as our booth.

I talked to Melissa every night and things were fine but the tension was building because we both thought something could explode again at any moment. She wanted me home. I wanted to be home. Garrett could show up at our house. Luis's friends might come calling. Cody could go on a bender. Moreland might decide three weeks was too long to wait.

I obsessively checked my watch during the show and in the hotel room at night, trying to chart what Melissa and Angelina would be doing eight hours behind me. The only highlight of those days was when Melissa put Angelina on the phone. I talked to her and heard silence back for several beats before she squealed "Da?" with absolute wonder that made me laugh out loud with joy.

ON THE NIGHT I was finally to meet with Harris, Melissa didn't answer the phone.

It was 10 A.M. in Denver, and no one was home. I felt something hot and sour rise up in my throat, and fought to keep it down. I didn't have enough information to panic.

I didn't leave a message, but went through the whole procedure again to call her cell. Again, straight to voice mail. What was going on?

Cody, I thought. So I went through the long procedure again, talking to long-distance operators, giving my phone card number . . . to find out his phone was off, too.

I was running out of time. Despite that, I called home again and got voice mail.

"Honey," I said, "what the hell is going on? I've been trying to reach you and Cody. Call me at my hotel and leave a message. I'm going to a business dinner but I'll call as soon as I get back. I want to make sure everything is okay. Love to you and Angelina. *You need to keep your phone on.*"

I SMOKED A CUBAN cigar for pure defense purposes—everybody else in the dark, cramped bar was smoking—in the Habana Haus off the hotel lobby and waited for Harris to arrive. He was a half hour late. Smoking the cigar and drinking a Berliner Kindle lager gave me something to do while I fretted, running scenarios through my mind explaining why Melissa didn't answer. I ran the gamut: Melissa and Cody were having a wonderful time together and decided to go shopping and take Angelina to the zoo and both had simply forgotten to turn their cell phones on; Melissa had taken Angelina to the pediatrician for a long-scheduled checkup she'd no doubt informed me of but I'd forgotten and she and Cody had obeyed the NO CELL PHONES sign in the waiting room (although it didn't make sense that Cody, for once, would obey a regulation); the power went out, rendering both the landline telephone and the cell towers useless.

Then the not-so-innocent explanations. Cody and Melissa had been arrested by the Denver PD in association with the beating and death of one Luis Cadena, and Melissa was being questioned in a spare room by detectives; Judge John Moreland and son Garrett had decided a month was too long and had shown up with a phalanx of cops to forcibly remove Baby Angelina and a fight had ensued, leading to the arrest of both Cody and Melissa; the two of them declared their long-smoldering love for one another and had bundled Angelina into the Honda and headed for Vegas.

SEVERAL HEADS TURNED when Malcolm Harris pushed through the heavily curtained entrance. He was recognized. At the travel show, he was a prize. Returning home with his business card impressed bosses. That he strode over toward me surprised a couple of the old female tourism warhorses from Florida, and one, a hatchet-faced woman who had likely once sold cars, was out of her chair with a quick movement that belied her bulk and started tugging at his sleeve. I noticed a little weave in his walk, probably because he'd been drinking already. Harris's face went cold when she hugged him, but he smiled gamely and hugged her in return with the enthusiasm of a twelve-year-old boy embracing a hated aunt, and she hung on his every word, which consisted of, "So, when did you get in?"

And she began to tell him, not only about her flight but about her luggage that hadn't yet arrived and her new condo and that she'd divorced and had been sick but was feeling much better now and she'd even lost sixteen pounds.

I rescued him by standing and clamping onto the back of his shoulder and pointing toward my watch with urgency.

"Are we late?" he asked, mock-surprised. "People have been buying me drinks all afternoon, and I've lost track of the time."

"I'm afraid so," I said. To the woman, I said, "I'm sorry, but they started serving at seven thirty." I lied, of course, having no idea who *they* were.

As Harris extricated himself, she followed him, poking her business card at him until he took it, pocketed it, and handed her one of his own, which instantly soothed her. She retreated to her table with the prize card as if she'd counted coup with her war club, waggling her eyebrows at her companions.

"God, thank you," he said when we were on the street. It was cold and damp, which felt good after the smoky closeness of the Habana Haus.

"You're welcome," I said, still brandishing the cigar.

"Florida people," he said, shaking his head. "They can be so obnoxious. It's as if they don't realize there is anything else in the world, you know, but Florida. Unfortunately for them, Florida is so over. But some of these marketing women will do anything for UK business, you know. That's where we got the phrase, '*Been there, done that, fucked the rep.*'"

I laughed politely. The lights of the Ku'Damm were ahead.

"Are we going the right direction?" I asked. "I don't know where we're going to dinner."

"Your treat," he said, reminding me. "This is the right way. First another drink, then dinner."

"Great," I said, not meaning it and tossing the cigar aside. Thinking, *Let's get this over with so I can get the hell home.*

THE RESTAURANT WAS A twenty-minute walk. Harris prided himself on having discovered it a few years before, and said it had the best schnitzel in Berlin.

"They make it the old way," he said, rubbing his hands together, "You can hear them pounding the veal with mallets in the back to tenderize it. They pound it *hard* with mallets."

The place was called Der Tiefe Brunnen, and it was located on Rankestraße. It was dark and old, lit by candles, looking very much like "The Deep Well" of its name. Black-and-white photos of un-known (to me) celebrities covered the walls. A cloud of cigarette smoke hung low in the room, but through it men and women eyed us from booths as we took our table up front near the bar. The owner, a severe man in muttonchop sideburns, greeted Harris in German. Harris shook the man's hand and pointed me out, obvi-ously telling the owner I was new to the place and would be paying the bill. A tray of schnapps shots was sent over immediately, brought by a woman dressed to showcase her massive breasts. She wore a see-through spandex support bra under a filmy shirt. Her hair was dyed German Red, a crimson/purple color not found in nature except for buckbrush in October when the leaves turned color. When she bent over the table to dispense the glasses, I was afraid her breasts would swing out of the confines of her shirt and hit me in the face like a pleasant one-two punch. The place re-minded me of something prewar, or at least pre–falling of the Wall, a throwback to the fatalistic island mentality of Berlin before that structure came down.

"I've already ordered for the both of us," Harris said, sitting down. "Schnitzel Cordon Bleu. And more beer, of course. This isn't like most places—it takes ten minutes to pour a proper beer, which is as it should be. But everything is worth the wait in here, believe me.

"Just listen to that," he said, smiling. There was indeed pounding going on in the kitchen behind the bar. The blows were so powerful that silver and glassware on the table jumped. "*That's* how you tenderize veal—the old-fashioned way."

Something about the way he said it hit me wrong.

He excused himself to find the toilet, he said, and on the way he had an animated conversation with the proprietor that I didn't track. The two of them laughed, and Harris followed the man through the back of the bar into his office. They closed the door. The proprietor returned to his place at the bar, but Harris remained in the office a long time. Maybe he was using a private bathroom? I checked out the photos on the walls and fought back exhaustion and sipped beer. I was sure I could lean back in my booth right there and sleep. Instead, I checked my wristwatch.

Nine o'clock in Berlin, one o'clock in Denver. I hoped Melissa and Cody were back from wherever they'd been, or at least had turned their phones on.

When Harris returned to our booth, his face was slightly flushed even in the candlelight, and the droplets of sweat had returned along his upper lip.

"Fritz let me use his computer to check my e-mail," he said, sliding back into the booth and taking a long pull from his beer. "It has to do with some urgent matters in London—the reason I had to postpone our dinner the other night. A minor crisis, it seems. The authorities are making my life miserable."

"Really?" I said. I hoped he wasn't going to tell me the relocation was off after all this time waiting for him.

"Nothing to worry about," he said, apparently reading my eyes. "Nothing I can't deal with. But you must know that in Europe, it's 1984. Big Brother is always watching, and they seem to be watching those of us who dare to be different."

I assumed he meant the entrepreneurs.

He called to Fritz, "Another round, my friend!"

As Fritz poured and rested the beers so the foam could subside, Harris leaned in to me and spoke sotto voce, "This is what I hate about Europe, Jack, the creeping fascism of the politically correct. It's everywhere, but most of it comes from the EU in Brussels in the form of edicts. They want to control what we eat and how we measure it, what we say and think, how we live, those bastards. They want to control bloody *everything*. And what Brussels doesn't decree, our own government takes care of."

Harris was getting animated, and his voice was rising. I had no idea what he was talking about, but I needed to act interested and hope—pray—he would state his intentions in regard to the reservations center.

"Is it really that bad?" I asked, surprised at his vehemence.

"Yes! In England these days, the worst thing you can be is a proper Englishman. Believe me, I know of what I speak, Jack. I wish I could say it's a cauldron, and it's going to blow up soon, that we're going to rise up and take our country back. But the sad thing is, I don't think we've got the balls anymore. I think we'll just sit there tut-tutting while the government assumes all control."

The waitress with the breasts brought our veal. It was tender, all right. In fact, it was fantastic—huge palm-sized pieces of meat breaded with crispy crust that was still sizzling and the whole thing covered with ham and cheese. I should not have been so hungry, but I was. I noticed a bit of a slur in his words. This was going to be one of those nights.

"You've probably heard I'm considering moving my headquarters," Harris said through a mouthful of veal. "I need to find a place where I can breathe again."

Finally.

"I have."

"I'm strongly considering Colorado," he said, watching me carefully for my reaction.

"That would be fantastic," I said, putting down my fork to shake his hand. "We'd love to have you."

He shook his head as if to say, *Of course you would.*

"It's a great place," I said. "The sun shines over three hundred days a year. We've got the mountains and the skiing, as well as a great airport and a mayor who really encourages international business . . ."

He interrupted, "I know all that. You don't need to sell it to me. I'm very familiar with the state and the powers that be. I've been in touch with several of them, although not yet officially."

The beer arrived, and he took a long draught before continuing. He didn't wipe the foam away from his upper lip, which I found distracting.

"It's a great place to raise a family," I offered. "The schools are pretty good, and there is lots of recreation. Here," I said. "Let me show you . . ." and reached back for my wallet for my photo of Angelina.

The look on his face was anticipatory. Most people will feign interest, but Harris was sincere. He smiled broadly at the photo of our daughter. "A new one, eh?" he said. "Recent?"

"A couple of weeks ago," I said. "She's almost walking now."

"She is still an angel, just like her name," Harris said, handing the photo back. I was confused.

"You probably get so many photos shoved at you that it's easy to lose track of which kid is which," I said.

"What are you talking about?" he asked.

"I don't remember showing you a picture of her before," I said.

"Of course you did," he said.

I shook my head. "I just can't remember it, I guess."

"Have another beer," he said, and laughed roughly. He seemed to be studying me all of a sudden.

When did I show him a photo before? I wanted to know. But I remembered, *This isn't about you.*

As discreetly as I could, I settled back into the booth and reached for my beer. Unaccountably, I seethed with a sudden rage. I had no idea where it came from, or why it was so intense. All Harris had done was contradict me, show that he had a better memory than I did. But big shot or not, it would have been very easy that moment to smash my fist into his face, to wipe the foam off his lip with my knuckles. I could feel an explosion just beneath the surface, anger that wildly outmatched the transgression itself. Maybe the past week was catching up to me, I thought, coming to a head. All this miserable waiting while my family was vulnerable thousands of miles away. I was ready to unload everything on a British tour operator who brought thousands of tourists and millions of dollars into my city and who might soon be moving his business there.

"Looks like you could use another one of those," he said, nodding toward my beer glass.

"That's okay," I said, tight-lipped.

"Meaning you'd like another one," he said, his face animated again. "Me too. Fritz!"

He paused. "Are you all right? You look pale."

"I'm okay. Just tired."

"Buck up, man. This is the world of international tourism. You've got to hit the ground running."

I agreed. I was grateful he was drunk enough—or self-absorbed enough, or both—to not pick up on my anger a moment before.

"You know"—he laughed—"you Americans seem to think your government is taking away your civil liberties, but you don't know what you're talking about. There aren't bureaucrats looking over your shoulder as you live your life, telling you how to speak and think and whom to associate with—taking your freedom away. My friends in Colorado say that compared to what I'm used to, I'll be bulletproof! That's the term they use, *bulletproof*. I love that."

"Really? Who says that?" I asked.

"Oh no," he said coyly, "I won't reveal my sources."

Suddenly, he was silent. He studied his empty and greasy plate. I didn't realize until that moment how drunk he was, and how he'd apparently ventured into territory he now wished he hadn't.

The restaurant was emptying out, which was good. I didn't want Harris—or me—to engage with anyone in any way, especially in the belligerent mood he was in. I called for the bill, always a frustratingly long experience. Fritz delivered it (finally) in person, and Harris raved about how good the food was, and I agreed.

Fritz leaned down conspiratorially, said to Harris, "Do you need to check your e-mail again?"

Harris laughed, squeezed Fritz on his arm, said, "I've seen enough for tonight."

Which I thought an odd choice of words at the time.

MY HEAD WAS SPINNING when I sat down on my bed. I had four messages. I fumbled through the codes and prompts, cursing the phone, the hotel, the German language, and Malcolm Harris for the condition I was in.

The first message was from Melissa.

"Oh Jack, I'm sorry I missed you. I'm so sorry. You won't believe who I met today—Kellie Moreland! Call me right away!"

The second and third messages were the same.

By the fourth, she was angry.

"Jack, are you even there? Are you checking your messages? I know it's two in the morning, so don't even call." She paused, then: "My God, I need to talk to you right away. I met Kellie Moreland today—Brian arranged it. And guess what? Are you sitting down? She doesn't know anything about Angelina!"

In the Air /
Denver / Wyoming

Friday, November 16
Nine Days to Go

Twelve

J ET LAG WORKS BOTH ways.

On the flight home, in the cocoon of the 737-400 with the lights dimmed, I couldn't sleep. I was preoccupied that Melissa—with help from Brian—had "run into" Kellie Moreland at a society fund-raiser at a local library and posed the question about Angelina only to be met with a blank stare.

"Angelina who?" Kellie had asked.

Which meant a lot of things. Either Kellie was stupid—Melissa swore she wasn't—or Judge Moreland was making a play with his son on their own for reasons that were unknown to us. When Melissa asked Kellie about Garrett, she said Kellie shrank back as if slapped, as if the mere mention of her stepson's name filled her with horror. As Melissa followed her, trying to engage her, Kellie walked away faster through the crowd until she was running. Melissa ran, too, until Kellie called for security, and my wife was stopped by two men who asked what her problem was.

"What my *problem* was," Melissa said, over and over that night on the telephone. "How could I explain what my *problem* was?"

Brian was back in Denver and fully engaged in our *problem*. And according to Melissa, he was waiting for the photos he'd referred to earlier.

"Once we have them," Melissa said, "Brian says the whole thing blows up. According to Brian, we'll have Judge Moreland and Garrett by the balls." She growled that last bit, and I'd never heard her do that before. The day at the fund-raiser and the encounter with Kellie had charged her up, given her hope again. If Kellie had no idea her husband and son where trying to gain custody of a baby, then something was seriously wrong with this picture, Melissa said. The judge was hiding something from his wife. And if he was hiding something, he couldn't be as cocksure about his position and his leverage as he'd led us to believe.

WHEN I LANDED AT DIA, I could barely wait for my luggage. On the other side of the frosted glass would be my wife and daughter and either Cody or Brian or both. The marble floors were gleaming and new. Despite the late hour, there was space, light, no cigarette smoke. So American. So not Berlin. My world.

Brian was with her, looking sharp. But the downcast of his eyes clued me in immediately that something was wrong. Melissa's face was puffy and red, her mouth downturned. Angelina saw me from her stroller and started clapping, though, oblivious to what was affecting Brian and Melissa.

"Harry," Melissa said, as I hugged her. She whispered in my ear. "Harry's dead."

The news made me go cold. "Harry?"

"Harry!" Angelina said, mimicking me and clapping her pudgy hands. "Harry dog!"

Brian tugged at my arm so we could distance ourselves from Melissa and Angelina in her stroller.

"The cops said someone threw raw hamburger into your backyard laced with rat poison and fishhooks," Brian said. "We found Harry coughing up blood on the back deck, but by the time we got him to the vet it was too late. The vet said there were a dozen hooks imbedded in his throat."

"When did this happen?" I asked, numb.

Brian looked at his wristwatch. "Five hours ago, I guess. We left the vet an hour ago to meet you, but it was over long before then. Melissa gave the okay to put him down because it was only a matter of time before he died."

"So," I said, "I was somewhere over Michigan when my dog died."

"I guess so."

Hot tears filled my eyes. I angrily wiped them away. I'm not a crier and was surprised by my reaction, but the news had hit me like a hammerblow.

"We know who did it," Brian said. "Remember how Garrett reacted to your dog?"

"Harry never hurt anyone," I said. "He wasn't capable of hurting anyone."

"Garrett got you back," Brian said. "And I don't think he's done with you."

"Jesus," I said, "this is so . . . depraved." I wiped at my face, not wanting Angelina to see me—or Melissa. I couldn't believe I was crying, especially because I hadn't cried after all of the things that had happened to us. But Harry? What had Harry done to anyone?

"I know how tough this is," Brian said, putting his arm around my shoulder. "But when we get home, Cody is ready to drive to Montana. I know you're tired, but are you up for that?"

"All of us?" I asked.

Brian said, "All but me. I can't afford to risk being out of town if my source calls with the photos. He could call anytime," he said, brandishing his cell phone. "Besides, Jeter Hoyt and I never really got along."

He whispered when he said the name Jeter Hoyt.

I said, "Are you going to tell me what these photos are? I'd like to know."

Brian shook his head. "I'm not positive myself—I'm leery of asking too many questions. My contact is jittery as it is. All I know is that he swears these photos will bring down the judge, or at least dissuade him from going forward with this thing with your daughter."

"And you're sure he's right?"

Brian said, "How can one ever be sure of anything? But I've told him I won't pay unless I've seen the photos and he's right. And believe me, brother, we're talking big bucks. So I don't want to be in the middle of nowhere when he calls."

I nodded.

"So, are you ready to go?" Brian asked.

"Right now?"

"Right now."

"Let's hit the road."

"Do you want to pay your respects to Harry so you have some closure?"

That hit me wrong. I guess it was the unreasonable but fashionable sensitivity of the question.

"I hate that word, 'closure,'" I snapped, shrugging off Brian's arm. "Like it's just a procedure, then we're all right. It's midnight. Do we break in to the vet clinic so I can cry, or what? Will that give me *closure?*"

Brian shrugged. "Sorry, Jack. Just trying to help."

"I know you are," I said. "I don't mean to take it out on you."

I paused for Melissa to catch up. She looked at me for some kind of guidance I didn't feel capable of providing. "I guess we're going to Montana," I said. "Are you up for that?"

She said, "I've been packing our stuff all day. Before this thing happened with Harry, I was getting us ready. Everything is in your Jeep. I guess we might as well go."

I turned her toward me and hugged her. I could tell by the way she went limp on my shoulder that she was exhausted. I buried my face in her hair. I loved the smell of her.

"God, I missed you," I said.

I squatted down and kissed Angelina. "You, too," I said.

As we walked out of the airport I thought about Harry. I wanted vengeance. I wanted blood.

WE PULSED NORTH through Wyoming in my Jeep in the dark, passing through Casper at four in the morning. Cody drove and I sat in the passenger seat. Melissa was in the backseat with Angelina in her car seat. There were no city lights, no southbound traffic. I slipped in and out of consciousness. When I slept, I slept hard and awoke groggy. It comforted me that Cody seemed alert, serious, and sober. I was very pleased to be *taking action*.

DAWN CAME SPLASHING across the Bighorn Mountains north of Sheridan, Wyoming, near the Montana border, the morning sunlight so intense Melissa pulled a blanket up over Angelina's sleeping face. We'd stopped for gas and coffee in Ranchester, and the smell of coffee filled the Jeep. The morning was cold and crisp. Spiderwebs of creeping frost headquartered in each corner of the windshield.

"Maybe we can get breakfast in Billings," Cody said.

"He speaks," Melissa said from the backseat.

"I've been thinking," Cody said.

"He thinks," I said, chiding him.

Cody didn't smile. Instead, he reached down and turned the defroster fan up a notch. The frost retreated.

He said, "We've got, what, nine days now before Judge Moreland's deadline? Before he said he'd come and take the baby away?"

"Yes," Melissa said.

"Not much time," Cody said, shaking his head.

"But that means nothing anymore," Melissa said. "We've got the photos coming anytime now. And this . . ." She indicated us, the Jeep, our purpose.

Cody cleared his throat and spoke softly so as not to awake Angelina. "I just want to be clear, so we're all on the same page. Every mile we drive takes us farther across the line. And the farther we get, the less likely you'll be able to use any legal options, like getting the baby awarded to your custody in court if it comes to that. That's because you're now tainted. We've left the land of the innocent and willingly entered the underworld. You understand that, right?"

I exchanged looks with Melissa, expecting at least some fear in her eyes. There was none.

"We understand that," I said, for both of us.

"Okay, then. So what we're trying to do here is hit the judge through his son. We want to scare Garrett into signing away custody."

After a few beats, I said, "Yes."

Cody nodded. "And you realize that whenever you choose to scare someone into doing something, there can be unintended consequences." He paused, then said, "It's not an exact science, being a criminal."

"Cody!" Melissa said from the backseat.

"I just want to make sure we all understand each other," Cody said. "It's better to use plain language."

"We're not the criminals," Melissa said. "We're not the people trying to take babies away from their parents!"

"The law is on his side," Cody said patiently. "I don't agree with it. There's a lot about the law I don't agree with. We've got Aubrey

Coates out on the street, for one thing. But the law is on Judge Moreland's side."

Melissa said, "But his wife doesn't even know about Angelina, so something really weird is going on. And his son, Garrett, killed our dog, not to mention what he and his friend did to Jack and in our house!"

Cody talked to her via the rearview mirror. "Melissa, his wife not knowing is not a crime. It's strange, yes. But it's not a crime. And we think we know who killed Harry, but we haven't proved it."

"What about Luis?" I said.

Cody smiled bitterly. "I'm the one who kicked the shit out of Luis. For what? For cruising through your neighborhood. Who is the criminal in this instance?"

"Garrett dumped him. That's a crime."

"And how do we know that?" Cody asked. "How do we know Luis didn't dump himself? I mean, Garrett could claim Luis wanted out of the car, that he didn't know how badly Luis was injured, that Luis just didn't want to go to the hospital. So Luis wanders off by himself in the dark and stumbles into the South Platte. How is Garrett liable for that?"

I said nothing.

"Why are you *doing* this?" Melissa asked, tears in her eyes.

"I want to make sure we all realize what we're doing," Cody said. "That's all."

"We realize," I said.

"Do you?" Cody asked.

"When Brian gets his hands on those photos, it might all go away," Melissa said. "Maybe this is as far as we need to go."

"You trust Brian and his photos?" Cody asked into the rearview. There was a pinch of sarcasm in the question and a dollop of pity. "Think about it. What are these photos supposed to show? Judge Moreland in bed with a girl? With a boy? What if they're doctored? What if the judge sees them as what they could be—amateur blackmail? Then where are you? And where is Brian when this happens? I'd guess he'd be long gone on one of his business trips.

"I'm just saying," Cody said. "Speculating, because that's what us cops do."

Melissa said, "I don't like your attitude about Brian."

Cody shrugged. "Jesus, this is why I *should* be suspended from the Denver PD, I guess: I can't keep my mouth shut."

"Why are you doing this?" Melissa asked again. I reached back for her hand, but she'd withdrawn, crossing her arms across her breasts.

"Because," Cody said, "once we unleash Jeter Hoyt, we don't know what the hell will happen."

I asked Cody to pull over, which he did, and I climbed into the backseat with Melissa. She was stiff at first, but finally let me hold her.

"We're doing the right thing," I whispered into her hair. "It'll be all right."

"I've got one more question for you," Cody said. He took our silence as assent. "If you had it all to do over again, would you still adopt?"

"Yes," we said simultaneously.

"Good," Cody said. "Good for you." His voice started trailing away. "Children need to be wanted . . ."

I noticed that as I'd held her, she'd slipped one of her hands out from beneath the blanket and she was holding the edge of Angelina's car seat in a white-knuckled death grip.

Montana

Saturday, November 17

Eight Days to Go

Thirteen

LINCOLN, MONTANA, POPULATION ELEVEN hundred, was a hamlet in the Helena National Forest on the bank of the Blackfoot River. The little community made the news in the 1990s when Theodore Kaczynski, known as the Unabomber, was arrested there in his hovel of a cabin, which was later shipped whole over Stemple Pass to the capital city of Helena fifty-nine miles to the southeast. It was a tough and sloppy little town that looked as if it had been dropped into the trees from a helicopter, and some of the buildings didn't land well.

It was also the home of Jeter Hoyt.

We arrived at 3:00 P.M. on Saturday. Fourteen hours. It was like driving across most of Western Europe, and all we'd done was cross one state and enter another.

Cody parked at a bar. Apparently, his cell-phone charge was depleted because it had spent seven or eight hours searching vainly for a signal to grab on to, so he'd need to use the phone inside. I got out with him, said, "You were a little rough back there."

He lit a cigarette. "I get like that when I'm not smoking or drink-ing," he said. "When all I've got is reality staring me in the fucking face."

"Thanks for driving, though," I said.

"My pleasure."

"What if your uncle isn't around?"

"Always a possibility," Cody said. "It's the tail end of hunting season. Remember hunting season?" he asked, his expression wistful.

"I do. But you talked to him a while ago, right?"

Cody nodded. "I told him we might be coming up. He didn't say he'd be here or not. He just grunted at me."

While Cody went inside, I leaned against the Cherokee with my hands in my pockets. There was snow on the tops of the peaks to the south and the Scapegoat Wilderness Area to the north. I could see a skiff of snow in the shadows of the pines behind the bar. Little mountain towns like this were especially unattractive during two periods of the year: now, when there was just enough early snow to muddy the ground but not enough to freeze and cover it, and again in the spring, when the snow melted and revealed all the garbage that had been tossed aside. But as if to offset the appearance, this is when a town like Lincoln smelled best, a heady mix of pine trees, the forest floor, woodsmoke. As I breathed it in, it reminded me of home, wherever that was.

I turned to see that Angelina was awake and grinning at me through the window. Melissa held her tightly. That smile filled me with such unabashed joy that I knew I was doing the right thing. I rapped at the window so she'd open it.

"Smell that," I said.

"It smells, um, woody," she said.

"If only these little places had jobs for international tourism specialists," I said, reaching inside the Jeep so Angelina could grab my finger. "What a great place to live, to raise little kids."

"Where her neighbor could be the Unabomber," Melissa said, and we both laughed. Angelina squealed with delight simply because her parents were laughing. We hadn't done enough of that lately, I decided.

Cody came out of the bar with a Coors Light in his hand and a cigarette.

"Some old high-school buddies in there," he said. "D'you remember the Browning brothers or Chad Kerr? They asked about you and Brian."

"They did?"

"Yeah," Cody said. "So much for coming up here incognito, eh? I forgot how everybody knows everybody's business in Montana."

"What about Uncle Jeter?"

"He's waiting for us out at his place. He said he'd disarm the trip wires so we could drive right up to his house."

"*What?*"

"I'm *joking*," Cody said, tossing his cigarette aside into the mud.

UNCLE JETER'S CABIN WAS tucked away in an alcove of pine and aspen trees and accessed via an ascending two-track road with potholes filled to the top with chocolate-milk-colored water. Cody said, "I *think* I still remember how to get there . . ."

We passed under an ancient sagging lodgepole-pine archway that was dark gray with moisture and crawling with bright green and white lichen. On one support pole was a tiny wood-burned sign that said HOYT OUTFITTING SERVICES. On the other was a rusted metallic sign that said NO WHINERS. Inside the archway, Uncle Jeter's cabin was shambling and low-slung, looking like a scene from 1880 except for the satellite dish mounted on a pole and aimed at a southern gap of cloudy sky to the south. I saw two four-wheel-drive vehicles—a Dodge Power Wagon from the 1960s and a new-model but beat-up Ford pickup—parked butt end first in an open garage. A cross pole high in the trees supported the hanging carcasses of an elk and what looked like a heavily muscled man.

I started to point when Cody said, "Bear. Skinned bears look like if you hung a linebacker. It always creeped me out. Melissa, if I were you, I'd not let Angelina see that."

"Luckily," Melissa said from the back, "she's looking out the other window at the horses." Three horses, two mules, and a couple of goats watched us from a corral.

"Quite a place," Melissa said, deadpan.

"About what I'd always expected," I said.

Uncle Jeter greeted us at the front door with a cheese plate: dozens of overlarge squares of Velveeta hastily cut up on a chipped dinner plate with Ritz crackers piled up in a couple of columns and colored toothpicks bunched together by a rubber band. It struck me as incongruous and sweet that this man, after receiving Cody's call, set about chopping little squares of cheese with a hunting knife for a snack.

Uncle Jeter was tall but not as tall as I remembered him, broad but not as wide as I recalled. In fact, he looked distressingly normal, except for the long beard striped with gray and the ponytail that fanned down half of his back. His eyes were the same, though— light blue-gray and piercing, set in hollows that were slightly red-tinged. His nose was large and beaky, complicated with hairlike blue veins. His hands were outsize and looked like mitts. He wore a heavy flannel shirt and a wool Filson vest so old it was shiny, tight Wranglers, and lace-up outfitter boots with heels for riding.

It was dark inside, the walls covered with tanned bear and elk hides. The antlers of mounted deer and elk served as gun racks for a dozen long rifles and shotguns. The place smelled of smoke, grease, and gun-cleaning solvent. Melissa, Angelina, and I sat on an ancient leather couch with three-quarter wagon wheels on the ends for armrests. Melissa had a tough time keeping our daughter on the couch and not scrambling to the floor. Jeter set the cheese plate sat next to a six-pack of Molson beer on a coffee table.

"I'm sorry," Uncle Jeter said in a gravelly voice to Melissa and Angelina as we entered. "This ain't no place for a lady and a baby."

"It's fine," Melissa said, flashing a tight-mouthed smile.

"No," he said, "no it ain't. Is there anything I can get the little one? Some milk or something?"

Melissa gestured to her overlarge baby bag, and said, "Not necessary—we came prepared."

To our surprise, Angelina seemed to be charming him. She'd give him her silly demure look, bat her eyelashes, then cover her face with her hands. It wouldn't be long before she'd spread her fingers and gaze at him through them, then giggle. I noticed that he had a tough time devoting his attention fully to Cody, who outlined our problem. Despite what Cody had said to us in the car, he didn't indicate any doubt at all as he told his uncle Hoyt how Garrett and Luis had fouled our house and shot me with paintballs, how Garrett said he owned us now. When Cody told him about Harry, I saw Hoyt's eyes turn hard.

When Cody was done, Uncle Jeter sat back and raked his fingers through his beard.

"So," he said, "you've got a boy who needs scared, and you came to me to do it. Why?"

Cody deferred to me.

"Because you scared *us*."

"That was twenty years ago, Jack."

Cody leaned forward and handed his uncle the envelope of reports and photos Torkleson had given us. Jeter took it and fanned through the photos of Garrett, while Cody said, "Because you're not known in Denver, Uncle Jeter. You've got no priors down there. I know how things work with the police—where they'd look if something went bad. They wouldn't look to Lincoln, Montana, unless you did something stupid like dropped your wallet."

Or if the Browning Brothers and Chad Kerr in Lincoln were questioned, I thought.

Uncle Jeter shot him a look that made me fear for Cody.

"Not that I'm saying something like that would happen," Cody said, backtracking. "Or even that Garrett would go to the police. The point is for him *not* to go to the police. The point is for you to persuade him to sign his custody rights away."

Hoyt raked his beard again, as if considering all of the odds. "I ain't done too many things like this in the last few years," he said. "I might be a little rusty. But you say this Garrett likes to associate with Mexicans, that it makes him feel like a big shot?"

Cody nodded. "Specifically, a gang called Sur-13."

Uncle Jeter turned to Melissa. "I'm sorry, ma'am, would you want to take a few minutes and show the baby the horses outside? I got some horses and two fine mules out there. And a goat, a good goat. He don't bite. Do you think that little angel might want to see them?"

Melissa looked at me, and I nodded.

As soon as the front door shut, Uncle Jeter said, "I got a problem with this illegal immigration. I got a big problem with the way them Mexicans are taking over our cities and flying the Mexican flag and all. A big problem, you understand me?"

Cody nodded.

Jeter said, "I called my bank in Helena a couple of weeks ago because they fouled up a deposit I made from a hunting client. They don't know what to do with cash anymore, it makes their eyes get all buggy. Well, when I called them, I got this recorded message that said press one for English and two for *Español*. This was Helena, Montana, fellows! I got so goddamned mad I drove down there and took all my money out. When the bank manager asked why I was doing it, I said, 'Press one for English and two for *Español,* you little prick!'

"As I was leaving town I drove by the hospital, and I saw these Mexicans lined up—lined up!—outside the emergency ward. They was carrying their little sick kids and just waiting in line because I guess the doctors have to treat them no matter what. I thought, whose country is this, anyway? What's wrong with our so-called leaders that sit by while we get infiltrated by our so-called neighbor from the south. Now I hear that some wannabe Mexican and his Mexican gang friends want that little angel out there." He glared at us and stabbed a long finger toward the front door. "It ain't right!"

Uncle Jeter was on such a frightening roll I didn't want to tell him the problem was the judge.

"Taking down a couple fucking Mexicans don't bother me at all," Uncle Jeter said. "Getting this Mexican wannabe to sign a piece of paper sounds like a piece of cake."

To demonstrate, he stood up swiftly—much quicker than I thought him capable of—and put an imaginary Garrett in a head-lock and fashioned his other hand into a pistol and cocked his thumb back.

"Remember that scene in *The Godfather*?" Jeter asked us.

"*Either your name goes on that agreement,*" Jeter said in a fake Mexican accent to imaginary Garrett, "*or your brains, senõr!*"

He continued to talk to imaginary Garrett, and his playacting was intense, unnerving, as if Garrett were truly in his hands.

Jeter snarled, "And if you think you can sign this paper, then run off and tell your daddy or the cops that you were coerced, you got another think coming, little *senõr*. 'Cause if that happens I'm com-ing back for you and I'm feeding your nuts to my goats. And that's just for starters, little *senõr!*"

He looked up. "Think that'd do it?"

"Maybe a little more subtle," Cody said.

"We've got eight days," I said.

Uncle Jeter nodded, let the imaginary Garrett drop to the floor, and took a breath to cool down. "Compensation?" he asked.

"You'll be working that out with Brian Eastman," I said. "He's handling the money."

"Brian Eastman?" Jeter asked, rubbing his chin beneath his beard, "Your old pal? Son of the minister?"

"Yes."

"He was queer, wasn't he?"

I sighed, "Yes. And he's helping us out with expenses. He's done well in Denver."

"I bet he has," Jeter said, sneering. "But fag money is as good as any, I guess."

I bit my tongue and glanced at Cody, who was rolling his eyes and shaking his head, embarrassed.

Jeter said, "Give me a day or two to get my poop in a group. There's supposed to be a hell of a storm coming first of next week, so I need to get out of here shortly, I guess. I can be in Denver by Tuesday or Wednesday latest. I ain't seen that city in years. I hear it's grown like crazy."

"It has," Cody said.

He turned to his nephew. "You regret leaving Montana and moving to a place like that?"

Cody nodded. "Lately I have."

Jeter nodded back. "Yeah, I can't see why anyone would want to leave Montana. Makes no sense to me. In my experience all cities are the fucking same—filled with undesirables."

I slapped my knees, stood up, and said, "Cody, a minute outside?"

After he'd shut the door, Cody said, "Second thoughts?"

"Yes. He's older and crazier than I remember. I don't think we can control him or count on him to stop what he's started."

Cody slowly nodded his head. "I agree. He's not the same guy we remember."

"Look, can you just tell him I got cold feet at the last minute, and we can get the hell out of here?"

Melissa walked up to us holding Angelina. She'd overheard. "He does seem unstable," she said.

Cody barked a short laugh. "He's always been unstable. It's hard to find a stable hit man these days. But yes, he's gotten worse. I guess I didn't realize how damned *old* he was."

Cody put his hands on our shoulders. "Look, you two get in the car. I'll go in and tell him you're reconsidering your options."

AS WE DROVE THROUGH LINCOLN, I asked, "How'd he take it?"

"He's hard to read," Cody said. "I think he's disappointed. He was really getting worked up there."

"It was the right choice," Melissa said from the backseat. "I just wish we had a ready option. Maybe Brian has one if we ask him."

Cody snorted. Then: "I wish the old fart had given me that envelope back."

Fourteen

HER VOICE WAS HESITANT. Who called on Saturday evening except telemarketers or someone complaining that there were cows on the road? "Hello?"

"Hi, mom."

"Jack!" Her voice was a mixture of excitement and trepidation. I called so rarely that when I did it must be bad news, I knew she was thinking. That tone unnerved me, sent me back in time.

"We're driving through Helena and I've got Melissa and your granddaughter with me. We'll be coming down through Townsend and thought maybe we'd stop by."

"*Oh my!* Why didn't you let us know you were coming?"

"I'm sorry. Don't worry about dinner or anything, and I mean that. We just thought you might want to see your granddaughter. Is Dad around?"

"Oh my, yes! He's outside doing something with the tractor. I was just starting dinner, and, oh, you've got me flustered. I don't know what to say. Why didn't you let us know sooner?"

"It's a long story," I said, feeling my face flush. "Look, if this isn't a convenient time . . ." I could feel Melissa's eyes on me from the backseat. How was it that even after seventeen years in the outside world, I instantly reverted back to my sullen high-school-senior self, when I had left the ranch—and them—for good? How quickly I was ready to call it off and go on down the road.

"No, no! You must come by! I was just so surprised you called. I was just opening a package of steaks and the phone rang and it was you. No, come by. When will you be here?"

"About forty-five minutes."

"Oh my!"

"Look, Mom . . ."

"Goodness. I'll open another package of steaks. Is it just you and Melissa and the baby?"

"Cody, too."

"Cody! Cody Hoyt?"

"Yes."

"*Oh my!* I'll go tell your father. Forty-five minutes, now more like forty, I suppose."

"Mom, we can grab something to eat. We can take you out to dinner. You don't have to fix anything. Really!"

"Don't be ridiculous," she said, a little angry I'd even suggested it.

I closed the cell and looked back at Melissa. "There, are you happy now?"

"Aren't you glad you called?" she said, smiling.

"I'm not sure. Mom's in a dither."

Cody said, "This is a good thing to establish some cover since everybody and their dog knows we're up here. If need be, we can always say you decided to visit your folks with Angelina for the last time. That makes perfect sense. And I drove because I don't have anything else to do." Then, sourly: "I just hope your old man doesn't put me to work fixing fence or some damn thing."

AS WE CLEARED EAST Helena en route to Townsend, and I saw Canyon Ferry Lake to the left—a few more houses on the banks than I remembered, but not many—I felt a twang of recognition.

"Hasn't changed much," Cody said, as if reading my thoughts.

"No."

"Not like Denver, where there's a new subdivision every few days," he said. "It's frozen in time here. I used to not like that, but now I do."

My anxiety grew. I was getting more nervous than I had been earlier in the day on the way to meet with Uncle Jeter.

"Maybe we should have gotten fast food in Helena," I said.

"Your mother would be furious," Melissa said. "Showing up and not eating? What are you thinking?"

Cody said, "Saturday night is steak night if I remember. Steak and baked potatoes. Every Saturday night. I wonder if that's changed?"

"It hasn't as far as I know," I said. "She said something about opening up another package of steaks."

"Good steaks, too," Cody said, nodding. "I can still remember the drill. Pork chops on Monday, spaghetti on Tuesday, hamburgers on Wednesday, cabbage rolls Thursday, pot roast Friday, steaks on Saturday, fried chicken on Sunday."

I nodded.

"Did it ever change?" Melissa asked.

"Never," I said. "If she tried something new, Dad would just sit at the table and just stare at his plate and pout."

"I really liked the cabbage rolls," Cody said. "Maybe next time we drive up here to hire a hit man we can come on Thursday."

"Cody!" Melissa said. "Stop that. What if Angelina starts using those words?"

Cody grinned as he slowed down and clicked the turn single, and we were soon on the gravel road that led to the ranch.

THE HOME RANCH LOOKED almost exactly as I'd left it. A few new things—a bigger gas tank, a larger Quonset for the equipment—but basically the same buildings, the same layout. A few inches of snow lay in the hayfields, and the Big Belt Mountains rose dark blue and snowy to the east. Between the ranch and the mountains, the foothills shimmered with the intense gold light of dusk, the kind that makes snow look like molten lava. I saw a small herd of mule deer hanging around the windmill and tin stock tank. A few hundred bald-faced Angus were bunched in the east meadow, massed and no doubt awaiting the cattle truck.

We swung into the ranch yard. Through Cody's window I got a glimpse of Dad in the Quonset working under a trouble light, tractor parts and tools scattered around his feet. On my side, Mom's face was framed in the kitchen window, looking out anxiously, and as soon as she saw us, she vanished and reappeared at the front door wearing the same apron she'd had on eighteen years before, the one with the blue ducks.

"Melissa!" she called out. "Bring that little darling in here!"

"She means Angelina," Cody deadpanned, "not you."

Mom gave me a quick cheek kiss and punched Cody affectionately in the arm to say hello, but both gestures were done en route to Angelina, who she scooped up in her arms. Angelina squealed happily, and Mom turned and took her in the house. Melissa followed with one of the diaper bags and gave me an amused over-the-shoulder look before going inside.

Cody and I walked over to the Quonset. Cows bawled in the

meadow, punctuating the otherwise complete silence. I had forgotten about silence.

Although they'd been to the wedding and to Denver to see Angelina when we brought her home, I hadn't been back. I didn't want to come back and feel like I was feeling now. I didn't know what to expect, but my heart was thumping, and my hands felt cold.

Dad stepped back from the tractor and wiped his hands on a rag with very little white left on it and watched us approach. His face had filled out some recently, and his lenses were so thick they distorted his eyes bigger. He looked old, which shocked me.

"Couldn't cut it in the big city, huh?" he said. "Coming back begging for your old jobs back, you two?"

My belly clenched, but Cody realized he was kidding and said, "Naw, Walt. We just want our wages. We don't want to have to *work* for 'em."

"Nothing's changed in that regard," Dad said, before breaking into a grin. "Good to see you, Jack," he said, reaching out. *My God,* I thought, *is he going to kiss me?* And he did! After a rough one-handed hug, he kissed me on the cheek before letting me go. I was left with a whisker burn and a lingering smell of engine oil in my nose. "You boys mind helping me put away these tools before we go in and eat?" he asked.

"See what I told you?" Cody joked.

"Hurry up," Dad said. "I want to go in the house and see my good-looking daughter-in-law and especially my granddaughter!"

"It's not like you haven't seen her, Dad," I said, gathering up from the floor scarred wrenches that were as familiar to me as my own fingers and toes.

"Yeah, but that's when you first brought her home. When she was just a little pink thing. I haven't seen her since she became a person."

"I'm sorry we just showed up without any warning," I said. "This was kind of a last-second trip."

He shrugged. "I'm just glad you're here. Besides, after dinner I got some fence that needs fixed." Again, I thought he was serious. Again, he was joking. What had happened to him?

"You sure you don't mind us crashing dinner?"

"As long as we've got enough steaks we're okay," he said, gesturing to the hundreds of bawling cattle out in the meadow. "I think we'll be okay."

DINNER WAS PLEASANT. No, it was more than pleasant. I was *joyous*. Angelina, as she had with Jeter Hoyt, spent most of the time trying to get Dad's attention. In turn, he doted on her, fed her, made funny faces that made her laugh. I looked at Melissa, and Melissa shook her head, as surprised with this new turn in both of them as I was.

Cody declined the offer of a beer with dinner since he was driving, which I thought admirable because I knew he wanted one.

Through a mouthful of steak, Dad said the ranch had sold, the result of a divorce settlement with the old owner. It was bought quickly by a hedge fund manager in New York City.

"This new bird, I don't know," he said, gesturing with his fork, "I'm not sure we're gonna see eye to eye."

"Give him a chance, Walter," Mom said. "We've been here a long time. I'm not sure I'm up to moving again."

"Hell, I'll give him a chance," Dad said, grumbling. "As long as he doesn't say the word 'bison' again in my presence, we might get along. There are too many goddamn buffalo in Montana as it is, and too many Ted Turners."

For the first time, I thought about what my parents would do when they finally left the ranch. Did they have retirement savings? Medical insurance? These were things that had never been discussed in my presence. Where would they live? I thought about the marriage they had, which, despite its flaws, had lasted forty years. Just the two of them, out here twenty miles from the nearest town on an expanse of land so big and raw it could have easily swallowed them up. *God,* I thought, *they're tough.*

The topic turned to Judge Moreland and Garrett. Melissa told the story but left out the most unpleasant details. Even with that, it was too much for Mom to handle, and she simply shook her head as if it were another of those big-city things she'd just never understand.

"Tell them to screw themselves, I like this one," Dad said, reaching over and mussing Angelina's hair, which resulted in a belly laugh that was contagious. "Keep her."

As if that were the end of the subject.

Angelina tried to reciprocate and stretched her arm out at him. Surprisingly, he bent forward and dipped his head so she could tousle his white hair.

"Yup," he said, sitting back while she laughed. "Keep *this* one."

"ARE YOU SURE YOU CAN'T STAY?" Mom begged. "Jack and Melissa can stay in Jack's old room. Cody can have the spare or the bunkhouse if he'd prefer. Jack's old crib is up in the attic for Angelina."

Looking past the fact that they'd kept my crib all these years, I explained that I had to go to work Monday, that I'd just returned from overseas the night before and had follow-up to do.

"I've never understood your job," Dad said. "What—you go to foreign countries and hand out maps? You get paid for that?"

Actually, I'd explained my job to him three or four times over the years. His eyes glazed over each time.

"Why don't you stay?" she said again.

He said, "I'm sure they can spare you for one day, for Christ's sake."

"I'm sorry," I said.

His face darkened, and I braced for it; *you sure are sorry* or something similar and cutting. He was still Walter McGuane in there. But he caught himself, held it in, let it pass. "I wish you weren't going to take this little one away from me," he said instead, tickling her, making her laugh.

"Isn't there supposed to be a big storm coming down from the north?" Melissa said. "I'm sure you wouldn't want us to be snowed in here." She was good at saying reasonable things.

"Hell," he said, "I wouldn't mind."

WHILE MELISSA AND MY MOTHER cleaned up dishes, Dad said he wanted to show me something out in the barn. He didn't. As we walked outside in the last gasp of dusk in the cold, he didn't look at me as he said, "I've realized something since you left this place, Jack. I was hard on you. I guess I didn't know how to be a father. My old man was a bastard, and he's the one supposed to teach you those things."

"You did okay," I said, a lump in my throat. All I remembered of my grandfather was a tall man with a full black beard that smelled of cigarette smoke and eyes that weren't kind.

"Naw. But that don't mean you shouldn't know how to be a son. Call your mother more. Hell, invite her to Denver. That little girl in there is her only grandchild. I'll survive if she comes down to see you. I know how to cook a steak."

We walked to the Quonset, crunching gravel. So much to say. "I'll do that, Dad. But didn't you hear what Melissa was saying about Angelina?"

"I did."

"We may not get to keep her."

"Bullshit. Fight it."

"We are."

"Good," he said. "And if you ever get the time from your busy damned job passing out maps of Denver, come back and stay a little while. I got fence to fix."

I laughed.

"I'm proud you done so well on your own," he said. "I was telling a cattle buyer about you just yesterday morning. He acted all interested, but you know you can't trust those bastards. But I am proud of you."

IN THE CAR, the lights of Bozeman looking like the last vestige of civilization in the pure dark of a cloudy, moonless night, Cody said, "We'll never figure 'em out, Jack. They are what they are. My old man's a drunk. I didn't fall very far from that fucking tree. This is a good place, Montana. I hope to come back someday."

"It is a good place," I said. "Or is it just because it isn't Denver right now?"

"Maybe for you. I just hope I can figure out a way to make it back."

Why did he say that as if he never would?

I WAS SLEEPING when Melissa's cell phone burred. I sat up, had no idea at all where we were in Wyoming. It was midnight.

"It's Brian," she said from the backseat, looking at the display.

She listened, mostly, saying, "That's great," and "You be careful, Brian."

She closed the phone, said, "Brian's meeting the guy with the photos tonight someplace downtown. By the time we get back, we'll have them."

"Everything's working," I said. "I'm glad we canceled that thing with Jeter."

"We'll see," Cody cautioned. "Brian could just as easily be on a wild-goose chase. That would be very Brian-like."

WE WERE APPROACHING CASPER at two in the morning when Melissa's phone rang again. She said "Brian again," and answered. A few seconds went by when she gasped, and said, "Who *are* you?"

"Give it to me," I said, and she quickly handed the phone over, as eager to get rid of it as I was to get it.

I could hear city noises and the sound of someone laughing in the background.

"Who is this?" I asked. "What are you doing with Brian's phone?"

"Brian?" the voice said. A young voice, Hispanic accent. "*Brian?* We kicked his ass."

Again the laugh in the background, and a phrase I'd heard before. My entire body went cold.

We fucking own you, man.

"Brian," the caller said before punching off, "is one dead faggot."

"Oh no," I said. "Someone called us on Brian's phone, and I think I heard Garrett in the background."

"Shit," Cody spit, and floored it.

Denver

Sunday, November 18
Seven Days to Go

Fifteen

WE HURTLED DOWN I-25, reaching speeds of 110 miles per hour, with Cody barking out the names of detectives he used to work with. I'd locate the numbers on his cell and speed-dial them and hand the phone over when someone answered. We woke up a lot of detectives. All were groggy from sleep. Cody asked whether the detective was aware of a homicide or attempted homicide in downtown Denver.

"Okay, thanks, man," Cody said three times in a row. "Sorry to wake you up," and handed the phone back to me to place the next call.

"Nothing?" I said. "Could it be a joke? A way of screwing with us?"

"That was Brian's phone they used," Melissa observed. "How would they have gotten it?"

"She's right," he said. "Goddammit, who was on shift? They won't tell me anything if I call the desk. I've got to find who might have worked it and talk to them personally. Jack, scroll down through the numbers. I can think of two other guys who might know something."

I found both numbers and called each in turn and switched on the speaker feature of the cell so Cody could talk and speed at the same time. It scared me when he held the phone to his ear and drove at the same time because he was incapable of talking without gesturing as well. The first detective didn't pick up, the second asked Cody if he was drunk to be calling at this hour.

"I'm fine," he said. "I need to know who was on shift tonight."

"The FNG—fucking new guy. Who else would be on midnights?"

"Torkleson?"

I felt a little trill of recognition.

"Yeah."

"Do you know his cell number?"

"It's fucking four in the morning, Cody. I don't know anything except that I want to go back to sleep. He's the FNG. I'm not sure I wrote his number down."

"Please, Dan, I really need to know it."

"Are you even working? Aren't you suspended?"

"Yeah."

"What the hell are you doing, Cody?"

"Checking on a friend. Please, Dan."

Dan sighed, and grumbled, "Hold on."

I was afraid we'd drive out of cell-phone range before Dan found the number. Wyoming was notorious for huge expanses where there was no signal. Luckily, it was also notorious for its lack of state troopers on the highway. Finally, Dan came back and gave Cody the number.

"Can I go back to sleep now?" Dan asked.

"Sure. Thanks. Good night."

To us, he asked, "Got it?"

"I do," Melissa said, and tore out the page of her check register that she'd used to write down the number.

I punched the numbers in, keeping the speaker on.

"Yeah?" the detective answered, no doubt leery of the late-night call.

"Jason, it's Cody Hoyt."

"Shit, I didn't recognize the number, and it's four in the morning. What can I do you for?"

"I need to know if you worked an incident tonight. The subject's a friend of mine named Brian Eastman. Tall, thin, Caucasian, midthirties. Probably somewhere downtown."

After a pause, Torkleson said, "He's a friend of yours?"

"Yeah."

"Oh man, I'm sorry to hear that, I really am. We took the call an hour ago—some drunk found a body in an alley. We just sent him to the trauma center at Denver General."

Melissa gasped in the backseat and buried her face in her hands.

"How bad?" Cody asked.

"Real fucking bad," Torkleson said.

"What happened?"

"Well, it looked like somebody tried to kick his face off. The paramedics weren't even sure at first if he was still alive, man. I've seen some beatings, but this one was really, really bad. I hate to tell you this considering he's a friend of yours and all."

"And I hate to hear it," Cody said softly.

Melissa began to cry.

"Hey, who's that with you?" Torkleson asked.

"My girlfriend," Cody said absently, obviously not wanting to explain our circumstances.

"Hey, I'm not sure your girlfriend wants to hear this."

"It's okay," Cody said. "Tell me, did you find anything on him?"

Torkleson's radar went up. "Like what?"

"You know," Cody said, tap-dancing. "His wallet, keys, phone, documents, anything?"

"You mean does it look like a robbery?"

"Yeah, that's what I mean."

"That's what it looks like. His ID was on him, and we found a cell phone in the alley. Nothing else unusual on him. What kind of documents?"

"Any kind."

Photos, I thought.

"No. His wallet had been cleaned out of cash and dumped. There's no way to know how much was in it."

Thousands, I thought, *to pay off his contact.*

"Denver General, you say?"

"Affirmative. I'm still at the scene, though. We've got the photographer and forensics team going over the alley, then I'll head over to the hospital myself to see if we can get any kind of statement. But from what I saw . . ."

"No witnesses?"

"None that have come forward, which isn't surprising. This is a crappy part of town. People don't tend to talk."

"It happened in an alley," Cody asked. "Any lighting? Any windows that overlook where he was found?"

I could hear Torkleson's voice tense up as he sensed Cody was trying to horn in on his investigation.

"There are overhead lights," he said, "but no lightbulbs. They've all been shot out. And yeah, a couple of windows but no residents in the buildings."

"Sounds like the Zuni Street area," Cody said.

I felt the hair on the back of my neck stand up. Near the Appaloosa Club, then.

"That's where it is," Torkleson said. "Hey, I've got a question for you. Where did you hear about this? I can't see you sitting at home with your girlfriend at four in the morning listening to a scanner."

Cody snorted. "No chance of that."

"So how did you hear about it?"

"The perp called us from Brian's phone."

"*What?*"

"I'll meet you at the hospital, Detective. Make sure you secure that phone you found and get somebody competent to download the call log and the text log. *Do it now!* And I hope to hell you dust that phone for prints, Jason, because whoever stomped Brian held it in his scummy fucking hand."

"Cody, can I ask you something? Aren't you suspended? Should we even be having this conversation?"

Cody deftly swerved to miss a pronghorn antelope on the highway. Melissa said, "My God, that was close."

He didn't miss a beat. He said, "Torkleson, that's my friend you found. We've been friends since grade school in Montana. I want to find out who did this, and you can either work with me or against me. Do you really want me pursuing this as a private citizen? Showing you up?"

"No."

"Then meet me at the hospital with those logs."

WE ARRIVED at Denver General at nine in the morning, after dropping Melissa and Angelina at our house. Not that Melissa didn't want to be there to be with Brian—she wanted to be there desperately—but she didn't think she could take the baby with us after twenty-eight hours in the car. Angelina was crabby and sleep-deprived but had been a good traveler overall.

As Cody and I walked down the humming, antiseptic hallways, I felt as if I were shell-shocked. I was sleep-deprived myself, but the visit with my parents and the news about Brian seemed to knock me sidewise. At the front desk, Cody asked about Brian and was told by a severe black woman the patient was in ICU, and there could be no visitors except immediate relatives.

"Damn it," Cody said, reaching back into his jacket, where he produced a wallet badge and flashed it at her. "We need to see him *now.*"

"Go right up," she said, eyes wide. "Seventh floor is ICU. There's one of your policemen up there already."

Cody nodded and pocketed the badge. In the elevator, I said, "I thought they took that away from you."

He nodded. "They took my real badge away. But any cop worth his salt has a couple of spares. You can buy 'em from cop catalogs. No one ever reads the details—they just see the flash."

The officer on the seventh floor wasn't Torkleson but a uniform assigned to Brian. He sat on a metal folding chair outside a pair of entry doors to the Intensive Care Unit signed ICU STAFF ONLY.

"How is he?" Cody asked the uniform, who was young with a crew cut and a wisp of a mustache.

"I haven't heard either way."

"Detective Torkleson assign you here?"

"Yes."

"I'm Detective Hoyt," Cody said, flashing the badge at a distance and pocketing it quickly. He was well practiced, I thought. *He could even fool cops.* Then he spoke with absolute authority. "We need to get in there and talk to the victim. This is Jack McGuane, an intimate of the victim. He's likely the only person he'll talk to."

The uniform shrugged. "From what I understand, he's hamburger. You aren't likely to get anything out of him."

"Let us by, please."

The uniform shrugged and sighed elaborately and called inside on the phone near the door. The door lock buzzed, and we were in.

"Mr. Eastman?" Cody asked the desk nurse.

"Room 738," she said. "Listen, he's scheduled for surgery any minute now. I'm not sure you . . ."

I followed Cody and braced myself. Even so, I wasn't prepared for what I saw when we went into 738.

"*Fuck!*" Cody said beneath his breath.

He was unrecognizable. He was a body beneath a sheet connected to what looked like dozens of chirping and humming machines and hanging bags of fluid. The bundles of tubing that connected his body to the hanging bags looked like exposed tree roots. His face was entirely covered with bandages. Thin gauze covered his nose—two dark spots of blood where his nostrils were—and a fogged-up oxygen mask covered his mouth and nose. His head beneath the wraps was misshapen, crushed in on one side and bulging out on the other. It didn't hit home to me that it was Brian in that bed. No way. This long bag of broken bones and bruised meat could not be him. I half expected the Brian I knew to stroll in from the hallway and say something cryptic or sarcastic.

If it weren't for a sockless ankle not covered by the sheets and a pile of clothing at the foot of the bed I recognized as his, I wouldn't have known it was Brian at all.

I felt something bitter rise in my throat, and I was unable to speak.

Cody approached the bed and fished through the sheets for Brian's hand. He found a ball the size of a mitten.

"They even broke his fingers, those bastards," he said.

He leaned down over the bed. "Brian, can you hear me? It's Cody. Can you hear me in there?"

No reaction of any kind.

"Brian, you'll be all right," Cody lied. "Help me get the people who did this. It was Garrett and his Sur-13 pals, right? Help me get them."

Nothing.

I stepped forward and touched Brian's naked ankle, the only piece of flesh not bandaged that I could see.

"Come on, Brian," I said. "You can do it. Was it Garrett?"

Not even a movement.

Suddenly, the room was filled with orderlies led by a nurse, who was angry we were there. "You two, out of here *now!* He's going straight into surgery, where we've got two trauma docs waiting. How did you get in here, anyway?"

Cody didn't badge her.

I said, "He's our friend."

"The best thing you can do for your friend is step aside," she said, and we did.

Once they were gone, I used Brian's dark bathroom to throw up.

"HE WAS SET UP," Cody said as we paced in the ICU lounge. "Whether Garrett—or his dad—started the communication with Brian about phony photos or came in later I can't say. But he was lured down there, and they jumped him."

"Can we prove it was Garrett?" I asked.

"I don't know," Cody said. "We can try." He stopped pacing and lowered his voice. "Jack, you're square in the middle of a police investigation. You're seeing it from the inside looking out, and it looks pretty fucking confusing, doesn't it? This is what we do when we don't have an eyewitness or a confession. There are rarely black-and-white circumstances. You and I are pretty sure Garrett Moreland and his *compadres* did this because you *think* you might have heard him in the background. That and all of this crap that's been going on between you and him. But we can't reveal everything, can we? Like why we were coming back from Montana when the call came in?"

I shook my head, confused. Instead, I said, "When you flashed your badge and lied to those people, it came pretty easy, didn't it?"

Cody glared at me. "What are you saying?"

I swallowed hard. "I'm not so sure lying comes as easily to me."

Cody shook his head. "I'm disappointed in you, Jack. You still don't get it. It's what I was trying to tell you a minute ago. *There are rarely black-and-white circumstances.* We want to get to the absolute truth, but most of the time we fall a little short. I mean, we know what we know—but sometimes we can't prove it to everyone's satisfaction because the bar is set too high. A good cop does his best to put the bad guys away. Sometimes we need a little help. Like from our partners"—meaning me in this instance—"or from a judge."

The Aubrey Coates case was obviously still very much on his mind.

He stepped toward me and reached out and grabbed me by the collar and pulled me into him. "As Margaret Thatcher once said, don't go wobbly on me now, Jack. Remember, this is all for you." His eyes shone, and his mouth curled down. I never really felt threatened. We'd fought before in high school, and I cleaned his clock at the time. Of course, that was before he became a cop and learned all kinds of tricks. I said, "I think it was Garrett."

"You think or you know?"

"It was Garrett."

He let me go. "That's what I needed to hear from you—some fucking *truth*."

"But there's so much that just doesn't make sense," I said. "The more I think about it, the less sense it makes. Why does the judge want our little girl? Is he in all of this with his son, or are they operating independently of each other? And how can his wife not even know? How is that possible? Or was she lying to Melissa?"

Cody shook his head and shrugged. "Don't think I haven't thought about all of those things for days since this all started. I know there's a thread that will tie it all together, but right now I come up with nothing."

"Are there even any photos?" I asked. "Will we ever know now?"

"Let's hope to hell Brian recovers," he said. "If he can tell us Garrett was there, it's a slam dunk. Everything changes. Brian testifies, and no judge would place a baby with a gangbanger convicted of trying to stomp an innocent man to death. We won't need any photos—it'll all be over, so think positive. It's amazing what these doctors can do."

Cody leaned in to me. "What's really important is that he comes out of it. Even if he's not sure who did it, can't remember—you know what I mean. If we talk to him first, *suggest* it was Garrett, he's smart enough to know to run with it."

At first I didn't get what he was saying. Then I did. I should have felt something, some physical manifestation of guilt.

"I understand," I said.

"There you go," Cody said, punching me in the arm. "There you go. It's what Brian would want, anyway."

I WAS ON MY CELL WITH MELISSA, telling her Brian was still in surgery and we hadn't heard anything from the doctors yet, when I saw Detective Torkleson in the hallway and heard Cody say, "It's about time!"

Ending the call, I walked over to join them. Torkleson looked tired—rumpled, unshaven. He'd been up for hours—all through the night and halfway into Sunday. He had a thick sheaf of papers in his hand.

"You've got to send a car over to Judge John Moreland's place," Cody told him, "pick up Garrett, and bring him in for questioning. He either participated in the attempted homicide or he was there to cheer it on. He probably lured Brian down there in that alley."

"Whoa, cowboy," Torkleson said. "You've got to give me something to link him to the crime before I send a cruiser. I know you've had this guy in your sights, but he doesn't have to talk. What I want is probable cause. Rock-solid PC. His old man's a judge, don't forget."

As if I could.

"What do you have there?" Cody asked.

Torkleson brandished the sheaf of papers. "Here are the call records from the victim's phone, as requested. Good thinking on your part." He shook the papers. "Your friend spent *a lot* of time on his cell, I can tell you that. The easy part was printing out the records. Now we've got to spend some quality time on these logs before we start sending out uniforms to pick people up."

"What about prints on Brian's phone?" Cody asked.

Torkleson made a face and held his hands out, palms up. "We're working on that."

"Meaning what?" Cody growled.

"We sort of screwed that up, Cody. The phone was handled by half a different cops and probably the derelicts in the alley who called it in. The prints on it are smudged. At some point someone must have put the phone in their pocket or something. There are no clean prints. I've got our tech guys looking for partials, but it doesn't look promising."

"Shit," Cody said, taking the papers and squinting at the small print. "How far do these go back?"

"That's just the past month," Torkleson said. "Like I said, he spent a lot of time on his cell."

"Jesus, what a talker," Cody said, looking at the most recent page. His finger jabbed the last number. "Melissa's cell number," he said to me. "It'll take days to get through all of this to find how Garrett set him up."

"You're leaping ahead again," Torkleson said. He paused, looked at me, then back to Cody. "And there's something else we need to consider before we put all of our eggs in the Garrett basket. Your friend Brian Eastman was very active in the gay community. I assume you know that fact."

"Of course we know it," Cody said.

Torkleson said, "Well, there are a couple of gay bars down in that district, you know. From what I've found out, he wasn't a stranger at either one. And if you look at a map, this alley we found him in is a natural off-the-street route from one to the other. We've got some officers checking at both bars to see if he was at either one last night, but it's hard to track down the bartenders or patrons on a Sunday morning. We'll do it, but it'll take a few days of good police work.

"But some of the uniforms were talking. They think maybe this was random. Maybe your friend was going from one bar to another when some gangbangers jumped him. He was a pretty good target, you know, the way he was dressed like the ultimate yuppie. Of course, they don't want to float this theory out loud because then it would be a hate crime, and if the mayor heard that, he'd go ballistic."

Cody leveled his gaze on Torkleson. "Most crimes are hate crimes," he said.

"You know what I mean. It could get political . . ."

"Fuck that," Cody said. "It doesn't fit. I'm not saying Brian didn't frequent those bars or know the route—he probably did. But when he called us earlier last night, he said he got a specific call to meet somebody. Maybe the caller picked the spot that would be familiar—I don't know. Or maybe he picked it because it was close enough to the Appaloosa Club that the gangbangers could run back there and clean up. But Brian wasn't out cruising—we know that."

Torkleson was slow on the take. "Hold it—*he* called you? When was that?"

"I don't know. Midnight, I guess."

"And what was he meeting this person for?"

Cody hesitated for a moment. I felt a chill go up my spine. Were we caught?

"Information," Cody said, finally.

"What kind of information?" Torkleson asked, stepping back half a step, distancing himself without realizing he was doing it.

"I don't know," Cody said. "Brian kept it all mysterious. He said he was going to meet someone tonight who was going to give us information that would help us in our case against Garrett and Judge Moreland. That's why he was downtown last night."

I thought, *Cody's high above the crowd on a wire without a net.*

"And that's why you asked me about documents earlier?"

Cody nodded.

"Anything else you've been keeping from me?"

"Not a thing," Cody said.

Torkleson swiveled his head, gave me the dead-eye. "What about you, McGuane?"

I knew I looked guilty. My face was burning up.

"What?" I asked. I tried not to look at Cody.

"You heard me."

I sighed. "The information was supposed to be photos," I said. "Photos with Judge Moreland in them. Something bad enough Moreland would back off."

"Ahhh," Torkleson said, nodding. "You two have been playing a little blackmail game on the side, eh?"

"No blackmail," Cody said. "You can't blackmail anyone if you don't have the photos to blackmail with."

"I see," Torkleson said. "I also think right now I don't want to hear much more. Later, though, I want the whole story."

"Thank you, brother," Cody said, then quickly changed the subject back to the call list. "I'll bet we've got incoming calls from Garrett on here. We've got to check all his numbers—his house, his cell, the Appaloosa Club, his fellow gangbanger's numbers against these."

"That's what I mean," Torkleson said. "We haven't had time to match up any of the incoming or outgoing numbers yet. My shop needs to spend some time on them, figure out who was talking to who."

I realized we were through the gathering storm. I let my breath out slowly.

Cody looked frustrated. "What if Garrett was using a burner?" he asked. "One of those damned Tracfones anyone can buy at Wal-Mart? Then the number doesn't mean anything at all because we can't link the owner to the phone."

Torkleson shrugged. "Unless we can prove Garrett bought it, with a credit-card receipt or something. You know how this works."

My heart dropped. I had thought for a few minutes it would be a matter of hours. Now I wasn't sure they had anything at all.

"You need to send that car," Cody insisted. "Send it *now,* and haul in Garrett's ass for questioning. We know he was there."

Torkleson was puzzled. "How do we know that?"

"Jack heard his voice in the background when they called," Cody said. "Didn't you, Jack?"

"I thought I did."

Torkleson took a moment to study me. "Are you sure?"

"I can't be absolutely positive," I said, "but I thought I heard his voice in the background."

"And you'd testify to that?"

I swallowed hard. "Yes."

"I'm confused," Torkleson said, turning to Cody. "You said you were with some woman named Melissa when you got the call. Now you're telling me this gentleman was there with you and actually took the call?"

Cody waggled his eyebrows, Groucho Marx style. "The three of us were together, if you know what I mean."

Torkleson looked dubious.

"Cody's kidding," I said quickly. "Melissa is my wife. The three of us were together, and Melissa's phone rang. Because it was Brian's phone calling but a voice she didn't recognize, she handed the phone to me. I swear to God."

"Look," Cody said, "if you haul Garrett downtown and start hammering him before he can manufacture a story, you might be able to get him to tell us some lies we can unravel."

"*We?*" Torkleson said. "Are you suggesting you be involved in the interrogation?"

"I can watch him from outside," Cody said, "feed you questions."

"And blow the whole case," Torkleson said. "A suspended cop actively involved in the interrogation. That'll play real well."

"Okay," Cody said, "I'll stay completely away. But I'm keeping these call logs. You can download another copy easy enough."

Torkleson wiped his forehead. He was sweating. He jabbed me in the breast. "The *only* reason I have to send a car to the Morelands' to request an interview with that kid is your statement. If it turns out he was in bed the whole evening or playing cards with his good judge daddy, my ass is grass. And so is yours."

"I understand."

He studied me a few more seconds, then looked to Cody.

"Do it," Cody said.

Torkleson stepped away from both of us to use his cell phone. I could have kissed him at that moment. I overheard enough to hear him caution the uniforms to be polite and respectful and to explain clearly that Garrett was being asked to come and talk because of my direct assertion, not because there was any physical evidence. As I heard him, the reason for them going to the Moreland house sounded flimsy even to me.

"You never know what he might say," Cody whispered to me, "once we get him in the box with a tape recorder running. He may give us five things we can disprove later. And if you heard his voice, you heard his voice.

"Good job back there, by the way. You gave him just enough. It sounded plausible. He bought it. Maybe you'd be a good cop."

"No," I said, "I don't think so."

WE SAT in the waiting area for the next hour not reading magazines. All three of us looked up every time a nurse or doctor walked by. Melissa called three times. Each time I had to tell her we hadn't heard anything yet regarding Brian's condition.

Torkleson was dozing when his cell burred. He sat up and patted all of his pockets in an unintentional imitation of Cody before he found his phone in his jacket pocket. He said his name and no more. As he listened, his face got red. The murderous glance he shot at Cody told me things had not gone well.

"Okay, sir," he said, biting his words off, "I'll be down there as soon as I know about our victim. Yes, I'll personally apologize."

He snapped his phone closed with such force I wondered if it would ever work again.

"You burned me," he said to both of us. "I'm in so much fucking trouble."

"What happened?" Cody asked, not affected by Torkleson's vehemence.

"My guys showed up at Judge Moreland's house. The judge was furious. He called the mayor, who called the chief, who just called me. The judge says Garrett was home all night with him, and he refused to send his son to answer questions. He said Mr. McGuane here is harassing him because of a legal matter and that Cody Hoyt is a rogue cop who is completely out of control. The chief asked me why I was even associating with you, Cody."

Cody shrugged.

"Fuck you two," Torkleson said, standing up. "I've got a wife and a little girl and a lot of years ahead of me. I can't let you screw that up."

"I've got a wife and a little girl, too," I said. "This is about trying to keep us together."

He wanted to launch into me, but Cody stood up and put his hand on Torkleson's shoulder.

"Look what this tells us," Cody said. "It tells us a lot. It means the judge is aware of what Garrett is up to. We've been wondering about that—are they working together or apart? Now we know. At last we have some clarity, even though this is about as bad a turn as we could get."

Torkleson shook Cody's arm off, his face still red. I felt sorry for him even as I contemplated what Cody had just said.

"Gentlemen, are you here for Brian Eastman?"

None of us had heard or seen the surgeon approach from the double doors down the hall. He was short and thin, wearing blood-soaked green scrubs.

"I'm sorry," he said, not looking any of us in the eye. "Mr. Eastman has passed."

"He's dead?" Torkleson asked.

"It was probably for the best, in a way," the doctor said. "With that kind of brain damage, he could have never functioned again."

I sat back in the chair and covered my face with my hands.

We'd lost our friend.

We'd lost our advocate.

We'd lost our friend.

Cody's eyes streamed tears. "Man," he said, "I wish I hadn't have been so hard on the guy earlier. He didn't deserve it."

Tuesday, November 20

Five Days to Go

Sixteen

There was something going on at the office. It wasn't a conspiracy of silence, where everyone seems to know what's up except the victim. It was simply that under the circumstances—a closed door meeting in the CEO's office that had started early before the staff arrived and was still going past 9:00 A.M.—some kind of trouble was indicated. The halls, offices, and cubicles were silent. No animated conversations, no laughing. Just tapping on keyboards from every office. I saw Pete Maxfield, the PR guy, walk down the hall to the break room tugging on his collar, as if the heat were turned up. He looked like he felt guilty for *something*. On my way to get coffee, I ducked into Linda Van Gear's office to ask her what was happening. She always knew, but she wasn't at her desk.

I asked Cissy the receptionist when Linda was expected back.

"Oh, she's here," she said. "She's in a meeting with Mr. Jones."

"Who else is in there?" I asked.

"Mr. Doogan from the mayor's office."

My mouth went dry.

BRIAN'S FUNERAL WAS SET for Friday. Because of his prominence in Denver, his murder was front-page news. Mayor Halladay appeared on the steps of city hall and said he was both mournful and angry at the same time and that the community had lost a great man. When a reporter from Channel 9 asked him if it was a hate crime because of Brian Eastman's well-known sexual orientation, Halladay exploded, saying if it was, he would personally make sure the DA charged whoever did it with the maximum penalty under the law. The mayor declared, "Denver will not tolerate hate!" He was followed by the Denver police chief, who said the department was pursuing every lead, and he was confident there would be arrests before the week was out. I knew through Cody that Torkleson and the cops had no more evidence than the day before, but the chief was assigning several more detectives to the case, and they were interviewing everyone they could find in LoDo who might have seen Brian or the assailants that night.

Melissa was in a stunned funk. Brian was her best friend, and he was simply *gone*. "He gave his life for us," she said through tears. I didn't know how to respond, so I simply held her. While I did, I looked at Angelina in her walker, wonderfully oblivious to what was going on. She'd never see her uncle Brian again, and there was no way to explain that to her.

Cody was splitting his time between our house and his. The media contingent that had been staking out his block had dispersed, likely so they could follow the Eastman murder. When I saw him, he seemed so quiet it was as if he wasn't really there at all. I couldn't tell whether Brian's murder had knocked him speechless or he was deep in thought formulating a plan—or both. I do know he was combing through Brian's call log one number at a time. He used our computer to cross-reference the numbers, and he kept a running list of numbers and names as he found them.

I worried that Jeter Hoyt might just show up since he'd kept the envelope, and was happy to hear that a terrific winter storm had hit Montana and dumped eighteen inches of snow.

CISSY LEANED INTO my office and whispered something I couldn't hear.

"Excuse me?"

"Mr. Jones would like to see you in his office."

I took a deep breath, pulled on my jacket, straightened my tie, and went to get fired.

"HAVE A SEAT, JACK," CEO H. R. "Tab" Jones said. I could tell by the way Linda smiled sadly at me when I entered the office that my assumption had been correct.

"You know Jim Doogan," Jones said, as Cissy stepped out and closed the door.

I nodded. Doogan shook my hand. He seemed almost kind. Despite it all, I still kind of liked him.

"Linda," Jones said, "do you want to tell Jack what we found out this morning?"

Jack, Linda would say, *the police say you've been implicated in the murder of a man named Pablo 'Luis' Cadena. They also say you went to Montana last weekend to hire a thug to intimidate an eighteen-year-old boy.*

Instead, she said, "Malcolm Harris was arrested this morning at Heathrow Airport before he boarded the direct London-to-Denver flight."

"*What?*" That one came out of nowhere.

Linda looked to Doogan to pick up the story.

Doogan said, "Your friend Malcolm Harris is suspected of being a very big fish in an international pedophilia ring. Apparently both Scotland Yard and Interpol have been working on this case for a couple of years, and today they pulled the trigger and made dozens of arrests all across Europe. Harris is considered to be a kingpin of these sickos. They're talking real bad stuff here, Jack. Buying and selling not just kiddie porn but actual children, group sex trips to Asia, about as bad as it can get."

I flashed back to Harris's long foray to the "office" behind the bar in Berlin, how he'd come back flushed. Did Fritz—no doubt a pedophile himself—have photos of children back there on his computer? Or maybe even a child? *Oh, God.* I cringed and felt physically sick.

"Are you okay?" Doogan asked me.

"He did seem a little off to me," I said. "I couldn't quite figure out what it was. And I had this urge to pound the crap out of him that sort of came from nowhere."

"A *little* off?" Jones said, raising his eyebrows.

"Give him a break, Tab," Linda cut in. "I knew Malcolm long before Jack came on board. I always thought he was strange, but I never would have suspected this." She laughed drily. "Lots of people we work with are strange."

I thought, *the way he looked at that picture of Angelina and thought he'd seen her before.* I didn't know what to make of it at the time, but now I figured he'd seen so many photos of little girls that he was simply confused, that bastard.

So many things Harris had said and done that night came flooding back:

"creeping fascism of the politically correct"

"There aren't bureaucrats looking over your shoulder as you live your life, telling you how to speak and think and whom to associate with—taking your freedom away."

"I've seen enough for tonight."

His outright joy in the way the restaurant tenderized the veal . . .

Jones was staring at me.

"Hold it," I said. "You don't think I knew about this in any way, do you?"

"Did you?" Jones asked, again with the eyebrows.

"For God's sake, no!" I was nauseated by the thought. "I have a nine-month-old daughter, Tab." It seemed ridiculous to have to defend myself to a forty-seven-year-old man called "Tab."

"I didn't think you did," Doogan said, "but we have a problem."

I shook my head, not getting it. Linda looked away.

"We—you—have been courting this guy," Doogan said. "The mayor himself has announced this new business coming to town. Channel 9, which is no friend of the administration, as you know, called for a statement. They're all over it. Even though it's unfair, this ain't beanbag we're playing. Imagine a headline that reads: MAYOR HALLADAY AND DENVER CVB COURTED INTERNATIONAL PEDO-PHILE."

"Jack," Jones said, "we're going to restructure the bureau. This international stuff is just too hot right now. The mayor's enemies and the press are always pointing to it as an extravagance we can't afford, and now we've got this. That's what we've been talking about in here. Linda's being moved over to conventions. We've got a position open there, and she's got seniority."

"Meaning I'm out?" I said.

Jones pursed his lips and nodded yes.

Doogan said, "The best way to deal with an issue like this is to get out in front of it. If Channel 9 presses the story, we'll respond by saying we've restructured our efforts and cut staff to avoid embarrassments like this in the future. Your name isn't likely to come up in any way."

"I'm sorry I can't take you with me," Linda said. "Maybe if something opens up down the road."

I sat back. Too much, too fast.

"Sorry it worked out this way," Doogan said.

"You don't know how much I need this job," I said. "You have *no* idea."

"You'll need to get with HR," Jones said. "We'll work out a generous severance package, and I believe you've got vacation and sick time coming."

Looks of strained sympathy all around. Linda, especially.

CISSY WAS SUDDENLY IMMERSED in whatever she was reading on her desk and kept her head down as I opened the door. Pete, who had been loitering in the break room the whole time, tried to thinly disguise his relief.

I went into my office and bent over my desk, my head spinning. How would I tell Melissa?

AS DOOGAN WALKED past my office, I said, "Jim!"

He came in. I said, "You might want to shut the door."

This was the first time I'd ever seen him look ill at ease.

I said, "How much of this has to do with Malcolm Harris and how much has to do with Judge Moreland? He knows I was in on the complaint the other night when the police went to talk to his son about Brian Eastman's murder. I wonder if this Malcolm Harris thing isn't just the excuse he was looking for."

He shrugged unconvincingly.

"You're not talking?"

He looked at my ceiling, my desk, his shoes, everywhere but at me. "Sometimes," he said, "I do things that keep me up at night. I just try and convince myself that running a big city can be messy at times. Sometimes things are done for the greater good, and they aren't necessarily fair or fun."

"I guess that answers my question."

"I've got to go."

"One more thing," I said. "I've got another problem for you, and this one's much bigger than me. I've been thinking about some of the things Malcolm Harris said to me. He's got connections here, Jim. That's why he was going to relocate. In fact, at one point he told me he would be *bulletproof. Bulletproof*. Any idea why he'd say that?"

Doogan looked puzzled. "No idea at all," he said.

"The mayor may have a much bigger problem than me."

Doogan shrugged. "Then we'll deal with it when it happens."

Seventeen

WITH THE PERSONAL ITEMS from my office in a box in the backseat of the Jeep, I roared out of the dark parking garage into a cold but sun-drenched day. I should have been devastated, but I wasn't. Instead, it was as if another burden had been lifted. I was charged up, filled with a full and dangerous kind of energy. I felt manic.

I called Melissa and told her what happened.

"Oh, Jack," she said. "Don't worry, you'll get another job. You're good at what you do."

"Yes," I said sarcastically, "there are openings for international tourism marketers all over town. I just need to snatch one up."

"We'll get by," she said. "I could go back to work after . . ."

"Don't say it," I said, cutting her off.

"Why us, Jack?" There was a catch in her voice.

"I don't know," I said. "It's like we're being tested. And I, for one, am getting damned sick of it."

"So does this mean you'll be home for lunch?"

We both found ourselves laughing at that one, the same kind of uncomfortable laugh one produces to a joke's punch line like, "Other than that, Mrs. Lincoln, how was the play?"

"So does it?" she asked.

"I'm going to go see Judge Moreland first," I said. "We need to have a talk."

She paused. "Is that a good idea?"

"What can it hurt?" I said. "What can happen? The mayor finds out and fires me?"

I FELT GUILTY for not feeling guilty. But in a strange way, my path had been cleared.

I parked on the street in front of the federal courthouse and took the steps two at a time. I would have charged through the lobby except for the guard who told me to slow down, empty my pockets, and walk slowly through the metal detector.

"Write down your name and who you're here to see so I can check you against the preapproved list," he said, handing me a clipboard.

I wrote, "Judge Moreland."

He took it back and asked if the judge was expecting me. "I don't see your name on the approved list."

I said, "Tell him Jack McGuane is here to see him."

I waited impatiently while the guard called upstairs, gave my name. Then shook his head while he listened and hung up. "They say he's not expecting you."

"I need to see him."

The guard narrowed his eyes and looked me over. This was one of those situations where my jacket and tie helped. "Are you a lawyer?"

"No. Judge Moreland is trying to take my child away."

"I'm sorry," he said warily. "You need to leave."

While I was putting my keys and change back into my pocket I looked up to see the man himself, Judge John Moreland, entering the building through a secure entrance accessed by a side street. He wore a suit and carried a briefcase, a long camel-hair coat draped over his arm. A vestibule of thick glass separated us.

"There he is," I said.

Just as the guard reached for his radio to call for help if necessary to get me out of there, Moreland looked up. I startled him. Our eyes locked.

I gestured, pointing to him and back to me. I mouthed, *I need to talk to you.*

Smoothly, oh so smoothly, he turned away and continued on to his private elevator. He stood there with his back to me, waiting for the elevator car to arrive.

"Sir," the guard said, rising to come around the counter. The public elevator on my side of the glass whooshed open and two more uniformed guards stepped out.

The three of them surrounded me.

"I'm going," I said, barely able to talk.

BACK OUTSIDE ON THE STREET, I seethed. As I approached my Jeep I turned and looked back at the courthouse. The three guards watched me from the double doors. And seven stories up, framed by a window, Moreland looked down on me with his hands on his hips. His face was impassive.

I WAS THREE BLOCKS away from the courthouse when I saw an open parking space and took it. My hands were trembling from anger as I opened my phone, got the number for the Alfred A. Arraj U.S. Courthouse from information, and punched the numbers in.

"Judge Moreland's office," a female receptionist said.

"This is Jim Doogan from the mayor's office," I said. "I need to talk with the judge."

"Just a moment."

In less than thirty seconds, I heard Moreland's mellifluous voice. "Hi, Jim."

"Why won't you talk to me?" I said.

It took him a moment, then he chuckled. "Using a ruse to get me on the phone, Mr. McGuane? That's not very sporting. Goodbye, Mr. McGuane . . ."

"Don't hang up! You need to hear what I'm going to say."

He paused.

"You've got three minutes," he said. His voice was all business now. "I need to be in court."

"Your son needs to sign that release," I said. "This can't go on any longer. Enough people have been hurt on both sides."

"I have no idea what you're talking about. Are you referring to having the police come to my house to question my son in regard to that murder? That was a really stupid, desperate play." God, how could he sound so rational?

"Garrett was involved," I said. "I heard him."

"Oh come now. He was at home with Kellie and me."

"I heard his voice. I know it was him. And I know you know it."

"You think you know a lot, Mr. McGuane. Look, I need to be going."

"I lost my job today," I said.

"I'm sorry to hear that, but it's no concern of mine."

"Actually, it is. It means I can fight you full-time."

He chuckled again.

"Why is it your wife doesn't know about Angelina?" I asked. "How can that be? What is your game?"

"Kellie?" He sounded genuinely surprised. "Kellie knows all about our granddaughter. She's been working for a month getting the baby's room ready."

"You're lying again. Melissa ran into her, and your wife didn't know a thing she was talking about."

Moreland sighed. "Mr. McGuane, I know this is tough on you. But it doesn't need to be so tough. My offer still stands. I'm more than willing to help you and your wife adopt another child. I'm surprised you've waited this long, actually. The sooner we can get the proceedings under way the sooner you can have a new baby."

"What is your game?" I said, nearly shouting. "*What is it?*"

"There's no game. I explained everything to you. My son needs to be accountable. Simple as that."

"I think you know everything your son is involved in," I said. "You two have some kind of unholy alliance."

"Oh please." Moreland sounded genuinely ticked off. "I'm beginning to think I made a mistake giving you and your wife so much time. It's given you weeks to martyr yourselves, and you've started to see conspiracies everywhere. I thought you were better than this, frankly."

"*You're trying to steal our daughter!*" I shouted. "Jesus, did you think we'd just *let* you?"

"You mean Garrett's daughter and my granddaughter," Moreland said wearily. "I'm afraid we've had this discussion before."

"Are you going to tell me you don't know your son is involved with Mexican gangs? With Sur-13?"

"I don't have any idea what you're talking about, Mr. McGuane."

"Deny, deny, deny," I said. "Where does the truth fit in all of this, or is that something you don't worry about anymore? Are you so used to handing down judgments that are obeyed that you think you're a god? That whatever you say just *is?*"

"You're embarrassing yourself, Mr. McGuane. And it's a pathetic thing to hear."

I paused. I was shaking. I could tell by his voice that he was going to hang up at any second. I wished I could be more coherent.

"Have your son sign the papers," I said, "so nothing else will happen."

His voice was maddeningly firm and reasonable. "Please think about what you're saying. Are you threatening me? Are you really threatening a sitting federal district court judge? I think we should both just pretend that you didn't just say that, Mr. McGuane, or otherwise you could be charged with a federal crime. Not that I'm threatening you—I'm not. I'm informing you. You don't know what you're saying. We can chalk it up to inexperience and runaway emotion."

"What are you hiding?" I said.

"This conversation is coming to a close, I'm afraid."

"*What is it?*"

"Goodbye, Mr. McGuane."

"Look," I said, "I may just be a rube from Montana who is in over my head. But Melissa is the most wonderful woman I've ever met. She's a fantastic mother, and she loves Angelina like no mother ever loved her child. You can't take our daughter away. I won't let it happen."

"You have five days, Mr. McGuane. Use them wisely. Now if you'll excuse me, I've got to go to work."

"Don't hang up!"

"Goodbye."

I DROVE TO SHELBY'S on 18th—the place Cody had taken me to—and pasted a fifty on the damp bar. "Keep 'em coming," I told the bartender. "Don't stop until this fifty is gone or I am."

CODY FOUND ME at about the time the place was filling up with cops after their eight-to-four shift. He slugged me in the arm hard enough to nearly knock me off my stool.

"Fucking idiot," he said. "Melissa's worried to death. What'd you do, turn off your phone?"

I left it in the car, I tried to say, but the words came out as gibberish.

"I'll give you a ride home," he said. "We can come back and get your Jeep tomorrow." He steered me out of the bar.

"You're a good friend," I said, but it came out *"You a goo fran."*

"Shut up. We'll grab some coffee on the way home."

"Bourbon."

"No bourbon."

"My head is splitting open." *My hay ish . . .*

We'd only been driving a short time when I gagged and belched.

"Not in my car, knucklehead," Cody said, whipping off the highway onto an exit so I could climb halfway out the window and throw up. It burned like acid coming up. I think I might have hit some of his door.

"I been there," he said, as I got back in and slumped in the seat. "It's our own special corner of hell, ain't it? But if anyone says it isn't fun getting there, I know they're lying because it is fun for a while." Then: "Wipe your mouth."

"I HAD A GOOD DAY," Cody said.

I opened my eyes. It felt like I'd been sleeping for hours, but we were barely out of downtown.

"What?"

"I said I had a good day. A rare good day. With Brian's call log. I think I'm getting somewhere."

It took a moment to register.

"You need to quit feeling sorry for yourself," he said. "You have to be alert and strong for Melissa these next few days. I hope you got this out of your system."

I nodded, afraid to talk and sound stupid.

"I take that as a yes," he said. "Now look, I'm going to have to

231

be gone soon. I may be gone a couple of days, I'm not sure yet. But there's something I need to follow up on, something in the call log. So if you and Melissa can't find me, don't worry. I'll be back."

I tried to talk. Couldn't.

"Yeah, I know we're running out of time," he said.

"SEE YOUR NEW FRIEND?" Cody asked as we drove down my street. I looked out the passenger window and saw three sheriff's cars parked across from our house, each stacked on top of the other. No, not three. As I focused it turned out to be just one.

"They're making sure you and Melissa don't take the baby and try to make a run for it. He's been there all afternoon. Hey, did you do something today to piss off the judge?"

"Yes."

"Thought so. He's calling in his chits with the sheriff."

MELISSA MET ME AT THE DOOR. I would have felt better if she'd scolded me, laid into me right there. Lord knows I deserved it.

She helped me get my clothes off, helped me get into bed. The ceiling spun, and I ran to the bathroom. There was very little left to throw up. I took a shower and cleared my head a little, gargled and outright drank several gulps of the mouthwash.

I was in bed when Melissa brought Angelina in to kiss me good night.

"I'm sorry," I said to both of them. "I'm so sorry."

"Get some sleep," Melissa said, taking Angelina to her bedroom.

THAT NIGHT, I had a dream. It was fused with alcohol. It was cinematic: *A pair of headlights snapped on in a dark garage. The light filled with hundreds of large swirling moths. No, not moths—snowflakes. A* deep-throated engine roared to life and the vehicle, its front grille looking like a mouthful of teeth, blasted out through a two-foot-high snowdrift. Snow exploded as the older-model pickup bucked drift after drift, going fast enough that it wouldn't get bogged down in the heavy and deep blanket of white.

Finally, the pickup swung onto a two-lane ribbon of black highway that was glazed with ice. The full moon lit up the snow in the meadows and sheened the ice on the road, but the pickup didn't slow down. Gradually, as the defroster cleared the windshield, I could see the driver.

He craned forward in his seat, leaning over the wheel. His eyes were dead as stones but there was a half smile on his face. On the seat of his truck was an arsenal of weapons: rifles, shotguns, Taser, bear spray, brass knuckles, leather saps, revolvers, semiautomatics.

The two-lane eventually melded into the interstate, which finally turned south. The ice cleared. The vehicle picked up speed and soon it was rocketing down the interstate, bathed in moonlight. There were no other cars on the road. As the truck hurtled into the night, chunks of ice broke off beneath it and skittered across the highway like comets leaving snow trails.

The heater was blasting, and the radio was up loud, alternating between archaic country western heavy with steel guitars and a Southern preacher who spoke in a mesmerizing cadence while his congregation urged him on. The cab smelled of gasoline, sweat, and gun oil.

At the rate the snow and ice was flying off the pickup, Jeter Hoyt figured it would be clean by time he hit Denver.

Wednesday, November 21

Four Days to Go

Eighteen

IT HAD BEEN A miserable day. I awoke with a monster of a headache and a terrible taste in my mouth. As I brushed my teeth, I stared at myself in the bathroom mirror and didn't like what looked back. My eyes were red coals in dark pools of blue. I looked ten years older than I was, and felt fifty years older. The guilt I hadn't felt the day before hammered me now, made me wonder why I'd drunk away a perfectly good afternoon feeling sorry for myself when I could have been home with my wife and daughter, could have been *doing* something.

By the time I got dressed, it was ten in the morning. After all, there was no place to go.

Melissa was playing with Angelina in the family room, making her giggle. When I saw the two of them there on the floor, I wondered how much I'd missed over the past year being at work. A lot, I knew. This was the place important things were happening, not at the office.

"Da!" Angelina cried happily. I picked her up off the floor and kissed her soft fat cheek. Damn, how babies smelled good. Again, I wondered at what age would they stop smelling so sweet? And I thought, *I may never find out.*

"I thought it best to let you sleep," Melissa said, taking Angelina back. "You were completely out of it."

"I'm sorry," I said.

"Except at one point when you sat up in bed and yelled, 'Here he comes!' That was interesting."

"I was dreaming that Jeter Hoyt was on his way," I said.

Melissa said, "Let's hope you weren't prescient." She shook her head and turned her attention back to Angelina.

I padded to the window and parted the curtain.

"He's still there," Melissa said. And he was: the black-and-white sheriff's vehicle. I vaguely remembered him from the night before. "There's another one around the corner in the alley."

"You're kidding!" I said.

"I wish I was. I saw him this morning when I took the garbage out. He's a nice man named Morales."

"Hmmm."

"I was thinking," she said, "since you're going to be home for a while if I couldn't ask *you* to take out the garbage."

"Sure."

"I may have some other chores as well. I know you're not at your best with time on your hands."

"True."

"And I don't want you just hanging around driving me crazy," she said.

"I've never not had a job. I don't think I know what to do."

"Look for another one, for starters. I left the employment section of the paper out for you. Who knows how quickly you can find something else? And I don't need to tell you it needs to be fast."

"Who knows," I echoed.

"If we need to move, we need to move," she said, bouncing Angelina on her knee, making her chuckle.

I looked at the two of them and felt my eyes mist up. I turned away.

AS I ATE cereal for breakfast, I watched them. I realized Melissa had taken no noticeable steps in preparation to turn our daughter over, even though it was just four days away. She'd packed no boxes, emptied no drawers. She behaved as if by denying the inevitability of it, the exchange wouldn't take place. I conceded I was doing the same thing.

Sheriff's cars in front of the house and down the block in the mouth of the cul-de-sac. There was no way we could slip past them even if we intended to do that. And where would we go anyway? Would we live in our car with the baby, constantly looking over our shoulders?

The obvious places for us to go were my parents' ranch or her parents—her mother's in Seattle or her father's in Phoenix. But because they were obvious, they would be the first places the authorities would look.

There was nowhere else I could think of. If we tried to live on the road, we'd burn through our meager bank account so quickly it would leave skid marks. My severance check and vacation/sick money wouldn't be processed for weeks. By then, if we had run, the sheriff would follow the check to us, wherever we were. Our credit cards would max out fast. We had no other income.

There was no way to sell the house for what little equity we had in it and use the money to escape. In the current Denver housing market, that could take months. I could get a few thousand from the Jeep and a couple thousand for Melissa's car, but what would we run away in?

Every damned option was bad. I felt like driving back to the cop bar and finding that friendly bartender and pasting down another fifty and starting over. I spent the rest of the day organizing the garage and the attic, generally staying out of Melissa's way. I kept my eye out for things we could sell if we had to. I watched a napping Angelina when Melissa went to King Soopers. She reported that she asked the deputy down the street—she described him as a very nice man—if he intended to follow her there and back. He told her no, their orders were to follow only if all three of us were in the vehicle, if it looked like we were attempting to flee our home with Angelina.

"Imagine that," she said, shaking her head.

WHEN THE PHONE RANG after dinner, I grabbed it because Melissa was changing Angelina in the living room.

"It's Jeter. It took me a while today to find that Appaloosa Club."

A rolling tremor went through me from the top of my head and my toes curled in my shoes.

"You're *here?*"

"Got in around noon. Found a place to stay. Took a nap. Now that it's dark out, I want to get to work. Damn—Denver got big on me. Used to be a glorified cow town. I don't hardly know my way around anymore. How many people live here now?"

"Two point four million."

He paused. "That's twice more than all of Montana."

"Yes."

"Where did all these folks come from?"

"All over," I said. "Where are you now?"

"Some fleabag joint on West Colfax. At least this part of town hasn't changed much. There are still hookers around, but I don't think I've seen a white person since I've been here. It's like some damned street in Tijuana."

I didn't know what to say.

"I called Cody, and he didn't pick up, so I'm calling you. I'm going to the club tonight."

"Jeter, please, no."

"What, you worried about my fee now that Brian's dead? Don't. This is a favor to you boys and to that little girl of yours."

"Wait, don't do anything until I get there . . ."

He hung up.

As I got my jacket, Melissa said, "Where are you going, Jack?"

"I don't think you want to know," I said. "That was Jeter Hoyt on the telephone."

Which told her everything, and she turned away. I wondered if she felt as unclean and panicky as I did at that moment.

AS I CLIMBED INTO my Jeep, I heard the motor start in the sheriff's car across the street. For a moment I closed my eyes and stood there with the door open. If he followed me down to Zuni Street . . .

I slammed the door and walked across the street. The deputy was young, fresh-faced, with brown hair and a blunt nose. He watched me approach with a practiced cop dead-eye stare, and I motioned for him to roll down his window. I saw him say something into his mike—probably notifying the cop down the block that I was there—and then his window descended halfway.

"Hello, Deputy."

"That's close enough," he said.

I stopped, put my hands up, and showed my palms to him. "I'm harmless."

He nodded.

"What's your name?"

"Sanders. Billy Sanders."

"And Morales is the name of the deputy down the street? We

might as well get to know you guys and be friends since we're spending so much time together."

He smiled. "Your wife met Gary Morales already."

"Look," I said, "I'm going to go downtown and have a few beers, just like last night. I was wondering if you'd like to go with me?"

"What?"

"Why sit here all night? I'll give you a ride with me, and that way you can keep an eye on me *and* have a couple of beers. I'd like the company because drinking alone is the shits. What do you say?"

He grinned, not unfriendly. "That sounds pretty good, but I'm on duty until my replacement gets here."

"I can be back by then," I offered.

For a second he considered it, then, "Nah, no can do."

"Are you sure? I'm buying."

He shook his head.

"Maybe tomorrow night?"

He laughed. "Maybe."

"I'm going down to a place called Shelby's. You know it?"

"Okay. Thanks for letting me know."

"It's on Eighteenth."

"I know where it is."

"Maybe I'll see you there later, I guess. And if I drink too much, maybe I can bum a ride back from you?"

He laughed. "I haven't done all that much surveillance, but you two are the only people I've ever watched who were so damned nice. You're making me suspicious, to tell you the truth."

"Sorry."

His window slid back up.

I turned and went back to my Jeep and eased out of the driveway. I watched him in my rearview mirror. If he did decide to follow me, I'd just go to Shelby's and read about Jeter in the *Rocky Mountain News* the next morning. In a way, I hoped Sanders *would* follow me. But, as I guessed, the sheriff's car didn't move. He didn't want to be stuck downtown when his shift ended with the possibility of having to give me a ride all the way back, and he knew that without Melissa and Angelina with me, there was no point in following.

Nineteen

ON ZUNI STREET I noticed two things simultaneously: the streetlights were out, and my headlights splashed on Garrett's H3 Hummer as well as a dirty four-by-four pickup with Montana plates.

"There he is," I said aloud.

Because it was so dark, the Appaloosa Club stood out, with its neon beer signs in the barred windows and the fact that it was surrounded by either boarded-up shells of structures or low-rent businesses closed for the night. The lights of the city washed like cream across the sky but didn't reach down into this dark hole not far from it.

Besides the H3 and what I assumed was Jeter's pickup, there were two or three others: classic seventies' Buick and Cadillac boats with gleaming chrome and fuzzy dice hanging from the rearview mirrors. One of the license plates I noticed was "13 13," framed by the green Colorado mountains. The thirteenth number in the alphabet was "M," so "M M," or Mexican Mafia.

I pulled to the curb, punched the light knob in, and the H3 went black.

I sat for a moment in scared silence. He was obviously already inside. I could hear thumping bass from the Appaloosa. My eyes adjusted to the darkness, and the shape of the club emerged. It was small and boxy. The *Pacifico, Corona,* and *Negra Modelo* beer signs seemed to increase in color and intensity. I considered going home.

"No!" I yelled inside the Jeep.

I launched outside in time to see a rectangle of light appear on the front of the club—the door opening—and the inverted "V" shape of Jeter Hoyt and his broad back in a long cowboy duster fill the doorway for a moment before the door closed behind him. He'd been scouting the club from the outside and just gone in.

I always traveled with a winter survival kit in my Jeep. I threw open the hatchback, unzipped the duffel bag in the back, and pulled out a navy watch cap. I thought if I pulled it low over my eyes that possibly—possibly—Garrett wouldn't recognize me. I wanted to follow Jeter inside and get him out before something awful happened. I'd keep my head down and, if necessary, drag him back outside before Garrett noticed him or recognized me.

As I strode toward the club I dug my cell phone out of my pocket and speed-dialed Cody. Not that I planned on a conversation, but I simply wanted to make contact. I didn't expect him to answer. I clutched the phone. I thought if I went inside and all hell broke loose, I wanted him to hear it later as a voice mail so he could get to our house to be with Melissa.

I eased the front door open and slipped inside. The thumping of the music—I didn't recognize the song or the artist but it was crude and raw—hit me in the face and made my heart beat even faster. I took it in quickly: The place was smaller than it looked from outside and both darker and emptier than I had imagined. A couple of morose Latinos in biker gear perched at the truncated front bar. A bald, obese bartender in a wife-beater was behind the bar. His thick arms and shoulders were covered in tattoos, and he had a soul patch under his lip grown long and braided. He was pointing a remote at the crappy single television mounted above the bar in the corner. There was a small cracked linoleum dance floor that was empty and a series of unoccupied booths along the far wall. In the back, beneath a black light, was a round table with five people under a thick halo of smoke.

Jeter was at the bar between the two bikers, trying to get the attention of the bartender with the remote. The duster he was wearing went down to his knees. It sagged beneath his arms. Hardware—and lots of it. He called again to the bartender and was ignored as the fat man rocketed through the channels so quickly it was like a malfunctioning slide show. He blasted through channel after channel until there was a glimpse of female flesh and one of the bikers yelled, "*There!*" and he slowly circumnavigated back to it, something on one of the premium cable channels.

I didn't want to stand next to Jeter and create more of a display than necessary. I took a stool ten feet away from him and kept my head down. I watched him peripherally, noted how agitated he was getting from being dissed. Finally, the bartender placed the remote under an ancient black-and-white movie poster of Anthony Quinn in *Viva, Zapata!* and turned to Jeter with bored contempt. I feared for the bartender.

I didn't turn around and look behind me at the table of five, but tried to see who was there via the filmed-over backbar mirror. Five people, three males and two slutty-looking Anglo females. The smoke they were creating and the dirty mirror distorted the view. There were dozens of empty glasses on the table and an overflowing ashtray. The black light behind them added a garish touch, lighting up dirty fingerprints on the empty glasses, the lipstick on the girls, and the brilliant white of overlarge T-shirts on the two Hispanic males. It was boy-girl-boy-girl-boy at the table. The dark man in the middle was grinning stupidly and bobbing his head to a rhythm while a blond girl next to him stared intently at his ear and rocked up and down and I realized she was giving him a hand job under the table. The other girl, whose hair was jet-black and spiked, fingered a silver ring on her bottom lip and shot glances at the action taking place next to her. Garrett sat on the far left end of the table with a coffee mug in front of him with the string and label of a tea bag hanging over the lip of the mug. For some reason, the bored look on his face and what he was drinking struck me most of all because he had the temerity and confidence to drink hot tea in a place like this. I almost admired him for a second, but only for a second. Again, I wondered what his connection was to these gangsters and why he wanted to be involved with them.

I was heartened by the fact that the five at the table didn't seem to notice Jeter at the bar. They were so self-absorbed that they hadn't even looked up. I knew it would be a matter of seconds, though, before they did. Jeter was hard to miss with that damned big coat.

Getting his attention wasn't easy. I wanted him to look at me so I could signal to him to get the hell out of there. He'd have to see me there, right?

"I'm looking for a shitbird named Garrett Moreland," Jeter asked the bartender loud enough for me to hear. I was shocked by his brazenness. "Is he in here?"

The bartender appeared not to have heard. I glanced into the backbar mirror to assure myself that Garrett hadn't, either.

"*Jeter!*" I hissed. "*Let's go.*"

The biker nearest to me looked up from his drink and scowled at me, but Jeter didn't acknowledge I was there.

"Garrett Moreland, I said," Jeter growled. "Is he in this shit hole?"

The bartender made a point of ignoring him. Instead, he waddled down the length of the bar, asking each biker if he needed anything and going by me as if I didn't exist. As he passed, I marveled at the quantity and misogyny of his tattoos; skulls with spikes driven through them, women impaled on the hood ornaments of late-seventies' Chryslers and daggerlike penises, the American flag dripping blood into the open mouth of a caricature of former VP Dick Cheney.

"*Jeter, goddammit!*" I yelled, trying to shout above the music. "*We need to leave!*"

The biker to my right wanted another beer. The fat bartender ambled back to where he'd started with the biker's empty glass to fill it from the tap. He never even glanced my way. While he filled the glass from the tap right in front of Jeter, I saw the Montanan do a frightening thing: He smiled.

"Either you tell me if Garrett-fucking-Moreland is in the building, you fat greaser," Jeter drawled, "or a particular kind of hell will break out all around you."

There was a beat of silence when the song ended. The bartender filled the glass. When it was full, he nodded almost imperceptibly toward the table in the back.

"Much obliged," Jeter said, turning slowly around while keeping one hand on the bar. I could see him squinting toward the table under the black light.

"Jeter . . ." I said.

Because I was concentrating on Jeter, I almost missed the movements of the bartender, who was fishing around under the counter. And with the deceptively quick movements of a fat man who for years has concentrated solely on the speed of his arms, the bartender stepped back with a black baseball bat and raised it above his head and smashed Jeter's hand with it. I could hear the bones break with the same muffled snapping sounds of dry branches underfoot.

I was frozen where I sat.

Jeter didn't cry out, didn't even pull his hand away. Instead, he turned back toward the bartender with an *I-can't-believe-you-did-that* look.

Surprised that the blow didn't bring this crazy Anglo in the silly coat to his knees, the bartender cocked back and swung again, smashing Jeter's misshapen hand on the bar, presumably breaking every bone that hadn't been broken by the first hit. I'll never forget the sound of contact, like hitting a Ziploc bag filled with pretzels.

I don't know why the bartender did it. I'll never know or understand. All I can guess is that he was reacting to the insult and that he'd done the same thing before in similar situations in order to drive people out of the club. But like my life those past two and a half weeks, what happened next was beyond analysis.

All of us have heard the phrase "He got his head blown off." I'm here to tell you that doesn't actually happen. I know because when Jeter reached into his duster with his right hand and came out with the sawed-off double-barreled ten-gauge shotgun that was once referred to as a coach gun because it was the weapon of choice for stagecoach drivers, and pressed the muzzle into the bartender's forehead with both hammers cocked and fired both barrels, well, the bartender's head was not actually blown off. The top right quarter of it disappeared, and what was left of the mirror behind the bar was spattered with blood, brains, and chunks of bone, skin, and hair. The bartender dropped to the floor as if his puppet strings had been clipped, taking a shelf of beer glasses with him.

The sound was tremendous, and my ears were ringing. The two bikers at the bar dismounted and scrambled and passed me, running toward the door. I watched them from above, detached, as if my own soul and perspective were removed from my body.

Jeter was enraged. He stared at his broken hand for a moment, saying "Why in the hell did he do that?" before recovering and breaking the shotgun open with his undamaged right hand. The two huge, spent, and smoking shells hurtled back over his shoulders on either side of his head. He transferred the weapon under his left arm and dug into his duster pocket for two fresh shells. He reloaded and he snapped the shotgun closed with an upward jerk, turning toward the back table while he cocked both barrels. His broken left hand hung uselessly by his side.

"WHICH ONE OF YOU SHITBIRDS IS GARRETT MORELAND?"

I realized that the high-pitched noise in my ears was one of the girls shrieking.

The gangster on the right end of the table farthest from Garrett pushed back so hard in his chair that he sent it flying behind him. He stood up next to the table. The dark boy in the middle, who had been getting serviced, stared openmouthed while he inexplicably felt the sudden need to button himself back up. The blond girl next to him screamed while holding her hands to the sides of her face. Garrett still had both of his hands on the table wrapped around his mug, his bearing remarkably calm, his eyes taking in the man with the shotgun, who was approaching him, as if trying to place him, trying to figure out why he'd called out his name.

"You the shitbird Garrett?" Jeter asked him.

Jeter didn't notice that the man who had stood up was bent slightly forward now, his arm behind his back digging for something in his pants.

Jeter pointed the shotgun with one hand, said again, "You Garrett Moreland?"

And the gangster pulled his weapon, a semiautomatic, and fired four quick rounds—*pop-pop-pop-pop*—with the weapon held sidewise out in front of him. Jeter's coat danced, and he stumbled back a step, then swung the shotgun over and it exploded again and kicked higher than Jeter's head. A great bloom of red spattered across the chest of the gangster, who fell back over the chair he'd previously sent skittering across the floor.

Patiently, Jeter slid the shotgun back into its sling inside his duster and came out with a stainless-steel .45 semiauto. He shot the dark boy in the middle point-blank in the neck before the gangster could rack the slide on the pistol he'd been fumbling for. The gangster's gun skittered across the table and fell to the dirty carpet.

"Run away, girls," Jeter said. "I've got business here with young Mr. Moreland."

The blonde kept screaming as she ran, her hands still pressed to the sides of her head. There was a moment when our eyes locked as she ran toward the door, and I wondered if she'd be able to identify me later.

Jeter stepped aside for the female with the spiked hair, not expecting her to stop, turn, pause, and shove a pistol into his armpit and pull the trigger three times with muffled *bangs*. He cried out with a yelping sound, the hand with the pistol dropped to his side, and he staggered several steps to his left before collapsing on the dance floor in a heap.

"*Goddammit!*" he bellowed, sounding more angry with himself than with the girl. He writhed on the floor, making himself a moving target for the girl with the spiked hair, who clumsily tried to aim at him. He rolled to his belly and came up with the .45 and took her down with three rapid shots.

Like a bear cub, Jeter rose to all fours and, with a grunt, he was back on his feet. The second gangster he'd shot was still sitting upright at the table, his hand clamped to his neck. Arterial blood squirted out between his fingers. Jeter staggered over to him and put the muzzle of his .45 to the man's forehead.

"*Sign your stupid name on them papers,*" Jeter said in his ridiculous Mexican accent, "*or you die, senõr!*"

I walked stunned through the acrid hanging gun smoke and put my hand on Jeter's shoulder. Shotgun shells and spent casings littered the floor.

"That's not him," I said.

"*Your signature or your brains, senõr!*" Jeter said, pressing hard with the gun.

"Jeter, that's not him!" I shouted. "Garrett ran out the back while you were on the floor!" I was fairly certain Garrett never saw me.

Jeter paused, letting that sink in. I could hear the rapid patter of blood on the floor from the wounds inside Jeter's coat.

"They all look alike to me," he said with a harsh laugh, and pulled the trigger. The gangster flopped backward, his eyes wide-open, a smoking hole in his forehead.

JETER STOOD UNSTEADILY and holstered the .45. His face was drawn and white, his eyes sallow.

"Man," he said, "I really fucked this one up."

I nodded.

"I shoulda played that different," he said. "I never would of thought that girl would have a gun. This is a rough damned place."

I didn't know what to do. Try to get him to the Jeep? Take him to a hospital? Leave him there? Wait for the police to show up? I didn't hear sirens yet.

"I don't want to die here," Jeter said. "I want to die in Montana. Not in Denver. Not in this shit hole with these shitbirds."

He tried to take a step toward the door, but he couldn't seem to get his legs to obey. Blood streamed from the hem of his coat and pooled on the floor.

"I'm really shot up," he said weakly. "It's like everything warm is pouring out of me. I'm gettin' real cold. Help me, Jack."

"Where do you want to go?"

That grin. "Montana."

"We can't go to . . ."

"I can hear Cody talking to me in my head," Jeter said suddenly. "I just can't hear what he's saying."

"Cody?"

"Yeah, I hear him."

And I remembered I was still clutching my cell phone. I looked at it, saw the call I'd placed had connected five minutes ago.

I lifted it to my mouth. "Cody?"

"Jack, are you all right? Jesus—all I could hear were gunshots."

"I'm okay, but your uncle Jeter . . ."

"I heard. I'm on my way. Hang tight for five more minutes." He clicked off.

Jeter chinned toward the bar. "See if you can find some different music on that stereo, Jack. Find some good old country I can die to. Hank Snow, Little Jimmy Dickens, Hank Williams, Bob Wills—something good. I can't stand the crap they play in this place."

With that, he pitched forward like a felled tree. His head hit the dance floor so hard, the fall alone might have killed him.

I WAS LEANING against the bar when Cody came in. I'd unplugged the beer signs in the windows and turned off all but the black light over the table so the Appaloosa Club looked closed from outside, and no patrons would come in. I was having an out-of-body experience again, thinking I wasn't really there.

Cody pulled on a pair of rubber gloves.

"Help me get him into my trunk," Cody said. "If we leave him here, the cops will eventually trace him to me."

"Where are you going to take him?"

Cody shook his head. "Up in the mountains. I've got a place in mind."

"He wanted to go to Montana," I said dumbly.

"I'll get him up there one of these days," Cody said, grasping Jeter's collar and dragging him toward the door.

Cody said, "Jesus, how much hardware does he have under that coat?"

"I've never seen anything like this before," I said, walking behind. "It was terrible, Cody. It was a slaughterhouse in here. The bartender broke Jeter's hand with a baseball bat, and Jeter started blasting. Garrett got away."

"I heard. You called me, remember?"

"We're going to go to prison," I said.

"I don't know," Cody said, looking around the club. "Looks gang-related to me. It looks like maybe a big fight over meth-distribution territory."

"Do you really think that's how the police will see it?"

Cody paused and looked up angry. "Are you going to help me, or what?"

"DON'T RACE OUT OF HERE," Cody said, after we'd lifted Jeter's body into his plastic-lined trunk and slammed the lid. "Take it slow and easy. The last thing you want is to be pulled over for speeding. Judging by that look in your eye, you'd confess."

I nodded.

"Go home," Cody said. "I'll catch up with you later."

He gave me a brotherly punch in the shoulder. "We probably should have kept Uncle Jeter out of this. He was past his prime and over his head. And he was too much of a bigot to think straight."

"You should have seen him in there," I said. "I'll have nightmares for the rest of my life."

Cody looked around. The street was dark and lifeless. "Let's get out of here, Jack."

I turned toward my Jeep.

"Jack," Cody called after me. I looked over my shoulder. "Until tonight, it's been another really good day."

I DROVE WEST TOWARD home on I-70 with the radio on KOA for sound but not hearing a word. I checked my rearview mirror every few minutes, expecting to see a squad car with wigwag lights flashing. My speed varied from forty to eighty, I couldn't concentrate. I set the cruise control at sixty-five so at least I wouldn't need to worry about *that*.

I felt dead inside, and my head was in a fog. Only then did I wonder what Cody meant when he said he'd had another good day. Had he meant with Brian's call log?

The scene at the Appaloosa replayed over and over like a loop of tape.

Did Garrett see me? Did he know why Jeter was there? Would he go to the police to tell them what he'd seen, or would he play it like he did with Luis—with silence?

Could the blonde ID my face? What about the two bikers? Did they get a good enough look? Would Cody get pulled over driving up to the mountains with his dead uncle in his trunk?

God.

I found myself drifting off the highway and nearly overcorrected into a pickup in the next lane. I tried to concentrate.

I didn't hear the first part of the report on the radio, maybe because I'd learned over the years to tune out much of what was on the radio. I caught it midway through. . . . *The police spokesman says there was a quadruple homicide tonight at a Zuni Street tavern . . . gang-related . . .*

Gang-related.

I WAVED at the new deputy in his black-and-white across the street from our house, and he waved back.

Inside, Melissa came down the stairs in her nightgown.

"Why didn't you call?"

I shook my head.

"Honey, are you okay?"

"No," I said. "No, I'm not."

"Did Garrett sign the papers?"

Thursday, November 22

Three Days to Go

Twenty

I FINALLY DRIFTED INTO an unforgiving sleep around four in the morning and when I woke up Melissa was standing over me with tears in her eyes. I expected her to say, "The police are here."

Instead, she said, "It's Thanksgiving Day, Jack. I *forgot*. Can you believe that?"

"I can," I said, rubbing sleep from my eyes, "because I forgot, too."

"How can a person forget it's Thanksgiving?" she said, and burst out crying.

I stood and held her. She seemed to dissolve into my arms, and I could feel her hot tears on my shoulder. I knew she wasn't truly crying about forgetting Thanksgiving.

IT WAS COLD and overcast. The mountains had no tops, and milky tendrils extended down into the valleys like cold fingers.

Winter had won again and was reclaiming lost territory, I thought. It was snowing hard in the high country. I thought of Cody having to drive up there somewhere, and hoped he'd made it back okay. I blew in my hands as I walked across the street to the sheriff's department black-and-white. Billy Sanders was back. His motor was running so he'd have heat. This time, he didn't caution me to keep my distance.

He lowered his window, and I bent over into it. I could feel a breath of warm air come out as well as the fake-cheese smell of Doritos. The bag was on his lap, and I could see several crumpled soft-drink cans on the floor. The morning *Denver Post* was beside him on the passenger seat. The headline shouted MASSACRE IN NORTH DENVER.

Man, oh man.

"Are you okay?" Sanders asked me. "You don't look so good." He closed one eye in puzzlement. "My replacement said you weren't out all *that* late."

"I wasn't," I said, and changed the subject. "So you have to work on a holiday, huh?"

Sanders nodded. There was a line of orange powder from the Doritos on his upper lip, and his fingertips were orange. "Yeah, kind of a bummer but that's part of the deal."

"I'm going to King Soopers to get groceries," I said. "My wife suggested we invite you in for a Thanksgiving meal. We won't have turkey and all the trimmings because we both forgot what day it was, but we'll have plenty of something else. I was thinking I'd bring back some roasted chickens and I need to know how many will be at the table. What do you say?"

He looked at me with suspicion for a moment. "Your wife really wants to invite me in?"

"She sent me out here to ask."

Melissa had surprised me with the suggestion. She'd said, "Thanksgiving isn't Thanksgiving unless we can share it with others. Since all our family is out-of-state, well, let's invite our watchers."

Sanders said, "What about Morales?"

"Melissa is out back talking to him now."

He shook his head and looked genuinely touched. "Man, that would be great. I was thinking I'd be sitting here all day feeling sorry for myself, and I guess technically we'd still be on the job since we'll be keeping an eye on you. Maybe we can even forget about those rules about drinking on duty just this once. Can we pitch in on dinner?"

"Sure, if you want. Why don't you call Morales, and the three of us can go to the store together?"

He laughed and reached for his mike. After talking to his partner, he called dispatch and asked for another car to watch our house while he and Morales "followed the suspect." After receiving a confirmation, he looked up at me, and said, "Sorry; we can't risk your wife taking off on us with that little girl while we're gone."

THE TWO DEPUTIES and I cruised the aisles of the grocery store like giddy teenage boys planning a camping trip. I pushed the cart, and they dropped items in it—canned cranberries, sweet potatoes, packaged mashed potatoes, jars of cream and brown gravy, a jar of CheezWhiz (Sanders!), two six-packs of beer, a couple *more* six-packs of beer. The aisles were empty except for a few desperate shoppers getting last-minute items. But no one was as desperate as the three of us because none of us had planned or shopped for a last-minute Thanksgiving meal before. There were four roasted chickens in the deli section. I didn't ask when they'd been roasted, and I bought them all.

"Better to get too much than not enough," I said.

"This is great." Billy Sanders laughed. "What about these dinner rolls? They look pretty good."

"Throw 'em in," I said.

"You are really nice people," Morales said, as we rung up.

"I've never had my surveillance targets invite me in for dinner before."

I thought, *We used to be good, too.*

THE DEPUTIES WERE AS inept in the kitchen as I was, so the three of us let Melissa shoo us out so we could drink beer and watch football. "Just one," Morales said, and so did Sanders. Just one turned into a lot more. Melissa didn't seem to mind doing everything herself. I heard her as she cooked and hummed happily. The smells coming from the kitchen were delicious. Angelina crawled between the three of us, offering up toys that we'd take and pretend to hide. She was once again a charmer and had both deputies giggling and mugging for her.

As I sat and watched them, the events of the evening before came rushing back, and I tried hard to steer them away. I jumped when my cell phone rang. Cody.

"Excuse me," I said to the deputies, who paid no attention to me. I took the phone into the kitchen and surprised Melissa, who quickly shoved something behind the microwave.

"Hey," I said into the phone.

His voice was grim. "Are you all right?"

"As much as I can be," I said.

"I mean now. I'm just down the street, and I can see two cruisers at your house."

"Oh that," I said. "We invited the deputies in for Thanksgiving. Why don't you come, too?"

I knew Cody had no place to go except his cop bar, where they put on a spread for single, divorced, and on-duty officers.

"Are you kidding?" he said.

"No. Come on—we've got plenty of food." I looked to Melissa, mouthed "Cody," and she nodded emphatically. She seemed to be enjoying this. She took a long drink from a glass of what looked like orange juice.

"Can I bring somebody?" Cody asked sheepishly.

"Of course you can. Who is she?"

"If only," he said. "I'm supposed to meet Torkleson. Can I bring him along? I guess his wife and daughter are in California."

"The more the merrier," I said. "Melissa loves cooking for a herd of cops, don't you, honey?"

"Oh yes," she said loudly enough Cody would hear.

Cody said, "Give me a half an hour."

I closed the phone and walked over to the stove to look inside some of the pots. "Smells good," I said to Melissa.

"Considering the eclectic mix of stuff you guys brought home, it's the best we can do," she said.

I reached behind the microwave and pulled out a half-full bottle of vodka.

"Since when do we keep this on hand?" I asked. Melissa had always been a "glass of wine with dinner" kind of woman. The last time I'd seen her with a drink was back in college, and even then she didn't appear to really like it.

She looked stricken that I'd found the bottle.

"It's okay," I said. "I'm just a little surprised you felt the need to hide it."

"You must be joking," she said. "I wouldn't leave it out in the open. What would everybody think?"

"They'd think we've had a really wicked month," I said.

"When you go to bed I sometimes come down here in the kitchen," she said. "I have a drink or two and try to figure out what we did to deserve this. Sometimes I take my drink upstairs and just sit by Angelina's crib and look at her and cry. Sometimes I come in and look at you, too. The only thing I can come up with is that we're cursed."

"No," I said, "we're being tested."

"Then I guess I'm flunking the test."

"Not at all," I said, brushing her cheek with the back of my fingers.

She asked me, "Are we disintegrating?"
I didn't know how to answer that.

I PAUSED for a moment before going back into the family room and looked through the angled slats on the kitchen door at Sanders and Morales. Both had their backs to me and were preoccupied with Angelina and the football game.

I thought: *I could knock them out from behind, and we could gather up our daughter and get in the Jeep and go.*

The kitchen was filled with heavy objects I could use—cast-iron skillets and pots, a rolling pin somewhere, that damned big mixer. For a few seconds my heart raced as I envisioned the scenario. I'd hit Sanders first because he was the closest, then go after Morales before he could stand and draw his gun. But knocking them out? I winced. That only happened on television and in the movies. What if the blows just opened up gashes, and one or both cops remained conscious?

No, I thought, the only way to ensure our escape would be to take them out. I glanced over my shoulder at the block of knives. That Santoku knife was sharp, substantial, and seven inches long. I could slit Sanders's throat and go for Morales's neck to cut it open or, if necessary, plunge the blade into his temple or heart. That might be possible, I thought. But could I do it in front of Angelina? Would she scream and be forever scarred?

That's when Sanders gathered Angelina up and sat her on his lap. And Melissa said, "Jack, could you go get the leaf for the table?"

CODY SHOWED UP with Torkleson, a baked ham, and a case of beer.

In the kitchen I whispered to Melissa, "What safer place for an

accessory to a quadruple homicide to be than at a dining table surrounded by policemen?"

She said, "I don't find that funny."

MELISSA THREW HERSELF INTO preparing the meal. The
glass of vodka and orange juice that always seemed to be full explained at least a measure of her vivacity. She clucked at me again
for our odd choices of canned food and the fact that we had enough
beer to serve a battalion. Cody and Torkleson seemed to get along
well with the two deputies, and the four of them talked shop, their
voices getting louder as they drank more and more beer. I felt
ashamed for my murderous thoughts, and for a while had trouble
looking Sanders and Morales in the eye.

Finally, Melissa announced to all of us that dinner was ready,
and we shambled in and took our places at the table. Melissa said
a prayer, and I glanced up to see all four men with their heads
bowed.

As for me, I wasn't on very good terms with God just then.

THE TALK AT THE table turned inevitably toward the multiple
homicides at the Appaloosa Club last night. I could feel my heart start
to beat harder, but I feigned uninformed interest and kept my head
down. The one time I looked up, Cody and I exchanged a fleeting
glance.

Torkleson said, "If I hadn't traded shifts with McCoy and
Scruggs, it would have been my case. Those poor guys. The mayor is
all over us because of the Eastman murder, and now this. Man, the
heat those guys are under."

"Any ideas who did it?" Morales asked.

Torkleson shrugged. "Some blond chick says she was there. She told the Scruggs it was a single shooter—a huge hairy guy with a beard and a long coat."

Meaning Garrett Moreland had not talked to the police, just like before. Either he was scared, or he had something serious to hide. I recalled how calmly he had sat there at the table cradling the mug in his hands when Jeter approached him and called out his name.

"Bullshit," Sanders said, then acknowledged Angelina in her high chair. "Sorry," he said to Melissa.

Torkleson agreed. "Yeah, I know what you mean. One guy doing all that? It's hard to believe. I don't know if the blonde is credible at all. She says the big hairy guy just pulled a shotgun out of his coat and started blasting."

Morales said, "She says this big hairy guy just let her leave? Her and nobody else? Come on . . ."

Torkleson said, "She claims she thought her friend was right behind her out the door, but it turns out her friend was one of the victims. Shot three times in the chest."

"A big hairy guy?" Sanders said. "Sounds like she's been watching too many movies. This thing has 'gang' written all over it."

Cody nodded. "You've got that right."

Torkleson said, "That's what we're thinking, too. Two of the victims were local leaders of Sur-13. It's like somebody was trying to cut the head off that beast, probably the 32 Crips or Varios. Maybe the Crenshaw Mafia, who are gangster Bloods—we've heard they're moving in from Southern California. No way this was random. It was a power play. And get this: One of the shooters used a ten-gauge shotgun. That's serious hardware. I thought those guys stuck to nines and the occasional AK-47."

But they didn't get Garrett, I thought. I wondered just how deep Garrett was involved with the gangsters. Then I thought: *He could be a leader, too. It could have been a meeting.* That made me think differently about Garrett.

"A ten-gauge. Jeez." Morales said. "I bet that made a mess."

Torkleson said, "From the photos I saw, well . . ." He glanced over at Melissa, who was rapt but very pale. I'd not told her any of the details of what had happened in the Appaloosa Club, only that things had gone horribly wrong, and Garrett got away. She looked at me, trying to read me.

". . . Let's just say there was a lot of blood," Torkleson continued.

"I'm sorry," Sanders said, "but I can't get all weepy about hearing that some big boys from *Sureños* 13 got hit."

Morales agreed.

"Two of the victims were bystanders, though," Torkleson said. "The friend of the blonde had a couple of priors, but nothing of note. The bartender was an ex-con and probably a member of Sur-13, but I'm sure he wasn't a prime target—he was just there."

"Nobody saw or heard anything?" Cody asked innocently.

Torkleson shook his head. "Nobody but the blond girl so far. You know the neighborhood—it's deserted at night, and not a lot of cops go by there even though they're supposed to. And from what I understand, gunshots at night aren't at all rare in that neighborhood."

"So who called it in?" Cody asked.

"A citizen," Torkleson said. "Some guy said he went to the bar for a drink, but the place looked closed, which was unusual. He looked in a window and saw the bodies."

"Anything else?" Cody bored in. I hoped he wasn't being too obvious, but I recognized the fact that he was just being Cody the relentless cop.

"One thing, and it's not much," Torkleson said. "A warehouse delivery driver called in and said he sometimes uses that street to get to his shop. He said he saw a light-colored Jeep parked in front of the place at about the time we figure it all went down, but that's all we've got."

"Hey," Morales said, gesturing toward me with a spoon, "Mr. McGuane here's got a light-colored Jeep. He was gone last night for a few hours."

"That's right," Sanders said.

I felt my insides clutch up. Melissa was dabbing at some sweet potatoes on Angelina's face, and I saw her freeze.

Sanders said, "Maybe on the way to the bar, you stopped at the Appaloosa Club and shot four people."

"Maybe," I said.

"Looks like we've solved the case," Morales said, digging into the mashed potatoes.

Sanders said, "Now we can get a commendation and a raise and be on TV standing next to the mayor. Excuse me, can you pass me the ham?"

I began to breathe again. When I looked over at Cody, he winked at me.

Melissa stood up unsteadily, but I assumed I was the only one who noticed. "Who wants dessert?" she asked. I could tell she wanted to top off her glass again when she went over to the counter.

WE WERE IN THE LIVING ROOM, and it had gotten dark outside. Tiny little hard balls of snow pinpricked the west windows and melted on impact and slimed down the glass, leaving snail tracks. The second Thanksgiving Day game was in the first minutes of the fourth quarter, with Dallas ahead by twenty and John Madden extolling the virtues of Turducken and eight-legged turkeys. I was frankly surprised the deputies and Torkleson had stayed so long. And they seemed in no hurry to leave. There was still plenty of beer, and Cody had cracked open the Jim Beam Black. I wondered if they'd stay until the end of the game or until the alcohol ran out, and I was pretty sure it would be the alcohol. Angelina was charged up by the company although she was starting to get wild since she'd refused to take her nap. Why nap when there were four men doting on her? Melissa was in the kitchen cleaning up and, I assumed, working a little on the bottle of vodka. I couldn't get the image of her sitting bedside with her glass, watching our daughter and me while we slept, out of my mind.

I loved Melissa, and now I knew the depths of her feelings were unfathomable. When—*if*—we turned Angelina over, I couldn't imagine Melissa not melting down, and me with her. She said we were disintegrating, and the loss of our daughter would no doubt push her over the edge. I wasn't even sure I'd know her anymore, just as I was starting to wonder what would happen to me, what I'd become with the loss. I could think of no scenario that wasn't terrifying.

I'd read where the loss of a child was the most devastating thing that could possibly happen to parents. I believed that. But presumably the loss in question was due to death or accident. No one had studied what it was like to hand over a child because of a legal anomaly. And to hand the child over to people who might just be monsters.

"THAT ENGLISH PERVERT," Torkleson said to Cody and the deputies. "Did you hear the latest about *him?*"

Of course that pulled me out of my reverie.

"What was that asshole's name?" Torkleson asked. "You know, the one who was going to move here? He was on 9 News."

"Malcolm Harris," I said.

Torkleson was obviously drunk. His words slurred, and he was talking too loudly. As were Sanders and Morales. They'd been practically shouting at each other for a half hour, telling cop stories, comparing cop notes. Cops, like ranchers and outfitters of my youth, were generally suspicious and taciturn men, except when they were around their own. Then the yapping began, and it was endless. I had only half listened, spending most of my time worrying about my wife and trying to keep Angelina from acting out. I was hoping Melissa would be done soon in the kitchen so she could take our daughter upstairs and calm her down and get her to bed. But when Malcolm Harris's name came up, I leaned forward in my chair.

"What about him?" Cody asked. Strangely, Cody seemed to be the most sober of them all. I'd noted that although he was drinking, he wasn't pounding them down like usual—or like the others were. I could only attribute his restraint to the "good days" he'd been having. Cody only drank when he was bored, which was most of the time. When he was wrapped up in a case or a project, he restrained himself.

"Who is he talking about?" Sanders asked Morales.

"That guy," Morales said. "Don't you watch the news or read the memos?"

"Fuck no," Sanders said before noting Angelina in my lap, and saying, "Sorry again."

I was thankful that at that moment Melissa came into the family room and scooped up Angelina. She said good night to everyone and was lavished with "thank-yous" and overdone praise. Her eyes misted as they thanked her—she cried so easily and quickly now—and she took our daughter to bed. I was grateful she didn't seem wobbly or lit up, and I made a note to check the level of the vodka bottle behind the microwave.

"You know that guy," Morales said. "The English guy. He was on his way here to move his company or something. I got a call to go to the airport just in case he was on the plane. If he landed, we were supposed to arrest him, but they got him before he boarded, I guess. He was some big-time pervert pedophile."

Sanders shook his head. "I never heard of him."

"Anyway," Torkleson said, as tired as I was of the deputy interplay, "it turns out he had a connection to somebody here."

That got Cody's attention, and mine.

"Aubrey Coates," Torkleson said. "Coates's e-mail address and phone number were all over his records. Scotland Yard thinks our man was part of this pervert's child porn and trafficking network. Can you believe that?"

"I wish he would have made it here," Sanders said, "so somebody could shoot the bastard. I hate those scumbags."

"I woulda shot him," Morales said, and I believed him.

"Hold it," I said, my head spinning. "Malcolm Harris had a connection to Aubrey Coates?"

I recalled Harris and the conversation:

My friends in Colorado say that compared to what I'm used to, I'll be bulletproof! That's the term they use, bulletproof. I love that.

Really? Who says that? I asked.

Oh no, he said coyly, I won't reveal my sources.

So his source was Aubrey Coates? What was Coates talking about? How was Coates bulletproof?

I looked to Cody for some kind of clarification, but Cody looked as mystified as I was.

Torkleson said, "But I heard the fucking U.S. Attorney won't go after Coates again. Not after Coates beat the rap the first time . . ." Torkleson lurched to a stop, realizing what he was saying and who he was saying it to. He looked over at Cody. "Sorry, man."

Cody glared at him with murderous eyes.

"What?" Sanders said. "What the fuck?"

Morales leaned back on the couch and beheld Cody and Torkleson. "Let's be cool, men," he said.

"What?" Sanders said again, completely confused.

"I wasn't thinking," Torkleson said to Cody. "My mouth was running away with me."

Cody said, "It sure fucking was."

"Be cool, brothers," Morales, the peacemaker said, standing up so he was between them. "Everything's cool here. We got women and babies in the house."

Sanders stomped a foot. "Would somebody please tell me what the fuck is going on here?"

Morales spun on his partner, said, "What's going on is Thanksgiving dinner is over. Our replacements will be here in twenty minutes, and it's time to go."

Melissa—thank God for Melissa—broke the tension by bringing

Angelina down the stairs. Our daughter was in her footie pajamas, and despite the fact that she was exhausted, she beamed at the cops, who were on the verge of going after each other.

"Angelina wants to say good night," Melissa said.

Sanders, Torkleson, and Morales stood up. They thanked Melissa once again and shook Angelina's chubby little hand. She rewarded them with a squeal each, which made them laugh.

"She's so tired, she's goofy," Melissa said. "So are you guys."

"What a darling," Morales said.

I kissed my daughter good night, but she was preoccupied with the men in the room whom she'd charmed to death.

"See you in a few minutes," I said to Melissa.

As she carried Angelina up the stairs, our daughter squirmed her way up over Melissa's shoulders so she could wave and laugh at the cops in the family room. Morales was smitten, as were Torkleson and Sanders.

Sanders, aware of why they were assigned to watching our house, said, "It just ain't right what's happening."

Morales shook his head, said, "No it isn't."

Torkleson quickly shook hands with me and thanked me for dinner, and was out the door into the snowstorm. Cody bored holes into Torkleson's back the whole way.

Sanders and Morales followed him. All I could think of was what in the hell Coates had told Harris—and why.

"THAT ASSHOLE," Cody said, seething, "showing me up like that.

"He wasn't thinking," I said, "he was just talking."

"Which is the problem with the whole fucking department. They don't think."

"Do you want a nightcap?" I asked.

Cody shook his head. "I'm done."

"The connection between Malcolm Harris and Aubrey Coates," I said. "There's something going on here I can't figure out. Something big and awful."

"Sometimes," Cody said, looking over my head, "I wish I had a license to just kill people. I'd kill a lot of them and make the world a better place. I'd start with Aubrey Coates and Malcolm Harris, and move to Garrett and John Moreland. There's about fifty others on the list I can think of."

"Cody . . ."

"Don't 'Cody' me," he said.

"Brian's funeral is tomorrow," I said. "Do you want to go with us?"

"It's tomorrow?"

"Yes."

"Jesus. I still can't believe he's gone. It hasn't sunk in yet."

"I know what you mean."

He looked at me. "No, I won't be there."

That troubled me.

"It has nothing to do with Brian," Cody said. He lifted his hand and pinched his thumb and index finger together. "I'm *this* close to cracking this thing."

I inadvertently took a step back. "You're kidding."

Cody's eyes blazed. "Nope. I think I've got it. I just needed to have the time to go through those call logs and do the police work. I think I've just about cracked it."

"Tell me," I said.

He smiled. His smile resembled—unfortunately—his Uncle Jeter's. "I'll tell you when I've got it," he said. "I can't put you two through any more false hopes or bad plans."

Cody grabbed his coat from where it was thrown over the couch. He gestured upstairs. "That Sanders guy is a doofus. But he's right when he says this ain't right, and it ain't."

He paused at the front door. Snow shot in. "Coates is a dead man walking, he just doesn't know it yet. But yes, I agree with you that there's more to it than what we know. This Malcolm Harris thing throws me for a loop, but somehow I think it all connects. I just don't know how yet."

"When will I see you?" I asked. "There's only three more days."

"Not soon," he said. "I'm going to New Mexico."

"Why?"

"Later," he said, waving me off. "Keep Melissa off the booze," he said. "I'm worried about her."

Friday, November 23

Two Days to Go

Twenty-one

THE FUNERAL FOR BRIAN took place in Capitol Hill at the largest chapel I'd ever been in, and the place was packed with mourners we didn't know. The décor was airy and sterile, all light pine and clean lines. Oh, and a small stylized cross hanging from a chain in a corner toward the front, as if placed there as an afterthought.

"A church designed by IKEA," I mumbled to Melissa, trying to make her smile. Didn't work.

If Brian were in charge of his own funeral—which in some ways he likely was—I thought it would look like this. It was larger-than-life, heavy on the hubris. An alt-rock band played contemporary dirges while a PowerPoint slide show presented shots of Brian skiing, swimming, speaking at a podium, clowning around, dancing, and costumed as both John Elway and Spider-Man at various parties. His remains were in a squarish marble urn on a velvet-covered riser at the front of the church. Brian's partner, Barry, spoke about Brian's loyalty, creativity, affection, and "ability to light up a room." Barry seemed like a calm counterpoint to Brian, and I could see how the two fit as a couple.

Barry was followed by Mayor Halladay, who gave not only a moving speech and tribute to Brian but vowed to those in attendance that he'd make sure the killer was caught and brought to justice. There was a swell of clapping when the mayor said Denver was no place for hate crimes, and that Brian's death would forever be remembered as the incident that ushered in a "hate-crime free zone." The mayor's assumption that Brian's murder was the result of his cruising downtown bars revealed where Mayor Halladay's head was. It also spoke to the lack of progress in the investigation.

I found myself looking around at the mourners as the mayor spoke. Many of the faces I'd seen in the society section of the *Denver Post* and *Rocky Mountain News,* and a few on television news. Brian always claimed he knew everybody who was anybody in town, and the outpouring at his funeral proved it. I was proud of him for making such an impact on this city while still remaining our small-town friend.

We sat near the back simply because there were so many people already there when we arrived. Sanders and Morales, of course, were with us but, thankfully, in street clothes. The two of them sat directly behind us at the service. I heard Sanders whisper, "World-class fruits and nuts in this place," to Morales.

Melissa whispered into my ear, "What bothers me is it's as if I didn't know Brian at all. Who are all of these people? The only one he'd ever mentioned was Barry. It seems like Brian had a secret life."

"We were his secret life," I said. "This room was his real life."

The mayor finally stepped aside. The band, somewhat inexplicably, played a cover version of REM's "Losing My Religion."

"Goodness," Melissa said. "Don't they know they're in a *church?*"

Although Cody said he wouldn't be there, I kept an eye out for him nevertheless. He'd left me with a strand of hope, and that strand was all I had.

When the band was through, a hip pastor with long hair and a stylish half beard and open shirt told us that we weren't there to mourn a death but to celebrate the life of an "awesome" human being. He began telling anecdotes about Brian—all from Denver, where he became public, none from Montana—that apparently had been gathered up by Barry and Barry and Brian's friends. Some were quite funny, but they were striking to Melissa and me because they were stories we'd never heard before about a friend we knew in a totally different context, and Melissa was soon both laughing and crying hard, which in turn made Angelina cry.

"I'll take her outside," I said, and Melissa willingly let me. Sanders followed.

The mountains were still shrouded in snow clouds. The ski resorts, from what I'd heard on the radio, were getting hammered. Marketing and PR spokesmen tried to outdo each other on the amount of "champagne powder" that had accumulated over the night. I knew most of the spokespeople personally from my work in tourism and knew they really weren't as breathless about falling snow as they sounded on the radio.

Angelina preferred being outside to inside, as she usually did. She pushed away from me as soon as we were outside, wanting to get down. I held her as she tried to push away. I couldn't let her down because Melissa had dressed her in a velvet dress, pink tights, and a heavy coat. As I struggled with her I found myself directly in front of Jim Doogan, who leaned against the trunk of a leafless tree and smoked a cigarette.

Doogan leveled his gaze at Sanders, who was a few steps behind me. He didn't say who he was but apparently he didn't need to.

"Give us a few minutes, will you?"

Sanders turned and walked back to the church and sprawled out on a bench.

"Is the mayor done in there?" Doogan asked.

"I think so."

"Was he good?"

I shrugged. "Good enough. He didn't say any bad things about Brian."

He laughed. "That Eastman guy caused us a lot of headaches. He used to drive the mayor out of his mind because he knew how to work the system and work the mayor. I always thought it was sort of personal."

"Brian was tough," I said.

"He was. And there's something I want to say to you. This is between us, okay?" Doogan said.

"Sure. I always confide with the guy who fires me. Not a problem."

Doogan snorted a small laugh. "You know I'm no more than the messenger boy, right? The mayor and the judge are close. The judge's wife is a major contributor, so the mayor has some obligations, if you catch my drift."

"I do." I fumbled with Angelina, held her tight to me. "But this is bigger than that."

"What do you mean?"

"Remember when we talked about Malcolm Harris?"

Doogan nodded.

"Do you know who his connection was here in Colorado?"

He shook his head.

"Aubrey Coates, the Monster of Desolation Canyon."

Doogan was lifting the cigarette to his mouth, but he froze.

I said, "Like I told you the other day, the mayor may have a bigger problem on his hands than he realized. If it turns out a major international pedophilia ring is headquartered in this city right under his nose, that won't help out his political ambitions, plus his pal the judge may be blamed for letting Coates walk. How will that one play on 9 News?"

Doogan said, "No, no. That wasn't the judge. That was lousy police work. No way that could be linked back to the mayor in any way. You're just throwing crap out there."

I *was* just throwing crap out there, but some of it stuck. I could tell his head was spinning a little. He was thinking how to mitigate the situation.

Said Doogan, "You're grasping at straws—anything to get back at that judge."

I didn't respond.

"I heard you tried to force your way in to see him the other day," Doogan said. "And when you couldn't get in, you called him, using my name with what could be construed to be vague threats. The mayor asked me to look into it, but I haven't gotten around to it yet."

"Thank you."

"I'd suggest not making a habit of that."

He turned his attention to Angelina, who was still struggling and had knocked my hat screwy on my head. "This is your little girl, eh?"

"This is her."

"She's the one . . ."

"*Yes.*"

He shook his head and looked away. He seemed genuinely moved.

I said, "Yes, she's the one the mayor's good friend Judge Moreland plans to take away from us Sunday."

Doogan took a long pull from his cigarette and blew the smoke out in an endless stream. "Judge Moreland, he's something else. He's a type, Jack, a rare type. I see his kind all the time, but he's a rare specimen."

I let him go on.

"You're looking at things the wrong way. You're making wrong assumptions. In my line of work, the politicos who are really going somewhere are never about the here and now. The good ones—and Moreland is a good one—think long-term. They *fixate* on the prize. Because they do, sometimes it isn't easy to figure out the moves they're making right in front of your eyes. You've gotta think long-term if you want to figure 'em out, and you haven't been thinking long-term."

I said, "What's he fixated on?"

Doogan said, "The Supreme Court."

I shook my head. "How can taking our little girl possibly help him get on the Supreme Court?"

"I don't know, Jack. You need to figure that one out. But I know that's what he wants."

I LEFT DOOGAN there by his tree. Sanders was a few feet behind again. As we approached the parking lot, I heard a powerful burbling engine fire up, and I instantly recognized it. The sound was like a straight razor to my throat.

Garrett's yellow H3 backed out away from us. I couldn't see inside well because of the dark-tinted windows, but I thought I saw two profiles—Garrett and his father.

"What, do you know who that is?" Sanders asked, noting my reaction.

So Garrett had come to the funeral of the man he'd stomped to death to what, gloat? And why would Judge Moreland have come? To see what?

Angelina squirmed in my arms and pointed toward a squirrel scrambling down a tree. She said, "Cat!"

I started to laugh when something hit me so hard my knees nearly buckled. I looked from my little girl to the departing H3 and back to my little girl. I thought, *He came hoping to see* her.

Which went back to the beginning, the simple unanswered question: Why did they want her?

And everything seemed to make sudden and terrible sense.

Bulletproof. What could be more bulletproof than a pedophile being a partner in crime with a judge? The judge in whose courtroom the Monster of Desolation Canyon—another participant in the international ring—had gone free?

Angelina cried out, and I realized I was squeezing her too hard. I eased up and looked at her. She was beautiful by all accounts, with her dark flashing eyes, her smile, her manner, and not just proud-parent beautiful.

I felt like I'd had the breath punched out of me.

I carried her toward the back parking lot of the chapel where I'd seen a couple of black-and-whites and Torkleson's nondescript Crown Victoria. The cops were there, no doubt, to see who came to the funeral because the case was still wide-open. Torkleson leaned against his Crown Vic talking with another detective—they stood out as cops even at a funeral where there were more suits and ties than usual—and a couple of uniforms.

Torkleson must have seen something in my face as I approached because he excused himself from his colleagues and met me on the sidewalk.

"Hello, Jack," Torkleson said.

"You said Malcolm Harris was connected with Aubrey Coates," I said. "How did you find that out?"

Torkleson shrugged. "Phone records, e-mails, uploads, downloads. A lot of technical evidence concerning ISPs and proxy servers and other stuff I really don't understand, but from what I was told, Coates transmitted big files and images overseas from that trailer of his. The Brits traced it back from Harris's computer. Unfortunately, we don't have the original files anymore, as you know." He shot a look over my shoulder to see if Cody was lurking anywhere and could attack.

"I don't know where Cody is," I said. "Don't worry about him."

"Why are you asking me this?" he said.

I said, "Because I'm pretty sure if you dug into the evidence for the charges, you'll find communication between Harris and Coates and someone else here in this city."

Torkleson looked at me closely. "We've got a team assigned to that," he said. "They're working with the Brits and Interpol. Perverts are getting arrested one by one all over the world. Are you talking about someone in particular?"

"Judge Moreland or his son Garrett," I said. "Or both."

Torkleson closed his eyes and took a deep breath and moaned. "Not again," he said. "You know what happened when I sent officers to his house based on your so-called tip."

"This is different," I said. "Of all the places he could relocate, Malcolm Harris chose Denver. He said he was coming here because he would be *bulletproof*. Somebody assured him it would be fine for him. And what better proof of it than when a child pornographer and molester like Aubrey Coates gets set free in Judge Moreland's own courtroom?"

Torkleson started to argue, but stopped. I could see wheels turning, things falling into place for him as they did for me.

"How do you know Harris?" Torkleson asked.

"I met with him on behalf of the CVB," I said. "Before we knew what he was."

"Jesus Christ," he whispered.

"Do you have access to the evidence against Harris?"

He nodded. "I'd have to get with one of our tech guys to interpret it," he said. "But I think we have all the supporting documentation that's been compiled. It's just a matter of cross-referencing phone calls, e-mail addresses, IP stuff—I *think*."

"Can you try?" I asked.

Torkleson looked over his shoulder to assure himself we hadn't been overheard by his colleagues. "I'll try," he said softly.

"Thank you," I said, wanting to kiss him.

"But I don't think it will pan out," he said, putting his hand on my shoulder. "If there are electronic trails from Coates and Harris to Moreland or his son, I think we'd already know it. This case has been in the works for a hell of a long time."

"I understand," I said. "But won't it be easier if you're specifically looking at a particular target—Moreland's or Garrett's computers or phones—than cross-referencing a whole city?"

"Maybe," he said. "I don't know."

By then Angelina had lost all patience and worked her arms free and was swinging at me, her little fists thumping against my topcoat lapels. "Down! *Down!*"

"*Angelina, no.*" The tone of my voice silenced her. She began to cry, and I was sorry I had snapped at her.

THAT NIGHT I ROLLED over in bed and opened my eyes and caught Melissa sitting there in the dark staring at me, a drink in her hand. No doubt wondering why she'd married a man who couldn't keep her family together.

Saturday, November 24

One Day to Go

Twenty-two

WHEN THE TELEPHONE RANG at seven thirty in the morning, I rolled over and grabbed it, rubbing my eyes and hoping it was Torkleson or Cody with news. After waking to find Melissa watching me the night before, I hadn't slept for hours and had just fallen asleep.

"Is everything ready for tomorrow?" Judge John Moreland asked.

I didn't respond.

Moreland said, "I know this has got to be tough. Please don't make it any tougher on either one of us than it needs to be."

I said, "I'm on to you."

There was a beat of silence. He said, "What?"

"You heard me. You'll be in prison, where you can never touch a little girl again. And you know what happens to your kind in prison."

When he spoke again he sounded angry and impatient. "I have no earthly idea what you're talking about." I had hoped he would act guilty and reveal himself. He was a good actor.

"Really?" I said.

"You've gone off the deep end. I hate to say it, but getting the baby out of that . . . environment can't be soon enough."

"You'll be wearing a jumpsuit and shoes without laces, and you'll spend all your time looking over your shoulder for the next attack," I said.

A heavy sigh. "I've done everything I can to be compassionate," Moreland said. "I never needed to give you the time, but I did. I've offered to help you and your wife with another placement, but you've spurned that offer. All I get from you is threats and paranoid rants. You accuse my son of murder and me of something I can't even say out loud. I would have hoped this entire painful thing could have been accomplished with some kind of maturity for the sake of the child, but I see that's just not the case."

Man, he *almost* convinced me with that one. He was damned good, I'll give him that.

"I'm on to you," I said again.

"Oh, for heaven's sake . . ."

I punched off and looked up to see Melissa in the doorway, holding Angelina in her arms.

"Was that him?" she asked.

"Yes."

"What did he want?"

"He wanted to make sure we were ready."

"Kind of him," she said, with a kind of hopeless sarcasm. She closed her eyes. I stood up in case I needed to steady her. Angelina reached out for me, cried, "Da!"

I COULDN'T EVEN EAT the toast I'd made and stuck to cup after cup of coffee. With the mug in hand, I wandered through the rooms in our house as if seeing them for the first time in a while. White winter light filtered through the blinds and curtains. It was a different quality of light than fall or summer, a more dispassionate hue. It was obviously cold outside because the heater clicked on and forced warm air through the registers with regularity. I thought, *Maybe this happens all the time, and I've just never noticed it before.* I tried to remember the last time I'd checked our furnace in the basement and couldn't recall when I'd done it.

Sanders and Morales were in their usual places. Wisps of exhaust from their running engines dissipated into the air.

I'd not told Melissa of my suspicion regarding Judge Moreland or my conversation with Detective Torkleson. Maybe I should have, but I was banking on the fact that Torkleson would call confirming the judge's links to the ring, and it would all be over.

MELISSA DECIDED the house was missing something and decided to bake bread. Soon, the smells of baking bread filled the place, taking the edge off the day. *Good call,* I thought.

In Angelina's room, there were boxes stacked up in the corner and marked SUMMER CLOTHES, WINTER CLOTHES, and TOYS AND GIFTS.

It was really happening.

For the fourth time that day, I pulled out my cell phone and speed-dialed Cody's number and heard, "The number you are calling is out of the service area at this time. Please leave a message . . ."

THERE WERE SEVERAL more phone calls throughout the day, none of them Torkleson or Cody. Melissa's mom and dad called from different places and she talked to each of them longer than I could remember her ever doing. Her face flushed as she talked to her father, and I could tell she was getting angry.

"We *had* a lawyer," she said, heatedly. "It's not like we didn't have a lawyer, Dad. It's that there wasn't anything he could do."

She scowled as he went on, and when she saw me watching, she rolled her eyes.

"Gee, Dad," she said, "it's really great you are suddenly so concerned and seem to have all of the answers. But where were you three weeks ago when we could have used some of your wisdom?"

My parents called shortly after, before Melissa had cooled off. She talked to them and told them the situation hadn't changed. After a while, she handed the phone to me.

My dad said, "Your mom is too busted up to talk anymore, sorry."

"I understand."

"I guess this is the kind of thing that can happen when we turn everything over to the government and to the lawyers," he said. "When a whole society abrogates personal responsibility, these kinds of situations come up." I'd heard his theory many times before that everything was better back in the pioneer days, when people dealt with each other fair and square, their word backed up personally by their reputations or their guns—without the involvement of third parties like lawyers or politicians.

"Dad, I can't sit on the front porch with a shotgun on my lap and keep them away."

"I know you can't," he said. "And it's a damned shame."

I thought of my grandfather's Colt .45 upstairs in the closet, and said, "Yes, it is."

Dad said, "I was joking to your mother that we ought to send somebody like Jeter Hoyt down there to straighten things out. That'd give those big-city types a dose of frontier justice, wouldn't it?"

I smiled bitterly to myself. *Frontier justice hadn't matched up real well with Sur-13.*

"Too bad we can't do that," he said.

I PACED. I called Cody's cell phone again and again, getting angrier with him each time. Same with Torkleson, who wouldn't answer his cell, either. I called the detective division, and the receptionist said Torkleson was out and she didn't know when he'd be back. She asked if there was anyone else who could help me, and I said no, I needed to talk to Torkleson.

I stayed away from both Melissa and Angelina because I didn't want my building anger and fear to effect them. I went upstairs and checked the loads in the .45, and went downstairs and looked at my furnace and wondered how in the hell it worked.

For once, what my father said made some sense. Why couldn't I sit outside on my porch with a shotgun across my knees and keep the world away from my family?

I couldn't stay home, but I couldn't leave Melissa and Angelina, either, so I threw on my parka and went outside. As I approached Sanders, he slid his window down and held out his hand, palm out.

"That's far enough, Jack."

"Why?"

"The sheriff didn't like our Thanksgiving dinner together. He told both of us to stop fraternizing with you and your family. You know what's happening tomorrow."

"And what would that be?" I said, angry.

"Jack, just stay back."

I turned around and stomped back to the house. As I did I whipped out my cell phone and called Cody.

Out of service range.

I called detective division again, and the receptionist said she'd put my message on his desk on top of the pile of my other messages.

DURING ANGELINA'S AFTERNOON NAP, I went into the kitchen as Melissa pulled more loaves of bread from the oven and put them on the counter to cool. I couldn't even count the number of loaves she'd baked during the day—maybe twenty-five, maybe more. The kitchen was overwhelmed with the smell of yeast and flour and golden crust. There was more dough on the table, and it was obvious she was going to keep baking bread until she ran out of ingredients. I took a cursory look around the hiding places in the kitchen and didn't see the bottle.

"You don't have to keep looking," she said. "I'm not drinking."

"JACK, IT'S DETECTIVE TORKLESON," Melissa said, shaking me awake. I'd fallen asleep in my chair in the living room out of exhaustion, and it took me a second to register what she'd said. When it did, my heart revved like a race-car motor, and I grabbed the phone and bounded up the stairs into our bedroom and shut the door.

He said, "I've been up all night since we talked. I hijacked our best tech gal and made her stay up all night with me in the basement of the building with her computers. We've been going over all of the evidence Scotland Yard and Interpol sent over . . ."

I tried to swallow, but my mouth was dry.

"Jack, we can't make any links at all between either Harris and Moreland or Coates and Moreland. We've got nothing to connect them."

I nearly blacked out and had to reach for the headboard to steady my legs.

"Can you keep looking?" I said. My voice was weak. I'd staked everything on this. "Maybe Garrett has a secret computer? Maybe they know how to mask their telephone numbers and IP addresses somehow? Hell, I don't know. All I know is that there has to be a connection."

Torkleson sighed. "Jack, I'm not saying there isn't a remote possibility. I'm not saying that. But the electronic trail between Coates and Harris is like a freeway. There's nothing like that with the judge—not even an old cow trail, if you know what I'm saying. There are some IP addresses my tech gal can't isolate, but nothing substantial, and nothing we could go to the DA with. It's a dry hole, Jack."

"It's got to be there," I said.

"Look, we've done all we could. It's an interesting theory you had that plays into your situation, but nothing we can pursue in any way, shape, or form. Maybe somewhere down the line Harris will say the judge is a known associate, or give up his name up for leniency. There's always that."

"It will be too late," I said.

"I know," Torkleson said.

I found myself looking out the window at Sanders's cruiser. It was dusk and getting colder. Exhaust puffed from his tailpipe.

I said, "When you lose all hope, what have you got left?"

"I can't answer that, Jack."

"Neither can I," I said, before thanking him and hanging up.

"HAVE WE DONE IT all wrong, honey?" I asked later that afternoon, as the sun dropped behind the mountains.

She stopped and looked at me, her eyes blinking oddly. "What do you mean?"

I shook my head. "Maybe we played it all wrong, because look where we are. Tomorrow they're coming to take her. Maybe we should have hired a new lawyer, tried to take the judge to court to stall this at least. I know everyone said we'd lose in the end, but at least we'd have had more time. Instead, we tried to get Garrett to sign the papers, and he never signed them." I didn't even want to mention all that had happened, all that had gone wrong.

I said, "We could have done that or we could have hit the road right away and decided to go out with guns blazing. Maybe we could have created a media spectacle, gotten the press and the public on our side. Maybe that would have scared the judge and Garrett away."

She took in a deep breath. "I've thought of those things. Believe me, Jack, I've never once stopped thinking of what we could do. Neither would have worked. I think you know that."

I wasn't so sure. "At least we could have tried."

"We *did* try," she said, her eyes tearing up. "We tried with the help of our best friends, and we did everything we could do. And I want you to stop speculating right now. All I've got in the world is the knowledge that we did all we could."

I sat down heavily at the table. She came over and put her hands on my shoulders, leaving flour handprints.

"And we still don't know why they really want her," I said.

But I had an inkling, a thought so dark I still couldn't share it, despite what Torkleson had said. And when I looked up at my wife, I could see by the emptiness in her eyes and expression that it had crossed her mind as well.

Sunday, November 25

The Day

Twenty-three

AND IT WAS OVER.

Even now the events of that morning are wispy and sharply painful and disconnected in my mind. I remember everything, but I have trouble putting the events in order. Even now, as I recall them, my heart palpitates and my breathing gets shallow and irregular and I find myself reaching out to steady myself.

It was early in the morning when the doorbell rang, I remember that clearly. The sun hadn't yet percolated through the clouds and, with an inch or two of fresh snow on the ground, it seemed ice blue outside. I remember my eyes shooting open and being instantly awake and thinking: *It's them.*

A BLAST OF WINTER as I opened the front door to find Sanders, Morales, the sheriff with his big gut and gunfighter's mustache, plus a female deputy I hadn't seen before. All of them crowded on my front porch wearing identical sheriff's department dark coats, condensation like smoke from their mouths haloing around their heads as they stood there like a small black army from hell. They stamped snow from their boots as they came into the living room.

Outside, parked in my driveway with the motor running, were Judge Moreland and Garrett. Waiting.

Behind me, Melissa came down the stairs holding Angelina. When she saw the cops she said, "Oh my God."

The female deputy was introducing herself, talking in I'm sure what she thought as competent and soothing tones. I didn't hear a word she said.

I can't recall if I lost it as she held out her arms for our daughter or when the sheriff said the Morelands "just want the child. They aren't interested in the boxes."

Something white-hot exploded behind my eyes and I was on them—punching, kicking, gouging, trying to get through them to the door so I could get outside and pull Moreland and Garrett from their car into the snow and kill them with my bare hands. Sanders went down with a surprised look on his face, and his fall took down the sheriff. The female deputy shouted while she unclipped her pepper spray and threatened me with it. Either Sanders or the sheriff clipped me hard in the jaw with a frozen fist and my teeth snapped together and my head snapped back and for a second I was staring at the ceiling. Then my arms were pinned to my sides and my feet left the ground as Morales picked me up in a bear hug and slammed me face-first into the couch. I saw spangles and little else for a moment. There was a knee in my spine and my arms were wrenched back. I heard the *zip* sound of flexcuffs being pulled tight around my wrists.

Through a fog, Melissa said, "I just can't hand her over to you. *I can't perform that act.*"

The female deputy said, "That's all right, I understand. Just put her in that swing, and I'll take her out. You don't have to hand her to me that way."

"I can't. I can't."

"Please, ma'am. We don't want to have to restrain you to take the child. Think of the girl, think of the girl in your arms. We don't want to risk hurting anyone."

Melissa did it.

I heard an animal roar that turned out to be me.

Deputies cried, looked away.

The female deputy wrapped Angelina in blankets she'd brought along and backed toward the door, flanked by Morales and Sanders.

Directly in front of me, inches away, was the hem of the sheriff's coat as he directed them. I could feel the cold emanating from it.

Angelina realized that she was being taken away and she screamed and her chubby hands shot out from beneath the blanket toward Melissa. The deputy quickly covered them back up.

Melissa shrieked and dropped to her knees.

The front door closed as the female deputy went outside with Angelina.

The sheriff said to Sanders, "Call the EMTs."

To me, "Can I trust you to help your wife if I cut you loose?"

"Yes," I said.

Melissa climbed back to her feet with the help of Morales, who was openly blubbering.

The sheriff watched the exchange outside through the front window, then said with grim finality, "It's done."

My cuffs were released, and I rolled off the couch to the floor, scrambling to all fours. Melissa was clutching herself, her eyes wild, her face bone white. I rushed to her.

She collapsed in my arms, but I held her body tight against mine so she wouldn't slide to the floor. I duckwalked with her that way to the couch.

They say that when a person dies, the body suddenly becomes lighter as the soul leaves, that it's been measured. Melissa didn't die, but I remember thinking that her soul had left her because she felt featherlight in my arms.

As I picked up her legs and put them on the couch, I heard the tires of Moreland's car crunch snow as it backed up and left.

A few moments later an EMT van, lights flashing, swung up into the driveway. The EMTs had no doubt been on call just down the street in case they'd be needed. Suddenly, there were more dark-clothed people in our house. They helped Melissa up the stairs into bed. I stood on the landing shell-shocked, my eyes burning. My jaw hurt.

There was a heated discussion as Morales and Sanders told the sheriff they refused to arrest me for assault, and if he insisted on it, he could do it himself, and they'd walk off the job. I heard him say, "Jesus, okay, *okay*. You guys are too damned close to this situation, that's for sure." While he talked, he sucked on a bloody front tooth that had been dislodged during the scuffle.

Sanders said, "You bet your ass we are."

I went upstairs.

Melissa was sedated. Her eyelids fluttered and her grip on my hand relaxed to nothing and her hand dropped away. I looked up at the EMTs and insisted I didn't need anything, didn't want anything.

When I went back downstairs, the sheriff had left. Morales and Sanders stood there with their heads down, staring at their boots.

Sanders said, "I hate my job."

Morales said to me, "Can we leave you? You won't do anything, will you? You won't hurt yourself or anyone else, will you?"

I shook my head no. Which meant *yes*.

And it was over.

THAT EVENING, as the sun set and suspended snow and ice crystals lit up with the cold fire of it and the temperature dropped to minus ten, I checked on Melissa in our dark bedroom. Still sleeping. The EMTs said she would likely be out all night. Nevertheless, I left her a note on the night table in a scrawl I didn't recognize. I wrote:

I'M GOING TO GO GET ANGELINA.
IF I DON'T COME BACK I WANT YOU TO KNOW I
   LOVE YOU WITH ALL OF MY HEART.
LOVE, JACK

I slipped the Colt .45 into the front right pocket of my parka. It was heavy. To balance out the load, I emptied the box of cartridges in the left.

THE COLD SLAPPED ME right in the face. When I breathed in, I could feel ice crystals form in my nose. The snow squeaked beneath my boots. That sound made me grit my teeth, and the hairs on the back of my neck stood up.

I'd forgotten gloves, and the metal of the door handle of my Jeep stung my fingers.

"Where do you think you're going, Jack?"

I froze. Cody.

I turned stiffly. He was walking across my lawn. His car was parked in front of the house, and I hadn't even noticed it.

"I'm going to kill Judge Moreland."

"So it's over? They took her?"

"Where were you? I've been trying to reach you for days."

"I broke my stupid phone on a guy's head."

"I need to go."

"He probably does need killing," Cody said. "But not now. Not by you."

"Stay out of my way, Cody."

He reached out and grabbed my coat sleeve. I wanted nothing

to do with him, had no desire to hear his words. He wasn't there when we needed him, and I had to do this myself.

Cody said, "What I'm saying is that you don't need to go over there right now. You won't get close anyway—the sheriff's got cars in front of Moreland's house just in case you thought of trying something like this. All this will do is land you in jail."

"I don't care."

"You should," said Cody. "Because I've fucking cracked this thing. We're going to be able to get that son of a bitch Moreland *and* get your daughter back."

I blinked.

"That's right," he said.

"How?"

"I've got somebody with me you'll want to meet."

I looked at Cody's car again. There was no one in it. But I noticed something I hadn't seen before. The car was trembling a bit, rocking slightly side to side.

"He's in the trunk," Cody said. "Let's go get him and have a little talk inside."

Twenty-four

INTRODUCE YOURSELF TO MR. McGUANE," Cody said to the disheveled little man he shoved roughly through my front door.

He mumbled something in a tight-lipped way that sounded like "My-wott."

"Where's Melissa?" Cody asked me.

I chinned upstairs. "Sedated."

Cody shook his head. "Bastards. Is she okay?"

"How could she be?"

"*Bastards.*"

"They came this morning. The sheriff and three deputies. The judge and Garrett stayed out in their car and didn't even come in."

My-wott stood there, watching us go back and forth as if he were observing a tennis match. By his blank expression I could tell he had no idea what we were talking about.

"Sit," Cody said to My-wott, indicating the couch. The little man shuffled over to it stiff-legged and sat down. I could see now why he couldn't talk and could barely move: He was freezing. His skin was sallow. His teeth were chattering so hard it sounded like popcorn popping. My-wott was thin, stooped, mousy. I guessed his build at five-four, 130. He had badly cut brown hair, thick horn-rimmed glasses, no chin but a prominent Adam's apple, and his face was a moonscape of old acne scars. He had furtive, darting eyes and a manner to him that was weak and annoying. I felt sorry for him but wanted to hit him at the same time. He wore a red-checked plaid shirt, baggy jeans, and Crocs shoes. His arms shot out when he sat down, and I noted a massive gold Rolex on his wrist that just didn't go with the rest of him. It looked like it weighed two pounds.

My-wott had a nasty-looking bruise right in the middle of a small bald spot on the back of his head. Cody saw me looking at it, and said, "That's how I broke my damn phone."

Cody dragged two chairs from the kitchen and placed them in front of him. He spun his around and straddled it, placing his arms on the top of the backrest. His eyes were gleaming, and his mouth was set in a sarcastic snarl. "I said, introduce yourself to Mr. McGuane." To me: "Jack, have a seat."

The little man looked down at his Crocs. His legs shook violently.

"Speak the fuck up," Cody said, and slapped him sharply on his face. I glared at Cody, who ignored me.

"Wyatt," the man said.

"Wyatt what?" Cody barked.

"Wyatt Henkel."

"And where are you from, Wyatt Henkel?"

"You mean now, or where I was born?"

Cody slapped him again.

"Jesus, Cody," I said.

Cody looked at me. "When you hear what he's going to say, you're going to want to do more than slap him."

"Still," I said.

"I was born in Greeley, Colorado," Henkel said, forcing the

words out through his chattering teeth. "I live now in Las Cruces, New Mexico."

"Good," Cody said. "Now tell Mr. McGuane why you're here. Why your telephone number was on Brian Eastman's call log from his cell phone."

Henkel looked away from Cody and stared at our gas fireplace, which I'd turned off a few minutes before as I left the house.

"I'm freezing to death," Henkel said, turning to me. "I've been in that trunk for eight hours."

"Seven hours, tops," Cody said. "Quit whining."

I got up and walked over to the fireplace to turn it on.

Cody said, "No—keep it off."

"Look at him," I said.

"Fuck him," Cody said. "We'll turn on the fireplace once he starts talking." To Henkel, Cody said, "*Fuck you.* Got that?"

Henkel avoided meeting his eyes.

To me, Cody said, "I noticed some weight in your coat pockets. Are you carrying?"

"Yes."

"Good. Get that gun out of your pocket. This is your grandpa's Colt .45 Peacemaker, right?"

I drew it out. It was heavy and cold, and it looked like a blunt instrument in my hand.

Cody said, "Cock it and put the muzzle against Wyatt Henkel's forehead. If he tells a lie, I'll ask you to pull the trigger. Don't worry about his brains splashing all over the wall because I don't think he has any. And don't worry about the body afterward, either. I'll just take it up to where I buried Uncle Jeter. It's a perfect place nobody will ever look. Maybe the coyotes will dig up their bones in 2025, but by then who gives a shit?"

Cody defused my look of horror with a barely perceptible wink that Henkel couldn't see because his head was still down. *Okay,* I nodded. *Now I get it.*

Henkel's head came up slowly. He was terrified.

I cocked the hammer and the cylinder rotated and I put the muzzle above his eyebrow.

Cody shifted in his chair and pulled his departmental .40 Glock semiauto. He held it loosely in his hand. "In case he misses," Cody said to Henkel.

"Let's start again," Cody said to Henkel. "State your occupation."

Henkel's voice was high and reedy. "I'm a janitor at Las Cruces High School."

"A janitor, eh?"

"Yes, sir."

"Yes, I like that. Call me 'sir.' And call Mr. McGuane here 'sir' as well. Now tell me how long you've had your job."

"Seven years."

"What is your salary?"

"I make $26,000. It's considered part-time."

"Interesting," Cody said. "You pull down 26K, but you live on five acres and you have two new vehicles. Is that correct?"

Henkel tried to swallow, and his Adam's apple bobbed up and down. "Yes," he said.

"And you have that big piece of gold on your wrist. Is it a fake? One of those Taiwanese knockoffs?"

"It's real," he said.

"And that Escalade you drive—was it stolen?"

"No, sir."

"You live well for a part-time janitor, don't you, Wyatt?"

"Not as well as some, but I do all right." His voice had gained some confidence. He was warming up both literally and figuratively. Which angered Cody.

"Shoot him," he said.

I pushed the gun harder into Henkel's brow.

"No!" he cried, his eyes round.

"Then answer me straight," Cody said. Cody even scared me.

"Okay," said Henkel.

"You weren't always a janitor, where you?"

"No."

"What other jobs have you held?"

"A lot of 'em. I'm not very smart, I guess." Although Cody was asking the questions, Henkel was answering them to me. Probably because despite my gun, Cody scared him more. "I do my best, but people just don't like me. No one's ever really liked me."

Said Cody, "I can see why. Again, what jobs have you had in your life?"

Henkel's eyes rolled up as if trying to remember. "Retail, mostly. Wal-Mart, Target, Pier One. I moved around a lot between New Mexico and Colorado."

"You didn't mention that one-hour photo place you used to work at," Cody said. "You know, that one in Canon City, Colorado."

"Oh, that one," Henkel said, his face getting even whiter. Cody'd struck a nerve.

"Tell Mr. McGuane when you worked there."

He thought for a second. "It was 2001."

"Before everybody went digital," Cody said. "Back at the end of the film-and-print days."

"Yes. I don't think that shop is even there anymore."

"Royal Gorge is outside of Canon City, right?"

"Yes."

"That's quite a spectacular place, isn't it?" Cody asked. "Lots of tourists go there to see it and walk across the footbridge and look down at the Arkansas River. There's even a state park there, right?"

I tried not to look at Cody to ask him where the hell this was going.

Henkel paused, then said, "Yes."

"In 2001, the caretaker of the state park brought in some film to have developed at your shop. Do you remember that?"

Henkel tried to swallow again but couldn't.

"Could I have a glass of water?" he asked me.

"You can have a bullet in your head," Cody said. "Again, do you remember when the caretaker of the state park brought some film in to you?"

"Yes."

"He brought in lots of film to be developed, didn't he?"

"Yes."

"You're not supposed to look at the prints that you develop, are you? And the way the equipment worked, there was no reason even to see them. The processor was automatic, right? The only time you even touched the prints was when you put them in the envelope for the customer, right?"

"That was the policy."

"But in this case you looked, didn't you, Wyatt?"

His voice was a croak. "I looked." As he said it his eyes darted to Cody and back to me.

"What was on the prints, Wyatt?"

"Nature stuff, mostly. But there were a lot of pictures of children with their families. The families were camping or hiking."

"Were photos of children pretty much all the customer took?"

"Yes."

Cody shot me a look. I still didn't know what the point was.

"And why did you run a second set of prints to keep for yourself?"

Henkel briefly closed his eyes.

"Wyatt?"

"There were four pictures I wanted to keep," he said.

Cody leaned back and reached into his coat with his free hand and brought out a manila envelope. "Are these the four photos you kept, Wyatt?"

"You know they are."

Cody handed the envelope to me.

310

Cody said, "Who has the originals and the negatives?"

"The customer."

Cody smiled sarcastically. "And who is the customer, Wyatt?"

"Aubrey Coates. He was the park caretaker at the time."

I felt an electric bolt shoot through my chest, and I almost pulled the trigger accidentally. Suddenly, it was as if all around me, for three weeks, there were dozens of sheets of clear plastic, each with a brush of color and several errant squiggles. Individually, none of the sheets made sense. But when they were placed one upon the other, a whole image emerged. It was as if everything we had learned and done over the last three weeks made horrifying sense.

I lowered the pistol and opened the envelope, knowing what I would find.

Brian was right. There *were* photos.

The first was of a young family of three hiking along a narrow trail. There was a rock wall behind them so it was obviously in a canyon—Royal Gorge Canyon. The photo was grainy, and there was a pine twig in the bottom corner of it, indicating to me that the shot was taken at a great distance, and the photographer was hiding in a stand of trees. The woman—plain, heavy, obviously pregnant—was in the lead. A boy of twelve or thirteen was last. It took me a moment to recognize him as a young Garrett. The man in the middle was John Moreland.

The second photo was slightly blurred, but it was obvious that Moreland was tugging on his wife's arm, and she was reaching out wildly to steady herself. Garrett stood in sharp focus, looking on with what looked like intense interest.

In the third photo, Dorrie Pence Moreland, the ultradevout Catholic homely homebody who was a drag on her husband's social and political climb and who was bringing another child into the world to compete with her monomaniacal and psychopathic first-born son, could be seen cartwheeling through the sky, her long black hair flying behind her like flames.

In the fourth, Garrett prepared to deliver the *coup de grace* with the large rock he held over his head to the broken body of his mother while his father looked on approvingly.

I went through the photos a second time, then a third.

"My God," I said. "So Coates owns the judge."

"That would be correct," Cody said.

"Which is why he was bulletproof."

"Bingo."

"So he's been blackmailing him all these years?"

Cody nodded his head and raised his Glock, pointing it at Wyatt Henkel's head. "Sort of. Tell him, Wyatt."

If possible, Henkel suddenly looked even smaller and more pathetic.

"It was me who blackmailed the judge," Henkel said. "I told him I had the pictures. I put them on a copy machine and sent a copy to him to prove it. So for years he's been paying up."

Cody said, "Hence the vehicles, the large spread, the Rolex. But you lied to the judge, didn't you, Wyatt? You told him you had the negatives."

Henkel nodded.

Cody said, "So when Brian Eastman started putting word out among all of his acquaintances that he was searching the country for someone who had some kind of photos on Judge Moreland, you contacted the judge again, right?"

"Yes."

"To tell him the price would be going up or you'd sell the photos to Brian, right?"

"Right."

Strangely, Henkel was warming to the revelations. It was obvious he was proud of himself. I really did want to shoot him, but not before I'd heard everything.

Cody said to me, "I'm speculating now, but it's speculation based on Henkel's role in this. When I was investigating Coates, I always wondered why Coates quit working at state parks five years ago and switched exclusively to campgrounds on federal land. It was just one of those little things that stuck out and didn't make sense to me. Now it makes sense. Coates's job switch corresponds with when Moreland was named to the federal bench. Henkel here had the photos and wanted money from the judge—and got it. Coates didn't want money—he needed security. Coates knew someday he'd get caught so he contacted Moreland and told him about his hole card. He wanted to make sure he was tried in a federal courtroom because he knew who the judge would be. Another thing: There are *nine* district court judges. Coates must have somehow made it known to Moreland that someday he might show up in his court-room and that he'd need a favor. So how did Moreland make sure he'd be the presiding judge if this unknown blackmailer got hauled before him? He worked the system from the inside, and made sure he'd be the judge for serious crimes committed on federal land. Moreland wanted to be in control of the situation for his own sake in case the second blackmailer ever needed that favor. That's why Coates was bulletproof."

"Son of a bitch," I said. Then: "Hold it. Why would Coates risk taking his film to Henkel? Wouldn't Coates be worried that Henkel or somebody would see the shots of the murder?"

"I can answer that," Henkel said. "I don't think at the time he realized what he had. Those photos are blown up, that's why they're so grainy. In the originals, the people look like ants against that wall. I think he may have gotten a shot of her falling, but I don't think he knew that the judge pushed her. I don't think he knew what he had until he got home and looked closely at the prints."

"And he never came after you?" I asked, skeptical.

He smiled for the first time. Rotten yellow stubs for teeth. "I was long gone if he ever did. I took those blowups and kept them with me when I moved from place to place, job to job. I think he tried to find me a couple of times. Once a man showed up at my store in Salida asking about me. I heard it from the other room and walked out the side door and never looked back. Another time I came home after work in Durango and saw some kids who looked like Mexican gangsters parked in front of my apartment building. I just drove right by and all the way to New Mexico."

Cody nodded, as if another piece of the puzzle had just fit into place. "So when you left the message about Brian Eastman, did the judge call you back?"

"No. It was the judge's son, Garrett. He's the boy in the pictures—the one with the rock."

"Right. And what did Garrett say?"

"You're going to kill me, aren't you?" Henkel asked us.

Cody screwed up his face. "I'm at ninety percent yes. But there's ten percent to play with, Wyatt. You need to convince me you're worth that ten percent by telling me the truth."

I could see Henkel thinking, running through the arguments. Finally, he said, "Garrett said they'd pay more but only if I called Eastman and told him I had the photos. I talked to him, and he agreed to meet me here in Denver. Garrett gave me the directions to give to Eastman, but he told me not to go. I guess Garrett met him instead."

I shot him.

The explosion was deafening. I don't know how Melissa slept through it, but she did. And Henkel was writhing on my couch, clutching his shoulder where the bullet hit, smearing bright red blood all over the fabric.

Cody wrenched the .45 out of my hand before I could cock it and finish Henkel off.

"For Christ's sake, Jack!" Cody yelled. "We're not done with him yet!"

"I am," I said, but what I'd just done shocked me.

Henkel grunted and moaned.

Cody grabbed him by the hair and sat him back up.

"Talk fast," Cody said, "and maybe you'll get to live."

"It hurts," Henkel said through bared teeth.

"It's gonna hurt a lot more!"

"I'm going to bleed to death."

"Maybe."

Cody leaned over him, his face inches away.

"As far as you knew, Coates never contacted the judge again until recently, correct?"

"As far as I know," Henkel said.

Cody looked to me, nodding. "When Coates found out I was closing in on him, he must have contacted the judge and reminded him what he had all these years. Imagine Moreland's surprise when he found out that one of the two people who knew about Dorrie's murder was the very pedophile we were closing in on. Moreland had the search and arrest warrants on his desk, of course, so he tipped Coates we were coming. That's how Coates knew to destroy everything ahead of time. And he made sure Coates walked."

A million thoughts were going through my mind. I tried to put them into some kind of order.

"But Cody," I said, "Coates walked because of what *you* did."

I instantly regretted saying it, and Cody's eyes flashed with pure rage.

"I'm sorry," I said. "But . . ."

Cody said, "Up until tonight there has always been one thing about that trial I couldn't figure out, and that was how Ludik knew everything there was to know about my movements after we arrested Coates. I mean, Ludik's smart, but he's not *that* smart. Somebody tipped him, and I think it was Moreland. He didn't do it with a phone call or anything that obvious, I'm sure. He probably told some court gossip something like, 'I just hope this is a solid case because there seems to be some real chain-of-evidence problems with it'— something like that. He probably heard about me through the DA or some blabbermouth cop. So Moreland put it out there so Ludik would hear it thirdhand and investigate. I'm not saying I didn't fuck up, Jack—I did. But Moreland set the whole clusterfuck in motion—from tipping Coates to the search warrant to suggesting to the defense they take a second look at the chain-of-evidence list."

It made sense.

Cody turned from me and shoved his Glock into Henkel's nose. His voice was flat. "When I came to your house in New Mexico, you were packing up your car. Where were you planning to go?"

Henkel said, "We were going to do the exchange."

"What are you talking about?"

"There was going to be an exchange. A big meeting, where everybody got what they wanted."

Cody slapped him again, and Henkel winced. The cushions were getting dark with lost blood. I could smell it, and it was sharp and metallic and it made me want to gag.

Henkel was fading. His eyelids were starting to drop.

"WHAT EXCHANGE?" Cody screamed.

"The judge was going to get all the photos and the negatives from Coates and me once and for all," Henkel said. "I was going to get my big payoff from the judge. We were going to meet at Coates's place up in the mountains tomorrow morning."

Cody said, "What was Coates going to get?"

Henkel coughed and nearly passed out. He said, "What he said he always wanted—his own little girl."

And at that moment I realized who had sent the photo of Angelina to his associate Malcolm Harris in London—Aubrey Coates. I recalled Moreland taking that photo the morning they came to visit when he went upstairs with Melissa. It was the reason he was so insistent that he see her, and the reason he asked Melissa to turn her over for a better look.

Monday, November 26
The Day After

Twenty-five

THERE WAS SNOW FALLING on I-70 that night as we drove to Desolation Canyon. It had started snowing around midnight and gotten progressively worse. The only vehicles our four-car caravan encountered on the two-hour drive from Denver were snowplows with yellow wigwag lights flashing and the occasional four-wheel-drive pickup. My nerves were shot, and I had trouble keeping coffee down. Cody had made three calls after dropping Henkel in a heap outside the emergency-room doors of Denver General: Sanders, Morales, and Torkleson. Torkleson had responded with a crime scene tech and a team of four SWAT officers in heavy black clothing. Morales and Sanders showed up in Morales's jacked-up four-wheel-drive pickup. Morales brought his wife along to watch over Melissa. Torkleson drove the lead vehicle, with Cody in the passenger seat and me in the backseat.

A panicked thought hit me. "What if they won't do the exchange without Henkel?" *Jesus,* I thought again, *I never should have shot him.*

"Good thinking," Torkleson said, and plucked his mike from the cradle on the dashboard. "I'm switching over to a nonpublic channel," he said as he called the state highway patrol. Locating a trooper he knew, Torkleson persuaded the man to put out a false report about a fiery head-on collision near the New Mexico border, and to identify one of the fatalities as a man named Wyatt Henkel. When the trooper agreed, Torkleson said to Cody and me, "We know Coates listens to police scanners, and if he hears that report, I'm sure he'll relay the info to the judge. That'll explain why he isn't there."

"You're the man," Cody said to Torkleson. "Both Coates and the judge will be happy to hear that Henkel—and his photos—are cooked."

I TRIED to sort out what we'd learned as we drove. Cody seemed to be doing the same thing.

I asked, "How did Coates learn about Angelina in order to pressure the judge for her?"

"I'd wondered that myself," Cody said. "Until I checked on the federal jail roster before the trial and found out that Coates shared a cell for two weeks with a slimeball named José Medina, who was in for trafficking. Medina is a big-shot Sur-13 gangster and a known associate of Garrett's. Garrett probably mentioned to Medina he had this adoption agency hounding him—bragged about it, most likely—and Coates overheard Medina talking about it. That's the kind of thing Coates would pick up on, especially since he had his deal going with the judge already. So he doubled down on his demands of the judge because Moreland had nothing to bargain with: the negatives and photos *and* a little girl of his own in exchange for an acquittal."

"It makes me sick," I said.

"No shit," Cody said. "What makes me even sicker is that the judge would go along. Or appear to go along."

"So why did Moreland and Garrett kill Dorrie?" I asked, guessing the answer.

"We'll probably never get a confession out of either of them," Cody said. "But I'm thinking Dorrie couldn't live with her guilt any longer for providing an alibi for John on the night John's parents were run off the road. The more she got to know him, the more she was *convinced* he'd done it—well, it was eating her up inside. She was going to church more, right? Pouring her heart out to God that she was married to a man who'd killed his own parents, and she'd provided the alibi. Maybe she asked John outright if he did it, or maybe he just guessed she wanted to tell somebody. Either way, John knew he had to get rid of her. Plus, he was probably already putting the hardwood to Kellie. So, if you're John Moreland, you have a heavy guilt-ridden wallflower who can bring you down on the one hand and a blond knockout with money on the other. Easy choice for John."

"But why did Garrett finish her off?"

"Because Garrett is a sick, twisted, evil little fuck," Cody said. "Your instincts were right about him. Plus, by helping his dad with the crime, Garrett knew he'd always have a bargaining chip and something to hold over his dad's head. In a way, killing Dorrie set Garrett free."

"And John knew what Garrett was from an early age," I said. "Imagine knowing your son is like that? And just living with it and covering up for him whenever possible. And the judge had to cover up for his son, or Garrett might confess what the both of them had done."

I said, "Jim Doogan told me something at Brian's funeral about men like Moreland. He said once a man likes that gets his eyes on a prize—in this case the U.S. Supreme Court—every move he makes is in preparation for it. I didn't realize what Doogan was saying at the time, and I don't think he did, either. But if you're John Moreland, and you want to be a Supreme, how can you even consider the possibility if your only son is a gangster?"

"Good question," Cody said. "How?"

"You mitigate the situation," I said. "You take in your bad son's illegitimate child and raise her as your own. You show the world that even though your bad-seed son has no responsibility, you do. You clean up the best you can for your son's indiscretion. You turn a negative into a positive. You also know that it's only a matter of time before your crazy-ass son goes down, and you don't have to worry about him anymore. It could have easily happened at the Appaloosa Club the other night. And when it does, you breathe a sigh of relief and go on."

Cody turned and smiled. I could see his teeth in the dark. "You might make a good detective after all, Jack. But there's something wrong with your theory."

"What?"

"Why would John hand over the child to a known pedophile? Aren't people going to find out?"

I thought about that for a while. Then it hit me hard. "Moreland is clever," I said. "Clever enough to figure out a way for Angelina to *disappear* after a short while, maybe even to stage a disappearance or a kidnapping. I could see him making a tearful plea on television to the kidnappers, turning Angelina into a new Lindbergh baby *who is never found*. He'd be a hell of a sympathetic figure. And someday, if a member of the Senate Judiciary Committee has the gall to question him about taking the child from our home all those years ago, he says he felt horrible about it and did all he could to help the young couple adopt another child, but not nearly as horrible as he feels about her fate at the hand of kidnappers and what an outrageous thing to ask! He comes off looking like a tragic saint."

Torkleson whistled, and said, "For the love of Pete."

"Now you're thinking like a Moreland, Jack," Cody said. "Ten steps ahead."

CODY KNEW THE LAYOUT and geography of the canyon because he had planned the raid on Coates months before, but he complained that it looked different in the dark and covered by snow. There was plenty of bitching when he said the only way to move in on the trailer was from behind it on foot because there was only one road into the campground, and we didn't want Coates to see us coming. So we parked on the shoulder of a gravel road on the other side of the mountain from the campground and plunged into the forest to climb. The snow was fluffy and knee deep. There was no wind at all, so the pine boughs sported three or four inches of snow looking like foam on the top of a beer mug. It was impossible to climb through the thick trees without hitting boughs and dumping snow down our necks. We all wore high-topped winter boots. The beams from our headlamps flew around in the trees as we climbed, and it was hallucinogenic, so I tried to keep my head down and concentrate on the trail in front of me. The SWAT guys carried automatic weapons with scopes, and Morales and Sanders had brought their hunting rifles. The .45 was in my parka pocket.

I was sweating hard by the time we reached the top, but my thoughts of Angelina and Melissa and Coates and Moreland propelled me. I finally stopped throwing up when there was nothing left in my stomach.

As we grunted and cursed our way down the other side of the mountain toward Desolation Canyon Campground, the eastern sky started to lighten into a dull, creamy gray. I doubted we would see the sun itself.

CODY GATHERED EVERYONE when it got light enough to see without headlamps. From where I stood, I could see a big opening below me and ahead of me: the empty campground. There were picnic tables stacked high with snow, and steel cooking grates mounted on metal posts. The roads to and from the individual campsites were untracked except from mule deer, as was the access road from the highway. Sheer canyon walls rose on either side, which made it darker than it should be at seven in the morning.

We all stood in the trees breathing hard, flushed from the climb and the descent. Billows of condensation rose from our labored breathing. One good thing about the falling snow was it muffled sounds.

Cody bent over and pointed out Coates's trailer. We could barely see the top of it through the trees a quarter of a mile away. As I'd heard about in the courtroom that day, the aluminum roof bristled with antennae and both satellite television and Internet-access dishes.

Cody and Torkleson debated the approach, and they decided to flank the park with two SWAT officers on each side of the trailer. Torkleson told his men to stay in the trees with clear shooting lanes. Cody reminded them the trailer had a back door as well.

Sanders and Morales agreed to split up, each going with two SWAT officers. Torkleson, Cody, the tech guy with his video camera, and I would move straight down the middle of the trees toward the back of the trailer, where Torkleson would establish a command post to direct traffic.

"Turn your radios down and put your earpieces in," Torkleson told his men. "*Communicate.* Report what you see so we all know. This exchange is supposed to happen at nine, so we have an hour and a half to wait."

"To freeze to death," one of the officers said sourly.

"To save a little girl and put three monsters away," Cody said.

As the men checked their weapons and equipment before splitting off into teams, I thanked each one of them for coming and I shook their hands. I hugged Morales and Sanders, and they hugged me back.

"We're glad we could make it," Sanders said. "We've got to square this thing."

"We'll get her back," Morales said, fire in his eyes.

WE FOUND a small clearing 150 yards from Coates's trailer and stamped the snow down with our boots. It gave us something to do, and the work kept me warm. We were on a steep hillside and could see out over the top of the trailer and the park and the access road. There was a thick U of four-foot-high juniper between us and the trailer to hide behind. Every few minutes Cody would raise his binoculars and study the trailer, watching for movement.

To me, Cody whispered, "I wish we could just go down there and cap the guy, believe me. But we have to do it this way, Jack." He looked up to make sure Torkleson was far enough away that he couldn't hear, and said, "You and I are dirty. We've got to get all these guys involved and let them make the arrest and the case. My name's got to be out of it, and so does yours. Henkel will make the case for them when he testifies. I wish you hadn't have shot him."

"Me too," I whispered back. "Something snapped inside."

"It happens." Cody grinned. I noted the frost on his eyebrows and three-day length of beard.

AT 8:45 we saw headlights coming down the access road into the park.

I couldn't hear what the SWAT team was saying to Torkleson through his earpiece, but Torkleson said, "Yes, we see it. Can anyone get the make?"

He listened, nodded, and turned to us. "A yellow H3 Hummer."

"Garrett's car," I said.

"Showtime," said Cody.

THE H3 WAS MOVING very slowly. It wasn't the snow that was holding it up but caution by the driver. I borrowed Cody's binoculars and tried to see who was inside. The smoked glass made it difficult, but I thought I saw the silhouettes of two heads.

"I still don't get Garrett," I whispered to Cody. "What is it with him? I can't figure him out."

"Psychopath," Cody said. "We may never understand. The kid crushed his mother's head in with a rock while his dad looked on. This is one gene pool that needs to be drained for good."

Realizing the implication of that statement, he said, "Jack, I'm sorry. I didn't mean Angelina, for Christ's sake."

I shook my head. "She's *our* daughter, Cody. She has nothing to do with Garrett."

But I can't lie and say what Cody suggested didn't shake me to my core.

GARRETT'S SUV SLOWED to a stop in front of the trailer. It was close enough I could hear the ratcheting sound of the emergency brake being pulled. I still couldn't see who was inside. They kept it running, and the headlights were still on. If Coates was inside he would have to know they had arrived.

The passenger door opened, and the dome light inside the H3 went on. I raised the binoculars. Garrett driving, the judge in the passenger seat. And between them, covered in blankets in the backseat in a car seat, was Angelina.

My heart filled my mouth. "Screw this! *We've got to go get her.*"

Cody reached out and put a gloved hand on my arm. "Not yet, Jack. At this point they might be able to come up with some kind of lie that explains why they're here. Remember who we're dealing with, Jack. We've got a judge with connections and a known pedophile who has never been to prison. They both know how to work the system. We've got to let this play out so we can get them *cold.*"

The crime-scene tech had set up a tripod and leaned into his camera eyepiece.

"Got 'em?" Torkleson asked.

"Perfect," the tech said.

Torkleson bent his head to the side, listening to his earpiece.

"Coates just opened the front door," he whispered.

The judge climbed out of the vehicle.

"He's having a stare-down with the judge," Torkleson reported. We couldn't see Coates yet because his trailer blocked our view, but I could follow his movements by watching the judge's eyes through my binoculars. Finally, the judge motioned toward the trailer and pointed at his car.

We couldn't see Coates until he approached the H3. He was lightly dressed in some kind of dark one-piece overall suit, and he wore a fur cap. When he bent over to look into the backseat, I could see him rub his hands together and hear him squeal with delight— an inhuman sound that made a shiver rocket up my spine and lodge at the base of my skull. He started to move closer to the car when Moreland blocked him.

"Kill them," I said.

"Wait," Cody cautioned again. "They still haven't done anything yet."

"Cody," my voice rose, "that's my *daughter* down there."

Torkleson looked away, concentrating on what he was hearing through his earpiece. "They're arguing about terms," he said. "The judge doesn't want to hand over the baby before he gets the photos and the negatives."

I could see the judge gesturing at Coates, and Coates crossing his arms and shaking his head. The words got heated, and I could hear shouting but couldn't make out what was being said.

At last, the judge nodded and turned to the car and barked something at Garrett, who was still behind the wheel. Garrett's door flew open, and the boy jumped out into the snow. He walked around the back of the H3 and opened the rear door and leaned in to unbuckle the car seat.

"Don't fucking touch her," I said.

"I can't believe he brought her," Cody mumbled.

Garrett freed the seat and swung the carry handle up. With one hand, he carried the seat away from the car and placed it in the snow between the judge and Coates. I raised the binoculars to my eyes so hard the eyepieces hit me in the forehead. I focused in on the car seat. She was covered in the same blanket the deputy had brought with her to our house. I couldn't see her face. I imagined that her dark eyes glistened and her mouth was screwed up and she would begin to cry, not knowing where she was.

"Behold, the exchange," Cody said, as Coates reached into his clothing and withdrew an envelope. He squatted and stuck it into the snow near the car seat.

"Hold it," I said, my panic rising. "*There's something screwy here. It's the wrong kind of seat,*" I said, and felt Cody and Torkleson look at me, puzzled. "I've helped her in and out of car seats so many times I know for a fact that Angelina outgrew an infant seat like that months ago."

I swung the binoculars over to Garrett. He had walked back to his car and was leaning against the grille, watching both men, smiling at how childish they looked negotiating terms.

The judge grabbed the envelope and tore it open. He rifled through what was inside several times. When Coates made a move to reach for the car seat, the judge warned him off until he was through. Apparently satisfied after a few moments, he nodded to Coates, who took a step forward to pick her up. I saw the judge mouth "no" and lift it himself to hand it over.

Then the judge raised the seat with one hand, using the other to tuck the blankets around Angelina. As Coates reached for the seat with a leer on his face, the judge seemed to shove it at him, one hand on the handle and the other in the blankets. Suddenly, the back of the seat blew open and there was a sharp *pop* and the snow from a thousand pine boughs across the face of the mountain dropped to the earth in a smoky white cascade.

Coates fell back, his arms outstretched.

Ripping out his earpiece, Torkleson screamed into his handheld, "Who the fuck did that?"

"Not me," Morales shouted. "It wasn't one of us, I don't think."

Cody and I flew through the brush we'd been hiding behind toward the trailer. A pine branch slapped me in the face and took my hat, and we were scrambling down the hillside in the deep snow. I could see two officers emerging from the trees on the right side of the trailer, hollering to Garrett and the judge to freeze.

Running, falling, a mouthful of snow and pine needles, back on my feet, Cody in front of me with his gun drawn.

Shouting from everywhere.

We ran around from the back of the trailer to where the judge and Garrett stood. The cops from both sides of the canyon were out of the trees now; so were Sanders and Morales, with their hunting rifles. The H3 and the father and son were surrounded.

Judge Moreland saw cops on both sides of him and raised the car seat in front of him so if anyone took a shot at him it would need to pass through it to hit him. His expression wasn't scared, or angry, but calculating.

"Thank God you got here, Officers," the judge said in the tone he used from the bench. "My son and I have a permit and we were up here trying to find a good Christmas tree, but we got lost. I realized we'd stumbled on Aubrey Coates . . ." And then he noticed Cody and me and he lost his train of thought and his ridiculous words tailed off.

I drew the .45, cocked it, and said, "Hand over that car seat and the gun in it or I'll kill you a thousand times."

I could see in his face that he was considering keeping it, using the seat as a shield.

"Drop the seat and the gun and hand over the negatives, Judge," Cody said, his weapon down along his thigh. "We've got Wyatt Henkel singing like a bird, and we've got the exchange on tape. You're fucked, so cooperate or die."

"Maybe you didn't hear me," the judge said, glaring at Cody and me with the righteousness of a true liar, "my son and I were going to cut down a Christmas tree . . ."

Cody laughed at him. "You don't understand, Judge. The camera's off. What happens now is your word against eight officers of the law and the father of the child you took."

That's when Coates moaned and thrashed in the snow.

"Son of a bitch," Cody said, wheeling. "I thought he was dead." And he raised the Glock and fired four times point-blank into Coates, who went still. That froze everyone. Cody dug into his parka and pulled out a nondescript revolver and flipped it at the body.

"This is why I always carry a throw-down," he said to Moreland.

The judge looked to Torkleson, who huffed and puffed his way from around the back of the trailer. "Aren't you going to arrest him? Didn't you all just see what he did?"

No one said a word. The judge lowered the smoking car seat into the snow. The blankets fell away to reveal a life-size baby doll. The large-caliber revolver lay across the doll's thighs.

Cody squared off, facing the judge. "Who's next? You," he said, then nodding toward Garrett, "or the fruit of your loins?"

Out of the corner of my eye I saw Garrett bolt for his father's gun. Before any of the cops could tackle him, I raised the .45 and shot him. I tried for his chest, but I hit him in the stomach, and he doubled over and sat back in the snow, holding his belly.

"Freeze," I said.

"You're supposed to do that the other way around," Cody said.

"I'm not a cop."

Garrett burned two holes in me with hate-filled eyes. "Aw, you don't really want her," he said. "She comes from me and him, don't forget. She's missing the same part I am. You'll see."

I shot him in the head, and he flopped back, his blood steaming and stinking and staining the snow. In my mind I severed the connection between Garrett Moreland and Angelina. Forever.

Torkleson stepped between the judge and me, and said, "That'll be enough, gentlemen." He gently took the gun out of my hand and slipped it into his jacket pocket. From the other pocket he drew a nickel-plated semiauto and tossed it at Garrett's body. To the judge, Torkleson said, "Too bad. He had such promise. He could have been a great gangster."

To his men and Deputies Sanders and Morales, he said, "We all saw the same thing, right, Officers? Both Coates and the boy here pulled weapons and were killed. And we'll all testify to that, my brothers?"

One by one everyone agreed. Morales wept with joy and dropped to his knees. Sanders stepped over and put a gloved hand on his partner's shoulder.

"But that's not true," Moreland cried. "I killed a known pedophile in self-defense! You all saw that, right?"

"Ha," Cody said, picking up the revolver from the car seat and sticking it into his belt. "I was wondering where my lost piece was. Now I've found it."

Canon City, Colorado

Tuesday, November 18

A Year After

Twenty-six

I WAS CONVICTED OF AGGRAVATED Assault with a Deadly Weapon for shooting Wyatt Henkel and was sentenced to one to three years in the Colorado State Penitentiary in, of all places, Canon City. The original charge had been for a class two felony, which could have been eight to twenty-four years, but the DA was sympathetic and knocked it down to a class five. The judge, also sympathetic, had no problem with that. When he sentenced me I said, "Thank you, Your Honor," but not because of the reduction. I said thank you because I deserved to go to prison, and I wouldn't have been able to live with myself for the things I'd done unless I did. I was also thankful that the worst of my actions were never discovered by the DA.

The judge said he'd write a letter to the parole board urging early release, but he said I should be prepared to serve a year. How does one prepare for that?

SO NOW I WEAR an orange jumpsuit and laceless boat shoes and every article of clothing I have is stenciled with CDOC—COLORADO DEPARTMENT OF CORRECTIONS.

The food is tolerable, but the scenery outside—when I can see it—is pretty nice. My Rocky Mountains are still there, although they're the southern Colorado version, and they aren't snowcapped. But they're with me, always, to the west, framing my days and nights and stretching all the way to Montana.

I'm in the general population. The guards protect me because they, like the judge and DA, are sympathetic. I've never asked them for favors, but they give them. I have my own cell with a bed, a washstand and a toilet, books, and this laptop computer. There are books in the library and decent medical care. I'm pleasant but not friendly with all the rest of the population. The only time I see the truly dangerous inmates is across the room at mealtimes.

YES, I'VE SEEN JOHN Moreland. Five times, to be exact. He saw me too, even though he pretended he didn't. Moreland wears a white jumpsuit, meaning he's on death row. All of us avoid the guys in white, and the corrections officers segregate them from us.

The judge was convicted in the trial some of you followed on truTV and the cable channels. Despite his investment in household names like Bertram Ludik as his defense attorneys and his earnest testimony—where he claimed both Aubrey Coates and his son Garrett were murdered in cold blood during a botched raid on the pedophile's residence that he mistakenly blundered into while looking for a perfect Christmas tree—the jury convicted him for murder in the first degree for killing Dorrie. Those four photos I first saw in my living room are among the most recognized images in America among those who follow murder trials, I've read. They were even printed in *People* magazine. Despite the photos and Henkel's testimony, John

Moreland has never admitted to either the murder of his parents or of his wife. He claims he was railroaded by rogue cops. He also insists it was he who shot Aubrey Coates, not the police.

During the trial, all of the officers who were there in Desolation Canyon that morning contradicted his allegation. One by one they told a version of events different from Moreland's. Why?

Because Cody, perhaps inspired by the judge himself, was thinking ahead. He knew that in prison, the lowest of the low was a child molester—considered even worse than a snitch. It was open season on child molesters, and even the guards looked the other way. In this case, the inmate was a judge who tried to aid a molester by letting him walk. Moreland is an ADSEG—Administrative Segregation. Despite that designation, I've heard he's been attacked several times, beaten, raped, and stabbed. I wonder if Dorrie's ghost approves. Maybe she has enough faith to forgive him. But I don't.

I sent him a note, via the guards. It read: I'M GETTING OUT IN A YEAR. HOW ABOUT YOU? MELISSA SENDS HER RE-GARDS.

There was no reply.

KELLIE MORELAND WAS INVESTIGATED and quickly cleared of being an accessory to her husband and her evil stepson's crimes. She claimed she was shocked and angry when John showed up that Sunday with a nine-month-old and announced she was now a part of their family. Kellie told police she accused him of ruining her life and in a quote compared to Butterfly McQueen in *Gone with the Wind,* said, "I know nothing about toddlers. Nothing." She said she fed Angelina grapes and toast and cried. When the police showed up the next morning with Melissa, she opened the door with Angelina in her arms and enthusiastically handed the baby to her mother.

—————

MELISSA AND ANGELINA come to see me every Saturday. Angelina is a chatterbox. She's still beautiful and charismatic. I must admit that each time I see her, I look for anything in her behavior or demeanor that would suggest what Garrett said or Cody inadvertently hinted about her was true. I've never told Melissa what either said, and I never will. But when I look at Angelina and play with her, I find a bright, loving, busy little girl. I see nothing that suggests Garrett was right. Nothing.

I've come to realize something that for three weeks of my life I'd begun to doubt: There are good people in the world. Good people, kind people. I think of Cody, Brian, Torkleson, Sanders, Morales, the SWAT team, my lawyers, the guards, the judge who sentenced me. They all could have chosen to be cold, cruel, indifferent. That would have been easy. Brutality, I think, comes naturally to human beings. But they chose to be good, even if what they did could be questioned within the strict confines of the law. I am not cynical.

But I am pragmatic. I know anyone is capable of anything, including me. It's a fine line between good and evil and, given the situation, the line moves. Oh, how it moves. It moved for me, but I still managed to cross it—repeatedly. And I've learned that once you cross it, bad acts become more effortless to commit because the moral restraints have loosened, and justifications cushion the implications of the crime. It becomes effortless to set things in motion, then stand by and let them happen, which is what I did. Effortless.

Which is why I'm here and why I should be.

And this is what I'll teach my daughter.

MELISSA IS WORKING FOR the Adam's Mark Hotel as general manager. They live in a condo on the fringe of downtown Denver because we had to sell the house without my income. Melissa insists the condo is perfect and she's shown me photos of it and it looks nice. The only thing she regrets, she insists, is that I'm in here and Angelina is in day care every day.

I guess we both have our keepers.

MY PARENTS DROVE all the way down from Montana to see me. I could tell by the way they entered the room they were as embarrassed as hell. I was embarrassed for them because I knew the security procedures probably set them back. I don't think my dad has ever walked a step in his life without his Leatherman tool, and my mother had to confess she had wire in her bra. As they sat at the table in the gen-pop visiting room, they held hands—the first time I'd ever seen them do that. I became fixated on their hands because they were so rough and knobby—the hands of hard workers—in a place where the supposedly tough guys had soft and smooth hands. My dad joked that he always thought I'd wind up in a place like this once I left the ranch, and my mom scolded him for saying that but didn't disagree.

"That was nice when you stopped by," she said. "I hope you'll do that more often."

"For Christ's sake," Dad said to her. "He's in prison!"

"But he won't always be," she said, turning red.

I promised to come visit. I told them it wouldn't be that long.

My dad said, "Good, I got fence to fix."

My mom said, "And I've got pies!"

CODY IS BACK in Montana, splitting his time between working as a detective in the Helena Police Department and helping my dad out on the ranch. He says he's happy, and I believe him. He has a steady girl and says he wants to bring her to Colorado to meet us. He's come to see me a few times when he drives south to visit his son, Justin. He urges me to move back to Montana when I'm released. I'm considering it, although there are no Adam's Mark Hotels in Montana.

Obviously, I've a lot of time on my hands to think about every-thing that happened during those three weeks. Some things became clearer in retrospect. I confirmed them during a conversation with Cody when he visited.

"You never really told Jeter to back off when we were in Mon-tana, did you?" I asked.

He hesitated, looked around, struck a match to light a cigarette under a sign that read ABSOLUTELY NO SMOKING. "No."

"Why did you mislead us?"

"Had to. You and Melissa got cold feet, Jack. You couldn't pull the trigger because you've got scruples. I don't have that problem. I knew we needed Jeter to force the issue and maybe take out Garrett. So when I went back into Jeter's, I asked him if I could use the bath-room and wished him good luck in Denver."

"That's why you were on the scene so fast after the incident in the Appaloosa," I said.

He nodded. "I was down the street. I wished I could have pre-vented you from following Jeter into that place. I had no idea you'd be that stupid."

Then he winked.

OH, AND ONE MORE thing. An amazing thing, a miracle. Melissa is seven months pregnant. The night of conception was our last night together before I went to prison. For once, I guess I had a live round in the chamber.

When I get out, we will have a daughter and a son. I wonder what our son will be like. I can't wait to find out. We've already de-cided his name, a long one. Cody Brian Torkleson Sanders Morales McGuane. After his uncles.

Don Hajicek

C. J. Box is the bestselling author of *Paradise Valley*, *The Highway*, and many other novels, including the award-winning Joe Pickett series. *Blue Heaven* won the Edgar Award for Best Novel in 2009, and Box has won the Anthony Award, the Macavity Award, the Barry Award (twice), the Western Heritage Award for Literature, and the Spur Award. Box's work has been translated into twenty-seven languages. He lives in Wyoming. Visit www.cjbox.net.